Sonia Florens is a British writer and translator who lives in London. She is active in the SF, fantasy and erotica fields. She was responsible for the bestselling *Mammoth Book of Women's Erotic Fantasies*.

The Mammoth Book of

Hot
ROMANCE

Edited by
SONIA FLORENS

ROBINSON

RUNNING PRESS
PHILADELPHIA · LONDON

Constable & Robinson Ltd
3 The Lanchesters
162 Fulham Palace Road
London W6 9ER
www.constablerobinson.com

First published in the UK by Robinson,
an imprint of Constable & Robinson, 2011

A copy of the British Library Cataloguing in Publication
Data is available from the British Library

UK ISBN 978-1-84901-467-0

1 3 5 7 9 10 8 6 4 2

First published in the United States in 2011 by Running Press Book Publishers.

US Library of Congress number: 2010941546
US ISBN 978-0-7624-4266-9

Running Press Book Publishers
2300 Chestnut Street
Philadelphia, PA 19103-4371

Visit us on the web!
www.runningpress.com

Printed and bound in the EU

Contents

Introduction

There's romance, and then there's romance. Let me rephrase that: there's old-style romance and new, modern romance.

In days of old, exemplified by the Golden Age of Mills & Boon and Harlequin, one of the great charms of romance stories was the sheer giddiness of the love stories they incorporated and the purity with which that love between male and female characters expressed itself. Few readers wanted to know more about what happened when the bedroom door closed and the happy ending reached its glorious conclusion. Things were better left to the imagination. Why spoil with unnecessary realism what was essentially a dream?

In recent years, as permissiveness has pervaded the society we live in, many fans now demand more grittiness in the stories they prefer to read. After all, we've long known about the birds and the bees, they feel, so why not find out more about the mysteries of love, once the mental epiphany has been reached and the time has rightly come for the heat and wonders of the flesh to manifest themselves in all their natural beauty? Which does not mean that there is anything wrong with the old style of romance where so much is left to the imagination; it is still here and available to all.

But for the readers in search of more modern material, with fewer euphemisms and added realism, the romance field has undergone a transformative tsunami. First of all, the bawdy world of the so-called bodice-rippers came into its own with shocking effect, both in a historical and contemporary context, soon followed within popular romance sub-genres by the fleshly romps of Native American romances with their ripple-chested Indian braves so often conquering the hearts and bodies of our heroines. And on and on. In the last decade, with the advent of supernatural and urban romances, realism has been at even more of a premium. After all, when vampires or werewolves bite, is it not a metaphor for sexual activity to say the least, and how could writers leave one crucial element in the equation out whilst delving on the other?

Fantasy? Wish fulfilment? Daydream? It's not for me to judge, but the fact that a frank and open manifestation of sexuality is now an essential component of romance writing is, I feel, a reason to rejoice, as it makes the literary genre we all cherish so much more relevant, and not as easy to be dismissed any longer as mere minor and derivative entertainment divorced from everyday reality.

Yes, many of the stories I've assembled here from the crème de la crème of modern romance authors, who were given a free hand to come up with fiercely hot stories involving human beings of flesh and blood and feelings, are explicit in their dealings with sexuality. But they have all come up trumps with torrid tales that will entrance, fascinate and beguile you, the reader.

Ladies, this is the premier division, no less, of new romance writing at work and play. So switch that fan on and start turning the pages. It's going to be hot, hot, hot!

Sonia Florens

(Like a) Virgin of the Spring

Susan Sizemore

Ginger was certain that there must have been a time when she found public fornication shocking. Now, crossing the courtyard between the baths and the sanctuary of the sacred spring, she barely glanced at the naked couple coupling on the altar at the centre. What the pair was doing was a sacred rite meant to please the gods. She did take a moment to glance their way and smile appreciatively, for the lad had a truly fine ass, the way his broad back narrowed down to his waist was truly a work of art. But the lust being shared out in the open did nothing to arouse her at the moment. Her attention was more on the upcoming meeting than on the pleasures of the flesh. Especially when those pleasures weren't hers to share.

It was spring, festival time, and people were crowding in from all over the countryside of southern Britain. It was a joyful time for most people, but for those with knowledge of the darkness moving towards them it was also worrying.

As priestess of the spring, Ginger was deeply concerned that the Lord of Ched had called for his senior people to gather in the precinct where she presided. She already knew that the next few days were going to be very hard on her, and she was certain that her talent as a seeress was going to be called upon on this day when she was supposed to be resting up for the festival.

Lord Ched was there when she arrived. He was a big man going to fat, his grizzled hair cut short in the Roman manner. Despite being near fifty he was still handsome. It was obvious where his daughter Morga got her beauty. Morga was chosen of the Mother and she and the year king should have been here instead of outside worshipping on the altar. Ginger wondered at the exclusion, but it wasn't a warning from her extrasensory perception that twisted her belly with apprehension. She hadn't always been the priestess of the well. The machinations of power and politics were as much a part of her original world as science and psychic research. Travelling back in time hadn't made life any simpler. Of course, back home she'd been more of an observer than a player. She was also well aware of the irony that the disaster of a time transfer gone wrong had turned her from the observer she was supposed to be into a person of importance in this time and place.

Not much importance, thank goodness. She wasn't trying to change history – even if she wasn't sure what the history was supposed to be. She was trying to survive in a dangerous, alien world where at least her psychic gift gave her a small edge. Well, a job to be more precise. She very rarely saw anything about her own future, but the seeress gig put a roof over her head, two meals a day and the protection of the most powerful person in the region. But all that could change soon if the invaders moved inland from their raids on the coast.

It seemed a certainty, really. Except that her recent visions had shown her fire and death, but no clear images of who the victors would be.

The steward of the manor followed Ginger into the sanctuary. After him came the harried-looking commander of the guard. The bishop visiting from Wales came inside as well. It was not a large space, though the entrance was wide and open to the courtyard. The four of them gathered around the tiled basin into which the waters of the sacred spring trickled from the back of the sanctuary. Ginger made up a quick prayer to the goddess of the water and to the new God of the cross and when she was done with the blessing they got down to business.

The guardsman did not wait for his lord to speak. "Can we make this quick? With the crowds coming in—"

"We need a new war leader," Lord Ched said, cutting him off. He looked around the gathering, expression hard, daring them to argue. "Right now. This very day would be good. Do you want the job?" he demanded of the guardsman.

A scar ran over the empty socket of the guard's left eye. He glanced towards the courtyard with his one good eye. They all followed his gaze. The couple was still busy on the altar. Morga's thighs were wrapped tightly around the year king's slender waist and the beautiful young man was pistoning away with hard, swift strokes. He was covered with a glowing sheen of sweat, his muscles bulging.

Damn, but that boy had stamina!

"He's perfect," the guard said. "How could I take his place?"

"He's not perfect," Lord Ched said. "He's an idiot, a fool and a braggart. He pleases my daughter and her belly's already swelling with a second brat, but he's useless for anything but fucking."

"In normal times that would be enough," the steward spoke up. He rubbed his jaw, the tough stubble on his cheeks made scratching sounds. "I suppose we could go back to the old ways and sacrifice him come the Planting Ceremony instead of just letting the lads wrestle for rights to Morga this year. The gods might like that. The crowd certainly would."

"Morga would not," Ginger said.

"Nor would I," added the bishop.

They were both ignored.

"Even if we return to the old ways," the lord said. "We need someone to replace the year king first. Someone who can fight. Someone who can lead. I'm too old. Morga's son is still with the wet nurse. Tradition dictates that the year king lead us into battle. A battle is coming, and that boy out there isn't up to the job."

All Ginger wanted was a little peace and quiet while trying to find a way home, but the invaders marching up from the coast weren't likely to leave anyone in peace. Or even alive if the rumours of complete slaughter proved to be true. The whole point of returning to the Dark Ages was to find out what happened, but, on the other hand, she was stuck in the Dark Ages where she didn't know what happened.

At least on a grand, historical scale. She was a board-certified psychic. But her gift only went so far, in certain directions, and after that she was as on her own as anyone else.

She found herself staring at the couple again. They were moaning and thrashing and happily rutting, unaware that the sacred pool was deciding their fate. She didn't like the year king or bitchy, vain Morga for that matter, but she was struck with a sudden burst of compassion for them.

Her thoughts were interrupted quickly enough by Lord Ched. "What shall we do, priestess? Look into the water and tell us what the gods say."

As she had suspected would happen all along, their fate was in her hands. Oh, she always tried to tell the truth of what she saw in water, but divination was one thing and politics was another. Right now it looked like she was going to have to find the right balance of both.

Ginger sighed, but didn't argue about her duty. She owed the lord of the manor her life as well as understanding his concerns. His world was threatening to fall apart; the people he was sworn to protect were in danger. She gestured for the men to stand back and knelt by the pool. They moved with great alacrity, obviously delighted the decision was in her hands and not theirs. If things turned out wrong later they could always claim that the priestess read the signs incorrectly.

Ginger brushed away any bitterness, in fact she put the men out of her mind altogether with easy practice. She looked into the crystal-clear water, her awareness going far deeper than the eight-inch depth of the pool. As always, she was amazed at how quickly her perceptions attuned to the energies present at this energy nexus.

From a long way away she heard herself ask, "Question?"

From even farther away the lord's voice came to her in an echoing whisper, "Who shall lead my people to war?"

Almost instantly a face appeared on the surface of the pool, though Ginger was aware she was the only one who could see it. A pair of piercing green eyes caught hers and she gasped, for she was certain that he could see her as clearly as she saw him. Nothing like this had ever happened before. "I see visions, I don't make contact."

"That's not my fault, is it?" his rough, deep voice answered. "Who are you? Where are you?" he demanded.

His gaze ate her alive but all she could do was continue to stare. She wanted to fall into the vision, into him, wanted him to fall into her. She wanted him the way a woman wanted a man and her body burned with a sudden need. She wanted his hands on her, all over her, though she knew they would be calloused from years of sword work. She wanted his mouth hard on hers. She wanted his cock thrusting between her thighs. She wanted possession – and to take.

He was as handsome as any year king should be, but for a small scar on one cheek. He couldn't be the man the lord wanted, then, for a year king must be perfect.

A crowd of men suddenly appeared behind the stranger's wide shoulders. They were a rough and dangerous-looking lot, with travel-stained clothes and heavy packs.

"Mercenaries," she said. He was their leader, the alpha among a pack of hungry wolves.

"Wolves mate for life," he said, then shook his head hard. His words made no more sense to him than they did to her.

"What do you see?" Ched's anxious voice came to her.

The question drew her away from the vision, but it was a sense of urgency that drew her to her feet. "He's here," she said. "Now. At the gate."

"What did you say, sir?"

Bern felt the weight of Sergeant Kaye's hand on his shoulder as the world came back into focus. "I hate it when that happens," he muttered. He frowned, and the sergeant stepped back. "Was I just talking to somebody, Kaye?"

"You spoke," Kaye answered. He glanced at the rest of the team, who were spread out across the road. "But you weren't talking to any of us."

"I was afraid of that."

Bern's rating on the psychic scale was a lowly little three, enough to get him transferred into the TTP's security force but not high enough to really interfere with his leading a normal, sane life. Except sometimes he heard voices, or had a flash of intuition. He'd learned to listen to the voices and trust his gut feelings. He'd just had one of those flashes though he couldn't remember the details – but it was an area lower down his gut that was demanding he pay attention.

"Something's up," he said. And in more ways than one.

He studied the lie of the land while he got the erection under control. It was spring, very close to the major seasonal fertility festival and the road they were on led to one of the holy sites scattered all over the southern part of the island. This particular temple to the local mother goddess was located on private property, and the pilgrims were camping out in cow pastures on either side of the road. The manor at the top of the hill had been built by a wealthy Roman colonist, but the local chieftain had taken over after the Romans abandoned all their foreign outposts a generation ago. Bern didn't care about the festival, but it was a good cover for checking out the place.

His holo map pinpointed this as one of the nexus locations and, despite growing doubts that any of them were going provide enough energy to work, it was his duty to check it out. Finding the right

door back to the future was only the second half of his assignment.
The first part was search and rescue for the science team that had
disappeared six months before his unit got the order to look for
them. In his opinion it had been stupid to send the eggheads back
in time without a whole team of sensible people to keep them out
of trouble. The whole thing had been fucked from the get-go. This
was the farthest back anyone had tried to travel, and to a time
period very little was known about. It was no wonder everything
had gone wrong – twice.

He gestured towards the crudely built wooden palisade surrounding the estate buildings. "Let's go see if we can get a look at what's
inside."

Ginger was used to the world around her going fuzzy and faded,
but she realized a moment before she fainted that this time it was
because she'd been holding her breath for far too long while
standing behind the men waiting at the gate. When the gate
opened, she simply blacked out, just as the man from her vision
walked in. Their gazes met for a moment, and then everything
went dark.

It was ridiculous, and she was so embarrassed that she scrunched
her eyes tightly closed when she woke up, not wanting the person
holding her to know that she'd come round. Those strong arms
were his, weren't they? Her head rested against a broad, hard chest,
and warmth and male scent engulfed her. Awareness of him sent a
wave of warmth through her, pooling deep in her belly. Her nipples
stiffened, scraping against the cloth of her dress, and her breasts
grew heavy.

"Oh, my," she whispered. Without any volition, her hand came
up to stroke his strong, stubbly jaw.

She could hear his heart rate pick up when she spoke, and the
deep sound of his laugh rumbled through his chest. For a moment
the arms around her tightened, pressing her body harder against
him.

Bern liked the weight of the woman in his arms; the touch of the
bare skin of her arms and the feel of the rest of her beneath her
dress made him ache, made him remember how long it had been
since he'd had a woman. It also made him thankful that women
didn't wear underwear in the Dark Ages. And this woman was a
perfect fit against him. He liked the softness of her curly red hair

tickling his neck and cheek. He wanted to bury his face in her thick hair, then follow the line of her throat all the way down to snuggle between the soft mounds of her breasts. He wanted—

Bern gave his head a stern shake. As stimulating as holding her was he didn't know why he'd rushed into the courtyard and automatically scooped her up off the ground when she fell. They weren't in the age of chivalry yet, and calling attention to himself and his men was stupid. Keeping a low profile was a matter of policy and survival among TTP teams. He had no idea who this woman was or what she meant to all the men staring at him. Though she did look familiar.

When she woke and spoke, he couldn't help but laugh; it was a triumphant sound, knowing that she was as aware of him as he was of her.

Then Bern realized that the words he'd heard hadn't been filtered through his translator implant: she'd spoken in English instead of the local lilting Celtic dialect. Now he knew who she was!

Her name was Virginia White, and though he'd never met her in the flesh he'd studied her holo image along with those of all the others on the missing team. Since he already held her, he was tempted to call for his men to cover his withdrawal and run back out the gate in order to ensure her safety now that he'd found her.

Since that wasn't the smart way to play it, he put her down, letting her body slide slowly down his until her feet touched the ground. She was tall and willowy, her height another clue that she wasn't from this time.

"You—" he began. But a hand landed on his shoulder and Bern whirled around, hand on sword. "What?" he demanded of the pot-bellied greybeard before him. The stranger wore a threadbare silk tunic. As silk was a luxury rare in these parts since the Roman withdrawal, Bern guessed this was the local chieftain. "My lord," he added, with a polite nod.

The chieftain's frown turned into an effusive smile. "You're quick, I see. Good. Good." He glanced towards the hand Bern still rested on the pommel of his sword. "Welcome to Ched," he went on. "Come to worship at the well, have you? Come for the festival?"

Bern nodded. He was aware that Virginia White had moved back into the shadow of an arched doorway. He wanted nothing more than to follow her, but he had to stay in character and deal with the master of the estate first.

Bern brought out a small leather pouch, heavy with gold and handed it over. "Please accept this small gift, in honour of the goddess and your hospitality."

The chieftain beamed, and glanced at Bern's people – an obvious unit of soldiers that waited by the gate, alert for Bern's orders. "Those are fine-looking lads you lead."

"We come in peace for the festival," Bern hastened to reassure the chieftain. He saw the speculative look in Ched's eyes and smiled. "But afterwards, our swords are for hire if you are interested."

He hoped that made him sound like a friendly and useful fellow to the chieftain, just in case his unit needed an excuse to stay on after the festival if he couldn't find out what Virginia White was up to before then.

Lord Ched's grin widened. He put his arm around Bern. "Join me for some wine. What's your name, lad?" he asked as he led Bern into the main hall.

Ginger considered going back to her duties at the spring, but curiosity got the better of her. That, and an irresistible craving not to let the man who named himself Bern out of her sight, made her follow the men into the hall. For some reason being close to Bern made her feel as if she were not alone any more, and she needed the nearness after all these months. She knew very well that any attraction to this man was foolish, and not even because intimacy with an indigenous resident was against Project rules. If Lord Ched had his way this dangerous stranger would soon be sharing the bed of his daughter Morga. Jealousy ripped through Ginger at the thought of Morga eagerly spreading her legs for Bern's cock, but she knew it would be for the best politically. They needed a warrior hero and Bern looked to have all the qualifications for the job.

And, Lordy, she liked how he looked, all tall, dark and handsome, with broad shoulders and big hands and the brightest, most beautiful eyes she'd ever seen. There was an aura of steely danger around him that should have scared her to death, but sent fireworks shooting through her instead. He wore a knee-length tunic that left his legs bare, bits of leather body armour and a light woollen cape. Her fingers itched to pull off all those layers and thoroughly explore what she found underneath.

Ched sent for Morga, then settled down to explain his plan to Bern over cups of strong wine. Business was usually conducted once the menfolk were well on the way to being drunk.

Ginger stayed in the background to listen and watch, taking a seat among a group of women working on spinning and embroidery. The men were barely into their second libation to the goddess and not yet into proper drinking when Morga came flouncing in. At least she's dressed, Ginger thought, for the priestess of the Mother frequently went around bare-breasted, and sometimes completely nude. Morga was beautiful, knew it and had no qualms about showing it, even if she wasn't lying on her back on the holy altar.

I live like a nun, Ginger thought, and she gets to whoop it up anywhere, any time.

Until a few minutes ago this hadn't bothered Ginger a bit, except for the missing sex part. Now she very nearly snarled as Morga caught sight of Bern and made a beeline to sit beside him.

"Daughter," Lord Ched announced once the girl was snuggled up against Bern's side, "meet your new husband."

Morga bounded to her feet. So did Bern.

"What?" Morga screamed.

"What?" Bern echoed.

His voice was quite calm, but anger crackled off him. For some reason this dichotomy sent hot shivers through Ginger. And several of the older women gave each other knowing looks as well.

Morga gave Bern another once-over, and her lips curled in disdain. "I don't mind a bit of flirting, but I like the husband I've got," she told her father.

Lord Ched banged a fist on the table. "You'll take the man I choose."

"The goddess chose for me already."

"Your year king has already reigned too long. When this warrior challenges, the younger man will lose. Be prepared for it – be prepared to do your duty by your father, your goddess and your people." He gestured towards Bern. "Now, be a proper priestess and take this fine bear of a man off to the bath."

"You sound like a Roman," the girl complained. "But this land is Celt again. And I'll do no such thing as bathe a stranger." She looked around haughtily, and pointed to Ginger. "There's a priestess who obeys you. Let her service this great bear of yours."

And, with that pronouncement, she flounced back out again – leaving everyone staring at Ginger.

Bern's initial impulse was to protest all this nonsense about marriage, and bathing with buxom young women, but he let it go when the girl suggested Virginia White as her replacement. It would be a good way to get White alone.

"Good idea!" he exclaimed, and stepped forwards to drag the missing TTP team member out of the crowd, his hand tight around her slender wrist. She looked at him with eyes wide with fright, and he had to fight off laughter as he caught an impression of her thinking about having a barbarian in her bathtub. He also noticed that she wasn't completely opposed to the idea as warmth spread between them from where they touched.

Hmmm . . . maybe they could turn this ridiculous situation into a bit of mutual fun. He was sure he'd communicated his moment of thoughtless lust from the contact of skin against skin because he noticed how her nipples hardened beneath the fabric of her dress.

"What are you waiting for, priestess?" the chieftain demanded. "Show the man the hospitality he deserves!"

"Come along," Bern said, and dragged White along with him out of the hall.

Once out in the courtyard she got her voice back. "You're in for a treat, warrior, for the Roman hypocaust is still working and the pool is deep, and hot. The baths draw as many visitors as the sacred spring, increasing the lord's prestige and—"

"I'm not interested in a hot bath."

She sniffed and wrinkled her pretty nose. "You should be."

He laughed. "I guess I am a bit ripe from a few days on the road. My tunic could probably use burning, besides."

"Where I come from that would be breaking a law against polluting the air."

For a moment he'd let attraction get in the way of professionalism. This reminder that she was no local priestess brought Bern back to his duty. "Lead on to this bathhouse," he growled.

Even with business uppermost in his mind, he couldn't help but appreciate the fine, pert shape of her ass, or the feminine sway of her hips as she walked ahead of him. He feared his body was going to overwhelm his brain at any moment.

Ginger was aware of the rough soldier's gaze. His intense energy devoured her and left her smouldering. She'd never been so instantly and dangerously attracted to a man before. All the recommendations about indigenous relations were overruled by the demands of her body. She didn't think she'd be able to keep her hands off this guy. In fact, to keep up her cover as a priestess she didn't have any choice but to scrape his naked body down with scented oil and rinse him off, now did she?

She grinned with anticipation as they entered the bath. But her grin was wiped away and replaced with a surge of fear an instant after they stepped into the room.

He grabbed her shoulders and spun her to face him. At the same time he growled, "Out!" to the pair of waiting bath attendants. She heard the slap of their bare feet on the mosaic as they hurried out.

"What the hell do you think you're doing?" he demanded the moment they were alone.

"Only what my lord order—" Then she realized. "You're speaking English!"

On a burst of sheer relief she grabbed him and kissed him. It took only an instant for relief to flash into pure lust.

What was a man to do when a woman flung herself against him and soft lips pressed against his own? Bern didn't care what anyone else might do when her hips ground enticingly against his. His cock took over the thinking for him and he grabbed her ass and pulled her closer. Her mouth was delicious, and his tongue delved possessively into the sweet warmth. Her breasts pushed against his chest and he brought a hand up to cup the soft roundness and stroked a thumb across the hard nipple he could feel beneath her dress. He'd never wanted anyone so much or so quickly. He picked her up and tossed her into the water, then took only a moment to unfasten his sword belt and toss off his leather armour before jumping in after her.

Though she was fully clothed the wet dress clung to her body and outlined her breasts and hips in a way Bern found utterly sexy. She shook her head, flinging water out of her thick red curls.

"People generally get undressed before bathing," she said.

"And before sex, too."

She laughed, and reached below the water to grab on to her soaked skirt. "Wet wool," she muttered. "Now I smell like a sheep." She gave him a leering once-over. "Does that make you a ram?"

She was holding the dress up around her thighs; he caught a glimpse of pale skin through the steaming water. "Don't stop now," he urged her. He wanted her naked.

She inched up the skirt some more and he caught a glimpse of springy, carrot-red curls at the juncture of milky pale thighs.

"Oh Lord," he groaned as his cock stiffened further. He splashed through the waist-deep pool and grabbed her around the waist. "Don't tease me, woman."

She threw back her head and laughed, and he took the opportunity to kiss the base of her throat then run his tongue across the tops of her breasts.

"Help me," she said. "This thing weighs a ton."

It took him a moment to realize that she was talking about her wet dress, but once he caught on he grabbed a double handful of soaking wool and yanked, while she pulled and squirmed, and soon he had her as naked as he wanted her. The water gave her skin a translucent shine.

"You look like milk in moonlight," he said. Then he remembered her name. White. "You look like your name, Dr Virginia White."

"Ginger," she answered instantly. "No one calls me Virgin – of course around here no one calls me Ginger, either."

He ran his hands up and down her flanks, pausing to cup the weight of her breasts before continuing to stroke her waist and hips and the outside of her thighs. "What do they call you if not Virgin?"

She drew back, lifting her head haughtily, or as haughtily as a panting, horny woman could. "Priestess," she answered. "Or the Lady of the White Bird Spring when they're being formal."

He needed to know how she'd gotten separated from her team, how she'd gotten here, and why she was part of the indigenous power structure. But he needed something else even more right now.

He pressed his hips against her, his cock straining against her belly. "Touch me," he demanded. He circled her nipples with his thumbs.

She found the hem of his tunic and pulled it above his hips. Once his cock was free her fingers closed around the base and stroked him slowly from his balls to the throbbing tip. Ginger loved the heat of his penis, the weight and thickness of it, the velvet over steel feel of it in her hand. She wanted it buried deep inside her body. Needed it.

She backed up a few steps to the edge of pool, bringing him with her as she continued to caress his penis and balls.

When they reached the side he cupped her ass and lifted her on to the mosaic edge. She tilted backwards on her arms and spread her legs. He kissed her belly and laved her navel with his tongue. Then his head moved down between her legs, where he found her clit and licked and nibbled the swollen nub. She came almost instantly, her hips bucking and her thighs clamping tight around his head as his mouth continued to explore her pussy with amazing skill and dexterity.

"Damn!" she shouted, and slapped her hands against the wet tiles. "More," she begged.

He lifted his head and gazed at her up the length of her body. "More?" His voice was low, and full of teasing promise.

Ginger arched her back, raising her body imploringly. "More."

She scooted backwards and he lifted himself out of the water. The length of his swollen cock swayed out in front of him. When he knelt over her she grasped it and guided him to the hungry wet entrance of her pussy. He filled her in one hard thrust.

The walls of her vagina closed tightly around him and Bern revelled in the pleasure of being within the grasp of her sweet heat. The salty, tangy taste of her sex lingered on his tongue and he bent his head to kiss her and share it with her. She moaned against his mouth, her tongue eagerly exploring his mouth. Her hands moved over his back and ass. She played with his balls, and teased the opening of his anus with one clever finger. His hips flexed involuntarily. Her inner muscles rippled around his erection and from that point on he was lost in pounding, pulsing sensation.

He lay on top of her for a long time afterwards, unwilling to move away from the feel of her soft breasts and the scent of her skin. He didn't know why, but the sound of her heartbeat against his ear made him feel like he was home.

Then she giggled and the sound brought Bern back into the here and now. He lifted his head to look at her. "What?"

"Lord Ched sent me in here with you to make Morga jealous. She'd really be jealous if she knew what we've been doing."

"What's with the chieftain wanting me to marry his daughter?" Bern asked.

"I suppose that's my fault," she answered. "He's looking for a warrior to replace the year king, and I saw you in the well. So—"

"I think we've both been in the past too long," he said. "Because what you just said seems to make sense to you, and it almost makes sense to me."

Tears suddenly welled in her big blue eyes. She reached out and stroked his temples and brushed hair off his forehead. "You're really from my time." The relief in her voice bordered on worship.

He wiped away her tears, then kissed her cheeks, leaving the taste of salt on his tongue.

"You're not from my team," she said. "I would have remembered you. How do you know my name? What are you doing here?"

He should have explained to her already. He should have gotten a debriefing from her. Duty should have come before sex. He'd never been hit so hard and fast and recklessly by lust before.

"I wanted you the moment I saw you in the vision, maybe I communicated my lust through a psychic link to you," she explained.

"I wanted you the instant I saw you as well, and stop reading my mind," he added.

"I get more impressions than actual thoughts from people. My gift is for scrying with water energy."

"Right," he answered. He knew that about her.

Frankly he wasn't all that comfortable with a scientific/military project needing to use psychics even if he was a low-level one. But the nature of time travel had turned out to need people whose minds worked on a different frequency than the majority of people's. No matter how much data time travellers collected on jaunts into the past, it was only the travellers with psychic gifts that were able to remember the actual experiences of the journey. So, Project teams took back all sorts of recording equipment, and that included the inclusion of a psychic to serve as a living, subjective memory of the events that were encountered.

Psychics also came along to study the energy nexuses, the doors as it were, where travellers could enter and leave different times. The scientists in charge of the TTP didn't approve of this use of psychic talent, it just wasn't scientific enough for them, but the people in charge of funding the project insisted on using every available research tool. Besides, as far as anyone could explain the process of time travel, it still seemed a hell of a lot more like magic than it did science.

"We ought to put on our clothes and get down to business," he said. He was still half-dressed. He got up and adjusted his tunic, then helped the lovely naked woman to her feet. "Sorry about soaking your dress."

"It needs a spring wash anyway," she answered. She picked up the sodden lump of cloth on the edge of the pool and began wringing it out into the bath water. "Give me a hand," she said, and together they managed to wind the dress tight enough to squeeze out most of the water. The whole time they worked Bern couldn't keep his eyes off her.

"You've got great tits," he told her. They were large and round and just as pale as the rest of her fine skin, but for the lovely dark circles of her large nipples. Nipples that grew peaked and hard when she noticed him looking at her. He grinned as a flush spread across her chest and throat. It wasn't only a smile that rose as he watched her.

"Ginger White, stop making me hard," he ordered teasingly.

She snatched her dress out of his hands. "I think maybe you'd better help me on with this."

He stepped close and ran his hands over her on the pretext of helping her manoeuvre the wet dress. She was cool to the touch, but she went warm where he touched.

"You feel like satin," he told her.

She smiled, and the blush spread to her cheeks, but she moved away from him and quickly finished dressing.

When she was done, she said, "Now that we're wet as drowned rats I suppose I should point out that what we did was a very un-Roman way of taking a bath."

"We weren't bathing, darlin'," he reminded her. "We were fucking."

"Yes, well – is your name really Bern?" she asked, suddenly anxious. "When are you from? Do you know what happened to the rest of my team? How did you find me? Where's the nexus? When can we go home?"

Bern held up his hands to halt her rush of words. "I'll answer yours if you'll answer mine." He spotted a stone bench against the wall and led her over to it. Once seated, he held her hands in his as they sat facing each other. "My team was sent out six months after yours, specifically to search for your team. When we came in through the Tintagel nexus it crashed behind us."

"Now your team is missing as well?"

He nodded. "At least the team all came through together. The theory is that some kind of hiccup in the time/dimensional energy field scattered your team in transit—"

"So that we all came through at different nexus points," she finished. "I'm no physicist but I've managed to figure that out on my own." She gave his hands a sympathetic squeeze. "So your team's as lost here as we are."

"Yeah. But we still had our mission. Along with hunting for your people we've been searching for a working exit point, but no luck yet with that. It hasn't been easy, since the energy hiccup shorted out most of your team's ID transponders. So far you're only the second team member we've found alive."

"Who else have you found?"

"Sergeant Kaye."

"Thank goodness! I've been so worried about them." Then she blanched. "You've found others – dead?"

He nodded. "We found Dr Bohrs' grave outside a village near Aquae Sulis. Gwayne had been enslaved on a Saxon farmstead on the coast. We got him out of the place alive, but he caught an arrow in the throat when we ran into a raiding party the next day."

"Damned Saxon invaders," she muttered.

"You've been hanging with the indigenous folks too long. Remember that the Saxons are supposed to have taken over the island after the Romans left."

"Yes, but the incursion seems to be happening far quicker than historians always supposed. There should be some factor slowing them down, giving the Roman influences that have overlaid the Celtic base culture time to fade. If the Saxons aren't halted soon the world we come from won't get a chance to develop. I've been starting to believe that maybe I'd transported into one of those alternate worlds the theorists worry about."

"I didn't think you were your team's historian."

"Nah, I'm just an Anglophile."

"Me, I just go where I'm sent and do what I'm told to do. And how is it you ended up as the local priestess?"

She looked down sheepishly, before looking him in the eye again. "I know such direct involvement with the locals is against the rules, but sometimes fate gets in the way of perfectly good intentions. I'm lucky that the holy spring's point of origin is in the woods behind the shrine and that's the nexus where I came through. The Romans channelled the spring into the sanctuary pool when they built the villa. So it was easier for the inhabitants to believe that I was the only survivor of a band of pilgrims attacked by bandits when I wandered bloody and burned out of the woods than it would have been if I'd appeared out of a blaze of light in the fountain."

She paused to take a deep breath, and Bern jumped in. "I understand how you arrived here, but how did you end up working for the chieftain?"

She shrugged. "A girl's got to eat."

"So, you decided to save yourself instead of searching for the rest of your team?"

She pulled her hands from his, and tapped a finger on her forehead. "How would I do that without any computer equipment? I'm too high level on the psi chart for any implant but the wrist chip."

"Right. Sorry,"

"I've tried scrying to hunt for them, but I've never seen anything."

"Because seers don't see things connected with themselves."

"At least not often. I thought about striking out on my own after they nursed me back to health, but it was the dead of winter, and there are plenty of bandits and barbarians outside Lord Ched's rather flimsy walls. Since this was the only safe place, I set about proving my usefulness so I could stay. The sanctuary hadn't had a resident seer for a long time, so I used my scrying abilities and got the job. Having a real fortune-teller at the holy spring increases the prestige and fame of the place. Which means a larger gathering of pilgrims bringing rich offerings for the goddess, and greater wealth for Lord Ched, at this year's fertility festival. Unfortunately, he's decided that the fertility part of the festivities needs a bit of re-arranging, and that's where you come in."

Bern thought about what he knew of the local customs, politics and religious practices, and concluded, "The chieftain wants a warrior to challenge the year king at tonight's ceremony."

She nodded.

He grimaced. "Ah, crap, he wants me to kill some kid for the right to fuck his daughter."

"And become the local war leader. He wants you to stop the Saxons." Ginger cleared her throat, and gave him an embarrassed smile. "This is my fault, really – I told him I saw you in the water when he asked who would be the next year king."

Bern shot to his feet. "Oh, for crying out loud, woman! I've got better things to do than interfere in local problems!" He pointed at her. "Rescuing you, for example, is more important."

She jumped up to face him. "Hey, I just report what the water shows me."

"You couldn't lie sometimes?"

"It's not like I knew who you were when I saw you. It's not my fault you're fated to be king! And sleep with Morga," she added.

He heard the jealousy in her voice, and he liked it. He noticed that they'd moved close together while they argued, and that arguing with her was arousing him all over again. The attraction between them was strong and hot, and driving him crazy. Being crazy was no way to run an op. Knowing that didn't stop him from putting his hands on her hips.

"There you are!" Lord Ched's voice boomed behind them before he could pull Ginger into his arms.

They turned to face the chieftain, and the trio of men that followed him into the bathhouse. Ched had a smile plastered on his face, but there was anger in his eyes. His hand was on the pommel of a dagger on his belt. Bern had been prepared to tell the man he had no interest in his game of kings and priestesses, but decided this might not be the right time to assert his opinions in the matter.

"What's wrong?" he asked instead. He put his arm protectively around Ginger's shoulders. He was aware of the way she leaned into him all down the length of his body.

"You're a clever one," Ched said, nodding approvingly.

"I know trouble when I see it."

His impulse was to gather his squad and see what was going on for himself, but he waited for an explanation. Even if the Saxons were attacking the gates it wasn't his problem unless the team he'd been sent to save was in immediate danger. He was not in charge of the indigenous situation here, and wasn't going to be despite the chieftain's plans or Ginger's visions.

Ched cleared his throat, and Bern realized he was embarrassed. "It's something to do with your daughter, isn't it?"

"Morga's run off," Ched blurted out. "And the year king ran with her."

"But she's the Mother's priestess!" Ginger gasped. "And he's—"

"You've been spending too much time with the locals," Bern whispered to her in English. "A pair of runaways is not our problem."

"But the ceremony is tonight."

Ched might not have understood what Ginger said, but he obviously recognized the desperation in her tone. "You see the problem, don't you, Lady of the Spring? Oh, we could raise the hue and cry and go after those foolish children. But if we drag them back I'll have to execute my own daughter to appease the crowd gathered for the festival. If the lad's not man enough to face you, it would offend your honour to hunt him down," he said to Bern. "Besides, you have more important things to concern you than a coward who doesn't deserve even to lose a fight to you."

"But what about the ceremony?" a one-eyed man asked. "Tradition—"

"We've changed tradition before," Ched said, cutting him off. He looked at one of the other men, a wizened, white-bearded fellow in rough brown robes. "Haven't we, Bishop Myrdyn?"

The old man was carrying a gnarled staff, and reminded Bern of Gandalf.

"You're not thinking of giving up your heathen fertility festival, are you?" the old man asked.

"Of course not!" Ched answered. "The people would riot for sure if we changed custom that far."

"There you go again – you promise to change your pagan ways, but you always find a way out of your promises."

"Didn't I say I'd let you baptize as many folk as wanted it tomorrow morning? And in our own sacred pool?"

"That you did," the Christian cleric conceded. He tugged thoughtfully on his ear lobe. "Once the people are sated and sore from the sex, and their heads are splitting from too much drink, I'll preach a sermon that will lure them to save their souls from the great sins they're going to commit this night. You'll make a fine year king," he added, looking Bern over. "I'll give my blessing to that."

"But we need a priestess for the king to mate with," the one-eyed man insisted. "The crops will wither without the spring mating."

"Well, if I'm going to turn the pool into a baptismal fount, it won't need a priestess any more, will it?" the bishop said, eyeing Ginger critically. He pointed at her. "Use this priestess instead of the one that's run off."

"Good idea," Lord Ched said, clapping Myrdyn on the shoulder. "One priestess is as good as another in the eyes of the goddess."

"But I'm not a virgin," Ginger blurted. "The priestess of the Mother must be a virgin when she lies with her first year king."

"Don't encourage them," Bern complained. Then he realized where she was going with this and spoke loudly. "We can't offend the goddess. I'm no virgin, either."

"Oh, that's all right," Lord Ched dismissed them. "The goddess won't mind." He waved his hand dismissively. "You were both virgins, once, after all. It's virility and fertility that matter most. You'll both do. I'm glad that's settled." He began to turn away.

"But I don't want to be king," Bern pointed out.

"What man doesn't want to be king?" Ched said, turning back. His expression turned hard. "Especially when the choice is between becoming king or going to the goddess with the priestess and all of your men sacrificed inside the burning belly of the wicker man?"

"Sex or death," Myrdyn said. "Either way, the crowd will be entertained."

Bern had seen the piles of kindling and a crudely woven straw statue in a field on his way into the stockade. He knew that criminals were often burned alive inside such structures during the spring fire festival. Lord Ched could probably get the mob angry enough at missing out on the orgy to attack his team. The ensuing massacre wouldn't look good on Bern's record. And there was the chance that some of his people could get hurt. He wasn't ready to risk any of them, especially Ginger, when there was another solution.

It wasn't like he minded having sex with Ginger White.

Besides, they could sneak off among the departing pilgrims after the festival, and get on with searching for a working nexus without any muss or fuss.

"King it is then," Bern said with a grin.

"Good," Lord Ched said, and he and his people marched away.

When they were gone, the horrified Ginger asked, "Now what are we going to do?"

Bern was still grinning as he took her in his arms. "Why, rehearse for the fertility ceremony, of course."

She took him to her room, and firmly closed the door behind them. "You can't really mean to go through with this," she said once they were alone. "Not that I have anything against public displays of fornication, per se – it's just that I don't think I'm up to being the star attraction in the local spring pageant."

"Sex show," he interpreted. "Do we really have a choice?"

She put her hands over her face. "Don't be so pragmatic." She peered at him between her fingers. "You'll have to wear a pair of stag horns, you know."

He grimaced. "And what will you be wearing?"

"Not a damn thing."

The grimace turned into a grin. "I can live with that."

"Yes, but—"

"My name's Andrew." He picked her up and carried her towards the narrow bed. "Colonel Andrew Bern. Just Bern to everybody." He kissed her before adding, "I thought we ought to be formally introduced."

She twined her arms around his neck. "Nice name. Kiss me again."

"All over," he promised, and set her down.

They took a few moments to help each other take off their damp clothing, then fell together on to the bed.

"You make me so horny I can't stand it," he told her as she pushed him on to his back and straddled him. He reached up to stroke her breasts.

Her back arched at the touch. Unbelievable heat rushed through her. For a moment everything but sensation went away. She could do this forever. But could she do it with anyone else looking?

The thought brought her back to reality.

"Oh, crap," she said. "I can't do this in public!"

When she tried to bolt off of him he grasped her waist and held on tight. "Look at me," he ordered. "Just look at me and we can do anything – together."

She'd just met this man. Why should she believe in him? But when she looked into his eyes, she did.

Those eyes were full of fire and passion that was just for her.

He took his hands away from her, and she moaned at the loss of his touch.

He responded with a deep, arrogant chuckle, and she responded to that by leaning forwards and nipping him lightly on the shoulder.

"Mean woman," he murmured, and ran his hands through her tangled hair.

Then she licked the spot she'd bitten, tasting the tang of fresh sweat. She breathed deeply, and kissed and licked her way across his throat while revelling in the male scent and heat of his naked body as he caressed her back and butt. His muscles were gloriously hard and sculpted. She sat up and ran her hands across his wide chest and down his flat belly.

"Look at me," he said again. This time his voice was rough with need.

When she did he turned her on to her back. His gaze never left hers as he urged her legs wide and guided his cock deep inside her. She rose to meet him, inner muscles closing around the hard, hot length that filled her. Soon his eyes, and the fire growing as they moved together was all there was in the world. Then even they were gone and only the fire remained.

"They've changed the rules because of the growing Christian influence. You won't have to kill anyone if you're challenged," Ginger explained. "We're in luck, because one of the local boys might fight you for Morga, but not over me."

"What? You don't want to have two knights fighting a tourney for my lady's hand?"

"Hell, no." She snorted. "And it's not my hand that's up for grabs." The part of her she referred to was still thrumming from what they'd been doing – for the third time – but hadn't had a chance to finish when they were called from her room for the ceremony.

"The only person that's going to be grabbing you anywhere is me."

She sighed and batted her eyelashes at him. "You're so romantic, Colonel Bern."

"It's not about romance, darlin', it's about sex." He squeezed her hand. "Are you sure you can go through with this?"

"No. You?"

"Me neither. Remember, all you have to do is look into my eyes and we'll be alone," he reminded her, sounding more confident after confessing he was as nervous as she was.

"And you look into mine."

"Good plan."

Night had fallen, sacred fires were lit, and hundreds of pilgrims were waiting within their glow just outside the front of the estate. The ceremony was ready to begin,

"I wasn't this nervous at my wedding," Bern confided. "Or my divorce hearing."

Ginger rounded on him. "You're married?"

"Was," he answered.

"You might have mentioned this earlier."

"Why?"

"Men." She spat the word like a curse.

He put his hands on the nervous woman's shoulders. "Don't go off on me, OK?"

"I do not have sex with married men."

"Then you're in luck, because I'm not married."

"Right. Divorced. Sorry." She rested her forehead against his bare chest. "I am so nervous that I don't know what I'm saying or doing."

"You look beautiful," he told her. "Like the bride of the summer god ought to look."

They had braided spring flowers into her thick red curls, and she was wearing Morga's most diaphanous white silk dress. He was wearing a doeskin loincloth. He had to claim the Summer King's sword, then be acclaimed by the people. After that they'd get naked and down to business.

Tightly holding hands they made their way through the watching crowd to where Lord Ched stood between two widely spaced bonfires. Ginger made herself look straight ahead, but she was deeply aware of the expectant mood of the hundreds of watching people. She made herself believe that Bern was the only thing that was real and everything else was a dream. She wasn't completely successful, but concentrating on the feel of him where his skin touched hers did help. Being near him truly did make her body ripe with need.

When they reached the chieftain, Ched held up a richly decorated sword and shouted, "Behold your priestess and her new Summer King!" While the crowd cheered, Ched plunged the tip of the sword into the soft, spring earth.

"Now what?" Bern whispered to Ginger.

"You say something about accepting the kingship for the love of the Mother and the fertility of the land, and pull the sword from the ground."

"OK, then." He began to step forwards, hand out to take the hilt of the sacred blade.

"Wait!" a man shouted from the crowd before Bern could touch the sword.

"Now, what?" Bern complained, turning towards the man who came rushing forwards.

"I challenge!" the man shouted, coming up to glare face to face with Bern.

"Oh, crap," Ginger muttered. "I forgot about Lanc."

"Who the hell is Lanc?" Bern demanded.

She pointed at the broad-shouldered, dark-haired man. "Oh, he's this Druid from Brittany that's been trying to get me to run off with him."

Bern rounded on her. "What? You weren't going to mention that there's this other guy?"

"You're jealous."

"Yes!"

She grinned. "Oh, that's so cute."

"I challenge!" Lanc shouted again. "Fight me for your kingship!"

Bern gestured at the challenger. "Hold on, I'll be right with you. What is this guy to you?" he demanded of Ginger.

"Nothing. He's one of a group of Druids going around trying to recruit psychics to come back to Brittany. They're trying to keep the old religion alive back home."

"So, he doesn't want to have sex with you?"

"Not as far as I—"

"Yes, I do!" Lanc cut her off.

"Oh, stop it," Ginger told him.

"Fight me for her!" Lanc insisted. The crowd was beginning to shout for the battle to begin as well.

"OK," Bern said, and turned around and hit the man in the jaw.

Lanc went down, but was up again almost instantly.

Bern took a step back and smiled, glad that the opposition had some fight in him. It was barbaric, but he was glad to have some competition so he could properly claim the woman as his. Deep in his gut, deep in his heart, he knew Ginger was a woman worth fighting for.

The Druid was a big, fit guy with some hand-to-hand skills. They sparred against each other, flesh and muscle straining, moving through firelight and shadow while the crowd cheered and shouted. Sweat stung Bern's eyes, and he tasted blood when Lanc got past his guard once to strike him in the face. Excitement built deep in Bern's gut and the clarity that only came with combat focused his whole attention on the struggle.

For a while he forgot the purpose of the challenge while he concentrated deeply on the fight. Then he caught sight of Ginger. She was flushed and her eyes were bright with excitement, which sent a zing of lust straight to Bern's groin. But her arms were tensely crossed, and she also looked annoyed.

"Enjoying yourself?" she called sarcastically when she had his attention.

The momentary distraction almost cost him but he caught Lanc's sudden kick out of the corner of his eye and quickly countered, though he ended up with a hard foot grazing his thigh as he turned. He returned the favour with a hard kick to Lanc's solar plexus, which brought the man down. When Lanc tried to struggle up, Bern knocked him unconscious.

Ginger rushed up to him. "Are you all right?"

"Oh, yeah." He grinned, and kissed her, pulling her tightly against him. The loincloth left nothing to her imagination about how he was feeling. He was vaguely aware of the cheering crowd.

Her hand brushed against the erection straining against the soft leather. Then she prised herself out of his tight embrace. "Not yet."

"Oh, come on!" he complained. But he understood when she pointed towards the sword buried in the ground. He laughed. "Right. Well, at least I don't have to pull it out of a stone."

She looked at him strangely, and asked, "Doesn't Bern mean 'Bear'?"

"Yeah . . ." He waved the question aside and quickly crossed to the sword. Bits of earth clung to the blade as he pulled it out and held it up for all to see. He waited for the cheering to die down, then shouted, "For Britain and the White Lady!"

The roar this time was deafening.

"Must have sounded good," he murmured.

Ched came up to them, took Ginger by the hand. A trio of young women accompanied him. One of the girls held a staghorn headdress. The girls made quick work of stripping off his and Ginger's clothes.

After fastening the headdress on Bern, Ched turned to the crowd and proclaimed, "Behold the Queen and King of Summer whose mating brings fertility to the land! Let the festival begin!"

"I don't think—"Ginger started.

But this was no time for thinking and Bern wasn't going to let her get started. He swung his naked lover up into his arms and covered her mouth with his. While his tongue probed inside that sweet, responsive warmth he carried her to the cloth-covered mound of grass and flowers that was to serve as both bed and altar for them to mate upon.

"Put me down!" she demanded.

"Don't chicken out on me now," he pleaded.

Ginger laughed wickedly. She remembered his directions to just look at him, but the crowd was the last thing on her mind at the moment. She wanted to taste him, and that was what she did, licking and kissing her way down his throat to his chest and belly. And then, on her knees, she put her lips on the tip of his penis, tasted a drop of pre-come on her tongue.

The crowd cheered when she took his cock deep into her mouth. A wave of raw sexual energy washed over her. The lust of the masses shot through her, and she projected it back to the people around them. In that moment the goddess filled her, and she worshipped the god of summer and king of the land with all the fervour and passion due him.

Bern's hips bucked and he tangled his hands in her hair. "God, woman!" he growled as she sucked and licked his hard shaft.

She would have gone on like this until he came, but Bern had other ideas. He pushed her gently away and on to her back on the soft, fragrant pile. He knelt over her, his cock poised at the moist opening of her vagina. He waited while her hips rose pleadingly.

"Now!" she demanded.

But he didn't move until her gaze finally met his. "The night is just beginning," he told her.

Then he entered her, and his worship of the goddess began in earnest

"Ahem."

The embarrassed sound, followed by a second voice demanding, "Cover your shame, woman!" was the last thing Ginger expected to hear.

Besides, she wasn't sure how shame was supposed to be covered, especially when what she felt was marvellous. All right, she was sore and tender in places, and rather hungover, though not in the having-drank-too-much-alcohol way. Who knew too much great sex could make you groggy? Could you have too much great sex?

"Colonel, sir," the embarrassed voice whispered. "Excuse me for waking you up, but—"

"Rouse yourself, man!" the other voice boomed.

Ginger giggled. "Please don't," she murmured. "Not on my account. Not just yet, anyway."

"What? What?" Bern muttered.

She felt his breath brush her cheek when he spoke, and realized that he was the warm weight lying half on top of her. The cool morning breeze skimmed across the rest of her, teasing one bare nipple to a hard peak. Maybe that was the shame the guy was talking about. Was that any way to talk to the goddess' own—

"Is that you, Dr White?"

Ginger's eyes flew open and she caught sight of a familiar, concerned face. "Sergeant Kaye?" Oh, good Lord, she was naked in front of a colleague! She didn't recognize the man standing next to him, but the stranger was frowning down at her with utter disgust written all over his face and tense posture.

"His name's Percy Perkins, and he's a jerk," Bern whispered. He sat up and said, "I hope you brought us some clothes, Kaye."

The sergeant held out the dress Ginger had worn last night, and a long tunic for Bern.

"Of course you realize that I intend to report this infraction," Percy said.

"Infraction of what?" Bern asked. "There's no rule against team members fraternizing."

"You led an orgy! Your disgusting behaviour roused the indigenous population to—"

"He didn't get any, sir," Kaye put in.

Bern scratched his jaw. "I can see how that might make him cranky."

"Not to mention being named Percy," Ginger added. "That alone has to have put the guy in years of therapy. Could you sue your parents for giving you a name like that?" she asked the fuming man. He declined to respond.

"I could use a shave," Bern said. "And a bath." He sprang to his feet and helped Ginger up. "How about you, sweetheart?"

"Definitely."

"Have the team meet us at the bath, Kaye."

She slipped the white dress over her head, and they walked arm in arm across the field towards the villa, frequently stepping over and around still sleeping revellers. Kaye went off to his assignment, and Percy followed behind them, making the occasional disapproving sound. The morning sun shone down, the sky was blue, the earth was green, birds sang, and Ginger was happier than she'd ever been before. They had the blessing of the goddess, she supposed.

They passed the old bishop preaching to a small group of revellers that looked thoroughly hangdog and hungover. Myrdyn gave them a pleasant nod when he saw them.

"We must be good for business," Bern said.

"If he baptizes all those people the energy in the pool is going to be whacked out for days," Ginger said.

"That is hardly a scientific explanation of a malfunction, Dr White," Percy complained.

They ignored him.

Once they reached the bathhouse, Ginger led them into the preparation room where scented oils and scrapers were stored. This was where the oil was used to clean a person's body before they got into the hot water of the bathing pool. Benches lined the walls, and the floor was tiled in a beautiful leaf-patterned mosaic.

"This is where I meant to bring you yesterday," she told Bern.

He pulled her close. They looked into each other's eyes. "It was worth the detour."

"You two are being disgusting," Percy said.

Bern sighed. "You know, this time I think I agree with him." He let her go.

"We do have work to do," she said.

"Do I detect some professionalism at last?"

"Shut up, Percy," Ginger and Bern said together.

"That's an order," Bern added.

Ginger took a seat on a bench against the back wall. Within a few minutes Kaye and the rest of the team joined them. Bern allowed his people a few minutes of teasing him before saying, "This is Gareth and Lamorak."

Ginger smiled. "Of course they are."

He didn't understand what amused her, and didn't ask. "Let's get down to business."

"Now that we have recovered Dr White, it's time to continue surveying the nexus points," Percy said immediately.

"Percy's a dowser," Bern explained to Ginger. "He's working on a new nexus map. But he hasn't yet found a spot with enough energy to get us home."

"It's hardly my fault that this island is swamped with more energy points than anywhere else on the planet, especially in this area. It was a mistake sending a team this far back, and especially to this geographic area."

"Yeah, I think we're all aware of that," Gareth said. "Since you tell us every chance we get."

"We have one more man to find," Lamorak said. "That's our mission."

"Finding the exit point is far more important for our own survival," Percy argued. "We should cut our losses and concentrate on finding a functioning nexus. Perhaps Dr White could conjure up a vision of where we should go," he added snidely.

"What did I ever do to you?" was Ginger's response to this rudeness.

Bern liked that she refused to be intimidated by the jerk. "No one gets left behind," he reminded Percy. "We're still looking for Owen."

"But his transpond—" Percy started.

"What does your gut tell you, sir?" Kaye jumped in. "You found me—"

"Your transponder was working," Percy said, cutting him off.

"Intermittently. It was Colonel Bern's instincts that really found me."

"Balderdash," Percy scoffed.

"Does anyone really say 'balderdash'?" Ginger asked.

"The colonel's gut led us here and we found Dr White," Gareth said. "What do you think about Owen, sir?"

Bern considered for a moment, sensing more than thinking. Finally, he said, "I think that most of the population in the area is camped out around this stronghold. If I was Owen, I'd be here too." He swept his gaze around his team. "Go look for him."

There were nods, and people turned to leave.

Before he left Percy just had to ask, "And what will you be doing while we're searching?"

Bern put his arm around Ginger's shoulders. "I'm going to be standing at the Lady of the White Bird Spring's side while she seeks a vision to help us find a way home."

"Good, Bishop Myrdyn hasn't used the place yet," Ginger said as they entered the empty shrine.

Now she didn't have to regret insisting that they get cleaned up before coming to the spring. Her skin felt fresh and tingly, and all the aches from strenuous bouts of sex were soothed. Her hair hung in a damp braid down her back, and Bern had shaved.

"If only we had coffee, we could face anything," she said.

"Find us the right nexus and I'll buy you your own Starbucks," he replied.

He wouldn't be able to do any such thing of course, even if she could somehow pull the right vision out of the sacred pool. It saddened her to know that she would return to her point of origin, and he would return to his, which was six months further along the main timeline than hers. She would remember what happened, and six months later he'd read a report filed by her, and learn what he'd done in the past. It wouldn't be proper to record their sexual encounters in the official record, even if the dry bureaucratic tone of reports could use spicing up a bit.

"What are you smiling about?" he asked.

"Nothing." She turned her smile briefly on him, and then dropped to her knees. "I doubt this will work," she warned. "I don't normally see anything dealing with my own future."

"You saw me, didn't you?"

"I saw you in response to Lord Ched asking who the next king would be. We need to talk about that," she added.

"No, we don't. As soon as we conclude the search for Owen, I'm taking you and the rest of my people out of here."

"But—"

"Look into the water. Calm yourself. Concentrate."

"I know how to summon the visions, Andrew."

He put his hands on her shoulders and gently began to massage them. He communicated his faith in her through his touch. Damn, but she was going to hate losing this man! She appreciated the moment, refused to feel sorry for herself, and set about doing her duty.

At first, of course, all she saw was a pool of water as still and clear as a looking glass. But the calm, peaceful water changed quickly enough.

Bern grew worried for Ginger when the muscles beneath his fingers went suddenly tense. "What?" he asked. "What do you see?"

"Fire," she answered, voice distant and dull. "Fire on the hill."

"What hill? What's burning?"

"There's a battle," she said. "You have to defeat them. It's your destiny."

He didn't like the sound of that. "What does any of that have to do with getting you safely home?"

Lord Ched came running into the sanctuary before she could respond. "They're coming!" he shouted. "The Saxons are coming." A guard followed him in, pushing a woman ahead of him. Ched looked at the woman. "Tell him," he commanded.

The woman was crying. "Mercy, my lord! I did come back to warn you."

"Yes, yes," the chieftain said. He pointed to Bern. "Tell the king what you told me."

Everybody looked at him. Bern wanted to yell at them to cut out the calling-him-king crap, but even Ginger had come out of her trance and was looking at him like he was the hero of the hour. And, damn it, the thought of disappointing her made him feel like a jerk. He gritted his teeth, and nodded for the woman to go on.

"It's true I helped my lady Morga and her man escape. I've taken care of the girl all her life, and I understood how she'd been with the last year king long enough to think of him as her husband and not want to bed a new man." She looked Bern over. "Though I think she would have gotten the better of the bargain had she stayed and done her duty."

"Get on to the important part," the chieftain urged.

"The pair of them were angry and affronted at being forced to run from their home. After we made camp last night they talked about how they would betray the secrets of the stronghold's defences to the Saxons."

Ched rubbed the back of his neck. "But that is the secret – we have no defences."

"The invaders weren't aware of how weak we are," the guard said. "They'll march straight for us now."

"They will be here soon," the woman said. "I had to come back to warn my people that their doom approaches."

Bern wished she hadn't put it like that. It made him feel sorry for the indigenous population. Even worse, the way they all looked to him to take command made him feel responsible for them. These people were going to be easy pickings without some help. Bern thought of all the defenceless people camped out around the stronghold. They'd come here for a religious celebration, not to be slaughtered.

"How will you defend us?" Lord Ched asked him.

Ginger came forwards and put her hand on his arm. "I was studying the pool for advice on that very subject when you arrived. If you would let us continue with the divination the king will meet with you afterwards, better prepared to save his people."

The chieftain and his people left without another word.

When they were alone, Ginger grabbed hold of the front of his tunic, held on tight, and talked fast. "Now you listen to me, Colonel Bern. I will not have you quoting rules and regs about non-interference and the possibility of changing history. We don't have any solid history of this era to go on. But we do have myths and legends, and, hon, I think I know what's going on here. You have to fight the invaders. You. You are the element necessary to slow down the incursions and give the native culture more time to recover from Roman rule. That way, when the Saxons do take over it'll be overlaying a British-based culture rather than a Roman one. In our time we'll have England the way we know it, but we won't if you don't take on the invaders here and now. You were meant to do this."

Bern gaped at her. "What the hell are you talking about? What makes me special?"

"You said it yourself, last night, 'at least I don't have to pull it out of a stone'. You pulled the sword from the soil of Britain and claimed the kingship. You are—"

"Don't you dare put that on me." He'd finally gotten where this was going.

"Bern means 'bear'," she went on. "One of the translations of—"

"No."

"And then there are your men's names. There's Kaye and—"

"You've been drinking that spring water as well as looking into it, haven't you?" His tone was harsh, but his instincts were shouting at him that she was right.

He knew he'd hurt her feelings, but they were interrupted once again. This time it was the rest of the team that came into the sanctuary.

"Look who we found, boss!" Kaye crowed. "Your gut was right again."

"Stop looking smug," he ordered Ginger before he said to the newcomer, "Welcome to your rescue, Professor Owen."

"I'm grateful the Project sent a team for us." He gave Ginger a nod and smile. She smiled back. "And if rumour is correct, you've come to the rescue just in the nick of time."

"We've heard that the Saxons are heading this way," Kaye said. "Time for us to bug out, right?"

Bern waited for Ginger to protest, but she crossed her arms and bit her lower lip instead of nagging him. Damn it! That made it even harder for him to say no to her.

"I took an oath to protect these people last night," he told the team. "The least we can do is give the locals a chance at getting away."

"What precisely to you mean by 'we'?" Percy spoke up. "At no point do I recall having signed a social contract with these people. Going native is not one of our options."

"What's wrong with helping people?" Owen demanded. "The locals have helped me survive for months. I owe them."

"So do I," Ginger said.

"Very touching, but irrelevant," Percy responded.

"You are such a wuss," Gareth said. "Come on, fighting a bunch of barbarians will be fun."

"No it won't," Bern said sternly. "And don't make the

assumption that I'm asking for a consensus, or volunteers. This is a military operation, and I'm in command."

His soldiers immediately snapped to attention, and he nodded to them. Percy didn't look happy, but at least this finally shut him up. Bern glanced at Ginger. She was looking at him with enough pride in her eyes to set his heart on fire. She made him feel like a hero. This wasn't the time to kiss her all over the way he wanted to, but he did put his arm around her waist and draw her close.

As they stood, hip to hip, he said, "Remember the hillside we crossed on the way here?" There were nods. "We're going to set up our perimeter there. It's time to break out the claymores, boys."

Ginger gave him a puzzled look, but her expression cleared before he could explain. "Oh, you're not talking about big Scottish swords, are you?"

"No, hon, I'm talking about things that blow up."

"Fire in the sky," she said. "Just what the vision showed me."

This had better work, Ginger thought. She hugged herself tightly. Please God let it work. And don't let anything happen to him – or any of the good guys – while you're at it. Please Lady, she added, since she was officially a priestess of the goddess.

Well, maybe not officially any more since soon she'd be leaving Lord Ched's villa forever. She was standing in the woods at the source of the spring with a bundle of provisions at her feet, waiting for the rest of the team to join her. The plan was for her to wait safely out of the way while the men carried out the op. Bern had insisted she stay out of harm's way, and she hadn't argued. She was no warrior.

Some of the other women had taken up arms to fight alongside their men after Bern gave a rousing speech to the gathered pilgrims. This was the ancient way of the Celts, and more proof as far as Ginger was concerned that this battle was going to slow the tide of invasion. The people were eager to follow Bern into battle. Their willingness to defend their homeland was a good sign, too. Right?

Please Horned God and Lady of the Spring, don't let me have started something that's going to get a lot of people killed. Especially not Bern.

She reminded herself that he was a competent professional soldier. He had a good strategy. He had explosives. He was going to win the day.

The plan for the TTP team was that after the battle was joined, and the good guys were winning, they'd withdraw and join Ginger in the woods. With their obligation to help the people fulfilled, the team could then continue their search for a working nexus that would take them home.

Home. Away from Bern. She dashed away tears. It had to be. If she went home with a broken heart and a deep ache for the way he made her body sing, she still had the memories to appreciate. At least they'd spent as much time as they could in the three days making love while waiting for the Saxons. And now the Saxons were here.

Ginger paced nervously. What if it didn't work? Was there something she could do to help?

She hated the quiet here in the woods. Maybe she was safer here, but the sudden need to know what was going on got the better of her. She cut through the woods rather than take the path that led towards the villa.

The perfect spring of the festival had been replaced by a pewter sky that threatened rain, and a wind that blew cooler than it should for this time of year. It was a grim day, fit for a battle, she supposed.

When she reached the south edge of the woods she got a good view down the valley to the hill beyond. Half of the British fighters were spread out below the hill, waiting there instead of occupying the high ground. She caught sight of chain mail and sword blades as grey as the day and the energy mixture of fear and anticipation hit her like a blow. She put herself behind a tree and waited, and watched.

The atmosphere grew even more tense, thunder rumbled in the distance, and very soon a large band of warriors appeared on the crest of the hill. They saw the Britons waiting for them and drew to a halt. More of the invaders came up behind them, and more, until there was an army of several hundred fierce barbarians looking down upon the several dozen not-quite-so-fierce barbarians below. The Saxons formed into a long line that stretched out along the top of the hill, but since they held the high ground they didn't seem to be in any hurry to rush the people below.

Which was what Bern had counted on.

A line of claymore mines had been set right where the Saxons were now standing. When the mines went off there was indeed fire bursting up towards the sky. And screaming, and blood, and flying body parts.

What was left of the Saxon invaders turned to flee, but that could not be allowed. Bern's team and the other half of the British force came out of hiding in the woods on the far side of the hill and drove the remainder of the Saxons down the hill on to the swords of those waiting there.

The reality was so much worse than her vision, but she never doubted the necessity of this battle. Ginger watched the carnage long enough to be assured that everything was going to turn out as planned. There was a victory here today at Camlan Hill. Legend would speak of magic making the very soil of Britain gape wide to send the enemy to the fires of hell.

Only witnessing it must have upset her more than she realized because she got lost in the thick woods making her way back to the spring. By the time she found her way to the rendezvous point it had started to rain. Bern and the team were waiting for her. They'd brought horses with them.

Bern stopped pacing and pulled her roughly to him by the elbows. "Where have you been, woman?"

She was so happy to see him that she kissed him. His hands kneaded her back and buttocks with forceful swiftness that told her that he'd been as worried about her as she was him. She began to cry with relief, and was glad to have the rain to cover this excess of emotion.

Except she knew it didn't work when he kissed her cheeks and said, "You taste salty."

"And you smell sweaty," she complained. "Let's get out of here."

He kept his arms around her when she would have gone for her pack. "But where do we go from here?" He glanced towards Percy.

The subject had been under discussion for days. The problem with this area was an overabundance of sites where energy concentrated. Ginger had stayed out of it, because she didn't want to be dismissed out of hand as a total loon. Now she had to speak up.

"We need to go to the Isle of Apples," she told them.

"Where's that?" Bern asked.

Gareth laughed. "So, I'm not the only one who's seen the parallels."

Kaye nodded thoughtfully.

Maybe she should have spoken up sooner.

Percy pulled a handheld computer out of a leather pouch on his belt. He checked a map screen and then frowned at her. "I've worked out the search grid very carefully. There's no reason to deviate from—"

"Where is this Apple Island?" Bern asked.

"Isle of Apples," Ginger corrected. She cleared her throat, took a deep breath, and made herself publicly say, "Avalon."

"Oh, for crying out loud!" Percy yelled in disgust.

She didn't blame him. "I admit it might seem a little far-fetched."

"A little?" He sneered. "Living among these people has made you as superstitious as they are. You've come to accept their mythology as—"

"It's not one of the local myths," Gareth said. "Not yet, anyway. It is one of our myths. Following it might lead us home."

"Gambling on what might happen is not a scientific or logical basis for finding the correct nexus," Percy argued.

Bern rubbed his jaw and chuckled. "Might doesn't always make right. I just remembered where that came from. But where is Avalon? Hasn't that always been a mystery?"

"It doesn't exist. You're not going along with this, are you, Colonel?" Percy demanded. He pointed accusingly at Ginger. "Why? Because she's good in bed?"

Ginger was rather pleased that several team members stepped forwards, but Bern got to Percy first, and punched him in the jaw. Percy hit the wet ground, and was wise enough to stay down. He sat in the mud, rubbed his jaw and kept his mouth shut.

"So, where do we go?" Bern asked her.

"Tradition points to Glastonbury," she answered.

"There's a nexus on top of that big hill there?" he asked.

She shook her head, and glanced at Percy. "Not on top of the tor, right?" He grimaced, but nodded. "There's a sacred spring called Chalice Well at the foot of Glastonbury Tor. I think that's where we have to go."

"Let's do it. Mount up," Bern ordered the team. "We need to get out of here before the locals come looking for us so they can throw a feast in our honour."

As the men moved to mount their animals, he snatched Ginger around the waist and put her up on the horse in front of him. She snuggled back against him, and he wrapped his cape around both of them. In this warm, intimate position he leaned forwards to whisper, "Being like this with you almost makes me like riding a horse."

She tilted her head against his shoulder, determined to draw every bit of nearness to him she could in the time they had left. "Then let's enjoy the ride."

*   *   *

"I don't believe it," Percy said. He double-checked his equipment as the water of the Glastonbury spring bubbled up at his feet. Then he gave Ginger a sour look. "She's right."

"The energy reading is right?" Kaye asked.

"It's off the scale," Percy answered.

"Enough to take both teams home?" Owen asked.

"Jump in and find out," Percy invited. He glanced around the green and lovely glade. "Before the priestesses we chased off come back."

"With an angry mob," Kaye added.

If at all possible TTP operatives were supposed to appear and vanish without any witnesses around. Scaring the locals with the sound and light show that accompanied time travel was considered not only impolite, but possibly dangerous to the primary time line TTP visits wove in and out of. And the problem with places like sacred springs as nexus points was that the places tended to be occupied with priests and pilgrims and such like. So, Bern had had his people approach this one with swords drawn and chase everyone away. Percy was right about their not having much time for goodbyes.

"Form up into teams," he said. He took Ginger's hand before she could join the people she'd travelled into the past with. He drew her away from the spring and tilted her chin up with his fingers. "You are so beautiful," he told her.

"In a pale, freckled sort of way," she answered. She tried to sound light, but her voice came out tight and strained.

"I'll miss you, Dr Virginia White." Words couldn't begin to describe what this was doing to him.

"Have I thanked you for rescuing me, yet?" she asked. She gave him a brief, hard embrace. "It's been a pleasure knowing you, Colonel Andrew Bern."

He kissed her then. It was hard and quick, and not enough. He ran the back of his hand across her cheek. "Hey, we made history."

"Or something like it."

He nodded, and his throat was too tight for him to manage to say more than, "Go."

She gave him a sad smile, and went over to join Kaye and Owen who were already standing in the spring's shallow pool. They each placed their left thumbs over the inside of their right wrists. Ginger's gaze didn't leave his.

"On my mark," Kaye said. "Activate."

Everyone pressed down hard on the retrieval implant.

The column of light that sprang from the water blinded him. The roar of the shock wave was deafening. Bern refused to look away. The last thing he saw was Ginger's face as she whispered, "Goodbye."

Ginger looked up from the photo before her on the desk, and sighed. A copper bowl filled with water sat on the desk, but she wasn't interested in looking into it. Being a psychic wasn't as much fun for her as it used to be. It had been six months since she'd got back to her own time. Six months and three days to be precise, not that she was counting. She'd done the debriefing and written up her report, and been sent back to her regular life until such time as the TTP deemed her special skills necessary again. For now her regular life consisted of working with law enforcement on cold case files, and being alone.

She sighed again, and stood up. It wasn't that she didn't appreciate being back. She loved her house and garden. She loved central heating and modern medicine and interactive holographic entertainment and regular meals of anything she wanted. She hadn't realized how much she'd missed shopping for shoes until she'd entered her first mall. She loved being home. It was just that . . .

She missed Bern.

Her body ached for him when she was alone in her bed at night, but the notion of taking another lover was anathema. Even trying a holo lover hadn't worked for her.

She got up and began to pace around her office. She was well aware that Bern had returned to the present three days before, and even more aware that it didn't matter. Maybe there was some way that she could introduce herself to him, but how fair would it be to him when she knew their past and he didn't? There was no way for them to pick up where they'd left off. There was a good chance he wouldn't even be interested in her under normal circumstances. Maybe she wouldn't be interested in him.

She laughed hollowly, still conscious of the ecstasy he'd brought her when his body joined with hers. "Yeah, right, sure I'm going to forget that."

Then again, she really wanted the man, why shouldn't she fight for what she wanted? She should find a way to introduce herself and see what—

"There is someone at the door," the house's security system announced. It was an old house with a very basic system, so it wasn't about to be more informative than that. So, unless the water in the scrying bowl suddenly showed her who it was – which it wasn't likely to do – she had to answer the door herself. A visitor, even someone looking to get their future read without an appointment, was better than pacing around feeling sorry for herself.

The man standing at the door was the last person she expected to be there. And the one person in all of space and time she wanted to see.

"Bern!"

He kissed her before she could say anything else. The fire that had been between them from the first moment sparked between them again. She clung to him with all her might, her body moulded against his. If he'd taken her there on the front porch she wouldn't have minded. Instead he swung her around into the house, and kicked the door closed behind them. They fell together on to the entryway carpet and clothes were quickly shed and pushed aside.

He was thrusting inside her, hard and strong and fast, before she managed to breathlessly say, "You remembered me!" Then she came for the first time and forgot about words for a long time afterwards.

"Of course I remembered," he said later, when they were lying together in a sweaty tangled heap. "You're unforgettable."

She stroked his cheek. "Oh, that's sweet . . . wait a minute . . . that means you're psychic."

He nodded.

"I thought Percy was your team psychic."

"He was, on the civilian side. The military side always tries to have someone who'll remember the op on a TTP team."

"Really? I didn't know that."

"That's because that information is on a need-to-know basis. This seems like a good time for you to need to know."

"Now I understand why Kaye kept talking about your gut feelings. I should have guessed he meant your psychic intuition."

"You should have guessed when we went for each other like we were in heat instantly. That kind of lust only comes when like meets like."

"So I've heard. Hey, the lust had me pretty distracted. That and starring in orgies and fighting the Saxons and that whole Matter of Britain thing we had going."

He sighed. "Matter of Britain, my ass."

She stroked his. "It's a very nice ass. I have a nice, big bed upstairs," she told him.

He licked and sucked her nipples for a while then he helped her to her feet, even though she groaned in protest when he stopped touching her breasts. "I'd be delighted to spend as much time as possible in your nice, big bed."

"Good."

"But first," he added, "I did come here to ask if you'd like to go on a date this evening. I've got tickets for a revival of an old musical I think you'll enjoy."

Curiosity nibbled away some of her lust. "What play would that be?"

He grinned. "Spamalot."

She hooted, and they held each other tight, shaking with laughter. What other production could possibly be more perfect for their first date?

Crimean Fairy Tale

Victoria Janssen

The Crimean Peninsula – 1854

Private Jonas Weston survived Balaclava without a scratch, then things got worse. He emerged from the brutal battle at Inkerman Heights with a shallow lance wound over a broken rib, bad dreams and hands that would never quite stop shaking. Three nights after the battle, when he'd once again woken screaming, Sergeant Jennings told him, "I've a certain cure for the shakes, lad."

Weston took another swig of coarse arrack and coughed into the embers of their shared campfire. It tasted miles worse than rum, but was thankfully stronger, and it helped numb the sharp pain in his side. If only he could get enough to make him sleep. He feared there wasn't enough in the world. "Need more of this," he said, shaking the flask.

"Not a bit of it. You need to dock a bobtail." In a conspiratorial tone, he added, "So long as you don't get yourself the crinkums, docking'll put you right. Keep your eyes open for shankers or blue boars in her notch; those're sure sign she's a fire ship and you'd be pissing pins and needles before a fortnight was out."

Private Dunn, who rarely said anything, piped up in agreement, nodding his head all the while. "Plenty of laced mutton here for no more'n tuppence. A healthy fuck's the best thing for nerves. My dad told me so."

Conversation erupted about the merits or otherwise of tossing off as opposed to tupping, and whether a threepenny upright was more or less likely to tip a man the token.

Weston wasn't much for women. He'd tupped a few, but only if his friends had talked him into it first, and then he had to get over worrying he would hurt the woman somehow with his big hands and big body. It felt wonderful if she encouraged him and he got going; he liked tupping because who wouldn't, but afterwards he always felt low for days.

His mother bore him out of wedlock, having been taken against her will, and though she'd never made him suffer for it in her short life thereafter, he'd never forgotten either. Even though they were paid and his mother had not been, he could never help wondering about the whores: what they thought about what they were doing, and if they really enjoyed it or were only pretending. If he'd had one, afterwards he would wonder if he was like his father had been, and that made him feel even sicker, even though he tried everything he knew not to get them with child.

It was an especially odd feeling because his father had another son, a legitimate one, serving as lieutenant of Hussars. Weston had even seen him, from a distance. He doubted the boy knew of his existence, and he certainly wished he didn't know of the boy's.

Aside from all that, Weston didn't like the risks of whoring – he thought most men were mad to risk being burned or poxed on a regular basis, and been called a cockquean because of his opinion – but Jennings had as good as ordered him, hadn't he? And, truth be told, he was like to die in the next few months, anyway, if the war continued as it had. He'd already escaped heatstroke and cholera, both of which had killed dozens of his mates before they'd even come near a Russian gun.

The thought of hiding his face in a woman's soft bosom made him shake even more, with longing. He'd forget then. Forget that after running out of bullets and losing his bayonet in a Cossack's ribcage, he'd beaten men's faces to pulp with his rifle butt. The stink of their blood and bowels wouldn't leave him, and he would catch himself looking at his hands to see if they were still gored.

He'd find a woman, hopefully a clean one, and then he'd forget it all for a bit and be as right as rain.

The wives and sutlers camped closest to the soldiers, followed by cooks, seamstresses, and laundresses. Clutching his greatcoat around him against the November chill, Weston weaved his way among wagons with chocked wheels, tents, campfires, pitiful attempts at vegetable gardens, coppers of boiling water. The cold had hardened the ever-present mud underfoot, but only a little. Everywhere were women, grubby children, and the occasional old man, hard at work. The women watched him as he passed, some warily, one or two with either undisguised interest or undisguised contempt. Either they knew where he was going and disapproved, or they didn't like his dark skin. He'd been asked more than once if he was a Turk, when in fact he was the cast-off bastard of a viscount. His mother had been his father's slave, from his sugar plantation in the West Indies; she'd died not long after she'd been emancipated.

The whores lived on the edges of the camp, most of them in shabby tents they'd made from army discards. Few had made any attempt to cheer up their muddy surroundings with gardens; the most decorative items Jonas saw were petticoats and chemises hung to dry and fluttering in the chilly breeze. He could hear distinctive sounds through the thin walls of one of the closer tents and, a few hundred feet away, caught a glimpse of a red coat as another soldier ducked into a tent.

He hadn't ventured far into their territory when several women converged on him, all talking at once and tugging his arms and the front of his coat. He didn't like this much but was too ashamed to protest, for fear his distaste would result in their mockery. "My, my," said a woman with bubbies like melons. "I'll dab it up with you for a smile. Or how about a couple tots of rum? All the jam tart you want, for a couple tots of rum."

'I've not seen you before, me fine cocksman," said a thin woman with a pointed chin. "Give my Lady Laycock a knock and your eyes'll cross until you see your own nancy."

A woman with greying hair grabbed his arm. "A lusty strong boy you are," she said. "Just what I need, after that lazy lobcock I had today. Want a hot buttered bun, laddie?"

Jonas didn't reply, but he looked at all of them, in search of a friendly countenance and one that was, hopefully, free of disease. Loitering behind the others was a little woman in a threadbare sparrow-coloured dress that buttoned up to her throat, with a thick wool shawl thrown over all. She was darker than the rest, her skin a warm brown that caught his eye and held it. Her hair, severely pulled back, looked thick and it curled around her neck. He wanted to touch it. Her face looked calm and smooth, her cheeks ruddy from cold and not from drink. She was watching him intently.

He had the feeling he'd seen her before, perhaps elsewhere in the camp. Not with one of the other men, he would have remembered that. Perhaps she worked at more than one job, and he'd seen her passing. Jonas wriggled free of grasping hands and called out, "What's your name?"

She sidled up next to him with the ease of long practice and said, "Betsy, love." Close to, he could see the shape of her nose and the soft curve of her lush lips. She was coloured, like him. His heart jolted. She snaked one arm around his waist and said, in a much softer voice, "Come along with me and I'll take care with your ribs." She smiled at him.

She must have seen him wince away from too importunate hands. "I'm Weston," he said. He breathed in deeply. She'd washed recently, and used something flowery on her hair. Her hand was gentle on his hip. It was enough.

Betsy's tent was on the outskirts even of the whores' camp, nearly to the mule pickets. She took his hand and drew him inside. It didn't hold anything but a pallet and a little jumble of miscellany that looked like clock parts, or . . . he wasn't sure. He'd never seen anything like it before in his life. Was it some kind of luck charm? Or . . . Heat rose in his cheeks. It was probably some kind of sex implement. He couldn't imagine to what use it could be put, and he wasn't sure he wanted to know. A moment later, though, he'd forgotten about the jumble because she was pushing his greatcoat off his shoulders and unfastening the stock at his throat before pressing a kiss against his skin. He hadn't even managed to get his coins out of his pocket yet.

Just that one touch of her full lips set him trembling all over. She was such a little woman she couldn't reach higher than his throat. He resisted the urge to just lift her up in his arms, and instead pushed her away. "I want your clothes off," he said. "Please." Wincing, he got his greatcoat the rest of the way off, then his belts and uniform coat.

It wasn't usual to unrig, but she didn't protest, even though it was cold in the tent. "Let me help you with your boots," she said.

Once he was naked, he took his time undressing her, kneeling first on her pallet to ease off her muddy half-boots and heavy woollen stockings. Her legs were long for her height, long enough to wrap around a man, long enough to hook over his shoulders and squeeze his ears. She didn't wear a corset under her gown, only a soft bodice that revealed more than it concealed, softness he could almost feel melting beneath his tongue. He shook harder as he got her last layers off, petticoats and much-mended chemise, no pantaloons; shaking not so much from cold but from the feel of her soft hands when she laid them on his bare skin; shaking from his need to cover her with his body and make her cry out for him.

When they were stretched out on the pallet together, snuggled close together beneath her blankets, he didn't do anything for a few moments but curl around her, his leg hooked over hers, his arms around her waist, his face buried in her loosened hair. Her curls tickled his cheek.

She said, "What do you want, soldier? Want me to take you in my mouth?" Her hand trailed lightly over his bandaged ribs, then gripped his naked hip, her nail caressing the thin skin over the bone.

"Weston," he said. "Use my name, Betsy."

"Weston then."

"I don't want that," he said.

"Do you want—" She stopped when he stroked her back, shoulders to softly cushioned arse.

"Hush," he said. Slowly, he warmed up and his trembling eased. He was taking too long with her, he knew that, but she didn't protest. He would pay extra, later, to make it up to her. Right now, he needed this. He needed to hold someone.

After a few minutes, he felt her relaxing against him, the cushiony weight of her small breasts easing against his chest, the shape of her nipples like fruit pips, only sweeter. He eased himself free of her embrace and slid lower to kiss her breasts and fondle her delicious little nipples, feeling something ease in him as she sighed and touched his shoulders. He slid lower still, pulling the blanket over his head so she wouldn't be left in the cold.

"Weston . . ."

He didn't think she was protesting, or not seriously. When he set to kissing her belly and thighs, another sigh eased out of her and her hands found his hair. Her fingers tangled in his curls, gently pulling and rubbing his scalp. She was going to let him take care of her. He closed his eyes, gripped her hips in his hands, and kissed her velvety skin until he could smell nothing but her arousal, rising around him like a fog; then he nuzzled through the hair covering her pussy. Her breath went ragged. He thumbed her lips open and blindly learned the shape of her inner creases with the tip of his tongue.

"You shouldn't," she said. "You shouldn't – you're not meant to . . ." Her voice trailed off in a small cry.

He pressed his lips tightly to her little knob and suckled. Her desperate sounds, her uncontrolled movements, flowed over him like the warmest summer wind. He brought her to her crisis, then stroked her down from it. She said, "Why are you . . . You don't have to . . ." but stopped when he eased his fingertip inside her cunny and licked across her little knob once more before closing his lips tight around it and sucking. He brought her back up to climax again, and again, until she sobbed with the pleasure of it, until she slid into sleep beneath his hands and mouth.

Only then did he pillow his cheek on her breasts, the tension sighing out of him. She breathed deeply, evenly, her hand slack on his shoulder. He dared to kiss her skin, softly so as not to wake her or leave a mark. Then he rested, until his own exhaustion forced him into sleep with her. He didn't dream.

She woke him, later, when it was dark, and he was momentarily afraid she meant to send him away post-haste. "Let me return the favour," she said next to his ear, and he relaxed. Her fingers traced his cheekbone, and he turned his head to kiss her hand. "You gave me such delight. I've skill with my mouth. I'd share it with you."

He was painfully hard and her breath on his ear sent warmth down to the ends of his toes. "Will you kiss me first?" he asked. "Please?"

She sat up. Before he could despair, she bent over him and feathered her mouth over his. His lips parted on a sigh. "One more?" he asked. The words had barely escaped him when she kissed him again, introducing his tongue to hers. He followed her when she would have retreated, sucking at her lower lip and stealing one last taste from inside her mouth. "Thank you," he said.

She didn't reply, and he wondered if she was angry that he'd overstepped. She ran her nails down his chest and belly, teasing him until his skin tightened all over his body. He touched her hair, threading his fingers through her thick curls. When her hot mouth closed over his cock, he gave himself up to her and the rising pleasure she drew from him. He could only last so long against her teasing tongue and wet lips. He lost control abruptly, with a hoarse cry, and came into her mouth.

Once more she didn't send him away. Perhaps she didn't like sleeping cold, either. Weston wasn't about to complain. He spooned up against her back and slept.

He woke, once. Not from a bad dream this time. Perhaps he'd heard a cry from one of the other tents. He stroked Betsy's cheek with his fingers. "So soft," he whispered, in wonderment. He wished he could see her, see his brown fingers against her brown cheek. He'd never been with a woman of his own colour before, and had never realized how beautiful she would be to his eyes. He'd be happy to look at such a woman for the rest of his life.

Her eyes opened. It was too dark to see, but he knew she was awake and watching him. It was like a warm touch on his face. He ran his thumb over her mouth. "Must I leave?" he asked. He didn't want to ask, but she might be afraid to ask it of him.

She smiled. He felt her lips curve beneath his fingers. "I've no desire to wander this cold night in search of custom," she said. "You're a lovely warm man, Private Weston."

He could feel her breath on his mouth. He cupped her cheek in his palm and used his other arm to draw her closer, curving his hand over her plush round arse. He wasn't much of a talker, but he wanted to talk to her. "Haven't been so warm in weeks," he said. It was the truth.

"I've never been so warm," she said. "You surprised me, you know."

"I did?" He stroked her bottom, trailing his fingers this way and that, for the pleasure of her softness against his own coarse callouses.

"Aye, you did. A paying customer tipping the velvet?"

He hadn't paid her yet, nor had she asked him to pay. She shifted a little, into his touch. Encouraged, he found the little dimples above her arse with his thumb, circled his hand on the small of her back, then down again, finding where her arse curved into her thigh. "Never touched anything so soft."

"I'm no more so than any other woman," she said, nuzzling his throat.

"You are," he said. "You tasted sweet, too. Sweeter than rum. Sweeter than sugar candy when you smiled at me."

She was silent for a long time. Twice, he felt her lips open against his throat, but close again before she spoke. She hadn't tensed or drawn away, but he could still sense that she wasn't as close as she'd been a few moments before.

He shouldn't have said that she was sweet. She might not like to hear his thoughts. He'd done it because he hadn't thought first, and because, he realized, he didn't want her to think of him as just another customer. It was ridiculous for him to feel that way; he'd just met her that day, and they hadn't even fucked properly. But he couldn't help how he felt. They had a connection he'd never felt to any woman before.

He certainly couldn't say that to her. For her sake, he changed the subject, at least a little. "Did you like it?"

"Hmmm?"

She sounded sleepy. Her muscles were too tense for her to be truly falling asleep. He rubbed his hands up and down her back, soothing and warming at once. He asked, "Did you like what I did for you?"

"You know I did," she said. Now she sounded cross, and for some reason that made him smile.

"I liked it, too," he said, truth but also pushing just a little, to see what she'd say.

"I should hope *so*," she said.

It should have made him jealous to be reminded she was a professional, but instead it made him laugh.

She slapped her hand on his chest, not hard enough to sting. "Stop that."

"What for?" He couldn't remember the last time he'd laughed. He growled and nipped at her throat, wiggling his fingers against her soft belly until she shrieked and squirmed away.

"You're mad!" she said. She'd begun laughing, too.

Once they'd quieted, he said, softly, "I must be."

Betsy crawled atop him, sprawling along his length like a blanket. "Does this hurt? Your ribs, I mean."

"Not a bit of it," he said. He put his hands on her hips and moved her a little. Now it was mostly true.

"Fancy another go?" she asked. "No charge." She fondled his prick, already half hard from their play.

"Don't know," he said. "Will you be gentle with me?"

"Do you want me to be?"

He reached up, wincing as his muscles pulled against his injuries. Luckily, it was dark and she wouldn't be able to see his expression. Her breasts were right where he'd expected them to be. They nestled into his palms and he squeezed them gently, lifted their round weight, swept his thumbs over her nipples until they tightened and her breathing changed. "Depends," he said.

"What do you mean?" she asked. She shivered. Before he could comment, she leaned to the side and he felt the fringes of her shawl brush his skin, as she draped it around her bare shoulders.

"Do *you* want another go?" he asked.

"How am I supposed to give you an answer to that?" she said.

"Would you like it?" he asked. "For you."

"You can't ask me questions like that," she said, cross again. "I offered myself to you, didn't I?"

"I'm sorry," he said, suddenly ashamed. He let go of her breasts, letting his hands fall to the pallet. Of course she couldn't tell him how she truly felt. Her livelihood depended on giving pleasure. It wasn't fair for him to ask her a question like that when he'd given – or would give – her money for what they'd done.

Men paid for their wives, it was true. They bought them clothes and housed them and fed them. How was that different?

It was respectable, that was how. Only a bastard like him would think maybe it was otherwise.

He said, "You don't have to. You pleased me right well."

She didn't speak or move for a long time. He waited for her to climb off him and send him away. Then she squeezed his hips between her thighs. "I want to," she said.

Her clever hands captured his cock, stroking him in tandem until he was as hard as stone. She enveloped his erection with her cunny in one long, luscious slide; they both groaned, and his fingers locked on her hips, holding on as she leaned forwards and rode him, grinding her little knob against him with each stroke.

Her cunny's suck and pull was even sweeter than her mouth. She made him feel safe, protected inside her body, even though he knew that wasn't true.

He didn't mind when her nails scratched his belly, accidentally drawing blood. He might still feel that scratch tomorrow, and it was as nothing to the wound on his ribs. He concentrated on the sting as long as he could, and the brush of her shawl against his skin, the scent of their combined sweat, any sensation not belonging to his cock as he tried not to climax, not to let this end. He almost lost control when she came, her cunny clenching desperately at his cock, but he thought of the cold and managed to hold off for a few precious seconds.

She started to ride him again, panting now, her fingers for sure leaving bruises. He dug his fingers into the muscles atop her thighs, encouraging her rocking motion, groaning deeply each time she ground forwards against him. He fumbled higher, found her breasts again, pulling and pinching more roughly than he had before. She rewarded him with cries that grew faster and louder, matching the increasing speed of her riding, then shattering into weak cries that told him she'd climaxed once more.

At her sounds, he could no longer stop himself from thrusting his hips. His rib stabbed him with pain each time, but his senses were so confused it felt like hot pleasure instead, and moments later he was spending in great spurts, every last ounce of fear and pain ripped loose from him, body and soul.

As they lay nestled together afterwards, she murmured, "Thank you. No one ever . . ."

She didn't finish her sentence. He waited for a long time, but she only turned her face into his chest. He tightened his arm around her and closed his eyes, listening to her breathe. For tonight, at least, he could keep someone safe.

This time, he didn't wake until sunlight filtered through a weak spot in the canvas above his head.

It was morning. She was gone, and he still hadn't paid her. He dressed and she didn't return. She'd taken the machine with her; he tried not to think about what she might be doing. A horrible fear rose in his throat that he'd offended her somehow. He waited as long as he could, but she still didn't return.

He left coins hidden beneath her pallet, all the shillings he had, and returned to camp. He was due for guard duty.

He tried to find her again, the next three times he was free, but she was never in her tent or anywhere in the vicinity. He feared she was avoiding him. One of the other women told him she wasn't often seen. "Pretty thing like her, probably hunts among the officers," she said, wisely. Weston supposed he ought to be happy for her, because maybe an officer could afford to keep her in style. Jealousy had no place in his feelings. She wasn't his, much as he wished she could be.

On his last visit, the whore with the huge bubbies finally took pity on him, and told him Betsy had taken up with a lieutenant of Hussars, describing the boy's uniform down to the last button. "A blue blood, even," she said. "How's about that rum now, lad?"

Betsy wouldn't even know she'd taken up with his half-brother. He couldn't be angry with her. But for the first time, he felt angry with the brother he'd never met, and experienced an unreasoning, clotted hatred for the father who'd abused his mother and done nothing for him.

The winter that followed struck the regiment hard. A terrible November storm destroyed the largest part of their supplies, blowing away tents and all their contents, blankets and clothing and even tables and chairs. Wagons were barely held to earth by the weight of the bellowing bullocks harnessed to them; the *Prince* and the *Resolute* and many more were sunk in the harbour. Weston was lucky to retain his clothing, as he was wearing most of it.

After the hurricane, he slipped away in the confusion and couldn't help himself, he went in search of Betsy, to see how she'd fared. He was unable to locate her, even when enquiring of the officers' servants. So far as he could tell, she wasn't with his half-brother any more, not that he'd had any evidence in the first place that she'd become the boy's convenient.

The whores to whom he spoke seemed sure Betsy wasn't dead, but none of them would tell him where she'd gone. Their looks at him were pitying. He hoped that meant she'd found another protector, someone with a roof to put over her head, maybe even away from this cursed Russian shore.

Soon his mind was taken over with more pressing concerns after an inflammation of the lungs brought him low. He wasn't surprised to finally fall ill. There'd been nothing to eat for a month but scant rations of salt pork, and everyone tried to sleep in the freezing open air, some without blankets; he was lucky to sleep for three hours in total.

Once he dreamed that his father came for him, raised him up from the ranks and took him to a house with a roaring fire. Betsy waited for him there, dressed in a fine gown with a jewelled pin at her throat, her hair dressed like ladies he'd seen shopping along the streets of London. Somehow he knew, in this dream, his brother had been cast off to wander and starve.

Weston woke shaking from that dream, which was as bad in its way as his dreams of killing.

The days blurred into constant numb cold, bouts of fever that were all he remembered of warmth, and ripping pain as he futilely tried to clear his chest. Weeks passed in this fashion. Men and animals died every day, frozen or starved or bayoneted while they slept in a trench.

Weston never remembered quite how he ended up in one of the hospital bell tents. Damp, chill wind wormed through the tent's seams and crept beneath. The stale hay on which he'd been laid did little to insulate him from the icy mud, and the blanket atop his shaking form did nothing but trap the sweat from his last bout of fever. His head reverberated with pain and his eyes burned; his throat felt like to crack from dryness. He couldn't feel his feet or hands. Every cough stabbed like a sword inside his chest.

If he could have summoned up the energy to move, he would have gotten up and crawled outside in the sleet to die. Anything was better than there. He didn't think he'd seen a doctor in more than a day, nor had any water or food in that time.

To his left, a private from the 55th Regiment of Foot died slowly from a gangrenous chest wound, bad enough that it could be smelled even in the cold. Weston couldn't remember when the man had last been awake, and from his stertorous breathing, thought he would never wake again. To Weston's right lay one of the Buffs, his cheeks sunken with whatever infection ate him from inside, staring blankly at the ceiling, too far gone even to shiver. The tent's fourth occupant had been dragged out for burial that morning. Weston had already dreamed that he'd been dragged out with the rest, unable to protest that he was still alive, gasping for breath as frozen clods of earth slapped stinging down on his face.

Outside, someone called out an obscene suggestion. A woman's voice responded cheerfully. Then the tent flap was thrust aside, and Betsy entered.

He was feverish, and dreaming. "How . . ." he whispered. His throat hurt too badly to say more, and a vision wouldn't hear him.

She wore the same dress and shawl as before, and carried a basket in both arms. Hallucination or not, Weston tried to smile at her. He wasn't sure if his face moved or not.

She dropped to her knees in the hay and laid a hand on his forehead. The warmth of her bare fingers was painful on his cold skin. He winced and closed his eyes, then realized a delusion wouldn't hurt him, and opened them again, drinking in the sight of her. She was much prettier than he'd remembered. "Angel," he whispered.

She smiled at him. "You'll be fine," she said.

When she removed her hand from his face, he cried out, a wordless croak.

She ducked her head beneath the cloth covering her basket and murmured softly.

"Can't hear you," he whispered.

She didn't reply. A moment later, she emerged with something in her hand. "Close your eyes, Jonas," she said.

He hadn't known that she knew his Christian name. He didn't close his eyes all the way, not quite. If he did, she might vanish. So he saw her hands approach him, saw the gleam of a pair of scissors. She snipped through his uniform trousers at the hip, then his drawers. Cold air rushed in and he began shuddering again. "What . . ."

"Hush, now. I'm not supposed to be here, or be doing this, so I have to be quick."

Something pierced his skin, a tiny hot pain that drew all his attention, followed by a wash of heat all over his body, and a physical ease he'd almost forgotten. Even his vision seemed to clear, though he felt woozy and confused, too. "Don't leave me," he whispered. "You're special to me. Don't go back to my brother." He wasn't sure if he actually said the last of it.

She stroked his cheek, a lingering touch. "I'm sorry," she said. Then another puncture, and he could no longer stay awake.

When he woke, she was gone. Or perhaps she had never been there. But he was covered with an extra blanket and he felt much better, stronger, and even less cold. Shortly after, Jennings arrived to bring him out. He spread his extra blanket over the Buff. He never learned if the man survived.

In January, materials to build wooden huts arrived, and in February winter clothing finally arrived. Weston found himself provided with woollen stockings and a woollen jersey, a shirt and drawers of soft flannel, a woollen hat and even a sheepskin coat. He'd never take being warm for granted again. Guard duty while wearing proper clothing was no longer such a misery, and he regained strength enough to work in the fatigue parties that carried supplies up from the harbour. Unlike some of the others, he didn't mind it. It was honest work. More honest, maybe, than fighting.

He thought of Betsy often. Though he tried to talk himself out of building castles in the air, it was difficult not to daydream they might have a future. He thought she might have feelings for him. Hadn't she come to him when he was ill? If that had been true and not a fever dream.

One more visit to the baggage train, sadly diminished after the hard winter, didn't help him, because Betsy was no longer there. He was told, vaguely, that she'd gone to the harbour camp. Further enquiries told him his brother still lived, but he wasn't able to discover if the viscount-in-waiting kept a mistress. If he didn't, and he could find her, Weston daydreamed then that Betsy might take up with him instead. He began to take every chance to visit the harbour camp, volunteering for sorties against the defences of Sevastopol.

It wasn't difficult to muffle one's straps and buckles, crawl through the mud in the dark, and then leap upon a pit's or trench's unwary occupants with a bayonet. It was hard work all the same.

Weston's hands shook all the time now, and his bad dreams now had his brother mixed up in them, and Betsy, and even sometimes his long-dead mother.

Because of that, the next time he was wounded, he thought he was dreaming when Betsy came to him. He was in hospital at Balaclava this time, propped on his side so the deep wound above his hip could drain. Occasionally, he'd fall into a fitful sleep when sheer exhaustion took him. When he woke in the wee hours to find Betsy standing over him with a basket and a lamp, he could only stare.

She stroked his cheek and said, "Jonas."

He could have said many things, but what came out was, "That boy's my brother. Did you know that? He got everything and I got nothing. You should go to him. He'll take good care of you. I want you to be safe."

She knelt on the floor beside his pallet, setting her lamp to the side when his eyes winced from its light. "Jonas," she said again. "This is important. Your brother – do you know him?"

So it was his brother, after all. Weston forced the words out. "He don't know about me, I don't think. And I'm sure not going to tell him. What would be the point?" His arm was shaky with weakness and pain, but he reached out and sighed in relief when she caught his hand and brought it to her lips. Her breath feathered over his knuckles, like moth's wings.

"What if you were in battle together?"

"That won't happen," he said, puzzled. "He'll never even see me."

"But if you were," she insisted, holding his hand to her face, kissing his fingertips. "If a Cossack was about to kill him, and you could save him, would you try?"

He didn't have to think about that one. "Course I would."

"Why?'

Weston considered. At last he said, "We're put on this earth to care for our fellow man, aren't we? There's too many as don't, but a soldier, he can't ignore that. And the man you save today might save you tomorrow." He thought a little more, staring at her face. Her gaze was fixed on him, her eyes huge and dark and soft in the lamplight.

He said, quieter than before, "He's not but a boy. Sixteen, I think. Only a boy. He's innocent of what his father did to my mum."

Betsy leaned down and kissed his forehead, lingering there.

Weston said, "Stay with me a little while, love. Before you go back to him."

"Oh, Jonas," she murmured, next to his ear. Then she stretched out beside him, laying one hand on his chest. He covered it with his own and took the chance to kiss her, not a deep kiss but a warm one, to show her how deeply he cared for her, this woman he'd met only a handful of times.

They lay there for a few minutes, Weston trying to memorize every instant. Betsy drew away a little then, and turned down the lamp to a glimmer so the room was full of darkness once again, and the sound of many injured men's laboured breathing. He could just barely see her face. She said, close to his ear, "Jonas, I can choose between you and your brother."

"Would it were so," he said. "I can't care for you, Betsy. Not like you deserve."

"It's not like you think." She petted his chest. "You're a good man, Jonas, and a kind one. You should live."

"God's will and I'll get back to England one day," he said.

She flung her arm over him and tugged him closer to her, so he could feel her bosom against his chest. "I can save you," she said.

"Can you then?" He smiled. It was a lovely dream, much better than the ones he'd been having. "We'd have a house of our own, plenty to eat and plenty to keep us warm. And children, maybe. Boys and girls both. And a cat. I'd like a cat that doesn't have to hunt mice for its livelihood." He kissed her forehead and inhaled the lavender scent of her hair.

"You're special," she said.

"You're special to me, too."

"No, you don't understand at all."

"Sure I do, love." He kissed her again. "Don't leave me yet. Please."

He was shocked when she pulled away from him and sat up. He reached for her, then stopped in mid-motion.

"Listen to me, Jonas."

Her voice sounded different. Like a commander. "Go on," he said.

"I meant it, when I said I could take you away from here."

"I'm sorry," he said. She really didn't understand. "I can't desert. Looking like I do, they'd catch me in a week. And you know what happens to deserters."

"I can take you where they'll never find you. And you'll live a long and happy life there."

"With you?"

She looked startled, then smiled, a slow beautiful smile. "Yes, with me."

He grinned back at her. If she wanted to play, then he would play along, so long as she stayed a little longer. "Let's go now," he said. "Tell me all about it."

"You're a special man," she said. "It's because of your father."

He wasn't sure he liked the way this was going, but said, "Then my brother's special, too. Like in a fairy tale."

"Yes, just like that." She touched his face, her fingers lingering near his mouth. "No one in your father's family has ever died from a wasting sickness. Not one. They all died from disease, or accident, or murder."

"Or in battle," he said.

"Yes." She paused. "You and your brother, you're both going to die in battle."

"Not yet," he said, soothingly. "I'm not dead yet."

She didn't reply to that. "A long, long time from now, people are still dying from wasting sicknesses. Even more than now. If you could go to them, you could help. Just by being who you are, you could help their doctors and surgeons and save people's lives."

"I always wished I could be a surgeon," he said. "Since my mum died. And here . . . I'd rather stitch someone up than cut them open."

"If you come with me, you can do that. You can learn to read and write and do sums, and you can learn to be a doctor."

He laughed, then stopped because it hurt. "I'd go anywhere to be with you," he said.

"I know you would," she said. "I know it." She kissed him again. "Would you leave everything behind? This world and all the people in it? Go to live with strangers?"

"And you," he added.

"And me." She drew back and stared into his eyes. "Say yes, Jonas. Say you give your consent."

Something about the seriousness of her gaze made him hesitate. Not for long. He wanted nothing here except her. "I consent," he said.

Her breath whooshed out, and she tipped her forehead against his. Then she sat up and reached into her basket.

Weston hoped she'd brought some bread. He hadn't had bread in months.

Instead, she brought out the little jumble of clock parts he remembered from his visit to her tent. She set it on the floor between them and fumbled with it, while Weston stared at it, confused. Did she think, somehow, that she could really take them away from here?

She produced a metal ring and slipped it on to his finger. He could have sworn it tightened itself. Then she put another ring on her own finger and asked, "Are you ready?"

He could make no answer but, "Yes."

She fumbled with the device again.

White light took his vision. His gut roiled, and desperately he grabbed for her in the nothingness. Her flesh was warm beneath his hands and he fell into the void gladly.

When he could see again, he lay on a bare floor, a floor that was warm and gave beneath his shifting weight. The room was warm, and smelled clean, not a trace of wood smoke or staleness. Betsy sat beside him. The ceiling was high, and covered with glorious colour, pictures of people's faces among bright flowers. He looked around, and there were others, more people standing behind a low barrier. The women were dressed just like the men in trousers and brightly coloured shirts, and only a few of them were white-skinned. They were all smiling.

Betsy kissed him. She said, "Welcome to the future. Welcome to our future."

Desperate Choices

Anna Windsor

One

Nothing could make Leah Mays consider asking a murdering, low-life bastard like Carson Taylor for help.

Nothing but this.

"We should call CARD." She shook on the inside but refused to let herself twitch on the outside. Rain spattered the griddle-hot pavement as black clouds cobwebbed across the spook-grey sky. "Child Abduction Rapid Deployment," she added, just in case Chief Oldham Simpson didn't get it.

Simpson ran his hand over the stubble of his white crew cut. His eyes never left the boy's bike lying on the road in front of his big feet. It was a cool bike with stickers and painted lightning bolts, ready to leap small dirt mounds in a single bound. The sight of it made Leah want to burst out sobbing, but her sister Alicia, barely restrained by her husband David at the kerb fifteen feet away, was doing enough of that for both of them.

"I ain't ready to involve the FBI." Simpson's drawl seemed even slower than usual. "What if the boy just got in a scrap with some bullies and ran off to lick his wounds, Major?"

Leah ground her teeth. She wasn't a major any more and hadn't been for six months, but Simpson didn't really know what to do with a retired female marine. Female marines, in Simpson's opinion, just weren't natural. God forbid a Citadel graduate and a former MP with four years of combat experience. He never would have hired her if the town council and her dead father's good name hadn't forced the issue. Leah had been raised to believe hate was wrong, but she was damned close to hating this man, and the two deputies hulking beside Simpson's nearby car weren't much better than him.

Mack Bennett had himself propped against the side of Simpson's cruiser, arms folded, black shades hiding his eyes even in the rain. With his tan face and thick brown hair, never mind his glory days as the Walker Valley high-school quarterback, a lot of women in town thought he was handsome. Bennett knew that. He more than knew it, and he'd been pissed for months that Leah hadn't fawned over him like all the other local females. Standing at Bennett's elbow – as usual – was Jeff Dale. Jeff had even more brown hair than Bennett and much better manners, but half the muscle mass and half the intellectual capacity, too. Dale had spent his life as Bennett's sidekick, and that obviously hadn't changed when they'd hired on with Walker Valley's finest.

Leah made herself breathe slowly and tried to keep her focus. She had gone to war while her classmates had stayed behind and built lives for themselves. She'd served her country with honour until circumstances forced her to walk back into the nightmare of her hometown. Something had always been wrong in Walker Valley, something deeper than Simpson and his two stooges. She'd been nuts to think she could make a difference.

But I have to make a difference. I'm Kevin's aunt.

Her eyes flicked back to the bike, but she made herself look away. A fault line formed in her gut, then fractured with bitter, clenching tremors. She had to work twice as hard to hide her fury and mounting terror.

I'm Kevin's aunt and he's missing and Simpson isn't going to do anything until it's too late.

Was it her fault Simpson was dragging his feet? He'd worked three child abductions in four years, all with bad outcomes – no findings, no body, just poof, kid gone, never to return. Would Simpson really slow-walk Kevin's case just to keep her in her place?

Behind Leah, Alicia sobbed with the rhythm of a ticking clock. Each gasp, each whimper hit Leah like a blow. How long had Kevin already been gone? Half an hour? Forty-five minutes? It was getting close to evening by now. Every second that slipped away made it less likely that they'd find Kevin alive – or at all. He'd gone missing halfway between Town Grocery and the safety of his own front

door. He'd left behind the bike and a bag with two candy bars and
a can of soda that had apparently exploded on impact. The dark
liquid had seeped under the fallen bike, looking way too much like
a bloodstain.

No one had seen a damned thing.

Keep it together. Don't lose it. Can't lose it now.

"I think the bully scenario is unlikely." Leah gestured to her
distraught sister and brother-in-law and the murmuring crowd.
"Every kid in town except Kevin is standing right over there on the
kerb. If you're convinced he fought with a bully, talk to them. If
you don't want to do it, send Bennett or Jeff, or let me start asking
questions."

Simpson's thick white eyebrows pinched together over his
sunburned nose. The lines around his mouth puckered until he
looked like a squinting, bad-tempered owl. "It's not even been an
hour, Officer Mays. You might not remember much from round
here since you've been away so long, but we take our time and
make careful decisions before frightening our kids, upsetting our
town's parents, or stirring up a hornet's nest like the FBI. I know
the boy's your nephew. Maybe that's clouding your judgment.
Maybe you ought to step back."

Me and the boys'll take care of this.

He didn't have to say that last sentence. Leah saw his meaning
etched across his angry face. He hitched up his brown pants and
adjusted his suspenders as his gaze swept over Alicia and David.
Leah imagined his thoughts all over again. *Another kidnapped
brat, and this one's gonna be more trouble than all the rest put
together.*

Because this one wasn't a brat. This one wasn't a reject trouble-
maker. Kevin had a family who loved him – a family who would
never stop looking, never stop asking questions and never let up on
the pressure.

Simpson ought to be panicked. Kidnapping wasn't standard
fare for small Southern towns, especially not Walker Valley, population 2,000 plus or minus a few donkeys, goats, sheep, horses
and a shitload of chickens. Simpson's list of troubles should
include petty theft, vandalism, public intoxication, fighting and
the occasional traffic accident. Instead, Walker Valley saw more
than its share of murders, assaults and rapes. They'd had home
invasions and ATM thefts, smash-and-grabs at the two local gas
stations, and five major drug busts in the year before Leah came

home. Then there were the kidnappings. Little boys, eight to fourteen years old.

Yeah.

Something was definitely wrong in Walker Valley.

Simpson might not be the cause of it, but he damned sure wasn't the solution, either. He must have seen the disgust on her face because he jerked his thumb in the general direction of the police station. "Go on, now, honey. We'll handle this."

Leah said nothing. She had no words left. Heat rising to her face, she turned away from the bike and away from Simpson and his two stooges. Sweating in the warm Southern rain, she headed straight to her sister.

Alicia's short blonde hair made her seem that much thinner and more frail as she turned David loose and launched herself into Leah's arms. "What's Simpson doing? What's happening? What do you know?"

"Nothing," Leah whispered, making sure nobody but Alicia could hear her. Damn it, she could feel her sister's ribs through the soft cotton of her yellow shirt. "Nothing, and nothing."

Alicia pulled back, blue eyes wide and horrified. "Is he calling the FBI? Please tell me he's calling the FBI."

Leah shook her head so that everyone could see, but she whispered, "I'll get help. Better than the FBI. We'll get Kevin back. I swear it."

"Better help than . . ." Alicia froze in her grip, and Leah knew her sister was processing her meaning. Alicia's breath caught, then she dug her fingers into Leah's shoulders. "Oh. Oh my God. Are you sure?"

She sounded worried but suddenly hopeful.

Leah knew she didn't have to answer. She gave her sister a quick kiss on the cheek, walked stiff-legged to her patrol car, and pulled slowly away from the crime scene. She didn't grace Simpson with a glance as she made like she was headed for the station. She went north instead, turning off on the winding mountain highway she had avoided since she came back to Walker Valley. It would be a while before Simpson understood she hadn't followed his directive to go to the station. It would be a little longer before he knew she was actively interfering in his non-investigation.

She figured she had at least an hour to get herself up Grace Mountain and knock on the one door she ought to leave closed.

Leah could only pray the devil himself would answer.

Two

From the minute Carson Taylor heard Leah Mays was back in town, he'd been steeling himself for their first meeting.

He figured he had himself under good control. He thought he was ready.

He was wrong.

His body came to full alert, and he heard his own pulse thumping in his ears. From the honey-coloured wisps escaping the tight weave of her braid to the summer-sky blue of her eyes, her beauty rattled his senses. Ten years. It had been ten years since the last time he saw her face to face, and she still smelled like honeysuckle in full bloom. He felt her nearness like a sudden storm, electrifying and dangerous and absolutely absorbing. Even standing in the rain wearing that idiotic Walker Valley cop costume, Leah Mays was the most incredible woman Carson had ever seen.

She was just a girl when I knew her, and I was nothing but a stupid kid. What he did to her, to himself – he didn't have any words for it. What it must have cost her to drive up Grace Mountain and knock on his door, he couldn't imagine. Thinking about the pain he caused her should have done something to ratchet down his arousal, but it didn't.

"Leah." *Yeah, good job.* He could still speak even though his tongue felt like dry concrete. "I heard you were back in Walker Valley but I didn't want to believe you'd do that to yourself."

Her blue eyes flickered from his black overshirt to his cotton T-shirt to the bulge of the Glock he kept snug against his ribs. He saw anger. Maybe fear. None of it stopped him from feeling her gaze like fingernails trailing across his skin.

Still staring at him, she opened her sensual mouth and said, "My nephew Kevin's missing."

Carson's own eyes went wide. Alicia's boy? A second set of senses fired into action, finally overriding his more primal instincts, and he stepped out of the doorway to let her inside. "Define 'missing'."

"Abducted approximately fifty-three minutes ago," she said as she slipped past him into the deliberately filthy living room with its whiskey bottles and hunting rifles in various stages of breakdown for cleaning. "Between Town Grocery and home."

Town Grocery and the old Mays place. The distance came to about two miles. Carson knew most Walker Valley parents kept their puppies on long leashes, but Alicia had always struck him as more careful than most. "Your sister OK with the kid running around town alone?"

"Christ, Carson." Flash fire blazed in the blue depths of Leah's eyes, jolting Carson's heart yet again despite the circumstances. She sounded pissed, but she gave herself away by wringing her hands just like she used to when they were seventeen and something scared her. "It's Walker Valley, not New York City – and Alicia's been sick. Breast cancer. David has to work double shifts to cover the expenses. Kevin's gotten pretty independent."

Carson added up Alicia's breast cancer with Leah's return to the hell they had both meant to escape, and things made a little more sense. He wanted to reach out, to touch Leah, hold her and comfort her – but he knew way better than to try a thick-headed stunt like that. "What's Simpson doing about the kidnapping?"

"Jacking off and pretending he's got a clue."

Her frown captured him just as much as her smile. Leah had known him once when they were so young it made him ache to remember those years. She had really known him, the truth of him, or at least he thought she did. But then he'd hurt her; he'd blown up his whole life and hers, too. Even after years in the military, years away from the dark spell of Walker Valley, Leah hadn't gotten over that betrayal, he could tell. And he didn't blame her.

Carson knew what Leah saw in him now, and it hurt like hell even though it was just what he wanted her to see. The same façade everyone in Walker Valley bought into, day after day after day. He was the heir to Walker Valley's lowest-class family of criminals, and the worst of the bunch in years. A man with a record. A man who had killed his own father. Everybody in Walker Valley had their opinion about Carson Taylor. Numbers runner, drug lord, killer for hire – the rumours – and the truths – never ended.

It took a mighty effort, but Carson mastered himself before he reached out to grab hold of this vision from his past, this reminder of what life might have been. She hadn't driven all the way up Grace Mountain because she wanted him, or anything to do with him. She came because she needed him. Her nephew was missing, the locals were idiots, and Leah probably knew she had one shot to get the boy back, even if it cost her a career in law enforcement and her whole non-future in Walker Valley. The best and fastest way to catch a monster was to do exactly what she was doing – set loose a bigger monster.

After all these years, Leah had knocked on his door again and, monster or not, Carson didn't plan to let her down.

"Wait here." He gestured to the living room and hated making her stay in the seedy mess. "I need to get a few things."

And make a call.

She nodded.

Carson tore his gaze from her, walked to his bedroom, and gave himself three seconds to stand there with his eyes closed to get his shit together.

Then he yanked his cell out of his pocket and hit the speed dial. The signal, boosted by a high-tech mini-tower concealed in the loft of his barn, went through without the usual rural hassles. Robert answered on the first ring.

"I'm taking down Preston," Carson said. "Right now. Tonight."

Silence on the other end. Carson almost hung up, but then Robert exploded with, "What the hell – no way! We've been working this angle for two fucking years. You absolutely will not—"

"I'm not asking permission, Robert. I'm telling you to send backup and body bags."

Carson punched off, shut down the phone, jammed it in his pocket, and grabbed his go-bag from his closet. After a second's consideration, he pulled a second bag from beneath his bed and double-checked the contents: two MP5s with under-barrel grenade launchers, three flashbangs, two sting grenades and a shitload of flex-cuffs. Yeah. Those might come in handy. He had body armour in a hidden compartment in his pickup toolbox, for himself and for Leah, too.

They were damned sure going to need it.

Three

Leah couldn't stop shaking.

Seeing Carson had pushed her straight to the edge, and the trembling finally came. Leah tried not to catalogue the bottles and guns and cards and dice, or the bookies' notes, or the little balance scales used to weigh God only knew what. She tried not to think about the perfectly carved arms, the broad-muscled chest, the deep, spine-tingling drawl, or the way Carson's black eyes never left her after he opened his door.

She had always had his full attention, from the moment she met him in sixth grade until the night she saw him dragged away, cuffed and smeared with his father's blood.

He hasn't changed.

Leah closed her eyes.

That was stupid. Prison always changed men. He'd only served a handful of years for manslaughter before the case got tossed on some technicality. Carson had needed reform and reshaping, but from everything Leah had heard since she left Walker Valley and since she came back, too, all of Carson's changes had been for the worse. She opened her eyes.

The old Taylor house hadn't been transformed, either. From the rotting walls to the dust in the living room's dark corners, the place looked just like it did when Carson's father held court over Walker Valley's criminal element. The Jack Daniel's bottles gave her the creeps because they reminded her of Judd Taylor. That craggy-faced shithead never spared her a leer, and he'd made a few drunken grabs for her late at night, when he thought nobody was watching. Heavy-handed with his wife, with Carson's older sister – Leah realized she didn't know what had become of Chelsea Taylor. The girl had left town, but nobody could say where she wound up or what she might be doing. As for Carson's mother, she had died about a year after Judd got killed.

Murdered by Carson. Murdered while he slept, if the gossip and news reports were accurate.

While the nasty old bastard was passed out, more likely. Leah didn't really know because she hadn't talked to Carson since his arrest. At first her parents hadn't allowed it. Then Carson had refused to see her when she showed up at the prison after his transfer. She had tried writing letters, but those got returned unanswered. Silence had killed whatever they'd had, if two stupid kids could have anything real.

But if it wasn't real, why did it still hurt so damned much to see him? I'm here for Kevin. That's the only reason.

Leah focused on the nearest Jack Daniel's bottle. Carson had never liked whiskey. When had he started drinking that stuff? When had he started drinking at all? It didn't feel right.

"Prison changes men," she muttered aloud, but the words sounded thick and flat in the dusty room.

Leah narrowed her eyes. The Jack Daniel's bottle had as much dust on it as everything else. She eased towards it. Touched the dry, warm glass. Yeah, that was a lot of dust. Curiosity drove her across the living room, examining the other bottles as she went. They were all dusty.

As she neared the back of the living room, she could hear Carson's voice. It sounded like he was talking on a phone, but there was no line service this far from the valley. Leah pulled out her own cell and checked. Full signal. That was weird. None of the rural areas had a consistent grid. How the hell did Carson get such good service halfway up a giant granite slab like Grace Mountain?

The few questions Carson had asked her when she showed up – those were pretty sharp. None of the swagger and attitude she had expected from a career criminal. She looked around the junky living room again. Yeah. Everything in the place screamed up-to-no-good and illegal, but . . .

But it felt staged. Not real, like Carson was hiding something else. Something bigger. Maybe something worse.

Christ, if this is his cover, how bad has he gone?

Leah's shaking got worse and she had to clench both fists to control herself. She might have made a terrible mistake coming here. If it hadn't been for Kevin and the fact she had no other option, she would have bolted.

Carson came back to the living room carrying two totes, both black, one small and one large enough to conceal assault rifles. His eyes, as black as the totes, studied her with an intensity that suffocated fear and doubt, instead kindling a fast, sizzling heat in her belly. Despite their history and his past, despite all the years and horrors separating them, in that moment, there was nothing but Carson and her – and Kevin, their common purpose.

Leah couldn't speak. She couldn't do anything but stare at Carson and wonder what the hell she was feeling.

He did the talking for both of them. "Let's move."

When Leah didn't head for the front door, his tone channelled desperados and drill sergeants. "We need to knock on a few doors and break a few jaws. You up for it, Marine?"

Marine. Shit. There it is again. Leah felt her stare turn to a glare. All the emotion inside her balled in her chest, and she almost took a swing at Carson.

He met her angry gaze without flinching. "Marine. Last time I checked, that word wasn't an insult."

Damn him and his drawl. His voice had hypnotic powers – arousing, calming – Carson could turn it whichever way he chose. He'd always had that talent.

"Simpson," Leah muttered, standing down as fast as she had flared to full alert. "He never served. It cramps his balls that I did."

Carson nodded like he understood. Then he pointed towards the door. His dark eyes commanded her, direct and concise without being overbearing.

Move out, soldier.

This time, Leah moved.

Four

Having Leah so close to him in the pickup cab made it hard to watch the road, but Carson kept his head in the game. The right head – and the right game. For now. He guided the big black Ford down Grace Mountain without looking left or right.

After a few miles of silence, he said, "You came back to Walker Valley because Alicia needed you."

Leah kept her eyes fixed on the windshield. Rain tapped against the tinted glass, and the evening sky bathed her pretty face in shades of grey. "David's a good guy, but he's not much in the care-taking department. With Mom and Dad gone, Alicia didn't have anyone else to call."

Carson left that alone because he understood. Leah and Alicia had always been close as kids, just a few years apart, and it was a damned shame that both their parents died so young – heart attack for Mr Mays and diabetic stroke for Mrs Mays. Heart disease and diabetes were two of the biggest killers in Walker Valley, if you didn't count drugs, running drugs, lowbrow human trafficking, and all the other sick bullshit that seemed to gravitate towards the town.

Leah didn't ask where they were going. Did that mean she trusted him?

Now you're dreaming. Keep your eyes on the road.

He knew Leah hadn't turned to him out of trust. She did it out of desperation, and he had to keep that in mind.

"All that crap in your living room – the bottles and scales and other stuff – it's crap." Her tone sounded strangely light and certain.

Carson glanced at Leah in spite of himself. He saw the shrewd eyes of a practised investigator staring back at him.

Well, shit. How did . . . Never mind. He tried to make his frown seem forbidding, to add a little menace and back-off to the silence now filling the truck cab. He would have liked to tell her everything, but that couldn't happen.

"You have cell signal," she added. "Where's the tower hidden?"

Son of a . . .

He calculated that a little truth would be better than a lie she could easily investigate. "Behind the barn in some tree cover."

"Standard equipment for rural drug runners these days?" Now she sounded triumphant and a little teasing. He didn't think he could take teasing from her on any level.

"The world's gone high-tech." Carson heard the rough edge in his own voice and hoped she took it for anger. "I had to keep up."

Fabric whispered as she turned to face him. "How did you get out of prison?"

Carson's frown got real in a hurry, and he gripped the wheel hard. How had he managed to forget this about Leah, how she wouldn't leave a thing alone when she got hold of it? She had always been like that.

I used to think it was attractive.

Still was.

It was part of what made her so strong and so determined. Hell, she'd made it out of Walker Valley once, survived the Citadel, survived Iraq – who knew what heights she could reach without their past and this God-awful town weighing her down?

"My lawyer got my conviction tossed over an invalid warrant," he said. "Fruit of the poisoned tree. You know the drill." His muscles tightened, waiting for the rest of her questions and hoping his rehearsed answers didn't sound like a total load of shit.

How did it happen, Carson?

Why did you kill your father?

Why did you turn your back on me? Didn't I mean anything to you at all?

He knew she hadn't been allowed to see him in jail. She was still a minor, and no way would her parents have gone for something like that. But after she turned eighteen and he cut her off – well. That was on him, wasn't it?

The questions never came, and Carson managed not to look at Leah. He sensed her studying him, felt her reading him and trying to understand. He knew if he so much as glanced in her direction, he'd pull the truck off the road, take her in his arms, and try to explain with his words, with his mouth, with his hands, with any type of communication she'd accept.

No time for that, asshole, and she deserves way better than you.

He turned off the main road without hitting the blinker and, a second or so later, she asked, "This is the Marsley farm, isn't it?"

"Used to be. Hank Preston bought it a few years back." Carson steered the truck into tall grass, parking behind a small tree-covered hill. "He's trash. Always has been, always will be, but now he's trash with money. Get out and wait by the toolbox on your side."

Five

Body armour. Military grade. Un-fucking-believable. Leah strapped on the chest protector, glad she couldn't see Carson's face in the growing darkness. He already had his body armour in place, and she could hear him checking clips on pistols and shoving them into holsters.

She was still in uniform and had her service Glock, and he held out a SIG. The barrel glittered in the emerging moonlight, and she took a deep breath of the hot, wet mountain air. No more rain, but the humidity lingered on, as stubborn as any bad memory. "Stow the SIG," he said. "Use it if you have to. It's not traceable, but I've got something else for you to carry."

Leah secured the SIG in her waistband, but her heart didn't start pounding until Carson switched on a flashlight and pulled two MP5s – with grenade launchers, no less – out of his tote. He handed her one.

She took it, feeling the familiar weight and pistol grips and automatically checking both safeties. She could tell by its weight that the clip was full and it was armed with a 40-millimetre grenade.

"I'm assuming you're friends with these," Carson murmured, checking his own submachine gun.

"Yeah." Leah had carried one for years in the desert. Signature weapon of her unit. Carson couldn't know that, right? "Now, will you tell me what the hell we're doing?"

He lowered his weapon.

Even in the moonlight, she could see the rising worry and harsh determination on his handsome face. "I can't go in alone and I can't involve anybody else. You're a soldier, so I'm going to respect that."

Leah's nerves jangled so badly she nearly choked on her own spit, but she tried to sound casual when she spoke. "I'm capable."

"I have no doubt." He left off the "Marine" this time, but Leah wouldn't have minded it if he'd used it. He handed her night-vision goggles, making her feel even more like she was back in the desert.

When he passed her a bunch of flex-cuffs, then rattled off their likely targets and his attack plan like a high-level field officer outlining an urban assault, she wondered when and how a convicted felon had managed to get himself in the service. Not marines, no. Army. Carson definitely sounded army.

When all of this was over, they had a lot to discuss.

Six

The world had gone phosphor green.

Carson lined up his shot using the night-vision goggles, squeezed his launch trigger, and blew Preston's outbuilding and weapons cache to smithereens. He heard Leah swear at the size of the explosion and the white-hot light no doubt searing her brain through the goggles. Smoke billowed like clouds straight out of hell, giving them cover as six big bastards with their own automatic firepower rolled out of Preston's main house and two more goons with rifles thundered out of the barn.

No body armour. No goggles.

Battle heat surged through Carson, narrowing his focus as he studied all the faces.

"Clear," he shouted over the roar of the nearby fire, so Leah would know none of these targets were Hank Preston. The fact that he'd talked to these men, shared six-packs with them when he had to, didn't matter. It was all a game. Everything was a game designed to lead up to a moment like this.

From the edge of the tool shed, Carson fired at the men in front of the house while Leah went to ground behind him and laid down two quick bursts to slow the barn guys. Dirt and rock kicked into the darkness. The barn guys howled from the shrapnel and fell hard.

Carson took his turn swearing. "I told you not to wound them – take them out or they'll come back swinging."

Leah put rounds in their legs and shooting arms. Their rifles went flying.

"Or not," Carson said through his teeth. Unbelievable she had that much control over aim with an MP5.

Guns chattered and bullets pelted against the tool shed. Carson reached for Leah, but he didn't have to. She had already rolled up from her firing position and taken shelter beside him. The shed's ancient wood was damn near petrified. It would shatter before it let through a slug. Fighting his instincts to protect Leah, Carson broke cover long enough to cut a wide path with his MP5, taking down half of Preston's thugs.

The other three hammered at the tool shed with steady, rapid fire. Chunks of wood and earth spewed in every direction. Leah edged along the back of the shed until she had position opposite Carson.

He gave her hand signals and, on three, they both opened up on the men still standing.

Leah didn't shoot to wound this time, and Carson never did. The three hit the ground and stayed down, just like the three Carson had taken down by himself. He signalled Leah to head for their next positions of strength – two oaks closer to the house, one on either side of the porch. She moved without question or hesitation.

"Preston," Carson bellowed as he ran. "Get out here."

His answer came in rifle shots, shattering window glass and thudding into his oak.

"Preston!" Carson taunted again, and more shots blasted from the house. Good sign. Just one shooter – Preston didn't have any assholes left to do his dirty work.

He glanced at Leah's tree. She was gone.

Carson's heart squeezed and he had to remind himself that this was his plan.

If anything happens to her, it's on my head.

He bolted from his oak, dropped, and rolled fast towards her tree as bullets cut into the ground right behind him.

Deploy. Distract.

On his feet. Behind the oak. Safe.

Leah isn't safe.

Fuck, he'd been an idiot to play it out this way. Why didn't he leave her out here behind the trees?

I'm taking the fire. Better this way.

He yanked a second grenade canister from his weapons belt, pushed it into the loader, and fired at the barn. When the explosive made contact with the meth lab inside, another unholy explosion rocked the dark side of Grace Mountain. Carson turned his face away from the blazing white glow. Waited. Waited another second.

His guts started to churn just as the rifle fire from inside the house stopped.

Carson threw himself towards the house's door, charging harder than he'd done since he shipped stateside. One kick and the half-rotten wood splintered and gave.

Carson ripped off the night-vision goggles, squinting through the bright indoor lights.

The first thing he saw was Preston's rifle lying near the far wall.

The next thing he saw was Leah on the floor in front of him, beside an overturned couch and table somebody had been using for cover.

She was crouched, one knee jammed into Preston's scrawny back. Her blue eyes looked calm and focused, and her braid, uniform and body armour were barely mussed. With very steady hands, she held the barrel of her SIG against Preston's temple. Good. At least if she had to shoot the meth-addled fucker, the bullet wouldn't trace straight back to her assigned weapon.

Preston had his toothpick arms stretched above his greasy brown hair. Sweat soaked through his white T-shirt, and the stench of urine rose from his perpetually dirty jeans. Carson saw that the man was shaking.

He strode over to the prone figure, crammed the barrel of his MP5 against Preston's other temple and said, "The kid that got snatched from the valley today. Where is he?"

"I don't know nothing about—aaaahhh!"

Carson knew Leah had used her leverage to increase the pressure on Preston's spine. He could almost hear bones grinding beneath her well-placed knee.

"He's my nephew," Leah said in the coldest voice Carson had ever heard. Shit, she could scare him in a blind alley, sounding that pissed.

"Who the fuck are you?" Preston whined.

Carson gave the bastard's head a little punch with the snout of the MP5. "She's with me."

Right about then, Preston must have processed just exactly how fucked he was, and his jaw came unhinged. "It's none of my guys

– Christ that hurts! Cut me a break here, Taylor. I didn't do nothing to your woman or her people. It wasn't me, I'm telling you. Not me or any of my guys."

"You don't have any guys," Carson told him. "They're gone."

Preston went silent for a second, then mumbled, "I thought you and me was tight, man."

"You don't need to think," Leah said. "Just talk. Who is it in Walker Valley that likes little boys? Who took my nephew?"

"Nobody." Preston talked so fast Carson figured he was pissing himself more with each word. "I mean – I don't think they're keeping the kids around here."

Not good. Carson moved the barrel of the MP5 back a fraction. "Selling them?"

Preston let out a little whimper of relief. "Yeah, maybe. Through the internet and stuff."

Leah didn't cut the man any slack. She pressed her knee in tighter, making Preston squeal. "Where do they hold them until they're bought?"

"I . . . I don't know! Christ on a cracker, Taylor, make her quit. Make her stop!"

Carson ignored him. "Who does know where the kids are held?" He nodded to Leah, who pressed harder.

"Simpson or one of his people!" Preston yelled each word louder than the last. "That's the talk. That's all I know!"

Leah bent down, her own words loud and sharp. "Which officer do you pay to never notice your meth cooking?"

Way past any games or attempts to protect himself, Preston's teeth chattered before he did. "Bennett. But just once, I swear it. Ah, fuck, Carson, did you really blow up my works?"

"The barn's gone, along with everything in it." Carson yanked a restraint cuff off his belt and fastened Preston's wrists behind his back. Leah moved almost as fast as he did, locking her flex-cuffs on the man's ankles.

"Do we call somebody?" she asked as she tightened the cuffs.

"Already did." Carson pointed to the ceiling and saw Leah's expression shift to one of surprise.

She could hear them.

Chopper blades slicing across the night sky, still a ways off but moving fast towards their position.

Carson jerked the nose of the MP5 towards the door. "Let's move, honey. Now."

Seven

Two minutes later, safely belted into Carson's truck and almost hidden behind her still-strapped body armour, Leah had so many questions she couldn't begin to ask them. Instead, she held tight to the panic grip above her window as Carson ploughed down the valley-side slope of Grace Mountain, sometimes taking roads and sometimes motoring through tree-choked short cuts that would have made her scream before Iraq.

Of course, throwing her career out the window, setting herself up for arrest on about a thousand different charges, and shooting a bunch of assholes running a meth lab would have made her scream back then, too. She'd grown up a lot since she and Carson melted the leather off the back seat of her mother's car.

Stupid, idiot kids. We were so careless. It was a plain wonder she didn't end up pregnant. But would that have been such a terrible fate?

Leah closed her eyes. Opened them. Enough of that shit. She had to keep her mind on nothing but Kevin, nothing but their next move. "How visible were those explosions?"

"The far side of Grace Mountain's always been no-man's-land." Carson's low voice cut beneath the roar of the truck's engine as he gunned down a long stretch of straight pavement. "The Walker Valley locals won't know unless somebody phones in to complain, and they won't come out to investigate unless God himself raises a stink."

"God." Leah sucked in a breath. "I did a lot of talking to God late at night in the desert. At the time, I thought nobody was listening."

Carson's hands visibly tightened on the wheel. "You got out alive. Somebody up there did you a favour." His soulful glance burned her like dark fire. "I'm glad."

Leah tried to take another breath but couldn't. Not for a long few seconds. The truck cab seemed way too small, and Carson felt way too close. As soon as this was over, she had to get the hell away from him.

Damn it. What's it been, an hour? And I'm already not sure how far away I want to get.

She had to be real about this. Whatever Carson was into, it was dangerous and deep and not something she wanted in her life. So why did sitting here next to him feel so natural?

Giddiness. Just a rush from the emergency, from the battle.
Yeah. Keep telling yourself that.

Leah couldn't believe Carson was affecting her like this after so much time and separate history, and with Kevin's safety occupying most of her mind. Maybe Walker Valley really was cursed land, with Carson as its relentless Witch King, watching his minions from on high.

The truth probably wasn't much better. "Back at the farmhouse with Preston, after we finished – the helicopters?"

Carson's face seemed to turn to chiselled granite in the eerie red light of the Ford's instrument panel. His dark eyes stayed fixed on the road, and instead of discussing who or what was coming to get Hank Preston and the wounded and dead they left behind, he said, "So, about Bennett. Are we going to have to shoot him?"

"I can handle Bennett." Shit, that came out fast. Leah wondered if she was lying. She kept herself motionless in the truck seat. One bounce of her knee and Carson would know she was uncertain. He'd make his own plan – and blood would definitely be involved. She didn't care what happened to her or to her career at this point, not if it brought Kevin home, but she didn't want Carson in the kind of trouble he couldn't escape. Busting up a meth operation was one thing, but firing on an officer of the law would be a whole different level of catastrophe.

Stay calm. Be confident. Bennett had weaknesses. Leah knew she could use those. "Park a block away and help me get out of this armour – but first, stop and get us a six-pack. Budweiser, OK? Cans, not bottles."

Carson arched an eyebrow. "When did you take up beer?"

Leah let go of the panic grip and started unfastening her body armour as best she could, given the seat belt. "About the same time you took up whiskey after swearing you'd cut your own throat first."

His frown came so fast she moved towards her door on instinct. This time, his knuckles turned stark white on the wheel, and Leah's throat went dry.

Good move, Mays. Piss off a murderer in his own truck.

But even with the anger boiling out of him, even with that harsh look on his face, Leah realized she wasn't afraid of him. Despite what she'd heard, despite what she knew, she couldn't see Carson as a murderer. That was a hell of a note, given that she was supposed to be able to read people, to judge their capacity for wrongdoing on the spur of the moment.

After a mile or so of high-octane silence, Carson said, "There's a lot I can't tell you, Leah. And a lot I shouldn't."

"You knew I was staying with my sister." Leah tried to bite back her words, but they spilled out despite her best efforts. "Why didn't you visit, or at least call?"

Carson's face shifted in the shadows. She saw tension and pain, even something like self-doubt. "You came back to Walker Valley clean and free. Seemed like the right thing to do, leaving you that way."

Leah pulled at the fasteners on the armour again, getting nowhere. "You act like you're toxic."

"I was always poison, honey. You were just too sweet to see it."

That drawl. It gave her chills, made her notice him even more, made him seem even closer – no. No way. "If you call me 'honey' again, I'll kick your ass so hard you'll have to watch the road through your butt cheeks."

Carson laughed. The son of a bitch actually laughed at her. Leah yanked twice as hard at her body armour. Jerk. He'd never taken her temper seriously.

Her hands went still on her chest protector.

It was one of the things she had loved about him.

Eight

Carson didn't like this one fucking bit.

He kept his right eye crammed against the MP5's night scope, using a couple of straggly pines for cover as Leah "handled" Mack Bennett.

Meaning, she had her gorgeous blonde hair down, her uniform shirt unbuttoned enough to show cleavage, a beer in one hand, and the rest of the six-pack dangling from the other as she backed the skanky bastard up against the tricked-out red Mustang in his driveway.

Bennett's driveway was tucked between his brick house and a fair-sized garage, private, lots of cover – good for their purposes. Bennett lived on a quiet cul-de-sac in the nicer section of town. Lots of manicured lawns, gazebos and porch swings, but nobody was out on such a dark, hot night. Too damned rainy and humid down here in the valley. Carson's scope kept fogging. Maybe the humidity, maybe seeing Leah pretending to be a vixen on the make.

All she needed was a slinky little evening dress, and the woman might kill a man just by walking past him.

From where Carson stood, he could watch from the side with a good line to Bennett if things got out of hand, and he could hear the conversation pretty clearly.

"I knew you'd come to see me sooner or later." Bennett sounded halfway to drunk, like he'd been hitting his own stash of Bud before Leah knocked on his door and lured him outside. "You upset about the kid?"

"Yeah. I need some comforting." Leah swayed, acting like she'd had a little too much herself.

"I'm your man." Bennett reached out and took the six-pack out of Leah's hand. She held on to the plastic rings just long enough to tease him, to let him pull her closer. Bennett put his free hand on Leah's waist, and Carson had to make himself hold his trigger finger very, very still.

The second Leah pressed herself against Bennett, she dropped her beer and pulled the SIG from where she'd tucked it near the small of her back. She had Bennett frozen against the Mustang, gun to his head, before the idiot even understood he'd been had.

Carson smiled. *Good play, honey.*

Leah's voice took on fresh force and clarity. "Know a man named Hank Preston?"

Bennett let the six-pack hit the ground beside his foot. "Yeah, I know him."

"His friends are full of bullets and his barn's on fire."

To this, Bennett said nothing. Through his scope, Carson saw the unspoken cursing in the deputy's expression.

"He said he paid you to leave his meth-cooking operation alone," Leah continued. "He said that somebody in the department knows where my nephew's being held."

"It's not me." Bennett's words came out in a gruff rush, but he didn't try to move. Maybe he was smarter than Carson thought.

Leah's laugh raised the hair on the back of Carson's neck. "This gun's not traceable. I'll be gone before anybody gets their curtains open to look."

"I don't know anything about Kevin, I swear to God." Bennett's voice dropped lower. More definite. More confident. He was sounding like an innocent man. Carson kept his aim steady, beginning to hope he wouldn't have to fire.

"I talked to God in Iraq." Leah pressed the SIG into Bennett's temple and got even closer to the deputy. "Funny. I was just telling a friend about that this evening."

Friend. Well, that's better than fucking bastard. I'll take what I can get.

"Do you know how many people I had to kill in the desert, Bennett? Just to stay alive. And my nephew's life and my sister's health and sanity weren't on the line then." Smooth and easy, Leah pulled her service pistol with her free hand and lodged the barrel between Bennett's legs. "I feel a little crazy from the stress."

Carson's lips twitched. He kept his sights fixed on Bennett's temple just in case, but now he was almost positive he wouldn't be shooting any cops tonight.

"Preston paid me once. Just once." Bennett's voice stayed steady, and he sounded more honest than ever. "I never should have taken it, but I had to send money to my parents. They lost their retirement in the stock crash." A pause, and then, "I swear I don't have a clue where Kevin is. If I did, I'd tell you. I'd drive you there myself."

Leah didn't let up or miss a beat. Through the scope, Carson thought he saw colour rising to her cheeks. "Who does know? Simpson?"

"He's an old shithead," Bennett said. "Incompetent and lazy, but he's not a criminal."

Leah's mouth opened in surprise. She jammed the Glock farther into Bennett's crotch, and he groaned. "Are you trying to tell me Jeff Dale's into snatching and selling little kids?"

"I don't know. Fuck! Back off, would you?"

Leah shook her head once. "No."

Bennett's jaw worked for a few seconds before he spoke again. "I've wondered, OK? Even poked around a little, but I didn't have any proof. Jeff's old man was a freak. A real perv. He tried to go after me once, and that kind of thing, it gets passed down, right?"

"Jeff Dale." Leah didn't look like she believed Bennett, but she eased back on the Glock between his legs. At the same moment, she shifted her grip on the SIG in her right hand and pistol-whipped Bennett so hard Carson winced at the crack.

Bennett crumpled like dropped laundry, and Carson had to lower his MP5 and hotfoot it to help Leah drag the deputy inside his house. She flex-cuffed him, but left his arms in front and his ankles free. He'd get help or get himself loose once he woke, if the poor bastard could even see with the headache he'd have.

Almost as fast, they were both back out of the house, Leah leading the way to the truck. She threw open the Ford's door and grabbed a piece of her body armour.

"Dale. Unbelievable." She struggled into her chest protector, and Carson reached out to help with the fasteners. She let him. Her blue eyes had gone from glittering to feral, and her expression conveyed gut-level worry that made his heart twist. "I'm getting a bad feeling, Carson. Worse than earlier. Worse than ever. I think we're running out of time.

Nine

Leah's heart jackhammered as Carson's truck jumped the kerb. Brakes squealed in front of the old Dale place, a clapboard monstrosity in a big field at the end of a tyre-littered road. This was the junky side of the valley, where nobody spoke to each other and nobody saw anything, ever, no matter what.

Damned good thing, because anybody looking was about to see plenty.

Both of them bailed out of the cab, MP5s fully loaded, ready for anything, ready for everything.

Leah saw Carson reach in his pocket. Wondered if he had another weapon. His hand reappeared empty, but he pulled a flashbang canister off his belt and held it out to her. "I'll get the door," he mouthed, and she understood him despite the earplugs they had inserted before they turned on to Dale's road.

Leah raced up the porch steps behind Carson, MP5 raised but trained slightly to Carson's left. They couldn't blow the door with serious explosives for fear Kevin or other kids or innocents might get hurt. "Police," Carson bellowed, then kicked the door so hard it ripped right off its hinges.

Leah lobbed the non-lethal grenade through the opening, and she and Carson ducked and squeezed their eyes shut.

She felt the impact of the flashbang, felt it in her skin and bones and teeth, and hoped like hell Kevin wasn't anywhere near the damned thing. It wouldn't do permanent damage, but the sound and light were enough to stun grown men for five or ten seconds.

Leah ripped out her earplugs and leaped through the ruined door, swinging her MP5 left, then right as she searched the dark living room for targets. *Wound and capture*, she repeated to herself.

They needed Jeff Dale and anyone who might be helping him alive in case the kids weren't stashed here. They had to watch out for kids being used as human shields. Her nerves jumped and burned, and her mind kept shifting to Iraq, to the hundreds of houses she'd helped clear, to the shouting insurgents, to the sobbing innocents.

Stay in now. Kevin needs you. Keep it together, damn it!

She didn't see anything in the house. "Kevin?" She stopped. Listened. Didn't hear anything. "Kevin! It's OK, honey. Answer me if you can."

Carson came through the door and stood beside her. Nothing. More nothing . . . and then running footsteps to her right. A figure darted through the blackness of the hallway, headed towards a dimly lit kitchen and, presumably, a back door. Big. An adult. Leah tried to track the running figure for a shot, but Carson stopped her with a quick, "Got it."

He hurled a sting grenade that hit the floor in front of the running man. The grenade blew, blasting hard rubber balls right into the guy's guts. He let out a howl and pitched forwards, grabbing his belly.

Leah couldn't think any more. Reason left her completely as she moved, pumping her legs like Satan himself was right on her ass. She reached the guy just as he hit the floor. Jeff Dale. Whimpering and crying like the coward he was.

"Where is he, you sick fuck?" Leah dropped to her knees and crammed her SIG into Dale's left eye. "Where's Kevin?"

She didn't have to tell Dale she'd kill him. He was wheezing from the stinger balls, his unobstructed eye wide and crazed with terror. Spit dribbled from the corner of his mouth.

"Tell me where Kevin is," Leah yelled in case the bastard still couldn't hear from the flashbang. "Tell me right now or so help me I'll make you hurt – and I'll make you hurt for ever."

Something was pounding. Was it her heart? Her brain? The noise pressed against her eardrums. Sounded like helicopters, swooping in close. She half-expected to hear strafing fire or explosions.

You're not in Iraq.

Keep it together.

The noise and her gun were freaking out the stupid ass on the floor beneath her. He was babbling about a barn in the next county. "But they're gone by now. In transit. The sale's over. The sale – an hour ago. It's over!"

Footsteps pounded up the porch. Leah heard men's voices, a few women. The living room. Friendlies? Foes? She didn't care if she took a bullet in the back. No way was Dale telling her it was too late to get to Kevin. She couldn't accept that, not for a single second.

Carson was talking to somebody. Sounded like he was giving orders.

Leah couldn't make sense of any of it. She wanted to kill Dale but knew she couldn't. She had gone too far, way past the point of no return, but she couldn't go the rest of the way. Fuck, she wanted to. Needed to.

A gentle hand gripped her shoulder. "It's OK." Carson's deep voice barely penetrated the battle fog shrouding Leah's senses. Lights came on everywhere. Two men in black body armour approached from the kitchen. Leah glanced up to see their chest protectors marked with three white letters: ATF. Alcohol, Tobacco, Firearms and Explosives officers were on the scene.

How was that possible?

"I turned on my phone and they followed the signal to us," Carson said, like he'd heard her thoughts. "We've got cars on the road and choppers in the air."

"Let us take him, ma'am," the nearest ATF officer said as he knelt to let her see his face, his earnest eyes and, more importantly, his weapon. "Let us have him so we can get routes and possible vehicles. It'll make retrieval easier."

Carson's hand stayed on her shoulder and, when Leah started to get up, he helped her to her feet. Dale didn't try to move as the ATF officers cuffed him and pulled him up, then shoved him through the kitchen, firing questions at him as they moved.

Leah tried to swallow as Carson steadied her, hands on her forearms, his dark eyes boring into her like he was trying to give her all his strength and magic, all his hope and certainty. She felt hot and miserable and lost, and like she had failed at the one thing that really mattered.

"Kevin." It was all she could say. She didn't cry even though she wanted to. Years on the battlefield had robbed her of that. No tears allowed, not for soldiers.

"We'll get him," Carson whispered, and his sureness made her hands shake. Carson gently took the SIG he'd given her and holstered it in his belt. Then he took her hands in his and held them.

She stared at him, confused and so twisted inside she thought she'd split at the middle. She opened her mouth to say something

– thanks, or fuck you, or we're too late, or do you really think your guys can get to Kevin in time – but what came out was, "Why did you kill your father?"

The centres of Carson's eyes seemed to go twice as dark, and he suddenly looked as sad and spent as she felt. "He tried to rape my sister. I took him down then cut a deal to serve and train in the army, then work with the ATF undercover in Walker Valley. In exchange, Chelsea got protective custody to keep her safe from the lowlifes my father knew."

Leah took this in, more amazed than surprised after everything they had been through since she drove up Grace Mountain. "The perfect cover. Nobody else could have gotten in like you did, not here. Not in Walker Valley."

Carson nodded. "Everybody assumed I went to prison and served my time until I got sprung. Nobody blinked when I came home and seemed to take up where good old Pops left off."

Leah let Carson keep hold of her hands even though she wanted to pull away. "All the times you sent me away, all the times I drove out to the prison to see you, you weren't even there."

His sadness seemed to multiply. "I wasn't, but I knew you'd try. I knew it would break your heart when the calls and visits got refused. I thought you'd move on and be a lot better off. I'm sorry, Leah. For all the pain. For all the lies. For everything."

After that, they just stood in silence, looking at each other. Leah had no understanding of time, no sense that she could do anything more than what she had done – about anything. Neither of them moved until a man in a suit with a cell phone came striding into the hallway.

Leah barely noticed him as she kept right on staring at Carson, trying to absorb everything, working to believe the words and accept the realities he had just presented.

"You're damned lucky you didn't fuck everything up, Taylor. We're putting out drug raid cover stories. We'll march you out of here in handcuffs – the valley will eat it up. A few weeks and you can be right back in action." To Leah, the man said, "We've got the boy. He's on route – five minutes. I don't need to tell you that none of this – and I mean *none* of it – can leak. Not ever. We'll figure some way to clean up the mess with Simpson and that prick Bennett."

Suit-man kept talking, but Leah stopped listening. At some point, the guy left the hallway, and Leah was glad.

Kevin was safe.

Kevin was on his way to her.

Leah knew she needed to go outside to wait for Kevin and take him home. That's what she'd set out to do, no matter the risks, no matter the cost. Desperate times called for desperate choices.

And this man holding her hands – Carson Taylor – had just proceeded to rock her world all over again. To find out the truth like this, about what and who he really was . . . to realize he'd laid his career on the line for her with no hesitation . . . to see the compassion and concern on his handsome face – she had no words. She had gone numb all over.

The man of my dreams really is . . . well, the man of my dreams.

Except for lying to her, abandoning her and leaving her totally in the dark.

She pulled her hands out of his grip and muttered, "You son of a bitch."

Then she hit him so hard she thought her fist had cracked at the knuckles. His head snapped to the side, and agony ricocheted from her hand to her elbow to her shoulder, then straight through her heart.

Carson didn't move to stop her when she raised her aching fist for a second blow. The tears got her first. Actual tears, hot and wet and real, coursed down her cheeks.

"Stay the hell away from me," she said, stronger than she felt, louder than she thought she could talk. "I mean it, Carson."

He still didn't move.

He just stood there like some figment of her imagination, like some handsome prince who forgot how to take the princess to live happily ever after.

A fantasy. That's all he ever was. That's all we ever were.

Leah wiped away her tears, then got herself away from Carson Taylor just like she knew she should.

Less than half an hour later, she had Kevin in her arms, in her lap, kissing his soft blond hair as an ATF helicopter whisked them towards the county hospital and Alicia and David, and something that might one day pretend to be a return to normal life.

Ten

Leah stood at the front window of her family home, in a living room that hadn't changed since she was five years old. Two recliners, a sofa, a loveseat a television, and three bookcases. Oak and leather, worn but functional. Even the order of the books on the shelves had stayed the same. She was gazing through gauzy curtains at the street where she'd skinned her knee for the first time, where she'd learned to roller-skate and skateboard and ride a bicycle. The slow summer sunset painted everything pink and yellow and orange, even the old oak in the long-vacant lot across the street.

I had my first kiss behind that tree.

It hadn't been Carson. Second grade. The boy's name was Simon Flynn, and his lips were huge and wet, and best Leah remembered, he had really needed to wipe his nose.

Carson had been her first real kiss though. His touch had kindled the first passion she had ever known. He hadn't been her first physically, but he'd been her first emotionally.

My first love.

And if she told herself the truth, her last.

Alicia bustled into the living room, humming and dusting the nearest bookcase. For a few seconds, she didn't even notice Leah. Alicia had colour in her cheeks now, and she seemed to be putting on a little weight. Leah thought her sister had more energy, as illustrated by her frantic dusting binge.

"What are you doing staring out that window again?" Alicia stopped dusting, her bright blue eyes going wide as she took in Leah's rumpled appearance. "It's been almost a month. Are you wanting Carson to come after you or something? He's bad news, Leah. He always was. Bad blood, that whole family."

Leah tried to smile and nod, but barely twitched her head forwards. She hated that she couldn't tell Alicia the truth about Carson, about what he was – and what he wasn't.

Do I even know? All I have are memories and one very dangerous, very intense night.

Alicia came around the living room coffee table and pointed her dust rag at Leah's nose. "You need to go back to work. I know they're paying you while you're on leave, but I think the boredom's getting to you."

"Boredom's not so bad." This time Leah succeeded in faking her smile. Boredom's fine with me, like cupcakes, and chocolate chip cookies, and this damned ratty blue bathrobe. OK, yeah, she really needed to get back to her regular workout schedule. A few good runs would wake up her mind. As for her body . . . well, she'd just have to control that on a day-to-day basis. It was possible if she didn't let herself think about Carson.

Alicia lowered the dust rag, but she wasn't finished. "Have you been reading the paper? A hold-up down at Second National. An assault on Main and Commerce with fifteen witnesses, all suffering from the same didn't-see-a-thing syndrome. Town Grocery is covering its windows with bars, for God's sake. We need every officer we can get in Walker Valley, and we need them on the streets."

Leah let out a breath and took another look at the sunset across the valley. She had been craving light and colour since that dark, rainy night with Carson. The bust-up of the child trafficking ring had made national headlines for a few days, but Alicia was right. Things in Walker Valley had gone slouching back towards normal the moment the out-of-town news vans had driven away.

"It's gorgeous out there." Alicia joined her, looking at the valley. "So perfect and beautiful, and so completely deceptive. It's like the town itself got cancer years ago, only it never got treated. Why is that, do you think?"

Old question, with no new answers. Leah sighed. "Sooner or later I'll escape Walker Valley again, and this time I'm taking all of you with me."

It would be a bitch to come up with the money, the opportunities, but she would find a way.

Her gaze wandered to the tree-lined base of Grace Mountain. Mist wreathed the slopes, hiding so many secrets, and somewhere in the grey, wet depths, Carson. His boss Robert Jenkins had been right. Walker Valley had swallowed the story of Carson's latest arrest without so much as a cough, and he was already "bailed out", waiting for a sham trial that would clear him, and right back in business. He could be infiltrating another meth operation, or breaking up an illegal weapons deal, or stalking some local prostitution and trafficking ring. Leah didn't know.

But, she had to admit, she worried.

She also had to admit she was a little jealous.

He was doing what she wanted to do – making a real difference in the troubled valley. Setting a few things to rights. Maybe treating some of the strange "cancer" Alicia had mentioned, or getting to the bottom of what made the place seem so dark and wrong and cursed.

He's doing the right thing, no matter what it cost him.

Leah closed her eyes and sighed again.

Carson and his life, they were fantasies. Dreams that used to be. She opened her eyes, and there was Grace Mountain, glowing like a beacon in the distance. She had a crazy thought that the old rock and all those trees wouldn't let go of the sun and let the last light run away from Walker Valley.

Something settled inside her then, and she finally stopped fighting what she knew she needed to do. It was a relief, really. And as scary as hell. She glanced at her sister to see if Alicia was watching, to see if Alicia had already guessed, but Alicia was gazing out at the horizon like she might be imagining some fantasy life of her own.

For now, Leah couldn't help her sister with those dreams. She gave Alicia a hug and kissed her on the cheek. Then she went to her room and got dressed, got her keys, and gave her sister another kiss. When she told Alicia she'd be back soon, she had no idea she was lying.

Night never snuck up on Grace Mountain. Dusk seemed to fight with daylight, then pounce. Carson had lived near the highest slopes most of his life, and he'd never gotten used to how fast darkness fell on the mountain. Somehow, it always annoyed him when the sun finally slipped behind the granite and pines and oaks, leaving the big yard and the hilly, steep fields with only the stars for light.

Tonight, though, he'd heard a car approaching on his way back from checking the cell tower behind the barn.

It wasn't an engine he recognized, and it made him hopeful.

Carson didn't want to hope. Hope hurt too badly. Until that night last month with Leah, he had managed to put concepts like hope and happiness behind him. Since that night . . . well . . .

He'd had trouble going back to business as usual.

Headlights swept up his long driveway, and a car parked in the shadows where Carson couldn't see the make or model. He stood motionless, ready to go for the pistol in his shoulder holster if he didn't recognize whoever stepped into the yellow glow of his porch lights.

Leah came walking out of the darkness like the answer to a midnight prayer. She had on a white cotton skirt and a white blouse, and she looked clean and perfect and unspoiled. For a few seconds, Carson couldn't move. If he took a step, he might shatter the dream. She'd vanish like some sweet, cruel fantasy, and he'd be back where he'd always been with nothing but a whole lot of emptiness on his horizon.

When she got to the porch and headed for the door, Carson finally got himself in gear and called out to her. She stopped and turned. Tiny white moths ringed her head and fluttered near her shoulders. She had her hair down, and the golden blonde strands seemed to glitter as he got closer, closer – and still, she didn't vanish. She waited, watching him as he came up the porch steps. Then she walked straight up to him and put her hands on his chest, and she looked him in the face as he put his arms around her.

She felt soft and fragile in his grip, but he couldn't deny the steel and fire in those gorgeous blue eyes. "If you ever hurt me again," she said, so calm it would have terrified a sane man, "I'll kill you in your sleep."

The smell of honeysuckle bathed Carson's senses. Sanity was overrated. He was happy with crazy. Crazy was fine by him. "I'll keep the SIG loaded for you. Just make it a merciful shot."

Leah moved closer, her body touching his, the swell of her full breasts pressing against his chest. Her fingers slid across the back of his neck, pulling him down, pulling him closer as she raised up to meet him.

"I'm not good at mercy," she whispered.

Just like when they were younger, she closed her eyes first, just before their lips touched.

Fire exploded in Carson's veins as he connected with the wet silk of her mouth. Every muscle tightened. He felt nothing but her heat, her nearness. He heard himself growl, couldn't stop the possessive tightening of his arms, didn't want to stop the hard proof of his arousal pressing against her belly. When he teased her lips with his tongue, she opened, let him in, joined with him—

But it wasn't like it used to be.

This was something new. Something like falling in love all over again.

After that first kiss, and a second, and a third, he touched her hair, her face. "I dreamed about you for a lot of years. This is better."

"Make it more." She ran her lips across his palm, then his thumb. "Make it everything."

Carson kissed her again, urgent, needing her as much as wanting her, and she moaned into the kiss. He lifted her off her feet and cradled her to him.

Oh, yeah. This was new and better. And it was right, and it was right damned now. "Just one thing," he murmured as he carried her through the dark, false part of the house to his bedroom, the only place neat, the only place orderly, the only place real in his life – tenfold now that she was there with him. "Don't shoot me 'til morning. I want a chance to earn my reprieve."

She bit at his bottom lip as he stretched her across the bed.

"Who knows –" he couldn't stop staring at her as he pulled off his shirt "– if I try hard enough, I might get myself a full pardon."

Eleven

Leah wondered if it was possible for two people to catch fire and burn to death without even caring.

The years were gone now. And all the darkness. And all of their clothes. The barriers were down, swept away, totally destroyed, and she was glad. Her heart hadn't pounded like this for anyone else. Her body hadn't responded to any man's touch like it did to Carson's. Just the sight of him left her shaking inside, and ready, and waiting.

His muscled chest felt rough against her fingertips, all man, just like his woods and pine scent. He studied her like she was his secret treasure, his most secret fantasy. He let her look at him, let her learn him fresh and new, and, when she raised her hands to his face, the hard stubble on his cheeks gave her sweet shivers everywhere.

"Don't wait any longer," she said, her voice barely audible, her skin a blazing misery waiting to be soothed.

Carson lowered his head.

Groaning, not wanting to survive another second, she pressed his face into her breast. He tasted her nipple, and her entire body throbbed in response.

"Harder," Leah murmured, wanting the flames, craving the rough bite as he nipped, then started to suck. She arched into his body and felt his cock against her leg, thick and warm, soft yet as hard as tempered steel.

Perfection.

She wanted him now. She wanted him fast. Then she wanted him all night and the next day, as much as she could take, as long as she could take it.

He toyed with her, switching nipples, then switching again and again. Leah couldn't stop the trembling, couldn't hold back the moans. His low growls of desire echoed through her centre, doubling her pleasure, pushing her towards frantic.

"Incredible," he said, quiet and definite, and bit her nipple, and bit it again, erotic pain, erotic pleasure blending until she had to run her fingers through his dark hair and grab and pull. Each time he sucked her breast, she pressed him closer.

She'd had other men, but she'd never had this – not even with Carson those first times so long ago.

This was passion. This was excitement. The words had meaning now.

I've been waiting for this man.

Carson bit her nipple again, shoving her right to that edge – then stopping. She moaned and pulled his hair harder.

He laughed at her, a deep rumble in his throat. Then he ran his tongue down her belly, all the way down. She spread her legs wide, and he pushed her thighs even farther apart as he tasted and teased, teased and tasted, leaving her gasping and damned close to begging.

"So good." She shifted her hips, taking more of his mouth, but he grabbed her thigh and held her still. She was so swollen, so ready, that the gentle brush of his lips and tongue almost made her scream.

"Sweet." His hot breath was almost the last straw. And then, "I have to have you. I have to have all of you."

Leah's thoughts lost coherence as Carson moved and settled between her legs. She didn't realize he was sitting on his knees until he lifted her hips and slid her tight, shaking body towards him.

Hanging on the sharp edge of need and want, Leah opened her eyes.

Carson's untamed stare rocked her essence as he held her absolutely motionless, then drove into her, deep, deeper, pulling her hips forwards. They moaned together, turning loose years of frustration with such a total union. Leah felt him inside her, felt him everywhere around her, felt the connection deepen as he brought her hard against his next thrust, and the next, and the next.

"Don't stop," she demanded. "Never stop."

Freedom. Release.

Finally.

Leah's back arched as he lifted her again, again, filling her, plunging into her, driving away everything but the heat, the joining, the ecstasy.

"More." Begging now. She didn't care. "Carson, more!"

On fire. Burning up. Closer. So close now.

When she looked at Carson, she saw a matching heat on his face. His muscles glistened like he'd been rubbed with oil. His dark eyes seemed to grow deeper with each movement, each breath.

When she felt herself clenching, Leah screamed and didn't feel shy about it.

"So right," Carson rumbled. "You're everything, Leah. Everything."

Grace Mountain could have crumbled around Leah. She wouldn't have known. She wouldn't have cared. All she could feel was Carson and the liquid fire searing every inch of her body, inside and out. All she could hear was him calling her name as he fell off the edge of the world with her, both of them tumbling and tumbling, and neither of them caring at all where they finally landed.

Twelve

"You're serious." Leah looked from Carson to Robert Jenkins.

In his suit and tie, Carson's ATF supervising special agent seemed totally out of place in Carson's "criminal decor" living room. It had only been a few weeks since Leah drove up Grace Mountain to spend one night and just sort of stayed, and it had taken all of her self-control not to clean the place from top to bottom and completely wreck Carson's whole badass motif.

Jenkins tugged at his collar and tie, fighting the summer heat. "I'm very serious. I think it's a natural."

Leah studied Carson for a few seconds, and he picked up her unspoken question. "Nothing changes. You're still here only as long as you want to be here. No strings. However things work out between us, we can play it off with my cover and yours, too, if you want to keep working with the ATF."

Jenkins nodded. "We need somebody in that police station. After Jeff Dale – well, you know we do."

"A lot of folks won't like me being hooked up with a known criminal." Leah gestured to Carson, not quite sure how Jenkins thought this would work.

"From all the gossip, half the valley's expecting it," Jenkins said with confidence. "The other half's surprised it didn't happen the day you got back to town. Trust me. It'll fly."

Leah wanted to believe the man. Her mind spun in big circles, trying to be sure she didn't miss any details, any catches in the offer Jenkins had made her. "Where will you send Alicia and her family?"

"They can choose Seattle, Phoenix or San Francisco. We've got potential positions for David in all three cities, decent schools for Kevin – and if your sister has a reoccurrence of her cancer, she'll be able to get first-rate care." Jenkins smiled at her, and he seemed sincere. "We'll manage all contacts and visits. It's not as restrictive as Witness Protection, but we have to be careful."

That sounded good to Leah. Better than good. "Just one more question, then. When do I start?"

Jenkins' smile got a lot bigger. "As soon as possible."

Carson shrugged. "How about now? You said we needed to go to the grocery store."

Leah felt her pulse pick up.

Could she really do this? Was she finally getting her chance to make a difference in Walker Valley?

"I'll try it," she told Jenkins.

He held out his hand, and they shook. "There's paperwork," he said. "I'll get it to you fast."

A few minutes later, as Leah and Carson watched Jenkins drive away, Leah couldn't quite believe she had just been hired on to work undercover with the ATF.

"Let me get this straight." She turned to Carson, keeping her eyes locked on his. "I play bitch to your bastard. We have lots of hot, sweaty sex. We act like bad guys, but we secretly get to take them down."

Doing his worst cowboy imitation, Carson drawled, "We'll clean up this town."

Then he grabbed her and kissed her until her knees got wobbly. When he pulled back, he grinned and raised an eyebrow. "Want to practise? Try this out."

He turned her loose and tried to look mean and rotten. "Get in the truck," he said, too loud, too harsh, but he winked when he said it. "Now."

She scuttled towards the big black Ford, jumped in and fastened her seat belt. When he got in, she said, "You take on the bastard role with gusto, don't you?"

"It'll be a pleasure, ruining your reputation. And it's all in a day's work, honey."

Leah pointed her finger and shook her head. "Oh, no. No, no, no. If you call me that again, I'll kick your balls through your nostrils."

Carson started the Ford. He hit the gas and sent them roaring down the driveway, no doubt planning to jump every kerb in Walker Valley to draw as much attention them as possible.

Leah held the panic grip, shaking her head.

He was laughing.

The jerk was actually laughing, but the best part was, she was laughing, too.

Sorcery

Cathy Clamp

The door knocker was heavy, a throwback to when the castle was built. I had to use two hands to lift it but it barely made a noise when it fell. Again I picked it up and put all of my frustration and fear into the downward strike.

The echoing boom that resulted made me want to run but my fear held my feet in place as surely as if they were part of the stone. The night seemed to close in around me and made me feel very small and lost.

Footsteps then, soft as a padding cat, but then louder as they grew closer. And still I stood, my heart beating like a trip hammer and a cold sweat springing from my brow. The door opened on oiled hinges, silent and smooth.

"Beth?" His name was Ethan and we'd gone to school together. He'd been rich, handsome and popular and I'd been poor and plain. But then his family's fortune took a nosedive and now he was a servant, tending to the needs of one who could afford the luxury.

He leaned out, looked around, panic and worry etched across his face. "What are you doing here? Go home before he sees you."

"I have to see him, Ethan. People are dying. I might be the only hope." He tried to shut the door, make my choice for me, but I put a foot and hand to stop it from happening.

A deep, accented voice came from down the hallway. "Who is at the door, Ethan?"

"Nobod—"

I called out over the top of him. "A witch, sir. From the village. I must speak to you."

In the pause that followed I could hear our heartbeats in coun-
terpoint, mine fast but Ethan's racing to catch up. Then the voice
again, filled with a warm and eager anticipation. "By all means,
come forth. Ethan, show her the way."

"Leave." His whisper urged, pleaded in just a few tones. The
grip of his hand on my wrist matched his wide eyes.

I shook off the hand. "I can't. Take me to him."

The pain on his face was real and there was no denying there was
cause. Anton Zell was a vampire – ancient as the pyramids. Legend
told of his fierce appetite and his equally terrible temper. But he
was also renowned to know everything there was to know about
spells and magic and I needed that knowledge tonight.

At whatever cost.

Ethan tugged his black butler's uniform and straightened his
bow tie before opening the door, his hands trembling enough
that I had to stop looking or I'd lose my nerve. Finally he turned
the knob with a deep breath. But before it opened he gave me
one last look, filled with compassion, empathy and . . . sympathy.
"Please?"

But I just looked straight ahead, clenching my hands so tight my
fingernails dug into my palms. I couldn't answer because I wanted
to scream, *Yes, please! Help me run away, push me out.*

But I didn't. I couldn't. I squared my shoulders and gave him a
simple nod. His eyes closed, defeated, and he opened the door.

Where the hallway had been dim and cold, the room was filled
with warmth. The fireplace blazed and lamps on the tables made
the room seem like any other house in town. I took two steps inside
and jumped a bit when the door closed behind me.

Movement caught my eye and I turned to see a tall, elegant older
man walking towards me. Dark hair with silver highlights crowned
a face that was sharply angular but not unattractive. He dipped his
head when he stood in front of me and held out a flattened palm.
"I am Anton Zell. Welcome to my home, Miss—" There was a
questioning lilt.

I put my palm on his, unsure of the proper custom. His hand was
soft and uncalloused, with long, tapered fingers that were nicely
manicured. "Beth Malus."

His fingers squeezed lightly and he lifted my hand to his lips.
The moment his lips touched a shock ran through me. I was
suddenly aware of the cooler temperature of his skin. He let his
mouth press down, and the pressure of lips and teeth against me,

the slight wetness of his saliva, caused a frantic fluttering of my heart. The bone under soft flesh was sharp, demanding. A long moment passed while he tasted me, smelled my skin and made my fear a living thing apart from me. "A distinct pleasure, Beth Malus. What can I do for you?"

He'd released my hand but I hadn't noticed and was still holding it in the air, as frozen as a statue. I shook my head and smiled, trying to get back in control of the moment. I tried to make my hand part of the conversation by pointing towards the door. "I'm hoping you'd allow me to look at your library."

He raised his brows and crossed his arms over his chest. "Indeed? For what purpose?" Reality seemed to coalesce around me once more and the room was just a room. I looked around for a place to sit. It was a long story.

He remembered propriety with an embarrassed expression. He instantly swept a hand to a pair of chairs near the fire, across from one another and separated by a thick wooden coffee table. "Please. Do sit down." A hand on my lower back to guide me brought the awareness again in a rush so strong I nearly gasped.

But then it disappeared once we were seated in chairs. I blinked and put my feet firmly on the floor and stared at him. His face was passive, interested – not at all terrible or frightening. Another deep breath and I was in control once more. "There have been deaths in my town. I don't know if you've heard."

He nodded, with what appeared to be an actual expression of sadness. "I have heard. Disease is a terrible, devastating thing. I am grateful some days I'm beyond such possibility. Is that what you hope to find in my books? I'm afraid you'll be disappointed. I have little in the way of medical texts."

"But you have books on sorcery. Is that right?"

His brows rose with interest and he crossed one leg over the other. "You're a sorceress?"

I nodded, feeling a little awkward at the interest. "I'm a witch, yes. One of a long line of healers. I believe that where there is no answer in the scientific world, there might be a cure in the magical."

His lips curled into a wide smile and now I could see the actual fangs. His canines were elongated and came to a sharp point. A thread of fear grabbed my stomach and made me squirm in the butter-soft leather seat. "Which are you? Witch or sorceress?"

I shook my head, not understanding. "They're the same thing."

"Are they?" He paused and stared at me, waiting. For what? I thought about it while his eyes bored holes into my head. My shirt began to itch and with it, my bra, making my skin twitch and move.

His arms were resting lightly on the padded rests, both thumbs pressing and rubbing against the index finger over and over. While he stared.

"I think so." Was that really my voice . . . so breathy and low? I shifted in my seat once more because now I was itching there too. And wet. What was happening to me?

"Tell me." It was similarly low, nearly a whisper, and I wasn't sure what we were talking about any more. His legs uncrossed and I couldn't keep my eyes from them, nor the way the tailored cloth created shadows that spoke of the fullness of flesh underneath. "Let's speak of witchcraft . . . and sorcery."

The fingers kept turning and twisting, creating a direct reaction in my breasts. It was as though I could feel his fingers kneading my nipples, making them tighten, harden. They began to ache. I shifted in the seat again and now the lacy bra abraded the sensitive nerves. A sudden contraction between my legs made me tense and shudder. And he watched.

I needed to get back to the subject, keep my mind on task. "Sorcery is just another word for witchcraft. Spells are spells. I've always been good at practising magic."

Another smile but this one more bemused. "You are indeed right in one respect. Witchcraft is the practising of magic. But—" He leaned forwards and let his lips open slightly, making my eyes follow as his tongue flicked out and slowly wet them. "What is sorcery?"

"It's the same," I breathed out and shifted again, the wetness between my legs causing my body to tighten and swell. My fingers dug into the leather, feeling very much like the skin of his palm. I rubbed it unconsciously and twisted my upper body, trying to find relief from the bra that had trapped my pebble-hard nipples in the holes of lace – captured them as surely as his movements mimicked. I couldn't keep my eyes from following his fingers because now he'd changed them slightly. One hand was rubbing, while the other thumb flicked incessantly against the middle finger, creating a new spasm inside me with each twitch. I swallowed hard, my mouth suddenly dry. He responded instantly by leaning forwards and pouring a glass of clear, chilled water for me.

It broke whatever spell was on me and I leaned forwards to grab the thick crystal like a lifeline. It poured down my throat, slowly at first and then in gulps until the icy temperature cleared my head. I put the cold goblet against my forehead, letting the cool seep into my skin. I held the glass long after the water was gone and it warmed to the touch.

Zell's eyes bored into me through the crystal and I couldn't escape the look of a predator lurking inside the innocent depth of blue.

What would those icy fingers feel like on my skin . . . my nipples, or inside me? How long to warm other parts of him to the touch?

He smiled slightly, as though reading my thoughts. Heat rose to my cheeks and I shook my head, trying to erase the image. I wasn't a virgin but the thought of letting myself run amuck with a man such as him . . . No. I let my voice return to normal. "Are you willing to let me borrow the books? It's for a good cause. I promise to bring them back when I'm done."

He raised his hands with a politely sad expression. "I'm very sorry, but I cannot allow the books to leave the house. Some of them are very ancient and all are irreplaceable. However, you're welcome to look at them here. Those, that is, that will *let* you look." He raised his brows significantly and I took the bait.

"I don't understand."

Zell stood up from his chair and skirted around the table towards me gracefully, his every movement smooth and slow. I felt trapped but it was more a heady sensation than panicky. While part of me wanted to leap to my feet and escape out of the door, another part watched him with languid contentment. He held out his hand and mine lifted and took it without conscious thought. He pulled backwards and I rose to my feet until I was standing mere inches from his slowly moving chest. The fast flutter of my heart was back and every hair stood on end. "Then I will . . . teach you." He leaned close enough that I could smell the soft cologne he'd splashed on his neck, along with the soap used to clean his clothes. His breath eased along my cheek into my ear and I shuddered deliciously. "Would you *like* that . . . Beth Malus?"

My eyes closed as another shudder overtook me. "Yes." It was a single word, innocently meant but his chuckle was low and satisfied in response.

He tucked my hand in the crook of his arm and pulled me along at his side to the double doors at the end of the room. He released my arm and opened one door and waved me inside.

The library was the size of a warehouse – thousands of books on hundreds of shelves. I looked up and around, to the ceiling at least two storeys up, to the ladders that attached to tracks and walkways between cases. *My God. The sheer volume of knowledge here – I could be the most powerful witch in the world.* I shook my head. "I wouldn't even know where to start."

He picked up my hand and backed up, pulling me forwards with him. He navigated the aisles effortlessly without looking. His eyes were on mine and I had to trust where he was leading because I couldn't pull my gaze away, no matter how hard I tried. When we stopped, I had no idea where we were. There were bookshelves everywhere and hallways leading off in all directions. He gestured to a shelf right at chest level. The books were elegantly bound in identical red leather, which matched the chairs in the sitting room. All bore a single number that increased from book to book but with no title. "Here are the books on witchcraft and sorcery. Witchcraft on the left; sorcery on the right. Which can you open?"

I pulled the first one at the far left and opened it. It was an elementary text that I had on my own shelf. But I'd already looked there before I arrived, so I slipped it back into the proper numerical slot. Then I stepped slightly past him and removed the furthest right book. I could feel his eyes on me as I laid it on my arm and tried to lift the cover.

But it wouldn't open. I pulled and then yanked at both covers but it was as though they were glued shut. "Is this a joke book or something?"

"Draw another one. Try again." His voice was right in my ear and created tingles that made my knees go suddenly weak.

I did. In fact, I tried all of the ones on the right side of the centre bar. But none would open. "What am I missing? If you're right and these can only be opened by a sorceress, what do I have to do?"

I turned around and looked up at him. But instead of backing up to a normal-speaking distance, he stepped forwards and pushed me back against the shelves until his body was against mine and I was trapped with nowhere to go. He leaned down, close enough to send shock waves through my body and breathed words into my mouth. "That is something you will have to discover. What *is* a sorceress and are you willing to become one? Are you willing to pay that price?"

"You could tell me . . . teach me as you said you would." Again my words came out breathy and I closed my eyes, not daring to look at what he might do. What was the price? Would he drink from my neck, strangle me, tear my body to pieces and then only tell me if I survived?

Did I care?

"*Yesss.* I could." Now his breath was on my neck, so close. So very close and as soft as down against my skin. Every nerve was alive, needing, wanting. His long, cool fingers curled around my forearms and I sucked in air as though I could never fill my lungs enough. He pressed himself hard against me, fingers tightening, until I gasped.

In that moment I wanted anything he would do to me. I was open, wet and hungry as never before. "*Please.*" The word was a whisper that destroyed every control I'd built in my life.

"It's morning," he said in a similar whisper. "You will have to wait until dark. Until then . . . sleep. Dream."

I knew I'd fallen bonelessly to the floor but couldn't seem to stop myself. Just like I knew he picked me up and carried me up a long flight of stairs. Then there was nothing for a long time, except the ache that wouldn't go away, the craving that hadn't been fulfilled. I squirmed under cool sheets. I wanted him inside me. His hands, his cock, his teeth. It didn't matter.

I reached up to touch my nipples, so hard and aching that I couldn't think straight. I plunged my own fingers between my legs, rubbing myself, thrusting my hips up – searching, straining. But it wouldn't relieve the tension. It only added to it.

I tossed and turned and could finally stand it no more. I got out of the massive four-poster bed and walked out into the hallway. "Ethan?" I'd always lusted after him and right now, I needed hands touching me, a hard cock inside me. If I waited until night, I'd go insane.

He didn't answer. I knew he lived here, was a round-the-clock servant but I couldn't find him.

I wandered the halls, the sumptuous furnishings and expensive artwork unappreciated in my need for something to ease the aching desire. Every door was opened, with Ethan's name being called louder and louder to no avail.

Finally I reached the last door, an elegantly carved oak artwork that would have taken a dozen men to install . . . or one vampire. I opened it cautiously. On a pedestal in the centre of the room was a black four-poster single bed.

Not a coffin.

Anton Zell was lying on the bed, face up, his breathing slow and steady, his hands by his sides. I'd thought vampires were dead in the day. Do they merely sleep? What would he do to me if I woke him?

I approached the bed without a sense of fear. I knew I should be afraid. There were too many stories of women who had met their end in the room with a waking vampire.

But he looked so peaceful, so beautifully pale and quiet. I put my palm on his chest, feeling the rise and fall of his chest. He didn't wake. I touched his hand then, the one that had captured me, held me motionless. It was as cool as the water I'd drunk. I raised the hand, feeling the limp weight of his arm try to steal it away. I kissed the hand as he'd kissed mine, with my whole mouth. Licked the skin, tasted him.

He'd removed his coat and tie and undone the first two pearl buttons. I let my painted fingernail trace down the smooth white cheek, then down the neck and into the open "V" of his shirt. My body was burning alive, throbbing to feel hands holding me down, roughly taking what they wanted from me.

I undid another button and then more until soon his whole chest was bare. I blew warm air on his nipples and watched them react, tighten. He let out a small sound and I froze, suddenly realizing what I was doing and how it would be seen. He'd never given any indication he wanted sex with me. What if all he'd wanted was blood, or nothing at all?

I leaned back from the bed, thinking to leave and find some other way to ease the ache. But then I looked down. The tailored fabric of his pants was taut against an erection. I hadn't anticipated that he might be able to . . . well, I just hadn't considered it. I tentatively touched the fabric and pressed. He moaned and his head flopped to the side with obvious pleasure.

He'd spoken of sleeping, of dreaming. Did vampires dream? Specifically, did they have *wet* dreams?

My brain tried to convince my hands it was wrong, that I shouldn't unbuckle his belt, unzip his pants. That I shouldn't stare with hungry awe as his cock sprang out and up proudly. But my hands wouldn't listen. They stroked along the cool length, feeling each ridge and vein throb with similar hunger. They gently caressed the heavy ball sacs inside the pants while he moaned and twisted on the bed.

What does a vampire taste like?

Once the question was in my mind, there was no stopping myself. I slowly lowered my face to the fragrant, musky thickness and slowly licked up the length of it. The moan became a growl of need that urged me on. I dropped my mouth on to his cock and let it slide in, cool and thick until it hit the back of my throat. I rested there, just feeling the delicious texture and taste of clean skin. Then I started to suck, slowly at first and then with more force, feeling the head respond, leak salty fluid.

"*Bethany!*" A horrified whisper pulled me straight up. I turned to see Ethan standing in the doorway with wide eyes. His mouth moved but didn't actually say anything until, "Oh my God!"

But he wasn't just horrified. I could see a growing erection as he watched me slowly stroking his employer's rigid cock. "Close the door, Ethan." His hand tensed on the knob, his eyes wide at my command. And it was a command. "Come in and close the door."

He did, with jerky movements that told of both fear and . . . something else. It was the something else that made his pants tent out even further. "He'll kill us."

I nodded with a glance at the vampire's face. "Probably. But I'm not stopping until it's done. Take off your pants."

Another twitch moved his belt. "Excuse me?"

I took my hand off Anton long enough to pull my shirt up over my head in one fluid movement. My breasts were hot, heavy and aching for hands on them. I stood and walked towards Ethan while his eyes went wide and his pants twitched. I knelt in front of him and undid his belt. He tried to push my hands away, but I pulled his hands down until one breast was in each one. I had to strain a little to get the angles right. The shock of the sensation of my hard nipples in his palms froze him like a statue. My hands returned to my work and in seconds his pants were around his ankles and my mouth was on his cock.

He moaned and nearly lost his footing, stumbling until he fell back against the wall. I leaned forwards and released his swollen member from my mouth's suction. "Tease me, Ethan. Pinch my nipples. Make me crazy."

His body overrode his brain and he did as instructed. He began to push himself into my mouth with desperation. Nobody ever visited the castle and I wondered how long it had been since he'd touched a woman. He worked his length in and out of my mouth while he squeezed and flicked my nipples just like I'd wanted Zell to do. "I want to fuck you, Beth."

I released his cock and smiled. "I know you do. And you will."

I stood up and led him by the hand towards the bed. He tried to pull away but I was insistent. Anton's cock had wilted a little but when I leaned over and put it again in my mouth it quickly regained its earlier hardness.

I repositioned myself so I was leaning over the bed and wiggled my butt at Ethan.

Would he? Would he drop my pants and shove himself inside me? It was what I wanted, needed.

He obeyed with a speed and near viciousness that almost pulled my mouth from Anton's length. In moments I had to steady myself on the bed from his frantic thrusts inside my desperately swollen folds. He grabbed my hips and slammed himself inside me until I could feel his balls slapping against my clit.

I wanted to climax. So badly it hurt. But the higher he took me, the more elusive it became. Finally he could stand it no more and, despite the fact I hadn't found relief, he moaned and pulled himself out. I felt him twitch against my lower back, spurting wetness to shiver my spine while I continued to stroke and tease the cool cock between my lips. It wasn't warming, despite the heat in my mouth. That interested me.

Ethan ran his fingers through my hair and leaned heavily on me with a whisper. "God, that was good, Beth."

"I need more." The words were fierce, from deep in my chest, and I felt the very beginnings of magic rumble in my stomach. I'd never had that happen before without a ritual. I kicked my way out of my pants and, despite Ethan's frantic hands trying to pull me back, I climbed on to the bed and straddled Anton's hips. I turned my head and stared at Ethan before commanding, "Kiss me. Kiss me hard." I adjusted myself and lowered on to the vampire's erection. The temperature difference was such a shock to my system that every muscle in my body spasmed and magic flared.

Ethan stared at the roiling magic around me with apprehension but watching me begin to slide up and down his master's dick was too much for him. He put one knee on the bed and pulled my face to his. The kiss was deep and powerful, hard thrusts of his tongue that matched the movements of my hips. His jaw worked against mine while his fingers tangled in my hair, keeping me tight against him.

The other hand went to my breast and pulled and rolled the nipple. Something started building inside me and I moaned. Ethan took that as a sign to continue to do the same thing, but even more. His hand tweaked and pulled at my breast while his mouth worked at me. But it was the chilled, twitching thickness inside me that was making me crazy.

Then the hips moved. Thrust upwards when I went down. I pulled away from Ethan's mouth to find Anton's eyes open, staring . . . watching.

Ethan let out a squeak and froze. So did I. Zell made a lazy motion of his hand for Ethan to back up. He did, with stumbling, scrambling quickness. He picked up his pants and fled.

The door slammed and then I was alone with the vampire. His cock was stuffed inside me and he was . . . what? His hips moved just a bit and I gasped. I was so close to climax I could barely think. My breathing was coming in short gasps and my blood pressure was making my head throb. After a long moment, he laced his fingers together on his chest. "Pray continue."

I started to lean forwards, to rest myself on his cool chest but he pushed me back to an upright position. "Just like that." The voice was heated with desire but he gave nothing away in his face. "Put your arms up and lift your hair."

I did, staring up at the ceiling with my chest thrust out. I could barely catch my breath as the knowledge of his gaze on me, his cold thickness inside me, drove me even higher.

"Now ride me. Take your pleasure."

My thighs tightened and I rose up slowly and then lowered back down. Right at the end, he gave an extra thrust and made me cry out. I opened my eyes but he reached up and closed them again with a smile that showed fangs. I jumped when his hands finally found my breasts and his fingers began to roll the nipples just as I'd needed. He teased around my crotch while I moved but wouldn't touch what needed to be touched. My desperate movements increased, with him changing the angle or the speed at will. I heard him whispering to me, urging me on. "Don't wait to have it given. *Take* what you need."

Fine then. I leaned forwards and he let me. I put one hand on Anton's broad, pale shoulders and continued to slam myself up and down on his cock. I toyed with my own clit, moving it this way and that while he stared with folded hands and let himself be used for my pleasure. I kissed him hard, opening his mouth as Ethan had done to me. The fangs were just teeth, not sharp enough to cut but I licked them and tangled my tongue with his.

I felt energy, heat build inside me, and I was suddenly apart from myself, letting the waves of pleasure wash over me as I kissed and fucked and finally eased the need.

My mouth moved away from his as my body tensed. At last. At long last. My cries caused him to grab my hips. He took back the reins and drove himself into me, further and faster than I could do myself. A second orgasm blossomed over the first and I was weightless, breathless and screaming his name. Power soared around us in an electric arc that stole my last ounce of resistance. I heard him moan and felt cool fingers dig into my skin as he thrust up one last time. I was so tight around him that I felt every twitching expansion as he released cool liquid into me.

"Do you ever warm?" It seemed an odd question, even to me, during a climax. But I had to know.

"I'm not dead. Just permanently near-dead. This is my normal temperature. I warm only when I've fed."

The thought should have panicked me but there was little left that could right now. I felt lazy, content and willing to make him feel the same. "Do you need to? Feed, that is?" I lifted my tangled hair and turned my head to bare my neck. I paused, a little worried he would, and terrified he wouldn't.

That fanged smile once more. "Perhaps some day. But I don't need to feed daily as the stories say. What's more important right now is to finish what you've started."

I was sated so I shook my head. "I'm done. Exhausted."

He raised his brows and lifted me off him. His clothing was a wreck but he didn't seem to mind. He simply stripped off his pants and shirt and I finally got to see him fully nude.

Anton was breathtaking, chiselled and slender with abs that men in the village struggled to achieve in a gym, but never did. He held out his hand. "You're not nearly done. Come."

I took the slender fingers, even though I didn't understand. "Where are we going?"

He led me to a wardrobe on the other side of the room. "Look and tell me what you see." The mirror showed an adequate body but nothing to write home about. My breasts were heavy and the nipples bright red from the teasing. My hips were a little . . . hippy, but I could still fit in clothes from high school. Still, I did look content and that was something.

"I look like I just had really good sex with an amazing lover. Have I thanked you?"

He frowned abruptly and it made me feel strange inside. "You should never feel the need to. Have you not yet learned the lesson?"

Apparently not. My brows furrowed and he sighed. He opened the wardrobe and pulled out a robe. Or at least I thought it was a robe. But it was completely transparent and pearlescent with a high stiff collar, wide sleeves and only a tie at the neck to hold it together. He took it off the hanger and held it out for me to put on. It seemed a little silly to put on a robe that covered nothing but I did it, to please him.

"It's . . . interesting." I looked in the mirror after he closed the door. I had to admit it made me look different. There was a wildness in my hair that the robe turned from just a tangled mess to something exotic and intentional.

"Now." He turned and pointed me towards the door. "Finish what you've started. Go downstairs and take what you will. Own this cloak, use it." His eyes glittered with power but not of the supernatural kind. "*Master* it."

I turned again and stared at myself in the mirror with a confused expression. He stood just slightly behind me and watched. Waited.

Master it.

My hand found his and I pulled it around me, putting it on my breast while I watched. He let me and kept it there when I removed my hand and encircled his cock again. He let out a small sound and it emboldened me to stroke his length again. It was probably too soon for sex again but while I stroked, I stared at him. "Kiss me."

He smiled and pulled my head back before closing his lips over mine. I nipped at his tongue and pulled his head closer while I continued to stroke him erect again. When I moved back at last, I smiled. "I think I understand."

"Yes? Then prove it."

I swept out of the room with the robe blowing in a breeze I created. Anton didn't follow but instead crawled back into bed. I shut the door behind me so he could rest. Walking down the hallway again, I was amazed I hadn't noticed some of the beautiful things he owned. Even the simplest of arrangements – a smooth, carved table, the coloured vase that spouted flowers – they were intended to entice the senses. Elevate the mind and body.

Yes. I understood now.

Ethan was at the bottom of the staircase, staring up at me with mingled terror and lust. "Are you OK? Did he hurt you?"

My bare feet stopped right in front of him and I guided his hands to my bare waist. He tried to pull back but the fire that had grown in my stomach had moved to my chest and to my hands. He was helpless against the magic, even as I leaned in and sucked his tongue into my mouth, nipped it.

Owned it.

When I ended the kiss, his eyes were wide and hungry and his fingers were digging deep into my hips. "No. He didn't hurt me. He *taught* me." I undid Ethan's bow tie and pulled him along by it. "And now it's time to teach you."

We went into the library, my feet remembering the path when I'd followed Anton. I selected a book from the far right side of the shelf and revelled in the weight of the embossed paper, the cool slick sensation of the leather against my bare skin. The heady knowledge of what I was going to do with it tightened my skin.

The magic in my stomach continued to guide Ethan as we walked back and it chose a very different part of clothing than his tie to pull him along by. He groaned and followed along obediently until we were inside the study. Had it only been last night? It felt so very different now.

I sat down in the big red chair and raised my legs until they were over the arms and the robe was spread to reveal my naked, restless body. "Lick me, Ethan, and then fuck me while I read."

What's difference between a witch and a sorceress?

A witch follows the magic and does what she can.

A sorceress owns the magic and does what she will.

Ethan had no choice but to kneel in front of me. I gave him no choice. I moaned as I felt his tongue flick against my once again hungry body and his hands caress my still-swollen breasts. I rested the book on his soft black hair and, without any effort at all, lifted the front cover.

It would be night again soon and I wanted to be prepared to show Anton the sorcery I'd learned before I went back to the village . . . and made it my own.

Blind Date

N. J. Walters

"I won't do it." Audra Simmons glared at her best friend. Make that her former best friend. "How could you do this to me?"

"Come on, Audra. It's just a blind date. He's a nice guy."

Audra rubbed her forehead. She had a nasty headache brewing and Joyce wasn't helping with her plug for Mr Nice Guy. She took a deep breath and tried again. "You know I don't date. Not since—" She abruptly shut her mouth, refusing to speak *his* name.

"Not since Tyson." The sympathy in Joyce's voice stiffened Audra's spine. No, she hadn't dated since Tyson Brewer had left her eight long months ago. Their relationship had gone from wonderful to disastrous in such a short time it had left her reeling, unwilling and unable to trust her instincts when it came to men. She'd had visions of them taking their relationship to the next level. She'd even begun to entertain thoughts of marrying the man. Instead, she'd ended up with a heartache that hadn't gone away. Not yet.

"That's beside the point," she pointed out to Joyce. "I'm busy. Starting my own law practice has taken up all my time." That was the one good thing that had come from the break-up. She'd taken stock of her life and redefined her priorities.

"I thought the whole point of leaving Barstow, Plimpton and Dyer was so that you would stop working yourself to death and actually have a life," Joyce pointed out.

Audra hated that her friend was right.

That was one of the few things she and Tyson had argued about – work. His and hers. She'd been pushing hard to make junior partner and he'd been putting in long hours with the engineering firm he worked for, which did a lot of overseas work. Near the end, they'd hardly had any time together, reduced to communicating by cell phone and email.

Audra took a deep breath and slowly released it. She glanced around her small office and smiled. This was one thing she'd done right in the past eight months. She'd left the corporate rat race behind and now spent her days working with small businesses and individual clients, taking care of their legal concerns. Even with starting her own small firm, she had more free hours than she was used to.

"Please, Audra. Tom already told him you'd go." Tom was Joyce's husband. A bear of a man, he ran his own construction company and loved his wife to distraction. He'd also done a lot of the work on Audra's new offices . . . for free. She owed him, owed both of them for being friends and supporting her through everything.

"What's his name?"

Joyce fidgeted with the strap of her purse. "His name?" she parroted.

Audra raised one eyebrow. "Mr Nice Guy does have a name, doesn't he?"

Her friend gave a small laugh. "Of course he does. It's David."

Audra waited, but when nothing more seemed to be forthcoming, she prompted Joyce. "David what?"

"Just David. We thought it was better to keep it to first names. No pressure. Just two people meeting one another. If you decide to exchange more information when you meet, that's entirely up to you."

She wasn't certain she liked the sound of that. Audra frowned at her friend as she sidled towards the door. "I was going to Google him." In this day and age a woman couldn't be too careful. Information was readily available at the click of a mouse. It only made sense to check out a potential date.

"Where's the romance in that?" Joyce huffed. She crossed her arms over her chest and glared at Audra. "I swear, there's no romance, no mystery left in the world. The man is perfectly safe and acceptable. I wouldn't have agreed to set up the date otherwise. Trust me."

Audra felt her resistance weakening. What would one short date hurt? Maybe she had been working too hard lately. It was an hour or so of her time in a public place. Perfectly safe. Plus, it would make her friend happy. "OK. I'll do it." She held up her hand as Joyce let out a small squeal. "But this is the first and last time. No more blind dates."

"I promise." Joyce made the sign of an "X" over her heart. "You won't regret this."

Famous last words, Audra thought hours later as she strode into the upscale jazz bar where she was meeting her date. She was already regretting it. "Not the right attitude," she muttered. She'd promised Joyce she'd keep an open mind and try to have fun. Easier said than done.

Work had run late and she'd had to hurry home in order to shower and change. In spite of the lack of time, she'd pulled out all the stops. It had been such a long time since she'd prepared for an evening out with a man that she'd almost forgotten how much she enjoyed the preparation, the entire ritual that came before the actual date.

She'd shaved her legs and slathered on her favourite vanilla-scented body lotion. She'd swept her shoulder-length brown hair into a sophisticated twist, anchoring it with a sterling silver clip. The long-sleeved black dress she wore was deceptively simple. It had a round neck but was cut extremely low in the back. She paired it with a pair of three-inch black pumps and a simple black purse with a gold-chain strap that she hooked over her shoulder. With her make-up done to perfection and her lips slicked with passionate plum lipstick, she knew she looked good.

She glanced at her reflection in the mirrored wall of the foyer. Yup. She looked hot. Not that she'd done it for her date. She had no idea who he was or if she'd even like him. No, she'd done it for herself.

Audra realized that Joyce was right. She hadn't gone on a date for months. Worse, she hadn't felt like a desirable woman. Just the simple act of rolling thigh-high stockings on over her smooth legs, of primping and pampering herself, had made her feel confident, womanly.

There was something sensual about rubbing her damp, naked skin with lotion, pulling on a sexy lace thong that only she knew she wore. It wasn't about attracting a man, it was about making herself feel like a sexual being once again. Like a woman.

Butterflies fluttered in her belly. Part nerves, part excitement. It was time to put the past behind her and make a fresh start. A date with this mystery man, David, was a step forwards. Tonight was all about new beginnings. It was only drinks, hardly even a real date, but it was a step in the right direction.

Confident in her appearance, she gripped the brass handle and pulled open the inner door. Voices assailed her, along with the low thrum of jazz. The place was full, but Joyce had told her that her date would be sitting just beyond the far end of the bar wearing a purple shirt.

Several attractive men tried to catch her eye as she made her way through the crowd. She smiled inwardly, even as she put a little more sway into her walk. Oh yeah, nothing like a few admiring glances to get the juices flowing again.

Audra relaxed and enjoyed the male attention. It was the first she'd had in months. She'd have a drink with her date, maybe stay an hour or so and then head home. But that didn't mean she couldn't enjoy that hour.

Letting her lips curve upwards, she pushed onwards to the end of the bar. Just beyond, she could see several small tables scattered around. They were as tall as the bar, with leather-backed stools surrounding them. Most were occupied by couples or groups of women or men scoping out the action. But there was one, mostly in shadow, that had only one patron. That had to be him.

The closer she got, the more butterflies fluttered in her stomach. She was actually nervous, which was utterly ridiculous. It was a drink. Nothing more. She took a deep breath when he stood and she caught a glimpse of the cuff of his shirt. It was purple. It was him.

His face was shrouded in shadows, but there was something about him that struck a chord deep inside her. Something familiar. She slowed her step, hesitant to take the final few that would bring her to the table.

He stilled. She could sense the rise in tension, even though she was surrounded by a throng of people. This was ridiculous. She squared her shoulders and walked forwards, sticking out her hand. "Hi, I'm Audra."

He captured her hand and she caught her breath as his fingers closed around hers. Her entire body quivered with anticipation, with dread. Her date leaned forwards and she caught her first glance of his rugged features. Long, black hair was pulled back with a leather thong, displaying his high cheekbones, crooked nose and strong jaw to perfection. She knew this face intimately. Had touched the rough, stubbled chin a thousand times, had kissed those firm, hard lips even more.

"Hello, Audra."

Tyson was surprised he could form a two-word sentence. He'd almost bitten off his tongue when he'd seen her coming towards him, her hips swaying in a sexy, come-hither roll. She was even more beautiful than he remembered. That poised, sophisticated exterior was just a sham. Beneath it lay the most passionate woman he'd ever met.

She tried to tug her fingers from his grasp, but he tightened his hold. He couldn't let her bolt. Not now. He'd spent months on regrets and plans. He had her here now and he wasn't letting her go.

"Let go, Tyson. Or should I say, David. I'd forgotten that was your middle name." She glared at him. "Why the subterfuge? Why did you have Joyce lie to me?"

His answer was simple. "I'm sorry about that, but I didn't think you'd agree to see me if I just picked up the phone and called."

"You were right about that." She started to pull away again, but he tugged on her hand, pulling her off-balance.

She stumbled, and he caught her against him. The feel of her lush breasts against his chest made him instantly hard. "We need to talk." He whispered the words in her ear, inhaling her unique scent. He'd missed her these past months.

She steadied herself and moved back a half-step. He hated even that slight distance between them. "We have nothing to say to one another."

He shook his head. "There's too much we never said." He used his free hand to trace the curve of her spine, almost groaning aloud when he felt nothing but soft skin. He skimmed his hand all the way to the upper swell of her ass before he felt fabric. Damn, this dress was hot. Just like her – sophisticated, yet simmering with passion.

"The time for talking is past." She gave him what he'd always thought of as her "lawyer" smile. All business, it was designed to put distance between them.

He let his hand slide lower, caressing the curve of her behind. She sucked in her breath. Though the light was dim, he could see the way she caught her breath. Her tongue came out to lick her lower lip and she unconsciously swayed towards him.

"Maybe it is," he conceded. "Maybe this calls for action instead." He used his hold on her to tug her closer. He lowered his mouth towards hers, giving her time to object, as he touched his lips to hers.

Audra couldn't think, couldn't breathe. Tyson was here. Tyson was her blind date. After all these months. What did he want? Why was he here? She was going to kill Joyce when she saw her again. What had her friend been thinking? She knew how much his leaving had hurt.

The feel of his large hands on her body sent her hormones spinning out of control. It had always been this way between them. The attraction hot and immediate. That had been part of the problem. Whenever they were together, they spent all their time in bed and no time talking about their future.

None of that mattered now. Not with his hands making slow forays up and down her bare spine. Not with his mouth on hers, his tongue probing for entry. She clasped her hands around his shoulders for support, feeling the hard muscles ripple beneath her fingers. He smelled good too. All hot male, tinged with the woodsy soap he favoured. It was a scent that fired her libido and made her nipples stand up and take notice.

It had been a long eight months. Passion flared as he stroked her tongue with his, enticing her to play. Her body tensed. What should she do?

He withdrew and took a deep breath. "Let's get out of here. Let's go somewhere we can talk."

Talk was the last thing on her mind. And why not? She was single and so was he. Why shouldn't she enjoy him one final time? When they were done, she'd be the one to walk away this time.

Determined on her course, she nodded. Tyson wrapped his arm around her waist and guided her swiftly towards the entrance. She could feel the hard bulge of his erection pressed against the small of her back as he guided her through the crowd.

Her body remembered his and just that small touch had her creaming her panties. She was glad when they finally left the bar behind and stepped out into the warm night air. "This way."

She didn't ask where they were going. Didn't care. She wanted, no needed, this. One final time, she promised herself. Then she'd tell him exactly what she thought of him before walking out. It would be the perfect revenge.

"I have a room here."

She glanced up, surprised to find they were entering a hotel a few doors down from the bar. "Sure of yourself, were you?"

His fingers tightened slightly, but other than that he gave no indication that her barb had hit home. "No. I'm staying here for a couple of days."

"I see." And she did. He was probably in town for a few days before jetting off to his next job. It didn't matter. She ignored the twist in her stomach and the pounding of her heart. She wanted to be the one to walk away this time.

Audra ignored his muttered, "I don't think you do," and concentrated on walking across the lobby to the bank of elevators. It seemed to take for ever. She was very aware of the metal strap of her purse digging into her clenched fingers and his broad palm resting against the small of her back. Finally, the bell gave a cheerful ding and they were inside.

It was just the two of them as the elevator lurched upwards. Tyson stood behind her and she could feel the heat rolling off his large body. She was a tall woman – five nine in her stocking feet. Even with her wearing heels, Tyson was taller. He lowered his head and feathered his lips over her nape. He knew just the spot to touch to make her skin tingle.

He worked his way towards her ear, tugging on her ear lobe before swirling his tongue over the whorl of her ear. Audra sucked in a breathy moan as his hand snaked around to cover her belly and pull her back towards him. His erection prodded her butt and she couldn't help but wiggle slightly.

Tyson swore and bit gently on the curve of her neck in retaliation. She released a soft cry of passion and let her head drop back on his shoulder. He knew exactly how to touch her to set her on fire.

"Tyson," she gasped.

The bell chimed and the elevator doors slid open. Tyson hustled her down the hallway. She didn't even notice what his room number was. All she cared was that they were finally in his room. The door closed with a thud. They were alone.

Tyson whirled her around and her back pressed firmly against the closed door. His lips sought hers in a blistering kiss. Audra clutched at his shirt, wanting, no needing him closer. How could she have forgotten just how primal sex was between them? Even her most vivid memories couldn't match the reality. It was no wonder she hadn't dated. No other man could compete.

"I've got to get you naked." His words were raw. Real. There
was no mistaking the fact that he wanted her as much as she wanted
him.

"Yes," she gasped. She gripped the edges of his shirt and yanked.
Buttons flew everywhere, pinging off the walls and floor. Audra
spread her fingers over his broad chest. The crisp thatch of hair in
the centre of his chest tickled her skin as her fingertips traced a path
down over his rock-solid abs.

He gave a low growl and pulled the strap of her purse off her
shoulder. The small bag fell to the floor, hitting the carpet with a
soft thud. He slid his fingers beneath the fabric at her shoulders
and slowly pulled it down to her elbows. The front of the dress
lowered, leaving her breasts bare.

Tyson cupped her breasts in his hands, moulding them as he
teased her already-taut nipples with his thumbs. "Beautiful." His
tone was reverent as he bent down and captured one straining peak
between his lips and sucked.

Audra's head fell back against the door as he used his teeth to
carefully tug on the tight nub. His nimble fingers teased the other
nipple. Her arms were trapped by her sides, caught in the fabric of
her dress. She wanted to touch him, to hold his head to her breasts
and tell him to never stop.

He pulled back and looked up at her. His hair had somehow
come free from the thong that had been confining it. Or maybe
she'd ripped it out. She honestly couldn't remember. It fell
around his shoulders like black silk. She wanted to run her
fingers through it.

"Help me get out of my dress. I want to touch you." She
squirmed, but it didn't help free her from the tangle.

He shook his head. "Not yet."

Tyson wrapped his fingers around her ankles and slowly slid his
hands over her calves. "You have the sexiest legs of any woman I've
ever seen. And when you wear heels, you're like a walking adver-
tisement for sex." His words made her sex clench with growing
need. Liquid arousal seeped from her core as his hands continued
their upwards journey.

He pushed the skirt of her dress up, exposing the lacy tops of her
stockings and her bare thighs. "Oh, yeah," he breathed. His hot
breath skimmed over her flesh, making her shiver with longing.

The heat in his eyes told her he was as aroused as she was. She
held her breath as he ran his finger over the small triangle of silk

covering her mound. A small, inarticulate sound of pleasure escaped her as his finger brushed her clitoris, sending a bolt of lightning flashing through her.

She was panting hard by the time he hooked his fingers in the thin string of her thong and slowly dragged it down her legs. "Lift," he commanded. She lifted one leg at a time and he swept her panties away.

"Just look at you, all hot and wet and ready for me." He raised her right leg, hooking it over his shoulder. It opened her sex wide, allowing him to see all of her. He inhaled as he shifted closer. "You even smell hot. Spicy and musky and sexy."

He leaned in and swiped his tongue over the slick folds of her sex. Up one side and down the other. Audra undulated her hips, wanting more. Her breasts swayed with every breath she took. They felt heavy and full and ached for his touch.

"Tyson." She groaned, needing more.

"Yes, my love."

She ignored the endearment and the twinge it caused in her heart. This was about sex, pure and simple. "Touch me."

"Here." He fingered the slick folds of her sex, rimming the opening of her sheath.

She was going to die if she couldn't feel him inside her. She dug the heel of her shoe into his shoulder and thrust her pelvis forwards. "Inside me," she ordered.

Tyson gave a low masculine laugh before pressing two thick fingers into her heated channel. Her inner muscles rippled and she gasped. He pulled his fingers almost all the way out before thrusting them in again. She rolled her hips, encouraging a rhythm she liked. He captured her clit between his lips and sucked. He used his tongue and fingers to push her until she was wound tight to breaking point.

He pulled back and stared up at her. "Come for me, Audra." Leaning forwards, he lapped at her clit, licking and sucking. His fingers continued to work in and out of her tight, heated core.

Her entire body tensed and then exploded. Hips pumping, she cried out as he continued to pleasure her. Her orgasm washed over her in waves. Months of wanting, of missing this man, were released. When it finally subsided, she slumped, unable to support her own body weight.

Tyson caught her and swung her into his arms. He stood and carried her to the bed, laying her on the crisp white sheets. He made quick work of her dress, dragging it off and tossing it aside. Her shoes were next. He left her stockings and went to work on his own clothing. She watched through half-open eyes as he toed off his shoes and yanked off his pants, underwear and socks. When he shrugged out of his shirt, he was totally naked.

Audra had never seen such a fine masculine specimen. He was even more ripped than he had been, his muscles more delineated. Whatever he'd been doing since he'd left her, he'd been working hard.

She'd missed more than just the sex these past months. She'd missed sharing the morning paper over breakfast and arguing about politics while they both worked in the kitchen preparing dinner. Tyson loved to cook and she loved to watch him, content to sip a glass of wine as they both unwound and shared the happenings of their day. She'd missed snuggling up on the sofa at the end of a long day and watching old movies. She'd missed hearing his voice, seeing his smile, hearing his laugh.

She pushed all those thoughts out of her head. The past didn't matter. Only now, this moment did. And it was all about sex. She'd deal with the consequences the following day.

Tyson came down on the bed beside her and gently pushed a lock of hair out of her eyes. Part of her hairdo had come down. He reached behind her head and undid the clip, tossing it on the night-stand. He sifted through her hair, spreading it over the pillow.

Neither of them spoke as he lowered his head and kissed her.

Tyson could still taste her arousal on his lips. When he kissed her, it mingled with the sweet taste of her mouth. His cock throbbed, liquid seeping from the tip. His balls ached for release. But not yet. He wanted to touch Audra, savour every second. It had been so long since he'd touched her and she was even more exquisite than he remembered.

He slowly released her lips and kissed her cheekbones, her nose and her stubborn chin, before working his way down her neck. She was extremely sensitive in that area and he used every bit of carnal knowledge he'd gained during their time together to give her the most pleasure.

She might think this was only for one night, but he was playing for keeps.

He used his fingers, his lips, his tongue to trace her collarbone, the curve of her breasts and lower. He ignored her pouting nipples as he followed the dip of her waist with his mouth. Her belly button invited him to dip his tongue inside, so he did. She whimpered softly when he nipped at her hip bones and kissed her mound.

She undulated sensually on the bed, rubbing her soft skin against his much harder frame. Digging her fingers into his shoulders, she urged him upwards. He worked his way quickly up her body, petting and caressing her, wanting to see what she would do. She didn't make him wait.

Audra pushed him on to his back and knelt beside him. "My turn now." A threat or a promise or both? He didn't care. Not as long as she touched him. He'd had other women in his life, but none of them compared to Audra. She had only to look at him and smile and he wanted her.

She gave him a small sensual smile that almost stopped his heart. It resumed beating a second later, pounding against his chest when she bent down and lapped delicately at one of his flat nipples. She dragged her fingers through his chest hair, teasing his flesh with her nails.

Tyson groaned and flexed his hips, unable to keep still under her tender ministrations. Audra sat back and licked her lips, her hot gaze trailing down his belly to his cock. It jerked, as if trying to get closer to her. He was in total agreement. The closer he could get to her the better.

She reached out, wrapping her hand over his hard shaft. "So soft and hard at the same time." Delight tinged her words as she dragged her fist up and down.

"Harder," he growled.

She ignored him, moving her hand at a leisurely pace. With her free hand, she touched his thigh, trailing her fingers up and down, moving closer to his testicles with each stroke. He gritted his teeth, determined to let her have her way. It wasn't easy. He was primed like a rocket ready to explode.

She dragged her fingers over his balls, rolling them carefully before finally cupping him with her hand. She squeezed gently and he sucked in a breath. "I'm close, Audra," he warned.

"Not close enough." That was all the warning he got before she bent down and licked at the head of his cock. Like a cat at a bowl of milk, she lapped daintily at the tip before dragging her tongue around the sensitive ridge.

Tyson's back bowed off the bed. He ran mathematical equations in his head, thought about his taxes, anything he could think of to keep from coming. He wasn't ready for her to stop her sensual torture. Not yet.

She gave a breathy laugh and closed her mouth over his erection. Moist heat closed around him as her hands continued to work their magic. It was too much. Tyson knew he couldn't last.

Audra closed her eyes and let the tang of Tyson's essence roll over her tongue. He was musky and salty and she loved the way his balls tightened beneath her fingers. She could feel his orgasm building at the base of his cock.

His arousal was firing hers and she leaned closer, rubbing her nipples against his side. It felt good, but it wasn't enough. She was empty. Aching. She needed to feel Tyson's cock buried deep inside her throbbing sex. She wanted to feel him, skin to skin, wanted to wrap herself around him and feel him pounding into her until they were both sweaty, exhausted and utterly replete.

She sucked harder on his cock, hollowing her cheeks to create the most suction. Tyson gave a low growl and pulled away. Her mouth came off him with a wet pop. Before she could ask why he'd stopped her, he flipped her on to her stomach and pulled her back towards him. His hands held her hips steady as the head of his cock probed at the entrance to her sex.

A fine sheen of sweat beaded her skin. Her arms quivered as she supported her weight and pushed her ass towards him, urging him on. With one smooth thrust, he filled her. She gasped and arched back.

"Take all of me," he groaned. He began to rock, pushing forwards with each stroke. She moved with him, wanting every inch of him inside her. Her channel softened and stretched as he forged inwards. When he was seated to the hilt, he dropped his head against her back and kissed her spine.

This was what she wanted, what she yearned for. Tyson filled her completely, pushing away all the lonely nights she'd spent since he'd been gone. The feeling of closeness that only comes when two bodies are so intimately entwined. He awoke nerve endings and volatile emotions, pushing both to the brink.

He started to move, short, hard stabs at first, gradually switching to long, slow strokes. He kept her off balance, her body teetering on the edge of orgasm but not quite going over. She bit on her bottom lip to keep from screaming at him to make her come.

He'd always been attuned to her wants and needs and that hadn't changed. He slipped his hands from her hips to her breasts, cupped them, tugging gently on her nipples with his thumbs and forefingers. A low moan escaped from between her lips.

"Tyson," she whispered. "Please."

He withdrew and she was momentarily stunned, her channel empty and poised on the brink of sexual satisfaction. How could he leave her when she was so close?

She started to turn over, but he was already shifting her on to her back. He hooked his arms beneath her thighs and lifted her hips. He met her eyes as he forged back inside her, hard and thick and hot.

His expression was one of determination as he began a slow game of advance and retreat. Audra looked into his bittersweet chocolate eyes and was lost. Her heart gave up the fight. She loved him. Probably always would. This had been a mistake. She would be months, maybe even years getting over this night.

"Audra." Her name slid off his tongue with such tenderness, tears pricked her eyes. She closed them, not wanting him to see her unsettled emotions. She was sure he'd be able to see the love she had for him shining in her eyes if he saw them at that moment. She couldn't allow that. It would make them both uncomfortable. He'd made it clear he didn't love her when he'd simply walked out after their last fight and gone to Japan without another word.

In spite of her best efforts, a lone tear trickled out of the corner of her eye and down her temple, disappearing into her hairline. "Ah, babe." Tyson lifted her into his arms, without dislodging himself. He wrapped his arms around her and kissed her temple, licking away the salty remains of her tear.

He ran his hands over her spine and cupped her ass, shifting her slightly. Her clit rubbed against his flat stomach, making her gasp. No matter her emotions, the arousal, the need was still there. It flared to life with that one simple touch. Audra didn't want this night to end, but it was too late for regrets.

She wrapped her legs around his waist and her arms around his broad shoulders as he lifted her slightly before dropping her back down over his erection. His chest hair abraded her sensitive nipples, making her shiver with growing need.

His skin was slick beneath her hands, his breathing laboured. She rotated her hips and used her grip on his shoulders to lift her weight. They couldn't get much motion in this position, but it was more than enough. She felt his shaft swell. His entire body tensed as he threw back his head and yelled. Hot pulses of semen pumped into her as he came.

Tyson buried his face in the curve of her neck and nipped. Hard. She gasped and ground her pelvis against his, stimulating her clit just enough to drive her over the edge. She cried out his name as her body spasmed. He banded his arms around her, holding her tight.

The world with all its problems spun away, leaving only the two of them. A man and a woman and the beauty of their physical joining. But eventually it had to end. Audra's heart slowed to a normal rhythm, her breathing became less laboured. The fine layer of sweat on her skin made her shiver now that the heat of passion had passed.

Tyson reached out and grabbed the bedspread, wrapped it around them both. He was still inside her, not as long and hard as he had been moments before, but still substantial in spite of his orgasm.

"I should get up." She didn't want to, but it seemed the sensible thing to do. Not that she'd exactly done the sensible thing tonight. Sleeping with her ex-boyfriend was definitely not a smart thing to do.

His arms tightened around her. "Stay. Please," he added, as if sensing her growing apprehension.

He released a deep sigh and shifted in bed so his back was resting against the headboard. Audra unlocked her legs from around his waist. She was still intimately joined to him, sitting on his lap, staring at him. It was amazing how comfortable she felt sitting naked in his arms with him still partially inside her. He hooked a stray lock of hair over her ear and trailed his fingers down the curve of her face.

"About what happened," he began.

She inwardly groaned. Did she really want to do a post-mortem on their failed relationship? The answer was no. They'd both been at different places in their lives, caught up with their careers. It wasn't his fault and it wasn't hers. It just was. She realized that now.

"I understand," she finally said. And she did. His travelling overseas to work was part of his job. He enjoyed it and excelled at it. "I just wish you'd told me about it sooner."

"Would it have made a difference?"

She honestly thought about it. "Yes. Yes, it would."

He raked his hand through his hair. She knew it was a gesture of frustration, one she was very familiar with. "I tried to tell you. Several times. You kept cancelling dinner with me because of work. I didn't want to talk about it over the phone. And then time just ran out. The date got moved up by my boss and I had to leave or give up the opportunity."

Audra thought back to that time and knew he was right. She winced at the memory. She had cancelled on him. Probably a half-dozen times before their final fight. She'd been in the midst of a case that she'd thought would push her over the top into junior partner at her firm.

"I'm sorry for that."

"Me too. I should have come to your office and made you listen."

She smiled ruefully. "Maybe you should have."

"I tried to call you several times, but you always seemed to be in court."

"You did? I only got one message that you called. " Surprise filled her and a sense of warmth surrounded her. She vividly remembered that time. Her assistant had been off sick for a month and they'd filled in with temps that hadn't always been as efficient as they should have been. She'd missed several messages, which had led to more than one headache for her as she'd soothed disgruntled clients. But it appeared she'd also missed the most important messages of all.

She nibbled on her lower lip, knowing she needed to be totally honest with him. "I called you back. I phoned your office the next day and then your apartment. Your phone was disconnected and the receptionist said you were already gone."

Pain flashed over his face, but quickly disappeared. "I didn't know." Tyson eased her closer, urging her head down on his shoulder. Neither of them spoke for a long while, content just to savour the closeness between them.

"You've left your old law firm and struck out on your own."

It wasn't a question but she answered him anyway. "Yeah, I did. After you left, I threw myself into my work. When the Anderson case was done, I expected a promotion. Instead, the new son-in-law of one of my bosses got promoted. I got a pat on the head. I realized then I'd given up any semblance of a life for nothing. They were never going to promote me. I quit and started my own firm. But you already know that." She pushed back and gave him a questioning look.

"Don't blame Joyce. I called her and begged when you didn't return my calls. It took a while, but she finally started giving me updates about how you were doing."

Audra was stunned. All this time, Tyson had been asking about her. "I don't understand."

He rubbed his hands over her arms and cupped her shoulders, easing the tension from her limbs. "Easy, babe. I finished my contract with my company and have gone freelance. From now on, I decide which contracts I take and where." He paused and cupped her face with his hands, staring deeply into her eyes. "That is, we will. If you'll give me another chance."

Her heart jumped and happiness soared. But it was quickly dampened by reality. They hadn't made it before, so what made him think they could make it now? She hadn't realized she'd voiced her concerns aloud until he answered her.

"I've lived this past eight months without you, babe, and nothing is worth that. I missed you every single day and every long, miserable night." His dark eyes were steady as he continued. "We've both changed these past months. I know what I want and am willing to do whatever it takes to make it work."

"I am too. Oh, Tyson. I missed you. So much." She captured his face with her hands and held him as she peppered his forehead, cheeks and chin with kisses. "When everything fell apart at the firm and I was left with nothing, I finally understood what really mattered. But it was too late."

He shifted and she noticed his erection was growing harder with each passing second. She squirmed and they both moaned. No doubt about it. All Tyson had to do was breathe to turn her on. But it went much deeper than that.

Taking a deep breath, she threw caution to the wind. "I love you. I never said it before because I was holding back. Protecting myself. Maybe if I had said it then, things might have been different."

He gave her a sad smile. "Maybe we weren't ready then. But we are now." He found her hands and held them, locking their fingers together so their palms were touching. "Marry me, Audra."

Stunned, all she could do was stare at him, her mouth wide open.

"I love you and I want to spend the rest of my life with you."

Hope and happiness bubbled up inside her, cracking through the hard, cynical shell she'd been building ever since he'd left. Did she dare take a chance? Did she really have a choice?

"Yes," she whispered, barely able to believe she was actually agreeing to marry Tyson. Less than twelve hours ago, she'd been trying to get over him. After tonight, she knew that would never happen. He was the man for her.

"Can you handle being married to a lawyer who works long hours?" She was still building her own practice and knew it would be a while before things settled down to anything resembling a normal schedule. "I promise to have at least several nights a week totally free." That was very different from when they were together before.

"As long as you come home to me." He chuckled. "I figure if we're married and living together, we'll at least see one another in bed at night." He sobered. "Can you handle me travelling from time to time? It won't be as far away or for as long as I used to."

She smiled at him, feeling her entire body heating, as she mimicked his words. "As long as you come home to me."

"That's a promise." He kissed her then, a deep passionate embrace that was steeped with all the loneliness of the lost months. Tongues twined, teeth clinked and deep moans echoed in the room. He cupped the back of her head with his broad palm, tilting it to the left so he could get better access to her mouth.

His shaft swelled inside her, filling her core. She lifted up on her knees and slowly lowered herself over his thick shaft. He cocked an eyebrow at her. "Again?"

She gave him a sexy smile. "Again and again and again."

Tyson threw back his head and laughed. "Never let it be said that I wouldn't satisfy a lady." His hands closed over her breasts. "My lady." Leaning down, he lapped at her distended nipples, wringing a whimper of pleasure from her.

"Oh yeah," he encouraged. "Moan for me again, babe. Move over me. Take whatever you want, whatever you need." His low, husky voice sent shivers from the roots of her hair to the tips of her toes. And she did as he asked.

Taking control, she moved over him with a sensual roll of her hips as he continued to pleasure her breasts. He nipped and licked and sucked at her sensitive nipples before sliding a hand between her spread thighs and finding the little bud of nerves at the apex. He stimulated and petted her clit until she was writhing with need.

His cock pulsed hard and hot inside her. She felt his shaft quiver and thicken. Knew they were both close. Audra squeezed her inner muscles tight, flexing around his thick length. He yelled her name and she felt the hot flood of his release. It set off her own orgasm, not as explosive as the last one, but somehow more fulfilling.

She slumped against his chest and they both lay there for a long time. When she tried to sit up, it took some effort. Their skin was stuck together with sweat. Tyson laughed and lifted her off him before hoisting her into his arms and carrying her towards the bathroom.

Audra wrapped her arms around his neck and smiled, feeling happier than she had in a long time. Second chances didn't always happen. They were lucky to have gotten one. Or maybe luck had nothing to do with it. Tyson had obviously worked hard to make this happen. He'd always been determined and focused when he wanted something. That was just one of the many things she loved about him.

And to think she'd almost said no to Joyce. "What would you have done if I'd said no to the blind date?"

Tyson paused just inside the bathroom door. "You wouldn't have gotten away from me that easily. I probably would have showed up at your front door and begged you to talk to me."

She snorted. Somehow she couldn't imagine Tyson begging and told him so.

He set her down on the counter and began to run a bath. "Don't kid yourself. I was desperate."

Any lingering concerns she had quieted. They'd both made mistakes and were ready to do what it took to make their relationship work. She smiled as he sauntered over to her. Every time she looked at him, she was seduced anew by his dark good looks. No doubt about it, her man was a hottie. But it was what was inside him that made the difference.

She linked her arms around his neck and dropped a quick kiss on his sexy mouth. "You can tell me how you would have grovelled while we take a bath."

He scooped her into his arms and carried her to the tub. He stepped inside and sat with her still in his arms. "I can think of better things to do."

She reached down between his legs and gave his testicles a squeeze. "I think I can too."

Hell's Fury

Jackie Kessler

With all that power, Alecto murmured in my mind, *you'd think the Light Bringer would be taller.*

Or brighter, said Tisiphone.

My sisters were both crazy, but I made sure not to share that thought. Alecto equated strength with physical presence, but Lucifer Morningstar didn't need to tower over others to prove he was one of the most powerful entities in all Creation. And whether Tisiphone was speaking of Lucifer's luminescence or his intelligence, it didn't matter – she was wrong.

He was perfect.

I slid my gaze his way, once again drinking in his form – first, the obsidian darkness of his thick hair, begging for me to run my fingers through it. Next, his spring-green eyes, which were narrowed as they focused on my liege lord. And then, his lips, which would have been sensually full if not for the way they were pressing together into a firm line, as if to trap words from escaping his tongue. Such tethered emotion; such careful restraint. Oh yes, this was a creature who knew the importance of patience. Considering that he could destroy most everyone in the room, that was extremely impressive.

Not that the other beings gathered here would ever admit such a thing – they all believed they were omnipotent. Gods tended to be deluded that way.

It had been quite the surprise to find that the Light Bringer had managed to persuade so many deities to come to Hell to negotiate treaty terms. It's difficult to get members of different pantheons together even for celebrations; there's simply too much rivalry among them for the gods to tolerate one another's presence. Humans may be fruitful and multiply until they fill the world, but there's only so much belief to go around – and a god without believers is nothing more than a name forgotten. To have two different pantheon members together in the same place takes quite the feat. Three is rarer than a phoenix. Four is all but unheard of.

More than twenty is unthinkable ... and yet, here we were, representatives of various pantheons, from the Aztecs to the Zoroastrians and nearly everyone in between, in a large room deep within the Light Bringer's palace in Hell. Somehow, Lucifer Morningstar had convinced them all to come in person, to discuss Jehovah's proposed treaty. Lucifer had to have a honeyed tongue to accomplish such a thing; gods were notoriously difficult to persuade.

Yes, a honeyed tongue, a silken voice, piercing eyes ...

My heartbeat quickened, and I forced myself to tear my gaze away from Lucifer. *Pay attention, Megaera.*

But really, if you've heard one deity pontificate, you've heard them all. Gods were all the same – in attitude, certainly, even if their physical forms were different. They all had dressed to impress, and so they sat in their finery, attempting to be regal in their high-backed chairs, around a massive table in the centre of the room. Along with the numerous divinities, their various entourages stood sentry, or sat beside them, or sprawled at their feet, whispering and cooing and stroking them, as if they couldn't get enough of their patron gods. As if they were lost without their touch.

Idiots. The only reason gods needed so many hangers-on was to look more important than they actually were.

Once again, I glanced at Lucifer. Although there were a handful of servants scattered through the chamber, Lucifer himself had no attendants. What was more, the Light Bringer was the sole representative of Jehovah's pantheon; no other so-called archangels sat by his side, and no demons capered behind him, waiting on his commands. He clearly felt no need to display his might, here in the heart of his power.

Or maybe he just didn't care about such things. The thought made me smile.

Utter nonsense, of course. He had to be just as arrogant as the other deities in the room; you didn't challenge your patron god, as he was rumoured to have done, without being a pompous ass. Still, I rather liked the notion that Lucifer felt no need to have his people fawning over him as he led the treaty negotiations.

I rather liked him, arrogance and all.

My liege lord's voice grew louder, until it was all but thundering in the large chamber. I checked myself from rolling my eyes. As usual, Zeus was overly dramatic. At least his breath didn't reek of fermented grapes. (He wasn't half as clever as he believed himself to be, and was more of a drunkard than was polite to acknowledge.) As far as gods went, Zeus wasn't horrible; he appreciated the importance of vengeance, and he wasn't a bad lover. (Usually.) What more could one such as I ask? Other than he not confuse me for one of my sisters, that is?

Stop that, Megaera. Don't complain about what you cannot change.

I schooled my face to impassive blankness as Zeus prattled on. And on. And I stole glances at the King of Hell.

From the little I could see of his body, which was swathed in an emerald toga, Lucifer was strongly built. More than the muscles of his neck and shoulders and arms, though, it was his skin that fascinated me. Given his title – which he still claimed, even though he no longer brought light to Jehovah's Heaven – I would have thought his flesh to be like alabaster, possibly even golden. Instead, Lucifer's skin was darker, swarthier . . . similar to my own. Though he sat in his chair with his back straight and his hands folded over the ends of the armrests, there was a restless energy about him, as if he couldn't wait to move.

I imagined him moving sinuously on a bed of pillows, the hem of his toga slowly riding up his thighs. And I imagined my hands on his thighs, stroking, working their way up to reach for what lay beneath his toga . . .

Uh-oh, Alecto said. *Megaera's got that look.*

She does, Tisiphone agreed. *Tell us, Meg. Which godling has drawn your attention?*

I bet it's Thor, said Alecto.

Oh, please, I said, flitting my glance to the Norse god. *Thor thinks he's skilled because he knows how to swing his mallet. If I want a thunder god, I'll stick with Zeus. At least he knows how to plant his lightning rod.*

That made my sisters giggle. Our liege lord frowned at us, but he didn't break from his painfully long speech. He simply couldn't; once he stopped speaking, he would have effectively yielded the floor, and then it would be another god's turn to explain to every-one why Jehovah's bold proposal was insane.

Then who? Alecto asked. *Maybe Seth?*

I know! Tisiphone said. *Yu-huang!*

No god of storm or sky, I insisted, shifting my gaze back to Lucifer. At that moment, the Morningstar looked over at us – no, at me. His green eyes flashed, perhaps due to wicked thoughts. I held his gaze, letting him know with only my eyes that I wanted to bed him right there in front of everyone. The corner of his mouth twitched almost imperceptibly before he glanced away.

Had that been a hint of a smile? What would it take to make that smile bloom properly?

Oh, Meg, squealed Tisiphone. *Not the Light Bringer!*

I've heard he's got some mortal woman, said Alecto. *He turned her into a demon just so he could have her.*

Tisiphone snorted. *So? As if our liege lord has never transformed human women when it suited him. Remember Io?*

He only did that because he was afraid of Hera catching him, said Alecto.

Which she did, anyway, Tisiphone replied with a shrug. *So what if Lucifer has another woman?*

I had to agree; creatures like us didn't worry about things like monogamy. Choosing to be with one lover for the rest of one's existence? Why would eternal creatures limit themselves in such a way? Especially when gods were so fickle? And their talent beneath the covers so very limited?

As my sisters gossiped about the Light Bringer, Zeus was finally getting to the point of his painfully long speech. My liege lord had just taken credit for bringing fire to humans, even though everyone knew that to be a lie – it was Prometheus who had stolen fire from Olympus to gift it to the hapless (and cold) mortals. But then, Zeus wasn't ruler of his pantheon for nothing; no good deed went uncredited to him.

Even when I brought him to orgasm, he acted like it was all his own doing.

Lucifer looked like he wanted to say something – emotions flashed behind his green eyes, and his jaw clenched. Even so, he kept his mouth firmly closed. I had a sudden urge to kiss that mouth, to feel his lips on mine, to see if I could make him forget such restraint.

As I pictured Lucifer's tongue darting against mine, Zeus finally made his play. It was not enough to tell the gathering of deities why he disagreed with Jehovah's proposition; Zeus aimed to become the new god of gods. He'd confided his plan to me before we'd travelled to Hell – locked in his embrace, smelling the sweat on his skin and old wine on his breath, I'd listened as he told me he'd convince everyone to bow to the Greek pantheon. I'd smiled blandly then, even as he'd called me "Alecto" . . . even as my sisters and I smiled now, as Zeus motioned to the three of us standing deferentially behind him.

Only the dim-witted entities in the room failed to understand what Zeus was actually saying: they must support Zeus as the Almighty – the one God above all other gods – or he would unleash we three Furies upon them.

My sisters and I, ever the loyal pets, kept smiling.

Gods usually don't take well to being threatened. But then, most gods can smite the ones that threaten them without thinking twice about it. Only a bare handful of creatures were strong enough to destroy me or one of my sisters; none was strong enough to destroy all three of us. So no one challenged Zeus on the spot in answer to his arrogance.

Disappointing. But not unexpected. Gods could turn self-preservation into an art form.

Megaera, Alecto hissed. *Keep smiling.*

Of course. I wasn't allowed to show anyone how I truly felt. I smiled until my cheeks burned.

Some of the entities in the chamber attempted to ignore us. Others, such as Quetzalcoatl and Brahma, appeared bored. Very few were openly afraid – in the Egyptian section, the cat goddess Bast stared wide-eyed at us, her fur puffed out. The other divinities, though, pretended that my sisters and I were nothing more than servants. Gods tended to wear pride like pearls, so the casual contempt in their eyes was almost innate – they were gods, after all, and used to being worshipped. They didn't like reminders that they weren't the strongest creatures in all existence.

In that way, they were similar to humans. But mortals had a healthy respect for my sisters and me, even if they were completely terrified of us. Gods? They didn't respect anyone, anything, other than themselves. Gods were self-interest personified. They disgusted me.

I'll have sex with them when I want to. And I'll serve them when I have to. But I'll never respect them, or consider them my equal.

Certainly not my liege lord, whom my sisters and I were bound to for all eternity. Zeus might hold my loyalty, but no god could ever hold my heart.

I darted a glance once again at Lucifer. He was no mere god, and not simply because he called himself an archangel. His power, like that of the divinity he served, was almost unrivalled. Surely, even one as powerful as the Light Bringer had a god's shortcomings: arrogance, pettiness, depravity.

Surely.

But I couldn't help noticing that unlike most of the other entities in the room, Lucifer hadn't feigned indifference when Zeus indelicately reminded everyone that the Greek gods had we three Erinyes in their corner. Instead, the Light Bringer had simply waited for Zeus to finish making his point.

That impressed me far more than Lucifer's lovely face. He didn't mind that we Furies were Zeus' personal enforcers. Everyone knew we were powerful enough to erase even a god's existence with only a thought . . . and Lucifer didn't seem to care.

What would it be like to have a lover who was truly as strong as I was, one who didn't want to use me other than for a night of pleasure? I wondered, and I imagined, and I felt my smile broaden.

A small eternity passed, and Zeus finally ended his speech. He sat heavily in his chair and murmured, "Wine."

My sisters and I had drawn lots before the gathering, and I had been the loser. So I offered Zeus an empty smile and an equally meaningless bow, and off I went to fill his goblet.

As I sought a cupbearer, Lucifer spoke. "Our brother the Greek lord has given us much to consider." His voice was deep, and richly musical, and it danced along my skin. "There will be an intermission before the next speaker has the floor." With those words, the King of Hell rose and strode out of the room.

His exit prompted a flurry of godly voices. Would Lucifer cast his allegiance with Zeus, or was he firmly committed to Jehovah? And what of this mad call for a treaty between pantheons – was that by Lucifer's design, or was this all the manipulation of Jehovah to cast himself as the one above all others? And so on.

None of them, from what I could hear, considered the possibility that Lucifer was tired of listening to gods scheme, and simply needed to escape the room.

While the deities murmured their suspicions, I approached one of the many cupbearers in the room and nearly gave her a heart attack before she understood what I wanted. She bowed and scraped as she poured wine into the goblet in my hands, without spilling a drop. I'd have to commend her to her master.

The thought of speaking with her master sent a tingle through my belly.

Hurry up, Meg, Alecto snapped. *Zeus is thirsty.*

Of course. Once I'm done playing fetch, maybe I should roll over and beg.

Pushing aside such thoughts, I returned to my liege lord and offered him the full goblet. His thick fingers stroked mine as he took the cup, and he said, "My thanks, Tisiphone."

Anger bubbled in my stomach. Blandly, oh so blandly, I smiled, and I thought of carving my name on Zeus' chest so that he would finally remember who I was.

He took a sip of his wine, declared it fit for Dionysus, then patted my bottom to dismiss me.

White-hot rage seared me, and blood roared in my ears. By my sides, my hands curled into fists.

I could remove him from the fabric of Creation with hardly a blink, and he dares to treat me like a human serving girl? Me?

Meg, Tisiphone whispered, *be calm.*

Oh, I was calm. I didn't destroy my liege lord, nor did I tear down the black walls of Hell's castle to show my rage. That proved I was calm.

Grinding my teeth as I smiled, smiled, smiled, I said, "By your leave, sire." I spun on my heel and marched out of the room before Zeus could say otherwise. My sisters immediately buzzed in my mind, but I pushed them out and created a shield, one that would keep my thoughts and actions private.

I am a Fury; it is my right to seethe in my rage alone.

I stormed down the hallway, not knowing or caring where it led. Various denizens of Hell scampered out of my way, all of them touching their heads to the ground as I passed. They, at least, gave me the respect I deserved. What did it say that Hell acknowledged what my own liege lord did not?

Why could even the basest of demons see my worth, where my own patron god was blind?

I paraded through the corridors of the palace, turning corners and rounding bends, until I came to a set of doors, slightly ajar. Red-tinted light poured through the crack, and odd sounds clamoured from beyond, as if trying to claw their way inside.

Curious, I nudged the doors apart . . . to find Lucifer Morningstar standing on a balcony, overlooking his dread kingdom as the sky bled fire and the land belched flame.

Even from behind, he was magnificent to behold – broad-backed and long of leg. One sandalled foot was planted on the balcony railing, and his arms rested over his bent knee as he peered into the distance. A hot breeze ruffled Lucifer's black hair, sending it crashing about his shoulders . . . and toying with the hem of his tunic.

"Lady Fury," he said in a deep baritone, without turning around.

"Lord Archangel," I replied, bowing my head. "I did not mean to interrupt."

"You haven't." He turned to regard me over his shoulder, a cautious look on his face. No surprise there – I was one of three weapons in Zeus' arsenal. As he appraised me, I listened to the strange music of Hell: the cries of the damned mixed with the chortles of the nefarious, blending to form a discordant tune that pierced my heart. Pain and pleasure. Agony and ecstasy. Fear and rapture. I hadn't realized that Hell embodied extremes.

It was oddly appealing to me . . . as was Hell's king.

His expression guarded, Lucifer asked, "What may I do for you?"

You may take me any way you wish.

I quashed that thought as I bowed again. "Nothing, my lord. I simply wished to take some air." Straightening, I added, "It was a little . . . stuffy in the meeting room."

"Stuffy." A smile quirked his lips, a flash and then gone, like heat lightning. "That's one way to describe a roomful of gods and their sycophants."

"A diplomatic way," I agreed, pleased by his frankness. "If I may be so bold, I don't know how you've kept your patience."

His eyes gleamed in the heat of Hell, bright green with tints of amber – the glow of his power, swimming deep. But even deeper were flecks of emotion: pride, anger, curiosity . . . at least a dozen more, flashing too quickly for me to name. He looked at me, taking in my face as if to memorize my features.

What do you see when you look at me, Lord Morningstar?

"Gods can be petty," he said, his gaze locked on mine. "I knew that well before Jehovah proposed his treaty and tasked me with leading negotiations." Another smile, one that he allowed to linger. "But after listening to countless deities as they recklessly cast stones, I'm all but ready to smite the lot of them and have done with it."

I chuckled softly. "If only it were that easy."

"Oh, it could be. But in the end, it would be more trouble than it's worth." He paused. "Smiting gods makes quite the mess. I'd never get the ash out of my fingernails."

I couldn't help myself – I threw back my head and laughed. The thought of my liege lord Zeus reduced to nothing but an annoyance beneath Lucifer's nails made me giddy.

When my laughter finally subsided to stray giggles, Lucifer murmured, "Lady Megaera, you have a delightful laugh."

My name on his lips stunned me, and not just because I enjoyed the sound. "Lord Lucifer," I said, "you can tell me apart from my sisters?"

He turned to face me fully. Slowly, he leaned against the railing, his arms back, his posture relaxed. His gaze, though, was not nearly as casual – it was both warm and wicked, brimming with humour.

Hinting at passion.

"Triplets you may be," he said, his voice low and lush, "but only a fool could fail to see that you are indeed Megaera Erinys."

His words lightened my heart . . . and heated me lower down. Lucifer Morningstar was a flatterer, to be sure.

It had been far too long since anyone had flattered me.

"With a single compliment," I said, marvelling, "you have scathingly insulted my liege lord."

"Did I? How very unintended."

Oh, I did so like this archangel, with his heated looks and laced words. I stepped on to the balcony and went to the guard rail . . . close enough to Lucifer for him to wrap his arms around me, had he wished. "Your Hell is an interesting place."

Lucifer turned so that he, too, faced his kingdom. The humour bled from his features until he was once more the powerful monarch. " 'Interesting'. Do you know, in all my years, I have never before heard the Underworld described as such? Terrifying, certainly. Upsetting, naturally. A place of wretched wonder, according to one prophet. But never interesting."

"It is, especially compared with the cold order of Tartarus," I said, gesturing to a cluster of demons below. "Hades would never allow his creatures to run amok as they tortured the damned."

A long pause before Lucifer replied: "I find the nefarious to be at their best when their leashes are long."

I arched a brow. "My lord?"

"Demons are given their boundaries, they're told what's expected, and then they're allowed to do their jobs as they see fit." He cast me a measured look. "They never assume they can do anything else. And so, they serve."

Heat burned my cheeks. I didn't know which embarrassed me more: Lucifer suggesting that I stayed with Zeus because I lacked imagination, or Lucifer comparing me to a demon. "Is that why you challenged your patron god?" I demanded. "Because you wanted to do something other than serve?"

Lucifer smiled, and this time there was no trace of humour to be found. "That is the popular story, is it not? That I wished to replace Jehovah and rule Heaven?"

I sniffed. "Indeed."

"Alas, Lady Fury, that is just a story. It was I who had suggested to Jehovah that he create Hell. And when he did, he appointed me its ruler." Lucifer chuckled, a bittersweet sound caught between humour and anger – a sound that numbed my own indignation. He said, "And so, I rule. The demons do their jobs well. The damned suffer until they are redeemed. And so Jehovah's will is done."

"Why would you suggest such a place as Hell?" I smiled wryly. "Were you bored in your god's Heaven, Lord Archangel?"

"I did so because it was better than the option. At the time, I had truly believed I was doing something important." Something dark passed behind his eyes, leaving storms in their wake. "But I have long since come to realize that Jehovah had already decided on creating Hell. He merely allowed me to voice the idea."

My smile had faded with his words. Lucifer, no longer relaxed, stood proudly outside of his palace, a look of raw pain in his eyes. "I don't understand," I said. "Was it your suggestion, or not?"

"Oh, it was. Not that it mattered. It was my idea, but he had already known what I would suggest." Lucifer's teeth flashed in a humourless grin. "Whether demon or angel, the creatures in Jehovah's pantheon know they're leashed."

Ah.

It was my turn to look away. "That is not unique to your pantheon," I said quietly. I knew very well how difficult it was for a proud creature to come when called.

Silence stretched between us, filled with the tension of Hell. My conversation with Lucifer was far more honest than my most intimate fantasies about him. And that honesty was painful. He was as angry with his patron god as I was with mine – no, more so. I, at least, had sisters to complain to. Who did Lucifer have to share his burden?

Who could truly know the mind and heart of the King of Hell?

"You and I, we are cut from the same cloth," Lucifer said. "We see the truth of things, and yet we are powerless to change them."

I had never been called powerless before. No one had ever dared. I stammered, "What truth?"

"Look at yourself. You are the sun, forced to dim your light so that a single bolt of lightning may outshine you." He paused, allowing his words to sink in. And they did; they burrowed under my skin, sucked at me like leeches. Lucifer asked, "Why do you allow it?"

Why indeed?

Numb, I replied, "I do what must be done."

"As do I. And so I allow rival gods to tramp about my home and squabble like geese." His eyes gleamed, reflecting the fires of Hell. "Don't you see, Megaera? Everything has already been decided. The treaty is nothing more than a pretence to allow the gods their dignity." Lucifer let out a bitter laugh. "Jehovah has got better at understanding pride."

I swallowed something thick and foul. "You are saying the negotiation is a sham?"

"Why would Jehovah propose a treaty among all pantheons, one that sets himself up as the Almighty god of gods, if he hasn't already decreed it to be so?" Anger heated Lucifer's words, and he spat, "We have no choice in the matter, Lady Fury. Heaven and Hell will absorb all pantheons, whether sooner or later. Jehovah will be the one God."

My head spun from his declaration. "You're insane."

"It will happen. It has already been decided." Lucifer closed his eyes. "It's not even the reasoning behind it that bothers me. I can understand Jehovah's desire to bond the pantheons together, to unite those worshipped so that any belief would affect all of us. I can understand him declaring himself as the god of gods; only a bare handful of us are even close to his level of power. It's the pretence of choice that I find so insulting."

"You make it sound as if the gods cannot make their own decisions."

"As I said before," he said softly, "at least the creatures in Jehovah's pantheon know they are leashed."

No.

No, this was too big. Too overwhelming. I couldn't accept that the gods themselves were nothing more than tools – that my own servitude, in the end, was nothing more than by some other deity's design.

Desperate and lost and needing things to make sense, I said, "Not everything has been decided."

"Everything," Lucifer said, his voice grating. "From large things to small, everything has already been set in stone. We simply don't know how to read the runes."

"You're wrong," I insisted. "Even ones such as you and I, beholden as we are to our deities, even we have choices!"

He closed his eyes and, when he sighed, I felt my heart breaking. "But we don't, Lady Fury. Humans have free will. You and I? We have only duty."

With those words, I suddenly knew how to prove him wrong.

"Not everything has been previously planned," I said firmly, reaching over to touch his hand. "Sometimes, things just happen."

"For a reason," he whispered, his voice tight. "Always for a reason."

"You're wrong, Lucifer. Let me show you." And with that, I kissed him.

At first, it was just my lips pressing against his, skin on skin, as I opened my mouth and swallowed the sound of his surprise. He stood there as I kissed him, unresponsive, unyielding . . . but neither did he push me away.

So rigid, Lord Archangel. My kiss is not deadly, I swear. Loosen yourself to me. Allow my heat to thaw your heart, my body to soothe your mind.

Let me in.

As if he'd heard my plea, he opened his mouth to mine, and now it was Lucifer who was kissing me, teasing a soft moan from my lips. He kissed me, and my body hummed from his touch. He kissed me, and my eyes slipped closed as he wrapped his strong arms around my back and embraced me. Lucifer Morningstar kissed me, and the world held its breath.

All too soon, he feathered smaller kisses on my mouth, then pulled away. I opened my eyes to see him searching my face, his green eyes darting, seeking answers to questions unasked. At that moment, he wasn't an archangel with the power to destroy most of Creation, nor was he a king with the burden of ruling.

He was a man, one who had lost his faith.

"Why?" he said, his voice rough.

"Because, as you said, we are cut from the same cloth." I stroked his cheek, tracing the outline of his chiselled jaw. "Because you are lonely, here in your underworld kingdom, and I am trapped in my Greek prison." I trailed my hand down his neck, softly brushing my fingertips over his skin. "Because I want to feel a connection to someone who understands me, who isn't afraid of me. Someone who sees me as a woman, not a Fury." Now both of my hands were on his shoulders, my fingers gently rubbing. "Do you?" I murmured. "See me as a woman?"

"Oh yes," he said. "By Sin and Salvation, yes."

And then he was kissing me again, and again, more passionate now, his mouth sealed on mine as he pulled me close. His tongue nudged between my lips, exploring, finding mine and coaxing it to dance. They rolled in slow circles as our mouths worked, and I delighted in the taste of him – heat and spice, as heady as mulled wine.

Yes, Lucifer. Yes. Inebriate me.

I trapped his head in my hands, threading my fingers through his hair, that glorious, thick hair. As we kissed I held him, pinned, even as his hands flowed down my back like water. More, I needed more of him. I sucked his lower lip, plumping it with my passion, then left his mouth to kiss the shape of his jaw, slowly, deliberately. I feasted on his ear lobe, using my lips and tongue and teeth to tell him without words how much I wanted him.

No plan, Lucifer. No reason other than a man and a woman wanting one another.

No reason other than because.

His hands skimmed my sides, whispered over the outer curves of my breasts, up over my arms. And then, with an animal growl, he captured my hands and turned me around, crushing my back against his torso. My fingers laced in his, he moved our arms down until they crossed over my chest.

His mouth by my ear; his voice playing along my skin. "Shall we love each other before all of Hell? Or does my lady prefer privacy?"

My voice husky, I said, "Whatever my lord desires."

"I desire you." He kissed my neck, the slope of my shoulder, darting his tongue to lap at my skin. Dizzy with need, I closed my eyes and leaned against him. "Tell me where we should go," he said between kisses. "The sky? The earth? The moon? Tell me what you want, and it shall be."

"You," I replied, breathless. "I want you."

"My lady, I am yours."

A ripple of power washed over me, through me, and then something deliciously soft cradled my head and back and bottom. I opened my eyes to find myself on a giant feather bed . . . and Lucifer leaning over me, one hand stroking my cheek.

"Here," he said, his eyes alight with passion, "in the privacy of my bedchamber, tell me how I should love you." His hand dipped lower, outlining the shape of my collarbone. "Slowly?" Now his fingers traced the folds of my tunic, from my right shoulder down to the top of my breast. "Forcefully? What does my Lady Fury want of her lover?"

His words made no sense. "My Lord Archangel, I want you. I want your body on mine." I reached up to touch his hip. "Your phallus in me. I want you to explode inside of me."

"What of you, Megaera?" He brought his hand down more, just enough for his fingers to brush over my nipple. Tiny shocks ran through me, heating me, waking my senses and making me want more than just a small touch. He murmured, "What do you want me to do to you? For you?"

"To come inside of me," I said, voice thick. "What more is there to say?"

He paused, his hand on my breast, his eyes like emeralds. "Lady," he said, "what of your own pleasure?"

"Your pleasure is my pleasure." I moved my hand, and now I felt him beneath his clothing, long and hard and eager for me.

"And yours," he said roughly, "is mine."

Another hum of power danced over me, and then I was naked before him . . . as was he, propped over me. His body was a work of art, every muscle sculpted to perfection, every angle just so, every plane defined. Fine black hair covered his broad chest, tapering to a line down his torso until it thickened just above his legs. And between them was proof of his arousal, fully erect, stiff with need.

"Megaera," he breathed, "you are beauty beyond words."

He leaned down to kiss me again, and again, and then he was moving down to my chin, my throat, kissing and licking and making my heart gallop. His tongue circled my right breast, maddeningly slow, tracing its curves, working so very carefully to its tip – and, once there, he took my nipple between his lips and began to suck.

I gasped from the twin sensations of wetness and heat, and the gasp became a groan as he flicked his tongue against my nub. He moved to my other breast, his teeth grazing my nipple, then his lips kissing away the small sting. Lucifer cast me a heated look as he suckled me, a look that went straight to my sex.

Oh my Lord Lucifer, what you do to me . . .

Awash with pleasure, I watched as he broke suction and kissed his way back up, over my breast, up more until now his mouth was on mine again and my eyes closed as I drank him in. As we kissed, I felt his hand on my cheek, then my neck, down lower, dangling now over my breast, his fingertips brushing its tender peak. I moaned against him, and he swallowed the sound.

His hand moved down, and down, slowly making its way to my belly – oh, so slowly. Teasingly slow. Excruciatingly slow. He kissed me once more, and his hand crept over my stomach. His mouth on my jaw, my ear now, his breath hot on my neck. Down went his fingers, even slower, and my hips began to rock. Down more, and I felt my body coil tight.

Yes . . . please, yes. Fill me.

He darted his hand between my legs, one stroke and then gone, and I cried out, needing more. He glided a finger over my sex, and back again, over and back, and I was lost in his touch.

"Megaera," he murmured, "your pleasure is my pleasure."

And then he slid a finger into me, and the world caught fire.

Rapture, primal and fiercely unforgiving, consumed me, burning away my past and my future, reducing me to nothing more than that moment. I floated, joyous. Ripple after ripple of bliss washed over me, eventually dousing the conflagration and leaving my body tingling.

Lucifer withdrew his finger and brought it to his mouth. "This," he said, licking my juices, "this is what I want. Your pleasure on my lips."

Oh . . . yes, Lucifer. Yes.

He leaned down to kiss me, and I tasted the barest hint of myself on his lips before he dived down, his hands on my breasts, squeezing, groping as he kissed down my stomach, coming to the mound of curls at the apex of my thighs. Now his hands were between my legs, nudging them apart to reveal my sex, and I cried out as he blew gently over me.

"Megaera, I want to taste you." And then his mouth was on me.

My head rocked back as he kissed me, licked me, made love to me with his mouth. He took me with his lips and his tongue, took me far away from Hell and Olympus and all of Creation as I spiralled further into ecstasy.

Between my legs, the Light Bringer made a sound of animal passion as I came.

Once the aftershocks ebbed, Lucifer kissed my sex once, twice, and then pulled himself over me. I smiled at him, too dazed to speak. His lips shone wetly, and I thought his mouth the most erotic thing I'd ever seen.

"My Lady Fury," he said. "You taste divine."

Oh, my Lord Morningstar. Let me show you divinity.

I placed my hands on his shoulders and pushed, rolling until I was straddled over him, his hips between my thighs, his erection poised under my sex. Looking into his eyes, I grinned, rubbing myself over him, slowly, making him slick with my arousal.

Your turn, my archangel.

I kissed my way down his chest, savouring first one small nipple and then the other, enjoying his sounds of pleasure. My hands toyed with the fine hairs on his stomach, tickling him as my fingers wound their way down to his thatch of pubic hair.

When I held his erection in my hands, he gasped.

When I placed my lips on his shaft, he groaned.

I kissed him and sucked him, took him deep in my mouth and lapped him with my tongue. His phallus throbbed, full of blood and restrained passion, and I stroked him harder, wanting to take him to the brink.

"Megaera," he growled. "Please . . ."

For you, my Lucifer. All for you.

His hands on my face, nudging me. I paused, looking at him as I kissed his tip. Desire shone in his eyes and, darker than that, need.

"Together," he said gruffly. "Let us come together."

I flicked my tongue against him once more. "Your pleasure," I said, "is my pleasure."

With a last kiss on his shaft, I moved up until I was poised over him, my sex on his, my hands in his. My gaze on his. In his eyes, I was no creature of vengeance to be feared, no weapon to be used. Lucifer Morningstar looked at me, and I was simply a woman, wishing to be loved.

And he was a man, wanting to love me.

"Together," I said, smiling as I lowered myself on to him. He slid into me perfectly, as if he'd been created just for me. I took him in completely, basking in his gaze, his grin, and we stayed like that for a small piece of forever, feeling, sharing, being. And then we moved, our bodies slowly undulating, smooth and rhythmic, faster now, making music as our bellies slapped together, skin on skin. Faster still, friction leading the way to rapturous release as something wild opened within me and swallowed me whole as Lucifer thrusted deep, bellowing as he came.

We shuddered, our climaxes roaring through us and, in that magical moment, we were one – joined forever in the action, the declaration, of love, of life itself: together.

And then the moment passed and we collapsed, limbs entangled, bodies spent, twin smiles on our faces.

Time stretched as we lay together, content, our sweat drying. There was no Zeus, no Jehovah, no gods or mortals or demands. There was only the two of us, and the bond that we had created. And it was good.

All too soon, the time came when we had to return to our lives. Lucifer pulled himself up and offered a hand to me, which I took. Standing, I looked up into his handsome face, into his eyes, and I smiled at what I saw.

He still was the Light Bringer, dread ruler of Hell, one of the most powerful creatures in all of Creation. That was all too clear in his eyes.

He was my lover, a man who gave me pleasure, who took his pleasure when I found bliss. And that, too, was in his eyes. It was that vision, that memory, which would stay with me whenever I would think of the king of the damned: Lucifer Morningstar holding my hand, his gaze lit with passion and something brighter – not in a flash like lightning, here and then gone, but instead a ray of sunlight, shining and constant.

With a touch of power – his, because he had been the one to disrobe us – we were once again clothed, girded once more for the war of politics. We kissed again, softly, tenderly. Lovingly.

"Megaera," he said, touching my face, "my Fury."

"My archangel," I murmured. "Do you believe me now, when I say that not everything is planned?"

Lucifer laughed softly. "My Lady, it is just as easy to say that Jehovah intended for us to steal this time for ourselves." He brought my hand to his lips and kissed it. "Whether this was spontaneity or serendipity, I am truly grateful."

"As am I." Suddenly shy, I whispered, "Thank you."

"Oh, lady," he said, squeezing my hand, "it is I who must thank you. You've given me something more precious than I ever could have wished for." He smiled, radiant. "You've given me hope."

"As have you," I said, breathless with the realization. For if he was right, and all the pantheons would become part of Jehovah's Heaven and Hell, then I would be free of Olympus' hold – and would be seeing much more of Lucifer Morningstar.

And if I was right, well, even with me bound to Zeus's pantheon, who was to say that there wouldn't be other such dalliances between Lucifer and me in our future?

"My Megaera," Lucifer murmured, kissing me again. I would feel the memory of his kiss on my lips long after he had pulled away. "My hope."

Spontaneity? Or serendipity?

And in the end, did it matter?

Another kiss, another lingering touch. And I decided that no, it didn't matter at all. Whether by design or just because, we had each other – to console, to share, to love.

And it was good.

Shelter from the Storm

Louisa Burton

Am I totally and completely nuts? Marianne wondered as she twisted the key in the lock of Alan's apartment door. He'd given her the key when he'd bought into this exclusive Upper East Side co-op six months ago, but she'd never used it because she'd never been to his apartment when he wasn't there – until now.

She let herself in, anticipating the look on Alan's face when he came home from his Friday night poker game and found her waiting in his bed. Every light in the gleaming penthouse was ablaze, of course; Alan tended to leave things on when he went out. A jazz saxophone moaned its ardent lament from the CD player in the sprawling, white-on-white living room. Given the muffled sounds from the bedroom down the hall, he evidently hadn't turned off that colossal new TV of his, either.

Unbuttoning her trench coat, Marianne thought back to the man Alan had been before last fall, when he'd been made the youngest partner ever at Swift, Banks and McKee, one of Manhattan's most high-powered law firms. He'd been more real, more down to earth when she'd met him, exactly a year ago today – 9 June – at a softball game in Central Park between his lawyer pals and her teacher pals. Could she thaw the corporate frostiness that had settled over him since then, she wondered, or was the old Alan gone for ever?

She held her trench coat open and scrutinized her reflection in the mirrored walls of Alan's foyer. *I am nuts. He'll laugh at me.*

No, he'll love it, she thought, regarding the seductive outfit she'd worn to surprise him on the first anniversary of their relationship – pink vinyl micro-miniskirt and matching angora cropped sweater, partially unzipped to expose most of the white lace push-up bra beneath, which yielded a cleavage of cartoonish proportions. She had on mile-high silver stilettos and white silk stockings, the lacy tops of which peeked out from below the hem of the minuscule skirt, along with the clasps connecting them to the garter belt.

Marianne smoothed down her carefully flat-ironed honey-blonde hair and rubbed away a smudge at the edge of her crimson lipstick, hearing in her mind the echoes of Alan's many discourses on the subject of their lukewarm sex life. *If you'd only loosen up a little, you'd get off once in a while. It's not my fault it's all over so fast. A woman's got to entice a man to keep him going. You'd know this if you had more experience.*

Marianne had been a twenty-two-year-old virgin when she'd met Alan. In many ways, she still felt like one. Or, as Alan sometimes put it, "a classic, frigid little kindergarten teacher".

I'll show him who's frigid tonight, she thought as she headed down the hall towards Alan's bedroom. The sounds from the TV grew more distinct as she neared the closed door. "Yeah, you like that, don't you, baby?" a man growled softly. There came a sound like a sharp slap, and then another. "You like that, too, don't you?"

Marianne heard a woman's shuddering moan, followed by a breathy, "Yes . . . oh yes . . ."

Had he left a porn video running? Marianne wondered.

She reached for the doorknob as the woman cried, "Yes! Oh, God, yes, Alan. *Yes!*"

Alan? The door swung open. Marianne's heart stopped.

A statuesque redhead, wearing a few artfully arranged strips of black leather and snugly laced boots, lay face down on Alan's colossal waterbed, her reddened bottom hoisted on a mound of pillows, her wrists secured behind her with a pair of chrome handcuffs. She squealed when she saw Marianne.

"Marianne?" Alan leaped off the bed, brandishing what appeared to be a doubled-up belt. He was naked except for something that looked more or less like a black leather jockstrap festooned with studs. "What the hell . . . What are you doing here?"

"Making a big, big mistake," she said tremulously as she backed out of the room.

"What have you done to yourself?" There came a little snort of laughter as he looked her up and down. "Oh, babe," he said, his expression both astonished and pitying. "You can't be serious."

Marianne turned and fled on quaking legs. Over the clicking of her heels on the marble floor, she heard the girl on the bed say, "Is that the kindergarten teacher? Oh my God, Alan, she looks like the Easter Bunny in drag."

Their laughter echoed through the big, chilly apartment as Marianne yanked open the door and bolted out into the hallway. Don't you dare cry, she admonished herself as she descended in the elevator, tugging her trench coat closed to hide her outlandish get-up even though she was alone. When the elevator opened, she sprinted past the nonplussed doorman and out into the night, driven by the need to put as much distance as possible between herself and Alan.

It was her own fault, of course. She had a history of falling fast and hard for the wrong guys, guys who were incapable of returning her supercharged feelings for them. Of course, she'd thought Alan was different, which was why she'd finally given up that precious virginity of hers. But she'd been wrong about him, too.

Well, if she couldn't trust her instincts when it came to men, she'd just have to unlearn them. What she needed was to take a break from relationships – a year, maybe – to concentrate on figuring out how not to fall in love at first sight the second she found herself unattached.

By the time she slowed down to a walk, her chest pumping, her mind whirling, she had only the vaguest idea where she was. It had gotten breezy, and the air prickled like it did right before a storm. She stopped and looked around at the buildings looming over the deserted cross-town street. If she could get to Lex and 53rd, she could catch the E or the F to her little studio apartment in Kew Gardens. The idea of taking the subway alone this late at night unnerved her, but she didn't have enough cash on her for a taxi, having just assumed, like an idiot, that Alan would drive her home as usual; he jumped at any excuse to get behind the wheel of that new white Porsche of his, which he loved to distraction. Probably the only thing he *did* love.

"Oh, God," she moaned, leaning against a broken street lamp and burying her face in her hands. "You idiot. You naive little dope." What had she been thinking, trying to remake the frigid little kindergarten teacher into a sex goddess? "You stupid, stupid, stupid . . ."

At the sound of a car turning the corner, Marianne raised her head to squint down the block, groaning when she saw the familiar flash of white. He'd followed her. She turned away from him and strode purposefully down the street, wondering what smooth line of bull he'd come up with to mollify her. Whatever it was, he'd find some way to blame it all on her, of course. *If only you were more responsive, this wouldn't have happened.*

Hearing the car come closer, she wheeled around and stalked up to it, trench coat billowing, hands on vinyl-clad hips, ready to tell Alan just what she thought of him and his lame, self-serving excuses.

The car glided to a stop as she approached, its front passenger window lowering. Leaning down, she peered inside . . . and froze.

It wasn't Alan at the wheel of the Porsche.

It wasn't even a Porsche; it was some nondescript middlebrow sedan. Marianne blinked at the driver.

He blinked back at her. From what she could see of him in the dark, he was fairly young, thirty maybe, with an open face and a head of thick dark hair that looked impossible to comb. His attire – a rumpled sports coat, polo shirt and jeans – was as comfortably nondescript as his car.

"Miss, are you all right?" he asked. "I saw you with your head in your hands. Do you need some help, or, uh . . . Oh." His gaze had lit on her breasts, of which he had an eye-popping vista, with her leaning over this way.

She straightened up, heat flooding her face, but that only gave him a better view of the rest of her.

"OK . . ." he murmured, contemplating the lace bands at the tops of her stockings. "Yeah, uh . . ." He raised big, dark eyes to hers. "Sorry, I, uh . . ." He shrugged. "I'm really not interested."

"Not . . . Wh–what do you . . ." With a gasp, Marianne yanked her coat closed. "Oh, my God, you think—"

"I mean, of course I'm *interested*," he corrected with a sheepish grin that made him look about fourteen. "How could I not be? I mean you're . . . you're . . ."

Was he blushing? It was too dark to tell for sure. "Look," she began, backing away. "I think there's been a little—"

"I didn't mean to imply . . ." He raked a hand through his hair. "I mean, you're incredibly . . ." He surveyed her head to toe, although her trench coat hid the Easter Bunny costume from view. "Wow. You've got to be just about the sexiest, most beautiful thing I've ever seen. But the thing is, I just don't . . . I've never . . ." He winced apologetically. "You know. Paid for it."

Marianne stared at him in wonderment as thunder rumbled overhead. The sexiest thing he'd ever seen? Was he serious?

"But, hey, if I was ever gonna . . ." His look of wistful desire was anything but boyish. "Anyway, sorry." He reached for the button to raise the window. "Uh, good luck, I guess."

It was as he was driving away that Marianne felt the first stinging shot of pain. She yelped and grabbed her shoulder as an ominous rattling filled the air.

Hail. Within seconds, thousands – millions – of marble-sized ice balls were plummeting out of the sky to bounce and roll on the pavement. From somewhere came a sirenlike wail, and then another, and another, as the hailstones set off car alarms for blocks around.

One struck her on the head, feeling like a bullet even through her hair. Shielding her face with her hands, she looked around frantically for shelter – a recessed doorway, an overhang, maybe – but the surrounding apartment buildings all had front doors that were flush with their façades.

The hail storm intensified, pinging like artillery all around her. Cowering at the side of a building, she tore off her trench coat and cloaked herself with it, but it was meagre protection from this hellish barrage.

"Miss!"

Peering out below the edge of the coat, Marianne saw the white car at the kerb again. The driver, leaning across the front seat to hold the door open for her, must have put it in reverse when the hail storm began.

"Get in!" he called out, gesturing to her. "Hurry!"

She stared at him through the icy torrent, relief warring with deeply ingrained trepidation at the prospect of getting into a car with a stranger. She cried out as a hailstone struck her hand.

He bolted out of the car and sprinted over to her through the onslaught, flinching as the hail pelted him. Crouching down, he yelled over the racket, "You're gonna get hurt if you stay out here!" He pulled her to her feet, holding the coat over her head. "Come on – you can sit in my car till it's over."

He grabbed her hand, and together they darted to the white sedan. After helping her into the passenger seat, he circled the vehicle, vaulted into the driver's seat and slammed the door shut.

"Whew!" With a diffident glance towards Marianne, he said, "Um, I'm Rob, by the way. Just thought, you know, since we're stuck here together, we might as well know each other's . . ."

"Marianne," she managed as she wrestled with her trench coat, which had got twisted around her.

"Pretty name." Rob's gaze lit fleetingly on her brazen display of cleavage as she squirmed free of the coat. Reaching for the keys, he killed the engine. "Guess we'll just have to wait this out."

Hail pummelled the windshield, the car, the street. The incessant bombardment, on top of everything else Marianne had endured tonight, made her shake so badly that she couldn't get her arms through the sleeves of the coat. Giving up in frustration, she draped it over herself like a blanket, aided by Rob, who solicitously tucked it around her.

"What a *night* I'm having!" She clawed her hands through her hair, ruining the sleek effect she'd gone to so much trouble to achieve. "Everything's gone wrong tonight, *everything*, and now this!" She gestured towards the windshield and the hailstones clattering against it.

"Hey . . . hey . . ." Lifting a hand to her hair, he brushed it off her face. "You're just rattled by the hail, that's all. It'll be over soon."

She hunkered down in the seat, pulling the coat up to her chin. "You think a hailstone could break a windshield?"

"Not these – they're too small."

"I hate this. This whole night, this whole stupid . . ." Her voice caught; her eyes stung. "I *hate* it!"

"Oh, hey, no. Don't cry. Please. I lose all perspective when women cry."

"I won't," she promised, trembling with the effort not to.

"Oh, man, this is even worse than if you were bawling your eyes out." He clambered awkwardly over the gearshift to wedge himself into the passenger seat with her. Gathering her into his embrace, he cupped her head against his chest. Beneath the age-softened cotton of his polo shirt, faintly redolent of laundry soap, she felt hard-packed muscle, heard the faint thump-thump of his heart. "So, uh . . . Marianne, is it?"

She nodded.

"Are you, like, prone to weather-related freak-outs, or is it just tonight?"

"Tonight," she sighed, "has been a nightmare."

"The nightmare is over now." He scooped her on to his lap as he shifted to settle his weight into the seat, his arms banding around her, his warmth seeping bone-deep into her. To be comforted in the arms of a stranger in this dark confined space, while outside the heavens unleashed their terrible fury . . . there was a dreamy unreality about it.

"Everything's OK now," Rob whispered as he nuzzled the top of her head. "Everything's fine." There came a soft pressure, a tickle through her hair. Had he kissed her?

Marianne grew very still. So did Rob.

She turned her head into the crook of his neck, inhaled his scent, his warmth. On impulse she touched her lips to the quickening pulse on the side of his throat.

His arms tightened around her, his mouth brushing her forehead, her temple, the crest of her cheekbone, her jaw, his breath coming hot and fast just like hers . . .

Their lips touched, parted, touched again.

"Oh God." He drew back. "I'm sorry, I'm . . . You're upset. I shouldn't be . . ."

"It's . . . it's all right," she whispered. *He thinks I'm beautiful, he thinks I'm sexy.*

"No, I should stop. Tell me to stop," he murmured, his gaze on her mouth.

"Don't stop."

He kissed her ravenously, one hand burrowing through her hair to grip the back of her head, the other fumbling with the coat in which she was wrapped. Marianne returned the kiss with a hunger that astounded her, pausing only long enough to yank the coat off and fling it on to the driver's seat.

His hands were everywhere on her, hot and demanding. "Yes," she breathed when he unzipped her sweater, flicked the front clasp of her bra, filled his hands with her. They both moaned as he kneaded the pliant flesh, her nipples tightening almost painfully as he fondled them.

And still he kissed her, their legs a restless tangle, their breath fogging the glass as hail continued to batter the car. Rob smoothed a hand up a stockinged thigh and over her lace-clad bottom, hiking up the little vinyl miniskirt as he went.

He slid a hand between them, growling deep in his throat when he discovered the panties to be crotchless. Marianne hitched in a breath as he pushed a finger deep into her, where she was already wet and ready, so ready, more ready than she'd ever been. She arched her back, thrusting against his hand, drunk with sensation, delirious with pleasure.

He took his time, enticing her slowly towards an ecstatic crisis of the senses – a crisis she had never reached with Alan. Where had it come from? she wondered dazedly. How could she feel this heat, this passion, this aching *need* for a man she'd just met?

It doesn't matter. Nothing mattered but this raw, ungovernable, astonishing desire. And it wasn't like she was violating her new moratorium on relationships. This wasn't a relationship, it was just . . . a fleeting encounter, two bodies uniting in the dark while fury rained from the skies.

Straddling Rob's lap, she unzipped his straining fly. He bucked beneath her when she closed her hand around him. "Yes . . . oh . . ." he murmured when she began to stroke him. He pumped into her fist, clutching at her, his eyes losing focus. "Marianne, I think I'm . . . you better . . ." He groaned. "Stop!" he said, clamping a hand around her wrist. "No, stop, *stop.*"

"Did I hurt you?"

"*Hurt* me?" He chuckled throatily. "It feels *too* good, that's the problem. I'm gonna end up going off in your hand, and that's . . . It's not what I had in mind."

"Me, neither." She smiled – a little bashfully, which was absurd under the circumstances, but there you go.

"What a pretty smile." He touched her mouth with fingertips that shook ever so slightly. I did that to him, she realized with amazement.

Reaching inside his sports coat, Rob withdrew a wallet from which he slid a little square packet.

Marianne closed her eyes, hearing the crackle of plastic over the hail still hammering the car, and thinking, This is happening. This is really going to happen.

"Marianne?"

She opened her eyes to find him regarding her with a look of concern.

"Are you OK with this?" he asked.

"I'm desperate for this," she whispered as she leaned down, claiming his mouth in another searing kiss. He lifted her up slightly, positioning her just so; she closed her hands over his shoulders to steady herself. Gripping her hips, he pulled her down, then came the hard, hot pressure of him stretching her open, pushing deep, deeper . . .

He groaned rawly as he drove into her. "I'm too close. I won't last."

"Just be still," she murmured into his ear, rising slowly up the length of him, then lowering herself just as gradually. "Don't move. Let me do it all."

"As long as I can touch you," he said, one hand lightly stroking her where they were joined, the other cupping a swollen breast as he leaned forwards to close his mouth over the rigid little nipple.

He suckled and caressed her as she made love to him, further and further into an utter delirium of the senses. She'd never taken control during sex, yet right now it seemed like the most natural thing in the world. Rob felt so hard and full inside her; his fingertips were so slick and clever, his mouth so hot.

She writhed and whimpered, panting as her climax gathered up. He moaned each time she sank on to him, the muscles in his thighs quivering with the strain of holding still.

"I can't . . ." he rasped. "I can't . . ." Seizing her hips, he rammed into her once, twice, and then stilled, his body taut and shuddering, his fingers digging painfully into her flesh. A guttural shout tore from his lungs as he throbbed inside her, igniting her own convulsive pleasure. It thundered through her with a violence that rocked her to the core. Dimly she was aware of a ragged groan, and realized it was her.

He pulled her close with quaking arms, laying her head on his shoulder, and covered them both with her coat. That was how they remained until their breathing steadied and their hearts slowed to normal.

"Wow," he whispered.

"Mmm."

"That was . . ."

"Mmm."

"I, uh . . . I'm sorry I couldn't make it last longer," he said.

Last longer? Alan was usually finished in half that time.

Before she could say something reassuring, he said, "Do you hear that?"

"I don't hear anything."

"Exactly," he said. "The hail storm is over."

Marianne sat up to look out the side window, but the glass was too steamed up to see through.

The hail storm was over. What now? Would they just shake hands and go their separate ways? That prospect filled her with a terrible sense of emptiness.

Not good, she thought as she and Rob clumsily uncoupled and righted their clothing in the cramped space. Not good at all. Half an hour ago she'd resolved to ignore that little devil on her shoulder that made her lose her heart to men she barely knew. The smartest thing she could do right now would be to walk away from here and not look back.

"I don't want this to end," he said, pulling her back into his arms.

Marianne's heart skittered in her chest.

He trailed his knuckles lightly down her cheek. "I'd like you to come back to my hotel with me."

"Hotel?"

"I'm in town on business. Just till tomorrow morning, then I'm flying back to Rochester, but I thought—"

"Rochester?" she said. "I grew up there. Is that where you live?"

"South of there, actually – Canandaigua. That's where *I* grew up, and I have no intention of ever moving. The Finger Lakes rule."

"They do – they're awesome." She raised her head to look at him. "We used to go down there every summer to go sailing on Canandaigua Lake, or sometimes Seneca. God, I loved it there." She shook her head as she lay it back on his shoulder. "I'd move upstate again in a heartbeat, but . . . circumstances have kept me here." Circumstances meaning Alan. Her job would never have kept her in New York. Fed up with teaching – or rather, babysitting – spoiled little rich girls in one of Manhattan's most exclusive parochial schools, she'd been all set last June to quit and apply to public schools upstate. But then she'd met Alan, and those plans had dissolved within days.

"Ah, yes, circumstances," he said thoughtfully. "So, uh . . . well. Like I said, I'm in town till tomorrow, and I was hoping . . ." He dragged a hand through his disheveled hair. "I, uh, I'm not used to this, so I guess I should just ask you . . . you know . . . how much it would be?"

"How much . . . oh." Oh God, that's right. He thought she was a hooker. *You idiot. You're falling for him at supersonic speed, and he's just trying to figure out your going rate.*

"For the night," he clarified. "If you came back to my hotel with me. How much would that be?"

It's just as well, she thought, steeling herself. You made a moratorium; you should stick to it. "You couldn't afford it."

She started to rise off him, but he stilled her with a hand on her shoulder. "How much?"

She'd heard something on TV once about a call girl who charged $1,000 an hour. "Ten thousand dollars."

"I can afford it," he said without missing a beat. She must have looked sceptical, because he smiled and said, "I'll give it to you in advance if you don't trust me."

"You've got that much on you?"

"On me? No, but I promise you—" he drew a cross on his chest "—cross my heart and hope to die, that there's ten grand in my hotel room safe with your name on it. What do you say?"

"Rob, it's . . . it's not the money. It's just this has been so . . . so incredible, so . . ."

"I know." Framing her face with his hands, he compelled her with his gaze to look at him. "It was . . . it was just like it's supposed to be and never really is. I completely lost myself in you. That's why I don't want it to be over. I want to spend the night with you, Marianne. I want to . . ." Closing his eyes, he pulled her towards him until their foreheads touched. "I want to lose myself in you again. And again and again. The thing is, I've never been with a woman like you before—"

"You mean a whore?" she asked, pulling away.

"I'm not talking about how you make your living, Marianne. I'm talking about who you are, *really* are. You're the most passionate, most responsive woman I've ever been with. I only lost myself in you because—" he shrugged "—you lost yourself in *me*."

"You . . . think I'm responsive?"

He laughed. "You're kidding, right?"

As he was driving her to his hotel, Rob said, "Do you mind my asking what you're doing here in New York? I mean, I know what you're *doing*. I know how you make your living." He said it casually and without any hint of judgment, as if he were referring to a perfectly respectable line of work. "I was just wondering why you left upstate, if you like it so much."

Marianne didn't know how to answer that. She'd been thrilled when Professor McGrath had hooked her up with the kindergarten position at Our Lady of Sorrows during the spring semester of her senior year at Nazareth. She'd moved to New York thinking it would be an adventure. Then came Alan.

Then came tonight.

But she couldn't reveal any of that to Rob without blowing her cover, as it were, and exposing herself to heartache all over again. His assumption that she was a prostitute was like an insurance policy against another precipitous relationship. By playing this role, she could enjoy a sexual adventure without risking her heart.

"Forget it," Rob said, reaching over to squeeze her hand. "I'm being nosy. It's none of my business and it's probably nothing you want to talk about. I mean, I know girls sometimes end up in your situation after . . . going through difficult times."

He thought she'd fallen into prostitution after a traumatic adolescence, Marianne realized. He assumed she'd been a runaway, maybe abused at home, maybe a drug addict: prostitute as victim, a heart of gold but a painful past.

She said, "You know what? Why don't we both just not talk about who we are and what we do and how we got here?"

"A gag order on our pasts?"

"The last few years, anyway. No questions, no explanations, just us, together, right now."

He nodded thoughtfully. "That's actually an excellent idea."

"It is, huh? Do you have some deep, dark secret I should know about before you get me alone in a hotel room?"

"A nefarious plot to chloroform you and sell you to Barbary pirates?" he asked with a grin.

"Barbary pirates?"

"I read a lot of boys' action adventure when I was a kid. Here we are," he said as he pulled the car to the kerb in front of an old and ornate-looking granite building with an awning over the front door. "This is a boutique hotel almost nobody knows about. The building dates from 1841. It was the mansion of a railroad tycoon, and it's an awesome example of Victorian Gothic Revival architecture. You can't see it in the dark, but there's the coolest gargoyle peering down from the roof."

"You sound like you're really into this stuff," Marianne said as a uniformed doorman sprinted up to the car.

"I'm a . . ." Rob hesitated.

"Never mind," she said. "I don't want to know."

The doorman eyed her with a tad too much interest as he was helping her from the car. Looking down, she saw that her trench coat was hanging open, revealing the sexpot garb beneath. She yanked it closed, but the damage was done. As Rob was guiding her into the elevator, she glanced over her shoulder and saw the doorman whispering to the desk clerk, a small, bespectacled, pointy-nosed man who looked like a cartoon rat. They were both looking in her direction.

Rob didn't notice. He had other things on his mind. No sooner did the old, oak-panelled elevator begin its ascent than he punched the stop button, making it groan to a halt. He lifted her against the wall and took her right there, fast and furious, bringing her to a volcanic climax in about half a minute. Slowing down, he used deep, grinding strokes that made her come again, even harder than the first time. He stopped moving and just held her there against the wall for a long moment while he caught his breath, and then he withdrew from her, set her on her feet, and straightened her skirt.

As he was zipping up his fly, she said, "Um . . . you didn't . . . Don't you want to . . . ?"

"Oh, yeah," he said as he pushed the button to make the elevator rumble to life, "but not here. I don't have another condom on me. I shouldn't have gone as far as I did. And I don't want you thinking I'm always as quick on the draw as I was before, during the hail storm."

"Rob, that was great. It was wonderful. You have nothing to apologize for."

"You *are* sweet, aren't you?" He sounded like a man who'd just discovered something fascinating. "I mean, for real."

"Too sweet," she said. "My boyfriend gave me no end of abuse when I cried during *Casablanca*. He laughed and emptied a whole box of tissues on to my lap and called me a simpering sentimentalist."

That seemed to give him pause. "You have a boyfriend? Wait, forget I asked. No questions, no—"

"It's OK. I meant my ex-boyfriend. I'm not seeing him any more." She smiled to herself when she realized that was true.

"Sounds like a smart move. There's no such thing as too sweet," Rob said as he ushered her out of the elevator into a Persian-carpeted hallway. "There *is* such a thing as being a cynical, arrogant, insulting dick, and it sounds like your ex had that role down pat."

Rob's hotel room was an opulent, Victorian-style enclave of dark polished wood and overstuffed furniture against a backdrop of cabbage rose wallpaper. He hung up her coat and offered her dinner from room service, which she declined, opting for a cold ginger ale from the minibar.

"Cross your fingers that I've got some condoms in here," Rob said as he went into the bathroom and flipped the light switch, igniting a pair of antique-looking sconces. He unzipped a leather Dopp kit sitting on the vanity beside the sink and started rummaging through its contents. "I can't recall the last time I packed any. My business trips are usually, well, all business."

Joining him in the bathroom, Marianne found it to be on the small side – not surprising, given the building's age – but quaint and cosy, with lots of marble and bevelled glass reflecting the soft amber glow of the sconces. The only modern touch was a whirlpool tub set into a marble surround within a little oak-panelled alcove.

"A whirlpool," she said. "You lucky duck."

"I'm a shower man, myself. Yes!" he said, brandishing a strip of condoms.

"My aunt and uncle had a hot tub when I was a teenager. They could never get me out of it when visiting. My parents didn't complain. They said it mellowed me out for about a day afterwards, took away that adolescent testiness and made me all sweet and obedient. I wouldn't complain about chores, just do what I was told without question."

"Do what you're told without question, eh?" With a villainous cackle, Rob stoppered the tub and turned on the faucets. "Maybe I won't need that chloroform after all."

Marianne fought off a twinge of embarrassment as he divested her of her pink angora sweater and bra and started tugging down the zipper of her miniskirt – an absurd reaction, considering what had transpired between them. Remember the role you're playing, she told herself. You're no bashful kindergarten teacher tonight.

He undressed her as the bathroom filled with steam, extolling her beauty with every inch of skin he uncovered, and then he stripped down in about five seconds and reached for her hand to help her into the tub. They settled together into the warm, roiling water, their arms and legs entwined, lips brushing, hands caressing and exploring. His body was well muscled and beautifully proportioned.

"Wow, you're in amazing shape," she murmured against his lips. "You must work out."

"Nah, I just do a lot of physical labour."

Doing what? she almost asked, but she held her tongue. No questions . . . but that didn't mean she had no curiosity. Rob was obviously pretty well heeled, even if you discounted his claim that he had ten grand in his hotel safe. Hotel rooms like this did not come cheap. And what kind of manual labourer came to New York "on business"?

Before long, they were moving together in a sinuous rhythm echoed by their tongues as they shared a long, breathless, heart-pounding kiss. He was as hard as marble, and groaned when she stroked him there.

"I hate to keep asking you to back off," he said as he gently removed her hand, "but I want you to come again first. You're so sensual, so beautiful. It's the most exciting thing in the world, just watching you. Here." Lifting her up, he turned her so that she was facing the foot of the tub and held her from behind, adjusting her position until she was kneeling on her haunches with one of the jets was aimed directly between her legs.

So intense was the carnal shock of water pulsing against her most sensitive flesh that she recoiled with a gasp, but he banded his arms around her, holding her in place as she gripped the edge of the tub.

"Easy," he said softly, wedging a leg between hers to keep them apart. "Just give in to it."

Her sense of helplessness as he held her crushed against him only intensified the erotic impact of the water thrumming against her. He squeezed her breasts and rubbed against her, his breath harsh in her ear. She moaned helplessly as her arousal escalated, her head thrown back, hips rocking.

A hoarse cry escaped her when the pleasure detonated, Rob holding her tight and kissing her cheek and throat as it ran its course. With an unsteady hand, he grabbed a folded towel and set it on the marble surround at the juncture of two of the oak walls. He lifted her on to it so that she was sitting facing him as he knelt between her legs.

Reaching for the strip of condoms, he tore one off and swiftly sheathed himself. She'd expected him to enter her then, but instead, he took her head in his hands and kissed her deeply and lingeringly. When he did release her, it was to pleasure her with lazy, curious hands until, when he finally did sink into her, she was once again at a fever pitch of arousal.

He renewed the kiss, bracing her hips with one hand while he caressed her with the other. His strokes, at first steady and measured, grew sharper, more urgent, the muscles of his shoulders and back and hips churning faster, faster . . . He cocked his hips, driving deep, as a strangled groan rumbled from his chest. They came together, holding each other tight through the explosive peak and the ensuing, gradually diminishing tremors.

"Wow." They both whispered it together, then laughed.

"I've got to tell you," he said, "the contrast between how sweet you seem most of the time, and how wild and sexy you are in the throes of passion, really slays me."

"You're kind of the same way. I mean, you come off as this really nice guy, a real gentleman . . ."

"Nice? Oh, no." He let out a chuckly groan. She felt the vibrations deep inside, where they were still intimately joined. "It's what every guy dreads being thought of by a beautiful, sexy woman. We all want to be Superman, not Clark Kent."

"No, but that's not all there is to you," she said, stroking the damp hair off his forehead. "When you're . . . you know, making love, you're a different man entirely – ravenous, uninhibited. It's like the caveman shoves Clark Kent aside and takes over."

"So Clark Kent turns into a caveman? I think you're mixing your analogies."

"Fine, then. You're Superman in the sack."

"Pure speculation on your part. I haven't even gotten you in the sack yet."

"The night's young."

"Indeed, it is," he said as he closed his mouth over hers.

Once they were dried off and wrapped in the hotel's plush terrycloth robes, she did let him order room service. They had champagne and cold shrimp and tiny, perfect raspberries in cream, after which they turned out the lights and slid naked between cool linen sheets.

And talked. Or, rather, whispered, in the sheltering darkness, of long-ago summers spent skimming across sun-spangled lakes in sailboats. In keeping with their agreement, they never ventured beyond childhood memories. She sensed he was surprised that she'd had such a happy family life, and she knew he must still be wondering how she'd ended up turning tricks in New York. Tempted though she was, she did not correct his assumption about how she made her living. To do so would have opened up a Pandora's box of feelings best left under lock and key.

They made love again, slow, drowsy, achingly sweet lovemaking that made her eyes burn and her throat tighten.

Afterwards, just as she was drifting off to sleep, she heard him murmur, "Which scene was it?"

"What?" She could just see him by the moonlight filtering in through the curtains. He was lying on his side looking at her.

"Which scene was it in *Casablanca* that made you cry? The last scene, on the tarmac?"

"No. I mean, I teared up a little then, too, but I was careful not to let Alan see. The scene he abused me about was the one at Rick's where the German officers start singing their anthem or whatever, and then all the French people get up and drown them out with 'La Marseillaise'."

"Yes!" Rob exclaimed, pushing himself up on an elbow. "Oh my God, what an amazing scene."

"So moving. I totally lost it."

"Me too. How could you not?"

"You cried?"

He blinked. "No," he said, lowering himself on to his back. The corner of his mouth twitched. He glanced at her, then away. "Maybe a little."

"Really? That's awesome," she said laughingly. "Oh my God, I love you." Now it was her turn to look away, her cheeks warming. "I mean . . . I don't mean . . ."

"I know what you mean," he said quietly as he rolled towards her, gathering her in his arms. He kissed her hair, whispering, "It's cool. It's all good."

She fell asleep like that, curled up with him. It was the first time she'd ever fallen asleep in someone's arms; Alan hadn't been big on cuddling. The warmth of Rob's skin, the weight of him, his increasingly steady breathing . . . She had never in her life felt such deep, dreamy contentment.

Marianne smiled even before she opened her eyes the next morning, when she remembered where she was – the king-size four-poster in Rob's hotel room. It had been an incredible night, a night that had changed everything.

Everything Alan had told her about herself, everything he'd made her believe about herself, had been much more a reflection of him than of her.

Rob thought she was beautiful, sensual, responsive . . .

He also thought she was a whore. She hated letting him think that, but it was the only way.

No relationships for a year. It was for her own good that she'd made herself that promise. If Rob found out who and what she really was, he might be tempted – as tempted as Marianne was, God help her – to get serious.

Who was she kidding? She already *was* serious. She'd done it again, fallen for someone new right on the heels of the last fiasco. The challenge now was to swallow down her feelings, say goodbye and walk away with the memory of this extraordinary night to nourish her sense of self-worth and sustain her over the next twelve loveless months.

You've got to be just about the sexiest, most beautiful thing I've ever seen . . . the most passionate, most responsive woman I've ever been with.

He lost himself in me, she thought with a warm surge of gratification. And God knew she'd lost herself in him.

Opening her eyes to the new day, she turned her head on the pillow to look at him.

The other side of the bed was empty.

She sat up and scanned the room, still shrouded in cool semi-darkness despite the mid-morning sunlight glowing through the heavy damask drapes. He's taking a shower. He must be in the . . .

The bathroom door was ajar, so she could see that his Dopp kit was missing from the vanity, where it had been last night. The sliding closet door was open as well; his luggage was gone, and the door to the little safe stood open.

None of his personal effects were lying around the room, no sign that he'd been there. Except . . .

Reaching over to the nightstand on his side on the bed, she lifted the oversized bubble envelope that lay there. Her stomach clutched when she opened it and dumped its contents – a stack of large bills secured with a rubber band – on to her lap.

A little handwritten note fluttered out as well.

My beautiful Marianne,
   I was just about to wake you up to say goodbye when I realized I couldn't do it. You probably think that's pretty goofy. You must have guys getting hung up on you all the time. So I thought it would be best if I just kind of snuck out. I hope you understand.
   There's almost $14,000 here. I would have given you ten times as much if I'd had it on hand. You were right when you said it wasn't about money – far from it – but I just wanted you to know I don't care about the money. What we shared was worth a lot more than this. It was priceless . . .

There was more, but Marianne was crying too hard to read it.

Just two more hours, Marianne thought as she herded her classful of squealing, uniformed hellspawn on to the sunny playground for after-lunch recess. Two more hours of servitude at Our Lady of the Criminally Pampered, and then the school year would be over and she'd be free of this bogus "teaching" job for ever.

She'd been a busy woman during the week that had passed since her momentous encounter with Rob. First thing Monday morning, she'd handed in her resignation to Scary Sister Ursula, and since then she'd lined up four interviews at public schools in the Finger Lakes Region. She'd told her landlord she'd be out of the apartment by September first, because with any luck, she'd have a job offer by then. She'd even started packing, two months early, desperate to keep herself occupied so that she wouldn't start thinking about *him* again, and wondering, if only they'd met under different circumstances . . .

Had she done the right thing, letting him go? When she thought it out logically in the cold light of day, the answer was yes. But every night, as she lay awake soaking the pillow with tears, she was all too sure it had been the mistake of a lifetime.

A chorus of shrieks and screeches jolted her out of her reverie. "Colleen! Jackie!" she yelled. "Stop pulling each other's hair before it all comes out!"

"That might be interesting to see," came a man's voice from behind her.

She wheeled around, her heart skidding. "Rob?"

He was standing about five yards away, on the other side of the seven-foot chain-link fence that separated the schoolyard from the street, wearing the same faded grey polo shirt and jeans he'd had on last week, sans sports coat. His hands were stuck in his pockets; his smile was as toothy and boyish as she remembered.

"What do you think?" he asked, nodding towards Colleen and Jackie as they tussled on the asphalt, having ignored her scolding as usual. "If they pull out all their hair, will you find the number six-six-six emblazoned on their scalps?"

"Without a doubt." Marianne walked towards him on rubbery legs, stopping a couple of feet away. "Rob, what are you doing here? How did you find me?"

"That was your fault, so if you're sorry to see me, you've only got yourself to blame." Before she could respond to that, he said, "I got the strangest package in the mail the other day."

"Ah." His $14,000. She'd been tempted to keep the money – very tempted – but she'd known that if she did, her memory of that enchanted night would be forever tainted. So she'd stopped at the front desk on her way out of the hotel that morning to ask the clerk – the rat-faced one from the night before – for Rob's full name and address so she could mail it back to him, only to be huffily informed that they didn't reveal personal information about their guests. The subtext – *especially not to the likes of you* – was all too evident from the way Ratface had focused in on her silver stilettos. He'd just smirked when she'd protested that she wasn't a hooker, she was a kindergarten teacher – in a Catholic school, no less! In the end, she'd had no option but to hand over the bubble envelope to the supercilious little turd, claiming it contained socks Rob had left in the room and asking him to mail it back.

"I called the hotel when I got the package," Rob said, "and they told me how you'd tried to pass yourself off as a parochial schoolteacher. That's when the light bulb went off. I called every Catholic school in New York till I found one that had a Marianne teaching kindergarten." He smiled as he took in her demure skirt and blouse. "You're even more beautiful like this. And I dig the ponytail."

She took a step forwards, holding on to the chain-link fencing to steady herself. "You're not mad at me for . . . misleading you?"

He shook his head as he closed his hands over hers. "I figure you had your reasons. I'd like to hear them, if you'd like to tell me. Say, over dinner tonight?"

She bit her lip. "You want to take me out on a date?"

"Oh, yeah," he said, his voice low and earnest. "And not 'cause I think I'm gonna get lucky, 'cause I'm not expecting anything like that, really I'm not. Just . . . you know, dinner, maybe a glass of wine, a little conversation. I, uh . . . I have an idea I'd like to run past you."

"An idea?"

This time *he* bit his lip. "I was gonna wait till tonight, but . . ." He shrugged. "What the hell. I know how much you love Canandaigua. I was wondering if you might want to come up and spend the summer there."

"W–with you?"

He nodded. "I've got a place right on the water, and it's 10,000 square feet, so you'll have all the privacy you want if that's an issue."

"Ten thousand square feet?" she exclaimed.

His smile was disarmingly ingenuous. "I built it myself. It's post-and-beam with fieldstone—"

"*Ten thousand square feet?* What are you, one of the more obscure Kennedy cousins?"

"You ever hear of Brix and Stones dot com?"

"That website where people can design and build their own dream houses? Didn't it just go public? I was reading in *Newsweek* where the guy who founded it, some architect, how he really . . ."

Rob was smiling.

". . . cleaned up," she finished in a small voice. "Oh, my God. You're . . ."

"The Brix and Stones guy – Robert Brixton, at your service. So, what do you say to a nice, relaxing summer on Canandaigua Lake? Although I'm not gonna lie to you. When it's time for you to come back here at the end of the summer, I'll probably make a fool out of myself trying to get you to stay."

"I'm not coming back here, Rob. I gave my notice Monday and applied to schools upstate." She paused, a smile tugging at her lips. "One of them's in Canandaigua."

"Seriously? That's excellent!"

"I'm . . . not so sure," she said.

"What do you mean? All the pieces are snapping into place."

"That's kind of the problem. I have a bad habit of falling head over heels for the wrong guy and ending up in a serious relationship that's only really serious on my end."

"Funny, I don't feel like the wrong guy, if by 'wrong guy' you mean some douche who laughs when you cry during *Casablanca*."

"You're not. You're not like that at all. I didn't mean that."

"Then what? You think I'm not as serious about you as you are about me? Seems to me you're the one who withheld her true identity from me and made me hunt her down like she was America's Most Wanted. I, on the other hand, am practically begging you to come spend the summer with me – and hopefully a lot longer, if this thing between us is the real deal. And it sure feels like that to me, even if it doesn't to you."

"Are you kidding?" she asked with an incredulous laugh. "I'm crazy about you. I'm just, you know, trying not to get hurt again."

Sobering, he said, "I get that. Look, we can take it slow; we can have any kind of arrangement you want. Just 'cause you'll be living in my house doesn't mean you can't have your own room. Hell, you can have your own guest wing. I just want to be with you. I want the chance to prove to you that I'm nothing like those other guys. We can wait as long as you want to, you know."

"*Wait?*" Marianne said. "I've replayed the other night in my mind about a million times since then. If there weren't a couple of dozen kindergartners watching, I probably climb over this fence right now and jump you."

With a laugh, Rob said, "Oh yeah, I think this is going to be an excellent arrangement." Reaching through the chain link, he ran a finger lightly across her bottom lip. "You really do have a very pretty smile," he said softly. "I'm never gonna get tired of looking at it."

We Were Lovers Once

Madelynne Ellis

We were lovers once . . .

I know that Ray is gone. I feel it inside me, as if a tight choking grip has suddenly been released. I knew it before the phone rang and a lady with a voice like splintered glass told me so. Twenty-five years. I hadn't seen him in twenty-five years and still I knew the moment he passed. It was as if in that moment all the bonds we'd formed were suddenly ripped away. And yet, I'm standing here in my black garb and sensible old lady shoes having read the numerous cards that adorn the wreaths and he's standing right in front of me, just exactly as I remember him – a pretty youth, sultry and self-possessed. Dark unruly hair casts shadows across his narrow face and partially masks the hypnotic silver of his eyes. He's slightly uncomfortable in his pinstriped suit. It's not black, I note, but dandyish navy blue with a black band around the sleeve. Ray would certainly have approved, particularly of the starched white hand-kerchief that peaks suggestively from the breast pocket.

"Mrs Melrose, it's so nice to meet you at last," this oddity extends a hand encased in black leather. Murderer's gloves. Ray always wore gloves in public too. He hated people touching his skin and leaving microscopic traces of themselves behind, as if such contact could somehow detract from his genius.

Ray was a genius, and a menace. And I loved him, for all his quirks and foibles, but like everything that burns so brightly, the passion between us was never destined to last. Ours wasn't a relationship built over time and mapped out over decades, merely a magnesium flare in the dark days of our fading youth.

I stare at this stranger with the sun blazing behind him, and I see Ray as he was years ago standing under the unforgiving blaze of a fluorescent strip light, while mist coiled around his shoulders from the steam-filled bathroom beyond.

We're in his apartment. What did we come back here to do? The details escape me, and my absent-mindedness leads me to drop the popcorn I hold within my hands, whereupon it scatters across the coarse woven carpet. I recall the film. How we sat side by side in the darkness, never touching as sounds and images bombarded us in an endless violent montage, and the gore washed over me as I sat captivated by the rise and fall of Ray's chest.

I've never wanted any man as much as I wanted Ray. Lust has never since bound me so tightly or ridden me so cruelly. I've never desired to possess anything so much as I desired to own him.

Ray's torso is bare and his trousers ride low upon his hips, so that every ripped muscle of his abdomen is perfectly displayed. I stand stock-still, in my 1980s post-punk chic, laughably out of my depth, with a man who is my mentor and my god, and whose floor I've just covered in sticky popcorn. He should be the older man, suave, sophisticated, a James Bond fantasy come to life in order to seduce me, but Ray is none of those things. He's still barely a man, four years younger than I am and in a position of power far beyond either of our years. He laughs at the mess, and swipes at the kernels stuck to his toes.

"I'm going to freshen up. It's been a long day." Still sporting a grin, he wafts me towards a seat. "Make yourself at home."

Twenty-five bars of Caramac are neatly stacked upon the table. I open one, when he retreats into the bathroom, and wolf it down. I'm too on edge to sit. Instead, I pace and gnaw upon my finger-nails, chipping the paint I so carefully applied three hours before. With each successive lap of the room I draw a little closer to the bathroom door, until I'm stood before it, and the image of him naked beneath the shower spray is so clear that I believe I have X-ray vision and can see through the wood.

I don't knock. I walk into the steam-filled bathroom fully clothed. My vision of him glittering with water droplets, completely nude is an unfortunate fallacy. All I can descry though the misted glass are shifting peach-toned shadows.

"Sophia, is that you?" There's little surprise in his voice, only a dash of laughter, which continues to purr in his throat when I throw open the shower cubicle door and climb in beside him. "You're all wet!" He traces a finger down the row of pearlescent buttons on my blouse. "Were you looking for the shower or the launderette?"

"You." It's the only word I can muster and sounds so husky it's a wonder he doesn't ask if I have a cold.

"Guess you're in luck. And now you've found me?" A bad boy gleam lights in his silver eyes. Instead of waiting for a reply, he turns his back, and then peeps coyly over his shoulder at me in order to pass the soap. "I reckon you can do the honours."

I take the square, off-whitish bar and sniff it suspiciously, my heart clenched impossibly tight within my chest. I have him cornered, and I'm already afraid of losing him. Instead of soaping his back, I stand with my elbows locked tight to my sides and turn the soap over and over in my hands until they are covered in a foamy lather.

It's then that Ray touches me. His hands lock around my wrists, and I realize that the pain I feel now will be nothing compared to what comes later, but that is still preferable to the hollowness of living without him.

"Stop thinking and act. You live too much in your head. You need to connect with the reality around you."

I need to connect with him. Temptation stares me in the face.

"Touch me." He places my hands upon his chest and sets them into motion, drawing concentric circles on the smooth slabs of muscle. I skirt around his tiny tightly puckered nipples, while he stands in perfect mock submission, his hands raised and pressed to the tiles at shoulder height. Nerves itching with suppressed desire, I hesitate over dipping any lower than his navel.

My clothes grow heavy with the weight of the water, until the hem of my skirt is distorted and my blouse sticks to my skin as transparent as cling film. Embarrassed, unused to being exposed, I try to tug it away from my breasts, but only succeed in having it inflate like a balloon. Why are all the insecurities and guilt about this mine? He's naked and I'm fully clothed. I should be in a position of power. What does it matter if he can see the outline of my bra?

"You're such a voyeur," Ray teases. He raises his hands and poses with them clasped above his head. "Art isn't only about looking. It's about contours and planes, contrasts and textures." His words as ever plant visuals in my head. I imagine him streaked with paint: vibrant carnelian, deep viridian, black and azure. He rolls across a huge canvas, giving himself up entirely to the painting, so that sunshine yellow mats in the close-cropped hairs around his groin, and his glossy black hair becomes streaked with silver. "You know, if you're ever going to get anywhere, you have to seize opportunities."

I do just that. I trace lower and lift his wet, slumbering cock.

"There is some drive in you," he laughs. "Suck me." His pose of submission transforms in the blink of an eye. Hands upon my shoulders, he forces me on to my knees, and presses his soft cock to my lips until I welcome him inside. He tastes of salt and soap, and I revel in my submission, until he grows hard and the forces of his thrusts drive me off balance and up against the glass door. I wait for him to leap, to tear off my clothes and transform into the rabid beast he's rumoured to be. Instead, he offers me a hand up and leads me from the shower.

Under the flickering electric light, he peels the layers of clothing from my skin until I stand before him completely naked. His cock is hard now. It stands tall and I try to commit its varying hues to memory.

"See with your mind. Not your eyes." He drags my gaze up from his genitals, and rubs his thumb across my parted lips, before pushing it inside my mouth to suck like a miniature cock.

For several minutes we stand there, me sucking, him watching, until he draws the saliva-wetted digit down over my chin to my bare breasts. The touch is electrifying. I jolt when it reaches a nipple. I'm all his, and he knows it.

"I'll paint you," he announces. No, "can I" or "if you don't mind", just a statement of intention. I don't know if that's down to arrogance or dominance. It's immaterial since the concept gives me a massive thrill. To pose for him is an honour.

Ray lures me into the living room and pushes me down upon the popcorn-covered carpet. It's a curious backdrop to be sure, but Ray's work often strays into the avant-garde. He gets a paintbrush, but no water or acrylics. Instead he draws the sable bristles down the length of my body and dips it into the thick arousal between my thighs, before using it to draw explicit doodles upon my stomach. Dip and paint, he works quickly, only infrequently sparing a flick of attention for my clit when he pauses for thought. "Turn over," he says, rolling me as soon as the words are spoken.

On all fours now, I present him with my naked rear, perhaps, my loveliest asset.

Ray casts aside the paintbrush. His next sketch is drawn with a different pen. The tip of his cock caresses the taut muscles of my rear, and I crane my neck to watch him work, so precise even with these mock instruments. When the thread of pre-ejaculate dries up, he dips his cock into my inkwell and starts over. And so the first sex we enjoy together is disjointed and yet more arousing than all the stealth fucks I've enjoyed in the dark. Ray stretches out our pleasure, until my nerves are in shreds and arousal drips from every pour. Two thrusts and a tickle, it's never enough. "Fuck painting," I want to yell. "Fuck me." I ache and grind my sex against my hand, coming twice in that way long before he finishes his drawings and buries himself deep in my cunt.

"Mrs Melrose."

Ray walks me home, and it's not until I lie in my bed that I realize that not once did he kiss me. Not once did he ever kiss me.

"Mrs Melrose."

"Mrs Melrose," the past life image says, breaking the memory spell. I give a small gasp and stare at his cascade of dark hair, shocked to find I'm still at Ray's graveside and the warmth of his presence is long flown. "Are you all right?" Ray's double reaches out to touch my shoulder.

"Perfectly."

The past seemed so real, that for a moment reality seems disjointed.

"I'm so pleased you came. Ray wanted you to be here."

I believe my stillness in response to that unnerves him, for he runs a finger around the inside of his shirt cuff, where the skin is surely warm and throbs with his pulse. Though, perhaps it isn't me he's unnerved by, but the grey shadows huddled around the embankment of flowers. A graveside is no place for his vibrancy and youth. He sees the people and the flotilla of carnations and surely recognizes them as the ghosts of his future. I turn away, in no mood for niceties, wanting only an escape from the memories that slide over one another like tectonic plates. It's time I returned to my cats and my books and my Women's Institute agendas.

"Wait!" His gloved hand cups my elbow, and again I'm forced to look him in the eyes, Ray's eyes. "I'm going over to the studio now, one last visit to say goodbye. I wondered if you'd like to come along."

The touch shocks me so much it sends a pulse of heat through my body. I stammer awkwardly for several seconds, trying to say no. I left Ray and all his foibles behind long ago. There's no need to go back and revisit what is already done. "You can say too many farewells."

He nods, but refuses to release me. "Then come with me and hold my hand, because my loss is far more recent."

I mean to refuse, but the way the words catch in his throat brings the sting of tears to my eyes. I haven't cried in years. I never cry any more. "Who are you?" I demand.

"Gabriel. I'm Gabriel Hawksmore."

He's Ray's son. Of course, he's Ray's son. I didn't even know Ray had a son. "Is your mother the woman who phoned?"

"That was Aunt Claire. My mother left when I was three." I don't enquire too deeply into his definition of left; whatever interpretation it surely spells tragedy.

"Will you come?"

I nod, and let Ray's protégé lead me.

I'm going back. My God, I'm going back.

The last time I saw Ray, he threw me from this place in little more than a gymslip and a camisole, my shoes rolling down the stairs behind me. I'd fallen from grace, and had been summarily banished. As if I gave a damn what he thought, or so I told myself and anyone else who would listen. I'd already made other arrangements, was headed for a life with someone who appreciated me, who offered marriage and stability, not an on and off relationship built on torment and ego stroking.

Slanted light from the skylight shows up the butterfly dance of the dust motes as Gabriel prowls across the pitted wooden boards of the garret studio. There's a certain familiar swagger to his gait as he grasps a large frame propped against the back wall and swings it around. I stare at the colours in disbelief, dazzled by their vibrancy – splashes of orange and violet, and a broad rainbow of creamy pearlescent flesh.

Twenty-five years ago I stood here and posed in that dress. I run my hands over my body recalling how the vivid violet fabric fanned out from my hips, and how I was so in love with the orange blooms dotted across the front.

"My Sophia", the painting is called, which depicts me rudely displaying my bottom in order to show the criss-crossed red welts left behind by his belt. I had no idea that he'd finished it. In truth I thought he'd probably dowsed it in alcohol and set it alight the night I left.

"You haven't changed," Gabriel remarks.

"Oh, but I have." Although, perhaps I've weathered a little better than most.

Gabriel lets the painting fall. When I jump, he grabs me, and his tongue, hot and invasive fills my mouth.

"Get off!" Shocked by his actions, I tear at his jacket lapels, but he only kisses me harder, until I feel it, a tiny long dead spark of arousal, which flickers into life and grows brighter, until instead of resisting, I'm responding.

Gabriel's gloved hands slide down my back. "I've wanted to see this image made flesh ever since I was old enough to understand its significance. What did Ray use to stripe you with?"

"His belt." I bite my lip until it hurts, and my first visit here flares like a beacon in my brain. Ray – with his artist's palette and brush – naked from the waist up, his feet bare, the toenails so shiny I'd swear they were lacquered, striding across the splintered boards to daub a cross upon my arse.

"There," he'd yelled. "Keep your fucking hand there, and don't move until I tell you to. I didn't hire you to preen." This from the man who'd taken forty minutes the previous night to fasten his bow tie. "I hired you to keep your damned arse still."

Hired! Oh, yes, Ray paid me both in cash and kind, but what exactly was my role, model or apprentice, girlfriend or whore?

Gabriel wrestles a hand below my skirt. His gloves are cool against my thighs. One finger flicks upwards and brushes the lace of my panties. Tremulously, I try to push him away, but he thrusts me up against the stacks of paintings, so that my bottom rests on the top of an ornate brass frame and my back arches towards the wall.

"Stop!"

"Is that really what you want?" He rests his hands lightly upon my knees as he lifts one eyebrow. "Don't you really long to give in. Weren't you wild once?"

"Never." Ray was the wild one, the instigator. I was just drawn to his flame. But looking back I know that's a lie I've been drip-feeding myself for over two decades. It's the way I've reconciled myself to the role I chose. I thought I wanted stability and a decent life in suburbia. I've made myself into a perfect wife. I've performed to the best of my ability, but this staid laced-up woman isn't me.

The real me is buried deep inside, screaming and flailing, now determined to get out. And like his father before him, Gabriel sees it. He slides his hands up my thighs again, until his thumb tip brushes the lace of my knickers, and presses between the lips of my slit.

"Take them off, I dare you."

This has gone too far! "What sort of pretence at mourning is this?"

And yet, even as I protest, my nerves zing with excitement.

Gabriel's silver eyes gleam with all the wickedness I could ever wish for. "Tell me to stop again, and maybe I'll believe you." One long finger hooks around the leg elastic and touches me intimately. I squirm, but not because of any desire to get away. No, I want more than this tease. I want to feel ecstasy again. I want the bliss a man's fingers working over my clit can bring. I desire sex that is dirty and crude. That is painful, irresistible and debauched.

"Are you going to take off yours?" I ask, when he tugs again at the lace.

"I don't have any on."

"Prove it." I shove him backwards, and this time I do not find him immobile. He retreats, whilst working open his belt buckle. God, he's so like Ray, right down to the way he snags his bottom lip with his tooth as he concentrates. Fly undone, he coyly teases the flap of fabric away from his loins, offering me only a momentary glimpse before he hides his assets again. Three times he repeats the gesture, before I shimmy down from my perch among the paintings and rip the fabric from his hand. His trousers pool around his feet, and I shove the hem of his shirt up to towards his breastbone.

Gabriel watches my reaction from under his eyebrows. It's a look of stubborn defiance that is both incredibly needy and fantastically hot. Unlike Ray, Gabriel is clean shaven. Ink decorates his skin in place of hair, the black lines extending in a bold pattern of knots along the length of his cock, the end of which is pierced with a silver hoop. I wrap a hand around his shaft, but he doesn't react, bar a subtle hiss when I deliberately squeeze, and then rotate the ring.

"Inked and silvered. I guess I can be pretty certain you're not a werewolf."

"I'm a changeling," he snarls back, and if I didn't know better I'd swear the gleam in his eyes was born of magic. "Your knickers," he demands holding out a hand. He steps free of his pooled trousers, and throws his jacket and tie over the hatstand before pulling his shirt over his head, so that he stands before me naked.

He's everything Ray ever was and more. His abdomen a study in ripped perfection, save for what looks like an appendix scar across one side. The silvered line is ten shades lighter than the surrounding skin.

The Celtic knotwork tattoo that adorns his loins also encompasses his hips, and the long muscles down his right thigh. It's a fascinating thing, which I picture myself spending long hours tracing in endless circles.

"Seen enough yet?"

I shake my head and continue to drink him down. It's a long time since I've seen a man this attuned to his body up close. I can't help but admire the hard globes of his backside, the breadth of his shoulders, and his delicate, tightly perked up nipples, the skin of which is so dark they seem pre-stained with blackberry juice or vampish lipstick.

"Now show me yours. Wasn't that the deal? It's not like I haven't seen it before." He turns another painting around, this one a watercolour of me lying naked by the edge of a lake, adorned with only two white blossoms, one of which pokes from my hair, while the other is captured between my thighs.

"Did he tease you with the stem?"

"I had to hold the stalk between my thighs. It wasn't erotic. It made my muscles ache."

"And afterwards?" he enquires, with a raised brow.

Afterwards. Yes, afterwards, Ray filled me with a different stalk. Actually, we took several breaks that day, so he could reinstate the flush upon my cheeks that he wanted to capture.

My smile tells Gabriel all he wishes to know. Hands on hips, he waits for me to do his bidding, and I admit to myself that the prospect of admiration thrills me. Miles, my husband, has only ever seen me naked in the dark. I don a nightgown before he comes to bed, and dress when he's left for work. Twenty-five years we've slept together, and our lovemaking remains as chaste and mechanical as it was on our honeymoon night, when I played the virginal bride and he took command of losing his cherry.

I wobble ungainly as I step out of my knickers, no longer used to making a performance of the act. Gabriel watches me with a predatory smile upon his face. "Ray always said you were atrociously bad at undressing. Said he kept a pair of scissors handy especially for you."

Were they just for me? I recall the scissors that Ray kept in the rainbow-splattered box in which he stored his paints. He'd use them to cut the sides of my panties, so he could strip them from me once he had me posed. You might imagine I'd have worn my most basic cotton briefs when I came to pose for him considering his disregard for my attire, but the truth is I sought ever-increasing luxury. Silks and ribbons, and lace studded with diamanté. Alas, none of them ever captured Ray's attention as completely as my bared pussy. Somewhere in this minefield of times past are in-depth studies of both my pussy and my arse.

Gabriel picks the shred of pearlescent pink fabric that comprises my current underwear from the floor. He brings them to his face and breathes in the scent of my body, covering both his mouth and nose.

"Fruity," he remarks. "Isn't pink a little frivolous for the occasion?"

"You can hardly comment." My gaze strays towards his discarded suit, and I remember why we are here. Not to flirt or play games but to say farewell. "What did Ray die of?" I ask, instantly sobered. A stab of pain pierces my chest. Ray is gone. Truly gone, and no amount of time or prayers will bring him back again.

Gabriel stills. "You realize that he loved you," he says in one breath.

To which I respond in the only way I can. With a laugh that rises up from my belly and explodes from my throat like a great rumbling bark. "Tosh, he did! How old are you? He must have sown his oats in your mother's belly almost the moment I left. He never loved me. I was a convenience, and a cheap one at that. He paid me less to pose than he did his students, and gave nothing for being his whore."

"His lover," Gabriel retaliates. We glare at one another. Strangers again, and for a moment bitter enemies. "I can prove it."

"How? How can you prove it? You can't conjure him up in order to confess. His paintings prove only that I was his one-time model, not that he felt anything remotely warm towards me."

"Perhaps not in person." With that cryptic remark, he turns, and strides towards the broken sash window that overlooks the chimneys and the street below. From the windowsill he claims a thick leather book, which he turns towards me and holds against his chest. "See."

I see my likeness peeking from the page, as radiant as only the young can be. Coy and sweet in one pose, and dashed with anger or irritation in the next. Around the numerous pictures words of the heart form an endless spiral of introspective thought. Declarations are made and crossed out. Only to be rewritten.

"He waited for you to come back. Waited his whole life for you to see sense. He knew you weren't happy."

"I'm happy."

Gabriel continues as if he hasn't heard my rebuff. "You're right. The episode with my mother came just after you left. It was his night of revenge, a blind fling in order to get over you. But he didn't get over you. He never got over you. 'Gabriel,' he told me, 'you have to be there for her, because one day she's going to wake up and realize what we could have had, and I'm not going to be around to give it.'"

My nose stings at his words. Tears cloud my vision. Gabriel moves in close, so that his naked body presses against the wool of my clothing. "He loved you. You were his muse and his greatest malady. He never forgave himself for letting you go."

"You still haven't told me how he died."

"It doesn't matter how he died. Only that you came back."

"He knew where I lived. All this time, he could have called."

"And begged?" Gabriel lifts an eyebrow in question. "Ray never begged, and he believed in the sanctity of marriage. If you strayed from your vows it would never be down to his cajoling. I, on the other hand, have no such qualms."

I tut at him in disgust. "You're arrogant, like him. You mean nothing to me. You're just an echo of the past."

"An echo that you're just dying to fuck."

He has me hooked at that. Disgusted and infuriated, but hooked. His voice softens, though his words still pack a punch. "Admit it, Sophia. The thought of me sliding my cock into you already has you wet. When was the last time you came by a method that didn't involve your own hand?"

How can he surmise that from looking at me? "Whether I come with my husband is none of your concern."

Gabriel shakes his head, so that his dark hair flutters around his shoulders. "Ray made it my concern."

"It was none of his concern."

"Just once." His voice drops to a lethal whisper, coaxing and smooth, the devil's voice whispering in my ear having kicked the good angel into a vat of tar. "We need never meet again if that's how you prefer it. But I made a promise, and I endeavour to always keep them."

Ray, his father, made him promise to fuck me. How twisted is that?

I think it over. One brief moment of passion and then I get to walk away and carry on as normal, only with a bright, new, shiny memory to cling to. If only I could stockpile sexual satisfaction from the encounter to support me through the next decade or two. It's a crazy, foolish idea, and I'm not quite a crazy old woman, yet. "What sort of screwed-up goodbye would that be?"

"It doesn't have to be a goodbye. It could be a beginning."

Fatal words. I feel my reservations crumbling, and a moist ache begins in my pussy. "I'm too old and too respectable." I protest.

"You're neither, Sophia Melrose. You're a beautiful woman who deserves to be herself."

I hurry away from him, low heels click-clacking on the floor-boards, but my flight path is too familiar and the pain of separation from Ray too raw. I don't want to go. I never wanted to go, and so I turn back at the door and stare at Gabriel in bewildered panic. "Don't make me do this," I say to Ray, not Gabriel, seeing the ghost of years ago, standing there in all his paint-splattered glory.

"I can't marry you, Sophia. I can only love you. I told you that."

I don't hear the love in Ray's voice, or the fear, only the rejection. "You don't want me. Miles wants me," I yell.

"He wants to own you. You'll be another piece of artwork to him, no more treasured than any of the rest. He wants you because you're a piece of me, you're my muse, and how incredible to own that. He's an obsessive. He loves art only because of the value others place on it, not because he admires it himself."

Truth. All Ray ever told me was the truth, but I didn't want to hear it, didn't want to acknowledge it.

"I'm going," I snap.

"Go then, but don't come back. I'm not interested in you if you're wearing his ring."

The words rage on inside my head, circular arguments, hope and fear rising and falling on a tide of twisting emotions.

"Why did you do it?" Gabriel asks, standing right before me again. I notice his hand is upon the doorknob. "Why did you leave him like that? And are you running from me for the same reason?"

"I wanted stability. Respect. Miles promised me a partnership, and I suppose I saw myself cheering on Ray's career as his sponsor, as an art hostess, instead of his fuck buddy. Only, it didn't quite work out like that. The moment we were married, Miles cut Ray's sponsorship. He moved on, said Ray's art had become passé, but none of his new fledglings had an iota of Ray's talent. Miles' collection turned into a riot of mediocrity. He took to golf and yachting instead."

"And cut your lifeline." Gabriel touches my face, bringing me out of the trance, and I realize he's still wearing his gloves.

"What's wrong with your hands?"

He grips the leather with his teeth and frees his fingers. Beneath them his skin is milk pale from lack of light, and the backs of them are scarred as if the flesh has been melted and smoothed into place with a butter knife. "Cleaning fluid. When I was twelve. It's much better than it once was. I was trying to be helpful."

"You should let the air get to it."

I study the scars, lifting his hand to rub my lips against their shiny surface as if I can somehow kiss them better.

That moment of closeness as he exposes himself to me, warms me inside. I catch a hint of his scent, and find myself pressing my nose to his skin to breathe it in more deeply. He's like Ray, and yet he isn't. I find myself aroused and yet tortured by him. I want to touch. I want to forget. I want Ray, but only Gabriel is on offer. Still, what forty-eight-year-old woman gets a treat like him everyday? My lips reach his wrist, tongue teasing over the pulse point where the skin is smooth and supple.

"Have you any scars?" he enquires.

"Only invisible ones."

Our eyes meet, and passion simmers. I crave passion and his vitality too much to refuse him. Hell, I've been circumspect for too long. Too scared of the hardship freedom might bring to flee my gilded prison.

Gabriel's hands stretch around my back and he unfastens my dress, which puddles around my feet. "Did Ray love to stripe you because the marks made you more interesting? He used to say to me constantly that it's our defects that make us unique." Gabriel's touch moves to my bottom, holding the fleshy cheeks, and squeezing them. And I find myself quietly chuckling and shaking my head.

"Nothing so cerebral. He liked the way I jumped and my breasts jiggled when he struck, and the fact that it made me so wet."

"I like the way you gasp," he says just before he warms my cheek with a smack.

"Ah!" I do gasp, and do so again when he strokes two fingers over the flat of my stomach and down into the springy curls at the apex of my thighs. He cups my mons. Then two fingers press into the slick heat of my pussy and his thumb completes a circuit with my clit. I ride his fingers, sandwiched between his hard body and the door. It feels so good that I realize that I've forgotten just how amazing sex can be, and just how wildly it makes my heart beat.

"Is it me or the place that turns you on, Sophia?"

Neither, I decide, but of course it's not true. With each passing minute since we left the graveside, I feel Ray's loss more keenly. Yet, his presence still fills this room, and Gabriel adds a sense of calm.

I look into Gabriel's silver-flecked eyes and know that he means to take me as I've never been taken in years.

"Not here," I say as his finger catches my clit, and that single caress sets me shivering.

"Absolutely here."

"I mean not against the door."

"Where then?"

I drop on to my hands and knees and crawl between his legs. Gabriel follows as I stalk across the boards, naked save for my bra. I pause when I reach the enormous Belfast sink and rise. God, it's so domestic, being fucked over the washing-up bowl. Gabriel laughs when I waggle my arse, and suddenly I feel alive. I know what I'm doing, my body, my instincts are in control instead of my screwed-up brain.

I quiver in anticipation as he wets his thumbs in my heat, and rise on to my toes as his cock nuzzles against my clit. The ring in his cock moves as he brushes against my nether lips.

"Tell me what you want, Sophia. Do you want my tattooed cock inside you? Are you going to frig like crazy as we fuck?"

"No, you're going to do it for me."

He snorts in amusement. Then leans over me as if to assess the angles. "Hard or soft?"

"I'll yell if you're a bit off."

The sound of his chuckles vibrates against my neck. I think he's about to enter me, but he doesn't and, when I crane my head to look back at him, he winks. "Do you think we're moving a little too fast?" In response, I push back against him, so that his erection nuzzles against my slit. "OK, easy." He slides in deep, and then crushes me tight to his body. We don't really move, at least not the parts that are joined. Instead, he traces his lips across my shoulder and slowly up the side of my neck. "Normally, I like to kiss before getting quite so intimate. It makes it more personal somehow."

"Ray never kissed me." My husband bestows chaste cheek pecks, or else breathes heavily into my ear.

"I'm not Ray," says Gabriel.

No, he's not. I can feel that he's not. His touch is softer, and more considerate than demanding.

He rolls his hips finding exactly the right angle to make me keen, while he strains to deliver that promised kiss. He's taller than Ray and suppler, so that when he twists so that our mouths meet he doesn't feel the need to break away immediately. His kiss is slow and giving. It begins as a gentle exploration, but the rush of it floods my senses causing tremors to stream down my throat and into my breasts. My nipples pucker and my breathing grows shallow. Greedily, I kiss him back. Demanding more. Receiving more. And somehow we manage to rock together as we engage in this tango of tongues.

When the kiss ends, it is only because we are both breathless and desperate for more friction down below. I brace my hands on the sink again, and Gabriel holds tight to my hips.

He slides back and forth, slow as you please, refusing to rush, until I'm so turned on that I yell in frustration. Only then, does he give me the pounding and rubbing I crave. Our bodies meet with a smack and the slick sounds of his cock fucking my wet pussy are just as loud as my whimpers.

My climax builds faster than I'd like. God, I want to savour this, but I've been too long without good sex and my body is too eager. "Oh, please. Please!" I mumble. Don't let this end so soon.

Gabriel presses a finger inside me alongside his cock, which rubs insistently on the tender spot inside of my pussy, causing it to clench tight in the first spasms of release. He continues to move from the hips, giving me everything, powering into me as if his intention is to knock me head first into the sink as I come. But I don't care because my body is shaking, and the orgasm is so sweet and joyous that nothing about it could be any more perfect. And as I push back and meet his delicious thrusts, I realize for the first time in a quarter of a century that I don't blame Ray for what happened. He remained true to himself. I was the one seeking the

streets of gold. He had no inkling of my life outside our relationship. Had no concept of my past and the desperate desire I had to
escape the poverty of my youth. Marriage to me seemed the perfect
answer. I loved Ray, but I was too afraid to let him take care of me.

Artists starve, that's what my folks told me all through college.
Best you go get yourself a checkout job. Money will be tight, but at
least ends will mostly meet.

Miles has more money than sense, the bills are always paid and
yet I've always been hungry.

Gabriel comes inside me, in six long shudders. He kisses his way
right down my spine before pulling out. We don't say a word, but I
watch him wash his cock in the sink. The ink and the ring fascinate
me. He holds my hand and lets me turn the silver loop through the
piercing, an action that quickly makes him stiffen again. He stalks
me around the studio, pounces and pins me down. We fuck again,
this time face to face, my legs spread wide, and my nails curled into
the firm globes of his bottom, guiding him, pulling him deeper.

"Isn't there a wake you're supposed to be attending?" I ask,
when we manage to separate ourselves long enough to pull on some
clothes.

"Oh, yes." A grin stretches his face from ear to ear. "Come with
me. It'll infuriate Aunt Claire. She banned you, or at least your
pictures, from the house."

I squeeze his scarred hand. "Sounds like an appropriate way to
say goodbye."

"Doesn't it."

And so begins the affair.

Long Time Coming

Bonnie Edwards

One

Pressure gathered in Kurt McCord's chest rose as he fought for composure. He hated needing anything, let alone help. "Damn it, Leigh, can't you just give us a weekend? Marion needs help. I'll hump furniture all day long, fix whatever needs fixed, but she's a wreck and I don't handle that stuff well."

"I leave for Japan at the end of next week." Leigh's sultry voice went soft as if she saw the futility of resistance. Her last gasp of denial.

Merciless, he went in for the kill. "She cried, Leigh. Marion cried. I don't know about you, but I never saw her cry about anything. It was over some photo albums and that old movie projector of hers. I haven't seen that thing in decades. I doubt it'll work any more." He hadn't been able to do more than give the old girl an awkward pat on the shoulder.

Females in emotional pain made his gut twist. He hated feeling helpless and he never understood what women in distress really needed. So he fixed things. Hauled whatever needed hauling, and ate whatever they cooked for him. Marion was a good cook and had loved to feed him and all the other foster kids she'd mothered. "Leigh, we owe her."

"Would next month work?" Her voice, silken and sexy, drew tight circles around his chest. He lost the battle with his breath and let it out. Dragged in another. He would win this.

He would.

He couldn't take another month of Marion's tears. Hearing

Leigh's voice brought back a whole lot of other stuff he thought was long over.

Things like desire. Need. Want.

Yes, he still wanted Leigh Douglas.

"Next month's too late. She's got to take the place right away." Retirement units in this building didn't come up often. "This one's a bottom floor corner. She can keep her cat and patio furniture."

"She can use her grill, too?"

Memories of Marion's legendary backyard grilling parties skipped through his mind. "Yes, she can even grill, too." He had her and they both knew it.

A sexy sigh and then, "This thing in Japan is an interview for a promotion. I can give you three days, no more." Her voice dripped capitulation. "I'll be there as soon as I can."

The crunch of tyres on gravel brought Kurt's head up to listen. He swiped his cuff across his forehead and leaned his axe against the woodpile at the side of his house. Splitting logs for firewood was great for stress relief. Leigh's arrival counted as stress. He scrubbed his fingers through his hair to clear his head then headed for the front of the house. He ran a mental checklist as he walked. Fridge was stocked. Guest room prepared. Wine was chilling. With any luck, she would agree to eat with him before they headed to Marion's.

A dark grey luxury sports car rolled to a stop by the rose bed he'd planted in the middle of his circular drive.

Sound fell away, his breath stalled while he watched one high-heeled boot, then another, descend to the ground. Butter-coloured boots. No woman he knew wore butter-coloured boots. Not in this town.

A blonde knot of hair appeared as she unfolded from the low-slung seat. Leigh had always been a beauty, but now, she had the profile of an angel.

He catalogued every glorious inch of her, from the topknot of blonde waves to the curve of her breasts to the flat plain of her belly. The car door hid her legs, but he had them memorized. Long, strong, shaped just right, they rose from perfect feet to thin ankles and thighs that led—

"Are you going to say hello?" she asked, her voice sultry and hot as asphalt in the sun. "Or will you stand and stare all day?" Her wide-open gut-busting grin hit him in the chest. Then she stepped away from the car and walked into his arms like a long-lost sister.

Yeah, that was it. As if he needed a reminder. She smelled of flowers and windswept hair and Leigh. Not the little-girl Leigh he remembered, but a woman. Her curvy body fitted against his as she gave him a perfunctory buss on the cheek.

He pulled his head back only to see her grin falter from open to hesitant. She was so damned appealing he could eat her up. "Good to see you, Leigh. I'm glad you made it. Have you been to Marion's yet?"

She nodded, stepped out of his arms and concern flashed across her face. "The doors were locked and lights all off. Where is she?"

Surprised, he said, "She was there this morning. I moved furniture for hours." Worry dampened his sexual focus. He shook his head because Marion wouldn't have left the house unless absolutely necessary, not with Leigh on the way. "She was excited to see you."

"So you have no idea where she's gone?"

"Come on in," he said as he dug his phone out of his pocket. "I'll call her cell."

But before he could pull her number up, his ring tone played. He checked call display, ready to hang up on the caller if need be. "It's her."

Leigh gave her car door a hip shot to close it, then stepped close enough for his nose to catch her scent again. He answered, relieved to hear Marion's normal, rushed voice. He passed Leigh the phone. "She wants to speak with you."

Thirty seconds into the conversation, Leigh's voice warmed with concern. A problem with Marion's sister. He straightened when Leigh said goodbye. She handed back his phone.

"Marion had to leave for her sister's place. Heart trouble. She won't be here all weekend. She said we could go over to the house in the morning and she'd call then." Her lips moved into a classic Leigh pout. He wanted to kiss it away. "I suspect she'd prefer we deal with a lot of the decisions for her. This can't be easy for a woman who's as vital and active as Marion."

"She was pretty racked up over that projector and the old film reels. I found the projector screen, but it's ruined."

"If it had been her choice to retire she might handle this better." She smiled, her wide blue eyes a symphony of kind memories. "In the meantime, we have an evening to kill."

"Stay here tonight, we can get caught up." And there it was. *Stay with me. Sleep in your big brother's house. Where you'll be safe.*

Her smile turned sultry. "Let me get my bag." She turned and gave him a view of her lush backside. Round, smooth, high and oh so inviting, his hands itched.

Unless and until, Leigh gave him the go-ahead to touch, he'd keep his hands to himself, even if it killed him.

Two

While Leigh settled into the guest room, Kurt opened a bottle of red wine to let it breathe. Then he called Marion.

Her sister had the constitution of a tank. Heart problems didn't ring true. Maybe this move into the retirement residence had been harder to accept than he thought. But Marion had faced too many angry and confused foster kids to be frightened by downsizing her home. He listened to her soft-voiced explanation of family duty and hung up, no more convinced than when he'd called.

Footsteps made him turn to watch Leigh's expression as she approached through the great room. What he read in her eyes pleased him. As did his home. He'd worked hard on the design and it showed.

Log walls, gleaming wood floors and high ceilings made for rustic luxury. French doors flanked the fieldstone fireplace and led to a lakeside deck that appeared to extend the width of the house.

"Your home's lovely, Kurt," she said as she took the wine he offered. She'd let her hair down into waves that tipped at her clavicle. He wanted to trace those fine bones out to her smooth shoulders. Trace her skin lightly, lightly, lightly, until she shivered with need.

"Thanks," he said, and pulled back from the errant thought. "I never seem to finish the place though." He grinned and nodded towards a walk-in pantry. The scent of fresh-cut pine filled the air. Shelves he had yet to install leaned against the inside wall.

She took in the granite counters, the breakfast bar, the view over the lakeside deck. "I'd love a kitchen like this."

"Feel free to cook whatever you'd like. I'll eat your cooking anytime." He'd eat *her* anytime.

"I may take you up on your offer. I don't cook much. Meals for one don't hold a lot of appeal."

"You're single? Hard to believe." *Down, boy.*

"Why? There's no evidence of a woman living here. If you're single, why shouldn't I be?"

"I've been busy building a business," he said, pleased she'd paid attention to his living arrangement. "Until now relationships have taken a back seat."

"Now?"

"Now, I'm ready to take care of other ambitions." He held the door to the deck open for her and motioned her outside to take in the view. "Marion's told me for years it's time to settle down, and I'm ready to give her that wish."

She stepped by him to the deck while he leaned in for a whiff of her shampoo. "When I lived here I never got to the private side of the lake," she murmured. "Only the public beaches." Her scent went to his head. Better than wine. Much better. "This is spectacular." Her eyes showed delight in his success. "Why have you waited so long to settle down?"

"My old man was decent enough, but he could never get himself off the ground. Never got life right. I swore I'd be different if I had a family. I wanted to be ready. Prepared."

"Not broke." A statement, not a question. "I swore I wouldn't get pregnant at fourteen."

"Which may have happened, given the way you looked much older."

Her smile went thoughtful. "But I had you running interference."

"Whether you wanted it or not."

She slipped her hand to his cheek, her warmth a balm. He tilted into it. "Thank you, Kurt. You were my champion, my guardian."

His hand burned with the need to touch. To take. So he clasped the deck rail and pretended to see the lake. He waved at his neighbours, out for their daily paddle. The red canoe skimmed over the water, graceful and silent.

"Sunset is my favourite time of day," she said with a sigh. "I don't see it often enough. Everything's pretty again." She tapped her temple. "My mind races through the day." She settled next to him at the rail, her shoulder grazing his.

"I like the long shadows, the deepening quiet as the birds settle and the lake turns pink and gold."

"Renewal, rest and reflection." She turned towards him, her eyes scanning his face, counting the years since they'd last seen each other. "You've changed some, but I still see you, Kurt McCord. Like no other man, I see you."

He had a sick feeling that maybe she always had. "When we were kids—"

"I'm sorry I was such a pest." She laughed. A light tinkling sound he'd looked for in every other woman he'd known.

"You weren't. I was a jerk."

She eyed him. "Only sometimes." Her grin set his mind at ease.

She still had no idea how sick he'd been. Still was. A brother wanting his sister. Correction. Foster sister.

Not that it made any difference. Marion would be appalled. And Leigh would look at him like a flyspeck.

Maybe that would set him free. He'd stop comparing women to Leigh. He could move on and work on those new ambitions. A wife. Family of his own.

Just as soon as he put this Leigh thing aside.

And then she looked at him; really looked and he looked back.

Damn, she was hot.

She nodded at the neighbours as they glided by. "They're still together? They were a couple back in high school."

He nodded. "Sometimes first loves are the only loves."

She took a sip of wine too fast. She coughed and he patted her back. "OK?"

"Fine. Thanks." After a moment of quiet reflection, she spoke again. She leaned over the rail to look around the lake. "That time I walked up to your car and you had some girl with you . . ." Her voice trailed away into an unspoken question.

"Diane Brown. I remember she was no girl." Older by at least eight years and already divorced, Diane held his interest for all of three weeks. Long enough to learn what he'd needed. "What about it?" But he knew what she'd seen, what he'd done.

"You saw me coming for the car, holding my report card."

He'd been such a prick. "I'm sorry about that."

She hadn't heard him, was trapped in the past. "You grabbed her and kissed her the way I wanted you to kiss me."

It was his turn to choke. If he thought he'd waited on pins and needles for Leigh to arrive, it was nothing compared to the absolute stillness of his body, his life, his world as her words sunk in. After a shocked moment he turned his face towards her.

"Don't look so shocked," she said. "I had a huge crush on you."

She blinked and seemed to pull out of wherever her memories had taken her. "You must have known."

The wind had been punched out of him and he dragged in a breath to replace it. "You were my little brat sister. Not possible." And he was four years older and had a lifetime worth of experience.

"You were *never* my brother, Kurt. No matter what the foster care system said. No matter how much Marion wanted us to call her Mom." She swallowed. Hard. Then slanted him a glance that spoke volumes. "You're not my brother, Kurt. You never were." She pressed her shoulder against his and tipped her wine glass towards him.

"Diane Brown," was all he could think to say. He'd seen Leigh running towards the car, eyes wide and happy, face aglow with pride. And he'd seen her falter when she'd realized he wasn't alone.

"You looked me right in the eyes. Then you pulled her into your arms and kissed her in a way—"

"In a way you were too young to see." He'd done it for her own good. He was older, a full-on raging-hormone-filled teenager with a car. Many times he could have picked her up on the walk home from school. He could have taken her anywhere and she'd have gone with him. The temptation had been powerful, but he'd been stronger. "It was safer to see you as a younger sister." He clinked their glasses and took a sip without looking at her.

"Safer? For whom?"

"Me," he murmured. "Safer for me. I wanted you, too, but you were a kid, a child. I felt sickened by my own thoughts."

"I'm not a child any longer, Kurt. And I'm here."

He looked at the way his wine rippled in his glass, a reaction to his trembling hand. "Are you sure?"

"I've been sure since I was twelve."

Three

Leigh faced Kurt. Desire and heat radiated from his tight jaw and hooded gaze. Male focus wrapped its sexual fingers in and around her body. *Thank you, God!* "I suggest it's time we find out what we missed out on back in the day."

He slipped his hand to her wine glass and set it on the deck rail. "I'm glad you're thinking the same way I am."

She leaned close, pressed her breasts to his chest and waited for his lips to take hers. She heard the same low hum that he'd used on the phone. It rolled and rumbled and churned her insides. She was about to be taken and taken well.

At sixteen, he'd been gangly and good-looking with an intensity about life that had sent her girlish heart into spins. "You've filled out."

One side of his mouth kicked up at her appreciation.

Broad shoulders tapered to a thick, muscular waist. His forearms would give her dreams for years. While she took inventory of his body, he studied her face. Her girlhood attraction blossomed into full adult lust.

She placed her palms on his chest to cop a feel of solid masculine muscle. Heat. Strength. Desire.

"Are we doing this or will we pretend we're not allowed to tear each other's clothes off?" she asked on a whisper of sound.

"This brother–sister thing's already old." His low sexy rumble sent warm shivers down her belly.

She raised her face but he cupped her cheeks and forestalled her kiss. "I want to take this slow. I've waited too long to hurry."

She nodded. Now that she was here, like this, with him, she had all the time in the world. "This has been a long time coming." She sighed against his mouth, thrilled by the deep desire in his voice. He'd been all too eager to see the last of her when she'd left town and she'd been too hurt to look back.

Until now.

He moved his hands down her neck, along her shoulders and then slowly down her ribs to her full hips. His eyes darkened with need and lust roared to life.

His lust.

Hers.

Yes.

He clasped her hips and kneaded flesh. "God, you're all woman. So soft. Lush. Made for—"

"Fucking? It's all right. I've heard it before." Her mother had passed along genes that gave her a woman's body too soon.

"No. Not for fucking. For loving. You were a kid, until one day, you walked towards me with the sun at your back. You wore a yellow sundress. On the outside it was baggy and shapeless, but outlined under the dress were curves I'd never seen before. I was so turned on I scared the crap out of myself."

Even now, he looked appalled at his teenaged reaction.

He pulled back to search her face. "You were an open book. Unmarked, unfettered and free. I could have touched you anywhere, anytime. You were so young you didn't understand the invitation you gave me. You scared me to death."

"That's why you scared off every boy in town."

At his nod, she said, "Here's a fresh invitation, Kurt. Let's go to bed." Her low belly went heavy. Needful.

Drawing her face to his, he settled them into their first kiss.

A brush of lips, a taste, a breath, while her belly swooped and her heart thudded a tattoo. She shuddered against his mouth until he pressed harder.

His tongue sparked an inferno as he slid into her mouth. Firm lips, deep tongue, a hard wall of hard man, Kurt was more than she'd imagined. Her nipples beaded as need gathered low and warm. She bloomed and softened between her legs. Moistness prepared her for him.

The first kiss ended when he lifted his head.

The next began as she pressed for more with a soft moan that said, *Finally!* "I've wanted this forever. You could have had me, been with me, I was so completely yours," she murmured between kisses.

"Too young, too ready. Too much." He bent and picked her up in his arms. "If I'd touched you then, we'd have been lost. I couldn't have stopped; you'd have been pregnant. Our lives would have been a repeat."

She slid her lips to his heated neck. He was right. They'd have been swamped by this need, overcome with youth and lust and foolish desire. His restraint had been their salvation. "Thank you, Kurt. Thank you for being a man when you were just a boy."

He paused at the foot of the staircase. "Ready?"

"You can't mean to carry me?" She squirmed, delighted to let him show off, if only for a moment.

He wasn't out of breath, his arms were still tight around her. He was indeed capable of carrying her to his room. He kissed her again to prove he had energy to spare.

She settled into the novel experience. At her height, no one had ever tried to carry her anywhere. Caring, generous and incurably macho. Where was the Kurt she used to know?

When he reached his room, he nibbled at the tender flesh of her lower lip as he released her to slide down the length of his body.

His hands roved across her back, streaking heat along every nerve ending they swept. She pressed tightly against him. The scent of fresh air rose from his hair and shirt. Taking deep draughts of his scent, she rolled her head to let him nuzzle at the spot behind her ear. His breath tickled, the rasp of his bristles sensuously rough against her collarbone.

She reached for the top button of her blouse.

"No," he whispered, "let me. I'll strip you bare and then—" he kissed her once more on the lips "—I'll do this all over you."

She shuddered as he trailed his hands from her shoulders to her fingertips so he could take over undressing her.

"Don't move. Don't speak," he demanded.

Nodding, she melted inside with a frustrated desire to reach for him.

He undid the first smooth, round button on her blouse with trembling fingers. He kissed the skin beneath. The second button fell open of its own accord and she shuddered in anticipation when he smiled slightly. Her nipples puckered as his tongue tentatively touched her again. The other buttons followed slowly, the skin under each one given his unique brand of reverence. She thought she would scream before he was through.

"Don't move," he said. "Don't speak."

She dragged in a deep breath and kept her hands at her sides. Silently she begged him to release her from this thrall but the chain of her promise kept her silent.

Pushing her sleeves down her arms he bit lightly at her shoulders. She tried to nip his ear without success. He was killing her. She squirmed with impatience.

"No moving." His guttural demand went urgent.

Through the thin lace of her bra, he caressed each nipple with his lips and tongue until they strained against the cups. A short sound of frustration tore from her throat as his lips left her.

He undid her bra and dropped it at her feet.

She shifted, as the heavy weight of desire settled deep and low. She'd get him for this. She stiffened against him and glared into his eyes with a demand to hurry. *Hurry!*

Kurt grinned. "You'll make me pay, right?"

She dipped her eyelids closed. *Yes.*

He knelt before her and blew hot puffs of air across her ribs and stomach. Her knees started to quake until he grasped them. He nuzzled her through the heavy denim of her jeans. The sound she made this time was louder, more desperate.

She was about to fall. Couldn't he see that?

"Don't move," he begged.

By the time he undid her zipper she flowered for him, open and wet.

He slid his large palms down her thighs, moving from back to front as he removed her jeans. When she stepped clear of them, she shifted closer. He drew in her scent and held it. "Mm, you smell delicious."

He nuzzled at her soft curls.

She arched into him and ached.

She threaded her fingers through his hair to hide the shift to widen her stance. Exquisite fire rushed and roared at the first touch of his finger as it trailed across her mons.

He found her clitoris and drew a circle around the bud. She crooned and shook with the fiery relief. Relief soon eclipsed by more need as he blew hot breath across her exposed nerve endings.

"Don't move." He sounded ragged.

She stood still, panting to gain some control as he tugged her panties to her ankles then off her feet. He kissed her lips once, hard, then returned to his knees to place one gentle kiss at the heart of her.

She sagged against his broad shoulders, mind reeling from the luxury of touching him.

"Don't move." His voice went hoarse.

"Aahhh," she sobbed raggedly, breath catching. "I'll get you for this."

"I hope so."

She glanced down and found him looking up at her. His gaze was so heated it scorched. She gave a soft sigh and waited.

He found her again, open and ready. Shock waves of intense arousal ricocheted through her lower abdomen and she collapsed on to the bed. Leigh closed her eyes against the frustration burning through to her fingertips. The soft rustle of clothing falling away filled the room.

She opened her eyes. He stood, broad at the shoulders, thick at the waist, and from a thatch of dark hair his cock rose like a stanchion, thick, wide and ready. As much as she'd suffered the ache of unfulfilled need, so had he.

The look of full dangerous arousal on Kurt's face thrilled her as she skittered backwards up the bed. When her head reached the pillow, she smiled, opened her legs and let him see the effect he'd had on her.

"Do that again."

Four

Leigh closed her legs, opened them. The light caught Kurt's hard gaze. "Again," he demanded.

She teased him with more as he prowled up to her pussy from her ankles, leaving soft wet kisses in his wake. By the time he'd settled at her apex, she was thrashing. The man was slow. And deliberate. And frustrating, but immovable.

He feathered her clitoris with his tongue, then pressed and retreated several times, bringing her closer and closer to implosion. The hard press of his penis on her calf promised the moon if only he'd go faster.

"Haven't we waited long enough?" she gasped between rolling waves of sensation. "Fuck me, Kurt! Now."

He chuckled.

"This is not amusing. It's torture."

"Teasing."

She lifted his head, saw his lips glistening with her juice. "This is over. Do me now."

He lifted an eyebrow then nodded. The press into her came swift and hard and she whooped with victory as her lips spread to take him. The fullness, the ripeness of his urgency, his weight on her felt too right. Perfect. Exquisite.

"Rock me," he urged, as he thrust deep.

Too late, she was shattering already, overcome by the sudden rush of freedom to touch, to feel, to love him.

When she floated back, he still held her. Small diamonds of perspiration shone on his brow as he clenched his jaw to maintain control. "Rock me, Leigh. I need you."

She rocked. Thrust and hold, thrust and hold, the rhythm meant to take him to release. He growled into her ear. She smiled into his.

Tension built as again and again she took him deep, holding him until he lifted her hips to surge into her.

"Kurt!" she cried as he slid into her, urgent, orgasmic. He strained against her hips, driving her body along the sheets. His heart pounded against her chest, his arms taut, his buttocks hollowed with each thrust. And then she was swept high, high on her own spearing release.

They held each other so tight, Leigh couldn't tell if the trembles she felt were hers or Kurt's.

*   *   *

In the bright morning light, she found the coffee maker had been preset and fresh-brewed coffee awaited her. She filled two mugs and returned to bed. Kurt sat up, and scrubbed his chest hair, looking more like a bear than ever. His dark-blond hair tufted all over his head.

She'd speared her fingers through the strands as she'd held his head between her thighs. She went juicy at the memory. "Good morning. Are you Happy Bear or Grumpy Bear this early?"

She stood by the door uncertain if she should stay or go.

"You look frightened, Goldilocks. Come here, I promise I won't hurt you." He patted the mattress and relief eased her into stepping forwards to offer him coffee.

She settled in beside him, let the warmth of his body heat her. "And for the record, you're not a hairy beast."

He stopped mid-sip and looked at her with humour. "Good to know."

"Actually, you're perfect." In too many ways.

His lips pursed as he held back a grin. "So are you." A sly hand slid up the inside of her thigh. "As much as I want to recharge and continue what we started last night, we need to get to Marion's."

"Agreed."

Five

They showered and ate a quick breakfast before setting off.

As they pulled into the familiar driveway, the weight of nostalgia settled in Leigh's chest. Kurt tugged her hand into his lap and gave it a squeeze. She blinked back moisture and gave him a breezy smile.

"I've got an appointment with the realtor," he said. "We could walk through the place with him while you make a list of things to sell."

"It'll be easier for me than Marion." A home sorted through and catalogued, pieces discarded. Her heart beat a tattoo as she looked at the lovely old home. "I want my own family to grow up in one just like this." The veranda beckoned, deep and cool in summer, protective in winter. The trees were large with limbs strong enough for tyre swings.

"This was a great place for children. I was too old when I came here to hang around much, but all the little kids loved the yard and the big kitchen table." He subsided as he, too, let nostalgia claim him.

As she walked through the place again, Leigh noted the flowered wallpaper in the upper hallway was exactly as she remembered: faded yellow roses growing in straight lines up the wall. The smell was different. She sniffed. Closed in at the least, musty at the worst.

"We'll have to put in some elbow grease to get the house ready," she'd told Kurt. He'd listened to decorating and staging ideas without interruption. In fact, he'd been extremely quiet throughout the tour with the realtor.

She went into Marion's room. She threw back Marion's heavy drapes and opened both windows that overlooked the street. Seeing Kurt in deep conversation with the realtor, she felt a stab of want so strong she could have swooned with it.

She grabbed a scatter rug and shook it out of the window. Kurt caught the motion and laughed up at her. "We'll need to clean from top to bottom," she called out to him.

He waved. "I'll be right up to help."

She shook the life out of the scatter rug, coughing with the dust. When she turned into the room again, she found Kurt against the door frame, grinning at her.

"I tried six months ago to get her a maid service but she wouldn't hear of it," he said in his rough sensual voice. An underlying burr of desire made her moisten.

"How about some hot teenage bedroom sex?"

"You mean the way I wanted back then?"

But she'd already grabbed his hand to tug him down the hall to her old room. The furniture was more scuffed, the paint and curtains updated by a decade, but memories of Kurt as a teenager were fresh and tart. "I thought of this when the realtor opened the door to this room."

"Me, too." He grinned when she kicked off her shoes and shucked her jeans. "Did you think of this back then?"

"Eventually. At first I wrote your name a million times in my journal, but by fifteen I'd moved into hot steamy dreams." She lifted the coverlet on the narrow bed. "Not a lot of room, but we'll manage."

He followed her down on to the mattress, each squeak of the bed frame a blatant reminder that they were both bigger now. Bigger, more needful, more aware and infinitely more in tune.

She giggled. "This is hot, but loud."

"I'll take your mind off loud, just let me slide down." His bristled chin started a firestorm between her legs. 'Yeah, that's right." His tongue found her. "So delicious, like strawberry cream . . ."

He swept her up and off the bed, out of the room, into the heavens with his tongue and fingers, while she let her teenaged fantasies play out behind her eyes: Kurt, climbing into her window; Kurt, stealing kisses in the kitchen; Kurt, taking her in dirty mysterious ways that thrilled her teenaged body into early panting orgasm.

"Some day, will you climb in through the bedroom window?"

He looked up her body, mouth still working her. His eyes crinkled at the corners as he grinned. He chuckled with his tongue on her clit.

Electric.

She shuddered into her orgasm and swore that one day, she'd pull out her old cheerleading costume and meet him under the bleachers.

An hour later, sated and relaxed, Kurt leaned over Leigh in the tiny, squeaky bed. She stretched out in languid satiation, her curves fitted against him. He didn't care that her feet were cold and tucked between his calves. He'd kept her feet in the air for most of the time spent in this bed, so payback was only fair. "Are you sure you want to leave?"

"It's a good promotion. But it would mean at least three years in Japan."

He studied her lovely, expressive face from her slight widow's peak to her determined chin. Her eyes clouded at the mention of three years.

She shifted to slide under him while awareness rose along with his cock. It wasn't their omnipresent attraction this time, but the knowledge that this would soon be over.

He couldn't see anything beyond her leaving. And he didn't want to lose her again. "What if I said I'd buy this house?"

"What? Why?"

As he spoke without thought, he filled in a new future. One with her in it. "The market's hit an all-time low and I'll pay more for the house than anyone else. Marion will be better off, and we'll keep the house in the family, so to speak."

"It might be nice to imagine you raising children here. You'll be a great dad." Again her eyes clouded and he heard a soft hitch in her voice she tried to cover with a smile.

"I said *we*, Leigh. To hell with Japan. Stay here. Let's give this a shot." He pulled back to see her reaction.

Her eyes couldn't go any wider. Knockout eyes, killer smile, a glow that lit her from the inside. He read her acceptance before her mouth could move.

And then he kissed her, deep, hard, gentle and coaxing. He kept his eyes shut tight so she wouldn't see the wetness he felt. His hand found her wetness, stroked those velvet petals until they blossomed.

"Kurt," she breathed in between kisses, "you know how to rock a girl's world."

He pressed his fingers into her, holding her deep, weeping channel. "Answer me, Leigh. I'll even climb in your window." Every week if he had to. He rubbed her until she caught her breath.

"Three years is a long time to be gone."

He nuzzled her ear. "And this has been a long time coming for us. Try with me, Leigh."

After her initial surprise, she leaned into him, angling her head for better contact. She reached around his back and held on, smoothing her hands across the muscles, heating him through.

Her scent rose, warm and flush and he laughed with the headiness. "Let me take you home, little girl," he murmured.

Home. Home is where the heart is. And her heart had always been here. But with Kurt making it clear he didn't want her, she'd forced herself to look for a future elsewhere.

"You're serious? You want me to stay?"

"We'll make a home together, a life in the house where it all started. I've never been more serious."

She shook her head no. His eyes turned dark at the negative shake. Thunder gathered in his expression, until she realized he'd misinterpreted. "I'm shaking my head because I can't believe it. You sent me away. I only left because I couldn't bear to be here without you."

"No Japan?"

"No Japan."

With that, he laughed from the bottom of his barrel chest and lifted her into his arms for a deep bear hug and whispered the words she'd longed to hear. "I love you. I have for years."

Her heart kicked back into even pumps. "Even when I was twelve?"

"Especially then. You were honest and funny and smart. The way you felt about me was written all over your face, all the time. But I was old enough to know the time wasn't right for us."

"So, you waited?"

"And waited, and waited. Then, when I heard about your promotion, I couldn't wait any longer. I may have exaggerated Marion's reaction to the move, but I had to take drastic measures."

"But you said she cried."

"She did. But I'm not sure she went to her sister's for any reason other than to give us time alone."

"Her sister was always fit and healthy so I wondered that, too."

"But just in case this move is difficult for her, I plan to have her old home movies transferred to DVD. We'll watch them together."

"Oh, Kurt. That's very sweet." She slid her hand to his ready cock. He shuddered with the contact. She squeezed the length until he groaned with need. "You made me wait a long time. You deserve to be punished." She squeezed him again and slid her hand up and down his stiff rod.

He kissed her deeply. "A long time . . ." He pulled her under him, eager and ready.

She opened her legs and felt the press of heated flesh between her moist lips and sighed with contentment as he slid inside. "But worth the wait."

Wolf at the Door

Charlene Teglia

One

Karen Smith stopped on the last leg of the trail below the Sol Duc falls, sat on the unforgiving ground, and leaned her back against a convenient Sitka spruce. She pulled off boots that her aching calves swore weighed four pounds apiece and pulled a bandage from her backpack to cover the blister that had formed above one heel. Then she leaned back and closed her eyes, just for a minute.

Just a minute to rest and then she'd shove her swollen feet back into her hiking boots, and walk the rest of the way to her car. After hours on the trail, she'd earned a breather.

Something made her eyes come open, some sound or sense that told her she was no longer alone. What she saw made her freeze.

A huge grey wolf sat on its haunches on the far side of the trail. Watching her. It was as big as a Shetland pony, easily six feet in length, maybe more. It outweighed her, outmuscled her, and Karen didn't doubt it could outrun her.

The sheer size told her what it was, but that was impossible. The Olympic grey timber wolves had been extinct since the 1920s. The impossibility combined with exhaustion made her blurt out loud, "You're extinct. You don't exist."

The wolf stood, stretched, turned to display all sides of itself to her, then sat down again with a shrug of its massive shoulders, as if to say, don't believe your eyes, then.

Maybe it was a spirit wolf, not a physical predator that couldn't exist anyway. Karen shut her eyes. "You're not real. I'm imagining you. Go away."

Feet padded towards her. She kept her eyes shut and refused to move, retreating into the childhood defence against monsters. If you don't see it, if you don't move, it can't see you. Fur brushed against her bare upper arm. A muzzle nosed against her cheek.

Oh, God, she wailed inside. But the physical contact soothed her and some inner certainty told her this wolf wouldn't harm her.

The wolf's breath huffed against her ear as it sniffed her. It gave her a gentle nudge. When she didn't move, she felt teeth nip at the fabric of her tank top. Karen's eyes flew wide open. Satisfied that it had her attention, the wolf grasped her boots in its jaws and dragged them to her. The action said, *Hurry up. Get moving.*

"You're not a normal wolf." Since she couldn't win an argument with a figment of her imagination, Karen fumbled her socks on, then the boots. While she laced them up, the wolf let out a soft yip. "OK, OK. I know when I'm not wanted."

The wolf gave her an indecipherable look and rubbed its great head against her bare leg. Then pushed her pack closer with its muzzle.

"So you don't mind my company, but for some reason you want me to haul ass out of here." Karen bent to pick up her backpack and slid it on again. She grimaced as she rotated her shoulders under the weight. "Fine. I'm going."

Time to get moving anyway. Twilight had crept up on her. She'd stayed out later than she'd meant to. Soon the northern summer extended daylight would give way to the rising full moon. Her animal guide hurried and worried her all the way to her car, and then it kept to the shadows while she took out her keys, lowered the backpack, unlocked her trunk and dropped it in.

She closed the lid with a thunk then opened the driver's side door. Habit made her scan the interior of the car for hidden dangers. Satisfied that no knife-wielding psychopath hid behind her seat, Karen gave the wolf a wave. "OK. Everything's fine. You can go now."

It let out a snarl that turned her blood to ice and launched itself towards her. No, not towards her, she realized, past her. Whirling to put her back to the car, Karen saw the wolf putting itself between her and the looming figures of five men. Where had they come from? She hadn't seen anybody near her parked car. Had they been waiting for her? Was this what the wolf had come to warn her about?

The men scattered, but Karen didn't wait to find out what they'd wanted. She jumped into the car, slammed the door shut and started the engine. By the time she had the car aimed down the road, the wolf and the men were gone. The only evidence that anything had happened was her pounding heart and the adrenaline that raced through her, fuelling the ancient reflex to fight or flee. Her feet voted on flight, since she was unarmed and outnumbered, and she let them carry her, stepping on the gas pedal and heading for home.

The invaders to his territory scattered and fled when he confronted them. He would have been content to watch and wait, to see why they'd come, what they wanted, but then he'd picked up the woman's scent. His senses told him what she was, if not who. And he hadn't been able to stay hidden when his mate was in harm's way. He'd shown himself to her, risking her terrified response. Counting on it to scare her into fleeing for safety. Because despite the undeniable instinct that identified her as his mate, she was human. Unchanged.

But she hadn't run from him.

The memory warmed him. Her chestnut hair, cut short in layers, invited touching. Her clear hazel eyes, flecked with brown, had a steady look that pleased him. Her angular features gave her a distinctive beauty. The faint vanilla scent of her lingered with him. The softness of her skin and her leggy, lean form entranced him. He wanted a string of uninterrupted days and nights to explore and discover all of her. To claim her.

He'd have to find her first. And fast. Because the group of strange wolves he'd been tracking since they entered his territory had been lying in wait for her. As men, not in their animal forms. In his wolf form, Sam was faster, stronger. He could catch up to her car and see which way she turned. He'd follow. He already knew her licence plate number. He would learn her name and where she was staying. That should be easy enough. She was a newcomer here or he would have discovered her before.

The knowledge that his mate was so close, and in danger, drove him to tireless pursuit. When he learned where she lived, the irony that she'd been directly under his nose while he remained oblivious made him want to howl.

Karen parked by her cabin overlooking Lake Crescent and nearly ran from her car to the front porch. Once she had the heavy wooden door bolted behind her, she did a quick visual check of the cabin's interior. The wood stove sat at the centre of the open floor plan. Her living space circled it, beginning with the kitchen area, which gave way to a trestle-style table with two benches on either side, then a faded couch next to two tall and overstuffed bookcases.

Nothing looked out of place. She checked the bathroom that was pretty much a closet on the far side of the kitchen, the only room with a door. It, too, was empty except for a small sink, toilet and shower stall.

She climbed the ladder up to the half-loft that served as her bedroom. The big log bed covered with a bright quilt, nightstand and dresser all looked just the way she'd left them before she'd headed out for a hike in an effort to find some peace or at least wear herself out. On impulse, she opened the deacon's bench at the foot of the bed. Tucked under neatly stacked clean sheets and an extra quilt, an antique dagger rested. She covered it back up and closed the bench, exhaling relief.

The cabin and its contents had been left to her when her employer, an eccentric collector and historian, passed away. Jobless and bereft at the loss of the man who had been more like a grandfather than a boss, Karen had left Seattle for the rustic location to mourn and regroup.

When she'd taken possession, the post office had delivered the package they'd been holding for her. A package addressed by the man she'd just buried. She'd found the dagger inside, along with some notes about its history, which read like the wildest fantasy.

Maybe Cyril Foster had started to suffer some insidious erosion of his brilliant mind towards the end of his life. Or maybe he really had left a genuine bone-handled Damascus dagger from the 1500s that contained the soul of a mad German werewolf in her keeping.

Since he'd also promised her that she'd be protected by a wolf guardian and warned her of dark forces that had hunted the dagger through the centuries, Alzheimer's seemed more likely. Except that she'd just been saved by a guardian wolf.

Coincidence? Maybe. But the odd phone calls with nobody on the end of the line that ended with a disconnection, the men who had been waiting by her car and the frequent sensation of being watched that had dogged her since shortly after she'd arrived at the cabin meant something was going on, and that dagger was probably in the middle of it.

Cyril's collection had been accounted for in his will. As his personal assistant, she'd helped catalogue it. This piece hadn't been included. She'd seen the dagger for the first time when she'd opened the package Cyril had mailed to the cabin the week he died. If nobody knew he'd had it, who would come looking for it? Somebody who knew it was in his possession, somehow. A piece that old, with a history that colourful, somebody must have known something about it. Maybe somebody suspected Cyril had kept it hidden even after his death.

"If you'd bothered to explain any of this while you were alive, it would make my life so much easier," Karen said out loud.

But he hadn't, and now he was beyond reach. She couldn't ask him to explain, couldn't demand that he tell her what was really going on. All she could do was carry out his final instructions to her and keep the dagger hidden.

The incident in the parking lot made her wish she'd rented a safe deposit box to stash it in. It had seemed safe enough hidden at the cabin before, when she'd believed nobody else knew about it.

She regretted her failure to find a more secure hiding place even more when the sound of an engine outside was followed by the crunch of booted feet on gravel and a knock at her door.

Two

Alarm made her heart race. Had one of those men managed to follow her here?

"Stop being paranoid," Karen muttered to herself. It was probably a neighbour.

Washington's sparsely populated Olympic Peninsula wasn't exactly the kind of place where she had to fear living alone. Still, she moved as quietly as she could coming down the ladder. She peeked out of the window to try to identify the visitor.

She didn't recognize the mud-spattered pickup. She could tell it was one of the expensive ones, designed like a luxury car with four-wheel drive and a truck bed. She wasn't sure if the evidence of money was a good sign or a bad one.

Her mysterious visitor knocked again, harder. "Miss Smith? Are you all right?"

The deep, throaty masculine voice was easy on her ears. If only it was equally easy on her nerves.

"Do you need assistance?" The voice took on a more urgent tone.

Karen hissed a short, foul word under her breath. Somebody must've seen her drive in like a bat out of hell and assumed she'd had an accident of some sort. If she didn't want an ambulance to follow on this man's boot heels, she'd better answer.

"I'm fine," she called back, pitching her voice to carry. "Give me a second to get to the door."

She eyed the safety chain on her door. If she undid the bolt, but left the chain on, it offered some measure of protection while she checked out her visitor. If he proved harmless, she could let him in. If he were a neighbour who just wanted to make sure she was all right, a glimpse would be enough to reassure him.

Karen unlocked the door and opened it the slight span allowed by the chain. "Hello."

"You are all right, then." The man on her front porch seemed to relax fractionally, but he didn't smile. He ran his fingers through the rumpled length of wavy blond hair that hadn't had a cut recently and regarded her with brown eyes that seemed to see too deeply into her. He had the kind of down-to-earth good looks that could have made him a movie star, but if he had been one, she would have recognized his face. He wore a short-sleeved white T-shirt that clung to his broad shoulders and muscular arms and chest before disappearing into the waistband of faded jeans. Cowboy boots completed the ensemble.

He wasn't dressed like a thug, or wearing the kind of clothing that might mark him as a wealthy collector who might be trying to acquire a Damascus dagger. And he appeared to be near her age, late twenties to early thirties.

"Yes, I'm fine. Thanks for checking." Karen gave him a polite half-smile.

"So you're the one who inherited this place from Cyril," her mystery man went on. "Pleasure to meet you."

"Did you know him?" Karen asked, the fine hairs at the nape of her neck stirring in alarm. She'd worked for Cyril for ten years. That provided ample opportunities for her to get acquainted with his friends, family, peers, business associates. This man was a stranger to her.

"Not really," the man said with a slight shake of his head. "We knew each other by reputation. And I knew the cabin was bequeathed to his long-time assistant. I got a letter from him asking me to keep an eye on the place."

Cyril had been a busy man at the end of his life. Busy putting events in motion that he'd kept secret from her until after he was gone.

"I see," Karen said, although she didn't.

He motioned towards the door with one hand. "Since you're all right, would you like to invite me in? I could use a cup of coffee."

Not subtle. But if he was some sort of thug, he could threaten her with a weapon through the partial opening in the door. He could break a window to get inside. If he meant her harm, unchaining the door wouldn't make matters much worse. And if he was even distantly familiar with Cyril, maybe he knew something that could help her put together the pieces of the puzzle she'd been left with.

"Sure." She closed the door, removed the chain and opened it all the way. "What did you say your name was?"

"I didn't. It's Sam. Sam Owen." He held out a hand, and Karen placed hers in it. As soon as she did, their hands gripped and a strange tingling buzz spread up her arm until her body seemed to vibrate with it. Her heart thudded unevenly in her chest. She stared into his eyes, unable to look away. Her breath seemed to stop.

His eyes darkened as he looked into hers. He stepped closer and raised his other hand to her hair. His fingers combed through the chunky layers, testing the texture before sliding down to curl under her chin. "Karen." His voice went lower, dropping into a husky timbre that shivered down her spine. He made her name sound like a caress.

"Sam." She said his name on a breath of sound and licked her lips in nervous reaction. What was wrong with her? She was holding on to his hand and staring at him like she'd never seen a man before. But she couldn't let go or look away. She had to fight the urge to move closer, to run her hands through his hair the way he'd touched hers and then run them lower to trace the lines of his shoulders, the wall of his chest and abdomen.

"I wish we could have met under different circumstances," Sam said. He moved closer, until only a few inches separated them, and closed the door behind him. She heard him shoot the bolt and restore the chain, all done without looking away from her.

"You mean, when Cyril was alive?" Karen asked.

"That might have helped. He could have introduced us. I wonder why he didn't."

The words were clear, but the meaning eluded her. Karen struggled with the sense that she was missing something, but it was hard to think when she wanted with all of her being to simply feel. She wanted to feel the press of his lips against hers. The press of his naked flesh against hers. Inside hers.

"You wanted coffee," she said, but made no effort to go make it.

"In a minute." Sam took another half-step forwards, which brought his body into contact with hers. The buzz under her skin increased. Her hands itched to touch him.

"Kiss me." She hadn't meant to say the words, but as soon as they were out, she felt the yearning sweep through her. Oh, God, she needed him to kiss her. Now.

"It won't stop with kissing," Sam said. A warning note sounded in his voice.

"I don't want it to." She let her palms rest on his upper arms, her fingers digging into the soft fabric of his T-shirt and had to fight the urge to rip it. She wanted bare skin under her hands. Which really wasn't right. She didn't make a habit of fucking strangers. "What's wrong with us?"

Even as she asked the question in a tremulous tone, she was trailing her lips along the curve of his neck. He tilted his head back, offering her the sensitive hollow of his throat. She shuddered as she pressed a kiss there, feeling the beat of his pulse against her lips.

"Nothing's wrong. Although the timing sucks." Sam's arms closed around her, holding her close. One hand rested between her shoulders. The other moved down to cup the curve of her butt. "We need to mate."

That was an odd way to word it, but it seemed fitting. She wanted to mate with this man, body to body, soul to soul. She wanted to get as close as it was possible to get within the limits defined by physical constraints. She didn't just want sex with him, she wanted to merge with him.

"I need you." Karen whispered the confession against his bare throat and felt his body react. His arms tightened around her and his hips rocked forwards, pressing the length of his erection against her.

"I'll give you everything you need," Sam promised in a throaty growl. "Where's your bed?"

She made a wordless gesture towards the loft. He lifted her in his arms and cradled her against his chest to carry her the short distance. Then he set her on the ladder. She climbed up with heavy limbs, achingly aware of him close behind her. She made it to the top and sank on to the bed as a languorous heat spread through her. Sam followed her on to the mattress and stretched out beside her. He tangled a hand in her hair and looked into her eyes. "You're beautiful."

Karen shook her head. "I'm average."

"Beautiful." He lowered his head until his lips touched hers. "I want to see all of you."

That worked for Karen. She was too hot; her clothes were too tight. They restricted her and she wanted them gone with a ferocity that took her by surprise. But she followed her body's urging, stripping down to her underwear and then to skin. Sam matched her for speed and his clothes tangled with hers on the floor beside the bed. Then he was pulling her close and Karen shut her eyes as she tried to imprint him on her bare body.

"Want you," she muttered. Her fingers dug into his back. She curled one leg over his, urging him even closer. Her sex clenched with need and anticipation.

"Want you, too." He reached down to cup her between her parted legs. His palm pressed into her, relieving the ache of arousal. He moved his hand in a circle, massaging her clit indirectly.

Karen bit into his shoulder and moaned her approval, rocking her hips into his hand. "Sam. More. Hurry." Her body thrummed with urgency.

He petted her sex then pushed a testing finger inside her. He made a low growling sound when he found her slick and ready, easily accepting the penetration. "So hot and wet."

She felt hot all over. And wild, crazed for him. He rolled her on to her back and slid on top of her. Her thighs shifted wider apart as his legs pressed between them. He rested in the cradle of her hips for a minute while her heart thundered in her chest. "Karen. Mine."

"Yours," Karen agreed mindlessly. She was on fire, her skin burning for him, her body taut and trembling.

Sam positioned his cock at her slick entry and drove into her, filling her with one long stroke. Karen arched up to meet his thrust with a wild cry. Her short nails raked his back as she bucked under him, fighting to take him deeper, to get more of him.

He took her hard and fast, driving her straight to the edge. She crashed over it as waves of pleasure racked her. Sam let out a low groan and came in a liquid jet she felt deep inside.

Afterwards she lay panting under him, still trembling with aftershocks from the intensity of the peak she'd reached with him. "Talk about zero to sixty," she muttered, trying for a light tone.

Sam rubbed his forehead against hers. "I think we can make it last a little longer the next time."

"Next time?" She could feel him, still hard inside her.

"Starting now." Sam kissed her, gently, deepening it by degrees. The sweetness of it stole her breath and made emotion well in her throat and sting her eyes. He kissed her as if there was nothing else in the world he wanted to do more, as if he could spend hours immersed in the exploration of joined mouths and tongues. When he ended the kiss and raised his head, she stared into his eyes, feeling shaken to the core.

"Who are you?" The real question she left unvoiced: why did she react to him this way?

"I'm yours." He rubbed the tip of his nose against hers. The caress disarmed her. Then he rolled with her, coming to rest on his back with her sprawled on top. His hands cupped her bare butt to hold her so their bodies stayed joined.

"That makes no sense." But it pleased something inside her anyway. She hadn't belonged anywhere or with anyone since Cyril died. Karen levered her torso up and arched her back so that he sank deeper into her.

Sam made a sound of approval and ran his hands up her sides, then covered the slight curves of her breasts with his palms. "I didn't take time to touch these before."

Karen made a wry face. "You didn't miss much."

"You're very elegantly shaped. But if it makes you feel better, I'm a leg and ass man."

She laughed, the humour bubbling up from deep within, making her blood effervesce. "Lucky me."

"I'm the lucky one." He pulled her back down so that their torsos met while he thrust harder into her. "Kiss me again."

She did, her lips clinging to his open-mouthed and greedy, while their bodies rocked together. They drew the pleasure out this time, savouring the joining of flesh and the slide of skin against skin, until the need for completion became a demand they couldn't prolong.

She ground herself against him, coming in pulsing waves while he spent himself in her. Then she collapsed on top of him and rested there, trying to catch her breath.

Sam stroked her back, long, lazy caresses that soothed her and fed the skin-hunger he'd awoken in her. She wanted nothing more than to stay right there with Sam touching her. She felt the oddest sense of homecoming, as if she'd always belonged in his arms.

"Sam." Karen stirred herself enough to raise her head so she could kiss his chest. "What are we doing?"

"Mating." He kissed her forehead, a butterfly caress that made her heart ache. "I recognized you as soon as I caught your scent. By joining our bodies, we completed the bond."

She went still. "That doesn't make any sense." Having a sudden attack of hormones and going sex-crazed for a stranger, that she could believe. The chemistry of attraction put the brain in an altered state. There was a scientific explanation for it. Recognizing people by scent, that wasn't believable. And what did he mean, "bond"?

"It makes perfect sense." Sam rolled her on to her back again and pinned her under him with his body. "I'm a werewolf. You are, too, or you would be if the antigen in your bloodstream had ever been triggered by exposure."

Karen rejected the bizarre explanation forcefully. "Bullshit."

Sam went on as if she hadn't spoken. "Cyril had to have known it. He was a lone wolf, but he knew I was the alpha here. He sent you to my territory and asked me to watch out for you. I don't know if he guessed what you were to me and played matchmaker from beyond the grave, or if he just wanted you to find the pack and home after he was gone."

Cyril had promised her a wolf guardian. He'd also written about werewolves and left her a silver dagger that he claimed had killed one.

Silver. The reminder cleared the fog from her brain. Would it save her from Sam and his insane claim that they could both turn furry? What might he do to her if he truly believed he was freeing the wolf inside her? Forget werewolves, her logic shrieked. It's a weapon. If you stab somebody with it, they'll bleed.

Three

Sam's eyes narrowed as he looked down at her. His nostrils flared, then he captured her wrists in a lightning-fast move, stretching her arms up and apart, pinning them to the sides. But when he spoke again, his tone was filled with gentle assurance. "You don't need to be afraid. I won't hurt you. You're human and you'll stay that way unless you choose to make the change; I won't force it on you."

"I'm not afraid." But her heart was beating too fast, and she was sure he could feel it. Under the alarm, though, a part of her understood that he could never pose a threat to her. His scent and his closeness relaxed her, soothed her. She was safe with him. He would protect her with his life.

"Yes, you are." He looked almost pained for a minute, and then his expression blanked. "You didn't know. I'm sorry for that, sorry you're not better prepared. But you need to listen to me, because I'm not the only werewolf in the area with an interest in you."

"Right," Karen said, her mouth dry. "Your pack. Are they coming?"

"They are. I sent in a call from my cell phone when I found you. But they're not the ones you should be worried about. Those men waiting for you to come back from your hike, they're not human and they're not mine."

The memory of strange men surrounding her car, scattered by the impossible wolf made her shiver. "How do you know about that?"

Sam blew out a soft breath. "I was there. I walked you to your car, and I drove them off so you could get away."

"On four legs," Karen said, disbelief plain in her voice.

"Yes." He studied her, his expression intent. "Cyril never mentioned anything about werewolves to you? You don't have any idea what they want with you?"

"Cyril said I'd have a wolf guardian," Karen said, choosing her words with care. "He left me a story about werewolves, but I assumed it was just that – a story."

"Did Cyril have a habit of telling stories?"

"No," Karen admitted. "No, if anything he had a talent for understatement." That, combined with his meticulous note-taking and vigorous corroboration of research, would have convinced her the dagger's history was fact, not fiction, if it hadn't included the bit about it holding the soul of the werewolf version of Vlad the

Impaler. She was certain he was right about its age and origin, though.

"Do you really think I'm lying to you?" Sam brushed his mouth across hers, a tiny gesture that pulled at her heart along with her body. "You're my mate. You can feel the bond between us. No matter how far apart we are, you'll feel me. I'll always be with you, as long as we live."

"I feel a lot of things I don't understand." Karen whispered the words against his lips.

"If you'd known what you were, you would have known that you had the instinctual ability to recognize your mate."

She let out a shaky laugh. "Must save a lot of wasted time dating. You know right off if the other person's the one." But somehow she believed he was the one.

"It also prevents divorce and heartbreak." Sam kissed the corner of her mouth. "The bond is physical, not just emotional. It joins us together for life."

"This is crazy." But it was all real. She knew it with unshakeable inner certainty. And that meant Cyril had told the truth about everything. "Sam, you said Cyril asked you to keep an eye on this place. Did he tell you what he wanted you to watch?"

Sam shook his head. "I assume he meant you."

She drew in a deep, steadying breath. "He asked me to watch something, too. I think he intended for you to be my backup, or bodyguard. To make sure it didn't fall into the wrong hands."

Sam went still over her. "What?"

Karen tugged against his hold. "Let me up and I'll show you."

He let her go, and she crawled down to the foot of the bed. She lifted the lid of the deacon's bench and uncovered the dagger for the second time that evening. She took it out, careful to hold it by the bone handle, and turned towards Sam, displaying it.

He drew in a sharp breath. "Do you know what that is?"

"I know what Cyril said it was." Karen looked down at it. "A Damascus dagger. The metal blade is repeatedly folded and welded to make it unbreakable. This one was dipped in silver to coat the blade after it was made and charmed by a witch to capture the spirit of one historic bad guy named Peter Stubbe who terrorized the German towns of Cologne and Bedburg in the 1500s. Cologne was Calvinist then, so they couldn't find a priest to bless it. The witch did the necessary work to make it a weapon capable of stopping a werewolf serial killer. Once it was driven through his heart, it captured his soul and returned him to human form so he could be killed."

For a thing with such a violent and bizarre history, it was beautiful. It gleamed in the light, but she had no desire to touch it. Holding it by the handle was more than she was comfortable with. The thing gave her the creeps and had from the first time she'd seen it.

"That's what they're after," Sam said. "They want the dagger. There's always been a lawless rogue faction who want to be humanity's nightmare. They want to bring Peter Stubbe back to lead them." His eyes met hers, burning with intensity. "Don't let them have it. No matter what."

His words were punctuated by the abrupt sound of glass breaking from the room below.

"Get behind me." Sam lunged in front of her, forming a protective wall. He didn't seem to notice that he was naked. Karen scrambled into her discarded hiking shorts and yanked his T-shirt over her head. It was backwards and inside out, but if a bunch of insane werewolves was breaking into her cabin, she didn't want to meet them nude.

"Come out, come out, wherever you are." A strange man's voice crooned in an eerie tone. Karen heard laughter and more masculine voices joined in, chanting, "Hide and seek."

She watched as Sam's back rippled. He seemed to blur in front of her eyes until she saw two shapes, man superimposed over wolf. And then the wolf took over, leaving a huge grey timber wolf she recognized standing four-footed on the end of her bed.

Knowing it with her head was one thing. Seeing it with her eyes was another. But if any doubt had remained, the sight ended it. It was all real. Her fated mate. The cursed dagger. And the pack of men below were wolves on two legs.

A chorus of howls sounded from below. No, not two legs – at least some of them had shifted shape. But the creaking ladder told her one was climbing up in human form. His head came up over the edge. He didn't seem surprised to meet Sam. His eyes narrowed and his mouth formed a snarl. He swung himself all the way up and leaped at Sam. He seemed to hang suspended in the air and Karen saw him with the same doubled vision. He completed his descent as a brown and white wolf in an arc that intersected with Sam's position. Karen stepped back, the dagger held by its bone handle behind to her side.

The two wolves fought viciously, moving too fast for her to gauge which one was winning. She could hear the others below, howling and knocking against the ladder. She sucked in a sharp breath. Even if Sam managed to subdue his opponent, they were badly outnumbered. Then she felt a tearing sensation in her rear with a loss of power in her legs and saw the brown and white wolf hamstringing the grey.

"Sam! No!" Karen moved forwards without thinking, hand raised. The silver dagger flashed down, found its target, bit deep. The wolf let out a cry that turned to a human shout. The transformation process reversed before her eyes, wolf fading into man, leaving a stranger collapsed on the floor of her loft, trying to grasp the bone handle of the dagger, which was buried in his torso.

The grey wolf ended the threat the man posed with merciless teeth. Below, she heard crashing sounds and realized another group of wolves had arrived to deal with the first. She hoped they were the good guys, but just in case, she was going to stay hidden in her loft.

Sam shifted back to human while she watched. He started to come towards her then gave a warning shout. Karen turned her head and, seemingly in slow motion, saw a wolf's body hurtling towards her, saw the jaws open, and then there was searing pain and darkness.

She woke up in her own bed. Alone. Karen scanned the loft, but didn't see any signs of either Sam or a fight. The thought of the fight reminded her of the dagger. She struggled upright and then managed to reach the deacon's bench at the foot of the bed. The dagger was once again safely hidden beneath the spare bedding. The silver looked darker, but that might have been her imagination. Downstairs she felt a stirring, a rise of emotion and energy. Sam's. She recognized it instantly, even though she couldn't see or hear him. She could sense him and his relief when his vigil over her ended with her return to consciousness.

"You're awake." Sam's voice sounded from below her. "Good. Don't try to get up yet. I'll be right there."

She heard his footsteps coming closer, the creak of the ladder, then saw his head appear as he came up.

"Hello," Karen said, feeling unsure now that she was faced with him again. A familiar stranger. Her mate. And despite the injury she remembered him gaining, he was moving with the same strength and grace he'd had before it happened.

"Hello yourself. How do you feel?" He came closer, sat on the edge of the bed, and took her hand between both of his, enfolding her in warmth with that simple gesture.

Karen took a quick inventory. "Fine." Her surprise sounded in her voice. "I seem to remember losing the fight."

Sam shook his head. "You helped win it, actually. You used the dagger on the leader of the group of renegades who wanted to reanimate Peter Stubbe to help them usher in a new dark age of terror. Once you trapped him in human form, I had him. And then one of the other renegades came up over the edge of the loft and bit you. My pack had arrived by then and they finished the fight, but the cavalry came too late for you."

What he'd told her about the supposed antigen in her blood came back to her. She'd been bitten by a werewolf, and now she was miraculously healed. "Does this mean I changed?"

Sam nodded. "The attack triggered the antigen. You survived. You'll change with the next full moon." He watched her carefully for her reaction, as if worried this wasn't good news.

"So, you're a werewolf, now I'm one too, we're mated, and the crazy wolves are dead?"

"That pretty much sums it up."

"Cyril and his damn secrets," Karen said, but without heat. "Would it have killed him to explain any of this while he was alive?"

"Maybe he didn't want to have to face your doubt and suspicion. Maybe he was afraid you'd hate him if you knew what he really was." Sam kept his expression blank as he spoke. But the intimacy of their bond told her he had the same concern.

"Sam." Karen reached for him, scooting into his arms. "I don't hate you for what you are. How could I? You saved me. And I don't hate myself for surviving, either." She rubbed her cheek against his chest, loving the scent and warmth of his skin. "Hate is the last thing I feel for you."

"What about love?" she heard him ask, his voice a deep rumble in his chest beneath her ear.

She flashed on the urgent sexual need he'd awoken in her, followed by the yearning emotional ache. She'd felt him below her in the cabin, and that proof of the bond between them filled her with wonder.

"I thought we were fated mates," Karen said, unable to resist teasing him. "Doesn't that mean never having to say I love you?"

"No." Sam's answer came swiftly with a ring of certainty. "Not when you nearly lose your mate as soon as you've found her. Then you need to hear the words."

She raised her face to his and let him see the truth in her eyes. "I love you. Kiss me again, Sam."

He did. And it was a very long time before either of them stirred from the big bed.

After Hours

Rosemary Laurey

One

"A Pixie?" Ella Carrack had been a high school teacher far too long to believe that for one second. Pixies – if they existed, which was highly unlikely in her opinion – were not six-foot hunks wearing police uniforms and lots of heavy-looking equipment hanging from shoulders and belt. In the dark, (she'd always thought the school had better perimeter lights) the shadowy figure looked vaguely familiar. A student celebrating Halloween far too early, no doubt.

"Yes, ma'am," he replied.

Might as well play along before handing out a Saturday detention. "And you're here, why?" She stepped forwards, wanting to see exactly whom she'd be writing up for trespass after school hours.

In reply, he grabbed her by the waist and threw her to the ground, his firm, powerful body landing directly on top of her as a bullet whined overhead. "Because somebody's shooting ahead of time."

Sounded like several somebodies but now wasn't the time to quibble. Nor was it the right moment to fully appreciate the male body that covered every inch of hers. This was clearly no adolescent.

"What the hell are you doing here?" he asked, his breath warm against her hair.

"I came in to pick up some ninth-grade maths tests," she muttered. Mid-term reports were due Monday. Mind you, if the bullets kept flying, she might not have to worry about getting her paperwork in on time. "What the hell's going on?" She didn't normally swear at a police officer but excused herself in the circumstances. "And would you please get off me." By the pressure against the small of her back, he was enjoying the closeness a lot more than she was.

"Didn't Mr Bryce request no one work late this evening?" the Pixie policeman asked. Not budging an inch.

"Nipping back for five minutes for something I forgot isn't working late."

"But just as dangerous," he said. She wasn't about to argue as another bullet whined overhead and pinged against the dumpster, followed by an unearthly yell. "You need to get out of here."

She wouldn't argue that point. "OK." He shifted halfway off her. She still couldn't move but at least she had full use of her lungs back. "What on earth's happening? And what are you doing here?" Shouldn't he be calling for backup?

"I'm here to adjudicate."

"Adjudicate what?" A loud bang and a whoop that could have been a yell of pain sounded a few yards away. "Why the hell are people shooting?"

He gave a little gasp, as if suddenly understanding. "Damn, you're a Mundane! What are you doing here?"

"I told you. I forgot some papers."

He muttered something but didn't budge much. She tried to wriggle from under him, but it was like trying to lift a car off her back. Not that she'd ever had to do that, but lying on the grimy ground of the school yard left her unable (or perhaps unwilling) to appreciate the fine male body mashed against hers.

"Will you get off me so I can go home?"

He paused as if pondering that possibility. The weight on her back eased, as if he'd moved, when he muttered, "Too late, I'm afraid." There were shouts and running feet coming toward them as he leaped up, grabbed her by the arm and lifted her up against his body, her face rubbing his shirt and his badge pressing against her left eye. "Don't say a freaking word," he whispered.

Speak? She was lucky to be breathing the way he held her. She was starting to worry about the health of her ribs, when he lifted her off her feet, took a few steps back towards the building and opened the door she'd just exited. How the heck did he do that? It didn't open from the outside and she knew darn well she'd latched it properly. No outside door was ever left unlocked in this neighbourhood.

Only the emergency lights lit the hallway. Ella couldn't see much in the gloom and being half slung over his shoulder didn't improve her line of vision but it was enough for her to see he had blond hair, a bit tousled after their roll on the ground, and he was minus his hat, no doubt left outside with her left shoe.

"What now?" She found herself snapping.

"I get you away before someone scents you."

"What?" His breath didn't smell of drink but he was certainly acting that way. "You just got me in here. I want to go home." That sounded a bit pathetic. "How about you put me down?"

"OK." She was almost vertical, toes brushing the ground when he muttered, "Shit," as shouts and yells came towards them from a hall-way to the right. He pushed open the door to the gym and pulled her in. "They're going to be coming this way any minute. Quick."

She blamed the shriek on nerves, as he ran the length of the gym dragging her with him. He paused at the end, pushed a door open and slammed it behind them.

"Don't make a sound!"

To late for that, as she stumbled and sent a drum set crashing. Someone turned on the gym lights and in a shaft of light from the transom, she looked into the face of her insane police officer.

No wonder his voice sounded vaguely familiar. It was their DARE officer. "Officer Willard? Leigh?"

He stared at her. "Miss Carrack? Ella? Sweet heaven! What the heck am I going to do with you?"

"Let me go home and finish my report cards?" Just a suggestion. With luck she might just manage to reason her way out of this.

"If you go out there, you're dead. They're never going to let a Mundane like you walk away to tell."

There was a way out of this. Had to be. This was Officer Willard. A sensible man. A reasonable man. OK, a sexy man, but that was irrelevant right now. An officer sworn to uphold the law. Or he had been last time she saw him. "What the blazes is going on out there."

"A turf war between the Vampires and the Wolves."

Two of the local gangs. The fact they were fighting wasn't surprising. Sad, worrisome, troubling, but not surprising. "Why are they fighting in the school building?"

"We try to keep them on school property. Easier to clean up afterwards and we have the area cleared to avoid the possibility of involving stray Mundanes. Usually," he added with a frown clearly aimed at her.

"And what is a 'Mundane'?"

"Someone like you. A plain, ordinary human with no special gifts."

"No special gifts? I've survived teaching here for ten years, when half the new teachers quit before Christmas." Bit of an exaggeration that, there were always a few who made it to spring break before throwing in their lesson plan and books.

"I'll concede that but you're still a Mundane. No special gifts."

"I don't know about that. I've run a marathon; have you?" He visibly bristled at her challenge. What made her say that? Stress at being imprisoned with a cop gone insane. A cop who'd claimed he was a Pixie but Pixie or madman, he had a gun on his hip, a pair of handcuffs dangling from his belt, and who knew what in his pockets.

"Ella, if I were you, I'd keep very, very quiet."

It sounded more like advice than threat but, either way, she followed his suggestion. He still blocked the only door, so she sat down on a stack of instrument cases and looked at her captor.

She'd always thought Officer Willard good-looking. He'd always seemed committed and down to earth, even sane. She'd obviously been misled by a nice exterior, a dark uniform and the scent of leather.

"If there's a gang war going on, shouldn't you call in backup and get out there and put a stop to it?"

He stepped away from the door and squatted to be eye level. "I told you. Best if they fight it out among themselves in a contained area. And yes, I should be out there, but if anyone found you, they'd eat you or tear you to pieces."

"Officer Willard. I've faced down a lot of recalcitrant students in my time. I don't scare easily."

"You've never faced rampaging Vampires at night or a Werewolf during full moon."

She gulped; he was definitely devoid of sanity. Had to be, but his face told her otherwise. He was serious and believed what he was saying. "Give me a break!" Vampires? Wolves at full moon? Sheesh, werewolves! Honestly! The stress of being a cop must have turned his brain. "So they come into school and fight it out regularly?"

"Every couple of months or so and only at full moon. The Wolves like to be able to shift." He gave a tsk of exasperation. "Why the heck am I telling a Mundane this?"

"Because you've got me prisoner and we're making conversation."

"Quiet!" There was a noise, shouts in the gym, then a scream as the door slammed and silence for a few seconds until the uproar started again

"What happened?"

"Sounds as though someone got smashed in the door."

"Wait a minute. You're serious, right? The Vamps and Werewolves really are fighting out there."

He nodded. "I told you, two local gangs. You must have heard of them."

"Of course I have but I thought they were just names. Not the real thing." Especially since Vampires and Werewolves didn't exist but then, of course, neither did Pixies and she was talking to one. Or so he claimed. "So, Pixies referee the fights?" Humour him. Only thing to do.

"Adjudicate. We make sure they stay within the permitted area and count the dead and injured when it's over."

"There's a bunch of you."

He nodded. "Twelve to cover the entire building. We're not all cops. Just Pixies."

Honestly. He really expected her to believe all this. "I thought Pixies had pointed ears?" His were smooth and pink with ear lobes close to his head.

"That's Fairies!" he said. Then he muttered, "Mundanes!" as he shook his head.

"Sorry," Ella replied, "my mistake. How am I supposed to know the difference?" He ignored that. Probably just as well. She could guess what his one-word answer would be.

Pity really that he was off his rocker. In better circumstances, she might have suggested they go out for coffee. Now she was beginning to wonder if she'd live long enough to have another cup.

A cacophony of yells and screams from the gym brought him to his feet. Faster than her eyes could follow, he was standing back to the door and mouthing, "Be quiet" at her.

She was tempted to yell for help, but the screams that gave new meaning to blood-curdling didn't inspire any hope of rescue. There was a growl. Definitely animal. More shrieks and thuds. And gunshots as a spray of bullets hit a wall.

"No guns in the gym!" a deep voice thundered. "Penalty! Penalty!" Followed by an awful scream.

Good rule that. It followed school board policy. The scream went on and on until it faded to a whimpering gurgle. "What did they do to him?" she asked.

"By the sound of things, they cut off a vampire's arm as a penalty."

"Sheesh!"

"Don't worry. It'll grow back. They always do."

She was going insane. Had to be. Because he was beginning to make sense.

The door burst open and Officer Willard lurched forwards, then leaped out of the way and spun to face them.

Ella decided to be as unobtrusive as possible.

It didn't work,

Half a dozen definitely unfriendly faces focused on her. "She's Mundane," a pale one said. Yup, fangs. He hadn't been kidding about vampires.

"She's ours! Rightful target!" another, even nastier, one said. The gleam in his eye matched the diamond in his fang.

She couldn't move anyway. She was already flat against the instrument cases. Besides, she'd never in her life backed down in front of a student. On the other hand, Washington High's worst thugs were fluffy kittens compared to this lot.

Of course if Officer Willard were right, some of these creatures were their worst thugs. She glared but sensed it was a total waste of effort. As a cluster they surged forwards, eyes glittering and fangs shining. There was even a hairy face among the mob. This was her reward for trying to get her paperwork in on time.

Officer Willard stood right in front of her. How the hell did he move like that? Of course, he was a Pixie.

"This Mundane is mine!"

Two

They backed off. A bit. Heck, at that tone she would have if she hadn't already moved as far from the door as she could.

"She's not yours," one of then said, sniffing the air. "She's not marked!"

"Yes! Fresh Mundane!" another said and stepped forwards. "Unmarked Mundane!"

Trails of cold sweat ran down Ella's back. She had to be dreaming. That was the only way it made sense. This mob was the stuff of nightmares after all. One pushed himself forwards and, dear heaven, he had a bloody stump at his shoulder. "I claim her as consolation."

"No!" They backed up again. But nowhere near far enough for comfort. "She is mine. If you hadn't blundered in like a lot of drunken Werewolves, she'd have been marked by now."

"You calling us Wolves?" one asked, sounding direly insulted.

"I'm saying you're acting like them. "Get out and don't bother me!"

They obeyed, with a variety of unfriendly snarls and hisses. Officer Willard, slammed the door behind them and, for good measure, blocked it with a cabinet. A large metal cabinet, which no doubt was filled with stacks of sheet music and weighed half a ton. Then brushed his hands together and turned to her. "They won't be back but we'll have to make good on my claim if you're to walk out of here alive."

Ella swallowed. Still stunned by his strength and way he'd routed those monsters. "They were Vampires?"

He nodded. "Nastier on the whole than the Wolves but Wolves tend to be tougher."

Information she could happily have lived without. "Hey!" He'd unbuckled his belt and set it, and all the bits clipped on to it, on an empty music stand. "What are you doing?"

"Taking my clothes off," he replied, as he lifted his foot and untied his shoe.

"Why?" Dumb question. There was only one reason she could think of why a man took off his clothes when alone with a woman. "Now, wait a minute."

He took off the other shoe and looked at her. "I'm sorry, but we don't have any time to waste if you're going to survive the night. The only way you'll get out of here alive is if I mark you as mine. Claim you. They won't bother you then. They wouldn't dare."

"I see." That was a lie if ever there was one.

"Look," he said, unbuttoning his shirt, "I know this isn't exactly what you want. Can't say I'm precisely thrilled about it myself, but it will keep you alive and my credibility with that lot hinges on you walking out of here with my spoor on you."

"That is the most original proposition I've ever received."

He actually chuckled. In better circumstances she might even have thought it a sexy laugh. Come to that any circumstances were better than this. "I'll work on it," he replied.

"You're serious, aren't you? You're not talking about a bit of hand holding and kissing."

He shook his head. "I'm afraid I have to fuck you."

"That's a new one. Never heard 'I have to fuck you to save your life' before. Forgive me if I'm not quite in the mood."

He crossed the four or five feet between them. "I can get you in the mood."

Assuming she wanted him to. Which she didn't. "There's no other way out of this?"

He cocked his head at the door towards the thuds and yells and screams the other side. It was far worse than before. Ella shut her eyes. Not with any great expectation of opening them and finding she was dreaming. She opened them; he was taking his arms out of his shirt.

"That's a bulletproof vest?" She'd never seen one before and really didn't care to see one right now, but she was just the weeniest bit curious. She swallowed as he smiled.

"Touch it. I won't bite."

It wasn't his bite that she was worried about. He took her hand and pressed her palm against his vest. The fabric was smooth under her fingers, but beneath the slick fabric was something harder, textured, not his skin. "Does it really stop bullets?"

He nodded. "Yes. Hurts like the dickens. The force knocks you over most times and you get one hell of a bruise, but yes, it stops them."

"It's awfully thin."

"That's the cover. Inside is the Kevlar. Let me show you"

Anything to delay and maybe talk herself out if this. He pulled down the zip and slipped his arms out. Underneath he wore a thin white T-shirt: a tight-fitting, chest-clinging, white T-shirt. He held out the vest to her. It was warm from his body, but the weight was a shock and she almost dropped it. "You wear it all the time you're on duty?" This was insane, he was stripping off, preparing to fuck her and they were discussing body armour.

He must have been thinking the same. He took the vest and tossed it aside, before putting his hands on her upper arms. He held her gently but there was no denying the strength in his fingers. Hell, she'd seen what he could move.

"Look," he said, his voice low, "I know this isn't what you want. Wasn't what I expected this evening either, but we don't have all night. I've got to get back out there and help keep order. I won't hurt you. I won't harm you and you're a hell of a lot better off in here with me than out there."

Given the continuing and escalating noise, to say nothing of the clear and outspoken threats a few minutes earlier, she wasn't about to argue that point.

"Damn it! All I did was nip into the building for five minutes."

"After Mr Bryce clearly requested no one linger in the building this evening."

Fair enough and she usually followed directives from the principal. "He said the floors were being waxed."

"That's what he was told to say."

Made sense, she supposed. He could hardly announce there was going to be bloodshed and mayhem. "So, no one knows what really happens here on these occasions?"

He gave a sigh. "Other than those who need to, no. Now, do you want me to take your clothes off or will you do it yourself?"

Her throat went dry. Bone dry. It hurt to swallow. He wasn't kidding. He was deadly serious. Wrong choice of adjective that. She shivered and looked into his deep blue eyes. She'd always rather liked Officer Willard. If she'd met him at a party she might well have gone home with him. She took a deep breath. "You know we could both lose our jobs if this ever comes out?"

Yes, his chuckle was sexy. "I sincerely doubt anyone in that lot outside will report us, and I won't tell a soul."

She had no alternative. "I'm not really in the mood."

"You will be," he promised, untucking his T-shirt and pulling it over his head.

Oh my! The tight fit of the cotton had implied a nice body underneath. It was stupendous, just enough muscle to ripple as he pulled off the shirt, then settle to lovely male curves as he tossed the garment aside. "Not too bad, is it?" he asked.

"No." Oh, what the heck? Here was a magnificent specimen of man offering to fuck her and save her life. She definitely had no desire (wrong word again) to be mauled and eaten by the vicious lot outside. What the dickens was she hesitating for? As he unzipped his pants, she took off her coat and kicked off her remaining shoe.

"Good." As she slipped of her jacket and started unbuttoning her blouse, he nodded with approval. Whether with approval over her acquiescence or admiration of her bra, she had no idea. Wasn't sure she wanted to know. At least he was personable, intelligent and clean. Best get this over and done with, insane as it was, and she'd go home for a stiff drink. Correction: several stiff drinks.

She took off her blouse, fumbled with the hook at the waist of her skirt and lowered the zip. Seemed she was wearing a lot more than he was. As she stepped out of her skirt, he was down to tightie whites that left virtually nothing to her imagination.

He crossed the room, giving her a good view of the tightest butt she'd ever tried to ignore, and came back, carrying a rolled-up gym mat over his shoulder.

Show-off.

"There," he said, as he pushed aside a stack of music stands and spread out the mat. "That'll be more comfortable than the floor." She was down to bra and panties now. Her fingers froze at a sudden piercing yell from the other side of the door. "Here, let me do that."

He reached behind her and unsnapped her bra with a flick of his fingers, tossed it aside, and covered her breasts with his long fingers. "I meant what I said," he told her. "I won't hurt you but I will fuck you hard until you climax under me. I'm marking you as mine." He leaned to whisper in her ear, his breath warm on her skin. "After I've had you, no one out there will ever dare touch you. Trust me." His lips came to the side of her neck and brushed against her skin. She let out a little gasp, as his hand slid down to her belly. "This is just the beginning. It's going to exceed your wildest imaginings, my dear Miss Carrack."

It already had. Just not quite in the way he intimated.

His hand traced soft circles on her belly as his lips brushed up the side of her neck and caressed her chin. Then they were on her mouth. His mouth pressed on hers, as one arm came around to support her shoulders. Her lips opened under his and the tip of his tongue touched hers. It was a gentle kiss, a sweet caress of lips and tongue that went on forever. His hand came up the back of her neck and held her head steady as his mouth played hers.

Despite her worry, hesitation and uncertainty, she responded, let out a little sigh and relaxed into his embrace as he kissed on, sliding his mouth off hers to kiss her chin, her cheeks, her eyelids and then return to tease her lips again.

Eyes shut, she blocked out the place, the time and the circumstances and gave herself over to the sweet seduction of his kisses.

He broke the embrace, lifting his mouth gently off hers. "Not so bad, was it?"

She smiled. Talking seemed an awful lot of effort.

He picked her up in his arms and carried her over to the gym mat. "You know," he said, as he lay her down on her back, "when Pixies mate we prefer out of doors, under a moonlight sky."

"Not in the band storeroom on a sweaty old gym mat left over from the last wrestling match?"

"No," he replied, stroking her breast, "but we do like a challenge."

One glance up and she decided it wouldn't be much of a challenge. Mind you, he was male and she was as good as naked, a fine upstanding erection was pretty much a given.

He lay down beside her, still wearing his tightie whites, but that was fine with her. Even if they didn't hide anything, he was still partially, or more accurately, sparsely clothed. A good thing too. She was still not quite convinced of the necessity of all-out, full-powered sex. But lying here, with his arms around her and his lips in her hair, beat facing the ravening mob in the gym.

He stroked up across her belly and gently caressed her breasts before leaning over and taking a nipple in his mouth.

If nothing else about this evening proved the world had shifted on her, this did. Never in her entire life had pure pleasure coursed through her veins in such a wild torrent.

She threw back her head, let out a long, slow groan and hoped he'd never stop.

She almost got her wish.

Seemed for an eternity that he kissed one nipple then the other as he stroked and caressed every inch of her body. At some point her panties went AWOL. She really didn't need them anyway.

Sensation built and peaked until it shot through her in wild, cascading ripples. It wasn't really possible to climax from kissing, was it? Apparently it was.

"Are you really a Pixie?" she asked, after she got her breath back and her heart slowed to somewhere near normal.

He leaned over her, grinning. "You doubt it?"

"I've not had much experience of Pixies to measure by."

"You don't need any," he replied, easing down her body and settling between her legs.

The next few minutes, hours, whatever, rather faded into a blur of gasping joy and more orgasms than even a maths teacher could count.

She actually passed out and came to, as a limp mass of humanity, looking up at him smiling above her.

"Wow!" Not very eloquent but he seemed quite satisfied. Except, he hadn't come. Unless it was after she'd passed out. One glance below the belt convinced her he hadn't. "What about you?" Fair was fair after all. He'd saved her from the ravening hordes, he deserved his turn.

He shook his head. "I don't think you're ready for that yet, Miss Carrack. Besides, I need to get you out of here."

Three

"Through there." She looked at the door where the hordes still ravened as ferociously as ever.

"Won't be a problem. Not now. They'll smell me on you and not one of them would dare."

"What really is going on there?"

"I told you: a turf war. The Vampires and the Werewolves never did get along and now they're in the close confines of the city, it's worse than ever. So we let them fight it out every couple of months. Helps defuse tensions all around."

"Who are 'we'?"

"I can't tell you that. It's not allowed."

But carnage in the school gym and wild sex in the storage room was. "Why the heck do they live here if they can't stand each other?"

"Come to that, why do you live here? There aren't many nice, middle-class families left in this neighbourhood these days."

That was the truth. "I grew up here. Until Dad remarried and we all moved to Virginia when he got a new job. After college, I moved back to help take care of my grandfather. I got a job here and, when he died, I inherited his house and stayed. I've a nice house on a rough street in a tough neighbourhood, but I'm known by a lot of people. No one has ever bothered me until tonight." A death threat from a stoned parent didn't really count.

"Better get dressed."

He was gentleman enough to help her. If "gentleman" was the precise term for a Pixie. He'd enjoyed it as much as she did. She should have been shocked, indignant, embarrassed. Instead she was . . . sated. "Who really organizes these turf wars?"

"Never give up do you?" Didn't need brilliance on her part to pick up his impatience. Well damn, if she'd risked her life, might be nice to know exactly why it had been in danger.

"I'm a nosy old teacher lady."

He put his arm around her and brushed the inside of his arm against hers. "We do. The Pixies. We're the peacekeepers around here. Ever wondered that for a run-down neighbourhood we have no street-corner drug dealers and the crime rate is pretty low?"

"Low" wasn't the adjective she'd have used, but it was nowhere near as bad as Moss Side or Hallowhill. "Not really."

"Don't think too much about it," he said, pulling away. Her arm stung as he brushed hers but eased off as she gave it a rub. Must have caught on his watch band.

"All set?"

"I'm still missing a shoe and a set of maths tests." If only she'd graded them last night. Of course then she'd never have come back tonight and would have missed the best sex of her life.

"I'll find them," he promised. "Let's get going."

The din amplified when he opened the door. There was blood on the floor. And the walls. A body missing both legs crawled towards them, and at least ten or eleven furry things were leaping and snarling at the pale ones that she guessed had to be the Vamps.

The entire lot stopped, froze and looked in their direction as he took her hand in his and raised her arm as they walked forwards.

This was many times worse than talking Billy Weston into handing over his butterfly knife.

"He's marked her," the one on the floor said, looking up at them.

The mob moved back, every single one of them, leaving a wide passage to the main door. She walked out, none too happy to have that lot at her back but if Officer Willard wasn't worried, she'd follow his lead.

Outside, in the now pitch dark that seemed to give him no problem, he found her tests scattered behind the dumpster. No luck on her other shoe but if that was her only loss of the evening, she'd not complain.

He walked her to her car and insisted on riding home with her. Parting with an absurdly formal, "Goodnight, Miss Carrack," and a handshake, of all things.

A handshake after what had gone between them was ridiculous, and probably the ultimate in smarts.

The next morning, she might have managed to pass the whole incident off as a wild dream. Apart from feeling incredibly relaxed – ridiculous after the horrors of the night, but there was no denying he'd given her one grandmother of an orgasm to say nothing of the extras, and she couldn't ignore the splatters of blood on a couple of the crumpled test papers. As she stood under the shower, she noticed an odd blue mark on the inside of her left forearm. A bruise? After last night, a pale bruise was hardly surprising. She must have knocked it, flailing her arms about during one of her many orgasms.

She dressed, grabbed her usual coffee and bowl of granola and realized she'd have to face Officer Willard at some point in the next seven hours.

She was tempted to call in sick. Then the thought flashed through her mind that she ought to wonder about the state of the building, but that wasn't her responsibility. Although it might make an interesting topic of conversation in the teachers' lounge.

The building looked the same as ever. Mr Paget, the custodian, was muttering about a toilet roll jammed in the second-floor boys' bathroom. Seemed any damage to the building was a secondary concern. Peter Brougham, the wrestling coach, was fussing down the office phone, seemingly far too het up about a wrestling match against Central High to be bothered by blood and guts on the gym floor.

Interesting. The Pixies really must have cleaned it all up and that was too much to worry about faced with a line for the copier and a message to call a particularly irritating parent ASAP.

Ella was tempted to go down to the gym and peep but, on reflection, decided it would be some time before she'd willingly go down the hallway to the gym. She encountered Officer Willard in the office, but got away with a smile and exchanged "good mornings".

But he caught up with her later. Didn't take much effort to check her schedule and figure out her planning period. She'd nipped out to the wide ledge that overlooked the cafeteria roof. In days past, it had been a gathering point for smokers, but since no one smoked in school any more, it was usually empty apart from a couple of rusty lawn chairs. She often popped out there for a few minutes of peace and quiet. Seemed he knew that and was waiting for her.

She could have backed out and left him leaning against the parapet, but that seemed churlish after he'd protected her from dismemberment and given her the best sex she'd ever known. Besides, she didn't want to leave. A wildness came over her and all she wanted was him.

As Ella met his eyes, he smiled. For a fleeting second she wondered if he would kiss in daylight as well as he did in the gloom of the storage room. A few seconds later, she was finding out for herself.

She crossed the few yards that separated them and threw herself at him, wrapping arms around him and pressing her mouth to his. She was beyond reason. Just as well. Reason would have held her back. Wild need and longing propelled her forwards.

Not that he needed a second urging. She was surrounded by him, enveloped in his arms and the heat of his body and as good as lost in the power of his kiss. For a second, the thought flashed through her mind that this was not professional behaviour, neither was last night come to that, and here she was lip to lip while she as good as plastered her body against his.

Not that he was fighting to get away. His arms wrapped around her, pulling her to him, as he backed her against the wall. His mouth was on hers, hard and hot and wondrous. His tongue caressed hers, his lips pressing hard as he enthusiastically stroked her hair, and his other hand was inside her blouse.

As she feverishly kissed back, reaching her tongue to curl against his, his knee came between her thighs and she spread her legs to rub against him.

Just rubbing was nowhere near enough. A wildness invaded her brain, engulfed her reason and completely eradicated common sense. With a deep moan, she held on to his thigh with hers and rode him. Her skirt shifted up and all she had between her clit and him was a thin pair of panties. Realizing her need, he pressed his thigh closer to her core and joined in the rhythm.

Insanity wasn't the word, but she didn't care. She needed him, lusted for him and ached for release.

It didn't take her long. Passion and sensation built as her blood thrummed in her ears and her body sang with pleasure. Nothing mattered but his arms supporting her and his leg between hers. She was barely conscious of her cries. His hand was on her breast and the wildness of skin on skin drove her higher. As his fingers found her nipple, she rode him harder and faster until her body burst into climax and she collapsed with a great groan.

His arms held her steady as she trembled against him.

"Are you OK?" he asked.

OK? She had to laugh. She doubted she could stand, her heart was racing and she suspected her blood pressure was near stroke level. "No! I'm way far from OK but it was incredible!"

He smiled at her, his blue eyes crinkling at the corners. "I agree," he said and dropped a kiss on her forehead. His lips, or maybe it was her skin, were so warm the touch seemed to burn into her brain.

Not that her brain responded very much. Thinking seemed too much effort, even speaking felt like forced labour, she just leaned into him and listened to the racing of his heart as he held her close.

She shut her eyes, to better absorb the scent of his heated shin and the sheer and utter maleness of him.

The bell rang.

Shit!

He looked as stunned as she felt. Shock hit her like a blow in the gut. "Oh, my God! We could get fired!" And that was just for starters.

He shook his head. "We won't."

Nuts to believe him but she did. And now she had a class to teach. "I have to go!" Not that she made any attempt to. "It'll be chaos if I'm not there." Even if her prime rabble-rousers were home growing back lost limbs.

"Yes," he said. "I find you incredible, Miss Carrack."

All very nice to get compliments on top of great sex but she had to go back to her classroom and, somehow, pretend this had never happened. And yesterday evening. Some hope.

She had to. She'd forget all of this. Except the mark on her arm. "One thing." She disentangled herself from his embrace to give enough distance to pull up her sleeve and hold out her arm. "What's this mark?"

His eyes widened. "You can see that?"

"Of course I can. It's not tender like a bruise. I don't feel it at all but it won't wash off." She went to move, after all she didn't have all morning. Just five minutes before the next bell.

"You shouldn't be able to see that." He looked up at her "What are you?"

"You know that. I'm the geometry and remedial maths teacher and what the heck is it?"

Leigh ran his hand through his hair as he shook his head. "I marked you last night. Remember?" As if she was likely to forget. He held her arm. "Touch exactly where you see it?"

His thumb covered part of it, so she nudged his hand lower and traced the mark. If anything he went even paler. "You really can see it but that's not supposed to happen."

She didn't have time to argue the point right now. "I have to go."
And start acting like a sane and rational professional.

"Yes," he agreed, sounding anything but happy. "I need to find out what you are. We have to talk. After school."

"Why?" Damn! She sounded like a petulant teenage.

"This is why." He stroked the mark on her arm. "This afternoon. Right after school."

No way was she walking out of the building with him, observed by half the population. "Make it later. I have a couple of errands to run."

"I'll be at your house at six."

Maybe she'd stay at the mall until closing. "Have to go."

She ran.

And, most surprisingly, made it through the day. She admitted, at least to herself, to being unnecessarily sharp with several students but they'd survive.

She only hoped she would. At least time spent controlling, and attempting to instruct, obstreperous teenagers was time not spent horrified about her behaviour. In the past twenty-four hours she'd turned into a ravening sex maniac and she'd been stupid enough to agree to meet her partner in unbridled sex after school. And damn, double damn, she lusted after him.

She was losing it. Big time.

Four

Ella hadn't lied about errands but a trip to the library, the bank and the dry cleaner's did nothing to cool her insane ardour.

At ten minutes to six, Ella was sitting on her front steps waiting for him. Not from neediness but because she was dead scared if she actually let him in the house, she'd be ripping his clothes off, and didn't think she could survive three sessions of wild Pixie sex in twenty-four hours.

Damn!

He was walking up the street, looking ten times sexier in blue jeans and a black turtleneck than even his cop uniform with all the creaking bits of leather.

She stood and watched. Wild heat and need swirled in her mind and she took a deep, calming breath. That proved useless. Whatever was between them was definitely not normal man–woman sexual attraction.

"Ella?" He stopped a good six feet away and smiled.

"Hi."

"Look," he said, taking a couple of steps closer, "I found out something that rather explains things. Want to talk here or should we go out and get a bite to eat?"

Out was the far, far better idea. "I'm not really hungry but a cup of coffee would be good." And what the heck had he "found out"?

Only one way to learn.

Ella walked down the three steps to street level and got into step beside him. "What did you learn?"

He smiled. Damn, it did wonderful things to his entire face. "You said you'd lived here as a small child and came back to take care of your grandfather. So, curious, I took the liberty of checking out your personal file."

"I thought they were confidential."

Seemed he ignored that. "I learned your first name."

Big deal. "Hardly a state secret. It's Margot. After my mother and grandmother."

He nodded. "It made everything clear."

"Really?"

Damn, even his chuckle was sexy. "If you give me a chance, I'll explain. Tell me this: your grandparents, maybe great-grandparents came from France? North-west France to be precise: Brittany?"

"Yes." Whatever the heck that had to do with anything.

He let out an exasperated sound and shook his head. "Didn't your mother or grandmother teach you anything?"

"My grandmother died before I was born. My mother when I was two. Dad remarried and we moved away. We didn't have much contact with my grandfather, apart from phone calls and letters, until I came up here for college, by then Grandpa had a stroke and I used to come at weekends to help out. I got a job here and, when he died, he left me the house." She could have sold the house or let it and moved away. But she hadn't.

He was silent for a good two minutes but the crease between his blue eyes suggested he was thinking hard. "You stayed. Drawn there. Feeling you belonged?"

"Because this school system pays a bonus to maths and science grads." And some of the rest. Maybe.

"You were the eldest girl in your family, weren't you?"

"The only one, as it happens." What the blazing Hades did that have to do with anything?

Obviously it made sense to him. "You're a true Margot."

"Yes, I was named after my maternal grandmother."

"That explains it. Sort of." He let out an impatient "tsk". "You're a Margot. A type of Fairy." He fisted his hand up in the air and grinned. "That's it! We didn't leave a gap in the magic last night. And you and I are not a pair of raving sex maniacs. But that's beside the point now." Not to her it wasn't. "You got through the magic because you have Margot blood. The mark on your arm is invisible to Mundanes but any Other can see it and would know you were not to be harmed or bothered."

"That's all cleared up then. So I'll pop back home and get on with my grading."

His hand closed on hers. "Not so fast, Ella. We've a lot to talk about."

"If it's just talking fine, but seems we don't get around to talking that much."

"Yes, that had me worried too."

"Was it that bad?" Where the hell had that come from?

"Not in the least, but the intensity of what happens to me when you're around threw me for a loop. Now I know it's magic not an insane libido . . ."

"Magic?"

"Yes, magic, Ella. Don't you come over all mathematical and logical and tell me you don't believe in magic. You have Margot blood in you, stands to reason you have magic, just as surely as you saw Werewolves and Vampires last night."

"And a Pixie."

"Right. Don't forget the Pixie."

As if she could.

Damn.

"Look," he went on, "I can help you some, but what I know is Pixie magic."

"What's Pixie magic for?" Was she really asking that?

"Mostly for hiding in the woods or around street corners and spinning unobtrusive spells." Unobtrusive? Him? "Comes in handy in police work."

"So you have Pixie magic. Lucky you. Doesn't mean I have any."

He took hold of her arm and turned it so the grey mark was uppermost. "I told you, only magic users and some Others could see that. You're not a Vamp or a Shifter. You're a Margot and you have magic. Heck, I've seen it myself."

"You have? Give me a break." This was getting all around too much.

"You can quell a class of reprobates with a look. Don't tell me that's not magic; you instinctively channel it when needed. Like getting through our spell last night. We hired the most expensive wizard in the city and you penetrated his barrier."

Something coiled inside her fear? Uncertainty? The sort of panic you feel watching a car running downhill without a driver. Her life was changing at full tilt and she had no idea how to stop it. "OK, maybe I do have magic, but what now? I get to go and start grading papers?"

"Later. You need to learn about your powers and how to control them. But first there's someone you need to meet."

"And where are we going?"

"Concetta's."

"Concetta's!" It was a sleazy dive a few blocks from her house. Sleazy was too polite. It was a den for the local thugs. "You really know how to impress a girl."

"It's where we, the Others, meet. We use magic to keep the Mundanes away."

"It works!"

She never went near Concetta's dive. Always took the round-about route by the main road if she wanted to go that way, and now she was heading for it and walking in the freaking door as Leigh held it open.

It was pretty much what she'd expected. Dark in the corners, rows of booths around two walls and a few Formica-topped tables in the middle of the room and a bar in one corner.

A tall, dark-haired woman came towards them. She was wearing red leather pants and a black sequined top. Stunning was one word for it. Cheap and nasty were others.

"Leigh," the woman said nodding at Ella, "what's this?"

"This is a friend of mine, Miss Carrack, from the school."

"I know who she is," the woman replied. "I asked what she was."

"She's a Margot."

"Really?" Sounded more interested that sceptical. "Can it talk?"

"I most certainly can," Ella replied.

"So, you're a Margot? We used to have bunch of them around here, fifty, sixty years back. Where did you come from?"

"I've lived here for years." How could this woman remember that far back? She didn't look that old. Cheap and tarty, yes, but she couldn't be much older than Ella was.

"Kept under that radar, did you? Interesting."

"We came in to see Mère Aurelia," Leigh said.

The woman laughed. "Of course you did."

Leigh nodded to the teenager behind the bar – could that child possibly be old enough to even be in a bar?) – and, with a hand in the small of her back, steered Ella to one of the booths, already occupied by an old woman. Correction: a very, very, old woman.

Ella eased into the seat and Leigh slipped in beside her. Took all she had not to stare at the wrinkled creature sitting across the table.

"This is she?" the old woman asked, looking at Leigh.

"Yes," he replied and Ella was stared at so hard the hair rose on the back of her neck. It wasn't so much that the old woman was looking at her or even through her, it felt as if she were taking the layers off to see into Ella's bones. "This is Margot Eleanor Carrack. Ella, this is Mère Aurelia."

Shaking hands didn't seem to part of the introduction here so Ella nodded. "Good to meet you." At least she hoped she was.

"Where did you find her?"

It would be nice to be treated as more than an interesting specimen, but that didn't seem about to happen so Ella sat and watched Mère Aurelia size her up. Then the young creature from behind the bar walked up. At close quarters it was easier to see the tattoos on her neck and shoulders. The purple leather bustier showed them off to advantage. "She's not been here before. What is she?" she asked Leigh.

"She's with me," he replied.

"I can see that! I asked what she was."

"Don't be cheeky, Charlotte," the old one said, or rather snapped. "She's at my table, that's all you need to know. Bring them both a Calvados!"

Calvados was what her grandfather used to drink, ordering a couple of bottles from France each Christmas. "A glass of ice water would be good too," Ella added. Dry was not the word for how her mouth felt, under all this scrutiny.

Charlotte (incredible name for the creature) walked away without a word and returned in moments with three shot glasses of golden liquid and a glass of ice water.

Mère Aurelia raised her glass. "*Santé*," she said and downed the lot.

Ella stared at her. No doubt gaped, but managed to lift her glass and sip. She knew enough not to down it in one gulp. The old woman must have a throat made of cast iron to chug it down like that.

Her wrinkled eyes fixed on Ella. "You look like your grandmother."

Good thing she'd only taken a sip. Calvados down the nose had to sting like blazes. Ella swallowed. "You knew her?"

Mère Aurelia nodded. "Oh, yes, I well remember when she married your grandfather. A good enough man for a Mundane but it wasn't to her benefit."

Having loved her grandfather intensely, that last comment caught Ella on the raw. "Oh? And how was that? My grandfather was a very kind and loving man. He loved Grandma and missed her until the day he died." Let her put that in her pipe and smoke it.

Seemed Mère Aurelia wasn't used to being snapped at. She raised a grey eyebrow and pursed her mouth. Leigh tensed; Ella could feel his anxiety. So, she'd contravened some local taboo. Tough titties.

"You've found a sharp one here, young Leigh," Mère Aurelia said after a long, pregnant silence. She didn't sound too put out as she went on, talking directly to Ella. "If one of the fey marries and lives with a human it reduces power and shortens life to mortal span. In Marie's case, her lifespan was less even than most humans."

"She was run over by a drunk driver."

Mère Aurelia nodded. "So I heard."

Ella wanted to ask what else she'd heard or knew about the family but Mère Aurelia reached across the table, her hand open palm uppermost holding a disc of dark metal. "Touch my hand," she said. "Let me judge your power."

None to sure she had any power, other than the ability to quell a roomful of potential reprobates at a glare, Ella was on the verge of pooh-poohing the whole thing, but she glanced at Leigh and his clear blue eyes and half-smile to say nothing of his encouraging nod, had her obeying.

She rested her palm on Mère Aurelia's.

Sensing the younger woman's reluctance, Aurelia waited, noted the glance that passed between her and young Leigh and as Ella's palm brushed hers, closed her eyes.

Unused to being called, the power came slowly, then burst in a rush. Dear mother, the chit had no notion of her strength. Her grandmother, Marie, had been strong, before she took a human as consort, but this girl . . . Aurelia met her eyes and smiled.

Ella didn't smile back. Just stared, eyes wide with anxiety. Tasting power for the first time was frightening, particularly when you'd spent thirty-odd years unaware of what coiled inside. Aurelia shook her head. What a tragedy that Marie died before she had a chance to train Ella's powers. Still wasn't too late. Seemed young Leigh Willard was prepared to do his bit for the cause. He'd do. Even if he was a Pixie.

Aurelia drew her hand back, slipping the now heated disc inside her skirt pocket.

Yes, the girl would be worth a bit of trouble. A teacher, Leigh had said. Well, that wasn't her fault and one more up at the school when needed was a blessing.

"Yes!" Aurelia said aloud. "You're Marie Curnow's offspring. No doubt about it." She looked at Leigh and smiled. "You know what you need to do." She stood. "Pixies don't hang back."

Crossing to the door she turned to Charlotte behind the bar. "Feed them. They both need it." And opened the door and walked out into the cool of the night.

Ella couldn't help staring. "What was all that about and who was she?" She had about a dozen questions but that was enough to start. She rather suspected even that was more than she could process right now and whatever that metal thing had been in Mère Aurelia's hand, it was worse than the joke handshake gizmos so beloved by certain students. Her arm still tingled like a massive case of pins and needles.

"Mère Aurelia," Leigh replied. "We call her the Unan, the one. She's the oldest creature around here. A Margot like you and now she's recognized you, we can pretty much go ahead."

"Ahead with what?"

He was delayed in replying as Charlotte brought two bowls of soup. Looked like a rich tomato and smelled fantastic but it wasn't enough to make Ella forget her question.

"Ahead with what?" she repeated, once Charlotte of the purple bustier was beyond earshot.

He nodded over the spoon he held to his mouth. Swallowed and replied, "Making you known to everyone. Not just as someone I've marked and claimed but as an equal member of the community."

"And a teacher isn't?"

"Not this community. You're now part of a world the Mundanes don't recognize, acknowledge or believe in. And . . ." He paused, handed her the basket of bread, before taking a roll himself and breaking it in two. "You need to learn to harness the magic within."

"And how do you propose I do that?" Sheesh, she knew the answer, it was written all over his face.

"With me, my dear Miss Carrack. Don't deny it. You want me as much as I want you. This wasn't what I envisioned last night, but we forged a bond by magic and sex."

"Taking a lot for granted, aren't you?

"Tell me," he asked, "could you really walk away from me and never want me again?"

It was on the tip of her tongue to tell him "yes" and do just that to prove the point, but she'd never been one to tell lies. "I find this whole nonsense rather terrifying."

"Terrifying, yes, but nonsense it isn't and I believe, my dear Ella, together we'll forge a power that satisfies us both and changes the course of both our lives."

She took another taste of soup as she mulled over his proposal. It was insane, incredible and beyond reason, but she couldn't ignore the heat and desire coursing through her veins.

It should be impossible, but the old Unan was right – what surged between Leigh and her was magical.

She looked him in the eyes, smiled. 'You said last night, I wasn't ready for full-on sex with a Pixie. Is that likely to change any time soon?"

"Oh, yes," he replied. "It most certainly will."

Good.

All the Time in the World

Shiloh Walker

Boston – 1915

He had worked with beautiful women before.

He had slept with beautiful women before.

He had loved beautiful women before.

He had known beautiful women before.

The woman before him now wasn't just beautiful – although she was lovely, very, very lovely. At least, she seemed so to him. Her skin was as pale as milk, her eyes clear and soft blue, and her hair silky and dark brown.

Many women he had worked with had a frail look to them, although frail they were not. Frailty had no place in the lives they had chosen.

Gretel did not look frail. She had a woman's body . . . a *strong* woman's body. She was petite in stature, the top of her head barely reaching his chin, but she had generous curves and an undeniable strength to her body.

But there were shadows in her eyes. Those shadows and a vulnerability to touch something deep inside him.

Rip wasn't entirely sure he cared for it.

Do the job, he told himself. Once it was done, he could leave Boston, and Gretel, behind.

But it was never as easy as that.

If she did not know better, Greta would think the universe, God, mankind and her friends conspired against her.

It should have been a simple assignment – the two of them were to retrieve a book from this warehouse on the docks. Retrieve the book, destroy it. The book's owner had already been dealt with.

It should have been simple.

But the life of a guardian angel was rarely simple – Greta should have known that by now. Nothing in her life had been simple . . . and she'd lived a very, very long life.

Of course, if she had wanted simple, she never should have accepted the choice to become a Grimm. One of God's guardian angels, a select band of warrior-bred guardian angels, named the Grimm by one of their leaders – a man with a strange, rather macabre sense of humour.

Born on the outskirts of the Black Forest in Germany some three hundred years before, she'd lived through a nightmarish childhood, only to be saved when she was about to give up hope. Saved, it would seem, by a guardian angel.

A few short years later, she had died a rather painful and unexpected death. As her soul was slipping away, she was offered a chance. A choice of her own – she could move on, or she could return, this time a guardian angel, herself.

Simple . . . if simple was what she sought, then she should have just passed on to the hereafter all those years ago.

Inwardly she chastised herself. She should have known this job wouldn't be simple, should have known she wouldn't get away from *him* so easily.

Him. A fellow Grimm by the name of Rip. An odd name, that, and, like her, he had a story of his own. How much of the "tale" behind his name was truth, how much was fiction, she didn't know.

What she did know was that the man disturbed her on a very basic level.

This assignment was proving anything but simple – they'd had not just one demon-possessed to deal with, but four. Now that those four were dealt with, the warehouse was burning around them and Rip was injured.

Greta had to figure out how to get her companion out of there before the two of them died in the fire. They might not be easy to kill, but Rip was bleeding out, too weak to move and if she didn't get them out soon, the roof might collapse.

The heat was intense, scalding her skin, though the flames weren't close enough to reach them. *Yet.* Smoke stung her eyes and her altered body had already slowed her breathing – she didn't need oxygen the way she had when she was mortal, so the smoke alone wouldn't present the danger.

But the flames . . . she was rather certain a fire *could* kill them.

The air was thick with smoke, ash and sulphur. Death, too. Mustn't forget the stink of death.

The man with her lay still and silent, despite the pain she knew he must feel. His eyes, dark and brooding, stared into hers. "Get the hell out of here, Gretel. Now. The ceiling is going to collapse."

His blood slicked her hands as she pressed them against the gaping wound on his side. "I'm not leaving you here and it's not like you can walk out of here alone. I'll thank you not to call me *Gretel*, Rip. The name is *Greta*."

She hadn't gone by that name for more than three hundred years.

Gretel . . . to some, the name evoked memories of breadcrumbs, witches, gingerbread houses. But for her, it brought nothing but dark, painful memories. They tried to rise up, tried to swamp her, as they always did in times of despair.

She battled them back. She had no time for them now. The scent of blood, hot and metallic, filled her head. He was losing too much blood, and healing far too slowly.

"Fool woman. Are you insane?" Rip reached up and shoved at her shoulder. It was a sign of his weakened state that he couldn't budge her. "Get out of here."

"And leave you to burn to death? I think not."

"I will not burn to death," he said. "We can't burn to death."

"Are you so sure of that?" she asked, cocking a brow. She shook her head. "I don't want to test the theory. Besides, whether we heal or not – burns *hurt*. Come on now . . . if you want me out, I'll leave. But only if you're with me. I'm not leaving you here to roast."

Those dark brown eyes flashed. Then he sighed. "Fine. You'll have to help me up. I cannot walk out on my own."

She had already figured that much out on her own. It took some doing, getting him to his feet, but once they'd managed, she was just the right height to wedge her shoulder against his body, supporting his weight. They'd managed to make it exactly five steps when she heard an ominous crack.

"Oh no."

Spinning towards the nearest window, she braced Rip's weight with hers and lunged.

When she'd come into this new existence, it had come with some rather extraordinary abilities ... she didn't age, she never fell ill and she had the strength to lift a horse.

Too bad she couldn't truly fly. There were rumours that some of her kind could. It was a shame she wasn't one of them.

But she could pray. As she propelled herself and Rip through a glass window into the freezing waters of the Boston Harbor, she prayed very, very hard.

Rip's last clear memory was hurtling through the shattering glass, driven by Gretel's not insubstantial strength. There were vague memories of cold water, her soft voice and pain. A great deal of pain.

Now he dreamed. Time passed so strangely in dreams. Had he been asleep for days? Hours? Weeks ... ?

He knew what it was like to lose time, after all.

But even then, he hadn't been plagued by these strange dreams. Gretel was there. No ... not Gretel. Greta. She called herself Greta, even though he knew who she was. The name "Gretel" brought shadows to her eyes, shadows and pain. He would have to remember that. He hated to be responsible for the pain he saw in those eyes, even if it was just the pain of memory.

Pain – damn, it was everywhere, it seemed. It chased him, haunted him, surrounded him. In her eyes, nipped at his flesh even in these dreams. That pain was horrid, some of the worst he could remember feeling, disturbing his sleep.

The stasis sleep – a healing sleep. If the pain chased him even there, he must have been hurt badly. Likely, he'd be dead, if he were still mortal.

He wasn't though.

He'd live through this and, for now, he had Greta at his side, with a soft hand to stroke his brow when the pain became too great.

It lessened when she touched him.

Such a strange thing. When she touched down, he forgot the fiery pain of a slowly healing wound in his side. Another flickering fire replaced that pain ... the burning heat of hunger, but he was weak, so weak even that fire couldn't burn for long.

During the times when the pain faded to nothing but a dull ache, he fell into fitful dreams. Dreams of flying, dream of death, dreams of ash and smoke.

Greta ... find her. Need to find her. But the thick smoke blinded him, choked him, slowed him down. When he found her, it was too late. Those soft blue eyes stared lifelessly at him, her face frozen in a mask of death.

Sorry. I'm so sorry, Greta.

Such tormenting dreams. Greta rose from the floor and propped one hip on the bed. Leaning forwards, she rested a hand on Rip's shoulder. "It is just a dream," she said softly. "I am fine. I am safe. You are safe."

He seemed to settle for a minute, turning his face into her hand. She stroked his cheek and waited a moment. Then, carefully, she checked his wound.

The sleep had allowed him to heal, but it was still ugly. Had he still been human, he'd be dead.

But Grimms were harder to kill – almost impossible, really. Designed that way by the Lord Almighty. What good was an army of guardian angels if a few paltry, possessed mortals could take them down?

When she dragged him out of the harbour last night, the hole in his side was gaping and huge – she could have put her fist inside it. When one had been alive a few hundred years, a great deal of knowledge could be learned about the human body and she had put that knowledge to use as she cared for him through the night.

As morning drew near and still he slept, she began to worry. She spent the hours pacing the floor of the private room she had secured when she had arrived in Boston a few days earlier. She'd long ago learned the need to make sure she had place to go to ground, and fast. Now, tucked in the small, dark room, she wished she had something better. The narrow, simple bed suited her fine, but his longer, lanky body barely fitted on it. He should have a soft bed to rest while he healed. A soft bed, warm blankets, a hot meal.

As his dreams turned troubled, she soothed him and continued to worry. No, he hadn't lost enough blood to die and she imagined that could kill him. All animals needed their lifeblood. But he had lost a great deal of blood and then there was the plunge into the harbour . . .

She shuddered as she remembered the icy cold water as it closed around them. The swim to shore seemed to take years and Rip had lapsed into unconsciousness. She was strong, but even with supernatural strength, towing a man who outweighed her through the icy cold waters of the Boston Harbor wasn't easy.

As the sun began to creep over the horizon, she checked Rip's wound once more and breathed a sigh of relief. Finally, the wound was smoothing out, closing in on itself.

He sighed and shifted in his sleep, bringing one arm up over his head. His bicep bulged and Greta found herself staring at the firm, tense line. Her heart skipped a beat, then started dancing in her chest.

"Enough. He needs his rest," she admonished herself. Turning away, she rubbed at her chest, disturbed by the odd ache there. So he had a lovely body.

She had seen many men with lovely bodies.

But how many of them would have insisted that she run away and leave them, alone and bleeding, with a burning building about to collapse?

He did something to her, something she wasn't entirely comfortable with. It was a truth she had hidden from the last few days. While they worked, hiding was easy enough. And while he was injured, worry had kept her mind occupied. But now that he was healing, her mind tried to wander.

He did something to her. He made her feel things . . . made her want things.

You don't need those things. You have lived centuries without them. Life is easier without those complications.

Yes. Life was easier.

"So what if your bed is empty? So what if you are lonely?" she muttered to herself.

Although lonely did not describe it. How could it? Lonely was just a word. *Lonely* could not describe the ache that often lived inside her. It could not describe the emptiness, the need, the longing for more.

Turning away from him, she returned to her solitary station by the door. With her back braced against the door, she sank to the floor, used her body to bar the entrance. Propping her arms on her upraised knees, she closed her eyes. She needed sleep.

The small room she had managed to secure for them had but the one bed. Rip needed it far more than she did. Besides, she had slept in worse places.

Far worse.

When Rip woke, he was immediately aware of three things.

One, it was dim in the room, though not quite dark, so he assumed it was either early morning, just after dawn, or sometime around sunset.

Two, his side itched abominably, so he knew the wound he'd taken was healing – which would mean he had slept for quite some time. It had been a bad wound.

Three, he wasn't alone . . . he could sense Greta's presence, though he couldn't hear her, couldn't see her.

Slowly, he stretched, taking a quick survey of his body – everything seemed to be working as it should, although there was some tightness, some tenderness lingering in his abdomen. Touching it, he could feel the faint, rough ridge of scar tissue. In a matter of hours, even that would be gone.

Greta was sitting in front of the door, her back pressed snug against it, her dark head pillowed on her arms, sleeping soundly.

On the floor. "Damn it," he muttered, his voice all but soundless.

He climbed from the bed and glanced around the room. It wasn't familiar – basic and Spartan, nothing but a bed, a simple chest of drawers and a washbasin on a stand. The bed was narrow, hardly more than a cot. It wasn't what he would call spacious, but there would have been room for the two of them.

Enough room that she wouldn't have had to sleep on the floor.

Crossing the room, he crouched beside her. "Greta," he said softly, tapping her shoulder lightly.

"Hmm." She made a soft, questioning sound under her breath, turning her face towards his. But her eyes didn't open and the slow, steady rhythm of her breathing didn't change.

She slept the sleep of the exhausted.

Rip paused only long enough to check his reserves and then slipped his arms under her body, lifted her in his arms. She snuggled close, rubbing her cheek against his chest. It wasn't until he felt the brush of her silken, soft skin against his that he realized he wore no shirt. Or trousers. The only thing he wore was a leather cord around his neck that held the silver medallion all Grimms wore. It was a round disc, etched with upswept wings – their mark.

But beyond that medallion, he wore nothing. The medallion did nothing to preserve his modesty – thankfully, he had little of that.

He closed his eyes and stifled a groan as she turned her face against him, sighing in her sleep. Her lips brushed against his skin and, despite the lingering weakness and heavy exhaustion, Rip wished she were awake. Wished she would open her eyes and look at him . . . *really* look.

Look at him and see him, the way he had been looking at her from the first moment he had laid eyes on her four days ago.

He set his jaw and carried her to the bed, tucked her inside, drawing the covers around her softly rounded curves. That body of hers – he adored all those rich, round curves, the kind of curves that would fill a man's hands, cradle his body.

If you wish to get through the night with any semblance of sanity, *stop* thinking about her body, he told himself.

But that was easier said than done. Turning away from Greta, he prowled the room until he found his clothes and one swift glance told him why she had stripped them away. They were wet. Clean – he caught the faint scent of soap on them – but wet. It would be hours before they dried.

Normally, the temperature had little effect on him. But he was oddly cold. Dimly, he had some recollection of plunging into icy waters. The harbour, he thought. Greta had plunged them into the harbour. Cold could hardly kill him. But he was still human enough that he would crave warmth for a while.

Unwilling to wear the wet clothes, he ignored them in favour of searching for food.

Greta would have something somewhere, he knew.

And he was right. On the short, squat chest of drawers, he found cheese, crackers, fruit and dried meat. He didn't eat it all, though he was ravenous. If he knew she'd eaten, he would have eaten every last crumb.

He lingered by the washstand long enough to clean up, although the water and cloth were a poor substitute for a hot tub of water.

He felt a bit closer to normal when he returned to the bed, though exhaustion continued to drag at him. Tired. So tired, he ached. With his eyes heavy, he returned to the bed, sliding in between the blanket and the pitiful excuse of a sheet. Perhaps if he kept that between them it might help. Between the sheet and his own exhaustion, perhaps he could even forget that he was lying in bed with Greta, a woman he was coming to want as much as he wanted his next breath.

Actually, more. Breathing wasn't quite as necessary for the Grimm as it was for mortals.

Heat.

It surrounded her. Cradled her.

She sighed and shifted, unconsciously pressing closer. Her lips brushed against a bare chest and she smiled.

A dream . . .

It must be a dream, because when she was awake, she knew she'd never be this relaxed, this at ease with a man so close. The warmth of his body, the scent of him, the feel of him, everything about him combined to flood her senses and overwhelm her, leaving her loose and limp.

When his hand skimmed up her back, she arched against him and, to her delight, she found herself pressing against him in a new, altogether delightful way. Her legs parted, one on either side of his hips and now he pressed snug against the sensitive flesh between her thighs. The full, firm length of his cock twitched. She groaned and rubbed against him.

He swore, his voice low and rough.

The dreamlike state around her shattered.

Greta tensed, driving her hands down against the lumpy, miserably uncomfortable mattress and lifted up. Eyes wide, she stared down at Rip's face in shock. She lay atop him, draped over him like a living, breathing blanket, with his hands on her waist and the only thing between them her clothes and one very thin, worn sheet.

His dark, dark brown eyes stared up at hers, burning hot – so hot and hungry, it scalded her.

Blood rushed to her face.

Shuddering under the raging weight of her own hunger, she licked her lips, tasted him on her mouth.

Beneath the hunger, old fears surfaced.

Always the problem.

She had never been able to get this close to a man without those fears rising to haunt her. None of them she'd been with had interested her enough to try and work past them. No . . . not entirely true, there had been a few. But upon learning the truth of her life, they had withdrawn, and it came to the point that Greta stopped reaching out.

She stopped *wanting* to reach out. But Rip . . .

Her hands flexed on the hard, yet yielding muscles of his chest. Her voice rigid and stiff, she said, "I beg your pardon."

"I'm willing to beg for a lot more," Rip said quietly, watching her from under his lashes. His hands rested on her hips, holding her loosely, but there was nothing confining about the way he held her, nothing imprisoning.

Move, you idiot, she chastised herself.

But she couldn't. She felt frozen. And she didn't *want* to move.

Her mouth dry, she licked her lips. Rip closed his eyes and groaned. "Darling girl, if you do not want me to turn into a slobbering fool and do something we might both regret, you really need to move."

"And what if we didn't regret it?"

Her eyes widened. Oh, no. The words . . . had they really just come from *her*?

Rip studied her with a narrowed gaze. She couldn't read anything from him. Nothing . . . and she sure wished to. When he lifted a hand from her hip and reached up, tracing the line of her mouth with his finger, she held still. As he stroked lower, hooking the tip of his finger in the silver chain that held her medallion, her breath caught in her lungs.

"But wouldn't you regret it, darling girl?" he asked, his voice soft and low, a stroke of velvet against her senses. "Even now, you watch me with this strange mix of fear and nerves. You do not seem to know if you want to remain where you are, or run as fast as you can."

"If I really wanted to run, I would."

He tugged on the chain, drawing her closer. Greta swallowed and let him. Her bound breasts pressed against his chest and she was acutely aware of the fact that the only thing separating them was her clothing and the sheet twisted somewhere around his hips.

His eyes remained on hers as he kissed her – a gentle, questing kiss, light and soft.

Greta felt blood rush to her cheeks and her lashes fluttered low.

"No," he murmured, quietly. "Look at me. Let me see you. I ache for you. Every day I see you, I ache more."

She ached, as well. It was the first time she'd truly understood that desire could be a sweet, sweet ache and she wasn't sure she knew how to handle it.

Start with this . . . stop thinking. As his mouth returned to hers, she kept her eyes open, staring into the dark, seductive depths of his eyes.

It was more intimate, she realized . . . made it so much harder to hide. Harder to hide from how it made her feel, and harder to hide from what it did to him as well. No way to hide from it, and no way to pretend she was still just dreaming.

But she didn't close her eyes.

★   ★   ★

Rip traced the line of her lips with his tongue and teased her into opening for him. She undid him, left him shaken by how much he needed her. Left him stunned and reeling by how much more he needed from her. Already.

He had loved before. Had wanted. Had needed.

But he had never needed like this before. Never wanted like this. And although they had known each other but a few days, he thought perhaps he already loved her.

She would fear that. All of them were gifted with special skills when they crossed through Death's door and back into to become a Grimm. Rip's skills were those of a hunter. He knew weaknesses and strengths – all he ever needed was a simple look.

One simple look was all he needed to size up his opponent, and although Greta was no opponent, he saw her strengths, her weaknesses just as easily.

Greta would fear anything she saw as intimacy, so until she could trust him, he would keep his feelings quiet.

Until she trusted him . . . until she needed him as much as he was coming to need her.

Her body relaxed against his as he kissed her, reining in his body's needs. He combed his hand through her dark hair and, when his fingertips brushed against her nape, she shivered. Sensitive, he discovered. She was so sensitive . . . the lightest touch could make her gasp, and the merest brush could make her moan.

He trailed his fingers down the centre of her torso, watching for any sign of fear, any sign of trepidation. Slipping the button of her trousers free, he paused . . . waited.

Her lashes fluttered low as he eased the trousers lower. They only went so low before catching on her thighs. He could see just the faintest glimpse of dark, tight curls, the pale curve of her hips. "We could have a bit more fun if you'd lose the trousers, darling girl," he murmured.

"Hmm? Oh. Oh . . ." She blushed, catching her lip between her teeth.

When she rolled to her side and started to shimmy out of them, Rip caught her hands. "Let me," he murmured, gathering the fabric in his hands and drawing it down, staring at the rich, ivory curves being revealed to him.

So perfect. So lush and soft. Catching her hips, he tugged her to the edge of the mattress and knelt before her. He wanted, *needed*, to touch her, taste her, feel her, but every instinct he had warned him she wouldn't take well to his weight crushing down on her, not yet. Not just yet. Kneeling on the floor, he reached for the simple buttons on her shirt, freeing them one at a time. "You're a lovely woman," he murmured, staring at her face, only her face. Though he could see the full, soft curves of her breasts now, pressed flat and straining against the binding she'd used, he wanted to see her, watch her. Let her see *him*.

Easing her upright, he smoothed the shirt from her shoulders and dealt with the thick cloth she'd wrapped around herself to press her breasts flat. Greta might look soft and gentle, but she had the strength to deal with any man who might try to take advantage of the picture she presented.

Still, such things often interfered with their work, which was why many of the women chose to dress as men. Greta had been dressed in the guise of a waifish boy when he'd first seen her. The disguise hadn't fooled him.

As he unwrapped the cloth, he saw the faint red marks the bindings had left on her skin and he brushed his thumb over them, then dipped his head to follow that path with his lips. "Such soft, delicate skin," he murmured.

When he kissed the hard, pointed tip of one nipple, she cried out.

Lifting his head, he studied her face. Her cheeks were flushed, her eyes wide and startled . . . and hungry.

Smiling, he dipped his head and kissed that pretty rose peak again and this time he sucked it into his mouth, lightly scoring the flesh with his teeth. She whimpered and arched, squirming closer.

Resting one hand against her thigh, he skimmed it higher. Between her thighs, he found her hot, wet . . . ready, so ready. When he touched the tip of his finger to her slick, sensitive folds, she cried out again, his name a surprised cry on her lips. Slowly, he circled the stiffened peak of her clitoris once, twice . . . but as he started to make the third rotation, she bucked against him and, to his utter shock, she started to come.

Her head fell back, her eyes staring blindly at him, as she rocked and moved against him, desperately riding the hand between her thighs.

She moved with blind, determined hunger and, as she pushed against him, Rip let her overbalance him, falling back to the floor, with her cradled against him. Her knees settled on either side of his hips and she shivered as that position had his cock rubbing against her sensitive sex.

"Put me inside you," he whispered, staring up at her.

For a moment, she looked confused. Arching his hips against her, he said, "Put me inside you . . . please, Greta . . . you're killing me."

Her fingers closed around his cock, cool, soft, strong.

Rip groaned at the light touch and, unable to hold still, reached down and closed his fingers around hers, tightening her grip as he drove himself into her fist. "Fuck, that feels perfect . . . just . . . like . . . that . . ."

"Is that how I'm supposed to have you inside me?" Greta asked, giving him a look of wide-eyed innocence. Then she shifted and rubbed against him, reminding him of a softer, slicker embrace.

"No. But it feels pretty damn good," Rip muttered, reluctantly drawing his hand away.

She gave him a cheeky smile. "But mostly one-sided."

"Then put me inside you, and I'll see to it that both of us feel pretty damn good," he promised. He just hoped he could keep that promise and not explode like a boy the moment he had his cock seated inside her.

Pretty damn good, he had said.

Oh. Oh, dear. Not even close, Greta thought as she slowly sank down on him. He stretched her, filled her. It hurt . . . a sweet, sweet pain. With his hands on her hips, he held her steady as she took him inch by slow inch.

He flooded her.

Filled her.

In so many ways . . .

Tears stung her eyes and she swayed forwards, gasping as the movement drove him deeper, but she couldn't continue to watch him, couldn't continue to let him watch her. Too intimate. He saw too much.

Burying her face against his neck, she shuddered, twisted her hips to relieve the aching fullness inside her.

Rip turned his head and pressed his lips to her temple. "Shhh," he murmured.

She lifted her hips, tried to move and he swore, a half-strangled sound. Pain sliced through Greta and he growled. "Damn it, you're hurting yourself," he snarled. One strong, elegant hand closed over her hip, holding her still even as he slipped the other between them.

When he touched that tight, aching bundle of nerves, Greta

gasped. As he started to move, slowly, keeping his thrusts easy and shallow, she shuddered.

In under a minute, he had her keening out his name and he was wrong. Pretty damn good did not quite describe how he had made her feel.

Amazing did not even touch it.

Nothing could describe it . . .

He stole the breath from her lungs with a hot, deep kiss and, as she struggled to get it back, he rolled them over on to their sides, his body half-poised over hers. He stared down at her, his dark gaze commanding, devouring.

"Look at me . . ." he rasped. "I want to see you."

She stared at him.

A slow smile curled his lips. "So lovely," he muttered. Her lashes fluttered down and he reached up, tangled a hand in her hair. "No. Do not close your eyes . . . see me. Look at me."

Even as the orgasm broke open inside her, Greta forced her lids up, staring at him. *Look at you? See you?*

Moaning out his name, she shuddered under the force of the pleasure cascading through her body. So good . . . he felt so good inside her. Over her. Within her.

Just being *near* him felt good. Felt right.

If ever in her life there was a night she wished would last for ever, it was this one. This one night, she thought. She wanted to preserve it, for ever, locked in crystalline clarity.

And not just the way he touched her, not just the heat he made her feel, although that was something miraculous.

He made her laugh. He made her feel. He made her think.

For the first time in several centuries, Greta actually felt complete.

And in just that moment, she felt slightly drunk. But it had nothing to do with the wine that he had produced from somewhere. While she dozed, he had slipped out of the room and managed to find more food – a meal, rather than the light fare she had gotten, dishes and wine.

She hadn't had good wine in an age.

With her back braced against the wall, a glass of wine in her hand, she stared down at the top of his head and tried not to blush as he trailed a juicy tip of a peach around her navel.

"If I had known you were going to play with your food," she told him, "I wouldn't have let you have the last one."

"Oh, I plan on eating it." He glanced at her from under his lashes and nipped a bite from the peach. After he swallowed, he dipped his head and licked the juice from her belly. "I can't decide which tastes better: the peach or you."

"Oh, the peach. Wherever did you find peaches this time of year? I haven't had peaches in months."

"A bit of money in the right hand will land you almost anything." He shrugged. "Fortunately, I didn't lose mine when we had our swim through the harbour."

Greta found herself enraptured by the play of muscle under his skin. Then she blushed as his eyes caught hers. As his lips curled, she realized her mouth had gone dry. Lifting her wine to her lips, she took a sip.

He ate some of his peach and then he lowered his head.

Greta's hand shook and she almost spilled what remained of the wine. As he parted the flesh between her thighs, she set the glass down before it fell. He licked her, slowly, thoroughly, taking his time, as though he was trying to commit her taste to memory.

A strangled moan escaped her lips and she reached down, fisted her hands in his hair.

"It's not the peach," he muttered against her flesh. "It's you."

"Peach?"

He lifted his head and stared at her with glittering eyes. "You . . . Fuck me, Greta, the taste of you. It's addictive." He tossed what was left of the fruit to the floor and cupped her hips in his hands, lifting her up to his mouth.

She bit her lip to keep from crying out, barely muffling the cries as he licked and stroked and teased her. But just when she knew *one more touch* was all she needed, he stopped.

Whimpering and desperate, she opened her eyes to glare at him, but he was sitting crouched between her thighs. "I want you," he muttered, a look of such naked, raw hunger on his face.

The sound of his voice sent a shiver down her spine. Greta lifted her hand. "Then have me."

"For how long?" he rasped, settling his long, lean weight against her body, tucking the head of his cock against the wet, soft folds of her sex.

Watching him through slitted eyes, she tried to ignore the flutter in her heart. There was a world of worry, a world of needs in that question. No simple answers . . .

But instead of answering him, she lifted her face to his. "Take me, Rip. We have now, don't we? Isn't that all that matters?"

He cupped her chin and, as he claimed her body, his tongue claimed her mouth. Part of her wondered at it . . . that she could take the weight of him without panic, without fear.

But another part of her revelled in it. Revelled in him.

Bringing her legs up, she wrapped them around his hips and arched against him.

"Little witch," he muttered against her mouth.

She was trying to drive him mad, even as she was breaking his heart, Rip suspected. Time . . . that was all she needed. Just some time. All they'd had together was a few days.

He worked a hand between them and pressed one finger against the sensitive bundle of nerves, teasing it, stroking the sensitive flesh where she stretched so tight around him.

She was so slick, so hot and tight. The taste of her was still on his tongue, a tangy, salty musk that was uniquely Greta – uniquely her.

The muscles in her sheath contracted around him, milking him, pushing him dangerously close – no. No – gritting his teeth, he eased back, tried to slow down and she tightened her legs, opening her eyes to stare at him.

"You're driving me mad."

A smile bowed her lips upwards. "You started it," she replied, licking the soft, full curve of her lower lip.

Pushing up to his knees, he gripped her hips. "You really are a witch," he muttered.

That teasing smile on her lips spread and she brought up her hand to rest it on her belly. With a glint in her eyes, she trailed her fingers lower and lower, until she could stroke the rigid flesh of her clit.

It was wholly unexpected – the sight of that teasing smile on her lips, and the wicked play of her fingers over her pink, wet flesh. Swearing, Rip fell back over her and, with a growl, he slammed into her.

Greta cried out, her voice a mixture of delight and shock.

Freezing, he stared at down at her. "Did I hurt you?"

"If you don't move, and soon, I will hurt you," she said.

Hooking his arms under her shoulders, he braced her body and drove into her. This time, when she cried out, he caught it with his lips. Moments later, when she fell blindly into orgasm, he swallowed those cries as well.

*   *   *

Long moments passed as they struggled to level their breathing out. Greta lay on her side, staring into Rip's dark, velvety eyes and tried not to think about what she had just done.

Wicked, wicked girl, she thought. She wanted to be ashamed – or at least, part of her felt she *should* be.

But all she could feel was a vague sense of disbelief . . . and pleasure.

She had teased him. Deliberately. Without even fully realizing what she was doing.

And he had loved it.

"What are you thinking about?" he murmured, his voice low and husky.

Greta frowned, perplexed. "Shouldn't it be the woman to ask that?"

Rip chuckled. "Are there rules? You just lie there, looking confused, and so I wondered why."

With a sigh, she inched forwards and rested her head on his chest. She tried to tell herself it was because she was tired, and this was a rather comfortable spot to be. Nice and warm . . . she was so tired of being cold. It seemed she had been cold since they'd arrived in Boston.

But the truth was that she needed a respite from those insightful, knowing eyes.

"I just don't know what to make of all of this," she said quietly.

"Who says you need to know that right now? Can't you figure it out as we go along?"

As we go along . . . like this was some journey they might take together.

But Greta wasn't ready to take this sort of journey with any man.

Not even with Rip. Although in her heart, she wanted to. Wanted to try, at least.

He stroked her back and she snuggled closer against him. "There's time enough to figure all that out, isn't there?" he murmured, pressing his lips to her temple.

Look at me, he said. *See me.*

Who says you need to know that right now? Can't you figure it out as we go along?

. . . time enough to figure all that out . . .

Greta lay in his arms, brooding as the sun rose high in the sky.

It was morning . . . the best time to go and take a peek around the warehouse, a chore she had avoided while she waited for Rip to recover.

She couldn't avoid it any more. But she couldn't work up the energy, or the interest to move.

See me.

How could she do anything but that?

She had a terrible feeling that she was going to see him in her mind each time she closed her eyes for a good long while.

It disturbed her, scared her even.

It was a vulnerability, one she wasn't equipped to handle. He thought they had time to figure it out, but she knew better.

No amount of time would ever lessen the fear she felt blooming inside. Now that the heat had passed, now her soul was quiet, and she could think, memories swamped and darkness threatened to choke her.

Time couldn't help her.

After all, if three hundred years hadn't eased her pain, why should she expect things to change now?

She was afraid. Rip sensed it, even as she slipped away.

He understood fear and, because he did, he didn't chase her down the street, the way he wanted. No, pursuit wouldn't work on this – getting her to trust him – *that* was what he needed.

He had to bring her to trust him. On her terms.

It would take time.

In the best scenario, they had all the time in the world.

Swinging his legs over the edge of the bed, Rip stood. He wasn't a patient man, though. He wasn't certain he could wait that long.

A note to my readers: I hope you enjoyed this prologue to Rip and Greta's story. You can read the rest of their story in Candy Houses. *You can find more information about their story and the rest of the Grimm series at my website www.shilohwalker.com*

Fire and Ice

Portia Da Costa

It's Christmas Eve, and I'm home alone, wrapped in my fleecy throw, and tucked up in front of the television with a lovely bottle of wine. Not for me the purgatory of fractious family shindigs that turn into Armageddon over the mince pies. I'm just happy on my own, doing my own thing, chilling out but toasty.

Of course, there is someone with whom I'd like to spend Christmas. Someone I'd gladly share my blanket and my wine with . . . but if he was here, you can forget about the television.

Innes McKenzie is my boss, my unbelievably gorgeous boss, and the one I can thank for the yummy wine. He's just the sort of guy to remember a casual conversation from months ago, and take note of my favourite tipple for future reference. He's like that, thoughtful and inventive.

The African Queen is on the box now, another Christmas favourite. I try to imagine Innes on a riverboat covered in grease like Bogart, but it's a reach. My boss is cool and immaculate and as beautiful as an angel. A very manly angel, naturally, and needless to say, I'm head over heels in love with him.

I can't help but wonder about his Christmas. I picture his apartment as a place as immaculate and elegant as he is, maybe done out in white with monochrome silver decorations. He and some groomed, smart-sexy woman are eating a gourmet Christmas dinner, and later, they'll retire to his wide, expensively sheeted bed for some intense, gourmet sex.

Mm, my mouth waters . . . Innes à la carte . . .

His rich fruity wine is slipping down a treat now, and in my mind it's me in that snowy bed with him, writhing and grappling with my hot, elegant boss. I've never seen Innes with his clothes off, of course, but imagining him is a pastime I often indulge in.

Inside my fleecy cocoon, I shimmy and wriggle, pretending that a naked and perfect Innes McKenzie is touching me . . . here . . . there . . . everywhere. His skin is warm, his blue eyes are as brilliant as lasers . . . and his rampant cock is as magnificent as the rest of him.

I open my legs, sliding in my own hand in lieu of his.

At work, he always moves in a very neat, spare, precise fashion, and I suspect that in bed he's just the same. No action wasted or overdone, everything efficient, full of meaning, accurate and fiery.

I'm wet now, thinking about him and mellowed by the wine. I start to moan, and Bogey and Hepburn are forgotten as my arousal circles around the imaginary totem of Innes McKenzie.

He likes me, I know that. But relationships in the same office are frowned on at work. For the hundredth time, I consider a transfer, but then I wouldn't see Innes every day.

"Innes . . . Innes . . ." I moan, my pleasure rising as dark desire burns in those blue, imagined eyes. They glitter in my mind and I'm moments from the brink, almost there, with him, in my dream world.

Then my mobile phone rings and snatches the orgasm from my grasp.

"Bugger, hell and damnation!"

Who can it be? I've told my family I'll visit at New Year, and everyone else that I'm having quiet, opt-out Christmas. But clearly somebody didn't get the message or thinks I'll change my mind. Maybe it's my mum, checking up to see if I've finally got the boyfriend she so wants for me.

My phone shrills again and I snatch it up. I wrinkle my nose because my fingers smell of me.

"Cally Hobbes." I try to inject a bit of peace and goodwill to all men into my voice, rather than sound like a young female Scrooge.

"Hello, Cally," croaks a voice I've never heard before.

I say I've never heard it before, but I have actually. Every working day. But I've never heard it sound quite like this. It's my Innes, but his vocal cords seem to have been recently sand-blasted.

"Hi, boss. Are you all right? You sound a bit husky . . ." He sounds more than husky. He sounds absolutely terrible.

"I'm OK," he lies, in a gravelly near-whisper so unlike his crisp, sexy tones. To me, he still sounds sexy in a backwards about ways.

"Thanks," he adds, in afterthought. He must be ill. His manners are usually unshakeable. "I was wondering if you could do me a gigantic favour, Cally? As I'm at home, I thought I'd do a bit of work on the Simpson merger, but I don't have my files here. Is there any way you could possibly pick them up and bring them round? You can just slide them into my letter box and I'll come down and get them. I've got a mild lurgy of some kind and I'd hate you to catch it too.'

It's no mild lurgy. It's a forty-eight-hour flu bug that's going round the company. I had it a fortnight ago, when Innes was at an overseas conference.

"It's OK, boss. It sounds like the flu . . . and I've had it. I'll collect the papers and bring them round. Is there anything I can get you? Aspirin? Cough mixture?"

"Don't worry, I'm fine, Cally . . . really I am." I detect a spark of life in his voice. "But are you really sure I'm not keeping you from anything? It's Christmas Eve. Shouldn't you be with your friends or family?" He pauses and, weirdly, it almost seems as if he's tentative . . . something that's totally unlike my super-confident boss. "Or your boyfriend . . ."

"Nope, I'm footloose and fancy-free at the moment, boss. And I'm visiting my family next week." My turn to pause . . . "So until then, I'm completely and utterly yours."

I wish.

"I can't thank you enough, Cally." He breaks off for a coughing fit, while I try to fool myself there are nuances of meaning in his shattered voice that have nothing to do with gratitude. "You're an angel," he gasps when the cataclysm is over. "A true Christmas angel. I don't know what I'd do without you."

And I know what I'd like to do with you, boss man.

After he gives me his address and rings off, I leap out of my fleecy burrow, thanking a fairy godmother I never knew I had.

This has got to be the best Christmas present ever and Cinders shall go to the ball!

Forty minutes later, my taxi pulls up outside the large old build-ing where Innes has his flat. I managed to catch the security man at work and get in for Innes' papers, and now I'm here with them, plus an emergency care package for my boss.

I've got lemons, honey and whisky to make toddies. I've got all the medicines that I dosed myself with when I had the same bug.

I've even got one or two Christmas snacks and treats for when he's feeling better and his appetite returns.

I'm ridiculously excited. I've never been to Innes' home, and I'm dying to see if it's as stylish as I imagine, as stylish as he is. Not that I'm really interested in his furnishings and décor . . .

As I ring his speakerphone, I'm actually trembling, stupid as it seems, and I have to wait for an answer, until Innes' hoarse voice growls out, "Cally, is that you?" He sounds crabby, but I make allowances. The man is ill.

"Yep, it's me, boss. I've got the papers and some other stuff."

"What other stuff?"

"Oh, nothing much . . . Can I come up?"

"It might be safer if you didn't. Just shove them in the letter box and I'll come down in a little while." I can almost hear him despairing of his own manners. "And thanks, Cally, really. You're a star. I hope you have a wonderful Christmas."

But I've come this far, and I'm not going to be fobbed off. It occurs to me for a moment that he might not consider himself presentable – he's so fastidious – but my desire to see him is too strong. I squelch my qualms and prepare to squelch his objections and his masculine pride. "They're too bulky for the letter box," I lie. I haven't even looked. "I'll just come up for a minute and leave them. I won't linger, if you're feeling ill."

Silence. Then, "OK . . . All right."

He sounds grumpy and ungracious. He must be really ill, this curmudgeon just isn't him. He's always composed and civil and friendly. For a boss, he's always on the side of us lesser mortals.

The lock uncouples and I push my way into the hall and make my way up the stairs. It's an old house, but elegantly appointed and at any other time I'd linger to admire it. But today, oh God, it's like an icebox. Bone-chillingly freezing, as cold as outdoors. A horrible thought occurs to me . . . Are the actual apartments as cold? If so, no wonder Innes sounds so rough. If he's ill and frozen, it's not surprising his temper is frayed.

On the landing, I locate his door. Raising my hand to knock, I pause then try the handle. The door's unlocked and I push it open and step inside – where the meat locker chill hits me in the face. Along with another shock . . .

I don't know what I was expecting. I'd been envisioning the sick Innes as looking suave and immaculate, as always. I've pictured him in jeans and a beautiful sweater, maybe with a scarf as a concession. Or maybe a sexy, high-end robe – thick and de luxe, very masculine, worn over classy sweatpants or something.

But in reality, he looks like a deranged wild man shambling through a disaster zone of tissues, abandoned blankets and empty coffee cups and half-drunk glasses of Lemsip. There's even a tangle of forlorn, un-hung Christmas decorations on the coffee table.

"Oh my God, boss, you look terrible!"

It's out of my mouth before I can stop it, and Innes scowls as if it's hit home. He does look dreadful, though. For him . . .

"Well, thanks for that."

To offset the biting cold, he's wrapped himself in the duvet off his bed, and he's padding around in his bare feet, the idiot. His usually immaculately groomed blond hair is all mad curls and tufts and his handsome face is frighteningly pale, but with hot flags of a fever flush across his cheekbones – yet somehow he still manages to look gorgeous, devastating virus or not.

"I'm sorry . . . I didn't mean it like that. It's just that I've never seen you ill and you look . . . different."

He hitches up his slithering duvet. Oh God, he's shaking . . . "Well, come on in and shut the door. Wouldn't want to let the heat out, would we?" he finishes savagely, grabbing me by the arm and hauling me inside.

"But this place is like a deep freeze. What's happened to the heating?" I set down my tote bag in a chair and move aside some cups and newspapers and a bunch of tinsel to put the files he asked for on the coffee table.

Innes throws himself down in another chair, as if he's finding it hard to stay on his feet. "Everyone in the building's gone away for Christmas, including the landlord." He rearranges himself inside his makeshift tent-come-shelter and pulls it up around his ears. "The guy who usually does the central heating has got an emergency job on, and none of the others I've rung will come out until after Christmas."

"But don't you have a gas or electric fire?" I look around. The place has obviously been remodelled from its original configuration and I can't see a fire.

"If I had one, I'd have it on, obviously." His voice sounds really odd, and I realize his teeth are chattering.

Poor thing, he looks so miserable. How awful it must be for a confident, self-sufficient man like Innes to be rendered so powerless by illness and circumstance. He shrugs in his cocoon and suddenly gives me a shamefaced grin that melts my heart and sends a sensation like warm honey seeping along my veins to pool in certain places.

Dear God, I'm a horrible person! I'm getting the hots for a man who's probably quite seriously ill!

"Sorry, I'm being such an ungrateful bastard," he rasps, 'Forgive me, Cally. You've been really helpful and I'm being an arse."

Helpful? I suppose so. But I've got other motives. I can't believe my luck that circumstances have brought me here, alone, and put me in this strange position of power over the very man I adore.

"You are a bit, but I'll forgive you because you're poorly." I stride across the room and take him by the arm. "Come on, where's the bedroom? Let's get you to bed."

Wearily he hauls himself up, but for a moment a brighter glimmer flares in his eyes, and they look even bluer than normal. It might be the fever . . . but it might be something else. He might be ill, but he's still a man. My heart thunders.

"Now that's a very tempting offer . . ." His voice doesn't have its usually strong, decisive ring, but there's a lot more life in it than there was a moment ago, and suddenly he waggles his sandy eyebrows at me. "Sorry, Cally. Must be the lurgy talking. Forget I said that."

"No problem . . . now show me where your bedroom is." I'm smiling as I follow his shuffling steps. Surely he wouldn't have said what he said, if deep down a part of him didn't mean it . . .

We navigate our way out of the living room, along a little corridor and into his only marginally tidier bedroom, where the denuded bed reveals the home of the duvet. I hustle Innes towards it, but he hesitates. He looks vaguely perplexed in the soft light from a couple of wall lamps.

"Come along then. What are you waiting for? Get in and I'll spread the quilt over you."

He gives me an odd, almost wicked look. "OK, Nurse Ratchet . . ."

I flap the sheets, still waiting for him to comply, but when he shucks off the duvet to climb underneath them, it's my turn to get a shock of chills and fever.

All this time, he's been stark-naked beneath his quilt.

My jaw drops and delicious guilt surges through me like a tidal wave.

Even in his flu-ridden state, naked Innes is spectacular: lean and athletic, with long limbs, long muscles and a crisply defined six-pack worthy of a male pin-up. He's a veritable feast of male pulchritude, but to my greedy shame I zero straight in on his cock, which is also long and crisply defined.

"Get under the sheet. You'll freeze to death," I command, my voice not quite steady. Innes complies, his moment of possible bravado a thing of the past as he flops on to the bed and bundles the sheet around him like an Eastern bloc washerwoman. Still stunned by what I've seen, I fling the duvet in his general direction, my aim so addled it goes over his head too.

"Thanks . . . I think," he groans, emerging. He's gritting his teeth to stop them chattering again.

"You're still cold. You need more bedding. Have you got any?"

"There's the summer duvet . . . It's in the top cupboard, over the wardrobe."

The cupboard is high, so I snag a chair, kick off my boots and climb up. In the low light, it's difficult to see what's in there, but amongst some old sports gear and other stuff, I spot the familiar white ticking cover of a duvet. I start to pull it, then experience the most peculiar sensation like a ray of heat flowing over me. Holding on to the edge of the cupboard, I whip around precariously on the chair.

Ah-hah, the weak and sickly patient still has enough energy to check out my bottom in my snug-fitting jeans.

I beetle my brows at him, and he mutters, "I'm ill," by way of an excuse.

"Thanks, I think . . ." I parrot back, vaguely cross with him as I spread the extra duvet over him. Why does he have to plead illness to admit he's susceptible to my body?

"I'm sorry . . . you know what I mean . . . it's very nice, your bottom. Very nice indeed . . ." He hunkers down beneath his bunched coverings and scrunches his eyes closed. "I've always thought so."

Part of me thinks, Cheeky buggar! But part of me is very, very pleased by his admission. He's finally confirmed what I've always hoped, despite the stupid codes of our workplace.

"I'll make you a hot toddy. Stay under the covers, and try to keep warm."

"Can you bring the files, please?"

I shake my head. "Absolutely not. How can you possibly work when you're nearly half dead?"

He makes a harrumphing sound as I hurry out of the bedroom.

En route to the kitchen, I have a little snoop round the rest of the apartment. It's nice, very nice: a gracious blend of modern and traditional beneath the temporary disorder and the frigid temperature. It's a bit like Innes himself. He's a contemporary man but with sweet old-fashioned values sometimes.

A few minutes later, I'm back in the bedroom, still wishing I was here under different circumstances. Innes is humped under the two duvets, barely visible, but in my imagination we're both there, engaged in a brand of humping. My breasts tingle at the thought, and desire grinds low in my sex, stirring my guilt. What kind of sex monster would want to ravage a shivering invalid? I've made myself a hot toddy too, but I'm wondering now whether I should have done ... I'm frisky enough already without the alcohol.

Innes struggles to sit up and, setting the mugs aside, I help him. His skin is burning hot when I put my arm around his shoulder so I can adjust his pillows, and it's almost electrified as his hand slides against it. I jump and, even in his feverish stupor, Innes starts too, his blue eyes wide with surprise. It's almost a relief when we split apart and I scuttle away to get his dressing gown to wrap around him.

After more struggling, and some coughing, he's sitting up, clutching his mug of toddy. He wrinkles his nose at the first sip, but then takes another longer one. "This isn't my whisky," he observes, still swigging the stuff down.

"No, it's mine." I taste my own drink, and the sharp/sweet tang of lemon and honey is delicious, despite the cheap and cheerful whisky. "I knew you'd buy good stuff, and it's no use drowning posh single malts in a whole bunch of other ingredients."

Innes manages a grin. "Quite right too. Good thinking, Batman."

We sip in silence for a while: Innes slumped back in his pillows, his cup cradled on his chest, me perched on a chair a few feet away. Despite the rigours of illness, he still looks irresistible, and it's not a good idea for me to be closer. The idea of that sleek naked body beneath the duvet is still making me feel crazy.

"So, why no boyfriend?" Innes enquires suddenly. We have the best of working relationships, but we never pry into each other's private lives. It'd be dangerous for me, and Innes is too sensible.

"I don't know ... nobody seems to be asking at the moment. Well, nobody who I'd be interested in." I drain my toddy, and its heat sinks down through my body to meet the heat rising up from my sex, the heat fired by Innes being so close.

"Men are fools," says Innes, setting his own drink aside.

I laugh, loving the strange closeness between us. It's sweet, even allowing for my sexual frustration. "Indeed they are, boss. Indeed they are."

He gives me an odd look, and mutters, "And I'm probably the biggest fool amongst them." Then his eyelids flutter, and he seems to drift off to sleep.

I wonder what to do. I know what I want to do, which is climb beneath the duvets with Innes and see if a bit of hands-on physical therapy can cure him. But instead I've got to find a distraction from those thoughts. I don't want to leave the room, but I can't risk turning on the flat-screen television on the wall in case I wake him. In the end, I switch off the lamp furthest away from me and, by the light of the closer one, I flick through a book that Innes appears to have been reading. It's a collection of pithy anecdotes by a controversial motoring journalist, and it's really funny when I get stuck into it. From time to time, I spring to red alert, when Innes stirs, but after a while, the toddy gets to me too, and I drift off to sleep, book on lap.

I don't know how long I doze, but I wake with a lurch, disturbed by a sound. I glance immediately towards Innes, and he's moving, tugging at his covers. He's obviously just shuffled back from the bathroom, because one of the quilts is on the floor, and he doesn't seem to have the energy to restore it to the bed. It's also colder than ever in the room, even though I'm still wearing my outdoor jacket. Darting across to check my patient, I find him half awake, half asleep, and muttering under his breath. Where he was hot before, he's now icy cold and clammy. I wonder whether he has a hot-water bottle somewhere, but he doesn't seem the type for one, and even if he was, I've no idea where he'd keep it. I conduct a cursory search while I'm in the bathroom, but I feel awkward rummaging about amongst his belongings without permission.

When I get back to the bedroom, I can tell he's deteriorated. Innes is shivering hard now, despite his heap of bedding. What the hell can I do? He doesn't appear to have any more duvets or blankets, but I've got to find a way to heat him up.

There is one, of course, and it's been staring me in the face all along as my heart's desire.

Body heat.

Nothing to do with sex at all, at least for him, but skin on skin is probably the most efficient way to warm him.

As if he's sensed my intentions, Innes rouses again when I peel off my jacket and throw it on top of the duvets. "What are you doing?" he whispers as I kick off my boots, then wiggle off my jeans, adding the latter to the heap.

"I'm about to administer emergency heat."

Just as I'm dimming the remaining lamp, his eyes snap open and, as I elevate the duvets a smidge and start to slide beneath them, he gives me a delicious, slightly perplexed and worried look. "Maybe I should put something on . . . some boxer shorts? I'm afraid I don't own any pyjamas."

At the moment, he doesn't look as if he has the strength to blow the skin off a rice pudding, much less put on underwear, and I'm in bed now anyway. God, his skin is so cold! It feels like marble. I snuggle up, as best I can, trying not to think too much about the sizeable knot of his genitalia pressing against my knicker-clad loins. He's not hard, but he's still big and the feel of him is monumental, swamping my senses.

And he knows what I'm thinking, I'm sure of it, because he tries to tug away.

"Look, Innes, astonishing as it may seem, I've been in bed with a naked man before, and during that time, I've managed to not have sex every single second I was there." He relaxes, and I even sense a smile, despite his shivers. "I'll do my best not to harass you, out of respect for your delicate condition."

He chuckles and edges closer, sliding his cold arms around me now, and suddenly he cracks open his self-imposed shell of propriety again – and comes to life. "I wasn't thinking of you harassing me . . . it was more the other way around, Cally."

Be still my stupid heart! And be quiet my stupid pussy! He's ill. He's probably delirious. He doesn't know what he's saying and he hasn't the energy to do anything anyway, even if he meant it.

"Indeed, boss . . . Well, we'll see . . . Given the state of you, I think I'm pretty safe from any advances. You're shaking too hard to even find my erogenous zones. Now stop talking nonsense and let me warm you up."

It's cruel and unusual torment being allowed to touch him and yet not really touch him, but I set to work rubbing his back and shoulders and arms, and even his bottom, in an attempt to heat his skin. He feels as if he's been carved from a glacier at first, but, eventually, he starts to thaw. Even his frigid feet start to warm up.

It isn't sexual, but even so, he sighs, as if just not being frozen is a pleasure. His limbs loosen and his breathing slows and steadies as his shivering subsides. Is he falling asleep again?

Great!

Proper rest is the best thing for Innes, but, irrationally, I feel a tiny bit insulted. Obviously my body isn't quite as drop-dead alluring as I'd hoped, and his libido isn't inclined to fight the flu germs.

But somehow, lying in the arms of the man I love, with his naked body pressed all along my clothed one, is relaxing despite the infernal temptation. I too feel drowsy, warmed by my clothes, by the duvets and beloved Innes.

Influenced by my wine at home, and the hot toddy, I drift in and out of a light sleep for a while, tired by my amateurish attempts at nursing, I suppose. But eventually I rise into wakefulness again. Not with a jerk this time, just a gradual awareness and a subconscious perception of change.

Innes is warm now, and it's a natural, healthy warmth, not a fever. And that's what's woken me. We've moved apart a bit, but I can sense his body close to me. He seems not to be restless any more, and neither too hot nor too cold, and I remember how quickly I felt better with this bug. But I'm scared to ask how he's feeling, lest I disturb his sleep. Holding my breath, I roll on to my side, facing him, then reach out and touch his chest, letting my fingertips rest with infinitesimal lightness against his smooth skin and the sexy dusting of hair across his breastbone and his pectorals.

To the touch, he feels recovered, almost well. And I squeak like a cornered mouse when his hand settles on mine, so I can't withdraw it.

"Sorry to wake you. I was just checking your temperature." The hand stays put, flat over mine, pressing my fingers against the firm muscular contours. "You seem a bit better."

"I feel better." His voice sounds clearer, still a little husky, but not weak or blurred by illness. "Thanks to you . . ." He moves, and the mattress rocks, making his thighs brush mine, almost as if his naked body is seeking naked parts of mine.

My heart thuds like a Kodo drummer's drum. Boom boom boom. It's a wonder it's not shaking the bed. I daren't open my eyes, and every nerve and instinct is telling me that Innes' health isn't the only thing that's changed. It's as if the whole configuration of the universe has suddenly shifted. A self-imposed structure that presided just a few hours ago has become fluid and mutable, opening doors of perception and possibility.

Here's my chance, a life-changing opportunity that might never come again. I wait, wondering, knowing I should withdraw, but unable to because I'm his for the taking.

Innes begins to direct my hand. Not forcibly, it feels more like a medium resting on the pointer of an Ouija board. Our nested fingers slide down, slowly, over his ribs, and his belly, until we encounter the inevitable, his warm, hard cock.

Oh boy . . . he's fully erect.

Rising on to my elbow, I risk a look at him. His face is all shadows and angles in the dim lamplight. I open my mouth to speak, drag in the necessary breath, but I can't frame words. The feel of his warm flesh cradled in my fingers steals away my ability to express myself in speech.

"I know, I know," murmurs Innes. He can still speak and, attuned to me, he voices my thoughts. "We're work colleagues and it'll make things complicated." He stares heavenwards for a moment, then draws in a breath, with effort, the way I did. The look on his face as he turns to me says he knows we're being crazy, but there's yearning there too as he launches onwards, "But, I care for you, Cally. I really do. And I know you like me. Maybe for Christmas, we can just forget work and be two people . . . take time out?'

The whole universe seems to be vibrating now, not just me. Anticipation pounds in my veins and my throat, reverberating in my brain, its beat synchronized to the pulsing blood in Innes' cock. Even though the air outside our haven of duvets is just as frigid as before, everything around us seems hot now, surging hot.

And though I still can't speak, I don't have to. Innes knows me, probably better than I do myself.

"Let's pretend you're Florence Nightingale and I'm a recovering soldier in need of a bit of TLC to enhance my treatment."

The sweet laughter in his voice releases the tension. I'm still bursting with excitement and months and years of suppressed desire, but I feel free now, and happy, to express it.

"Well, I don't have the benefit of a history degree." I chuckle too as I lean in towards Innes and kiss the corner of his mouth while I move my hand on his erection. He gasps as I go on, "But as far as

I know Florence didn't shag the soldiers. She just waved her lamp about a bit and gave them laudanum and all that."

"You can give me more of the medicine you gave me last night . . . body heat works for me." He rocks his hips, thrusting into my grasp. "It's far more effective than Lemsip or Night Nurse. I feel much better now. . . and parts of me are a hundred per cent again."

No need to single out which parts, obviously. The thick, hard, hot shaft in my hand feels like a a thousand per cent to me.

I thought I was besotted with Innes before I walked into his flat tonight, but suddenly I adore him more than ever. He's a sexy, playful man who's somehow reborn, like a phoenix, from the ashes of forty-eight-hour influenza.

Why not have him? Just for Christmas? A gift to myself. At work, things are never going to be the same anyway. Looks like a new job is on the cards now, so why not grasp these moments of crazy para-dise while I can? Come the New Year, Innes might well be all business once again . . .

"But what if the treatment's too rigorous? What if you have a relapse?" I ask, letting my thumbprint slide over the fine, silky skin of his penis. "I'd be slacking in my nursing duties if I made you ill again."

"I'll risk it," he growls, sounding more energetic now than he has done since I walked in the door, "and I can always have a nice rest afterwards, can't I, Florence?"

"Yes, you certainly could do that." I try to sound airy, but it's difficult when Innes slithers his free arm around me beneath the covers and pulls me down towards him, squashing our two hands, still holding his cock, warm and hot between us. It's not the most elegant of clinches, but it's infinitely erotic as I kiss him hard and hungrily.

Innes' cheeks are stubbly, and the feel of that is unexpectedly piquant. He's such an immaculate man, so smooth and groomed, and here in bed, he's all kinds of raw, delicious and primitive. As we kiss like wild things, I feel a pang of disquiet, wondering what my middle of the night breath tastes like, but it doesn't seem to bother Innes or quell his sudden voraciousness. His own mouth still tastes of whisky toddy, all spicy and honeyed. We wriggle about beneath the weight of bedding, and I'm forced to relinquish his cock as he tips me on to my back and starts to explore me. His hand feels like a firebrand on my midriff as he works it under my jumper and T-shirt, slithering upwards. He cups my breast through the soft fabric of my bra, squeezing gently, his thumb flicking around my nipple through the cotton. I suspect that usually he's a far more sophisticated and circumspect lover, but who needs a virtuoso at a time like this? I start to wiggle and drag my heels as energy builds.

We don't say much as we fondle and kiss. We're totally focused, and I sense that Innes wants to channel all his depleted strength into pleasuring me. His hand feels like feverish magic as he sneaks it beneath my bra and strokes bare skin at last, exploring and pleasing. He swaps from breast to breast and back again, toying and teasing my nipples until I can't think straight, and can't stop twisting around and rubbing my crotch against his hip, his thigh and his cock. I've never been so excited before a man's even touched my pussy. I usually need quite a bit of extended foreplay. But with Innes I'm all afire from the very beginning.

Expertly, he presses a strong athletic thigh between mine, and starts to work himself against me, to and fro, to and fro, rubbing me with hard muscle and warm skin, stirring my clitoris. I'm almost embarrassed how wet I am. I'm a simmering pond down there, a pool of needy moisture that's soaked right through the flimsy cotton of my knickers.

"God, I want you so much, Cally," Innes gasps, the words blurred because his mouth is still pressed to mine, "I want you so much."

Overcome, I howl out in my mind, Then have me!

As if he's heard me, he rocks faster against me, despite all the constriction from the sheets and quilts. His hands slide down and around me, grip my bottom to hold me closer, work me harder. I slide my arms around him, reciprocating, helping him to help me towards my climax. I can't help but smile. We're as good a team in bed as we are at the office. Maybe better.

Pretty soon, I can't hold out any longer. Not that I want to. My pussy clenches in a hard, deep rhythm and I come. Innes feels my spasms through my knickers and growls and laughs in primitive triumph. My nails dig into his back as the pleasure surges.

While I'm still gasping for air, he rolls away from me, pausing to give my pussy a friendly squeeze, then wiggles an arm out of the covers in the general direction of his bedside cabinet. Ah, condoms, I presume . . .

He fishes around blindly for a moment, while still trying to kiss my neck at the same time, then lets out a curse as it becomes apparent he can't find them. Goddamn it!

"Haven't you got any?"

"Yes, I have some, but it's a while since I had a need for them and they must have got buried."

"Let me look." With my sex still simmering, I half roll, half clamber over him, and my thigh brushes his hot erection as I go. I edge a little way out of the cave of duvet heat and lean over to look in the drawer. It's full of typical male detritus: passport, car documents, an old iPod, but, underneath them, I find an open twelve-pack of condoms, barely touched. I'll ponder what this might mean about his recent sex life another time. For now, I just want get a contraceptive on him, so I rip the foil off and set to my task.

Innes' efforts seem to have tired him, and he lies inert as I enrobe him in latex. "Are you sure you want to do this?" I ask, even though it's blatantly obvious his cock wants to do it, even if the rest of him is flagging.

"Hell, yes," he says fiercely, and, as if regenerated by a moment's respite, he surges up again, rolls me on to my back again and rears up over me, duvets and all. "There's still a bit of life in me yet, Florence, so don't you worry!" He pauses to give me a rough but pussy-melting kiss. "I'll probably be completely knackered afterwards, but it'll be worth it! I've wanted you far too long to let anything stop me now."

For a moment, I feel sad, thinking of months and months of lost opportunities. Then there's no time and no reason to feel sad, because first I'm wriggling and squirming out of my panties, and then Innes' lovely erection is nudging at my pussy. After a few moments of the manual adjustment dance, he pushes on into me.

And pushes and pushes . . . God, he's big. Just the way I imagined him during idle moments at the office spent fantasizing about what lay inside his elegantly tailored trousers. He's everything he promised to be and more.

Finally, he's right in. Deep. To the hilt. And we both lie still as if adjusting to a whole new world. My mind keeps chanting, This is Innes. This is Innes. Oh my God, this is Innes, while my heart just croons, Thank you, thank you, thank you . . .

But pretty soon, my body instinctively rises, pushing against him, wanting to be closer, closer . . .

"Cally," he groans, not really thrusting, just pushing back. Despite his claims, I know he's still fighting the illness, but desire gives him strength from out of nowhere and enough to give me pleasure, through pressure and friction. As I strain against him, he jerks his hips, and the action knocks my simmering, needy clit.

"Ah . . . Oh . . . Oh, Innes." I croon his name as orgasm claims me again, so soon, so quick, so deep, so intense . . . No need for a long extenuated dance of the flesh. He's in me. I love him. So I come.

Gasping and whimpering a lot of wordless nonsense, I arch even harder against him, my body working of its own accord, while my mind is blank but for the white world of pleasure and the single word "Innes". He moves too, kissing my face and my neck, his chest heaving as he drags in long breaths. Bracing himself with one arm, he slides a hand beneath my bottom to hold me closer.

"Oh hell, I wanted this to last. I told myself if it ever happened, I'd make it good for you.' His narrow hips buck fast, faster, then furiously, as I cling on, gripping his back and his bottom, just as he grips me. "Cally . . . Oh my Cally," he gasps through gritted teeth as he jerks in a desperate rhythm and comes inside me.

The feel of him pulsing sends me soaring yet again.

Afterwards, it's like having survived a cyclone. I haven't got the flu. I'm in rude good health at the moment. But even I'm completely exhausted by our efforts, so heaven knows how Innes feels.

After he climaxed, he hauled himself off me with an obvious effort, then collapsed beside me, his fingers searching blindly beneath the duvets to lace with mine. There was still strength left in him to hold on tight, really tight. "Oh God," he sighed, then promptly fell asleep.

Not that I can blame him. If ever a man deserved to sleep after sex, it was Innes, now. His performance was above and beyond the call of duty for a man as sick as he's been.

I lie for a while, just holding on to his now relaxed hand like it's the Holy Grail. Either that or the greatest Christmas gift ever, barring none. And it is Christmas now. We've slept and made love through Christmas Eve and now it's the early hours of Christmas Day.

I'm tired. In fact I'm exhausted. But I fight to cling on to consciousness.

This is Innes. I made love with Innes. What's to become of us?

I squelch all thoughts of the future, kiss his shoulder . . . then drift off myself.

Actual morning rolls around, and I'm awake again. The room is still cold when I poke out an experimental limb, but fortunately Innes feels comfortably warm beneath the covers, neither feverish nor chilled. Sleeping easily, he looks like an adorable rumpled angel.

Staring down at his beautiful, sexily stubble-clad face, I make an executive decision. While he sleeps on soundly, I wriggle into the various bits of clothing I took off then drop a kiss on his cheek, preparing to go.

As I turn away from the bed, his hand shoots out from beneath the duvets and clamps around my wrist, his grip ferocious for a recovering invalid.

"Don't go . . . please." His eyes snap open, blue and clear and luminous. "I know it's going to be a crap Christmas here in this icebox, but we can always keep warm by staying in bed." His smile is as wicked and playful as I've ever seen it.

I place my free hand over his, on my wrist. "Don't worry. I'm coming back. I'm only going for supplies. I've got a fan heater, and some hot-water bottles, and some Christmas dinner stuff I want to bring round.' His smile widens, and there's real relief in his eyes. "If we combine our assets, I think we can have a decent little Christmas between us."

Innes draws my hand to his lips and kisses it in a way that makes my knees go wobbly and the rest of me just wants to crawl back beneath the duvets with him, double quick. "Good thinking, Florence." He winks at me. "I'm all for combining our assets, if last night was a taster." He kisses my hand again, with evident meaning, then releases me. "Hurry back though. I'll miss you while you're gone."

I give him a little wave and dash out of the room, before I say something really, really stupid. He's fond of me, I know, but this is probably the Christmas equivalent of a "holiday romance" to him. To me, it's a treasured dream, despite the cold, and his flu.

Trying not to think too deeply, I summon a taxi, ride back to my flat, and have a quick shower and change before gathering together the things I think we'll need. Then I stuff everything, along with my weekend bag, into the boot of my car, and hurtle back to Innes' place as fast as I dare on the icy Christmas roads.

Innes sounds bright when I buzz up to be let in and, when I reach his flat, I find him up and shaved and showered. He's bundled up in his dressing gown over a sweatshirt and track pants, and his complexion is a still little bit pale and wan, but his smile is happy.

"You idiot, have you had a cold shower? You'll have a relapse!" I upbraid him as he grabs me for a quick kiss.

"Don't fret, woman. The bathroom's a bit cold, but it's a power shower, so we can get any hot water we need by using that." He hugs me hard.

"Very civilized. But I wish you'd get back to bed and rest. You're still poorly, despite having –" he quirks a blond brow at me "– recovered some of your . . . er . . . capabilities." Speaking of which, the way he's holding me tells me that wasn't a fluke.

"Everything's in perfect working order, nurse," he whispers, sliding his hands down to my bottom and holding me against him. "Would you like to check?"

Tempting . . . oh so tempting . . .

But I resist. "I've got stuff to bring in from the car, then I'll see about an inspection, maybe." I give him a stern look as I pull away from him, then wink.

"Let me get my coat and I'll help you."

"No way! There isn't that much. You need to save your strength!"

I see the decisive, always in control Innes of the office longing to assert himself, but then he smiles and shrugs, abandoning macho stubbornness. "OK, boss," he says, with a twinkling wink. "But is it OK then if I make us a cup of tea and some breakfast while you're bringing in the hoard?"

I give him an old-fashioned look. "All right then, but don't overdo it."

Not long afterwards, we're back in bed, under the covers, eating toast and marmalade and watching a silly film on TV. The fan heater is coughing gently in the corner of the room, and though it's not tropical, the worst of the chill has left the air.

What follows is the strangest Christmas Day ever spent . . . and the best. Some of it's spent platonically, scuttling between the kitchen and the bedroom, preparing and eating rich but jumbled meals and getting slightly tipsy on seasonal beverages, then goggling mindlessly at daft but traditional television programmes.

But it's not all platonic. In between there are giggly but beautiful bouts of cuddly, fumbling, duvet-bound sex, also slightly tipsy and rich with kisses and pleasure.

Innes mostly sleeps afterwards, revealing that he's still not fully recovered, but I salve my conscience by telling myself that sex is the perfect light exercise and good for his spirits. Bloody hell, it's doing wonders for mine!

Every now and then I wonder what'll happen when we return to normal life after Christmas. Innes doesn't speak of it, and I guess he's putting it out of mind, like me, but as he lies sleeping, he stirs and frowns once or twice.

Boxing Day morning brings a trill on Innes' entryphone and, as he's still sleeping, I swathe myself in his dressing gown and answer the call. To both my delight and my suppressed dismay, it's the central heating engineer.

While Innes sleeps on, I deal with him. The cheery craftsman quickly sees the problem and, miracle of miracles, has the right parts to fix it. I offer him tea, and while we chat I discover something that makes me feel fonder and prouder of Innes than ever. It seems that he gave up his priority place on the central heating man's worksheet in favour of an old folks' home where the heating had broken too – and then told the guy not to spoil his Christmas by coming out afterwards.

When I return to the flat, the rumbling radiators are already warming up and, as Innes sits up, he smiles from ear to ear as if he's kid and Santa's brought him a bicycle.

"Wahey, let there be heat!" His blue eyes cruise slowly over me from top to toe. "Maybe now I'll get to see a bit more of your gorgeous body. It's been a crying shame to keep it covered up with jumpers and duvets."

"Well, it's early days yet. I'm not stripping off until the radiators are right up to temperature."

Innes is unabashed. "That just gives me something to look forward to, Florence." He waggles his sandy eyebrows again. "So, what's for breakfast?"

It's strange to be able to walk round the apartment without cringing and shivering beneath layers of clothes and blankets, but pretty soon, the central heating does its job and the atmosphere is toasty. Innes allows me some private me time in the newly warm bathroom, then takes his turn while I make phone calls and tidy up. It's lovely not to be cold, but perversely I'm also a bit nostalgic for it. Our arctic Christmas experience is almost over now, and we'll both soon be heading elsewhere to our separate New Year celebrations.

And after that, it's back to work and we'll either assume our normal roles or everything will change.

So, there's all the more reason to make the most of our last day and the possibilities afforded by central heating. I knock on the bathroom door, hoping Innes will let me in.

He does, though his "Come in!" is muffled.

Inside, a sumptuous sight greets my eyes. He's standing stark-naked in the steamy air, drying his blond curls vigorously with a small towel.

Desire twists hard in my gut. He's beyond beautiful and this is the first time I've seen his remarkable physique in its entirety since that moment I ordered him back to bed, what seems like a lifetime ago. I've explored his body by touch, beneath the duvets, but here in the light and warmth he's more magnificent than ever. He's a poem of smooth, athletic musculature, a dusting of tawny body hair and a long thick penis, already awake and taking interest.

"J–just came to check if you were OK," I stammer as if I haven't fucked him and touched him goodness knows how many times in the last couple of days, "hoping you hadn't had a relapse."

"Do I look as if I'm having a relapse?" His smirk is roguish and the way he drops his towel then casually frisks his cock is nothing short of boastful.

"You look fine, actually."

"Just 'fine'?" He advances towards me. "Cheeky madam ... weren't you supposed to be showing me all the goodies I've blindly been fondling under the covers all this time?" When he reaches me, he pulls me hard against his body so I can feel every magnificent inch of him. Intoxicated, I wish my clothes would just dissolve.

His kiss is long and thorough, expressing the desire of a man who's now fully recovered and ready to exert his full powers; something that thrills me and at the same time piques my own sense of devilment. So he thinks he can start throwing his weight about now, eh?

I push away from him. "I still think you should take things easy, boss." The endearment is pointed. "If I'm going to strip off, I think it's safest if you lie down, you know. I wouldn't want you to pass out from the magnificence of my beauty."

Innes laughs, and nods. "All right, Ms Nightingale ..." Gracefully, he subsides on to the fluffy bath mat and stretches out like a pasha in his harem. The sleek way he moves is as much Innes putting on a display for me, as the other way around, and the sway of his heavy penis has me hypnotized. I just stare as he takes a hold of it and gently pumps.

My own strip isn't very graceful, but Innes seems to like it. He gives a low growl of appreciation and grabs my ankle to pull me down. "You are magnificent, Cally, but I've no intention of passing out just yet. Maybe when I come inside you, yes, but for the moment, I'm staying conscious, believe me."

We roll and rock on the mat, our bare bodies rubbing against each other while Innes strokes and kisses me. Within moments, my heels kick and I arch in a quick, hard orgasm, before running my fingers over every inch of him I can reach, including his cock. "Oh, hell, yes," he grunts, and pushes me over firmly on to my back, "I think we're going to need a condom, Nurse Florence."

I push on his shoulder with force of my own, and smilingly he concedes and settles on to his back. "We are," I confirm, throwing a leg across him and settling over his thighs while I scrabble for the pocket of my abandoned jeans and the condom in it.

His cock is a rosy, delicious pole nestling against my belly. He's hot and hard, his glans stretched and juicy. He gouges at the rug, then grabs my thighs as I roll the thin latex down his length.

"Oh, Cally," he moans as I fondle him, his bottom shifting against rug, rocking me to and fro, "please don't tease me . . . God, I've got to be inside you.'

"Anything to oblige, boss." It comes out flippant, but that's not the way I'm feeling. Every moment is precious beyond words, and I rise up, and up, to position my body over him. Then, between us, our fingers jostling, we ease the tip of his cock inside me, and I sink down again, and down and down and down.

I gasp. It's like he's pushing into every cell in my body and every corner of my mind. He totally engulfs my heart, and I have to close my eyes to hide the tears.

Oh, how I love him. Life will never be the same again.

I blink hard and dash at my eyes, praying he won't notice, but when I look down at him, his own eyes are closed and his beautiful face is a mask of taut sensation. We settle into a rhythm, slapping against each other, Innes' hands at my waist guiding my movements as I incline over him, my hands braced upon his shoulders. When the gathering of tension becomes too intense, I arch back, supporting myself one-handed on his thigh. With my free hand, I reach for my clit, but he's already there, seeking it out, wanting to give.

After that, all is mad crazy beauty, a chain of orgasms, several of mine, and one of his. There are moments when I'm not sure where I end and Innes begins. It's the closest thing to paradise upon this earth, but in the aftermath, cuddled against him, the tears return.

After this, nobody else will ever reach me quite the same, and though Innes murmurs my name, I sense his thoughts are as troubled as mine.

Christmas is over. The New Year has begun. It's my first day back at work, but no sign of Innes yet. He must have been in yesterday though, because there are papers to file from the Simpson deal. Or maybe he worked on them while staying with his family.

We haven't spoken since our strange, slightly awkward parting. He seemed to hug me as hard as I hugged him, but neither of us could think of anything much to say. He's texted me a few times since – odd, funny, strangely intimate little missives from his family home, nothing about "us" but feeling like messages from a friend.

But now we're back to being working colleagues, although I'm not really sure I'll be able to hack it.

How shall I greet him? How shall I be with him? Do I even refer to our chilly idyll? I just wish he were here, so we could face the situation head on.

I make coffee. I get on with routine tasks. I watch the door, my eyes yearning for a glimpse of him, no matter how problematical our new relationship is.

After half an hour, the door swings open. He's here!

Innes strides in, so handsome and familiar, yet so different from my beloved Christmas "patient". Restored to full health, he's immaculately suited and groomed in the way that's always taken my breath away. But having seen him naked adds an amazing new dimension. Having touched him makes me flutter with instant desire.

He comes straight over to my desk, and pauses, not saying anything, just pursing his lips. I can see complex emotions on his face, shadows in his eyes. Oh hell, this is awkward.

"Look, this is uncomfortable, isn't it?" I blurt out, standing up. Innes' eyes widen as if he was about to say the very same thing. "What happened, happened, but we can be adult about it. I can pretend it never happened, if you can. If that's what you want. We never have talk about it ever again." Once it's out, I feel deflated and ready to sit down again. Innes looks first thunderstruck, and then a bit angry.

"Well, I can't pretend it never happened and I want to talk about it. I want to talk about it right now!" He grasps me by the arm, his fingers firm and strong as I remember them from bed. "Let's have some coffee and sort this out, get it over with."

A few minutes later, we're in his office, sitting in the little conversation area where he chats with important visitors. Innes is on the sofa beside me, instead of the chair opposite. He's far too close for comfort, and just being near to him is both agony and ecstasy. He looks as tense as I feel, and he seems to be missing his usual poise and self-possession.

He launches into it, just as I did. "Look, Cally, I've just been over to Woodburn House and spoken to Philip Hastings. He's looking for a new PA because his girl is going overseas with her husband." He reaches towards his coffee on the low table in front of us then snatches back his hand. I've never seen him nervous before, and if this wasn't such awkward situation, I'd almost find it funny. "It's a step up, with some management responsibilities. but the job's yours if you want it. Starting immediately." He plucks at the knee of his beautifully tailored trousers. "It's a nice salary hike too – a great opportunity."

I reach for my coffee and sip it. I'm trying to stay calm, trying to focus on a hopeful gleam in his eyes and pray that I've interpreted it correctly.

"Ah, so you're getting rid of me." I eye him levelly, watching his dear face and the little telltales of stress and . . . and understanding. "Well, that'll work. With me over at Woodburn House, and working in a different division, we'll rarely see each other, possibly never. No awkward moments at all."

His eyes narrow, but he's smiling. "We won't see each other during the day, Florence –" he suddenly winks "– but I was rather hoping that we'd see a lot of each other . . . a hell of lot of each other, the rest of the time." He reaches across, takes the coffee cup out of my hand, then lifts my fingers to his lips and dusts a kiss on them. "I might have a flu relapse if I don't get regular nursing . . . and therapy."

This was what I was hoping for, dreaming of. I love working with Innes but I love being with him, and simply loving him, much, much more.

"You've got it all worked out, boss, haven't you?" I give him a narrow, teasing look. "So sure I'll fall in with your schemes."

"But I'm not your boss any more . . . Or I soon won't be." He kisses my palm, then tugs on my hand, drawing me closer and closer to him. "The choice is yours, Cally, believe me, always yours."

Our faces are almost touching. I can kiss the cool, firm line of his jaw, the arc of his cheekbone, or the plush curve of his lower lip, if I want to.

And I want to. I hook my hand around the back of his head, and kiss him hard. This is fraternization, office romance, but who cares now?

"OK, I choose you," I gasp against his hot mouth as we part, just barely. Time to go for broke, now or never. "Because whether you like it or not, boss, I love you."

"Consider me chosen, Nurse Florence," he growls and kisses back, just as hard. "I love you too."

From now on, it'll be Christmas every day.

Lust on Set

Sèphera Girón

When I heard that I was going to be in a movie with a rather well-known up and coming actor, Paul McKenzie, I looked him up on the internet. Funny how I was familiar with his work and had been hanging in the same circles as him for many years, yet our paths had never actually crossed.

The realm of the fantastic spreads wide and there are many opportunities to meet people. There are conventions, readings, screenings, award ceremonies, message boards, Twitter and other social network sites. As a result, we had a mutual friend who was making a low-budget movie and was looking for peers who had acting experience as well as casting bona fide "real" actors. I was surprised to get the call that he wanted me in the movie and was excited as hell to do it. I'd done a couple of small movies, been an extra in some big ones and had decades of community theatre under my belt.

It was easy to see why Paul had been cast for the movie. His twenty-nine-year-old countenance was not hard on the eyes at all. His MySpace profile picture showed a lean angular face with the twitch of a smirk and playful blue eyes. Well, at first those eyes looked playful, but, on closer examination, I was distracted by a distant longing. There were other pictures of him on his site. He had a good portfolio of model shots with him darkly brooding or boyishly grinning. In all of them, there was something going on behind his eyes that spoke of seeing too much. Like someone who has gone through a war. Painful secrets and broken hearts.

I was mostly known for my four-book vampire series, Eternal Crypt. Other creepy renderings had made me rather notorious in the dark fiction crowd, but tenacity and decades of consistently publishing also gives me cred. He had fans, I had fans. Our director was wise in pooling talent with fan bases from different aspects of the fantastical genre.

Paul at twenty-nine was roaring into life. I myself had been around the block a few times and, though not quite as enamoured of some experiences I had been part of in the past, I still was looking for that elusive something that could make my blood sing. Complacency leads to death.

Although I enjoyed his online looks, I never really considered that anything would come of my appreciation, as I was substantially older than him and not the hottest broad on the block. Perhaps I could squeak by as voluptuous but I'm a rather fleshy lady at the best of times. I never was sure if wearing baggy T-shirts was better or worse for my appeal, although I have been known to squish myself into a corset with excellent results.

After weeks of admiring him online, the star of many a self-induced, multi-orgasmic fantasy, it was at last time to meet.

The first moment I saw him, when I was walking in from the hotel parking lot, he was leaning against a wall, smoking a cigarette. His tall lean form slouched like Jimmy Dean and he had bad boy written all over him. Even though I was prepared for who he was, my legs trembled just the same. I grinned as I shook his hand and looked into those troubled blue eyes for real.

Clear and vibrant, that sad haunting was just as clear in real life as it was in the photos. I wanted to hug him in my arms and kiss him better. I wanted to press my naked body against his, taking away whatever sorrow he was hiding. I was horny for him already and he had barely said hello. Poor guy. But I pushed my lusty thoughts down.

His eyes belied his infectious enthusiasm. We quickly discussed how excited we were to be in the movie. It was a low-budget horror flick and other assorted scream queens and dark fantasy artists, writers, and special effects artists were involved. We talked about the movie and our work and how many mutual friends we had. Our director returned with other actors and we all piled into the van to go to lunch.

We were to eventually meet with several other actors for a rehearsal at the director's house. Both Paul and I were from out of town, and quite distant by several states. We'd been brought in for a day of meetings and rehearsals before several weeks of gruelling filming were to begin a couple of months later.

After lunch, the director took us to one of the warehouse locations and we walked through it as he pointed out which scenes would happen where. All of us spent the afternoon bonding and discussing set-ups and despite how I tried to make friends with the others, my attention was always drawn back to Paul.

The rehearsal went well but I was dismayed to discover that we'd never have scenes together and, in fact, wouldn't even be in town at the same time. It seemed like it was one of those things where perhaps we would just be ships that passed in the night once more.

After the rehearsal, a bunch of us went out for drinks, and stood around the bar as we had a great time telling stories. I was being billeted at someone's house, as was Paul. But not the same house. And I had to leave in the morning.

I'm sure he noticed me staring at him, hanging on to his every word, as I wondered why the laughter didn't quite reach his eyes. His arm did brush against mine a few times as we stood around the bar and, as jaded as I am, the warmth of his touch fluttered through me, stirring up my libido against my better judgment. I wanted to believe that some of our more playful glances at each other contained a deeper subtext, but despite our enthusiasm, the reality was that I was about fifteen years older than him.

With his rising fame as an artist, he already had the pick of the hottest babes. An older vampire writer likely wasn't on the menu when there was fresh, tender, tight flesh.

The more animated he became, the more quiet I grew. I didn't even try to captivate him, letting the beer flow through me, and settled into observances much like a cat patiently surveying the lie of the land. Of course, writers tend to do that anyway. We'll suddenly stop engaging in a group scene only to ponder some quirk of human nature that inspires attention. He commanded centre stage easily with boisterous stories and was admired by women and men alike for both his wit and charisma. He was just funny enough for the entertainment industry, still fresh enough to be amusing and not over-rehearsed like the more jaded actors I've met over the years.

I sipped and observed, working my way through several glasses of draught interspersed with water. A girl needs to keep her flesh hydrated so water was always consumed after every beer or two. As he spoke, I stared at him, imagining his mouth pressed against mine, pushing me back on to some large fluffy pillows somewhere. I'm sure my eyes betrayed the nasty thoughts I conjured while I

watched the evening's activities unfold. I wondered if it was possible to simply will a man to kiss you, but I knew from decades of
experience that it wasn't likely.

By the time I said goodnight to him, I was in full-blown lust and
wished that it wouldn't be too forward to ask him back to my place.
However, it wasn't my place to ask him to and I had no idea if he
felt any connection to me besides being "that vampire writer"
who's also in the movie. I didn't even have any beer to lure him
over with. So that was the end of that.

Of course, now that I'd actually met Paul in the flesh, felt his
charisma wash over me, his intellect intrigue me, and wondering
when I'd hear the story about what haunted him, thoughts of him
flitted through my head with new vim; while I was writing, while I
was at the grocery store, while I was driving. I'd go to his website
and look at the rehearsal pictures, and wonder if he ever thought
about me at all.

By the time filming started a few weeks later, the shooting list
was out and my scenes were to be shot a couple of days before his
were to start. I did learn there would be one day of our presence in
the same city, as he came in early to prepare and I had the next day
to unwind before I left.

There were several homes where people were crashing, which is
rather the norm for a B-movie experience. I was set up with other
people from my scene in one house. Other actors who appeared in
the other section of the movie were staying at another house about
a mile away. Paul was one of them.

As the days ticked by and my scenes were shot, I lamented over
ever seeing him at all during my time on the set. If he was able to
get to the set to see what it was like, how on earth would I ever get
him to stay? There wasn't really a place where everyone went to
unwind together. Since most people were local and the days were
so long, they just went home to bed.

Lunch was late because there were difficult lighting issues for
each shot. As I stood around the green room, munching on a sandwich, I saw him come in. He was escorted by a couple of the PAs
and was being introduced around. When they came to me, I hugged
him close to me. He was so thin and so real.

I stepped back and welcomed him to the set. We chit-chatted a
little while and I asked if he wanted to see if a bunch of us could go
for drinks later. He seemed up for that. Before long, the PAs were
ready to escort him to another one of the locations that he would

be working in. We exchanged cell phone numbers just in case we didn't meet again.

During one of my last scenes, he came back to the set to see what was going on. He watched the last of the scenes wind up and a small group of us decided to go out for drinks to celebrate a successful wrap. Well, for those of us that had finished our scenes. Paul had yet to begin his days on the set.

We ordered dinner and soon the beer was poured in abundance. The more we drank, the more we laughed. I found myself catching Paul's eye as we shared in the joviality. My confidence was higher, likely inspired by my successful delivery on set. I played a predatory temptress in the movie and it was hard to switch gears after living it for days though I have to admit, it wasn't a very big stretch for me.

After I watched him going outside for a cigarette for the third or fourth time, I decided to join him. He was chatting to someone from the pub about the movie and I approached them. A quick round of introductions, a bit of movie chatter and, soon, the stranger left.

"I just came out for some air," I told him.

"It's a beautiful night," he said, and it was. We stared up at the sky and he started to talk about how excited he was to start the movie. I told him how I had had a great experience and he would too. I watched him speak, the way he grinned, the way he told stories effortlessly and his ability to make me laugh. His eyes glinted in the street light and I thought of the darkness of a bedroom.

"I love this time of year," he sighed as he put out his cigarette. "Seems a shame to go back in, but we must."

He took my hand as we returned to our friends who were starting to leave.

Four of us stayed until long after hours, one of them being Randy, our designated driver. The bartender had taken a shine to the movie people and let us continue to party with him and his buddies until the wee hours. The tequila shooters came out and my confidence magnified.

By then, I was sitting close to Paul and I casually draped my hand into his lap. He didn't flinch away. I turned to look at him and smiled. He grinned back and leaned over to kiss me.

"You're beautiful," he said. His lips were softer than I would have expected and I eagerly sucked on his for a pulse or two before pushing him away.

"Now, now," I said. He winked at me and drank his beer. My heart raced at the thrill of his impulsiveness. I vaguely wondered what the others thought but several pints of beer had rendered me incapable of caring. As I thought about a harmless kiss, he kissed me again, fully and completely. This time he did take my breath away.

I excused myself to go to the washroom. Once in the ladies' room, I washed my hands and stared at my face. I figured the beer goggles must be working for the poor boy. I wasn't looking exactly young for my age at this hour of the morning. I freshened up my lipstick and fixed my hair. I returned to the table where everyone was laughing about something Paul was saying. I sat back down and Paul's attention turned back to me. I was to regale the barkeep with tales of my days of shooting, which I did rather easily.

The night began to shift into morning, slashes of the coming dawn filtering through the blinds.

"Can you believe how late it is?" I asked my friends. Everyone nodded and continued to drink.

There came that point where we didn't want to leave but knew that we should since Paul began shooting the next day, that day, in a few hours. I was sad that I wouldn't see him again or at least for a few months until the movie premiere or some convention.

I sat in the back of the car with him, saying that our tall friend with long legs should sit in the front. I scooted close to Paul and we kissed some more. By then, I didn't care what our friends in the front seat had to say.

I wondered how we could stay together for the rest of the night, despite the late hour. Even cuddling together on a cot would be heavenly. My hands cupped his face, wishing that there was some way we didn't have to part so soon, wishing I could tell him what I wanted to say but couldn't.

We pulled up to the house where he was staying, and we all said our goodbyes. He reached into his jeans and pulled out his key for the front door and I leaned into him. It fell from his fingers and on to the floor of the car. We both bent over to pick it up, nearly smashing our heads together like the Three Stooges. I spotted the key before him and quickly picked it up. I cupped it in my hand before he could see that I had found it. I pretended to continue to look for it as he lifted the mat. Our designated driving friend, Randy, turned on the dome light but try as we might, there was no key to be found by our feet.

I slipped the key into my pocket while we all left the car and tried to find a way into the locked house where everyone was asleep. We didn't want to make too much noise and upset the actors but tried to find a loose window. There was no way to break in so we all piled back into the car.

When we returned to the house where I was staying, I wondered if it would be possible to entice him. My room was upstairs, along with two other bedrooms with occupants. There was someone already asleep on the folding couch in the living room. The other living room couch was the spot for one of our friends and Randy had another small room just off the kitchen that was someone's home office. While I tiptoed into the kitchen and poured myself a glass of water, Randy whisked Paul into a little porch room off the other side of the kitchen and blew up an airbed for him.

When Randy returned to the living room without Paul, I assumed Paul was safely tucked away for the night. Randy gave me a look, as if he dared me to disturb the actor due on set in a few hours. I sighed and crept upstairs in the darkness, trying not to disturb anyone in what was now a strangely silent house.

I changed into my nightgown and went into the bathroom to brush my teeth. The dawn was filtering through the bathroom window and my heart was pounding. Paul was right below me, no doubt asleep already. I hadn't even had a chance to kiss him goodnight.

I lay down on my air mattress, turning the events of the past few days over in my mind. I was high with drink and euphoric with lust. There was no way I was ready to sleep. My thighs trembled at the thought of Paul downstairs, alone in that little room.

Before common sense could talk me out of it, I grabbed a condom from my purse and crept down the stairs, through the snoring bodies on the couches. I felt like Sylvester sneaking through the sleeping dogs in a Warner Bros cartoon, hoping they wouldn't wake. Randy was rattling around in the kitchen but I ignored him as I was now on a mission to the sunroom.

I opened the door without knocking, boldness channelling through me in a manner I've never experienced. Before Paul even realized that someone was in the room with him, I crawled on top of him where he lay on his air mattress and I kissed him. The radiance of dawn seeped through the blinds, but it was still dark enough for us to be mysterious shapes, and light enough to see the glow of his surprised eyes.

I expected him to tell me to go away, to leave him to sleep since he had to be on set soon, but his arms pulled me into him, his lips hungrily seeking out mine. Whether it was the booze, the fun of the evening, the urgency of a warm body, I didn't care; I only knew that I ached for him and wanted to take a chance.

My heart raced as I kissed him more, my hands searching out his face, his chest, his body. I wanted to feel him, to engulf him, to be one with him inside and out.

He pushed me back and sat up and, for a moment, my heart fell as I waited for the inevitable rejection. To my surprise, he lifted my nightie and buried his face between my legs.

It was all I could do to keep from moaning as his tongue found that most delicious spot. I nearly came the moment he touched me, but instead spread my legs wider with a gasp. He enthusiastically licked my rigid little clit, his fingers sliding in and out of me in an emphatic and steady rhythm. I put my hand over my mouth to keep from crying out in excitement and pleasure. I didn't want the whole house to hear us, for the other guys to think that I would sleep with just any guy. I could imagine the rumours that would spread like wildfire. They didn't know that the lust had started long before this day. And my head was swimming with dreams come true, as misguided as they might be. A woman infatuated with art can be a power to reckon with.

I gave my body over to him and he was every bit as attentive as I had ever hoped he'd be. He licked and sucked me to orgasm, I couldn't help myself, and then again. Months of lust flooded through me and on to his fingers and into his mouth. It was so hard to be quiet, but the secrecy turned me on even more. Were they listening on the other side of the door to the moans that had escaped from my lips?

I knew time was short and the sun was rising and I still hadn't done what I came to do. I didn't know if he was too drunk to enjoy himself or if he could enjoy himself with me at all. I lifted his head and made him lie back. Quickly his pants were down and I found his cock. I was surprised at how erect he was and delighted that he was bigger than he had been in my masturbatory fantasies.

My mouth opened wide to take him slowly into my mouth. I perched above him to accommodate his length down into my throat. I slowly drew back up again and proceeded to suck on him. I licked him up and down, circling his fleshy head with my tongue, slurping his shaft with wet eager lips. His firmness had me dripping and wanting once more. I stroked him with my hand, my mouth sliding up and down his length.

My thighs trembling, I slipped off my nightie and hurriedly unwrapped the condom that I had tossed beside the mattress. He sighed a little when I lowered myself on to him. I sat, letting the sensation of him filling me right up linger. My body twitched a bit but I didn't want to come again just yet. I leaned forwards on to my hands and fucked him slowly at first, enjoying the sensation of him so large and hard inside of me.

Again, I wanted to moan and tell him how much I was enjoying him, but fear of the people just outside the door hearing us kept me mute.

He pulled my face to his, kissing me while I ground into him. Our pace was pleasurably rhythmic and another swell of orgasm was so close. Suddenly, he raised his hips and tipped me back. His hands grabbed mine so that my arms were pinned behind my back. The firmness and aggressiveness of him turned me on more as he thrust into me rapidly. My breasts bobbed up and down and my pussy throbbed hungrily. I threw my head back, riding him as he ploughed into me, his grip on my hands firmly holding me how he wanted me adding another layer of exhilaration to my already overstimulated body. I wanted to shout and scream as my body released once more on to my lovely fantasy lover.

He flipped me over so that I was on my back and he was above me, his eyes glimmering as they looked into mine. His eyes were wide with heat and lust, like a lion studying his prey.

I moaned with anticipation. He entered me slowly, parting my flesh with his warm, stiff dick and I raised my legs so that my feet hooked around his back. He kissed me as he pumped into me, his lips firm around mine. My hands held on to his shoulders, my fingers dancing along his back. I moaned softly into his mouth as his cock plunged into me time and again, each stroke more ardent than the one before.

He pinned my hands above my head, fucking me hard, staring at me with those gorgeous blue eyes. I trembled and quivered, orgasm melting into another orgasm; the sensation of being held down and fucked cranked the notch of excitement up yet another level as he vigorously thrust into me.

Then, he was the one trying not moan, as he pumped his enthusiastic ecstasy into me.

He held me tightly for a few minutes, and I savoured the beating of his heart against mine. At last, he withdrew from me and turned on to his back. He shut his eyes, his mouth turned up in a satisfied smile. The birds were singing loudly outside of the window and I pulled my nightie back on. I kissed him goodbye on the cheek and quietly left his room.

Randy was still in the kitchen and I'm sure he heard every squeak of the air mattress, every muffled moan and sigh and, for all I knew, he'd been jerking off to us but I didn't care. I said goodnight to him and went up to bed.

The next day, I watched the movie being filmed for a few hours. I wanted to spend a few more minutes with Paul and, though we hung out with the other actors and crew between takes, I never had a chance to speak with him alone.

I had to catch my plane home and the PAs were ready to take me to the airport. It was time to say my goodbyes to all the lovely people I had befriended over the past few days. My movie adventure had come to a close. At least the filming part.

When I kissed Paul goodbye, I stared into his large blue eyes. They stared back at me with warmth and comfort. I looked for the haunted part, that secret part of him behind his eyes, but it wasn't there in that instant. There was a glow of comprehension, a slit parted in the curtain of his secret life, and the idea of possible penetration seized me. I smiled and he smiled back and, this time, the smile reached his eyes.

I hoped that one day our paths would cross again. Maybe even at the movie premiere. In the meantime, I just had to look at the key lying on my desk to remind me of a fantasy come true.

After a couple of weeks, I decided to go visit the set and see how it was going. Last-minute seat sales were in my favour and off I went.

One good thing about being a full-time author and part-time actor is that my schedule is more or less my own. Have laptop, will travel. Sometimes I get more done on trips than I do around the house.

I found a cheap hotel and rented a car. I stocked my room with beer, condoms, lube and some snacks, just in case I had company later. Then off I went to the set.

When I arrived they were filming a suspense scene. Paul and six other actors carefully made their way down a dark corridor, stealthily hunting an unseen monster that would be added later in CGI. I held still until the director called cut then I found a place among some of the other watchers and sat down on a folding chair beside an adorable young dark-eyed man.

When the final take was done, I was greeted by everyone with hugs and kisses. Paul rushed over.

"What are you doing here?" He had a gleam in his eye. The excitement of filming gave him a wondrous joie de vivre.

I smiled. "I figured I could take a couple of days to hang out on set. Maybe I'll write about it."

"That would be good for everyone," he said taking my hands in his firm warm ones. "I missed you."

"I missed you too," I said. Our eyes locked and my heart raced as I saw lust in his.

"I haven't had a chance to call you, I'm sorry," he said.

"Nonsense, you've been pretty busy."

"And you've been on my mind," he said, widening his eyes.

"Back on set," a PA called. Paul turned to me. "You going to stay all day?"

"You bet."

"Maybe drinks later?" he said. "A bunch of us go to a place around the corner from where I'm staying."

"Sounds good to me,"

The day passed quickly and I made notes and took a few pictures. While I was there, I struck up a conversation with the young man I had sat beside earlier. His name was Ben and he had deep dark eyes and shaggy dark hair. He wasn't thin like Paul but he was a solid man with nice arms and long fingers. An enticing contrast to Paul's fairness, he was around the same age. He had been sent by a film magazine to hang around on set for a few days to work on a story.

"I'm . . . I'm a writer too," I told him as I stuck out my hand. His grip was warm and I found myself lost in his eyes.

"I've read your books," he said, a slight flush creeping along his cheeks. "I like them."

"Thank you," I said.

Paul noticed us getting friendly and, with every short break between takes, he made sure to come over and flirt with me. I was enjoying the attention from both the young men and was glad I had made the trip.

It was early evening by the time the day was wrapped. Most of the production team was exhausted and ready to go home. The talent and journalists on the other hand, were aching to break out.

"Want to go for drinks with us, Ben?" Paul asked, as everyone was gathering up their things to leave.

"Sure," Ben replied and the three of us left the set together. I gave them a ride to the pub and we joined the other ten or so people at the table.

It was a beautiful summer night and the three of us found ourselves on the patio more than in the bar. We talked about the movie and how fun it was to shoot. Ben said he had some good coverage for his magazine. We talked about films and books and then silly jokes. As the drinks flowed, talk turned to sex, as it inevitably does.

"What's the craziest thing you've ever done?" I asked them. They both laughed and stories came out. Paul once had sex on the terrace of a restaurant behind a potted palm tree. Ben's escapades included a parked car after a rock concert and a hay mound in a barn. I grinned at them, my gaze flitting from blue eyes to brown eyes.

"Any orgies?" I asked.

Paul laughed. "Orgies . . . oh for sure. Well, parties where it seems anything goes. Mostly cast party type events," he told us.

"I've been in a couple of experiences like that," I told them. "It's so fun and spontaneous. You never know what's going to happen."

"I had a threesome once. Two girls and me," Ben offered. "That was one hell of a night."

"Mmm, threesomes. I've always wanted two guys," I said with a grin.

Paul stared at me, his eyes twinkling mischievously. "Never had a threesome?" he asked.

"Not with two guys. One of those things on my list of experiences I want to try before I die."

The waitress came around and we ordered more beer and some shooters. I excused myself to go to the bathroom and, when I returned, both the boys were staring at me intensely.

"What?" I asked as I sat down.

Paul reached over and took my hand. "Do you want your fantasy to come true?" he asked.

"What fantasy?"

"Two guys." He grinned.

My thighs trembled as I stared into his eyes. "Today?" I asked.

Paul looked over at Ben who had the biggest smile I'd ever seen. "Today," Paul said. "Now, if you want."

"I want . . ."

We left my car at the pub and took a cab to my hotel. Once inside the door, I realized I was shivering with anticipation and anxiety. I was glad I had had the foresight to have some beer on hand and offered the boys one.

As I handed Paul his beer, he took me in his arms and kissed me fully and passionately on the mouth.

"I've missed you," he whispered. My lips met his again, our tongues darting and entwining.

"I've missed you too," I said.

"I can't stop thinking about you," he said. "I'm glad you showed up."

"Me, too."

The three of us settled on the bed, clutching our beers.

"So, here we are," Paul said as he pulled some condoms from his pocket and put them on the bed. I took out the condoms and lube I had brought and added them to the collection.

"Yes, here we all are," I said. Ben raised his beer sheepishly, staring at the condoms. We drank our beer in awkward silence for a few moments.

"Why don't we all take a shower?" Paul suggested.

I nodded eagerly. "Let's!"

We all stripped off our clothes, the boys eagerly helping me remove my T-shirt and jeans. As my large breasts were released from my bra, they each took one, eagerly touching them and suckling on my nipples. I stroked both of their heads, staring down at the blond and the brunette kneeling before me. At last, I took their hands, helping them to their feet.

"Let's go," I said.

We went into the tiny bathroom and I turned on the shower. It wasn't very strong but it would do. One by one we carefully stepped into the tub, helping each other from slipping. Paul's lean form accentuated his growing erection. Ben's broader body boasted a firm and pleasing-sized expanding cock as well. I licked my lips.

The boys took care soaping me up. Their strong firm fingers rubbed across my shoulders, my back, across my breasts, along my thighs and down to my feet. Paul spread my legs and knelt down to lick my throbbing clit. I leaned back against Ben for support and his hands cupped my soapy breasts. Between Ben rubbing my breasts in a slow circular motion and Paul licking at my clit, I was in ecstasy already and we'd just begun.

Paul slipped his fingers into my warm waiting pussy and fingered my G-spot, his tongue still dancing on my clit.

My head pressed back into Ben's chest, my eyes closed as they touched and massaged my most erogenous zones. I spread my legs wider, pushing my pussy towards Paul as he fingered and sucked me to climax. I cried out, not afraid of anyone hearing me this time.

When I stopped trembling, I helped Paul stand up and, this time, I was the one kneeling. The shower pulsed against my back as I took their cocks in my hands. I stroked them together, savouring the differences in length and thickness, either one of them a wonderful specimen for any woman.

I wrapped my lips around the head of Paul's cock, teasing it lightly with my tongue, my hand stroking him as I stroked Ben. I looked up and saw them both watching me, eyes glazed with lust and my pussy was warm again.

Grabbing Ben's cock firmly, I turned my attention to him, licking his shaft and mouthing his balls. He groaned as I suckled him, teasing him and then took his cock fully in my mouth and deep in my throat.

After I sucked them both again, I slowly stood up.

"I think we've all washed enough, don't you?" I asked coyly. They both nodded and we all stepped out of the shower. The boys dried me, towelling me carefully and briskly.

Paul lay down on the bed, his arms outstretched towards me. "Kiss me," he said, and took me in his arms.

Our bodies pressed together, warm from the shower, and I remembered our night of passion a few weeks earlier. I entwined my legs around his, feeling his hardness pressed against me.

I broke the kiss and turned over to Ben who stood shyly watching. I held my hand out to him and he took it. I pulled him into me and we kissed. A soft passionate kiss, different from Paul's but exciting just the same.

Their hands roamed across me, strong manly hands that firmly touched and probed and spread and wiggled. Squirming beneath their touches, I found their cocks again and stroked them firmly. They took turns kissing me, as they fondled me in stereo.

I knelt and took Paul's cock into my mouth. As I crouched over him, Ben slipped his fingers into my pussy. My juices were slick as he thrust his hand in and out of me, his thumb pressing on my clit. My hips wiggled in glee, allowing me to take more of Paul's cock into my mouth. Paul moaned as I slurped up and down his enormous shaft.

Paul pulled me on top of him and he slid into me. I gasped at his size and grabbed for Ben's cock. As Paul fucked me, I sucked on Ben's cock. Ben grabbed my hair, pulling my head up and down in rhythm to Paul's fucking. I moaned around Ben's cock, the excitement of two beautiful men making my pussy slicker than ever.

"Fuck my ass," I said to Ben. He pulled his cock from my mouth and put a condom on it.

He crouched behind me and, though it took a bit of pressure because of Paul's size already in me, he managed to work his way in.

The sensation of being doubly penetrated caused me to moan.

"Am I hurting you?" Ben asked.

"No. You feel exquisite. Both of you feel so good inside of me," I sighed.

They fucked me, slowly, all of us trying to reach a good rhythm. Paul's lips were on mine as his hardness pierced into me and withdrew repeatedly. Ben kept a good rhythm and soon I was coming again.

"Oh, God, fill me up," I cried out. "That feels so good."

My moans filled the room as they eagerly took me to ecstasy. As I caught my breath, Ben withdrew and sat back on the bed. I disengaged from Paul as Ben put another condom on.

Paul stood up and lifted me from the bed. He held me in the air as he impaled me on his cock again. Ben stood on the other side of me, helping to hold up my legs as his cock found my eager asshole once more. They held me up, fucking me as I'd always seen on the porn sites but had never tried. I wanted to cry, the sensation was so amazing.

Slowly, they lowered me down so that Ben was lying on the bed with his cock still up my ass. Paul held up my legs as his cock found my pussy once more.

Paul leaned over me, fucking me hard, his elbows looped around my legs as his hands gripped my waist, moving me up and down on both of them.

I stared into his bright blue eyes. He grinned at me as he thrust.

"Are you enjoying your fantasy?" he asked.

"Most definitely," I sighed.

He leaned forwards to kiss me again. His teeth lightly bit my lips. "Good. So am I."

My hands touched his chest, stroking his little firm nipples. I ran my fingers across his shoulders and down his arms. The magic these men were invoking in my body was beyond my wildest dreams and I moaned and sobbed with every thrust.

"I like to hear you," Paul whispered. "It's good to hear you."

"No one spying on us today!" I gasped with a grin.

Paul angled himself so that he hit my G-spot. The slight difference in pressure sent me over the edge and a gush of warm liquid flooded from my pussy as I came all over them. As my juices ran down Ben's legs, Paul withdrew.

"I want to come on your tits," Paul said as Ben continued to fuck my ass.

I held my tits up, pulling on my nipples, as he peeled off his condom and stroked on his cock. His eyes stared intensely as my fingers tweaked and toyed with my breasts. His hand moved faster up and down his shaft until he cried out. His come spurted across my tits in a warm pulsing stream.

"Jesus," he cried out, his body trembling.

I disengaged myself from Ben and rolled over. Paul went into the bathroom and cleaned himself up and returned with a washcloth. He gently washed his come from my breasts as Ben watched.

Paul kissed me fully on the mouth.

"Now, for you," he said turning to Ben.

"How do you want to come?" I asked him.

"I want to fuck your beautiful pussy," Ben said, pulling on another condom. He manoeuvred me so that I was on my hands and knees. He squatted behind me and slowly eased his thick cock into me.

I groaned with the newness of him and pushed back. He filled me up for a moment, his cock hot and throbbing inside of my warm tingling flesh.

His hands clutched my hips and soon he was fucking me hard and fast. The bed shook with his thrusts and I watched Paul watching us with a lusty look on his face as he sipped on a beer.

Ben fucked me hard and my head was spinning. His hands moved from my hips to my breasts and I sat up higher, taking him deeper, my hands reaching behind me to hold on to him for balance. Paul reached over and fingered my clit. More shudders throbbed through my body, lost in the frantic thrusting of Ben. My moans were soon joined by his, as he pumped his pleasure into me. He stiffened and cried out, and soon the pulse of his orgasm met with my own.

Ben collapsed on top of me and I lay under him for a while, enjoying the masculine warmth of his body pressed against mine, his panting breath loud in my ears.

As I slowly regained my senses, Ben rolled off me. Paul sat on the bed, holding out a beer for us.

"Thank you," I said, as I took a bottle and drank deeply from it.

The next morning, we all went to the set. It was Ben's last day and, when filming was finished, Paul and I said our goodbyes to him.

"It was lovely to meet you," I said as I hugged him.

"I hope we meet again," Ben said with a shy smile.

"I'm sure we will."

That night I took Paul back to my hotel room and that was our routine for the next two days. We talked and fucked and drank lots of beer. It was a wonderful time to forget the reality of daily life back home. We talked about our threesome and other adventures we were curious to try. But fantasy can last only so long. I had to return home.

As I dropped Paul off at the set on my way to the airport, my heart ached.

"I guess this is goodbye, again," I said sadly as we sat in the car.

"Yes, it is, for now," he said.

"I guess I'll see you at the premiere." I averted my eyes.

He took my chin in his hand and tilted my face up towards his. His eyes were staring intensely at me. "You aren't getting rid of me that easily. I'm going to come and see you once this movie wraps."

I smiled as he kissed me fully on the mouth.

"Oh, I almost forgot," I said with a laugh.

"What?"

I fumbled in my purse and brought out the key. I handed it to him. "I think this belongs to you."

He took it and held it up. After a moment, he laughed. "Why you . . ." He kissed me fully on the mouth, his tongue darting against mine.

"I can hardly wait for this movie to be over," he said. He slid out of the seat and closed the door. He peeked into the window one last time and winked.

I watched his tall lean form saunter away and I smiled.

Hot Out Here

Delilah Devlin

Beads of condensation, glittering jewel-like in the sputtering candlelight, ran in rivulets down the sides of Jason's ice-cold beer.

Detail I shouldn't have been able to note, given the fact I wasn't anywhere near him.

As I lowered my nephew's toy binoculars, I reflected that I had indeed sunk to a new low. You see, my bedroom window conveniently overlooks Jason and Robert's fenced backyard. A fact that never registered with the previous tenants, but one that proved too delicious to ignore after the arrival of the handsome duo.

I began a furtive surveillance at once. One that had me cringing in embarrassment each time I greeted them in passing and feeling even more ashamed when we struck up a friendship.

We'd shared meals, drinks, watched football games together on their wide-screen TV. And still, I peeked into their backyard, waiting for those moments when they popped outside to mow it or catch a few summer rays. Their bodies gleamed with sweat while raw lust warred inside me along with the fear that I'd mess up our relationship if I let the guys know how I really felt.

My convenient perch on the windowsill afforded me a window into their private lives, and I was hooked from the very beginning. They'd become an obsession, one frustrated by the fact they treated me like a kid sister rather than a woman one of them might desire.

And therein lay another problem. I'd resisted the urge to seek a deeper relationship because then I'd have to choose. My libido was completely fickle, lusting after Jason's muscled physique, then sighing over the possibilities of what Robert's tall, bony frame and large feet hinted at. That their personalities were perfect bookends, fierce and funny, confused my heart as well.

Lucky me, I licked the sweat gathering on my upper lip while this night one of the handsome men living next door tilted his bottle and took several long sips. The look of pure bliss that softened his otherwise stern features made my chest ache.

I watched the movement of Jason's throat as he worked it down, imagining him sipping at my overheated flesh. My skin began to tingle. My nipples beaded, crowding uncomfortably against my lace bra. My thighs clenched as a delicious wash of arousal seeped to wet the crotch of my plain panties.

The sigh he emitted as he set the bottle on the table was echoed by my own painful groan. Watching either of them had never caused my heart to skip a beat like that hint of a moan sliding on the tail of Jason's long exhalation.

Sure, it was hotter than hell out there. I too felt the effects of the enervating heat. Record temperatures had strained the region's resources and planned service interruptions began that night. But something about that sigh felt . . . unsubtle, exaggerated, maybe even dramatic. And Jason was too straightforward a man for that.

I blotted sweat from my forehead, asking myself again, What am I doing?

Only this time, my peeping hadn't been deliberate. I'd rushed home from work and showered quickly to beat the brownout. Then I'd put on my underwear, pulled back the curtains and opened the window, hoping for a breeze to cool my skin. Sitting limply on the sill, I waited for the world to flicker into life again.

That's when I'd noticed him, sitting in a lounge chair alone in the dark.

He wore his usual work "uniform" – khaki trousers, white shirt and a tie. Tonight, the tie hung loosened and askew, his collar opened beneath it.

I could see it all despite the lack of electricity. Moonlight silvered his dark hair and reflected bright as a beacon against the white shirt. The golden light from the large citronella candle lent warmth to his skin and the amber bottle he held between his hands.

As always, he was lovely to watch, but tonight his expression drew my attention more than his breath-stealing features. A sullen slanting of his brows, a bit of pout plumping his masculine lips, an edgy energy to his slight movements – he was either irritated or aroused.

Wanting an answer to the "either-or", I watched. My forte is observation; my people-radar exquisitely tuned to body language and a voice's tonal cues. My curiosity and my lust were caught. No way could I back away from my window now.

The bottle tapped the table as he set it aside. A long-fingered hand tugged the knot of his tie, dragging it from his neck.

When he began to undo the row of buttons down the front of his shirt, I settled deeper on the sill, leaning closer, but taking care to keep my pale body hidden behind the sheer curtain.

The edges of the shirt parted over a broad, nicely muscled chest. My gaze zeroed in on taut, lean abs dusted with dense fur the same colour as his close-cropped black hair that stretched nipple to nipple then ran along a thin dark line to slip beneath his zipper.

His hand stroked his chest, scratching through the hair, the faint crinkling sound causing my own chest to tighten, my nipples to surge.

A light sheen of sweat glimmered on his chest and belly. Again, my tongue swept my lips, tasting salt, and I imagined I lapped the dew right off his skin.

When a lazily roaming hand slid over his belly, I tensed, fascinated, as he swept the flat plane. Would he be hard or desk-soft? He looked firm. So, I enjoyed fantasizing that he was and touched my own stomach, following his path.

His hand slid down to the knot bulging behind his fly, and he cupped it. Squeezed.

My own hands itched to replace his and grew still, clenching against the fantasy of holding his burgeoning cock as it roused. My cheeks heated and my breaths shortened. No need to tease my own body into arousal, moisture already soaked my panties.

The buckle opened, and the belt slid sinuously from the loops as he lifted his hips and pulled it free. A flick of his thumb and the button at the waistband of his trousers opened. His zipper rasped as it slid down.

Dark fabric formed a V-like shadow as his hand rooted beneath his waist, and then he slipped the long, gleaming column of his semi-aroused sex from the flap at the front of his boxers and wrapped his fingers around it.

I swallowed the liquid pooling in my mouth. I blinked to moisten eyes that had grown dry and scratchy as I stared, wide-eyed. My breaths grew ragged, a little choked, and I must have made a noise, because suddenly his head swung my way. His eyes narrowed on my bedroom window.

I froze, hoping his gaze couldn't penetrate the darkness.

But a crooked smile slowly stretched his lips, and his hand tightened around himself and began to pump up and down the thickening rod, all the while staring up at me.

Jason knew I watched but didn't seem to mind. I let out a deep, trembling breath and continued to stare, my own body heating, growing increasingly aroused in tandem with his hardening cock.

His head turned away, and his hand dropped from his engorged cock. It fell against his belly with a soft, muffled thud. Heavy, hot, thick – I knew its girth would stretch my mouth.

Another sound intruded. The chime of my doorbell. I bit back a curse and drew away from the window, slung on my robe, then headed downstairs to the front door.

Robert stood in on the stoop, a lazy grin on his face, a sweep of lank blond hair covering one eye and two beers dangling from his fingers. He was shirtless. Low-riding blue jeans encased his slender hips and long legs. His large feet were bare. "Thought you might like to join us."

"Us?" I repeated stupidly, dragging my glance upwards again to lock with his.

"Jason and me?" His head tilted, and his pale-blue eyes studied me.

Did he know what Jason was up to? He hadn't been in the backyard. Maybe he didn't know and the invitation was issued without a carnal subtext.

It wasn't like I hadn't enjoyed a beer or dinner at their place before, but it had always been a "friend thing".

"Are you OK? You look a little flushed." The teasing glint in his eyes, and more, the narrowed focus of his stare, told me he knew exactly what I'd seen. His gaze slid beyond my shoulder into my darkened living room. "Keep us company until the lights come on?"

I nodded, afraid to attempt a verbal assent with my tongue glued to the roof of my dry mouth.

The cool beer slid into my hand, and he clasped my wrist to lead me through his house and into the backyard.

My heart pounded hard. I was afraid but also a little giddy to approach Jason after seeing so much of his naked body. When I stepped through the glass, I found him lying on the lounge chair completely nude except for a towel draped across his lap.

"Excuse me for not rising," he said, a mocking smile curling the corners of his lips while a hard stare bored into me.

Unnerved, my chin came up and I rounded on Robert, whose watchful gaze narrowed on me. "So you both know I peeked. Did you bring me here to make fun of me?"

"Not at all," Robert replied smoothly. "We thought you might be as hot as we are. Might like to cool off with a beer."

"And that's all?"

"If that's all you want . . ." Jason dragged the towel from his hips and placed an arm beneath his head, a relaxed pose completely at odds with the extreme angle of his cock.

I couldn't help thinking how nicely angled it was – nearly perpendicular to his hips, a seventy-five-degree angle at the very least.

Once again, with me watching, Jason wrapped his fingers around his shaft, just under the crown, and stroked towards his groin. The pull dragged the skin downwards, emphasizing the elegant shape of the tapered head, the gleaming satin that cloaked the hard column and the bluish veins that tracked all around it.

My gaze whipped back to Robert, but I couldn't meet his eyes. I'd come, knowing something would happen, having been seduced by the heat and the promise of hard cock.

Robert's hand still clasped my wrist, and his thumb smoothed over the thin skin.

Did he note the rapid beat of my heart as my excitement spiked? The hand holding the beer lifted, and he slid it into the opening of my robe, snuggling it between my breasts.

I gasped as cool moisture met my hot, flushed skin. A hand slipped up the inside of one thigh and I glanced down at Jason, whose expression held a hint of challenge. His fingers slid upwards, halting where my thighs clenched together, waiting . . .

"You trust us, don't you?" Robert said softly. "We're friends. That won't change. But wouldn't you like us to be . . . more?"

Wordlessly, I widened my stance, allowing Jason to smooth upwards until his fingers met the edge of the elastic banding at the top of my thigh. My gaze shot back to Robert's who studied my reactions to Jason's intimate touch.

"Open your robe, sweetheart," Robert whispered, sliding the bottle up and down the centre of my chest.

My lips parted. I meant to say something to ease my embarrassment, something light and witty, but Jason's fingers traced the
damp cotton, burrowing into the fabric and between my swelling
folds. I remained mute, knowing I couldn't push a single word past
my tightening throat. With my free hand, I pulled at the cord tied
around my waist, loosening it. The edges of the robe fell open.
Warm, muggy air brushed over my body.

Robert rolled the cold bottle across the tops of my hot breasts,
then over the thin cups of my bra, lingering over my nipples until
they began to sprout. He set aside the beer and pulled mine from
my cramped fingers, then pushed the robe from my shoulders until
it fell behind me to the ground. Standing in my underwear, two
male gazes sweeping my curves, my uneasy qualms disappeared.

An opportunity presented itself. One of extraordinary appeal.
Jason's thickly muscled body gleamed with health and an alluring
power. Robert's long, lean frame was just as appealing, but in a
very different way. So tall, I could rise on tiptoe and not meet his
lips; his height overwhelmed me.

I liked the feeling of helpless femininity that swamped me. I was
theirs for the taking. Even with Jason's fingers strumming my pussy,
I knew they were waiting for me to make the first move, to give
them permission to proceed.

"How sturdy is that lounge chair?" I asked Jason.

His lips curved into a wicked smile. "Climb over me, and we'll
find out."

"Not so fast, Jace," Robert murmured. "She's been spying on us."

I pressed my lips together, but wondered why I no longer felt
ashamed at the accusation. Jason's fingers slid inside my underwear
and between my slick folds.

I rocked on the balls of my feet, fighting the need to sway beneath
his coaxing, sliding assault. Robert's hand cupped my jaw, lifting
my gaze, but I closed my eyes halfway, not wanting to meet his
steady stare.

"Haven't you, Emily? Haven't you been watching us?"

I bit my lip, and then released it around a ragged exhalation.
"Yes. I've been spying."

"What should we do with you? Do you think we should ignore it?
Award your transgression by giving you pleasure?"

I sure hoped so, but the sharp edge of his quiet whisper excited
me. I wanted more of that rasping disdain. "I should be punished,"
I said softly, wondering where that came from.

Robert's glance sliced to Jason, whose lips thinned.

Was he hiding a smile, or was he really disapproving? Jason swung his legs over the side of the lounger and stood.

With both men flanking each other, standing so close I could feel the heat radiating from their bodies, I began to quiver. Excitement shivered through me, plucking at my nipples, releasing a gush of arousal that soaked the crotch of the panties Jason had abandoned.

"Maybe she needs a spanking?" Jason said, crossing his arms over his chest.

My downcast gaze clung to the cock that remained rigid, thrusting upwards from a nest of wiry, black hair at his groin.

"Maybe she should service us," Robert said softly.

I swallowed, liking that suggestion even more, but unwilling to let them see how much.

"I'd like to warm her bottom a bit, first," Jason said, grit in his tone.

Oh. My. God. Both suggestions appealed. I shifted my feet, fighting the tension curling in my womb. I fisted my hands at my sides to keep from reaching out.

"We've been exposed, ogled, our privacy invaded to serve her perversion."

"Uh-huh," Jason murmured, his hand petting his long, ridged shaft.

He knew I stared at him still. I darted him a glance and found his narrowed gaze fixed on my face. "First, I think she needs to be as exposed as I am." He lifted his chin. "Strip," he ordered.

I didn't hesitate. I reached behind me and struggled with the hooks of my bra until it sagged in front and I let it drop. Then I slid my panties down my legs and stepped out of them.

When I straightened, both male chests in front of me rose as they pulled in deep breaths. My confidence reinforced, I squared my shoulders and faced them with my chin raised.

"Turn around," Jason rasped.

I turned slowly, glancing over my shoulder.

"Don't watch us," he reprimanded. "Haven't you done enough of that already?"

"Bend over and clasp your ankles," Robert murmured.

I balked, lowering my brows. "Is that really necessary?"

"Bend over," Jason repeated. "Or we send you home."

His implacable stare ate away at my resistance. I didn't want to leave. I turned away and widened my stance, then bent at the waist, curving downwards, as the muscles in the backs of my thighs stretched.

Air whistled between teeth behind me.

Blood rushed towards my head, and I found it hard to breathe. "Has this been long enough?"

"I'm really liking the idea of that spanking," Jason said, his voice more hard-edged than before.

"Widen your stance," Robert said quickly.

"Lord protect me from sadists," I muttered. I heard the rasp of a zipper and watched between my legs as Robert's jeans sagged around his ankles. He pushed them off and kicked them to the side.

"I'm getting dizzy with all the blood rushing to my head." What really made my head swim was the thought of looking at Robert's cock, but I couldn't see high enough up his legs from this angle.

"Then go to the chair and bend over it."

"Good idea," Jason said.

Laughter caught me by surprise. They sounded like two boys arranging their soldiers for battle. Only I was a life-sized toy especially for their pleasure.

The thought didn't dampen my arousal one bit. I straightened, shaking my head as blood drained south, gave them a sullen pout and stomped towards the chair. Keeping my back to them, I made quite a display of myself as I knelt in the grass and bent slowly over the chair, widening my knees to give them another glimpse of moist pussy. Maybe they'd get the hint and get down to business.

"A spanking would be awfully loud, don't you think?" Robert said. "Neighbours might hear."

"But they won't see. She's the only one whose upstairs windows look into our yard."

"True. She'd have to keep her howls quiet."

"I don't howl." But I did growl.

"Not yet you don't."

I snuggled my breasts against the seat cushions and rubbed. If they weren't going to do more than talk I might have to take matters into my own hands.

"Better get on with it. Suspense is always the worst part of punishment." Robert sounded so cheerful, I gritted my teeth. Their soft footfalls brought them closer to me.

Jason sighed loudly as he knelt. Fingers slid into my folds, then withdrew. "Just a taste to tide me over."

A slap landed on one fleshy globe, and I gasped. "That was a little hard."

A soft masculine grunt gusted. "Supposed to sting," Robert said. "It's punishment."

Another harder slap landed, this one muffled by the weight of the hand. "See? That's how it's done," Jason said, satisfaction lacing his words. "Firm, but not harsh."

"Don't spare the goddamn rod," I muttered.

"Exactly."

Slaps landed, one after the other, on my upturned buttocks, so fast my breaths came in shattered little gulps. As the flesh of my ass warmed beneath their strokes I wriggled, trying to avoid them, really trying to invite a sharp slap against the hot flesh between my legs.

One of them finally got the hint and rapid slaps landed directly on my pussy – taps that jolted me forwards until I lay over the chair, groaning.

Something hard and cold rolled over my bottom. A beer bottle. When it rolled between my legs, air hissed between my clenched teeth.

"She liked that, Robert."

"Get the ice chest."

I buried my head against my folded arms and waited while the rustling movements drew further away, and then returned.

Something small and stingingly cold was slipped inside me. An ice cube!

"Sweet Jesus," I groaned as it slid deeper and began to melt. Another cube rubbed lower, over my distended clit, cupped against me by a broad hot palm.

Hot and cold stroked over me, leaving a wet trail over my slit then my ass.

"Feel better, now?" Robert asked. A soothing hand continued to stroke over my sensitized skin.

I jerked a nod, afraid to say anything that sounded like a complaint.

"Do you think you've been punished enough?" Robert's long fingers slid between my buttocks, glancing over my back entrance.

Although fleeting, the painful intimacy of it left me breathless. "I don't know," I replied, wanting to be fucked, but also deeply curious about what the two men might come up with next. "What do you think?"

"I think she hasn't learned her lesson at all," Jason bit out, his fingers sinking deep into my pussy. "She's drenched. I think she liked our punishment a bit too much."

"Emily, Emily," Robert said, pretending disappointment.

I aimed a hot glare over my shoulder and caught Jason's widening grin. Damn!

"See what I mean? She hasn't learned a damn thing," he said, looking smug.

"Perhaps we should make her ache a bit."

"Sore throat?"

"And jaws."

"A little tennis elbow?" Jason's eyebrows lifted in a wicked arch. Then his gaze dropped to his cock. "You know what I want."

I growled deep in my throat, but secretly I was more than willing. I'd envisioned sucking his cock until he quivered a thousand times. My gaze landed on Robert's cock for the first time, and my breath left in a rush. "Holy fu—!"

"We'll get there," Robert purred. "Promise, sweetheart."

With a deep, resentful sigh, I faced them on my knees, my head down, hands clasped together.

"I'm not buying her show of obedience."

Jason's gravelled tone, and the way his fingers tapped his cock, caused my supplicant's mask to slip a notch. Irritation drew my brows together.

"Maybe she thinks we'll go easy on her if she plays it up a bit," Robert said in an exaggerated aside.

"I'm way past easy. That mouth of hers has been driving me crazy for months."

Suddenly, I didn't mind that they teased me, drawing out my patience. Jason loved my big mouth.

"Since the very first day she showed up with a casserole dish in her arms." Robert earned brownie points for his quiet agreement.

"Didn't buy the Suzy Homemaker act, either," Jason rumbled.

"Too much passion in those lips."

"Can't cook worth a damn."

My gaze shot up to find them both pressing their lips together to fight smiles. A challenge was tossed as I flipped my red hair behind my shoulders.

I reached out my hands to encircle both of their impressive cocks and tugged them closer. The men flanked me, standing slightly to my side. Beneath my lashes I appraised their excitement. Jason's cheeks and square jaw sharpened. Robert's eyes glinted in the darkness.

I brought them closer and rubbed the tips of their cocks over my pursed lips, gratified when moisture painted them in salty streaks. Drawing back, I licked my lips, closing my eyes as a genuine groan crept from my throat.

All humour bled away from their expressions. Sharply honed tension gripped their faces and bodies as I stuck out my tongue and swabbed first one soft crown then the other, taking care to poke the tip into their tiny slotted openings before sitting back again and gauging my next actions by how rapidly they breathed.

Jason's nostrils flared and his hands fisted on his hips.

Robert's arms lifted away from his sides, as though he meant to fly or perhaps just because he didn't know what to do with his hands.

I rubbed my cheeks along their shafts, purring like a kitten, then pointed their cocks upwards and dived first towards Robert's balls, opening wide to gobble them with my lips while my tongue painted them with moisture.

"Goddamn," he breathed.

I turned quickly to Jason and suckled him hard, surrounding him in heat, tugging his hard stones with my lips until he lifted on the balls of his feet and began to rock.

When I released him, I stroked my tongue up his length, holding his hot gaze with mine, until I reached the head atop his thick shaft. I opened wide . . . but backed away.

Again, I switched, ignoring Jason's deep growl and swallowed Robert's round, blunt head, my lips stretching around him and sinking lower as I swirled my tongue up and down the steamy sides of his cock.

At last, he figured out what to grasp and sank his fingers in my hair, guiding me slowly forwards and back until I began to suction hard on each upstroke and his hips flexed forwards, stroking deep into my mouth, faster and faster.

I squeezed my fingers around him and pumped up when he pulled away, stroked away when he sank into my mouth. Over and over, faster and faster, while the wet, juicy strokes grew louder.

"Fucking hell, Rob," Jason rumbled.

I gave Jason's cock a rough tug. His hand closed around mine. He guided it up and down once, and then he stepped back.

Robert's mouth opened around a deep, agonized groan. He tugged my hair hard until I came off his cock, gasping for breath. He too stepped back and then Jason moved in, placed his hands beneath my arms and lifted me off my feet.

He walked me backwards, my legs dangling until he reached the chair, sat me on the end then shoved me down until I lay with legs hanging over the edge. When he dropped to his knees and buried his face between my thighs, I laughed, low and throaty, enjoying the fact I'd turned his "punishment" against him. But my victory was short-lived.

His mouth closed around my clit, his fingers slid between my damp folds, and suddenly, my back arched as he drew hard, suckling until pinpricks of pleasure crackled all over my damp, sweaty skin. Rough hands lifted my thighs over his shoulders; he cupped my ass, controlling my movements, impeding me from rocking against his mouth.

He tugged, licked and sucked me until I squirmed. When Robert came at me, lowering himself over my head to latch his lips around one nipple, I knew they'd taken back control.

I trembled beneath their joint assault, quivering uncontrollably. Completely overwhelmed.

With Jason's face swirling, his whiskers scraping my inner thighs, his tongue fluttering against my clit, his fingers plunging deep, I couldn't concentrate on just one sensation – so many bombarded me, ratcheting up my pleasure to a painful peak.

When my arousal curled tight, I dug my heels into Jason's back and bucked.

Robert pulled away.

Then Jason. Licking his lips and smiling, as I came back down, disgruntled because I'd almost climaxed, and the delicious tension was quickly ebbing away.

"Think you've learned your lesson, now?" Jason whispered.

I hiccoughed, which surprised me because it sounded like a sob. I couldn't muster a scowl, could only stare as he rose in front of me.

His gaze tore away from me, landing on Robert who sidled up beside him. "Let's cool her down. I don't want this over too quick."

I jackknifed upwards, ready to leave. Suddenly, I felt weepy, knowing I couldn't take much more before I flew at them. My emotions were raw, my pussy throbbing. I'd rather take a cold shower than let either of them tease me to the edge of the precipice again, because I'd scream. To hell with the neighbours.

"Where do you think you're going?" Robert said, his voice dead even.

The corners of Jason's lips quirked upwards.

I could barely stand to look at either of them, their cocks engorged, rising thick and straight from their groins. "I'm through playing. I'd like to go home."

Robert's gaze lifted to Jason, and then he leaned towards me and wrapped a hand around the back of my neck, forcing me forwards. Our lips met. A soft melding. It struck me that they'd touched my entire body, but never kissed me. I mewled against Robert's lips and wrapped my arms around his neck.

He drew back and kissed my forehead, then turned me in a circle with his hands on my shoulders until I faced Jason.

My gaze lowered to the broad, furred chest and a deep moan slipped between my lips.

Jason closed the space between us and his hand lifted my chin. Our mouths mated.

At the first stab of his tongue I melted against him, sighing when his arms wrapped around me. This was what I'd craved. A hint of tenderness. Something to reassure me I was more than just a convenient fuck.

His fingers combed through my hair, cupping my head. My hands lifted to glide up his hard, muscled chest until I clung to his shoulders, while our mouths and tongues moved in endless circles.

When he broke the kiss, he rested his forehead against mine. "Still want to leave?"

I shook my head.

"Let us finish this my way?"

Without hesitating, I nodded.

His smile was slow, warm – and approving.

An inner glow suffused my body, warming me again.

"Bend over the lounge chair, sweetheart."

He stepped back, and I closed my eyes for just a brief moment, hating the loss of his caresses. I walked directly to the chair and knelt, bending once again until my torso lay on the chair and my ass rose in the air.

The rattle of ice in the chest told me the boys weren't done playing. Fingers stroked my pussy and another cube was inserted.

A sharp hiss sounded behind me. "Seemed like a good idea," Jason said, his voice tight, "but goddamn that's cold!"

"Warm it up," Robert said with snicker.

A broad, blunt tip prodded my opening and a thick column of cock slid into me, strangely chilled. "What did you do?" I asked, as my cunt clasped it, contracting tightly around him as he drove deeper.

"Thought I'd cool down my dick with ice. Not a good feeling. But this is better, don't you think?"

It was. The ice cube melting inside me was shoved deeper with each firm stroke. Friction built between the walls of my channel and his thick cock heated me up from the inside. I snuggled closer to the chair, raising my ass for him to tunnel deeper.

Liquid from the melted ice churned with my own cream and his thrusts, resulting in juicy-wet laps of molten honey that dripped down my inner thighs as he continued to pump.

"Watching's fine, but I'm wondering when you're going to remember I'm here," Robert said, irony flavouring his words.

"Emily," Jason said, gritted out, "time to perform more community service. Lean up and let's get rid of this chair."

Jason's arms enfolded my waist, and he leaned back, taking me up with him. Staked on his cock, I bounced against his lap, unwilling to lose the escalating tension winding at my core, while Robert pulled away the chair and knelt in front of me.

His lopsided smile invited as he threaded his fingers through my hair and brought my face towards his lap.

My lips opened to accept his thrust while Jason lifted me to my knees, never breaking our connection.

With Jason pumping into my pussy and Robert driving towards my throat, I began to moan loudly as the tension curled tighter inside me.

"Shhh, Emily," Jason whispered.

Robert shoved deeper into my throat, effectively cutting off my voice, as I opened my jaws wider to accept him and swallowed around his head to give him a wet, sexy caress.

Jason's hands smoothed over my back then around my sides to clutch my shivering breasts. "Not gonna last," he ground out.

I gave a garbled shout which vibrated all along Robert's cock, then began to suction hard.

Robert's thighs tensed beneath my hands then his hips lifted, and he stroked into my mouth. "Damn, damn, damn," he chanted.

Jason hammered hard, slapping the cradle of my sex, the sound moist and unmistakable in the heavy night air.

I couldn't worry about the whole neighbourhood listening in, couldn't think beyond the hard body pounding behind me and the lean, long muscled one thrusting towards my face.

Tension coiled deep inside me, and then suddenly unwound. My pussy convulsed, pulsing around Jason's shaft. My muffled shout accompanied a tightening of my throat and mouth. Agonizing pleasure exploded, blinding me as I shuddered and writhed. Molten liquid bathed my womb in scalding spurts; thick ropes of salty come coated my tongue. As the churning, rocking motions slowed, hands caressed my face and breasts, arms enfolded me.

Jason brought me up, pulling me from Robert's cock, and hugging me against his chest. Robert bent to kiss and nuzzle my breasts as I fought for breath. A fine sheen of sweat coated all our bodies. Our rasping breaths lengthened and slowly eased.

"Do you think she's had enough punishment?"

I blinked my eyes open to find Robert's expression schooled once again into stern condemnation. Only now I knew it was part of the game. A game I was only too eager to play.

I bit my lower lip and cast my gaze downwards. "I'm still not sorry."

The lights flickered on and the ceiling fan whined as it started to whir. The hand lying on my hip squeezed and I pushed my bottom against Robert's groin. He wasn't aroused. Just needed a little comfort. Which was why we'd moved from the yard to Jason's bed.

Fingers curved around my chin, forcing my face towards his. Jason's dark gaze landed on my lips as he rubbed his thumb over the lower edge of my pout. "Power's back."

I didn't know how to take that. Did he mean the fun was over and it was time for me to go home? "Yeah, I suppose I should head back to my place."

Robert's hand grew still on my hip and he shifted behind me, rising.

Jason's gaze narrowed. "Is that what you want?"

"No," I said, wanting to be honest, but wanting them to take away my fear that I hadn't made a huge mistake.

"What do you want, Emily?"

I took a chance. "I don't want to fuck this up. We've been friends. I don't want to lose that. But when I leave, the next time I see you guys, it'll be different."

"Because you've seen us nekkid?" Robert said, kissing my shoulder.

I turned my head and kissed his cheek. "Because we've all seen each other come. And because I'm a girl. This might be something you do for fun, but I've never played like this."

Jason tweaked my nipple hard. "You think this is a game?"

"See there?" I said, trying to keep a tremor out of my voice but failing. "I'm afraid to answer that. I don't want things to change."

"But we do."

Robert turned my face. His features were tight, his expression worried. "Do you think we've ever been friends with a woman like we are with you? That was our first clue. We liked having you around. But we both paid hell trying to keep our dicks from scaring you away."

Jason snorted. "He was afraid. I wanted to jump you from day one."

"So what is it you want?" I asked, turning the question on them both.

Jason's eyebrows furrowed. "You here. Under me."

"Ugh," I quipped, then let him see my grin.

"I'm willing to share," Robert said. "I want us getting closer."

"You wanna see where this goes? I'm OK with that. It'll give us time to see if it can work."

Jason cupped my breast and scooted closer. "Through talking?"

Robert and I both laughed.

Jason shoved Robert back then rolled over me. "I'm not much of a talker when I'm horny. Get used to it."

Jason's aggression, I was beginning to suspect, masked his own insecurity. I opened my legs and wrapped them around his hips. Then I reached up to kiss him.

He slid inside me and groaned, tucking his head into the corner of my shoulder.

I met Robert's crooked smile and he lifted a hand from Jason's back and gave it a kiss. "Hungry?"

"I think I will be."

His loose-jointed frame ambled away, and Jason turned the power on, angling deep, his strokes sharp and quickening. He brought us both to completion in moments.

As he slowed the motion of his hips, he opened his eyes. "Think you can get out of your lease?"

While Robert might have been the more skilled at conversation, Jason got straight to the point with a precision that took my breath away. "Do you both want me here?"

"We already talked."

"When?"

"Months ago."

"What took you so long to include me in the conversation?"

"We wanted to do everything right. Get you to like us first. To trust us. Then seduce your pants off. I got a little impatient tonight."

I cupped his cheek and smiled. "I'm glad you did. But I'll never look at a beer the same way again . . . or an ice cube."

He leaned down and kissed me hard, lips sucking at mine, tongue thrusting deep.

When we both came up for air, he groaned and pulled away. "Hate that part."

"Me too. I should shower."

"After you eat. Smell dinner?" He reached down and grabbed my hand, then tugged me up.

Wearing one of the guys' T-shirts, I followed him downstairs to the kitchen. Robert looked up. "Like what you're not wearing, sweets."

I laughed. "Jason insisted."

The meal wasn't an ordeal. Wasn't awkward in the least. We talked about football, about work, about where we wanted to vacation. It was the same as it had always been between us . . . only better. We were connected now. Sex added a new dimension to the friendship.

The house was still warm, so we headed out to the backyard with a blanket. Watching the stars overhead and listening to the hum of ACs from the row of houses stretching down the road, we cuddled and explored, fingers searching out all those lovely "joy" spots until the tension built and we shucked our clothes again.

This time, straddling Robert's hips with Jason pressed against my back, I didn't hold a thing back. Not my moans. Not the emotions flowing through me. When I got a little weepy towards the end because they'd pushed me too far, Jason's arms encircled my waist, Robert's hands stroked over my shoulders and breasts.

"You OK?" Jason asked, kissing the sensitive spot behind my ear.

"Never better."

A breeze kicked up, licking at the sweat drying on our skin.

We settled to the blanket, spooned together.

"I'm thinking we should move," Jason said, his voice a deep, rumbling growl that tickled my ear.

Robert snorted. "We need some property. No neighbours."

"I like the way you two think," I said. They were making plans for a future. Tentative ones, but I was all right with taking baby steps if they wanted to slow down. I had a feeling, one that warmed me from the inside out, that we were on the right track. They'd wanted to be friends first. Wanted to know me and for me to know them.

"I'm gonna give my nephew's binoculars back."

Love Under Will

Adrianne Brennan

The grey, rocky landscape made Aliyael cringe. Her eyes burned and she longed for some splash of colour, some vague semblance of cheery reality. It made her long for her physical assignments on Earth.

I hate dream sequences. They never stop being all grey tones until the person starts to be a bit more aware.

The angel surveyed the woman nearby with a critical eye. Brown hair in knots all over her tense shoulders, worry lines around her mouth . . . she looked a mess. In short, this looked to be one hell of an angelic assignment, even for a seraph-ranking angel like herself.

Sighing, Aliyael sat down on the ground next to her. *Better get this over with before she wakes.* Walking into people's dreams could be sometimes fun, and sometimes not. She hoped this wouldn't turn into bad. Seeing humans' nightmares was the closest Aliyael had ever come to feeling the absence of the Powers That Be. "Petrifying" couldn't even come close to describing the sensation which chilled her to the core.

I can never truly understand humans, nor am I sure I want to.

Fighting back a tremor, she brought her attention back to her appointed task.

"Well, hello there, Claire."

The brunette turned to Aliyael with a start. "Oh, hi." Her quiet voice sounded strained.

"You look like a lot's on your mind. Life got you down?"

Claire shrugged.

"Well, that's all right. But, you know, you have to stick with what makes you happy. Follow your dreams. Let them guide you."

"But what if they're wrong? Danny says—"

"Screw what Danny says." Claire's eyes widened. "He doesn't understand. You've got to *make* him understand. If he cares about you, he'll support you. It's that simple."

The brunette's expression became sceptical, then . . . curious. The angel felt Claire's gaze wash over her.

Ah, she's aware. This might be . . . interesting.

"Who are you?"

"I'm Aliyael. You can call me Leeya."

"Um, Leeya . . . how do you know me? And about all of . . . ?" Claire waved her hand around her.

The angel smiled. "You mean your music? The audition? And how you've kept it all a secret from your fiancé this whole time because you're afraid he won't approve and it won't pay the bills?"

Claire's jaw fell open. "But he won't, I know it! It's too impractical, and what if I don't make it? What if I fail? And he wants to start a family soon after we're married, and—"

"You're not ready yet," Aliyael finished. Watching the brunette's face turn scarlet, she tried to keep the smug grin off her face. *I may have this assignment in the bag yet.*

"Wh–what *are* you?" Now it was the angel's turn to be startled. Did Claire . . .? "Seriously."

"Seriously?"

"Seriously."

Oh well. Aliyael gave a little shrug. "I'm an angel, sent to you from the Powers That Be."

Claire blinked. "'Powers That Be'? You mean to say there are many?"

"Yes."

"But . . . I thought the angels only served God?"

"Yes."

"So . . . do you serve one god . . . or many?"

"Yes."

Claire shook her head. "Wait, which?"

"It's all the same." Trying to explain divinity to humans gave Aliyael a migraine. She didn't want to go there. "Look, Claire, take my advice or you'll regret it for the rest of your life: follow your heart and go to that audition. If Danny's with you for the long haul, he'll support you too. All right?"

Groaning, Claire put her face in her hands. "I–I don't know what to do . . . What do I say?"

"Just say 'yes', you'll go. And do it."

The brunette's eyes brightened. "OK then, I will. I'll give it a try." Then she frowned. "You know . . . you look a bit different than I'd expect an angel to look like."

She snorted. "What, the lack of wings? Or that I'm not blonde?" Claire's gaze shifted away from hers. *Ah-ha. Of course.*

"Well, I didn't mean *that* . . . I mean, um . . ."

"My last body was blonde, if it helps." Aliyael winked, watching the confusion spread on to Claire's face. Aliyael felt a small prickling sensation. *Ah, my time here's nearly up.*

"Remember what I said: follow your heart. You won't be sorry."

She could see the myriad of questions on Claire's face, and a part of her longed to answer them. But this was a short-term assignment, limited only to this dream and this dream alone. Not much of a chance to explain how angels over time shed bodies like snakes shed skin, or how each one was determined only by the whims of the Powers That Be. In her current body, Aliyael towered over the average human female and possessed short, very curly toffee-coloured hair, dark eyes and cocoa skin.

Claire's surprise at her appearance as an angel still amused her. *Sorry, not going to be a white-lily princess angel. I'm just me.*

She grinned at the brunette and watched the grey scenery fade out to be replaced by her own inner landscape.

I think that went well. Nothing in the world I can't handle, right?

She smiled up at the blue sky. Claire, no doubt, would go to that audition as instructed. Her marriage to Danny remained unscathed – after all, the poor girl had no way of knowing that her fiancé would decide to hide money away to help support her music as part of her wedding gift. All he needed to see was that she was serious, and how happy her music made her. Overall, she could count the mission as a success. Even the little background detail on her visit hadn't gone too wrong.

At least I didn't have to explain that we sometimes can even change gender. Although that might've been fun . . .

With a chuckle, she transported herself back to the Sanctuary with the rest of the seraphim.

"They want me to rescue *what*?" Aliyael was glad for being back at the Sanctuary; had she still been manifested in the physical world on Earth, her voice would've hurt her throat.

To Loriel's credit, if her reaction startled her she didn't show it. "An angel who fell." Loriel tossed her long, light-brown hair over one shoulder. Aliyael had noticed the hair thing became a nervous habit for the other angel. *She's still not used to that hair, or her body . . .*

"Look, it's a major assignment," her friend continued, "a huge deal. You've proven in the past you can handle the most impossible cases, surely this one wouldn't be beyond your means?"

Aliyael shuddered, unable to reply. One of the fallen. Once an angel had fallen, no telling where they'd go. Some went mad, some tried to go mortal, others . . . demonic. Sorrow and terror welled up in her every time they were mentioned. Mostly terror, really, she admitted. Once removed from grace, powerful angels could transform into dangerous, deadly creatures.

But Loriel was right; this was a fantastic chance to prove herself further to higher-ranking seraphim. Taking on more challenging assignments meant evolving and moving up further in the Sanctuary – not to mention the possibility of serving the Powers That Be better than before. She might even wind up someday serving among the ranks of the archangels. How could she turn such an opportunity down?

Then again, how could she not? Convince one of the fallen to return? What if it backfired and he joined Lucifer against them? What if they themselves fought?

I can't be Michael, and I wouldn't dare even try.

"Leeya, c'mon. Look at me. You know you can do it."

She tried to smile at Loriel, who had been her good friend for countless ages. Aliyael had befriended her back in her earlier male body before it was shed into the one he – she – bore now. With her support, Loriel's adjustment from male to female occurred with both grace and humour. It was still *him*, after all – still the Loriel she always knew – just in a different body, a different mode of expression. It changed him – well, her – in ways which fascinated her.

Aliyael remembered her words to Loriel at the time: *"The Powers That Be don't give us anything we can't handle, and we must remember that as we serve them."*

My turn now to heed them, I guess. Squaring her shoulders, she resolved to march in there and take the job. *Right then. One fallen angel back to the fold, coming up!*

A wide grin spread across Aliyael's face. "Sure thing, why not? What's this fallen angel's name and where can I find him?"

"That's my girl! His name's Julael, although I hear he's calling himself Julian now. You'll find him among the humans roaming the streets of Boston."

Hm. Boston? She hadn't been anywhere near there in a while. Her last assignment before Claire's dream was to prevent someone from walking out of their house underneath a rather large, falling icicle. Prior to that, she was tasked to Los Angeles.

City of Angels, ha!

Aliyael nodded. "All right. Guess I'm Boston-bound, then."

"Good luck!"

I'll be needing it. "Thanks!"

"Chin up! At least you can have a bit of fun, pretend to be a human while you're there. Rumour has it that's what he's up to. You're authorized full use of your powers, of course, provided the usual discretion."

Full use of her powers. That meant the Powers That Be considered him to be a potential threat, either to the Sanctuary or to humans. Or worse yet, both.

Oh great, he probably wants to become mortal. No telling what a desperate angel might to do achieve that end – or the amount of destruction he could cause given he had been one of the seraphim like her and Loriel. Last thing they wanted was an imploding angel manifesting as a terrible disaster among the humans, most likely in the form of a massive fire or earthquake. Sometimes even a flood.

Would be at least somewhat better than him being bat-shit bonkers, right? Although each possibility could prove extremely dangerous, and it was quite possible this fallen angel would be both. An angel didn't have the power alone to become human; that right was reserved for the Powers That Be to decide. Very few angels were permitted to incarnate as human beings, and such fates couldn't be predicted. There appeared to be no pattern or commonality among those who had been chosen that Aliyael could determine. Like many things, knowing the Will of the Powers That Be was sometimes impossible.

Even for a seraph, the highest-ranking angel in the Sanctuary.

So what was Julael's deal? Why was he fallen and wandering among humans? Aliyael couldn't help but be curious in spite of her innate revulsion at the idea of having fallen from the grace of the Powers That Be.

And why Boston? Was it random? Was he sent there? Maybe he just likes the city. And where in Boston? It wasn't exactly a small town. How would she find one fallen angel in it? Frustrated, she ran her fingers through her thick, light-brown hair and sighed.

"Loriel, do you know where in Boston he was last seen?" *Good question to start with, right?*

"Sort of. We have a report placing him somewhere in the Back Bay. He's been spotted in Boston Common and on the subway."

How odd. "Maybe he's sightseeing?" Aliyael gave a little laugh.

"Or he's passing for one of the homeless. But his clothes sure don't look it. You'll see what I mean. Oh, and Aliyael . . . ?"

"Yeah?"

"Don't get too close to him. Stick with the assignment. Do what you can to convince him to come home, but be careful. All right?"

She nodded. "You got it."

"Good. See you back here soon . . . with Julael. Got faith in you, kid. I know you can do it."

Aliyael gave her a wry grin. *Kid, eh?* Loriel had been an angel a few millennia longer and had a few ranks on her in the seraphim as a result. She sometimes wondered if her friend saw her as more of a younger sister.

"Thanks, Lore. Be seeing ya."

A whirling of air, the blowing of papers and leaves, and Aliyael materialized behind a few trees within Boston Common. She stepped out and towards the path, breathing in the cool, dry wind. *Glad I chose to wear a jacket.* The colourful array of trees told her it was autumn. She wasn't sure of the calendar year, but figured she had been sent to whenever Julael was hiding out.

From the looks of things, early twenty-first century for sure. She guessed 2010, which had been where her last cases had taken place. That made sense; angels rarely travelled through time during their assignments and tended to live alongside the humans as their centuries progressed. Each case was received in chronological order according to the human timeline.

However, with a fallen angel, that predictability could've gone right out the window.

Aliyael brushed her hands along her worn, light-blue jeans. Clothing, but her usual attire. It almost was her human uniform at this point: long, black trench coat, blue jeans and a purple blouse. She gazed down at the front of her shirt. *Yup, still there.* Hanging from her neck was a set of black Buddhist beads that one of her assignments had given to her as a gift before he passed on. She continued to wear them in memory of him.

What a wonderful guy Tom was. And still is, no doubt. She didn't know what became of his soul, but was certain it was something fantastic, glorious. He deserved no less.

She reached into her back pocket and took out her Charlie card. Her senses tingled. *Time to investigate the subway.* Maybe he was riding the T somewhere around here. But which line? Orange? Green?

I'll try Green first. Maybe I'll get lucky.

Shoving her hands into her pockets, Aliyael walked towards the main public area ahead. She eyed the vendors in their carts along the sidewalk. Jewellery, hot dogs, pretzels, sausages. A whiff of grilled onions mingled with the odour of dirt and exhaust from the traffic on Tremont Street. She glanced at a sign above the nearby entrance to the T stop: PARK STREET, repeated twice, once with a red background and next to it in green. Beneath was the legend: ALL TRAINS.

There we go. Clutching her Charlie card, Aliyael ducked into the entrance and down the stairs. She swiped her card at the gate and, once she passed through, made her way through the crowds of people. In the middle of the platform she came to a halt, glancing back and forth at the different signs for the B, C, D and E trains.

Great, which train do I take?

Behind her on the left the sound of a horn blew, startling her out of her thoughts. On the front car the brightly lit "B" answered her dilemma.

Heh, are they making this easy for me or what? Or at least she hoped as she ran towards the swarm of people boarding the train.

Clunk, squeak. With a false start, the train lurched forwards. Grasping for a nearby rail, Aliyael managed not to fall into the person standing beside her.

Oh, hi there, gravity. We don't have you where I come from.

At the next stop more people piled into the train car. A fluttering sensation emerged in her stomach, and her hair stood on end.

It's him. He's one of them. But who? The mere sight of Julael should trigger the proper intuitive response from her. All angels possessed the ability to sense when another was near, and the power to detect became more potent upon viewing. Depending on the strength and rank of the angel relative to the other, the psychic impact could be immense. Running into Gabriel in Los Angeles demonstrated that for her. Aliyael still remembered almost learning what the experience for a human to throw up was like.

A small smile sprang to her lips. *The quickening ain't got nothing on what we've got.*

Her smile faded when she spotted the back of a man's head. Shoulder-length, glossy black hair. Brown suit jacket over a slim but muscular build. Her gaze travelled downwards to get a better look at his appearance. She stared at the lower half of his body, which his dark navy jeans showed off quite well. *Nice ass, definitely a looker. The Powers That Be did well with that form.* But that impudent thought dissolved once she comprehended what her reaction to his presence meant. Then she picked it up: that distinct signature embedded in his energy of one of the fallen. She could distinguish it out from the stream, an off-key note in the music.

Aliyael's stomach churned. *It's him. Julael.*

With great speed, the man's head spun around. In moments her gaze met and locked with a rather intense pair of light-blue eyes. The shock sent a bolt of white-hot lightning into her core.

She gulped. *Whoa.*

When she recovered from the jolt, the man had vanished from view. Yet the faint spiritual essence lingering within told her Julael was still near. Did he hide somewhere in the crowd? How did she miss him moving from the spot where he had stood?

Leeya, you idiot. She felt like a new angel on her first assignment all over again. Had she learned nothing at all? Where had all of her training gone? How careless!

The memory of those powerful eyes branded into her mind, and she could just remember the details of his face. Strong chin and high cheekbones framed by ebony hair, and the hue of his eyes had melted against the glow of his skin. *Who was this guy? Whoever he may be, he had an awful lot going on upstairs, even for a fallen. Oh, Light, what is wrong with me?*

Her arm ached, and she realized she had been clutching the rail. Aliyael relaxed her tight grip and forced herself to breathe. *Remember, you have lungs now. And they work.* Eyes burning with frustration and shame, she knew she had to find Julael again, and soon. Only this time, however, the uncertainty of how much she wanted to find him remained.

But beyond any doubt in her angelic mind whatsoever, she knew that in spite of her trepidation, she wanted to see him again.

* * *

Think, Leeya, think. Where did he go? Desperate, Aliyah rummaged through her mind to remember all of her lessons on tracking energy. She could still sense Julael onboard the train, but where had he gone? She would need to follow him to his destination if she wanted the chance to speak with him.

If. She clenched and unclenched her free hand, willing herself to calm down. A trickle of sweat made its way down her back.

This would not be an easy assignment.

Nervous, she fingered the prayer beads around her neck. *Think I could use a bit of help here . . .*

"And what stop are you getting off at?" The smooth baritone voice broke through her concentration. She whirled around to see that it came from Julael, who now stood behind her. *Holy hell, how did he* do *that? Light, he's good.* Too good, she figured, given he was capable of sneaking up behind her. She swallowed, her insides turning into fire and ice. *Breathe, Leeya, breathe. Not your first time in a body.*

Aliyael tried to keep her tone light. "Just wandering around, enjoying the day. And you?"

"Same. You like tea?" His voice reminded her of melted caramel. When was the last time she had a caramel candy, anyhow? A number of assignments ago, perhaps. Maybe in that small town outside of Seattle? Or was it in that shop in London? She couldn't remember. Then she realized he was still waiting for an answer.

What was he asking her again? Something about his eyes distracted her. *I . . . what? Do I what?* She fought to comprehend the question. *Right, tea. Tea's good.* "Um, yeah. Why?"

"There's a good tea café place at the next stop. You should try it."

She blinked. Here stood one of the fallen beside her on the subway, and he was chatting with her about *tea*? Claire's dream seemed more real to her than this.

"C'mon, I'll take you there if you don't believe me."

Fighting to keep from stammering, Aliyael blurted out, "Are you asking me out for *tea*? You for real?"

Julael laughed. "What else are you going to do while you're here on Earth? Get drunk? Go to a Red Sox game?"

He's got a strange sense of humour, this one. She chuckled. "OK, you've got a point. But there's decent beer at Fenway." Aliyael dared a glance at his face and into those amazing eyes. Sure enough, she saw amusement twinkling in the icy-blue depths.

"And here was I thinking angels didn't know how to have fun any more."

She didn't know how to reply to that. The train crunched to a halt, and the doors swung open.

Julael gestured towards the open door. "After you." Loriel's warning echoed in her mind. *Don't get too close.*

She settled for a smile. "Thanks."

They exited the train and made their way through the station to the street above.

"Name's Julian. You can call me Jule."

"Aliyael. Leeya for short." She added, "If you like."

"Sure thing, Leeya." He smirked, and the strange tang to his energy sharpened. At once Aliyael recalled what her purpose in being here entailed, and her stomach fell into her shoes.

Oh wow, this assignment is nuts. What were the Powers That Be thinking? For that matter, what was *she* thinking? This line of thought would wrap itself around her head over and over again once they sat across from each other with a mug of tea in each hand, the seraph and the fallen angel. The sole conclusion that bubbled up from the tangle of ideas assured her that while the Powers That Be may know what they were doing, they also possessed a very bizarre, twisted notion of what passed as comedy.

Aliyael glanced at his mug, then at back at hers. Julael ordered Earl Grey; she chose chai. Two bags of sugar went into his tea, which he stirred with a thoughtful air while she put soy milk and brown sugar into hers. From the outside, the entire exchange looked . . . normal. Two people ordering tea and sitting down for a chat together. Perhaps people watching them thought they were here on business or were friends.

Maybe they think we're out on a date. She smothered a fit of the giggles and took a sip of her chai.

"So! Don't keep me in suspense." He put his mug down on the table, and his long slender fingers drew her attention while he folded his hands in front of him. "I'd love to hear why you think I should rejoin the seraphim."

Choking on her tea, she almost dropped her cup on the table. While she continued to cough, Julael continued to speak. "Oh, I know that's why you're here. I figured that much out. They don't send a seraph into a major metropolitan area just for giggles, after all."

Light, now what? "Well, um." Aliyael coughed again. "I was more hoping you could tell me first how you, um . . . well . . ."

"How I fell?"

Not trusting her voice, she nodded.

Julael grinned. "Not liking that term, are you?"

Averting her eyes from his forceful gaze, Aliyael chose that moment to take a slow sip of her chai before replying. "I can't say it's a pleasant one."

"Nor are my reasons for it. But I'll tell you what." He leaned in towards her, and she could smell some sort of spice mixed in with an earthy fragrance. Sandalwood? A hint of clove? Maybe some cinnamon. Or was that her chai? Dizziness overwhelmed her.

"You strike me as being a bit different from the others, Leeya. So I'm going to tell you the more important part of my journey."

After a few moments she found her voice, and was surprised to hear how clear it sounded to her ears. "Oh?"

"Yes. I'm not just going to tell you how I fell. I'm going to tell you why."

Oh, this ought to be interesting . . . "All right then, Jule," she answered, surprised at how easily his name fell off her lips. "Go ahead. Shoot."

Julael fell back into his chair with a grin, and once again the table served as a comfortable distance between them. Somehow this proved to be disappointing to Aliyael, which confused her even further.

"What's the difference between us," he pointed at himself and Aliyael, "and them?" He gestured wildly towards the rest of the café patrons seated around them.

The corners of her mouth began to turn downwards. She had a bad feeling as to where this conversation was leading them, had heard similar arguments before.

With a small shrug of her shoulders, Aliyael opted for what she hoped proved to be a sane response. "We're angels, and they're humans."

"Mm-hm. And how do angels differ from humans?"

Oh dear. She knew this was coming. Her reply was given in a careful, measured tone. "They have free will. We do not."

"And why is that?"

"Because our priority is to serve the Powers That Be. Our whole beings, everything that we are, what we do . . . it all goes into it." She chugged the rest of her mug, wishing the liquid inside were a bit stronger. Perhaps of another variety altogether. *Maybe I should've gone for the beer at Fenway after all . . .*

"Say we were to choose something they didn't want us to do. What would happen?"

Her brow furrowed. "Um, doesn't that question suggest we have free will to begin with?"

Julael laughed. "Oh, I think I like you, Leeya!" He picked up his mug to take a sip. Peering at her over the top, he asked in a sly tone, "So, would that mean that every choice we make is technically something either the Powers That Be want us to do, or leads us towards doing something which is in line with serving them?"

A glint in his eyes made her hesitate in responding. "I . . . I guess."

"All right then. So tell me, Leeya . . . why did I fall?"

She froze, her mind reeling. "You're telling me you think that the Powers That Be *wanted* you to—"

Driving his pointed finger in the air, he exclaimed, "Precisely! Which is why I think I'm going to enjoy the rest of this wonderful tea, apologize to you for failing your assignment, and offer you the chance to come back to my place afterwards."

Her mouth dropped open. "You can't be serious."

"At which?"

"All of it. I mean, what?" She folded her arms in front of her chest. "Jule, you are some kinda crazy. Are you listening to yourself? If they wanted you this way, then why did they send me here?"

"No idea, Leeya, no idea." He winked at her. "Wanna find out?"

She arched an eyebrow at him. "And how do you propose I do that?"

"You done with your tea?" She nodded. "So am I. Come, follow me."

Perplexed but curious, Aliyael did.

Julael lived in a rather small one-bedroom apartment in the Back Bay, but knowing the rents in the area Aliyael knew he must be spending a small fortune. *Where is he getting the money? If he's abusing his powers, that's not cool.*

Not even bothering to hide her reaction, she folded her arms and glared at him. "Very nice. So, aside from the high cost of living, what did you wanna to show me?"

He made a small noise. It sounded like a cross between a snort and a tsk. Shooting a disapproving look in her direction, he replied, "It's not what you think."

"It better not be."

"It's in my bedroom."

Oh, Light. "You're not going to hit on me, are you?"

His sole response was to laugh and open the bedroom door. In a slow, cautious fashion, she peered her head in.

The small room contained within it a bed, a nightstand . . . and a million pieces of artwork surrounding the bed. The paintings on each canvas depicted scenes of Boston, the Sanctuary – but all of it from an angel's perspective. The brilliant hues of people's energy shone in the paint, giving each detail an almost surrealistic look. Each piece of art was unlike anything Aliyael had seen before.

She gasped aloud. "When did you start doing these?"

"Not sure, really. But they sell pretty well. I've made enough to live here and save a bit extra."

"You're saving money? For what?" She couldn't fathom what an angel would do with money. What would they buy with it? A yacht? DVDs? Angels had no need for such things, no desire.

Julael threw his hands up in the air and beamed at her. "I have no idea. Absolutely no idea. But think! That's the beauty of it! What would I do with the money? How would I spend it? Anything!"

Staring at him in silence, it hit Aliyael what these paintings meant to him: they were his freedom. She couldn't deny the fact that they were splendid. The exquisiteness contained within each detail stunned her and filled her with awe. How can one of the fallen have such a beautiful mind? She didn't understand. It went against everything she understood about angels after they fell.

"These must really . . . inspire people. Tell me," she asked, turning towards him, "what have others said about them?"

"They love them and they're buying them, so I hope they're inspirational. But you know, I think the whole thing about being 'fallen' is funny, you know that?"

Aliyael did her best not to grimace. "How so?"

"Well, let's take the previous conversation we had about that, for instance. So let's say we as angels have no free will. I fall. Ergo, it was Divine Will which made me fall, correct?"

She gave him a slow nod.

"All right then. So if any one of us could fall at any given time due to Divine Will, how are we best serving the Powers That Be?

What does it mean to fall?" He sat on the bed, and waited for her response.

"It means you were . . . exiled. Banished from the Sanctuary." Seating herself next to him, Aliyael began to wonder what she was now in for.

"And thus cast out of the presence of the Powers That Be."

"Correct."

"All due to Divine Will."

"Right."

"So . . . is it possible none of us are actually serving the Powers That Be at all? Why would we not be given free will, but still be able to exhibit traits which allow us to be banished?"

"I . . ." Her voice trailed off.

"Simple: either we have free will – which is something the angels are said not to have – or none of us are serving the Powers That Be."

She shook her head. "That can't be right. Not having free will doesn't mean we don't make choices on our own."

"Ah! But it does. It implies that our choices come from a Higher Power, Divine Will. See? It's the ultimate paradox, isn't it?"

All Aliyael could do was laugh. "Well, I guess it's the Will of the Powers That Be that you be brought back, or I wouldn't be here." She grinned at him. "Maybe this was the opportunity for you to see how the other half lives, so to speak. I don't know."

"And to be honest, I rather like it." Julael reached out and clasped her hand in his. "Tell me, what is it like for you, having your body turned into form and flesh while here?"

The contact of his warm, smooth skin against hers did odd things to her insides, none of which was unpleasant. She cleared her throat. "I like tea. And I was right: you're hitting on me, aren't you?"

"Is the question bad? Tell me, am I making you uncomfortable?"

"No, but—"

"It's an experience the Powers That Be gave you, right? In allowing you to come here, take on physical form . . . have you been given any objections to it or what you do here?"

His gaze locked with hers, and it took Aliyael all of her strength not to lose herself in his eyes. She struggled to reply. "Beyond not compromising the life or well-being of any human, acting with discretion . . ."

"All right. And wouldn't you say that your stay here is good? Enjoyable, even?"

"Well, sure. But I—"

"Then I don't see what the fuss is all about." Removing one of his hands from hers, he placed it on her cheek. Despite herself she closed her eyes, savouring the touch of his fingers.

A million thoughts popped into her head. *This is wrong, I need to leave. What am I doing here?* Before she could attempt to remove his hand and leave the room, a most delightful sensation met her lips – the soft but firm pressure of his own lips. A ray of light cascaded through her, and her world exploded when his tongue entered her mouth.

The pleasure became unbearable, and she broke away with a gasp.

"What's wrong? This isn't harming you, is it?"

Unable to bring herself to speak aloud, she shook her head.

"This isn't harming anyone else, is it?"

She hesitated, fighting to think through the haze of joy still coursing through her. "No," she said at last.

Smiling, Julael stroked her cheek, the contact setting her skin ablaze. His fingers trailed down her face to her throat, her chest . . . Aliyael let loose a huge breath she didn't realize she had been holding.

"Then I still don't see the problem." He bent down and kissed the nape of her neck, and her gut clenched with desire. Her hands leaped up towards his head, her fingers tangling themselves in his hair. Teeth grazed her throat as he nibbled and sucked at the sensitive flesh. Her eyes rolled back into her head. What were these sensations? And how could she possibly deny them? The unfamiliar heat between her legs made her mad. What *was* Julael, and what sort of strange power did he have over her?

With great care he removed her coat and began to unbutton her blouse. Every ounce of self-control ingrained in her had fled while a part of her stood on the outside, watching the entire scene in shock. When his thumb made slow circling movements around her nipple, Aliyael was glad for not having worn a bra. She often chose not to; she hated them. The silken touch of his fingers on her body brought noises to the back of her throat she had never made before and didn't know she could.

Moisture seeped between her legs, and a fire raged within her. Her hands sought comfort in his bare skin. The barrier of his clothing served but as a frustration. Fumbling with the fabric of his shirt, she reached underneath, sliding her hands over his bare chest. Skin on skin, and nothing but joy between them. Julael raised his arms and she yanked his shirt off, tossing it on the floor. She didn't know where it landed, and she didn't care.

It started to dawn on her why humans believed in enjoying the comforts of the flesh, as she discovered she shared it. At one point, this idea would've frightened her. In the ecstasy of the moment, it received but a dim acknowledgment. All she wanted was to savour the sensation of his skin with her fingertips. A part of her concluded that all she was experiencing was some form of madness brought on by this wild, new thrill. She was bewitched, seduced by one of the fallen . . . how had she come to this?

But these thoughts fled when his fingers trailed down from her breasts to her bare stomach, leaving a searing trail in their wake. Aliyael hissed, longing to feel his touch on her legs, her thighs, against the hot wetness inside of her . . . *Oh those jeans, damn those jeans.* All this silken skin, his body against hers, and too much fabric to be bothered with – they had to come off. As if he read her mind, Julael undid the top button of her jeans and pulled down the zipper. With both hands he began to slide them off, and instinct made her raise her hips to help him in their removal. Once the jeans were gone she lay on the bed, naked.

She didn't wear underwear either.

Her gaze slid to the paintings around them. *I wonder how you would paint something like this.* She didn't think anyone could. The delights of physical contact, hands and fingers and lips and tongue and body and skin . . . it was a whole other art. A different world of beauty. Then she looked at his hands, his elegant, long fingers against her skin, cream on chocolate. Gorgeous.

Then she stared into his light, sky-blue eyes. Was there a devilish spark in them?

He lowered his head and the delicious contact of his rough, wet tongue met the heat between her legs. A cry tore from her throat, and she arched her back, lifting her hips closer to the source of the bliss. Lips, mouth, tongue all over her swollen, sensitive clit. She could barely stand it. Clawing at the bed sheets beneath her, she drowned in the powerful sensations that shook her body and gave it a life she didn't know existed.

Holy, this is holy . . . How could one see anything but good come from such mutual delights? Why did she object to this earlier? If she had known . . .

Something overwhelming, fast and potent slammed into her. She saw stars and light, gasping as he brought her to the brink and over the edge.

But it wasn't enough; inside she still ached. Aliyael reached out towards him, but he was already removing his jeans. She marvelled at the sight of his erection, hard and swollen once freed from the bondage of clothing. Her hands stroked its head, revelling in the texture.

Julael groaned. "Damn you."

She couldn't resist. "A little ironic coming from you, hm?"

With a low growl, he grabbed her wrists with his hands and with a fierceness she wasn't expecting, kissed her. Positioning himself between her legs, he found her soaking wet entrance and thrust himself inside of her. A mingling of pain and ecstasy pierced her, and she screamed. His chest against hers, his lips on hers, their hands clasped together, she couldn't get enough of it. When she came again, she almost blacked out. They lay on the bed together, drenched in sweat and silent save for their breathing.

I remembered to breathe, she thought with a smile.

Hours, then days passed. Weeks, perhaps – Aliyael wasn't certain. They talked over tea, kissed, laughed. One morning she turned towards Julael and stared at his profile in the sunlight. She could see the shine of his skin, but also see him glowing with an inner light as well.

When he spoke his voice was quiet, measured. "I guessed it when you first showed up, I think. But I know now why you're here."

"Oh?"

"I get it now. At least, I think I do. If you can love, you can serve the Powers That Be. There is no other Divine Will." He took her hand into his and squeezed it. "I think . . . I think I'm ready to come back now. But only for you, if you're ready. I mean . . . if you want."

She smiled, and handed him the parchment Loriel had given her.

"What's this?" He took it with trembling hands. When he finished reading it, he yelped. With a laugh, he picked up Aliyael and spun her around.

"Guess who wants us to stay here and finish this art project I started?"

Assigned to work as partners together. Oh, Light, I'm so glad. Her heart filled with such happiness she thought it would burst. Aliyael knew Loriel had pulled a few strings, but she didn't know quite how many nor to what extent – and she never would've guessed staying here would be granted to them.

Julael carried her into the bedroom and tossed her on to the bed. With a gleeful laugh, she pulled him close and gave him a passionate, heated kiss while she undid the buckle of his belt.

He broke off their kiss with a gasp when her soft hands slid down towards his rapidly swelling member. "That isn't very angelic of you."

"Is that a complaint?"

"No, but I think I've corrupted you. This isn't good."

"Oh, damn. There goes my halo." Aliyael took him into her mouth, flicking her tongue on his hard shaft, delighting in the sounds he made when she gave him pleasure. Everything about him was a miracle. When he lay her on the bed afterwards and she felt the paradise of his lips and tongue all over her skin, she knew that the Powers That Be had chosen her for the assignment for very good reasons. She remembered the advice she had given Claire: *"Follow your heart."*

I guess it's time to follow mine as well. Closing her eyes, she smiled and abandoned herself to ecstasy.

In between the sessions of mutual bliss, Aliyael turned to him with a smile. "So what do you think, Jule," she asked with a teasing tone, "is this by choice or Divine Will?"

"Both." He grinned. "And I'm fine with that."

"I guess I'm back, then. Congrats on finishing your assignment. "

"I guess you are. And you're quite welcome."

Fly by Night

Selah March

It's possible to drive the fifteen hundred miles from Jacksonville, Florida to the tiny border town of Presidio, Texas in under twenty-four hours. That doesn't make it a good idea.

If you keep to the back roads and avoid most major cities, the trip will be longer, lonelier and more dangerous – also not a good idea. But when you're skipping out on your loan-shark ex-boyfriend with a suitcase full of stolen cash, it's the only way to go.

Kate pulled into the outskirts of Presidio ten minutes ahead of the sunset. Just as her internet search had promised, the Big River Motel stood waiting for her by the side of the highway, and although she couldn't see the bridge that crossed the Rio Grande into Mexico, she could smell the water flowing dark and dirty a mile or two away.

Almost there.

She reached for the large leather shoulder bag on the seat beside her – a gift from Phillip on their first Christmas together and the only thing she hadn't ditched along the way. She set her boots on the dusty surface of the otherwise empty parking lot. The over-stuffed suitcase bumped solidly against her thigh as she walked through the front doors of the motel.

"Can I see some identification?" the desk clerk asked when she requested a room for the night.

Instead, she pushed a wad of $100 bills across the counter. She'd used the same tactic with a used car dealer in Alabama (where she'd traded her convertible for the beige sedan out front) and again in a pawnshop in Mississippi (where she'd sold her jewellery and picked up the small handgun and box of bullets that lay hidden beneath a single change of clothes in the bottom of her bag).

It worked then, and it worked now. The clerk pocketed the cash and only asked under what name she wanted to register.

"Katharine Hollis." She liked the way it tasted so clean and strong on her tongue. It belonged to a woman who could hold her own in any situation.

Ten minutes later, she stood in the shower of room 222 – the kind of room with a condom dispenser bolted to the wall above the toilet – and washed 500 miles' worth of West Texas out of her hair. Her stomach grumbled for food that didn't come from a vending machine. She wondered if she could risk a hot meal. If and when Phillip picked up her trail, would anyone recall details about a random brunette in a T-shirt and jeans? And did it matter? Especially considering the last time Phillip saw her, she was a blonde in designer beachwear.

After she'd dried off and dressed, she peeked between the dust-coloured drapes and spied a roadhouse across the street. Its neon signs blinked OPEN, and BEST BBQ IN TEXAS. Although she suspected the latter was an exaggeration, her stomach didn't care. She pinned up her hair, shoved the suitcase under the bed, grabbed her bag and left the room.

Another vehicle had pulled into the motel's parking lot since she'd checked in – a vintage Chevy pickup painted shiny black, with Oklahoma plates, Yosemite Sam mudflaps and an empty gun rack in the back window. She was too distracted by hunger and weariness to think much of it. She crossed the street and entered the nameless roadhouse.

At first glance, it seemed as deserted as the motel. Stale smoke clung to the low-hung ceiling in a fog. Dirty sawdust lay across the floor, as grey as an old washrag.

She approached the middle-aged, Mexican-American woman standing behind the bar. "I'll have a half-rack of ribs with a salad on the side and a bottle of water, please."

The woman had the same used-up look as the sawdust under Kate's feet, but she made up for her lack of youth and beauty with her unprovoked hostility.

"You'll take a full rack with a pickle and sweet tea and be happy about it."

"Yes, ma'am. Thank you, ma'am." For all Kate knew, the woman kept a loaded shotgun stashed behind the bar for use on smart-mouthed customers with a taste for iceberg lettuce.

She settled herself on a nearby stool to wait for her meal. The crack and roll of a game of pool in progress rose above the twang of the jukebox. With nothing more interesting to look at, she turned to watch.

The only other patron in the roadhouse turned out to be a man dressed in a white T-shirt, scuffed boots and faded jeans, the standard uniform of small-town Texas. He didn't appear to be a day over twenty-five, which made him at least five years younger than Kate. Six feet tall and broad through the shoulders, he sported sandy hair striped with gold and a few days' worth of stubble across his sharp jaw.

Kate hadn't been able to focus on anything for more than a minute at a time in weeks – not since the night she'd drunk too much wine, stumbled into the wrong room of her beach house and discovered she'd spent the past three years sleeping with a violent felon. The days that followed had blurred into a wash of muddy shadows shot through with the occasional streak of blood-red panic, like a badly done oil painting. Yet this man caught and held her attention.

He turned in profile and bent over the table. The glow from the low-hanging lamp revealed a sunburned complexion. His thick, shaggy hair glistened in the mellow light. He sank his shot, bouncing the cue ball off the bumper hard enough to make it jump three inches into the air and hit the felt with an echoing thud. Kate expected him to smile in triumph, but he only straightened and moved to the other side of the table. He executed his game with a careful, self-critical air, as if playing alone for practice deserved the single-mindedness of a professional.

In him Kate saw some of Phillip's all-American good looks. And although she was willing to bet half the cash in her suitcase that the streaks in his hair weren't $500 highlights, there was enough of Phillip in this man's careless confidence to make her wish she'd stayed in her room after all.

The grey lady reappeared and set the rack of ribs on the bar. The man with the pool cue lifted his head and levelled his gaze in Kate's direction. He didn't look away. Despite the poor light, she could see his eyes were a very pale shade of blue. When she turned to eat her meal, his continued scrutiny made the skin over her shoulders twitch like a plucked piano wire.

She tried to concentrate on the ribs. As she tossed the last denuded bone on to the smeared plate, the pool player ambled up to the bar. From the corner of her eye, Kate caught sight of his rolling gait and did her best not to cower at his approach. She was a strong, confident woman with nothing to hide and less to fear from random strangers. Besides, the grey lady would be back with her check at any second, and she'd be on her way.

"You know," the man said, his voice deeper than Kate expected, "if I'd been playin' for money, you would've lost that game for me."

"How do you figure that?" She didn't look up as she spoke, determined to keep conversation to a minimum and eye contact to zero.

He edged closer, plainly just as determined to catch her attention. "I could feel you watching. Made me nervous, to tell the truth."

Kate looked.

She couldn't help it – he'd surprised her. She hadn't made a man nervous in a very long time. The up-close view of his smile, so wholesome and bright, made her wonder how she'd confused him with her glib bastard of an ex-boyfriend. It was more than the small differences between cerulean-coloured contact lenses and eyes the bleached-out blue of the desert sky, or between a tanning bed glow and a spray of freckles across the bridge of a sun-kissed nose. It was the light years between fast-talking insincerity and sweet-talking charm, between a know-it-all smirk and a cocky grin. This cowboy was nothing like Phillip.

Her previous snap-judgment shamed her. "I'm . . . sorry?"

He smiled wider. "What's your name, darlin'?" he asked in an exaggerated drawl out of every bad Western ever made.

She didn't know why she answered. Maybe she was desperate for real conversation after ten days and nights of the most minimal human contact. Convenience store clerks so rarely wanted to shoot the breeze.

"Katharine." She swallowed the last of her tea and set the glass on the bar. "Most people call me Kate."

He nodded. "I'm Elijah, like the prophet. You can call me Eli." He used the heavy silver ring on the second finger of his right hand to rap on the bar. "What're you drinking, Kate?"

"Tequila." She'd always wanted to try it straight from the bottle, with no fruity mixer or melting ice to cut the burn, and now was as good a time as any. One drink wouldn't hurt her, or ruin her plans. One drink, and then she was out of there. Back to her room and straight to bed, so she could cross the border and be well into Mexico before the sun had cleared the horizon.

"Good choice," Eli said. The grey lady appeared, and he ordered two shots. Then he turned to Kate. "You know, they say agave nectar don't mix well with secrets."

"Secrets?"

He inclined his head. "There's two kinds that cross the border in a town like Presidio – tourists looking to go native, and folks with secrets."

The woman slapped the shots on the bar along with a dish of lime wedges and a salt shaker. Eli ignored the garnish, picked up his glass and tossed back the tequila. He wiped his mouth with the back of his hand and said, "You, Katie, are no *turista*."

She tried to mimic his action – the flick of the wrist, the toss of the head, the quick swallow. She managed all but the last part, gagging on the alkaline sear. Eli pounded her back with a good-natured grin.

When she'd caught her breath, she asked, "What makes you so sure I'm not a tourist?"

He signalled for a second round. "Seems to me, you're a woman on a mission. Running to or from something. Am I right?"

Somewhere Kate had read that the way to make a tall tale convincing was to add elements of the truth. No time like the present to start.

"Bad relationship," she said. "Turns out I make a lousy trophy mistress."

And that's where the irony came in, because if Phillip had married her, she probably would've made an excellent trophy wife – well groomed and easily placated, if a trifle too inquisitive for her own good.

"Phillip? What's going on?"

"It's nothing. Go back to bed."

"Who is this man? My God, Phillip, where did you get that gun?"

"You see? Now you've involved my girlfriend in this nasty business. How many innocent bystanders have to get hurt before you pay what you owe?"

She could still feel the cold press of the muzzle against her temple, and see how the strange man's eyes widened in horror as her lover threatened to splatter her brains all over the tasteful, cream-coloured carpet of her TV room if the debt wasn't paid.

Phillip apologized later, of course. He swore he'd never meant to go through with it. It all had been a spur-of-the-moment charade.

"Baby, you inspired me, looking so innocent in your white nightgown, with your hair down around your shoulders."

"But Phillip—"

"Hush. We won't speak of this again, will we, baby? That's my good girl."

That's when she knew she'd always be less a prize than a hostage. There weren't enough beach houses and diamond tennis bracelets in the world to make up for that.

The grey lady returned with their drinks. This time, Kate mastered the flick–toss–swallow. When she set the glass on the bar, she caught Eli staring at her mouth. Not the cleavage in the V of her T-shirt, or her ass where it rested on the stool, but her mouth. Another surprise.

He shook his head as if to clear it, and his browline dipped in a frown. "There's gotta be more to your story than that."

"Not really."

"Confession's good for the soul." He rapped his ring on the bar for a third round that Kate knew was a very bad idea.

"And you're a priest now?" she asked him, the sarcasm tasting as bitter as the tequila.

He shrugged. "Just an interested bystander."

A little too interested. What the hell was she thinking, engaging in even the most mundane bar chat with a stranger? She fumbled for her bag. "Time for me to go. Thanks for the drinks."

Eli dropped a large, square hand on her shoulder. Her heart skipped two beats and raced forwards like a sports car slipping into fourth on a straightaway.

"Don't le me scare you off," he said. "I'm just talkin' to hear my own voice."

"I need to go." But she didn't move, couldn't seem to find the floor with her feet.

"You're staying at the motel across the road."

It wasn't a question, and there didn't seem much point in denying it. She nodded.

The grey lady set the third round of shots on the bar in front of them.

"Drink up," Eli said. "I'll walk you back to your room."

"That's not necessary."

"Sure it is." He looked genuinely puzzled, as if he couldn't fathom why she'd reject a simple offer of safe passage from one side of the highway to the other.

"I don't suppose you'd tell me if you were planning to kidnap me and sell me as a sex slave, would you?"

He shook his head. "I don't suppose I would."

The sharp edges had worn off his smile, and his face glowed with a warm, open expression she found herself wanting to trust. Purely as a distraction, she fiddled with her shot glass, sloshing drops of tequila over her fingertips.

Eli bumped his shoulder against hers. "I'm harmless. Ask anybody."

She looked towards the grey lady, dimly hoping she'd suddenly become protective and maternal, and tell this pushy, pool-playing cowboy to let Kate alone. The woman stood at the other end of the bar, wiping out the inside of a glass. At Kate's glance, she lifted one eyebrow in a perfect arch, spit into the sawdust and turned away.

Kate laughed and tossed back the shot.

The alcohol was making the muscles in her legs feel warm and loose, but she wasn't drunk – not with her well-developed tolerance built on parasol drinks and half-carafes of wine with lunch. So what happened next couldn't be blamed on the tequila.

She stood and reached for her bag where it had fallen beneath the stool. Eli stopped her with a hand cupped around the nape of her neck like a collar made of new-forged iron. In contrast, his silver ring felt icy against her skin. A spray of goosebumps blossomed where it touched. Her mouth went dry, and sweat sprouted along her hairline. It wasn't all fear.

He leaned in close. "I could use some good company tonight. How 'bout you?"

It was a reckless thing to do. More reckless than leaving her loan-shark boyfriend. More reckless, even, than stealing her loan-shark boyfriend's secret stash of cash on her way out the door.

But desperation bred recklessness, and Kate had been desperate since the night she found out her entire life was a lie. That same desperation had grown more urgent over the following weeks as she quietly unearthed what a vicious, cold-hearted blight on society she'd been living with for the past three years.

It was the discovery of another beach-housed girlfriend in Miami and one more in Key West – both younger and blonder than she – that transformed a big chunk of her desperation into rage. As it turned out, desperation, rage and recklessness went together like salt, tequila and lime.

Now she only needed a durable target. Something or someone resilient enough to withstand the force of her anger as she worked it out of her heart and mind. Then she could be free of it. Then she could move on.

This smooth-talking cowboy looked like he was up to the job.

It wasn't supposed to go like this.

Eli had been doing this kind of work for a while now, ever since he'd quit the rodeo circuit after busting both arms and a collarbone in a single afternoon. Other guys in the business called themselves "retrieval specialists", but Eli always said his job was to find misplaced items and return them to their proper owners. Mostly, the items were money or jewellery. Sometimes they were documents or computer files. He'd never before been hired to find and return a human being. So far, he didn't like it much.

She wasn't anything like how she'd been described. He'd been told to expect a spoiled bimbo prone to tantrums and tears. His assignment was to keep her in one place till her boyfriend showed up and dragged her back to Florida. For that he'd get ten per cent of the hundred grand she was carrying with her.

Before Eli met the lady in question, it had seemed like an easy piece of work with a damned generous payday. Now, as he watched her exit the bathroom, walk across the mud-coloured carpet and drop a plastic-wrapped condom on the bedside table, he wondered if maybe he hadn't ought to reconsider.

Because this was no bimbo. This woman had both smarts and guts – two things that didn't bode well for the success of the operation. In Eli's experience, smart, gutsy women didn't much care for being told to sit down, shut up and wait for their men to come fetch them home.

On top of that, he liked her.

Sweat beaded along his upper lip. "You mind if I turn on the air conditioner?"

She jumped like she'd forgotten he was in the room. "I'll do it."

She turned her back to him and fiddled with the ancient unit. Her random turning of knobs and pressing of buttons told Eli she was nervous, as if inviting strangers into her motel room wasn't an everyday occurrence. The dim light from the single lamp gave her skin a golden glow.

He moved towards her till he stood close enough to lay a hand on her shoulder. She went dead still at his touch. He saw the leap of her pulse in her throat and thought of a skittish horse. Would she stand for him, or bolt?

The air conditioner came to life with an unhealthy whine. She turned, dislodging his hand from her shoulder, but she didn't move away.

"We don't have to . . ." he started, but the pleading way she lifted her pretty brown eyes to his face told him they most surely did. Even if he hadn't liked her so much, he was never one to disappoint a lady.

Their first kiss was more like an experiment, both of them licking quick and light into each other's mouth for a taste of salty skin and the last traces of tequila. He took charge of their second kiss and found her lips hot and plush, just as he'd known they'd be. He slid his fingers into her hair, pulling it loose, and cupped the back of her skull. Pleasure already throbbed like a bass line under his skin.

He went slow, teasing her with the barest of touches along the line of her jaw, the curve of her breast. Allowing the tension to build between them till it burst like a too-full rain cloud. She grappled with him then, pushing at his chest and clawing at his neck in plain frustration.

He caught both her wrists in one hand and used the other to urge her backwards till her shoulders thumped against the ugly, faded wallpaper.

"Easy now," he said. "There's no call to draw blood."

She glared at him. "I'm not some delicate damsel in distress."

"Well, that works out fine, 'cause I'm nobody's knight in shining armour."

He released her wrists. She didn't fight, so he bent and ran his lips along the line of her collarbone. When he slid his thigh between her legs and pressed his palm against the small of her back, she began to tremble. Right about then, he figured they'd both had enough of taking it easy.

He stepped back, pulled off his shirt and unbuckled his belt. She kept her hands on him, kept reeling him in for more kisses, interrupting his quest to get them both as naked as they could be in as little time as possible. He broke away and yanked her shirt over her head and down her arms to her wrists, trapping them a second time.

She arched off the wall and hissed in his ear like a scalded cat, "Get on with it, already."

He twisted the fabric tighter and used the other hand to unbutton her jeans and shove them to her ankles. Then he slid his fingers up her spine to the clasp of her bra. She lifted a single, well-groomed brow – a challenge if he'd ever seen one.

"I can pick a lock in fifteen seconds flat," he told her.

Her bra fell open before she had a chance to answer.

He tossed her shirt away, and the bra with it, and closed his lips over the peak of one pale breast. Her skin had a peppery bite that made his mouth water. He pulled off slow to see her nipple flush dusky pink and hard, and watched with satisfaction as her eyes fell closed. He continued like that, alternating between her breasts with lips and teeth and tongue, till her sighs trailed off into moans and her chest heaved under his mouth. Then he started working his way down.

The scrap of silk between his tongue and her flesh didn't keep him from finding all her sweet spots. He licked and nibbled till her panties were soaked through and her thighs quivered under his hands. He slid the waistband past her hips and down to join her jeans in a puddle at her feet, then leaned in for a real taste.

She was as ripe as a late August peach and twice as wet. His head buzzed with the liquid sounds of his lips and tongue on her swollen clit. He exhaled, and her scent washed over him, mixed up with the faint smell of perfume and a hint of gasoline.

She buried her fingers in his hair to urge him on, but he took his time over it till she pushed against his mouth in greedy, helpless little thrusts. He pulled back and grinned up at her.

"Give it up, darlin'," he said. "I'll make you pop like a firecracker."

He was off-balance – down on one knee and not expecting the sudden shove that knocked him back on his ass. That's what he told himself as he watched her kick off her boots and what was left of her clothes and reach for the condom on the bedside table. Then she was on him, yanking his jeans to his knees and straddling him like she was born to ride.

"Oh, it's like that, huh?" he asked, half-laughing and altogether amazed at how easily she'd overpowered him. The crinkle of the plastic wrapper was almost drowned out by the sound of their breathing. He clenched his jaw at the touch of her fingers, praying he wouldn't embarrass himself with a too-quick finish.

"Yeah," she said and dropped down, sheathing his cock in her body with one quick, hot slide. She braced her hands on his chest and smiled, looking pleased with herself. "That's what it's like, cowboy."

He bucked, not so much trying to throw her off as give her a reason to hang on. She went one better and twisted her hips in a hard figure eight that made his blood roar in his ears.

The cheap carpet burned his bare ass as she rode him. The air around them felt heated, as if it had passed through a brushfire. Her fingertips bit hard into his chest, but her mouth was the same soft, sulky pout that caught his eye in the roadhouse. He stared, hypnotized. There was a cut-loose feeling in his chest, like he'd jumped off a cliff of his own free will.

But at the back of his mind, he knew how it was supposed to go. And this wasn't it.

She loved the way he stared at her mouth. The way his gaze roamed over her, but always returned to her lips. The way his face creased in a frown of perfect concentration, as if she were the only thing in the world worth watching. It detonated pulse after pulse between her straining thighs.

Every shift of her body brought her down hard on his cock. She rocked and bounced, full to the edge of discomfort with a sticky-sweet friction that shot jets of pleasure out to her toes and fingertips and the ends of her hair.

But pleasure wasn't the point of this encounter. Where had all her anger gone? She was supposed to be working out her fury and desperation on this rugged cowboy, but all she felt desperate for was more of his skin against hers, more of his lips and teeth and tongue, more of his clever, calloused hands. More of that look on his face when she ground herself against him and felt herself throb around him.

The light caught the sweat forming along his collarbone and the stretch of muscles in his throat as he pulled one ragged breath after another. His half-closed eyes looked lazy, but they glittered behind the dark sweep of his lashes, and she knew he could see right down to the black, murderous rage in the tar pits of her soul.

"Harder," he muttered and curled upright to grip her tight around the waist. "You do me hard as you like, darlin'. No shame in it. Go on and ride," he said, one staccato thrust of his hips for each diamond-cut syllable. She let go with a wild, spooky laugh and took him at his word, glorying in the slap of skin on skin.

She was thinking how this change of angle rubbed her clit just right when her orgasm crept up on her like a dirty thought in church. It started as a slow pulling apart deep in her belly and spread outwards, shredding every cell till she was blind and deaf with it, lost in a storm of pure sensation.

She fell forwards, her face tucking into the crook of his neck like the spot was crafted for her. Beneath her, his body stiffened. He groaned low in her ear, the tremble and twitch of his fingers along her spine telling her everything she needed to know.

"Thank you," she whispered when she'd caught her breath.

"I'm much obliged, myself," he returned, and she could feel him grinning against her cheek. "You make real good company."

They moved to the bed, sore and sated and propping each other up like the last two cards in a fallen deck. She turned her back to the windows and let him curl around her. His breath was warm on the back of her neck. She felt safe.

The last thing she saw before closing her eyes was the red glow of the roadhouse sign reflected on the opposite wall.

Sometime after dawn, sleep slithered off Kate like a shed skin, leaving her mouth dry and her head clear. She slipped out of bed and into the bathroom. Her hands shook as she splashed water on her face.

"Stupid," she told the mirror. "What an unbelievably stupid thing to do. He could've hurt you. He could've killed you." She paused as the worst occurred to her. "He could've taken the money."

She crept back into the bedroom on her hands and knees, pausing to peer beneath the bed. The suitcase was right where she'd left it. Relieved, she crawled to where they'd dropped their clothes.

In the bed, the cowboy didn't stir.

She pulled his wallet out of the back pocket of his jeans. Inside it she found a few small bills, a driver's licence photo that didn't quite match his face, and a handful of credit cards emblazoned with an odd assortment of names.

A torn scrap of paper fell to the carpet. She unfolded it. Five words, in neat blue ink: "Melissa – tall, blonde, good body."

She was fumbling in the bottom of her leather bag before she made it to her feet.

"Eli," she said. "Wake up."

He rumbled low in his throat. Sprawled on his stomach, he reached across the sheets, long fingers searching out the place

where she'd slept. When they didn't find her, he flipped over on to
his back. A buttery spill of sunlight through an opening in the
drapes highlighted the smooth planes of his chest and the golden
streaks in his hair.

He was beautiful, not to mention the best lover she'd ever had.
On the other hand, he was obviously a criminal and undoubtedly
dangerous. But the word that described him at the moment – the
word that pounded in her head and chest like a second heartbeat
– was liar. The one thing she couldn't bring herself to forgive.

"Mornin'," he said and brushed his hair out of his face. His smile
was no less inviting for being slow and sleepy. But when his eyes lit
on the gun in her hands, that smile faded like an unfixed photo-
graph exposed to light. He pushed himself up to lean against the
headboard and lifted his hands at either side of his head.

She clutched the gun in front of her in a two-fisted grip, aimed at
the centre of his bare chest. Her entire body shook, but mostly her
finger where it was poised over the trigger.

"I don't want to shoot you."

"I don't reckon I care to be shot."

"Cut the cowboy crap."

"Yes, ma'am." He shook his head and let his hands drop. "Shoot
if you're gonna do it, but you'd better be ready to run. That bitty
snub-nose don't have a silencer. It'll make one hell of a bang."

She glanced at the door. Could she make it? Throw down the
gun, snatch up her bag and drag the suitcase from under the bed
before he got his hands on her? No, it wasn't possible. But neither
was killing him in cold blood.

Still, she raised the gun a few inches higher and straightened her
stance. "What's your story?"

To his credit, he didn't pretend to misunderstand. "Your
boyfriend hired a guy in New Orleans. He sub-contracted the job
to me."

"What's the job, exactly?"

He shifted a little, and the ratty motel blanket slid a few inches to
expose the line of dark hair leading down from his navel. "I find
lost things and put 'em back where they belong."

So that's what it came down to. In the end, she was just another
misplaced object to be collected and returned to its owner. But this
particular misplaced object had more questions.

"I was careful. I took every possible precaution. How did you
find me?"

His face twisted like he knew some bad news and didn't want to be the one to share it. "There's a GPS inside the lining of your bag. I've been trackin' you since you blew past Houston." He heaved a sigh and gave her a pitying look. "I guess your boyfriend's been trackin' you a lot longer than that."

The leather bag – the one that never left her side. Phillip's very first gift, which he'd undoubtedly used to follow her every movement for the past three years. She loved that bag.

This is what I get for being sentimental.

She heard a loud buzzing, like an especially obnoxious doorbell. It took her several seconds to figure out it was coming from inside her own head. A few seconds after that, she found herself sitting on the corner of the bed, the gun pointed at the floor.

Eli approached her, clutching a glass of water. He moved slowly, with his free hand raised in front of him, as if she were still likely to shoot him through heart. She saw he was naked, and realized she was naked, too.

He handed her the water. "If it makes you feel better, I've been hangin' around El Paso for days, waiting to see where you'd finally decide to cross the border."

"Why would that make me feel better?"

"You ever been to El Paso?" He smiled as he said it, and she felt the corners of her mouth wanting to lift.

"I made it easy for you, didn't I?"

He shrugged. "I didn't expect you to stroll into the roadhouse like you did. That was a piece of luck."

"The paper in your wallet says I'm a blonde. How did you know it was me?"

"It also says you're tall with a good body. I played the odds."

He was also playing at being honest. She knew better. "You said you were harmless."

"Have I hurt you yet?"

She set the gun on the bed next to her, drank the water and handed him the glass. It was all the answer she was willing to give. "Now what?"

"Now I'm supposed to hold you till your boyfriend gets here." He reached for his jeans.

She watched the stretch and roll of muscle in his back as he dressed. "You could take the money and let me go."

"It ain't the money he's after, I reckon." He pulled on his socks and boots. "Besides, how far do you think you'd get on your own, Melissa?"

She flinched. "I got this far. And don't call me that."

He paused in the middle of pulling on his wrinkled T-shirt. "Rumour has it there was quite the little bidding war over this job. Your boyfriend made you sound like easy pickins.' Said you were as soft and brainless as a new-hatched chick."

"I don't want to hear it."

"You deserve to know. He said you'd answer to just about anything, includin' 'baby', or 'bitch'.'"

The words seemed to hook into her flesh like tiny barbs that caught and tugged. She rose from the bed and gathered her clothes. On her way to the bathroom, she gave the leather bag a kick that sent it into the opposite wall with a thud.

Baby or bitch. Baby or bitch. It repeated in an endless loop as she brushed her teeth and pinned up her hair. Her reflection in the mirror was pale, as if she'd been washed in milk, except where the stubble across Eli's jaw had left its mark. The rug burns on her knees throbbed in time with her pulse. She couldn't think past the noise in her head.

When she looked up again, Eli was leaning in the doorway of the bathroom. He met her eyes in the mirror. "If you run, he'll set somebody else on your tail, sure as cold iron. Somebody not nearly as nice as me."

"It doesn't matter. I can't go back to him. He's . . ." She stopped. There were no words to describe the monster Phillip had grown to be in her imagination. No words for how much she despised him – or how much she despised herself for being such a clueless dupe.

"I can't go back."

Eli crowded in behind her. He rested his hands on the sink at either side of her hips and hooked his chin over her shoulder. Lit by the overhead fluorescent light, his grin had all the deadly charm of a rattlesnake's.

"Who said anything about goin' back?"

"So," Eli said, trying to keep his voice level and reasonable, "what you're tellin' me is you've never actually fired a gun."

"Right. But how hard can it be?" Her crooked smile said she'd recovered from her little spell of shell shock and come to grips with the situation.

Gotta admire an adaptable woman.

He sighed. "I guess we'll find out, won't we?"

He'd already contacted the client – Phillip, she called him, but

Eli didn't like the taste of it on his tongue – and told him where and when to take delivery of his wayward property. The man's voice had sounded tinny in Eli's ear, like the whine of a blowfly.

"Sweet Melissa," he said. "Feel free to try her out. Be sure she knows I gave you permission. You won't be sorry. Consider it a tip for excellent service."

The man laughed, and Eli had to hold the cell phone away from his ear to keep from dropping it in the dust and smashing it with the heel of his boot.

Over a vending machine breakfast shared on the wrinkled sheets of the motel bed, they'd put together a plan. Now it was a few minutes past noon. They were driving north, into the wind-carved landscape of the Chihuahuan Desert. Mountains rose in the distance, beyond mile after mile of straw-coloured dirt blowing in the gullies and a sky the bleached-out white of old tombstones. The un-air-conditioned cab of the truck felt like the inside of a kiln. The radio gave nothing but static. Eli did what he could to fill the sweaty silence with local trivia.

"This area has a population density of two people per square mile. The average income is only about nine grand, makin' it one of the poorest counties in the country."

"Why do you know all this?" she asked him.

He shrugged. "Part of the job."

She watched him drive. It made him nervous, like when she'd watched him at the pool table. He'd told the truth about that. In fact, he'd only told her a single, small lie. In the greater scheme of things, it wasn't worth much. So why did he feel so damned guilty about it?

"I'm sorry," he muttered, half-hoping she wouldn't hear. No such luck.

"For what?"

The tips of his ears were on fire. "For when I said I was just an interested bystander."

"You're not interested?"

He turned and found her looking at him with expectation on her face, like it was a serious question. He shook his head. "It's the bystander part that's the lie."

The answer seemed to satisfy her.

They pulled off the road next to an abandoned gas station. The small, saggy building stood up to its knees in yellow weeds. He set up a row of empty beer bottles on the fender of an old Dodge and taught her to shoot her bitty gun.

"A weapon that size is tricky. You wanna get as close as you can before you draw, 'cause it ain't easy to aim when the wind's blowin' dirt in your eyes." He showed her how to squeeze the trigger and stepped back, out of her way. "Watch out for the recoil."

She turned out to be a quick study. He wasn't surprised.

All at once, he wanted her – wanted to take her down in the dust and feel her fight against his hold. Wanted to feel her give in, and not because he'd overpowered her, but because she wanted him right back.

It crackled through him like lightning, and he had to look away.

He wondered how far he'd go for her. He'd never killed a man in his life, but it didn't seem like such a long fall from where he stood to the place where he'd be willing to shed blood just to keep her safe and at his side, where she belonged.

Kate watched Eli's hands as he cleaned and reassembled his rifle. His frown of concentration and his sure touch on the gleaming barrel sent distracting jolts of sense-memory through her body.

That's how he looked at me. That's how he touched me.

She turned away and squinted into the bone-coloured sky.

They were standing on the shoulder of a nameless road with nothing – not a tree or a boulder or even a mile marker – to dignify the spot. Eli lifted the rifle to his shoulder and checked the sight. He glanced at her. "Last chance to make a run for it."

She shook her head. "You're the one who said he'd never let me go."

"Just makin' sure we're on the same page."

She wanted to tell him she was with him all the way. Instead she asked, "Are you scared?"

The question seemed to catch him by surprise. He laughed. "Damn straight. Scared is what keeps you breathin', so long as you don't let it get in your way."

It seemed like a sound philosophy. Also, it made her feel better about the lump of terror in her throat that kept threatening to choke her to death.

"He's late," Eli said.

"He'll be here. He likes to make people wait."

The heat tightened like a tourniquet. As the seconds ticked down, they didn't touch or look at each other. They didn't talk about their plan, or what they'd do if they succeeded. But for the first time in recent memory she didn't feel alone.

Phillip arrived twenty minutes later. He drove a rented Mercedes, the colour indistinguishable beneath a layer of dust. He pulled off the road fifty feet from where they stood and got out of the car.

"Let him make the first move," Eli had told her when they were discussing strategy on the rumpled motel bed. "Let him come to us."

The gun tucked in the back of her jeans felt hot and hard and slick against her sweaty skin. She pressed her hand against the scorching fender of the truck to steady herself and observed how Phillip's hair didn't move in the breeze.

"Hello there!" he called and walked towards them, moving like he had sand in his joints. The salmon-orange polo shirt beneath his linen jacket flashed like neon against the empty desert. Even at this distance, his grinning, clean-shaven face looked insincere – full of artfully veneered teeth and bogus good cheer.

In sharp contrast, Eli lounged against the tailgate, working several days' worth of beard and dust-caked jeans. His rifle hung from the fingertips of one hand. The suitcase sat on the ground between his feet.

He smiled his rattlesnake smile. "Welcome to Texas."

Phillip ignored him. "Melissa? Is that you?" He stopped twenty feet away and squinted in the hazy sunlight. "Come out where I can see you, baby."

Hating herself for the involuntary urge to obey, she stepped forwards. When she came even with the tailgate, Eli stopped her with a whispered, "That's plenty far enough."

"You changed your hair," Phillip said. His lip curled in disgust. "It makes you look your age."

She stared at him, struggling to process the insult. He wanted to talk about her hair?

When she didn't respond, he shrugged. "That's all right. We can change it back again. Everything can go right back the way it was, baby, as soon as we get home."

Now Eli straightened and shifted his grip on the rifle. "There's been a change of plans." He kicked the suitcase forwards. "You take the money. She stays here."

Phillip chuckled. "Took her for a spin, did you? I told you she's a good lay."

Despite the heat, a sickening chill washed over her, raising goose-flesh down her arms and back. Eli shot her a look out of the corner of his eye and shook his head ever so slightly.

Phillip advanced on them, still moving stiffly, as if he couldn't bear to ruin the perfect crease in his $1,000 trousers. "I can't blame you for wanting to keep her a while, but let me tell you, friend, she's got some bad habits. Always asking questions, for one. Isn't that right, baby?"

"You should take the cash, mister," Eli said. "It's all there. I counted it."

Shock rocked Kate back on her heels. He counted the money? When?

Phillip didn't appear to be listening. "Of course, she's already past her prime, but I'm sentimental. I like to keep what belongs to me until I have no more use for it. Then I pass it along to someone with less discerning tastes." He waved his hand in a dismissive gesture. "She'll be a hand-me-down inside of a year. You can do better, friend. For a handful of pesos, you can rent better."

Beneath the constant rush of the wind, she heard Eli's teeth grind together. But when he spoke, it was all easygoing cowboy twang.

"I reckon you hadn't ought to talk about her that way, mister."

"Really? Is that what you reckon?" The smug grin dropped away from Phillip's face. "Because I reckon I'll talk about her any way I want. Now kindly hand that suitcase to Melissa and send her over here. I'll count out your cut and we'll be on our way. We've got a flight to catch."

Eli shook his head. "Sorry, mister."

Phillip rolled his eyes. "Melissa? Tell this fly-by-night cowboy to quit fucking around, will you? Tell him you want to go home."

Kate said nothing. She stood perfectly still and watched as Phillip's assumptions caught up with reality. First he looked betrayed, like a kid deprived of a promised treat. Then his handsome face hardened, and he muttered something that sounded like, "Bitch."

He reached inside his jacket and pulled out a gun. It was somewhat larger than the one tucked against the small of Kate's back. At the same time, Eli lifted his rifle to his shoulder and took aim.

"Melissa, grab that suitcase and get your ass over here."

"Get in the truck, Kate."

She laughed. She couldn't help it. It had been a long day. "Why don't you both settle down before you drop dead of testosterone poisoning?"

Phillip's eyes flickered in surprise. He wasn't accustomed to being spoken to that way – especially by her – and she knew she'd scored a point. Eli said nothing, but a muscle in his jaw twitched and he lowered the rifle a fraction of an inch.

Phillip cleared his throat. "I suppose we can come to some kind of compromise."

"Put your weapon on the ground, mister, and kick it away," Eli said. "Then I'll drop mine."

"That hardly seems fair."

Eli shrugged. "I've got the money and the girl. The way I see it, you've got nothin' to lose."

Phillip appeared to think it over. Then he bent at the waist, set the gun on the ground and gave it a kick. It slid several feet on the pebbled surface of the shoulder.

Eli lowered his rifle and leaned it against the bumper of the truck. He picked up the suitcase and started towards Phillip.

Phillip had shoved his hands into the pockets of his trousers. Instead of watching Eli's approach, he stared at Kate, his face fixed in a smirk. She knew that expression. He wore it when he was feeding her lies and expecting her to swallow them without complaint. When he was underestimating her completely – her intelligence, her strength of will, everything that made her a person.

Eli came to a stop three feet from where Phillip stood. His stance remained loose and amiable.

"Don't let Phillip make you angry," she'd told him that morning over pork rinds and lemon-lime soda. "Don't let him get under your skin. He's good at that. He knows how to take advantage."

Now, without ever taking his eyes off Kate, Phillip leaned in close and said something to Eli. She couldn't read Phillip's lips, and his words were blown away in the breeze, but she saw Eli react. She saw his back stiffen and his hand rise. She was too far away to stop it.

The crack of Eli's fist connecting with Phillip's jaw made her jump. Phillip grunted and fell back. A second later he straightened. He winked at Kate over Eli's shoulder.

You and me, baby, that wink said. *You and me, until I decide to toss you out like last week's trash. I can do it because I own you, and I'll keep doing it to anyone I please until someone stops me.*

It was the only warning she got. Then Phillip's hand slid out of his pocket. Sunlight glinted off the blade of his knife, and Kate knew he'd underestimated her for the last time.

The shots sounded louder than she remembered – much bigger bangs than when she'd been picking bottles off a fender. She heard at least two bullets ping off the rented Mercedes and realized she was firing with her eyes closed.

The recoils were stronger, too. No doubt she'd be feeling them in her shoulder for days.

The gun itself felt hot and slippery in her hand, as if someone had dipped it in simmering oil. She let it slide off her palm and drop to the ground. She stared at it, lying there in the dust, black as a moonless midnight. Had it always been so small? It hardly seemed like it could put a hole in a paper bag, much less—

"Look at me," Eli said, standing near enough to touch. She'd been certain she'd never get the chance to touch him again. But now here he was, well within arm's reach.

"C'mon, now," he said. "Look at me."

When she lifted her eyes, the expression on his face told her that he'd been standing there a while. She tried to focus.

"Is he . . . ?" She peered around Eli's shoulder. "Did I . . . ?"

"You did fine, darlin'." He pressed a kiss to her forehead and helped her into the cab of the truck. Then he retrieved her gun from where it lay and cleaned it with the hem of his shirt. She watched him, understanding he was wiping away her fingerprints, noting for what felt like the hundredth time how careful and thorough and competent he seemed. All that effort, just for her. Too bad she was too numb to appreciate it.

He tossed the gun away, climbed into the truck and pulled out on to the road. Only then did she notice the suitcase on the floor at her feet. There was a bullet hole in one corner.

He leaned across her and pulled a canteen from the glovebox. "Drink this."

She tried, but her trembling hands slopped lukewarm water down the front of her shirt. Instead, she observed the passing scenery and waited for her ears to stop ringing. After a while, she turned to look at Eli.

"We're just going to leave him there?"

He shrugged. "Buzzards need to eat, too."

By the time they reached Presidio, she'd stopped shaking. She could feel Eli watching her, waiting for her to break down, throw up or jump out of the moving truck. When it didn't happen, he visibly relaxed his grip on the wheel.

They stopped for gas and supplies, then headed for the border crossing. She sat upright and rigid, staring straight ahead, afraid to make eye contact with the uniformed guards. Could they smell the gunpowder on her hands? See the fear in her face?

Eli tried to make conversation while they waited in line. "Sorry I lost my cool back there. You warned me not to let the bastard get to me."

She thought about asking him what Phillip had said to make him throw that punch, and decided she didn't need to know. Not now. Maybe not ever.

"It's over," she said, meaning all of it – Phillip's casual malice, her own rage, all the ugly details. Finished. "It doesn't matter now."

Aside from the standard questions and requests for identification, no one gave them a second look, and they crossed into Mexico without incident.

They drove south-west till the bottom edge of the sun kissed the horizon. Eli turned off the highway on to another nameless dirt road. Fifteen miles into the desert, he pulled over. They climbed into the bed of the truck to watch the reds and golds and purples play over the landscape. The wind blew in arid gusts, and somewhere behind them a crescent moon rose above the mountains.

She took a deep breath and started what she thought might be the most important conversation of her life. "You still think I can't make it on my own?"

Eli inclined his head, considering. "You're smart, you've got guts and you're not lookin' for a fight. That's enough to keep you out of most trouble."

"But not all."

"No," he said. "Not all."

"So you're offering to look after me? What's your price?"

He squinted at her. "If I wanted to, I could drive off with the money right now and leave you standin' by the side of the road."

"But you won't."

He shook his head. "I won't."

She thought about it. After a minute or two, she said, "Phillip was right about one thing. I do ask a lot of questions."

He looked at her expectantly. "Go on."

"You knew the money was there all along? You counted it while I was sleeping?"

He nodded.

"And instead of sneaking out in the middle of the night with the suitcase, you came back to bed." It wasn't so much a question as a statement of obvious fact.

He nodded again.

"You know, I never wanted to hurt Phillip," she said. "I only wanted to get away."

"I know."

"And I'd never hurt you. Not on purpose." She turned her head and looked him square in the eye. "In case you were wondering."

"I don't intend to give you any cause," he said and smiled, no trace of rattlesnake now. "In case you were wonderin'."

She wanted to trust him. She wanted it like clean air to breathe and cool water to drink. "Why?" she asked. "What's in it for you?"

He shrugged. "I've been alone a long while, and you're real good company."

His voice was honey and gasoline – everything she'd never known she needed.

She thought about all the things neither one of them was saying. About what they'd already proven they were willing to do for each other on less than twenty-four hours' acquaintance. About the crackling heat between them, and how it might consume them – might build to a fever pitch and flame over into a desperate, dangerous thing.

She lay back and stared up at the sky, and wondered why none of that scared her.

He kissed her then, quick and hungry and deep, all prickly stubble and rough edges ragged with want. He lowered himself on her, pressing her into the hot metal of the truck bed. He was heavy, but it didn't matter. His weight held all her jagged bits and pieces in place. She tangled her legs with his, the harsh scrape of denim on denim the loudest sound in the desert.

They tore at each other's clothes. She heard a seam give way and willed her hands to go slow. The night before she'd been too frantic. Now she wanted to know the fluid way his muscles moved under her palms. She wanted to learn every inch of him – the way his breath hitched when she trailed her fingertips down his back, the way he groaned when she sucked at the skin where the curve of his neck met his collarbone.

She squirmed out of her boots and jeans. Together they slid along the surface of the truck bed, grabbing for leverage where they could find it. She turned her head to let him bite at her throat and saw his fingertips whiten as they pressed against the black metal, haloes of perspiration around each one. The tendons in the back of his hand worked under his skin as he leaned into her with sharp teeth and greedy kisses.

She let him flip her on to her stomach. He took her that way – gripped her hips and pushed the thick length of his cock into her with a grunt, slipping his hand down to pinch her clit between a calloused thumb and forefinger. She felt strung out and brittle, as if one more wrenching wave of sensation might snap her spine. He took a shuddering breath, pulled back and drove into her, hard. She didn't break. At least, not like she thought she would.

Then they were galloping at full speed, caught in a punishing pace that would leave bruises and welts in its wake. Her thoughts began to scorch at the edges, the promise of release like smoke before fire. She reached back and grabbed a handful of his hair to urge him on. The fingernails of her other hand scraped against the truck bed so hard she half-expected sparks. Her panting sobs spiralled into a howl as the world went red behind her eyelids and the sweet sizzle of pleasure burned through her core.

He didn't stop or even slow down. A roar rose from deep in his chest and cut off with a wounded cry. She felt him grind to a halt, his fingers digging into the flesh of her hips as he came. She kept rocking against him, enjoying how the aftershocks broke his voice and stole his breath.

He rolled off and fell to one side. Beneath them, the truck made a hollow bang and swayed on its tyres, as if applauding their efforts.

"We really ought to try that on a bed sometime, darlin'."

She laughed. It felt good, so she did it again.

He slept, and she counted stars. The cooling breeze made her shiver under the span of his hand, tanned and veined in contrast to the pale smoothness of her skin. His ring felt warm on her breast.

She closed her eyes and thought about another motel room somewhere down the line, maybe tonight, maybe tomorrow. A better one this time. Maybe something with a pool – or not. It didn't matter. She heard the rough timbre of his voice in the morning over coffee, saw his toothbrush on the sink next to hers, saw his boots by the door.

A twitch of his fingers told her he'd awakened. "We'd best get on the road."

They dressed and climbed into the cab of the truck. As he reached for the keys, she lay a hand on his arm. "One last question?"

"Shoot."

She licked her dry lips. "Are we bad guys now?"

"Nah," he said, and gave her a crooked smile. "We're outlaws. That's a whole other animal."

She sank back into the seat, satisfied.

It's possible to drive the four hundred and fifty miles from the Texas border at Presidio to the Pacific coast of Mexico in under seven hours. That doesn't make it a good idea.

If you keep to the back roads, travelling under a lemon-rind moon in an inky desert sky, the trip will be longer and more dangerous – also not a good idea. But when you're skipping the country with a suitcase full of stolen cash and a fly-by-night cowboy who has the answers to a lifetime's worth of questions, it's the only way to go.

Stolen Hours

Michelle M. Pillow

One

"Get out, get out, get out!" Helen covered her ears, trying to block out the rush of voices that punctured her thoughts like tiny needles. The chorus of words seemed to rain down on her, an omniscient presence she couldn't quite block out and the harder she tried to, the louder her house guests became – all three dozen or so of them. Well, "guests" wasn't exactly accurate. In truth, some had lived in the house before her and some were those who'd died nearby. The house was built near limestone and an underground stream. Both elements attracted the spirits and gave them energy. Now that the ghosts were enjoying their afterlives, they still believed they had a right to the place and she was their new caretaker. Apparently to some, caretaker equalled indentured servant.

Though she couldn't see them all, she knew they were there. They appeared as shadows and white mists, as tiny orbs of light, as full intelligent apparitions and as an endless looping of a single unaware activity. She heard them giggling and running, singing and dancing, usually just beyond the corner of her sight. They moved her belongings, creaked floorboards, jingled the crystal chandelier, made her paranoid to use the bathroom and essentially killed any chance she had of bringing a man home – not that there was a man to be found in the town of Nowhere, Oklahoma with its population of about eighty-three. Before she knew about the house's quirks she had tried to sell the place, but the economy was in the toilet and the realtor couldn't even get prospective buyers to tour the property. The money attached to the house drew enough interest to cover taxes each year and little else. That was why it was so important she kept her online blogger job and she couldn't work with the constant demands on her time.

Not bothering to look up from her desk to the transparent people before her, Helen said, "Fiona, I've already told you I can't do anything about the big band music. You have to fight it out with Bella, quietly and outside. Every time I throw the radio out, you all just bring it back. If you don't stop bringing this argument to me, I'll introduce you to heavy metal and turn it up so loud I won't be able to hear you ever again."

Helen knew the girls didn't know what heavy metal was but was beyond the point of caring. One of the girls whispered to the other, "She said she was going to drop metal on herself so she can be dead, too."

"Oh, no," the other answered. "Then who will be the caretaker?"

Helen kept her eyes on the desk, continuing on to the next of the house guests' list of demands, "Jack, I won't cook liver and onions for you the next time you take corporeal form. You never eat them and they stink up the house. Plus, the last thing I want to be doing in the middle of the night while you all run around and party is cook. It's bad enough that you all only become corporeal in the middle of the night and without forewarning.

"Winston, I'm sure running a machine that removes the fuzz off peaches was a fine career, but you're no longer in the north-east. This is Oklahoma. I need a job I can do in Oklahoma. So, for the last time, I am not rejecting your suggestion, it is merely impossible."

This time she did raise her eyes to a crotchety old ghost. He had his thumbs tucked into the sides of his overalls while he rocked on his bare feet. Every time he got worked up, scorch marks appeared on his wrinkled features. They were a reminder of the night his moonshine still exploded. "As for you, Jerry, please stop telling everyone there are demonic ghosts moving into the attic. We all know you died three sheets to the wind and when you get worked up you go into alcoholic delusions."

Jerry's face was blistered down the side of his cheek and neck, the horrific sight disturbing but no longer scary. He stumbled to the side and then disappeared through a wall. Next to him, twins Bella and Fiona giggled. The two eternally ten-year-old girls were always arguing over who was technically older. Bella was born first, but also died of scarlet fever first. Fiona, having lived ten days longer than her sister, tried to claim elder status. They chimed in cherubic unison, "We love you, Miss Gettsman." At Helen's stern look, they ran through the door, the sound of their giggles and loud footsteps echoing behind them.

The snow had begun to melt and the constant beat of dripping water tapped outside the window as it fell from the roof. Beyond the window, old trees and thick shrubs dotted the rolling hills. They were shaded with the light of late evening. Normally, when the ground wasn't a vast puddle of mud, the surrounding landscape looked like something off a postcard. Inside, the isolated three-storey mansion appeared close to what it must have looked like when it was built at the turn of the twentieth century, though the long years had taken their toll. Her late aunt had updated very few things, but luckily electricity and plumbing had been among them.

There wasn't much by the way of furniture. When she first came to the mansion, Helen had moved a lot of the old furniture to the barn to be refinished. A few of the spirits had some skill in that department. Though getting them to work was another thing altogether and the progress they were making was very slow. She supposed when one had an eternity ahead of them, they weren't in such a hurry. Her redecorating was another point of contention in the house.

Pictures of her ancestors and their friends lined the walls and fireplace mantel. She studied their faces, recognizing several of them as residents. Wryly, she muttered, "From living alone to over thirty vocal room-mates. Thanks for the inheritance, Aunt Susan. You couldn't have just been the crazy recluse we all thought you to be and left me a normal house?"

Strangely, Aunt Susan was one ghost who hadn't appeared.

"What do you mean normal? There is absolutely nothing wrong with my house. The design is perfect."

Helen couldn't help the small smile that formed on her lips. She couldn't see him, but she knew that British accent well. One of the pictures caught and held her attention. It was of the house during its construction. In the foreground a man stood, smiling in a way that made her heart flutter just a little. The happy expression shone from his dark eyes, radiating in such a way that whoever looked found themselves smiling back. He'd been a friend of her great-grandfather.

Henry Gregory, Architect, 1909.

"Hello, Gregory," she said softly. An orange light flickered, as if coming from a candle that wasn't there. The floorboards creaked and the faint sound of violins drifted in from far away only to fade. She pushed up from her desk, reaching to close her laptop's lid. "Where have you been? I missed you."

"Have I been gone?" The sound was fuller than before and more directional. She found Gregory standing in the doorway leading into the dining room. The turn of the twentieth-century Edwardian-style dinner jacket, stark white shirt and dark tie were the same as the day he'd died. Laced-up leather boots and a felt bowler hat with rounded crown completed the look.

Helen could see a chair through his transparent waist and caught herself staring at it. When her eyes darted up to his face, his crooked smile sent a shiver over her. Since the very first moment he appeared . . . well, no, to be fair, the first moment he appeared had been a little surreal. To be more accurate, since the first time she could look at him without freaking out about the fact ghosts existed, her house was haunted and she was what they called a caretaker, he'd made her pulse quicken. She was a fool and she knew it. Though he was an intelligent haunting, aware of her and their surroundings, he was a hundred years dead. She was thirty years alive. Nothing could come of them and she wasn't even sure how he felt about it, or if he could even feel as she did. Gregory was a gentleman from a lost era. His polite charm, the very thing that made her legs tremble and her desires rise, was merely a by-product of his time.

Gregory pulled the hat from his head, holding it with strong, tapering fingers. Energy snapped from his movements, as if life was there beneath the surface waiting to burst forth. He smoothed his brown hair back from his face and stared at her with even browner eyes. When he was near the other voices seemed to fade. She suspected his spirit had been here the longest, as he died the day the last stone was set on the house. Helen's great-grandfather moved in the next day.

Gregory looked at his hand, lifting it as if to reassure himself he was still materialized. "I'm still here."

She'd been staring again. Clearing her throat, Helen said, "Sorry. I was wondering about something, ah . . ."

"Yes." His body blurred, drifting gracefully only to pause once he stood before her. Her breath caught slightly and she wondered if he knew what his presence did to her. The very subtle hint of cologne wafted over her. He must have been wearing it the day he died, just like the fine suit.

"I know this might be a sensitive subject and . . ." Helen took a deep breath, trying to concentrate. She wondered if he knew how her body heated or that an ache low in her belly begged for release. "And if you don't want to answer, I'll understand."

"You want to know why I didn't kiss you last time I was corporeal." His hand cupped her cheek and, for a moment, she stood stunned by the somewhat intimate touch. She had thought he might, as he'd stared at her with fading eyes, but she'd convinced herself she'd imagined the moment.

"Can you feel such things being that you are a . . . ?" Her words were low and halting. But, now, as the tortured depths of his gaze, raw with emotion, bore into her and begged her to give him an answer to some unasked question, she knew what she'd seen was real.

"A ghost?" he finished when she couldn't. "Yes. I can feel things as deeply as I did in life. Some of the others are locked in an emotion, as was I for a time. But, now, I can feel emotions. I can feel sensations against my body, though I can't feel as I do when I'm corporeal. I have come to believe that death is merely a transfer of energy. I am still me, but not as I was."

Helen longed for the solid feel of flesh, for the heat that radiated between two people. She longed for him to be of flesh and bone. However, those corporeal moments were fleeting, stolen hours in the night. Some people called it the witching hour, those brief minutes when the dead could play upon the earth once again – not every night, not every ghost, but some. Her nerves tingled in awareness, but she couldn't feel him, not like she could a live man, not now while daylight still found its way inside. She wanted to grab him, have him press her against a wall, have his lips against hers. Closing her eyes, she answered belatedly, "I wasn't going to ask about that. I was going to ask about something else."

"I wish to explain." His words had grown softer. "I need to explain. I haven't been able to rest since I saw that look in your eyes as I disappeared. I never meant to hurt you."

The sensation of him surrounded her, like hands hovering over her flesh refusing to touch. Frustration mingled with sharp awareness. If she concentrated, she could tell exactly where his essence brushed over her flesh. His hand touched her arm, slid up her shoulder and along her throat. She moved her head to the side, allowing him access. A thumb drew along her cheek, dipping beneath the surface.

"I didn't kiss you because it would be torture to stop and my time was at an end," Gregory whispered. She blinked, opening her eyes. His face was close, but he had no breath to hit upon her lips. "Since you arrived a little over a year ago to be our new caretaker, I have tried to . . ." He looked away, before briefly finishing, "I tried."

Helen wasn't sure how to answer. All she knew was that her heart pounded in her chest and she felt hot and cold at the same time. A shadow moved through the corner of her vision, but she ignored it.

"I don't know if you can even feel me now." He moved his fingers through her lips. "When I touch you, it's like an electric current that draws me in." He reached for her hand and she lifted it, holding it between them. Gregory pushed his hand through hers. Helen curled her fingers, desperate to hold him but unable to. Her senses were heightened, focused completely on him. "There, yet just beyond my grasp, real but fleeting."

"I can feel you." She swallowed nervously. The chandelier crystals crashed together in the next room, reminding her of a wind chime. "You're tingling and cool."

Helen's entire body ached with the need to feel. To touch was such a simple thing, often taken for granted, and she couldn't even manage that. His nearness only made the rising desires worse, but she didn't ask him to leave. Where his fingers traced hers, a shiver travelled down her hand. It drew a wayward line through her arm, across her breasts to peak her nipples, only to centre deep in her belly. Her legs trembled. Her breath deepened. Her heart raced.

Wanting. Needing.

Denial.

Helen almost cried out. Instead, she whispered, "When will you become corporeal?"

"Shh," he said. "We can't talk here. Not about this. The others are watching us. They're always around. They're trying to listen even now. We must find a place away from them."

Helen turned her head as another shadow passed by.

"Look at her," a disembodied woman's voice whispered. "I told you she wasn't a good fit."

"She is no caretaker," a male answered. Helen recognized Samuel, which meant the whispering woman was probably Rebecca. The spirit followed Rebecca around like a supernatural henchman. "She doesn't understand the rules."

"Gregory is one of us," Rebecca responded. "It is time she learns that. This goes too far." A nauseatingly disgusting laugh followed the comment.

"What are they talking about?" Helen asked. When she turned her attention back to Gregory, she realized he was gone.

Two

Helen retreated to the only place in the house the ghosts couldn't materialize – her second-storey bedroom. The Victorian four-poster bed, antique furniture and lavishly woven rugs over the wood slat floors created an opulent feel. When she first spent the night in the bedroom, she'd had visions of being a fine lady. That was until she'd woken up to find two men playing cards at the foot of her bed. They'd looked at her like it was the most normal thing in the world. She'd screamed so loud and long that the two of them hadn't reappeared for nearly six months. A salt barrier went down the next day.

A grandmotherly spirit had been kind enough to point out the instructions Aunt Susan had left Helen on how to protect her bedroom and keep the house guests out. Apparently, she wasn't the first caretaker to have privacy issues. Though sounds of footsteps and whispers sometimes drifted in, the salt she'd poured kept the others out. There were times when she considered salting the entire estate. Only, to do so would banish Gregory with the others.

Helen glanced into the hall, placing her hands on the door frame as she leaned out. The lady in white walked past, not noticing anything around her before fading mid-stride. Telling time by the consistency of the lady's daily stroll, Helen knew it would be just after five o'clock. "Gregory? Are you here? Where did you go?"

She felt him before she saw him. It was a brush of cool air against cheek. She pulled back into the room. He stood on the threshold, unable to enter. Without speaking, she knelt down on the floor and brushed her hand over the thin line of salt to sweep it away. Before she could stand, he passed over her, entering. Helen drew her finger, redrawing a crooked line with the salt.

"You're trapping me in your room?" Gregory asked, though he hardly appeared concerned. The thud of running feet sounded overhead followed by a hard crash.

Helen pushed the door closed as she stood and listened for the latch to click. The room suddenly felt very small. "I can't believe we're alone." Heat warmed her cheeks. "It seems strange. I wasn't sure you'd come in here, but you said we needed a place the others couldn't see so we could talk."

He looked around the room. His features blurred slightly. "Why would you think that? You've never asked me to come in here."

"You being a gentleman and all." Helen motioned at his clothing, noting the way he carried himself. These traits were a constant reminder. "I feel myself compelled to act like a lady, only I'm not sure how a lady acts."

At that he chuckled. "I've been around for quite some time. Just because I only own one suit during my afterlife, doesn't mean I haven't changed. I don't expect women to be like the ladies of my time and I don't expect you to be anything but you."

"There is something I've been dying to know. Earlier, I was going to ask about your death. The family legend says you died of foul play because my great-grandfather owed you money. Is that true?"

"You think Frank killed me?" He chuckled. "No, it wasn't that, it was an accident. I was pushing the workers to finish on time and stopped to check on the progress before going to a dinner party with your great-grandfather. One second I was looking up at my creation, the next I was standing dazed in the middle of the parlour watching people walk right by who couldn't see me. They say the suddenness of my death is what kept me here, just like the others. Those who die naturally seem to take the option to move on to wherever it is spirits go."

"Honestly, it's kind of a relief. I couldn't stand the thought of a relative of mine having killed you over money." She gave a nervous laugh.

Within a breath, he was close. Tingling erupted on her flesh. She tried to steady her nerves, but her hands trembled. A thought whispered through the back of her mind, telling her this was insane. It didn't matter. Her entire life she'd felt like she was sleepwalking through the world. Now, in this secluded place in Oklahoma surrounded by ghosts, she felt more real than ever before. Gregory made her feel alive. She could no more banish him from her than she could stop breathing.

"I need to sit down," she whispered. "I have to hold on to something or I'll fall."

Helen walked weak-kneed to the bed. Gregory appeared next to her. His weight didn't shift the mattress, but the bed did shake a little. The harsh pant of her breath echoed around them. She reached for his face, her fingers tingling as they went through his neck. "I don't know if I can do this." He began to pull away. "I meant not being able to grab a hold of you. I can't remember wanting anything more. Tell me this isn't crazy, that I'm not locked away in some mental institution due to hallucinations."

Gregory shook his head. "As I've told you before, this is all very real. Though, I cannot attest to this place not being an asylum. You have met the residents."

Helen laughed.

"Lie back and close your eyes," Gregory urged. She slowly obeyed.

Sensations filled her, overwhelming her senses. He stretched out next to her, his body pushing into hers and causing it to tingle. A hand swept over her hip and down her outer thigh, the caress like a teasing feather over her skin. Her breath caught and she focused on his touch. There was no need to remove her clothes, she felt him as if she were naked. Parting her lips, she took a deep breath. With each weightless caress, her body heated more until she was squirming beneath him.

Moisture gathered between her thighs. Helen ground her heels into the bed, longing to have something firm pressing into her. She wanted to run her hands into his hair, to hear his breath echoing hers, to feel his lips and tongue and teeth against her mouth. The sensation of his hand slid along her inner thigh, bringing pleasurable torment with it. She tensed as he drew close to her sex, wondering what it would feel like to have him there.

Helen felt a tug at her shirt. At first it didn't register, as her mind stayed focused on her stomach and thighs. He tugged again. This time more insistently as he tried to pull the shirt over her head. She blinked, focusing on his face. The colour of pale flesh had begun to fill in the transparency of his expression. He pulled at her shirt, trying to grasp the material with fingers that could not hold them. Helen made a move to help, tugging the shirt over her head and tossing it aside. As soon as she'd finished, Gregory touched her skin. The sensation felt warmer, thicker.

"What's happening?" Helen reached for his face and met with solidifying flesh. The colour of tanned flesh replaced the pale, as if painted across his features. It filled in his lips, darkened his eyes until his gaze penetrated her with the full force of his desire. His hand pressed into her stomach. She gasped. It answered the call of her desires and was the most wondrous thing she'd ever felt.

Without questioning further, she knocked the bowler hat from his head and reached for his tie, pulling his mouth to hers. She sighed against the firm press of his lips. This was the moment she'd waited so desperately for. Her passion grew with each brush of their bodies. She pulled off his tie and slid her hands into the front of his jacket, pushing it from his shoulders. It fell next to them on the bed. The subtle musk of cologne emanated from his neck as she kissed a trail from his mouth to his ear.

Her hands fumbled as she unbuttoned first his shirt and then his old-fashioned under garments. Helen wasn't sure why she was so nervous. She'd known him for over a year, talked to him for endless hours. They'd discussed old books and customs. She'd told him of movies and the marvels of technology. They relayed stories of youth, of past loves, of all those little things friends talk about and can't really remember discussing later. She knew his face, his smile – though normally she knew them to be transparent. She knew the sound of his voice, how it sent chills over her each time she heard it.

And, now, as the material of his clothes parted, she knew the feel of his stomach against hers. Breath rushed against her cheek as he inhaled against her. Heat radiated from his chest. Fingers revealed muscles, finding dips and curves once hidden. Their legs tangled and hips pressed until the unmistakable feel of his desire moulded against her.

"How long will this last?" Helen rubbed her hand down his cheek and neck to travel over his shoulder. He leaned back and drew his arms out of his sleeves. A long scar cut across the smooth, strong flesh of his chest. He was a man who had worked during his lifetime, not only designing homes, but building them with his hands. She liked his hands – sure and steady with the callouses of hard work.

"I do not know," he answered. Lids fell heavy over his eyes as he looked at her. His gaze lingered on her light-green bra. "I have not done this since before my death."

Helen unbuttoned her pants and pushed them from her hips. Gregory leaned back on the bed, jerking them off her legs. Her lacy green panties matched the bra. He bit his lip to see them. Reaching for her hip, he pulled at the lacy barrier covering her sex. The panties glided down her legs and he dropped them next to the bed.

Urgency filled them. She had never seen him corporeal during the daylight hours and wasn't sure how much time they had until he disappeared again. His eyes focused on the thin line of hair standing guard over the slick folds of her sex. Gregory undid his pants. The material slung low on his tight hips, revealing the full length of his arousal. He caressed her legs, pulling them open so he could settle between her thighs. Helen reached for him, tugging his arm to draw him forwards. His hand ventured up her inner thigh, moving until his fingers glided along her pussy.

Helen gasped, arching her hips into his hand. His finger tested her response, dipping beyond the barrier of her sex. He entered her slowly before moving to rub the tight bundle of nerves hidden within the moist folds. Her hips jerked in response, a wholly involuntary movement that sent pleasure washing over her body.

His hair was soft as she ran her fingers into it. Her gaze travelled over his chest, following the thin scar, watching its subtle movements. She pulled his mouth to hers, moaning as she kissed him. Their tongues met eagerly. Gregory braced his weight on one arm and the sheer force of his solid body to hers made her shiver in anticipation.

He dipped another finger inside her and Helen thrust herself against his hand, trying to end the ache he stirred within her. She wanted him like she'd never wanted another. Her kiss became rough as she pushed up from the bed. The large bulge of his arousal brushed against her thigh and she tensed. Almost mindless in her desperation, she flung his hand away from her sex and grabbed hold of his hips.

He held his body tense. The first intimate touch forced a small cry from Helen's lips. The hard length of his cock filled her, slow and deep. Pleasure erupted, but it was bittersweet as tension and neediness soon followed. Gregory bit his lip, his entire body strained. He stayed embedded inside her, as if afraid to move.

Helen dug her hands into his shoulders, drawing her ass down into the mattress before pushing up. Her legs worked against his hips. Taking his cue, Gregory moved. He pulled out only to thrust deep. Helen needed more. She bucked beneath him, her body urging him with every subtle and not-so-subtle movement to give her more. They rocked their hips, seeking a natural rhythm that would alleviate their yearning desires.

Helen groaned. Her body was so close. She needed release so badly. Flipping him on to his back, she took over, riding him as she sought fulfilment. The new position gave her control over their movements. Gregory's fingers dislodged her bra as he grabbed her breasts. Electric sensations filled the hard peaks of her nipples as he pinched them lightly between his fingers. She lifted up only to fall down upon his lap.

Gregory groaned, grabbing her hips to keep the now frantic pace of her thrusts from slowing. His gorgeous body strained beneath hers as he rocked up into her. His feet dug into the bed, forcing his cock deep. She gasped, panted, moaned. Clawing at his chest, she circled her hips. The tension became almost unbearable. Release was close, so close, so . . .

Helen cried out as she reached her climax. Her body jerked violently and she felt as if she couldn't catch her breath. Gregory thrust a few more times before he too found his release. Inside her sex a tingling sensation erupted where his body intimately touched hers. Before she could pull off him, she fell on to the mattress. She gasped, looking at the empty bed beneath her. Gone, too, were his dishevelled clothing. He'd disappeared.

Breathing hard, she rolled on to her back. Her limbs tangled in her discarded clothes and mussed-up bedding. Her heart thudded hard in her chest and sanity took a long time coming back. Helen stared at the ceiling, barely seeing it. The best sex of her life had been with a ghost who came so hard he'd disappeared. She gave a slight laugh, unsure whether or not she should be worried.

Three

Helen glanced around the living room to make sure she was alone before she quickly finished her purchase. She'd done her research and according to the ghost-hunting websites she'd found, a device called an EMF pump would work as an energy source for ghosts. The theory was that entities could use the electromagnetic field to manifest more easily. It might be a long shot, but if she put one in her bedroom, maybe Gregory could . . .

She didn't finish the thought. Hearing an unfamiliar scraping noise, she frowned and shut the lid to her laptop. Someone was dragging something heavy across the floor. Suddenly, she was hit with a cold blast of air and her breath turned into a white puff as she exhaled. It had been a while since the spirits affected her in such a way. Shivering, she rubbed her arms.

"Who is that?" she called. The hairs on the back of her neck pricked up. Remembering the conversation she'd heard earlier, she asked, "Samuel? Rebecca? Is that you?"

The lights flickered. The dragging noise stopped.

"This isn't funny!" Helen yelled, making her way into the dining room. "Stop! I mean it."

Everything stopped for a brief couple of seconds. But, just as she was starting to breathe a sigh of relief, the lights began to turn on and off. Cabinets and doors opened and closed, banging loudly. The chandelier's crystals crashed together as the fixture swung violently on its base. A chair lifted off the ground, spinning in slow circles. Helen watched it as she edged towards the nearby stairwell. Suddenly, it was launched at her. She screamed, ducking as she ran. The chair crashed into the wall, splintering into several pieces.

"Who is this?" she cried stumbling to crawl up the stairs. Beneath her the first storey floorboards creaked. "What do you want?"

Though, Helen suspected she knew what this was about. Gregory. They'd taken their relationship to the next level, defying the laws of mortality and afterlife. Even as they'd made love she'd worried about what it would mean. She hadn't seen him since it happened. Had the others done something to him because of her? A knot of fear and worry tightened in her stomach.

The midnight hour fast approached and the spirits would only become stronger. A bitter wind whipped through the house as the front door flew open. The only thing she could think to do was get to the protection of her bedroom. Outside the country would go on for miles and the spirits could follow her if she tried to make a run for it.

As she neared the second-floor hall, the noise suddenly stopped. The silence was even eerier than the noises. Each of her steps was punctuated by the harsh sound of her breath. She pressed her arm against the wall, stepping as lightly as she could. A light glow appeared, slowly growing to form the lady in white. The ghost stepped silently through the hall. The midnight hour was here. When she reached the end of the hall, she disappeared, only to reappear and begin the walk again. The loop of her walk would last for about an hour. Though she knew the lady wouldn't deviate from her stroll, Helen pulled away from her as she passed.

The bedroom door was closed. Helen reached for the doorknob.

She studied the lady's serene face as she passed. The woman's eyes shifted, finding Helen against the wall. That had never happened. Without warning, the woman's mouth opened in a blur of movement. A loud screech blasted from the ghost's mouth as shadowed hands emerged from her chest. Whoever looked at her was not the lady. The lady in white kept walking as another figure emerged from within her.

Helen reached for the doorknob, shaking it as she tried to get it open. At first, the door didn't move. When she let go, it swung open. Gregory stood on the other side. His features suddenly turned white. A loud thwack sounded, denting his skull and sending blood streaming down his face. She automatically reached for him, but she felt something holding her back. He stumbled, falling to his knees and tipping over on to the floor. Helen breathed hard as his lifeless eyes faded. The door slammed in her face.

Helen stumbled to try to open it again, but the shadow creature flew towards her, hitting her body hard enough to knock her over as it passed through her. Dizzy, she grabbed her head, trying not to throw up as a wave of nausea washed over her. The shadow came at her again and again, draining her energy each time it passed through her body.

"Stop," she croaked. Helen crawled towards the stairwell leading to the third floor. She reached the bottom stair and the entity stopped. Tears streamed down her face. She tried to lift her body, but it was too hard to move. The hallway floorboards creaked. Helen pulled her knees towards her chest. Above her, someone stepped down the stairs, coming towards her head. A frozen breeze brushed over her, stinging her eyes.

"I knew you didn't fit here." Rebecca leaned over her, a dark-red slash across her throat. Helen felt more than saw the others gathering around them. Samuel's dirty, transparent boots appeared by her head. "Gregory belongs to us. You are not one of us."

"So, what? You're going to kill me and make me one of you?" Helen asked, finding her strength. She pushed up. A horrifically disfigured gathering stared back, crowding into the hall and stairwell. It was hard to see past burned flesh and bleeding gunshot wounds to the people beneath. Each one's story could be seen in their gaunt expressions and markings of death.

"Kill you?" Rebecca frowned. "We want you to leave here. Go. We don't need you. Gregory belongs to me. He's . . ."

"You?" Helen finally understood. Rebecca's jealousy washed over her. She'd suspected it once or twice, but Gregory never paid the woman much mind.

"Us," Rebecca corrected. It came a little too late. Fiona and Bella giggled. Jerry grunted and stumbled from behind Rebecca's back, falling through a wall. A young boy threw an invisible ball and ran away, chased by his ghostly parents.

"You're losing them," Helen said. A few of the grotesque figures mended, replaced by the peaceful countenance of the ghosts who normally roamed her halls.

Rebecca looked at the others, her throat reddening as she shouted, "She's trying to take Gregory from us. She trapped him in her room. She's using him!"

Rebecca's anger washed over Helen and she grasped at her chest. "Don't listen to her. Look at her. She's jealous. Don't let her hatred fuel you." Then, turning her full attention towards Rebecca, she stood, getting into the woman's transparent face. "You want Gregory for yourself. You're mad that he chose to come to my room. You're mad that he chose me. You want me gone, but I'm not leaving. You'll have to kill me first. But then you know I'll only be with him. He chose me, Rebecca."

"I can make your life here hell," Rebecca hissed. "You think tonight was bad, just wait."

"It's not right, caretaker," a normally quiet farmer said from behind Rebecca. He'd been shot in the chest. "You ought to stick to the living."

"Rebecca?" Samuel questioned, the sound slow. "What does she mean you want Gregory?"

Helen almost felt sorry for the brute. She heard the heartache in his voice.

"Shut your trap," Rebecca ordered the man.

Helen still felt weak but tried not to let it show. She stepped forwards, past Rebecca into the remaining crowd of onlookers. The air was chilled, but not as bad as before.

"Let me by," she demanded, keeping her voice low and exact. "This is my home now. If you want to remain welcome here, you will act with civility and respect towards me and each other. Otherwise, pack your supernatural bags and get out." A few bowed their heads and disappeared. A young woman in a party dress and an old man in his long pyjamas stepped out of Helen's way.

"Then you must respect us and leave Gregory alone," Rebecca said. Samuel stared at Rebecca, his face a strange blue as water dripped out of his lips. Helen turned, meeting the woman's eyes.

"I can't do that," Helen answered. "I love him."

The door to her bedroom opened. The sound caused her to glance over her shoulder. More ghosts disappeared, clearing a pathway to her room.

"No!" Rebecca screamed, but the sound wasn't sustained as she disappeared.

Helen walked towards the room and peered through the opened door. Gregory stood on the other side. The late hour had given him enough energy to take shape. He looked as he had when she first saw him, standing with a crooked smile on his lips, hat in hand. He took a step as if to come to her, but stopped, staring at the floor. She glanced down to the line of salt, realizing he was indeed trapped.

Helen didn't step past the threshold.

"I am sorry for this. I tried to warn you but I couldn't leave this room." He lifted his hand, but couldn't touch her. "I didn't mean to leave you earlier. I couldn't maintain form. If I hurt you, I'm sorry."

"You didn't hurt me," she said, nervous.

"If you command it, I will leave and not come back, not during your lifetime. I have no right to steal the years of your life with my death. You deserve more than I can give you." He stepped away from the door. "First you must release me from this room."

"Did you hear what I said in the hall?" she asked, stepping carefully over the salt. She shut the door behind her, trapping them both in.

"I tried to warn you—"

"I said I love you, Gregory. I know this isn't conventional, but I love you. I don't know where we go from here, or how we make it work, but I do know I want it to work." She closed the distance between them and reached for his jacket. His body solidified as she touched him. "I've tried to deny any pull I feel towards you because I didn't know if you could feel anything for me. But, after today, after what we shared, I never want to be without you again."

"I'm dead," he said hesitantly. "You're alive."

"No relationship is perfect." She gave him a small smile. "Besides, I won't always be alive. Eventually, I'll die and then you'll be stuck with me for an eternity."

"Eternity," he repeated, dropping the hat. It landed with a thud on the floor. He pulled at his tie, loosening it. "I like the sound of that."

Helen backed slowly to the bed, beckoning him with her eyes. "People are going to think I'm a crazy recluse just like my aunt."

"What do you think?"

"I think I've finally found a place to call home. Let the world think what it likes about me." Helen pulled him into her embrace. "This is what I want. You are what I want."

"And I want–" he glanced down "–you to be sure when you do die that you're wearing that green lacy thing you had on earlier."

Helen gasped, hitting his shoulder as she pretended to be shocked. Grabbing hold of him, she fell back on to the mattress taking him with her. His body settled against hers and she felt his interest poking against her hip. She nipped at his ear lobe. "Oh, I think you might change your mind when you see the other options available. Underwear has changed a lot since your time."

Gregory captured her mouth with his, silencing her with his passionate kiss. Happiness bubbled inside of her. Everything she could ever want was right here within the stolen hours in his arms.

Coming Home

Justine Elyot

The village had always worn Christmas well and, although Felicity had not been there for over ten years, the illuminated candles and stars on the grey stone walls gave her the impression of stepping back into her late adolescence, when possibilities had been as endless as the dark skies above.

Once the taxi driver had been duly tipped and sent on his way, she let herself into the tiny cottage she was renting for the fortnight, shivering as she lugged the suitcase over the threshold into the low-ceilinged living room, then felt about the side of the door for the light switch.

It was not furnished the way her parents had had it any more; it was over-chintzy and anonymously old-fashioned, as if to satisfy the tastes of a person whose idea of English country living had been gleaned from costume dramas and romantic comedies. But then, her parents were long gone, having given the place over to a letting agency and fled to the Costa del Sol, to live the expatriate karaoke-bar dream.

A big basket of logs lay next to the open fireplace, but Felicity was too tired from the journey to contemplate anything so strenuous as the setting of a fire. She looked around at the tiny shelf-mounted television, the fan shape of horse and dog magazines on the coffee table, the unfamiliar watercolours depicting hunting and fishing scenes on the wall. It was home, but not home. It needed adjustment. Adjustment was best achieved at the Bevis Arms, with the aid of a glass of wine or two.

"It's as if I never went away," she said to herself, walking slowly along the winding street to the village square, noticing the same curtains in the windows, or a Christmas ornament familiar from times past. "Are all the same people here? Will anyone recognize me?"

She threw off the disquieting thought. Young people never stayed in the village – they had all gone off to university, or to Bournemouth or Poole, to make their fortunes. And a considerable fortune it would have to be, if they ever wanted to own property in their childhood playground, for the village was fiercely expensive and the new breed of villager was the London weekender with money to spend in the delicatessen and knick-knack shops that had replaced the butcher's and the post office. She supposed she was just such a person herself now.

The Bevis Arms was warm and cosy, smelling of wood smoke and mulled wine spices. It was busy too – Christmas was a few days away and all the rental cottages and weekend residences were full, even though the campsites were closed. Glancing around as she waited to be served at the bar, Felicity was heartened to recognize nobody. Smartly dressed city types, mainly, plus a few bearded old men, listening to a fiddle and squeezebox duo cramped up in a corner.

She bought a glass of red wine, passing on the spicy festive variety, and perched herself on a windowsill, seats being at a premium. Sipping and listening vaguely to the folksy music, it was hard to resist the temptations of nostalgia. The last time she had been in this pub she was a starry-eyed eighteen-year-old, waiting for a boy who never turned up. Well, not a boy – she had thought of him as a man, for nine years was quite a gap at that age. She pretended to forget his name, but it burned at the back of her mind all the same. In her protective memory, he was the Man from Poole Quay. It had been nothing really. Half a dozen dates, a few hand-in-hand walks on the beach, a trip around the harbour on a sunny, windy day. Just a silly, girlish thing. Oh, and her virginity. There had been that, of course. But men were men and she had offered, after all. It was silly to feel hurt, particularly after all these years.

It was just that she was vulnerable, that was all. The divorce had been heartbreaking and soul-destroying and she needed recovery time, alone, somewhere with no memories of Tom. She could not have envisaged that her stupid sentimental brain would play this trick on her, replacing the bad memories of Tom with the earlier bad memories of Richard. Not that they were all bad. Just that last one . . . waiting at the table, spinning the beer mat, looking over to

the door, once, twice, three times a minute. Checking her phone –
those old ones with the bleeping ring tones and hardly any decent
features. No messages. Still no messages. His number going straight
to voicemail, every time. God, why did young girls do this to
themselves?

The red wine was a large one, and Felicity could feel her eyelids
slipping down, lending an even more golden glow to the twinkle-lit
bar room. She ought to go back and face the fireplace; unpack; run
a nice long hot bath. Nostalgia was strictly for the birds. She needed
a long sleep, a hearty breakfast and a good brisk walk, in that order.

In the doorway, she stood aside to allow a group of carousers
through, the first of their number so tall that his cold-smelling
waxed jacket brushed her cheek, followed by his scarf. The scarf
didn't smell of cold, though, it smelled of something that triggered
a sudden and shocking response along the line of every nerve. She
looked up and almost screamed, clapping a hand over her mouth to
prevent the rogue exclamation. Then she shoved past the rest of the
group and crossed the square at a run. As she pelted around the
corner to the winding main street, she thought she heard a cry of
"Fliss! Fliss?" but she kept up her pace, arriving at the cottage
breathless and red-faced, having to double over and clutch her
stomach for a long time before the cold reminded her that she
needed to sort out the fire.

In her dream, he came to her, as he had done on certain nights for
the last eleven years. Brushing that hank of dark hair that hung
eternally over his brow back with an irritated hand, grinning, eyes
full of the devil. Richard Wainwright, the bad boy, the latter-day
smuggler, no longer wrecking ships off the rocks like his forebears,
but carrying on the modern equivalent of their trade. She should
have known he'd let her down but he was so . . . salvageable. A bad
man she could have made good, in time. But only eighteen-year-
olds thought like that, didn't they? It served her right for being so
hopelessly naive.

In her dreams, though, he was Just Bad Enough. They rolled on
the heath as they had done, breaking the heather stalks, getting
them in their hair and stuck to their jeans, noticing nothing until
the kissing and touching and wheedling and half-hearted coy refusing was over and the sun setting to a cold clear dusk. He would
drive her home in time for tea, lurking on the corner out of sight of
her parents to make sure she got home safely.

Felicity gave her head a vigorous shake to dissolve the dream, then filled the kettle and set it on the hob to boil. From the farm shop next door she had bought bacon and eggs and butter, enough to clog her arteries, even if it didn't quite push out the intrusive thoughts of her lost lover. She pottered about with the frying pan, making plans for the day, which was cold, clear and sunny. Perhaps a day for going up to the castle, or maybe a trip into Poole to look at the shops. The fry-up gave her the energy she needed to negotiate the steep climb up to the ruins that lowered over the village like a sinister giant, so she dumped the plate in the sink, pulled on boots, scarf, coat and gloves and flung open the front door.

"Jesus!" she half-yelped, almost tripping over the man who stood on the pavement outside.

"No, I think you must be mistaken." He put out a hand to steady her, holding her at the elbow, smiling down roguishly, although the misty eyes gave a different reading of his emotions. "I recognize you though. It's good to see you, Fliss. How have you been?"

She was, for a moment, speechless, so he filled the silence.

"I knew it was you. Last night in the Bevis Arms. I thought you'd left the village years ago."

"You . . . you . . . don't tell me you've given me a second thought. All these years." Her tone was belligerent and she tried to yank her arm away from him, but he held on to it steadily.

"Actually, I have. I owe you an apology, I know. And you don't owe me anything. I'd like to have the chance to make it up to you though."

"Fuck you, Richard Wainwright!" The words spilled from Felicity's lips before she even knew they were coming. "Fuck you and your dodgy dealings and your . . . oh, just go away."

She managed to tear her arm away from him and marched up the street, hot tears gathering at the corners of her eyes. This was not what she was here for! This was the last thing she needed.

She could hear his footsteps behind her, following her, but she refused to turn back to face him or speak to him again. Instead she almost ran up to the small chalet at the foot of the hill, where visitors paid for access to the castle ruins.

"One adult, please," she huffed, her breath steaming out in front of her, shoving a ten-pound note at the cashier and not waiting for change. Surely Richard would not follow her past the turnstile, unless he was willing to pay for the privilege of pestering her and being sent away with a flea in her ear.

Yet it seemed he was, for taking great strides up the green slopes behind her he came, that evocatively scented scarf streaming out behind him, his face pale with cold, contrasting with the still luxuriant darkness of his hair.

"Fliss," he called, that voice still so warm and rich and deep, halting her in her tracks. "Please."

She spun around and barked a sardonic laugh. "You paid to stalk me? You must be serious."

"No, I didn't pay," he said, holding up a National Trust membership card with a somewhat sheepish grin.

"What? You? A member of the National Trust? No way! You must have stolen that!"

"Times change, Fliss, and so do people."

"You really are a member?"

"Are you calling me a prick?"

Felicity laughed, genuinely this time. She had forgotten that earthy, wicked wit of his.

"You've probably got a point," he said with a shrug. "I've done some twattish things in my time. Letting you get away being possibly the most twattish of the lot."

"Oh, come on, Richard, you can't think a bit of sweet-talk is going to . . ."

"I don't. I don't think that."

"You didn't let me get away. You disappeared. You did a runner. I tried to get in touch for days."

"Days, eh?" Richard smiled ruefully. "I was in a French jail for longer than that."

"What?"

"Come on. Let's walk up to the castle together. I'll give you my pathetic excuse for standing you up eleven years ago, and then you can decide if you want to kick me in my richly deserving bollocks or . . . not."

He put a hand on a hip, clearly inviting Felicity to link her arm with his. Hesitantly, she laid her hand on his wool-clad forearm and allowed him to steer her up towards the looming pile on the horizon.

"So you're saying you were in prison? While I was waiting for you in the Bevis Arms?"

"I was. I was caught loading Jug-Ears' boat with moody cigarettes at Cherbourg harbour and kept in the cells until it got sorted out. Took ages – but that was my fault for being a stroppy idiot. I don't think they wanted to let me go. I think they wanted to teach me a lesson, to be honest. And I can't say I blame them, looking back."

"Wow. Did you have to go to court?"

"No, not in the end. I got fined and sent home. It was a wake-up call though. I haven't smuggled since, Your Honour. I have turned my life around and am now a jolly decent, respectable chap with a National Trust membership."

"And a wife?"

"No. An ex-wife." He grimaced.

"Oh, I'm sorry. I know how that feels."

"Really? You're divorced?"

"Freshly on the shelf."

"Oh no, was it a bad one?"

"Are there good divorces?"

He walked on in silence for a moment before speaking again, quietly. "The Wainwright timing strikes again then."

"What do you mean?"

"You'll be . . . I dunno . . . on the rebound, or wanting some time to think. I've come and gatecrashed your retreat, haven't I?"

Felicity made a non-committal face and thought about this proposition. Was his presence unwelcome? Did she really want to sit and brood about Tom in her chilly cottage for the next ten days? And was she on the rebound? If she was completely honest, she had been on the rebound – badly – when she met Tom in her first week at university. Perhaps her whole life was a rebound from Richard, in which case . . . did it make a kind of sense to bounce back to him?

"You haven't changed that much then," she offered, giving him a subtle clue that she might want him to take this conversation in the direction he wanted. "And you do owe me an apology."

Unexpectedly, he clutched at her hands, threading his fingers with hers in a tight cat's cradle.

"I know. I'm sorry. Truly, I am. If I could make the past play out differently . . ."

"Don't worry about it, Richard," she said lightly, trying not to betray the racing pulse, the heightened colour brought about by his nearness and warmth. "You didn't ruin my life. You knew I was going to university anyway. I expect you already had my successor lined up."

"Felicity!" he reproached and she shivered, remembering how he had only used her full name when she had said or done

something outrageous. "That's not even close to the truth. I was
. . . I had a real thing for you."

"Really? Wideboy Wainwright? With every girl from Poole to
Lyme after you?"

"Wasn't interested in those girls."

"You found one to be interested in in the end though?"

"Yeah." They were at the top of the hill now, leaning against a
ruined stump of castle stone, looking down over the patchwork
fields and woodlands, across to the dark-blue sea. Richard smiled
wistfully. "Fiona. It worked out, for a while. She did a lot for me.
Calmed me down. Showed me that there was more to life than
thrill-seeking on the boats."

"She sounds great." Felicity kept the dash of jealousy out of her
voice, barely.

"She was. I managed to get a job after the France fiasco – just
labouring on Breaker Island. Fiona was the warden – she got me on a
college course. It changed my life. I found something I really wanted
to do, and that I was good at. Now, I'm the warden on Breaker Island."

"You never are! Seriously?" Felicity laughed. "So that's why
you've got the National Trust card. You work for them!"

"I am the picture of respectability." Richard took an ironic little
bow.

"And Fiona?"

"She got a promotion to the Peak District. I didn't want to go. I
couldn't leave this place."

"Gosh." Felicity was sombrely silent for a moment. Richard was
a son of this soil, of these hedgerows and the chalky cliffs at their
edges. He reminded her how much she loved this land, and the
land reminded her how much she loved Richard. It was as if they
were part of each other. Somehow it made sense that he would not
leave it, even for a loved wife.

"Silly romantic notion, probably, but it's in my blood," he said,
expressing her thought for her. "I know I'm a sentimental fool."

"That's not such a bad thing to be," she murmured. "Sometimes,
you can't get things out of your system."

He turned to her, hot coals for eyes, that long sweep of dark hair
over them, the incipient stubble that no razor could ever quite
defeat, the strength and solidity she had missed, almost without
knowing it, for these last eleven years.

"I shouldn't," he whispered, touching the pads of his fingers to
her cheek. "But I can't seem to help myself."

Help yourself, help yourself, urged every fibre in Felicity's body. He took her up on the invitation, bending low to brush her lips, pushing her gently but inescapably up against the weather-worn stone that supported her. Her skin sang, collapsing into grateful recognition, revelling in its sense memory of the careless rapture of a decade before. Coming home, I'm coming home, I'm home now, the familiar lips, the fondly remembered weight of him, the way their faces fitted together, the way his heat cancelled out the whipping wind on the hilltop . . . How had she ever given this up? And would she ever be able to do it again?

She banished the intrusive worries that threatened to derail this sensual abandon, giving herself up to the probing excursions of Richard's tongue. It was like listening to an old favourite song again, or tasting something divine that had been unobtainable for years. All the kisses of yesteryear flooded back into her mind, all the rolling in the heather, all the passionate clinches on the beach, all the slow dances and stolen moments when their friends weren't looking. And then her shaky legs, and the building heat and moisture between them, reminded her of what all that had led to.

She remembered his dark head, haloed by the sun above it, looming above her in the golden corn, his teeth grinning white, his hair full of broken straw, his voice rumpled and wicked. "You could come back to mine. Flatmates are out on a trip."

"Back to your place? In Poole?"

"Yeah. Stay the night."

"You mean . . . ?"

"I love you, Fliss. And you're going away soon. I want to be with you . . . properly."

Properly. How nervous she had been, and yet how completely unable to resist him. She had knocked over the bottled alcopop he had served her in his squalid living room and then flustered around with kitchen towels and disinfectant spray until he had removed them from her hands and said, "Never mind – leave it. Let's go upstairs."

She had thought he might be demanding and intense and a little bit rough, the way he was when they tumbled in the heather, but he was gentle her first time, and so considerate. He made sure she was ready, made sure she was happy, made sure she came before he did, and when she dissolved into emotional tears afterwards he held her and shushed and stroked her hair and said he loved her and she was special and always would be.

And the next day he didn't show up at the pub.

Felicity broke the kiss with a tiny mewl, suddenly realizing how very, very cold it was at the top of the hill.

"Perhaps we should continue this elsewhere," suggested Richard, noticing the indignant glares of a couple of elderly visitors.

"Perhaps." Felicity did not want to leave the sheltering warmth of his wool-coated chest, outside which reality appeared frozen and uninviting, but she drew back anyway, unable to meet his eyes, feeling as shy as a schoolgirl again.

"If you want . . . I don't mean to presume . . ."

"You can. You can presume. Presume away."

He laughed delightedly and kissed her on the cheek. "Let's go somewhere warmer."

They ran, hand in hand, down the hill and mooched through the village, looking in shop windows and reminiscing, until they arrived at the Bevis Arms, where Richard bought lunch for them both.

He really is different, thought Felicity, listening to his tales of life on Breaker Island, observing the annual patterns of the seasons and preserving the natural wonders there. He has grown up. He is a man, not a Bad Boy.

"And does London life suit you?" he asked, almost as if hoping for a negative response.

"I . . . well. It did. It really did, for a long time. And Tom was a Londoner through and through – could never bear to be away from the action. But I'm finding it difficult now we've split. I'm at work most of the time, and I don't see a lot of the friends we shared. I'm . . . you know, I actually considered joining a dating agency."

"It's lonely?"

"Yes. In a nutshell. I know a lot of it's to do with grieving for my marriage but . . . God, it's hard sometimes. Sometimes I just want to stop having to be so bloody grown up all the time and just retreat to somewhere I was young and happy and naive and unspoiled."

"You were all those things when I knew you."

"Yes. I was, wasn't I." She looked at him directly. "I'm not now. And you've changed too. Do you think we can ever . . . ?"

He put a hand over hers. "I think we can try."

Tumbling out on to the street, insulated by steak and kidney pie and bright with two glasses of wine, they bought a holly wreath at the florist in the square and went to install it on Felicity's front door.

Richard hammered it into place and they stood back on the pavement, admiring its verdant cheerfulness, before Felicity turned to him and asked if he wanted to come in. For coffee.

Slipping an arm around her, he kissed the tiny scrap of her neck that was exposed between her knitted scarf and her coat collar and spoke softly into her ear.

"Can't, love. I have to get to work. I wish I didn't, but I drew up the rota myself! Can I come round tomorrow? Will you be in?"

Felicity's heart hammered. She had hoped never to have to do this again – to say goodbye to him and trust that he would be as good as his word.

"I . . . expect so. If you aren't too late."

"Oh, I get off at lunchtime. Could be here for about two, is that all right?"

Felicity nodded. It would give her the morning to get provisions in for Christmas. And what better than a busy supermarket full of grumbling, sniping shoppers to take her mind off the waiting?

"OK," she said. "I'll see you tomorrow then."

He scooped her up and ravished her with kisses beneath the holly wreath. "Get some mistletoe in," he advised, turning to go with a wave.

"I will. Oh, and Richard . . ."

"Yes?"

"Don't get arrested."

She was on overdrive for the rest of the day, barely able to sit still for two minutes at a time. Her book failed to draw her away from the excited babblings of her mind, so she opted for an early night, huddling under the old-fashioned candlewick bedspread, listening to the sigh of the wind with its promise of snow, and giving herself up to her fantasies. The one she'd had as a teenager, of him being kidnapped and imprisoned by foreign pirates and her rescuing him from his terrible plight. But before she untied him, she teased him into a frenzy, taking advantage of the pirates' absence, for they were all insensible with rum next door and would not be roused for hours. He sat in a corner of the old-fashioned brig, rope looped around his chest, clamping his arms to his sides, his ankles similarly fast. He tried to appeal to her through his gag, his red-rimmed eyes lighting up at the sight of her, his thick black hair matted and dishevelled – but in a sexy way, not a greasy horrible way. He expected her to rush over and free him straight away, but instead of that, she flitted across and dropped to a crouch in front of him, placing a finger on the outline of his mouth through that red-spotted handkerchief gag.

"Don't worry, Richard. I'm here to save you," she said, and she would slip her hands either side of his neck, on to his shoulders, and kiss his scratchy face, his eyelids, his ear lobes, his forehead, all the sweet, sweet lines and planes of his handsome face while he stiffened and tried to speak, tried to urge her to let him go.

"Oh, not yet, not yet, Richard. You never keep still, and just this once, you are going to keep still for me." Her fingers raked his hair, massaged his scalp, and, although he still struggled, she could feel his muscles loosening, feel his forehead uncrease and his knots unravel, watch the rise and fall of his chest slow and his shoulders slump. He was hers, to do with as she pleased, until she decided it was time for them to leave.

He was wearing one of those big billowing shirts from olden days; it was a little torn and there were bloodstains where he had valiantly fought the pirates. The tantalizing glimpse of bare chest tempted her lips downwards and she tore the stained linen just a little more, to reveal a nipple which she sucked on with eager gratitude.

Now he was moaning through the gag and, when she settled herself in his helpless lap with her knees either side of his thighs, she could feel the itchy jiggle of his pelvis and pressed herself against the hard heat in his breeches. If his arms had been free, he would have overpowered her, crushed her into him, flipped her over and fucked her hard, to scratch that itch as quickly as possible and fly to safety. But his arms were not free, and Felicity was going to dictate the pace. She licked a slow trail, using the very tip of her tongue, around his nipples and then down the line towards his navel, until the confining ropes halted her explorations. She could go up or she could go down. By now, it was tumescently obvious that Richard was hoping for the latter decision – and after all, she loved him. So she would please him in this regard.

She bent to unlace his crotch – somehow it was 1759, which was how the fantasy worked – and, with a gentle hand, finessed the awoken beast from its casing. Oh, he was writhing now, and making incoherent sounds of near pain into his gag, trying to jerk his pelvis towards her, to say "More! More! More!" Lovingly, she stroked the shaft and cupped the tight-packed balls, smiling up into his pleading eyes before lowering her head and kissing his dark-red cock tip. This now was her gift to him. The gift of giving him what he wanted, even when he had no choice in the matter. The gift of showing him that she knew what he wanted. The gift of showing him that she was right for him. She plunged down over the erection, sealing it with velvet lips then sucking it, tickling it with her tongue, lapping and tasting and breathing vocal vibrations along its length. She waited until the rest of his body was completely limp and acquiescent in her hands, then she withdrew, stood up, stepped back. He lunged, as much as a man in bondage can lunge, roaring through his gag, and then the ropes around his arms snapped and he broke free, ripping off the gag, swearing great oaths, freeing his feet and catching her before she could retreat to the other side of the brig.

Beside himself, he slapped her bottom hard before wrestling her to the floor, wrenching her skirts aside and giving her the hard, hot, bone-shaking ride of her life, vowing all the time that she would only ever belong to him.

They must escape from the pirates in the end, Felicity supposed, removing her sticky fingers from between her legs, but somehow the fantasy never got any further than that. The clock said 11.03. And now she could sleep.

She decked the halls with boughs of holly, and mistletoe – plenty of mistletoe – before placing lights in the front window and putting a clove and cinnamon candle on to burn. "Falalalala," she hummed to herself, watching the clock, nearly two, nearly time, nearly Richard Time.

"He won't come," she told herself severely. "Don't get your hopes up. You know what that leads to."

At five to two, she decided to go out.

If he came, if he was serious, he would wait. If he didn't . . . she would have achieved something. Though really, she had no reason to go out.

"I need wine," she decided. "That's a good reason to go out."

She grabbed her coat and scarf and half-skated along the icy uneven pavements towards the small market in the square. The sky was iron grey, presaging a heavy snowfall, and the stallholders clapped their gloved hands and shifted from foot to foot, blowing out copious wafts of white steam into the air.

Felicity bought a bottle of red wine and some spices for mulling it at home, figuring that it was a day for making sure you were warm all over, inside as well as out. She deliberately dawdled back through the village, intending to be as late as possible, contemplating a detour into one of the chichi little craft shops to further draw out the agony – until she saw, in the distance, a huge tree leaning against the wall of her cottage. A Christmas tree, probably slightly too big to even fit inside the bijou living room – was this something to do with Richard?

She picked up her pace, ignoring the craft boutique and skidding onwards, through the first flakes of snow, until she arrived at her front stoop. Yes, it was a Christmas tree all right, its top branch pointing up almost to the bedroom window – but where was . . . ?

"Ah! Where were you?" Richard rounded the corner between her cottage and the farm next door, hacksaw in hand.

"I thought wine . . ." said Felicity, holding up the bottle, staring at the rusty-toothed implement in her ex-lover's hand. "Whereas you thought the occasion called for . . . a hacksaw."

Richard laughed. "I think I miscalculated the dimensions of your cottage," he said. "We had a few trees left over on Breaker Island, so I thought you might like one. But it'll never fit inside there. Come on, let's take it round the back and cut it down to size."

Felicity hugged her arms to her chest, glowing with more than the cold. Richard, here, for her, and doing everyday manly things like sawing wood – because he wanted to do this for her. It was better than a dream.

Tiny dots of snow kissed his eyelashes and cheeks as he sawed through the excess branches, gripping the tree firmly in a leather-gloved hand. "Why don't you get inside and do something with that wine?" he suggested, but Felicity did not want to miss a second of him. The wine could wait.

"I want to help you," she demurred, meaning "I want to look at you". Richard seemed to understand, half-smiling roguishly at her and finishing his tree surgery with a flourish.

"Thanks for your help," he teased, lifting the tree and manoeuvring it through Felicity's tiny kitchen door. "Don't know what I'd have done without you."

"Oi!" Felicity laughed, setting the bottle on the worktop and following him into the living room. "I'm not sure I've got a pot or bucket for that thing."

"Leave it to me," he said. "For God's sake, sort out the wine, woman. And do you have anything to eat? I came straight from work without having lunch."

"I've got sausages. Can do sausage sandwiches. Oh, and mince pies. And lots of Christmassy stuff – if it isn't too early to crack it open."

"If the snow keeps up, you might need to ration the provisions." Richard grinned, looking about for the best spot to pot the tree. "Let's go with the sausage sandwiches, shall we?"

Felicity felt light-footed as she twirled around the kitchen, putting sausages under the grill and slicing thick hunks of bread. He didn't seem the kind of man that would relish dainty triangular sandwiches without crusts. No, a big doorstep wedge for Richard, thickly buttered and with lashings of ketchup on the sausages. By the time the meal was ready, Richard had potted the tree and installed it in a nook between the fireplace and the front window. Pine needles scattered every surface of the room, but the heavenly fresh scent of them was enough to light a festive flame in Felicity's heart.

"You kept this candle burning while you were out," said Richard, frowning at the source of the clove-and-cinnamon scent that dovetailed so deliciously with the forest pine. "Jesus, Fliss, you always had your head in the clouds. It's a wonder you're still alive."

"Shit!" Felicity clapped a hand to her mouth. "I completely forgot." She gave Richard a sheepish look. He had always been taking her to task about things like this back in those far-off days when they were lovers. She was not as scatty or impractical now as she had been then, but she still had her moments.

"It's a good thing I'm here, isn't it?" said Richard softly, taking the plate of sandwiches from her and putting it aside on the coffee table.

She could not answer, full of a complex of emotions, not one of which could claim the upper hand. Indignation at his assumption that she was helpless, which could be traced back further to an unhealed anger at his leaving her in the first place, all those years ago, but also a kindling spark of desire for the protection he seemed to offer, even as she felt she should repudiate it. She wanted him, but she did not want to want him quite so much as this. She should hold back, keep her heart safe.

"For now," she said, almost inaudibly, but he heard her, and took her by the wrist and pulled her down to where he knelt, on the sheepskin rug in front of the fire, framed by the green fronds of the tree.

"I know I hurt you," he said, holding her hands in his, keeping her captive in his clear grey gaze. "I know you probably want to shy away. Protect yourself. And I can't blame you. But will you give me a chance to give you a Christmas you'll remember? And perhaps, who knows, perhaps something more?"

This was good. No extravagant promises, of the kind he used to make; no offering of the moon on a plate. Just an honest statement of intent, and one she found intoxicating. The perfect Christmas, with a warm fire, warm mince pies and cream, and a hot man to curl up beside – who could turn that down? Certainly she would have to be made of sterner stuff than Felicity Partridge.

"A Christmas to remember," she repeated, and she put her head against his shoulder, allowing him to fold his arms around her and hold her for a long time, until the sausages grew as cold as the grate, and the fire really needed to be lit.

"Should light that fire," said Felicity half-heartedly, feeling she could live forever with her face breathing in the manly musk of Richard's scarf and the skin beneath.

"Should eat that sandwich," sighed Richard, lost in the nostalgia the scent of Felicity's hair had evoked. "But I'd rather . . ." He unwrapped one arm, freeing the hand to break the seal of her cheek and his shoulder hollow and angle her chin upwards, so she had to look at him. And where the eyes led, the lips had to follow. There seemed no other option but to fall into kissing, to collapse sideways on the sheepskin and bury themselves in the intimate excavations of lips, teeth, tongues, hands, fingers. Still wearing heavy coats and gloves, the pair of lovers strove to dig deep, under the zips and buttons that held them apart, until Richard raised his tousled head with a laugh and suggested moving upstairs.

"If you want to," he stressed.

"I do. Can't we light the fire though? It will be nice to come down to."

"Tell you what. You go upstairs. I'll eat this sandwich – think I might need the calories. And I'll light your fire. Wait for me. Have some wine or something. I won't be long."

Felicity left him fumbling with the firelighters, hotfooting it upstairs with the bottle and two glasses. Up in the small room, with its dense floral prints and lily-of-the-valley scent – so unmanly! – she took a moment to peer out of the casement window at the street outside. The snow was settling now and everyone who passed had scarlet cheeks and ten layers of clothing on. The skies were so dark that some villagers had lit their tree lights and colourful twinkling could be seen in many of the windows. Even the castle ruins, high on the hill, had a string of rainbow-hued bulbs hung between the crumbling remnants of the gatehouse. Perhaps, after all, this was some kind of fairy-tale alternative reality. Anyone would forgive her for thinking so. Too good to be true, too good to be true – the words beat a dispiriting tattoo in her head.

But she had to stop thinking like this. Just because one chance taken didn't work out, did that mean that all other chances had to be left in the dust? No. It was almost a new year; it was time to be brave.

She took off her coat, scarf and gloves and then sat on the bed, wondering what would be appropriate now. Should she take off her boots? Her jumper? Everything? No, that would be too much! He should work for it, just a little. She grinned and poured the wine, sipping at her glass, lying back against the pillows and watching the flakes fly outside. Downstairs, Richard would be tearing into the sandwich. She hoped he was ravenous for more than food.

Her hopes were not disappointed. She dashed her glass down on the bedside table as soon as the thunder of his boots on the stairs became audible. A few drops of wine spilled on to the snow-white cloth beneath the table lamp. Damn! But this was just too exciting. He is coming. He is here.

He threw open the door, his teeth bared in the widest wolf grin she had ever seen, his hair all over the place, warm outer clothing all discarded downstairs.

"You look comfortable," he said, his breath short, eyes glowing. "Mind if I join you?" He pulled off the big work boots, chucked them outside to the landing, then, not waiting for Felicity's answer, took a dive on to the bedspread, leaping on top of her so that she squealed into giggles.

"God, you're gorgeous!" he exclaimed, like a greedy boy with a fistful of sweets, wanting to eat them all at once. He could not decide where to put his hands or his lips, putting them everywhere, seemingly all at once, catching the squirming Felicity between strong legs and holding her down so escape was not a possibility. Determined fingers swarmed up beneath her jumper and tugged at the waistband of her jeans; they found the outer edges of her bra and the lace of her knickers as if following a scent. It had been so long since she had felt a man's large, hot hand on her skin and Felicity cursed the hours wasted, waiting. She should have come and got this sooner, much sooner.

"Missed . . . this . . ." he gasped between starved kisses, "so . . . much. Missed you . . . so much . . ." She was clutching at his hair and at the perfectly shapely curve of his behind in those tight jeans he always wore, her small fists kneading the taut flesh, wanting to sink into it, to possess it, to drive it into her.

"D'you still fancy me, then, Fliss?" he muttered into her ear, having now managed to yank her jumper up over her bra and unbutton her jeans.

"Ah, God, I always did," she moaned. "Never fancied anyone more."

"Same here," he averred, rearing up a little so that he could lift the jumper clean off over her head. "My Fliss." He sank back down, his head bending over the cups of her bra, wrenching them down over hard pink nipples with his teeth. "The taste of you, oh God." He began to suck at the tempting buds that stood so stiff for him, nuzzling her collarbone with his sweep of hair, so that she felt tickled and devoured and aroused and wild with want for him. She lifted her pelvis, wanting to cram herself into the hard knot beneath his jeans, rubbing and rotating, both hands now squeezing his bottom as if it were particularly springy dough. She reached blindly for the fly of his jeans, scrabbling at the metal buttons, pulling them from the buttonholes one by one. He nipped at a nipple, making her yelp, then sat up, a magnificent tower of man growing upwards from her hips, stretching out his arms, throwing back his head and growling.

"Did you want something, Fliss?" he asked with a dangerous glint, bringing his face back down towards her. "Is there something I can give you?"

She squeezed her hands inside the unbuttoned jeans, feeling the heat and weight and iron hardness there.

"This will do nicely." She grinned, trying her hardest to dint the stiffness, and failing. "Along with the rest of you."

"Sold," he hissed, with a nip of her ear lobe that made her squeak. He made short work of removing her bra, then the jeans were wrenched off, with quite a struggle, until Fliss had only a cotton thong and a pair of woolly socks protecting her modesty.

"Sexy as these are," said Richard, standing at the end of the bed to ease off the rainbow-knitted footwear, "I might have to let them go."

Felicity wriggled her bare toes, then prodded the hot crotch that stood so close to them, almost completely exposed now by the waistband that crept lower and lower, introducing red paisley boxers to the interested eye.

Richard snatched the errant foot and held it aloft.

"You need to keep a tighter rein on these toes," he reproved. "I could have them done for sexual harassment."

Felicity yelped as he kissed each varnished toenail in turn.

"Well, seeing as you've just ripped my clothes off – eep! – I'm not sure any – wah! – court in the land would – no! don't tickle me! – convict – argh!" Richard was stroking Felicity's sensitive instep with the tip of one torturing finger, a crooked grin playing on his face as he watched his victim thrash and writhe and howl for mercy until the covers were thoroughly mussed.

"Still ticklish then?" he said, testing the statement with another diabolical circuit of her left foot.

"Oh STOP! NO! PLEASE!"

"Nothing's changed there in eleven years. God, I've missed this!"

"I . . . haven't . . ." Felicity began to scream and Richard took pity, though he kept a firm hold of her ankle and began kissing a trail up the suffering foot and then along the calf, taking his time, enjoying every patch of skin that met his lips until, at the underside of her knee – an area that made her squirm almost as much as the foot-tickling – he knelt on the bed, for an easier route to the inevitable end of this journey.

Slowly now, past the knee and on to the succulent flesh of her thigh, kissing and licking, getting closer and closer to that small part of her that was still covered, but smelling it now, breathing in its scent of arousal, feeling its heat and moisture, so close to the target . . . He paused to switch thighs, subjecting the other to the same treatment while Felicity began to wonder if her white thong was transparent with her wetness by now – it certainly felt that way.

Now Richard's mouth and tongue had reached the crease along which the elastic of her thong lay like a border between territories, a crossing to the promised land. He licked a path along it, as if looking for the secret door that would grant him access, then crossed to repeat the process on the other side. Then, unexpectedly, the flat of his tongue pressed against the central panel that covered Felicity's drenched pussy, pushing at it, licking and nipping the cotton, soaking the entire area in their mingled juices. The rubbing of the wet material against Felicity's clit, together with the hot pressure of Richard's tongue, drove her mad with want and she bucked on the duvet, pushing herself into him, urging him word-lessly to dispense with the thong and eat her until she could take no more.

He half-obeyed, sliding his tongue up underneath the elastic, letting it bathe her puffy lips and clit, adding his fingers for extra stimulation, using them to wrench aside the thong and leave her naked to his ravenous mouth. One, then two long fingers pene-trated her, feeling how easy it would be for his cock to follow, how wet and hot and willing she was. He did not stop feasting on her until she came, jiggling and wiggling and clamping his head between her thighs as if they were nutcrackers, spending liberally on his wicked tongue.

"You still like that, I see," said Richard softly, extricating himself and throwing off the rest of his clothes in a furious rush. "Remember how I used to do that to you on the heath? Just lift up your skirt, or pull down your jeans, and lick you in the open air until you came? You do remember, don't you?"

"Pretty often," sighed Felicity, stretching out like a satisfied cat, arms above her head, before ridding herself of the thong and presenting herself in the nude.

"And do you remember what we did in Jug Ears' boat when we borrowed it that day? How you helped me with the steering?"

Felicity laughed and sat up on her elbow, grinning saucily at her newly rediscovered swain.

"Oh, yes, I remember that now."

"Don't tell me you'd forgotten." He brought his magnificent nakedness over to the bed and sat down beside Felicity, grabbing one of her hands and moving it down to enclose his cock, which seemed to surge with energy beneath her palm. "There I was, trying my best to steer a straight course and keep us off the rocks, and you go and drop on to your knees under the wheel and take down my trousers . . . and . . . what did you do then, eh?"

"You know what I did!"

"It's slipped my mind. Tell me. Go on."

"I put your cock in my mouth."

"That's it! That's what you did. Ummm, it felt so good. How the hell we didn't crash, though . . . anyway. I've taken you down memory lane. Now I think I've earned a little trip of my own. Haven't I?"

Felicity melted at his face, momentarily doggy-eyed and full of hope, and repositioned herself carefully between his powerful thighs, still holding that fat, hard cock in her fist and bringing her mouth down, low and slow, licking her lips in anticipation.

He arched his back and murmured something unintelligible as rounded lips met red curved tip, sliding down, gently as syrup, enclosing him in her wet, warm hollow.

"Ohhhh, Fliiiisssss." Her nickname leaked from his lips like air from a punctured balloon and an upwards flick of her eyes revealed the rewarding sight of his face, distant in an individual heaven somewhere, a heaven of her making.

She kept the movements small and slow to begin with, keeping that grip around the base, using her tongue to enhance the measured up and down slide of her mouth. It was difficult not to speed up too much in response to the tiny catching sounds at the back of his throat – she wanted to thrill him as much as he thrilled her, draw it out, make him beg. But only five minutes had passed before his hand grabbed at her hair and he seemed genuinely alarmed.

"No, no," he whispered, the words strangulated. "I can't come yet. Stop or I'll come right now. I want to . . ."

"Fuck me?"

"How do you read my mind?" he muttered, regaining a few ounces of composure and flipping her on to her back again.

She beamed and reached out for him, as if to say, Go on then! It was hard, watching him kneel at the foot of the bed and fidget with a condom wrapper, to keep her eyes off that upward-pointing weapon that meant to do its worst inside her, but she tried to drink in the whole of him, from the shaggy black hair to the toned thighs, and all that lay between. Shoulders and arms that seemed hewn from years of woodcutting tapered down to well-defined abdominal muscles; it was clear that Richard's work as a nature reserve warden kept him in tip-top condition.

His cock, though, was the same one that had taken her virginity, no different in size or width than it had been eleven years ago. And now it was ready for her. And she was ready for it.

As soon as he lunged forwards, braced on his elbows, she clasped eager hands around his neck and brought his face down for a long, smoochy kiss. Whilst locked to his lips, she felt his hardness probe the inside of her thigh, seeking its target with single-minded purpose. Joyously lustful, she widened the spread of her legs, bringing them around his hips, kneading her heels into the firm flesh of his arse, urging him onwards.

Now he was there, blunt and smooth, at the edge of her sex lips; now he was gathering her natural lubrication, rubbing himself up and down and around her clit and now he was using that extra coating of juice to make a single swift plunge down inside her, making her cry out.

It had never felt this way with Tom; there had never been that feeling of fullness, of perfect fit, of all being right with the world. He was inside her again, at last, and it was like a homecoming – the right hand in the glove, the right key in the door, the right man for the job.

"Ahh, you feel . . . like . . . so good," raved Richard, inarticulate with overwhelmingness, into Felicity's ear. "I didn't know how much I'd missed you . . . but God, I missed you. Don't go away again."

"I want you, want you always," she responded, settling into a slow, sensual rhythm, raising her bottom to meet his deep, unhurried thrusts. Their skins pressed and rubbed together, her nipples brushing his chest, her thighs clamping his hips, their faces mashing and kissing and spreading hot breath all over. Their sexes worked in harmony, a give and take, a cut and thrust, a push and pull, taking them on a pleasure trip whose destination they were not too impatient to reach. They savoured each stage of the journey, using the unforgotten intimacy with each other's body to maximize their enjoyment. But it was more than a meeting of skins and sexes. There were deep emotions at play as well – the emotions of nostalgia, of affection, of loss and love regained, and hope paramount, all boiling beneath the surface of their coupling.

"I want to make you . . ." hissed Richard, short of breath now, beginning to jerk and strengthen his thrusting, putting a hand beneath Felicity's bottom to find the perfect angle for her climax. There, yes, that was the spot, he was sure – and Felicity's widening eyes and heaving chest backed him up. She felt the flicker of panic that had always preceded her orgasms with Richard – would it be too much? Would it knock her out? – then she let herself fall over that cliff side, down, down, with wailing and flailing and all hope of ever resisting him again abandoned, while he cried, "Yesss! I've got you!" shortly prior to surrendering to his own rush of release.

Felicity, burrowed deep in the hollow of Richard's arm, shed a few tears. It was exhaustion, she told herself, but it wasn't really. It was happiness, but a happiness tinged with fear and regret. Perhaps this was it now. Perhaps Richard would get up, and say how nice it had been to catch up, and kiss her and leave. For ever.

"Say something," he said, after ten long minutes of sighing and breath-catching. "Are you OK? Was that good?"

"You know it was," she muffled into his chest.

"If the earth moved, it didn't do anything to stop the snow," he said, shuffling to a sitting position and bringing Felicity up with him. She moved her face to look at the window. He was right. Everything outside was white, white, white.

"Can I ask you something?" he said, breaking another contemplative silence.

"Of course."

"That wasn't the last time, was it? You aren't going to . . . get my hat and scarf for me and send me on my way? I mean, if that's what you want, I won't stop you, but . . ."

She turned and gave him a long, impulsive smacker of a kiss.

"You idiot," she said, the tears springing forth again. "That's exactly what I've been wondering . . . well, I mean, it's my place, so you wouldn't send me away but . . . no. I hope, more than anything, that that wasn't the last time. God, why would I want to throw away something that amazing?"

"Amazing, eh?" Richard smiled crookedly, preening. "You weren't so bad yourself."

Felicity giggled, burying her face in his neck, before an almighty rumbling from her stomach brought her up short.

"Oh my God!" she exclaimed in wonder, biting her lip at Richard. "I'm starving!"

"Didn't I fill you up?"

"I think it's a different type of sausage I need."

"I'll make you a sandwich. You stay there. Keep that wine ready. You're going to need it."

"Oh? Why?"

Richard was pulling on his jeans, preparing to making a barefoot foray into the kitchen.

"Because we haven't discussed the way you left that candle burning while you were out yet. I think your bottom might be in grave danger."

"Oh, you!" Felicity squeaked and took refuge beneath the bedclothes, shivering pleasurably at his arched eyebrow and folded arms. "You wouldn't dare!"

"Oh, I love a challenge." He chuckled menacingly and went to supervise the grill.

An hour and a half later, Felicity lay snuggled up in bed with a full stomach, a slightly sore bottom and a warm, drowsy feeling from toes to fingertips.

Richard, wrapped in a blanket, crouched by the tiny dormer window, watching the village turn slowly but inexorably into a Christmas card.

'Much as I could murder a glass of that wine,' he said, 'I think I'm going to have to get back to the island while I can. This snow isn't going to stop and the roads are going to be hell later.'

Felicity sat up and let the corners of her mouth droop. "Oh," was all she could think of to say. "Yeah. It's settling now."

"I'm working the Christmas shift," he said. "Won't get any more time off the island till the day after Boxing Day."

"Oh," said Felicity again. *That only leaves five days for us.*

He turned and did a double take at her dramatically despondent face. "Fliss! You look so sad!"

"I'll miss you."

He came over to the bed and sat down, taking her hands in his. "No you won't," he said. "Because you're coming with me."

"What?"

"I've more than enough room. And I could use the company! Had planned to have my sister and her family round for Christmas dinner, but with this weather . . . who knows? Please say you'll come. I really don't want to leave you now."

"I . . . Yes. I'd love to. I'd love to see your house and the island – I haven't been there since I was a child! Are there still red squirrels there?"

"Oh yes! I'll find some for you. Come on then. Pack a bag and let's hit the road, while we still can. Shouldn't take long – you won't need much in the way of clothes."

Laughing, Felicity threw a few essentials into her case while Richard dealt with the tragically unused fire downstairs.

"Shame about the tree," she said. "Why did you bring it, if you planned to spirit me away?"

"I dunno. Wasn't thinking straight. You have that effect on me."

The snow was lying thick now, and Richard's car drove in the deep tyre tracks left by the preceding vehicles. The fields were pristine bright – no heather was visible on the heath and the distant cliffs looked as if they had sugar icing peaks.

"Don't you miss this land?" Richard asked her. "Don't you ever think of coming back?"

"All the time," said Felicity dreamily, looking out at the place she still thought of as home.

"It never lets you go," he said. "It'll never let me go. I know that much. I hope I never have to let you go either."

He put a hand on Felicity's knee and she covered it with hers.

"I hope so too." A lone sheep wandered in front of the car, bleating bleakly, causing them to stop suddenly on the lonely road.

"Fucking sheep!" cursed Richard, and Felicity burst into a peal of delighted laughter.

"It's so good to be home."

The Devil You Know

Saskia Walker

Leonie Carlton watched the hulking shape of the Land Rover as it weaved along the rough dirt track towards the plantation house. Her heart was racing. Despite her preparations for this moment, she could barely keep her emotions in check. Mike Racine – the lover she'd wanted to be with so badly, but had failed to understand – was about to arrive on her doorstep.

Leonie would have fought tooth and nail to keep him away – even though she'd dreamed about the man every night since she'd escaped to Australia, twelve months earlier. Thank God she'd been warned he was coming. Mike hadn't wanted her to know. Luckily, Tansy, her old friend back at HQ, had emailed her. Apparently he'd insisted on making the trip. Mike Racine himself was coming to approve their coffee beans. *No kidding.*

She gave a wry smile and watched as the Land Rover drew to a halt in the gravel drive. With her hands wrapped around the balustrade on the long veranda to anchor herself, she tried not to react. She hadn't even allowed herself to dress any differently, just because it was him.

The sun blazed low on the horizon behind the parked vehicle as the afternoon turned to evening. The windscreen was tinted, hiding the occupant from her gaze, but she could feel the weight of his stare nonetheless. She took a deep breath, walked along the wooden veranda until she got to the steps he would have to walk up, and folded her arms across her chest. The sound of the crickets seemed to grow louder in her ears, her skin prickling with awareness and anticipation.

"Come on, Mike," she whispered. "Give me your best shot."

After what seemed an eternity the vehicle door opened.

Unfurling his tall, limber frame, Mike climbed out, a leather backpack in his hand. He slammed the door behind him, threw the backpack over his shoulder, and walked up the path to the house.

Each step he took made her body tighten with anticipation.

Dressed in boots and faded black jeans, his khaki shirt outlined the breadth of his shoulders and the lean line of his waist and hips. He wore a baseball cap pulled low on his brow. It was a poor disguise – she'd have known it was Mike from his posture alone.

He drew to a halt at the foot of the steps.

She shook her head at him. "You should have let someone else come. You promised you would leave me alone."

He shrugged. "I lied."

Taking off his hat, he eyed her from top to toe, and ruffled his shaggy black hair. It brushed the edge of his collar, longer than it had been. He wore a teasing smile that was so familiar it tugged at something deep inside of her. What struck her most of all was that his expression left her in no doubt of his intentions towards her. He'd come for what had been so good between them – that which hadn't been enough for her, in the end. She'd put it behind her, half a world behind. Why then, did her heart race in response to his nonchalance? Why did her traitorous skin tingle under his scrutiny?

"Damn you, Mike."

"You always did look bloody sexy when you're angry," he commented.

Arrogant prick. It was as if the intervening year hadn't even happened. This was the way it had always been. He used to come to her place late at night. He'd just walk in after some function or other and assume he could have her. But she couldn't resist when he rested his hands on her and walked her back against the wall. They'd be at it, right there in the hallway, before she even had a chance to tell him to leave. He overwhelmed her and made her need him badly, until one day she got fed up with being his convenient part-time lover and decided to put some serious distance between them.

She shook her head, warning him off. "Things have changed."

He lifted his eyebrows, accusingly. "Nothing has changed, that is quite obvious." He always did have the cheek of the devil. "I can see you still want me every bit as much as I want you."

How dare he just throw that out there? She sighed aloud, but her very centre was heavy and aching for him, her pussy fast growing damp. "We're not in London now. You can't just come here and expect everything to be the same between us."

"Everything is the same, except for one thing." He paused, and he did it deliberately, emphasizing every word. "I've come a whole lot further for you this time."

Her breath caught in her throat.

It was true. He had come further. But that didn't mean she was just going to fall on her back. Her body, however, seemed to be at odds with her brain on that particular point. His very proximity had unleashed her libido, as if he were a match to her fuse.

"Don't make any assumptions," she snapped.

There it was – that devilish smile, the dark twinkle in his eyes. He scanned her chosen outfit, shorts and a shirt with rolled-up sleeves, practical but close fitting. His inquisitive stare brought back too many memories, memories of how good it had been between them, and between the sheets. He had a thing about licking her breasts, the entirety of them, after they'd made love. Right now her breasts were aching at the very memory of it.

He walked up the wide wooden steps on to the veranda, closing the gap between them.

"Let's just get this over with, shall we?" she said, her heart racing. "The owners of the plantation, Frank and Sherri, are waiting inside to hear what you've got to say about the harvest."

He stepped nearer, until he was right up against her. "That's not the only reason I came, and you know it."

He ran the back of his hand down her neck, and the brush of his knuckles against her throat made her shiver. His touch was so startling that it set her adrift on a tide of emotions.

"I never stopped thinking about you, never stopped wanting you. You're looking good, Leonie. Better than ever, in fact."

Maybe I look good because I haven't had to deal with you. She managed to turn away, and led him inside the house. As she did, she once again vowed to remain professional throughout the encounter, although she was beginning to see that was going to be easier said than done, especially as he seemed determined to push it. Then there was the fact that his presence strolling behind her was totally magnetic.

It's a year since you've had sex, that's all it is, she told herself, annoyed beyond belief. But she wanted him, always had. And he was so bad for her. When she had failed to understand him – and he'd failed to help her do so – she'd walked away. *Far away.* Queensland, Australia. She had exchanged a desk job at a leading fair trade coffee importer in London for a hard, hands-on job helping to stabilize and expand a struggling plantation. Working with the owners, she put her years of theory and training into practice at grass roots level. And she'd worked Mike out of her system, or so she thought.

She strode down the hallway and into the family kitchen, measuring each breath to calm herself. Frank and his wife, Sherri, the plantation owners, were standing by expectantly. That made it easier. This was incredibly important to them, and Leonie swung into hostess mode, ushering Mike over to meet them. Once she'd made the introductions, she stepped away. They'd prepared for this moment for so long, and she had helped Frank to choose the finest beans they'd harvested, making sure the mix was perfect.

Mike met them warmly and within moments he made Sherri laugh at length with an amusing anecdote about his long journey. He had that kind of magnetic personality – he could win anyone over. Leonie noticed that the intervening time had added a few more laughter lines around his sardonic smile, and a more relaxed twinkle to those luscious dark-brown eyes of his. He looked so bloody attractive. Leonie couldn't keep her eyes off him while he chatted. His broad chest made her fingers ache to touch him, to lock her hands over his shoulders while she pressed her whole body to his in a true physical reunion – the sort she'd only allowed in her dreams.

When she'd first met him, over three years earlier, he'd been the same way, charming people. Her gaze drifted over the body she knew so well. It made her long to gravitate to him, to touch him as a lover might, and she swayed. She was remembering. Remembering this one time when he'd walked into her office and closed the door behind him.

Her office door always stayed open. The very fact he closed it sent up a warning flare.

Then he folded his arms across his chest and nodded at her, his mouth lifting at one corner. Dressed in a fine suit he was a wolf in sheep's clothing – polished but predatory. His expression was positively wicked, and he just stood there and looked at her, making sure she knew what he'd come for.

Unable to resist, she rose to her feet, her legs weak under her.

When she stepped out from behind her desk, he walked over and urged her behind the filing cabinet, where he hiked her skirt up around her waist and touched her through the flimsy barrier of her French lace panties.

"You can't mean to—"

"Oh yes," he interrupted, "I do mean to. I've been thinking about this all afternoon." Inserting one finger under her panties, he drew them to one side. Then he reached inside with his free hand, and slid a finger into her slit, making her gasp aloud.

Lifting one foot then the other, she grabbed his shoulders and held on for dear life while he stroked her into a frenzy of arousal. She flashed her eyes at him, and he cinched her swollen clit between his knuckles, rocking his fingers gently until she climaxed. Lethal, he was thoroughly lethal. She was still clinging to him – her thighs taut and shuddering, her pussy slick with her juices – when he issued his next instruction.

"Turn around." The look in his eyes spoke of pure mastery.

Following his command, she latched her fingers over the edge of the cabinet. He pulled her panties down her thighs, letting them trail around her ankles where they looked strangely obscene draped over her expensive designer heels. Slowly, lovingly, he'd stroked the outline of her bottom, as if savouring the shape of it, and then moved his hand lower. Even as his fingers opened her up, she grew damper, anticipating him.

A moment later came the merciful sound of his zipper, and his command. "Bend over."

Bent at the waist, she clung to the cabinet as he probed inside her, his cock opening her up, stretching her and filling her to capacity. Leonie kept her eyes on the door, willing it not to open, her grateful pussy clutching his erection as she thought about the humiliation she would experience if someone walked in on them. The threat made her even hornier.

Mike knew that, because he loved pushing her, exploring her boundaries and then edging her over them. And he'd prepared her well. His cock slid easily against her slippery walls, over and over, until he had to put his hand over her mouth when she cried out at her peak, saving her honour amongst those who had offices along the corridor.

He threw her every time. She never knew where she stood.

*   *   *

One day, that was too much. It also wasn't enough.

I wanted more than he could give me, she reflected, staring across Frank and Sherri's kitchen at her ex-lover with a rueful sense of acceptance. She was fated to love a man who couldn't settle.

It was then that she noticed he had his hand latched over his belt. With a sharp intake of breath, she realized it was the same belt she had given him as a gift, two years earlier. And he'd used it for more than holding his jeans up. He'd used it to stop her struggling against him during sex, which had made her struggle all the more.

Leonie shivered at the memory.

Mike stopped speaking.

Her gaze shot up to meet his.

He was smiling at her accusingly. He knew she'd been looking. He must have been keeping a subtle watch on her. She glanced away from his knowing stare, but images of what he used to do with that belt still flashed through her mind. He'd worn it on purpose today, she was sure of it. He'd worn it to remind her of what they used to be like together.

Sherri was pouring him a cup of fresh brew. The aroma reached Leonie, rich and intoxicating. Pride blossomed in her chest, levelling her head somewhat.

Mike took the cup, breathed the scent in, and then drank heavily. He had a way of holding his cup, ring finger through the handle, cup cradled in his palm. He nodded as he put the cup down. "The sample you sent tasted superb, undoubtedly one of the finest harvests of the year, but there's something really special about tasting it where it's grown, with the people who made it this way."

He put his hand out to shake Frank's all over again.

Sherri was beaming. "Dinner will be ready in about an hour. If you'd like to freshen up after your journey, I'll show you to the guest lodge."

Mike nodded, but turned to Leonie. "Leonie could show me." His gaze raked over her. "I need to go over some facts and figures with her anyway."

Bastard.

"Of course," Sherri replied, and winked over at Leonie.

Had she sensed there was something between them? She looked from Sherri's smiling face to Frank's startled one. The atmosphere had shifted, yes, and their attention was fully on her. They must have guessed.

"This way." She led him out of the back door, down the steps and along the path to the annexed lodge. It was a prefab building with a dozen rooms used for guests, and for the workers in the busy harvesting season. It was here in this simple place that she'd made her home for the past year, and here where Sherri had made Mike a room up, right next to hers.

"They seem to be good people," he commented, as their footsteps crunched on the gravel path.

"They are, and they worked hard for this. I think they'll be fine when I leave."

"It was an ambitious project, but you've helped them on their way. You put your stamp on the franchise. That was obvious from England."

He must have been watching her reports, and he wasn't even on the overseeing panel. His job was in marketing, unless that had changed and Tansy hadn't told her.

"Overseeing the plantation has been good for me. I needed to strike out on my own, prove I could do what I was preaching to others about."

She put her hand on the screen door of the lodge, pausing, and met his gaze. "The board seemed pleased with my work." Two weeks before, she'd indicated that she was ready to move on. "Do they want me back in London, or elsewhere?"

He didn't answer her question. He merely smiled.

She opened the door and went inside, her back to him as she paused and waited for him to follow.

The narrow corridor had twelve doors off it, and a storage cupboard at the far end. Plain and utility, the building smelled of citronella. Leonie had long since learned that the underlying citrus insect repellent was barely combated by her most expensive perfume. Once the screen door shut behind him, she heard his bag drop to the floor and felt his breath on her neck. Then she couldn't smell the citronella any more, because he was so close to her that she could smell him, his cologne, the same one he always wore, and, beneath it, his scent. Her eyes closed, savouring it.

He stroked her hair. "Be honest," he whispered against her ear, "you missed me."

She couldn't deny it, so she said nothing.

His hands closed over her shoulders and he turned her around, forcing her to look at him. "Tansy told me you always ask about me when you email her."

Tansy had a lot to answer for.

"Idle curiosity." His proximity overwhelmed her body with need, but her will defied it. She backed away and out of his grasp.

He closed again, reached out and touched one finger against her neck.

A stifled whimper escaped her lips. She tried to shift, but found herself backed against the wall.

"Idle curiosity? Is that all it was?" He rested the palm of his hand at her collarbone, capturing her, holding her still with his fingers on her collarbone.

She tried to quell her erratic breathing, aware that he could see and feel her reactions. He always had this effect on her. A master of seduction, he could push her buttons so easily. Nothing had changed. The only way to deal with it was to ignore him and not rise to his leading comments.

He lifted a strand of hair from her neck and looped it where the rest was clipped on top of her head. The intimate act threw her, fuelling her desires for him and him alone.

Ignore him.

He bent his head and brushed his mouth along her neck.

Shivers of sensation undermined her resolve. He unravelled her so easily, leaving her thoughts and desires naked and vulnerable. "Don't test me, please," she begged, but her body gravitated towards his.

"Always so ready for this, aren't you, Leonie?"

Heat raced over her. He exposed her, thoroughly. She should demand he stop touching her, but she couldn't. "You promised me. Back in London, you promised that you'd leave me alone. Try at least to be professional."

"We're not in London now."

She rounded her eyes at him. "You're infuriating!"

"And you're so beautiful when you're aroused."

"I'm not aroused. I'm annoyed."

He stroked her cheek. "Your eyes flash and your lower lip trembles. Just the way I remembered."

"Did you come all this way to humiliate me?"

"No. I came all this way because I wanted to be inside you again."

Her breath caught in her chest, her core contracting with need.

"I came because I wanted to hold you, to taste you . . . to make you come." He smiled. "There's nothing in the whole wide world that feels like that . . . nothing in the whole world like you, lover."

He wants me. He'd come for her. But wasn't that what he was always like? Always pitching up unannounced, expecting her to fall flat on her back. They never even did normal stuff, like dating. It was work, and sex. She needed more than that.

"You can't just walk in here and treat me as if we were still in a . . . well, relationship . . . if you could even call it that. It was far from a normal relationship."

He shrugged one shoulder. "What's so good about normal? If you honestly preferred that you'd be safe at home in London now, not willing to take on the world."

He had an answer for everything. And still he stroked her collarbone, making her traitorous body yearn for him all the more.

"Besides," he added, "I seem to recall you liked being pushed out of your normal, comfortable zones . . ."

"It always comes back to sex."

"I can't help wanting you," he whispered. "I've missed you so much, that's why I had to come." He brushed his thumb over her lower lip, his expression growing more serious. "Don't fight it, Leonie. You know it's going to happen as much as I do."

She couldn't quite comprehend what he'd put into words, cheeky devil. And yet – *yes* – now that he was here, there was such an over-whelming sense of inevitability about it. She'd been longing for his touch since she'd heard he was coming. Would it hurt to have sex, just one more time? Maybe it would, but she'd already done enough hurting without it. *Don't let him take anything for granted.*

"Once more for old times' sake, huh?" sarcasm rang in her voice, because that's what he'd said to her when she'd announced she was leaving London.

"Old times were good times."

They were heady days, for sure, but that didn't give him the excuse to barge in and take over after she'd managed to pull away and reshape her life. "Shame you didn't realize that back then."

"I did." He locked eyes with her, holding her gaze. "Just because we didn't do everything by the numbers . . . what we shared was the best."

She glared at him, hating that he said that now, when he'd been so flippant a year ago.

He gave her a knowing look. "Don't be bitter. It doesn't suit you."

"What do you care?"

"I'll show you how much I care." He pulled his shirt free from his jeans, and undid his belt.

Oh, how her blood rushed, annoyance and lust burning her up from the inside. "Thinking with your cock, as usual?" she snapped.

"You never used to complain."

Images flashed through her mind, images of him over her, back in her flat in Kensington. They rarely ever slept, even when they spent a whole night together. "Arrogant bastard."

"Maybe, but I'd like to point out I've thought about this a whole lot, and not just with my cock." His eyebrows lifted and he shifted his weight from one foot to the other, his hips rolling. The belt hung from his hand, a constant reminder of his power over her. "Although I have to admit, it likes thinking about you too . . . every day, and every night, when I was alone in my bed."

The very thought of him masturbating made her damp. Had he really thought about her? Had he stroked his cock while he was thinking about her, the way she had sometimes coaxed herself to guilty orgasm with his image in her mind?

His jeans were now hanging low on his hips. She could see the waistband of his jockeys and the growing bulge inside them. Her hands ached to hold him, to run her fingers around the edge of his waistband, to feel his warm skin and hard abs against the back of her knuckles as she slid her hands inside to reach for him. Blinking, she rocked on her heels.

"Which is your room? I want to be on your bed while I make love to you." He ran his nose against her hair. "I want to smell your pillow. I've missed your scent. Missed it. Badly."

She let out a long withheld breath, her will to resist him weakening by the moment. He was whispering against her skin, seducing her.

"We need to do this, Leonie, and you know it. If we don't, we'll only be putting it off until later." He drew back and gave her a knowing smile. "Meanwhile, your friends here will have to deal with the tension between us."

Her blood hit boiling point. She'd been about to give in and let him melt away every tension in her body, but the reference to the plantation owners slapped some sense into her. "Jesus, you're saying we can't behave professionally until we've had sex?"

He lifted one shoulder. "It was always like this between us. As far as I can see, nothing has changed."

Her heart was pounding. But he was right, damn him. Even though she hadn't touched him, their need for one another was in charge. It was a hurdle they never could get past until they'd given in to the overwhelming chemical reaction that was triggered whenever they were together. *Why the hell not,* her body screamed.

"Fuck me then," she blurted, "if you think it's the only way to get past it and act like civilized people."

He didn't even blink. "Lead the way."

"I hate you."

"No, you don't."

"Smug bastard." She turned on her heels and strode to the end of the corridor, then turned right into her room. Her heart was beating so hard she could hear her blood rushing in her ears. With one hand, she steadied herself on the chest of drawers just inside the door and watched as he followed.

He shut the door behind him, and then nodded at her shirt. "Take it off."

Apparently he didn't plan to waste any time. *I swore I wouldn't do this.*

But his control over her hadn't diminished an iota. Her fingers were automatically on the buttons, doing as he commanded. "I hate you for this."

"Why?"

"Because I can't say no to you!"

"Just me?" One eyebrow lifted, he gave her a teasing glance.

"You are insufferable. Yes, just you. Bastard." He'd wanted to know, though. Did he think there had been others? A legion of fit Aussie harvesters who kept her company in bed at night? Perhaps she should have let him believe that, but she never was very good at lying, hence the predicament she currently found herself in. The plan was to say no and pretend she meant it. What a ludicrous notion.

When she dropped the shirt to the floor, he nodded at her bra.

Reaching around, she undid the clasp, muttering curse words under her breath. Whether she was cursing him, or herself, she wasn't quite sure any more.

When the bra joined the shirt on the floor, he smiled appreciatively. "I've missed your breasts."

Her nipples were already peaked, and they quickly knotted under his gaze. He didn't touch her, he just ate her up with his eyes, and that made her even more edgy. It was his way – making her desperate for him by doing next to nothing and yet controlling her so thoroughly with his words and actions. She inwardly cursed herself, but she wanted him, there was no denying it.

"And the rest." The belt snaked in his grasp.

Her core clenched. Kicking off her shoes, she undid the button and zipper on her shorts, dropping them to the floor and stepping out of them. She paused. He didn't even have to say the words. She felt the weight of his command, and rolled her panties down her thighs, abandoning them too.

Stepping closer, he lifted her wrists into one strong hand and bound them together with his belt, securing them by buckling the belt into the extra hole he'd cut for this very task, so that the loop fitted her bound wrists perfectly.

The restraint melted away her last shred of resistance. She was his now, if only for this moment. Her eyes shut, savouring the freedom in that, savouring the tight bondage around her wrists and how it made her feel.

Mike sighed heavily. "It's a dire situation when a man has to travel halfway around the world for a good lay."

He spoke as if to himself, but it turned her on even more because it was like a raw confession, one that her ego needed to here, one that he had never uttered before. She gave a husky laugh, but her heart soared – anticipation, and sheer, heady delight at his comment making her dizzy. "Is that what I am, a good lay?"

He nodded. "The best."

Her head dropped back. Her body felt boneless. He'd never said anything like that to her before.

Leading her to the bedside with a tug on the belt, he gestured, indicating that she lie down. She sat, and then lay flat out. It was getting difficult to breathe. He lifted her hands with the belt, jerking them at the wrist so that her arms were straight and her breasts rolled together. He seemed to like the way that looked, and strapped her to the metal bedpost, bending the soft leather belt over on itself and looping it through the buckle, to hold her in place with her arms above her head. When it was done, he rested a kiss on one nipple, making her arch against the surface of the bed.

She watched as he stripped off. His body, so familiar, made her ache. The sight of his naked, erect cock set her on fire, and she wriggled against the restraints.

He shook his head, ran his hand over her belly and then lower, pushing a finger into her slit. "Open your legs, let me see you."

She did as he said and he watched while he stroked his cock with one hand. The way he was looking at her was so blatant. With her legs splayed, her burning pussy was exposed. Liquid dribbled down in between her buttocks. Her clit was buzzing with the need to be touched, her sex gaping and yet contracting inside.

He climbed over her, landing with his hot cockhead against her splayed pussy. Her clit leaped, the contact making her legs thrash wildly. "Always so eager," he murmured, pushing her loosed hair back as he looked down at her with curiosity in his expression.

Had he doubted she'd still want him? It was there, ever so briefly, in his eyes. And then he was nudging inside her and thoughts melted into sensation.

He pushed. The walls of her aching sex stretched to accommodate him, her pulse pounding, silently screaming: *So good.* Being filled by this man – who she loved so desperately – was even better than she had remembered during all those nights tossing and turning. It didn't matter if it was a day or a year, there was no memory or dream as stunning as that feeling of being suddenly filled, his hard shaft ploughing her deep. Then he hit home, brushing her core, and she moaned loudly and lifted within her restraints, her back arching, her shoulders jerking up from the surface of the bed.

"Oh yes," he murmured, and kissed her mouth.

All that pent-up regret and longing, all that frustration poured out of her, and she locked eyes with him and ground her hips to meet his.

He thrust his cock deep inside her.

"You didn't come all the way here . . . for this," she managed to accuse, with a gasp for air on his thrust, "surely?"

He nodded, his brow drawn down with the effort.

"It's a long way to . . . come . . . for a shag, Mike."

He gave a hoarse laugh, and pulled out, urging her to chase after him. Her hips reacted of their own accord, reaching for him, angled up from the bed. Her pussy brushed fleetingly against his cock. Her hands moved helplessly in the belt.

With a soft chuckle, he thrust home again, making her gasp. "Oh yes, I came here for this, but not just for a one-off. For you, all of you. I want you to be mine."

A tight fist contracted in her chest. Her gaze searched his, looking for the truth.

He eased back inside. "Yes, I love you, you crazy diamond," he whispered, and his eyes shone.

Tears of relief blurred her vision. Her heart beat frantically, the ache in her chest blossoming into joy.

He nodded at her, reinforcing his words. Then he lifted on his arms and started to thrust hard and fast, massaging her most sensitive places, sending hot tides of sensation over her entire body.

She cried out, trying to hold back to gain the measure of his words, but it was too much. Her whole body had been ready for this for far too long, and now he was inside her and she couldn't help shouting her joy. Her body met his, her hands wrapped around the leather belt for purchase.

Hard and fast, they thrashed out their longing, their differences and their desires. The bed rattled and shunted on the tiled floor, creaking loudly.

Her core spasmed. Relief was imminent.

"You feel so good." The words were wrenched from his lungs. "I want be here for ever."

He was close, and she knew that because she knew this man so well.

Her climax hit, her whole body shuddered with the force of it. She held him deep inside and squeezed his cock hard with her inner muscles. He clutched at her, his cock jerking hard, his fingers in her hair and words of love on his lips as he came.

Mike was kissing her.

Leonie was in heaven.

He kissed her eyelids, her forehead and then the tip of her nose. He rubbed his face against hers, grazing her with his stubble, then he teased his lips against hers while he cupped her face in his hands.

"Untie me," she pleaded, aching to hold him.

"Maybe." He smiled, as if to himself. "I like you this way," he added, and his voice was hoarse with emotion, "because you can't run away from me again while I've got you tied up."

"I didn't run away."

His eyelids lowered but not before she saw it – she'd hurt him. He masked it quickly and reached for the belt. When he unbound her, she touched him, holding him eagerly.

Am I dreaming? His hard body under her fingers seemed to deny that. Running her hands along his flank, she drew back and looked at him, needing the constant reassurance this had really happened.

He rested alongside her and ran his hand up the length of her arm. "You're different, leaner."

"I've been working hard."

"You have. It suits you." His expression seemed to soften, and yet his fingers lingered around her biceps, stroking her as if he was acquainting himself with the physical changes that had been brought about by hard labour.

"You are different too, more wrinkles." She touched her finger over his face.

"That's your fault." He smiled.

"Oh, right, my fault." She laughed softly.

They continued to explore the newness they found in each other. Leonie wanted to savour every moment. She didn't want to ask him if he really meant what he'd said, not yet.

He turned his attention to her chest, and licked her right breast, long and slow, eking out her afterglow, making her even more warm and languid. Her hips stirred against the bed, heavy and yet warming for more action. Her fingers latched over the abandoned belt, anchoring her. "Why the belt?"

"Thought you might not be so willing." He moved to her left breast. "Thought that I'd have to convince you."

He had doubted her need for him. But still he came . . .

"Willing?" she teased, on an intake of breath, when he pleasured her sensitive breast with his kisses.

Then his cock began to stir against her and he seemed to make an effort to gather his thoughts. "There is something else I need to say, a few things actually."

"What?"

"It's about work." He drew away, ever so slightly, but she noticed.

If this was about work did that mean he had moved on already – that he had already shelved the intimacies said in the heat of the moment?

His expression grew more serious. "The board of directors suggested a new post for you. They like what you've done here. You gave a new franchise confidence. The board wants you to do it again, with a bigger project. They haven't given all the details yet, just wanted me to run it past you, in theory." There was a certain sense of misgiving in his tone. "I can tell you it's in South America. The plantation is big, up to five times the size of this, and the conditions are harsher."

It sounded like the sort of new challenge she wanted, but he was wary. Maybe he didn't want her to go. Was this an either/or situation?

"I've learned a lot," she said, cautiously. "I'm willing to think about it."

His eyelids lowered. "They are offering it to you under one condition." His mouth twitched, and she sensed he was trying to play it deadpan.

"Condition?"

"Just one. You work with someone else." He met her stare and the twinkle in his eyes made her heart thud in her chest. Curiosity and hope gripped her.

"Who?" Her voice was barely a whisper.

He shrugged. "Yours truly."

"But you said you'd never leave London, you said you'd never tie yourself to anyone or anything—"

The words tumbled out, but he put his finger against her lips, hushing her. "I changed my mind. If you agree, we'll do it together, and you'll be the expert." He stroked his hand down her flank, his expression serious. "I'll just be the newbie who wants to be alongside you."

She knew that was hard for him, and she knew that he was offering the sort of commitment he'd never been able to offer before. "Are you sure you've thought this through?"

He nodded. "I've thought about nothing else for the last twelve months, since the moment you left. I love you, Leonie." He paused. "I couldn't be what you wanted, back then. I know that I let you down. But now, it's different. I had a nasty shock when you went away. I thought I could handle it, but it tore me apart. I realized what an idiot I'd been."

She almost couldn't stand it. His confession made her ache.

He drew her hands to his mouth and kissed them both reverently. "You did the right thing. I needed a kick up the arse. You're the best thing that has ever happened to me. If you'll have me, we can go on together. I want new challenges too, and I want to be with you, always."

She tried to keep the smile from her face, but failed. "Hmm, now let's see . . . a new assignment." She latched her hands over his shoulders. "I'd have to give it some serious consideration."

"Don't make me wait too long, or I might have to force the issue." He prized her legs open again, his cock hard against her thigh, his mouth nuzzling her throat hungrily.

A sense of heady, heady bliss saturated her. She lifted her hips and encouraged him back in.

A tentative knock sounded.

Sherri coughed outside the door, in the corridor. "Hey folks, I just wanted to let you know, dinner is just about ready."

"I'll be right there," Mike managed to respond, as he eased his cock inside her. "I'm just freshening up."

"You're in *my* room, idiot," Leonie whispered. She couldn't help laughing. When she did, his cock buoyed up against her most sensitive place. "Oh, oh, oh," she murmured.

"OK," Sherri called out. "No rush, it'll keep. I figured you guys had some . . . freshening . . . to do. I put your bag outside the door, Mike. You left it in the hallway." They heard her chuckling as she walked away.

Mike fixed Leonie's gaze with his, his hips pinning her to bed. "Well?"

"What if I ask for it to be someone else, for the sake of my sanity?"

"I want us to be together." He pulled back and then thrust inside her, demanding. "Stop toying with me and agree, damn it!"

He was actually fretting about her response. She could see it in his eyes. She could also feel it in his needy thrust. "Oh," she said, in between gasping for breath. "I suppose it might be better to be with the devil I know . . ."

"Agree. Or we'll never make it to dinner."

She gasped as he rolled his hips from side to side, his shaft massaging her. "Looks like you've me got over a barrel," she managed to reply.

"Now that I'd like to see." He plied her with kisses. He reached down and stroked his one finger back and forth over her clit, brusquely, demandingly. "Agree," he urged again, taking shallow thrusts.

This time she met his gaze on every move, watching him in wonder as he made every part of her sing. She felt herself fluttering open deep within, each internal kiss like a seal on what had been said. Crying out, she climaxed suddenly and unexpectedly.

"It's a deal," she managed to blurt out, and then wrapped her legs around his hips, locking him in place while he poured himself into her and his cock jerked in release.

"I love you, Mike," she whispered, as he rolled her into his arms.

Even if she could have resisted him for a moment longer, it didn't matter any more. The devil she knew was right where she wanted him to be – in her heart, in her soul, and in her bed.

Afternoon in Paradise

Rebecca York

It should have been a perfect afternoon in paradise, yet Jenna Brockhurst sensed something unsettling in the air as she stepped on to the marble terrace of the tropical resort. A gentle breeze played through her blonde hair and the gauzy shirt she wore over her bikini top and beach wrap skirt. Raising her head, she scanned the terrace, then the wide beach and the bay beyond where sailboats skimmed across the blue water of Honeycomb Bay.

Was she looking for danger? Or looking for *him*? The lean, dark-haired guy with the broad shoulders and eyes so dark they were almost black, except for the touch of fire in their depths. The same guy who radiated a leashed power that made her want to run. Towards him or away? She wasn't exactly sure. He'd met her gaze that first night in the elegant dining room where they'd both been eating alone at separate tables. In those first seconds of eye contact, she'd thought he might ask to join her. Instead, he'd turned back to the slab of steak on his plate and left the baked potato before signing the check and disappearing.

Over the next two days, she'd seen him around the resort. Always alone. One time he'd been out on a jet ski. Another time, he'd been pumping iron in the gym. And always with a look on his face that warned he didn't want company. Yet she sensed that he was interested in her.

She'd heard one of the hotel employees call him Señor Marshall. And from the sign-up sheet in the gym, she knew that his first name was Zack.

Had he looked at her name, too?

Maybe she should walk up to him the next time they encountered each other. What was the worst thing he could do? Send a
letter bomb to her room? Tell her that slim blue-eyed blondes
weren't his type at all?

She'd come to San Marcos because she'd known that if she
didn't get out of the US and away from her high-pressure medical
research job, she was going to snap. Luban, the company where
she worked, was pressing for a breakthrough on the cancer vaccine
project, and she'd just run into another dead end.

If they fired her for a two-week escape, so be it. But she'd had to
get out of the lab and into a totally different environment. So far
the peaceful atmosphere of the resort had helped to rejuvenate
her. The only thing missing was a romantic adventure. Apparently
that was too much to ask. There were maybe 100 guests at El Sol y
Enrolla, but few singles, as it turned out.

Except for Mr Mysterious Marshall. She'd dreamed about him,
sensuous and disturbing fantasies that had left her lying in bed with
her nipples tight and her sex wet and swollen. Thinking of the
dreams brought back the hot sensations that had accompanied
them. With a silent curse, she sat down at one of the glass-topped,
umbrella-shaded tables that dotted the patio and took a sip of the
iced latte she'd brought outside. Perfect as usual. Maybe the cold
drink would cool her down.

Exotic vegetation and flowering shrubs screened the patio. From
hidden speakers, the hotel sound system played light sixties
rock. Stretching out her legs, she examined their hue. She'd gotten
a little tan since she'd been here, but not enough to wipe away her
lab-pale skin.

She had just taken another sip of her latte when a sound that was
totally wrong made her head jerk up.

It came again, and she realized it was gunfire. From an automatic weapon.

Two dark-haired men dressed in black T-shirts and jeans were
running across the beach, firing machine guns as they went.

To her horror, she saw a man and woman in bathing suits go
down, then one of the beach attendants.

The men with the guns were heading her way, speaking to each
other in Spanish. Instinctively, she slid off her chair and crouched
behind the low wall that separated the terrace from the sand. Footsteps
pounded towards her, and every muscle in her body tensed as she
waited for one of the men to round the wall and start blasting away

at her. But they kept going, into the hotel, where she heard screams and more gunfire. From more than the two guns.

Lord, what was happening? She'd heard murmurs of political unrest in San Marcos, but she'd never thought it would reach her out here at this isolated resort.

Apparently she'd been wrong.

Every instinct urged her to run for her life. But where?

El Sol y Enrolla was a small resort on an island off the coast. You could only get here by boat or small plane. Which meant that she couldn't make for the road and get anywhere besides the other side of the island. The road was a bad idea, anyway, because she'd be exposed.

From inside the hotel, she heard more sounds of carnage. She'd seen two men, but there must be more. Or maybe somebody was shooting back. Either way, horrible images leaped into her mind. How long before men returned and found her?

Knowing she couldn't stay where she was, she raised her head and looked around. The beach was clear, except for the dead bodies. She said a silent prayer, then crawled to the other side of the wall. Keeping low, a screen of foliage between her and the terrace, she made for the little hut where white fluffy towels were piled for hotel guests.

As she reached the shelter, someone streaked to her side, and she froze, thinking that one of the invaders had lingered on the beach, waiting for guests trying to escape.

But it wasn't one of the gunmen. It was Zack Marshall, dressed in jeans and a blue polo shirt, coming up beside her.

"Keep down," he said, his tone low and hard.

"I am." She heard the quaver in her voice, felt herself trembling. When he pulled her close, she closed her eyes and leaned into his strength. He stroked his hand up and down the goosebumps on her arm.

"What are you doing out here?" she whispered.

"I was walking. I heard the gunfire. Then I saw you."

She nodded against his chest, pressing closer, wishing she could sink into his warmth.

"We'll get out of this."

She wanted to believe it. "Who are they?"

"My guess? Opponents of the government who want to make a statement by wiping out a bunch of Americans. Which means we've got to get out of here."

"There's nowhere to go."

"Into the jungle. Until help arrives."

"Does anyone know what's happening here?"

"Somebody must have gotten out a call. The emergency number is posted in every room," he said, but he didn't sound perfectly confident, and she wondered how long it would be before anyone realized the situation on the island.

He looked around the side of the towel stand and gestured. "The gazebo's about thirty yards away. We'll make that our next stop."

It was on the lawn, closer to the hotel. But there wasn't any other cover.

"OK." She'd let him take charge because she had no idea what else to do.

"I'll go first. If I make it, you follow me. Keep low."

She winced at the way he put it, but she told herself that if anyone was going to make it, he would.

He cupped his hand around her shoulder, and she reached up to cover his fingers with hers. For long moments, neither one of them moved.

"Zack," she murmured.

He stiffened. "You know my name?"

"I saw it on the sign-in book at the gym."

He laughed. "And I saw yours. Jenna. Too bad we're meeting this way."

She wanted to ask if they would have met at all under other circumstances, but he muttered, "Gotta go."

Her heart leaped into her throat as she watched him dash across the open space between her hiding place and the white gazebo surrounded by hibiscus bushes. When he made it without any gunfire, she breathed out a sigh of relief.

Then he motioned to her, and she gathered up her courage to make the dash. Following his example, she ducked low, running flat out for the back of the gazebo, tumbling into Zack Marshall's arms. He gathered her close, sliding his hands up and down her back and shoulder. She had wanted to be this close to him and never expected it. Now it felt like the most natural thing in the world to raise her face to his.

Their lips were so close. She could have kissed him. Wanted to kiss him. Out of gratitude or because the danger was heightening her emotions? She saw from the look in his eyes that his thoughts were travelling the same path.

But instead of kissing her, he raised his head and looked towards the jungle. "We're not safe here. Got to get into the trees."

This time, they had only twenty yards to safety. She hoped it was safety.

"You go first," Zack whispered. "I'll keep guard."

Her heart pounding, she took off towards the jungle, saying a prayer of thanks as she plunged into the darkness under a grove of low palms.

She'd made it!

She expected Zack to follow, but when she peeked out from behind a tree, he wasn't there.

Oh Lord, what had happened to him? Had he changed his mind? Was he leaving her here to fend for herself?

When she heard an explosion of gunfire, she went rigid. As her eyes searched the expanse of the lawn, she saw one of the gunmen moving towards the jungle, gun in hand, and she knew he must have seen her plunge into the underbrush. She froze, unable to move. Then she saw something so out of place that at first she couldn't believe her eyes. A grey shape was moving slowly across the lawn, following the man with the gun. It was a large dog or a maybe a wolf, although she'd never heard of wolves in San Marcos.

As she watched, she knew the moment when the gunman realized there was something behind him. He whirled, the weapon aimed at the animal. When he fired, Jenna screamed. But the wolf was already in motion, taking a giant leap at the invader. The man tried to fight him off, but the animal continued the fierce attack, biting and mauling him until he went still.

The wolf stepped away, looking down at the attacker. Then, to her astonishment, it came back and pulled the gun from the man's hands, dragging the weapon towards the jungle.

For long seconds she stood frozen, wondering if she had really witnessed the violent scene. But the gunman was still lying on the lawn where the wolf had left him.

She was still trying to come to grips with that, when she heard the crackle of foliage behind her. Her heart pounding, she turned and saw Zack coming towards her.

Wide-eyed, she stared at him. "Where were you?"

"I saw the gunman and ducked back."

"Did you see the . . . wolf?" she asked in a strangled voice.

"Yeah. I stayed where I was until the fight was over."

She nodded, wondering if that really dovetailed with the facts. "They have wolves in San Marcos?"

He shrugged. "I guess you saw him."

"But why did he attack?"

"Maybe he's trained to go after a man with a gun."

"Maybe," she answered slowly, wondering if her mind was playing tricks on her. Yet it wasn't just her. Zack had seen the animal, too.

"We'd better get out of here," he muttered. "Before they come looking for the guy – or us." Knitting his fingers with hers, he led her further into the vegetation.

They kept going, every step putting distance between themselves and the danger. Finally, she paused, her breath coming in small gasps as she looked helplessly around.

Zack stopped beside her. "It's all right. We're going to be all right."

"Maybe not," she answered. She could have been killed in the first few minutes of the attack. Then again just now – if the wolf hadn't taken the gunman down.

Zack turned her towards him, and she felt a jolt of sensations she'd never experienced before, as he pulled her into his arms.

It was the desperate circumstances making her feel this way, she told herself, when she knew deep within that it had as much to do with the man.

With a low rumble in his chest, he pulled her more tightly into his arms, crushing her breasts against his chest, and she was suddenly overwhelmed by lust. Or maybe need was a more polite word. What she called it didn't matter. Not when she craved this man in ways that she'd never even imagined.

Raising her head, she stared at him, wondering what he would see in her face. Probably a mixture of intense heat and fear.

Her throat was so tight she could barely speak, but she managed to say, "I don't . . ."

"Make love with a guy you just met?"

"Yes." But she stayed where she was and, when he lowered his mouth to hers, she felt another jolt of sensation that crackled between them like heat lightning.

She still didn't understand what was happening between them. All she knew was that the physical contact, the arousal was more than she could have imagined. And more dangerous, because she knew on some deep, subconscious level that she was vulnerable to this man in a profoundly elemental way. If this went any further, there was no going back. Ever.

"At the hotel, you stayed away from me because you were afraid this would happen," she choked out, not even sure what she meant.

"Yes," he answered, his voice strong and deep. "But now I know I have to make love to you – or go insane."

That was a dramatic way to put it, yet she understood the truth of his words. He was as vulnerable to her as she was to him.

He lowered his head, his mouth coming down on her for a kiss that sent a jolt of heat through her. He turned his head one way and then the other, drinking her in, nibbling at her, breaching the barrier of her lips with his tongue for an invasion that might have been savage if she hadn't been a full participant.

When he finally lifted his head, they were both breathing hard.

He looked back the way they'd come. "We can't stay here."

She'd forgotten where they were and why they were standing in the jungle. The knowledge zinged back to her as he took her hand and led her further from the resort, into the wilderness.

The sun was high overhead, but the trees blocked out much of the light as they came to a little hut almost hidden from view. The walls were made of bamboo slats, and the roof was thatched with palm fronds.

Beside her, Zack dragged in a deep breath through his nose and let it out.

"What are you doing?"

"Making sure nobody's here."

"How?"

"I'd smell them."

It was a strange conversation, but she didn't stop to ponder it as he led her forwards. "Some of the locals must use this place from time to time, but nobody's home now."

"You've been here before?"

"I found it while I was exploring."

He draped an arm over her shoulder and led her inside. Looking around, she saw shelves along one wall with various supplies and a bed of blankets on the floor. No doubt where they were headed. And no doubt that her behaviour was totally out of kilter. From the sudden danger of the gunmen's attack. And from her reaction to this man.

She stopped trying to fathom her motives when arousal made her legs unsteady. He solved the problem by scooping her up and bringing her down to the bed, turning so that she was sprawled on top of him.

As he stroked his hands up and down her back and over her butt, she closed her eyes, absorbing sensations, loving the feeling of him under her and the way the length of her body fitted against his – starting with her breasts flattened against his chest and moving downwards to her hips cradling his cock. It was full and hard, ready for lovemaking, and she couldn't stop herself from moving against him, thinking she was in danger of coming just from this contact.

As he stroked one hand down her body, pressing her hips more tightly to his, he tangled his other hand in her hair, bringing her mouth back to his for another scorching kiss.

She had been obsessed with him since the moment she'd seen him at the resort. It felt like that had been months ago – and she had been waiting to make love with him all this time.

"I want you naked," he muttered, echoing her thoughts.

Both of them sat up, and began tearing at clothing. She shrugged out of her gauzy shirt. As he reached around her to unfasten her bikini top, she leaned into him so that he could untie the knot at the back and toss the garment away.

When he was done, she found the snap at the top of his jeans, then lowered the zipper. She'd never thought of herself as a bold lover, but now she reached inside his undershorts and wrapped her hand around his erection, feeling the strength and the power of him.

He dragged in a sharp breath. "Lord, that's good. Too good. I don't want this to go too fast for you."

She was thinking that nothing would be too fast for her. Not with him. But he eased her to her back and kicked away his jeans then lay down beside her and studied her.

"You are so beautiful," he breathed as he trailed a hand between her breasts, down to her navel, then lower, to play with the blonde hair at the juncture of her legs. She wanted him to slide his hand even lower, but she wasn't going to beg.

"So are you," she said instead.

She lifted her hand and ran her fingers through the thick hair that covered his chest, then found his flat nipples and circled them with her fingers before plucking on them.

Again he drew in a breath, then grinned as he cupped her breasts in his hands, running his thumbs over the tips, driving her mad with wanting more. He knew it, too, because he captured her nipples between his thumbs and fingers, twisting and squeezing them, sending hot currents downwards through her body, where they coalesced in her clit.

He lowered his head and swirled his tongue around one of her nipples, then sucked it into his mouth as he kept teasing its mate with his hand.

She arched into the caress, feeling urgency wrapping itself around them, making it hard to breathe. Hard to think. All she could do was surrender to the power of the moment.

She reached down and clasped his cock again, deliberately pushing him past the point of no return.

In response, his hand slid down her body again. This time his fingers parted her slick, swollen folds, lingering there before dipping inside her.

She gasped, moving her hips to create friction, but it wasn't enough. Not for either of them.

He circled her clit with one finger, then slid lower again to circle the finger just inside the sensitive opening of her vagina, sending jolts of heat through her.

"Please. Now."

He covered her body with his as she grabbed his cock and guided him to her, crying out as he slipped inside. She felt more than physical pleasure. She was open to him, body and soul, and, in that moment, a kind of terror overtook her.

He must have sensed her panic because he whispered, "Trust me."

Could she? Did she have a choice?

She felt herself settle into the rhythm of lovemaking, her hips moving with his, her need for orgasm spiralling out of control. Conscious thought fled, driven out by the hot, greedy desire created by the friction of his cock moving in and out of her.

He reached between them, pressing his fingers over her clit, giving her the extra jolt of stimulation that triggered her first spasm of release. As she reached the peak of sensation, he followed her, his hot semen pumping into her.

She heard his shout of satisfaction. Heard herself cry out in wonder as the pleasure of it went on and on.

When it was over, he cradled her against himself, holding her tenderly as she struggled to absorb the wonder of their lovemaking. Reaching to stroke damp hair back from his forehead, she was caught by an incredible feeling of closeness that she had never experienced before. Yet she knew so little about him.

They lay together for long moments, until she finally broke the silence.

"That was . . . more . . ." Words failed her, but he seemed to know what she meant.

"Yes, it was."

"I don't even know where you live," she murmured.

He laughed. "I guess we should have exchanged some information first. I'm from Maryland. Not too far from you. And I had to come all this way to find you."

She blinked. "How do you know where I live?"

"I looked you up, after I found out your name. It turned into an obsession. Maybe you didn't see me around because I was in the business centre on the computers, finding out everything I could about you. I know you went to high school in Bethesda. I know your political affiliation. You're a physician who works for a drug company. You own your own home. Your parents are in Florida. You're in the middle of a big project, but you needed to get away."

She laughed softly. "I guess I should have been doing the same thing."

"You wouldn't have found much. I try to keep a low profile. I live in rural Howard County. I'm an environmental advocate. And I lead some wilderness expeditions when I want to get away."

"You researched me. Did you find out something you didn't like? Is that why you kept avoiding me?" she forced herself to ask, because that was the most logical conclusion.

He stroked his hand down her arm. "Not at all. I was trying to avoid my destiny."

"Which is?"

"You."

She stared at him, trying to figure that out. "What do you mean?"

"I know you felt the power of our making love."

She nodded. "I felt it. What does it mean?"

"That you belong to me."

The matter of fact way he said it sent a cold chill skittering over her skin, and she shivered.

"You're sounding like a caveman or something," she said, wondering what she had gotten into. They'd run away from a massacre and ended up in each other's arms. She wasn't the kind of woman who fell into bed with a man she hardly knew, yet they'd done it, and now she was thinking she'd made a reckless mistake.

"Or something." He rolled to his back, staring at the thatched ceiling of the hut.

"I think you'd better explain."

"I'm working my way up to it."

The flat tone of his voice didn't help the situation. And since they'd started the conversation, she didn't feel quite so cosy with him in bed. After shrugging into her bikini top, she grabbed her shorts and wiggled into them. He stayed where he was, watching her dress.

"You're not going anywhere," he said.

He was right, of course. They'd run from danger, and the situation back at the resort hadn't changed, as far as she knew.

"Tell me what's going on with you."

"It's something that happens to the men in my family."

She was about to speak, when he suddenly sat up.

"Christ," he whispered.

"What?"

"Someone's tracked us here."

To confirm the statement, she heard harsh voices approaching. Men speaking in Spanish.

He glanced towards the shelves along the wall. "There's an axe handle. Use it to defend yourself if you have to." He might have added, "If you can." As he spoke, he leaped from the bed and faced the door. Naked. He didn't even reach for his pants, only stood with his muscles tense.

Then something happened that made goosebumps rise on her arms. He began to chant words that sounded ancient and, as she watched, his body went through a rapid change. Fur began to spring up on his skin. A tail grew from the crack above his ass. His entire shape transmuted so that in seconds he was no longer a man but . . . a wolf.

As she sat there in shock, she realized she had seen the animal before – when the gunman had come after her. A large dog or a wolf had sprung towards him, taking him down before he could catch up with her.

Now it was happening again. Only she was watching in horrible fascination as Zack Marshall changed from man to beast. She had just made love with him. And now . . . She couldn't allow herself to finish the thought.

Too shocked to turn away, she watched as he came down on all fours and sprang through the door, streaking away, leaving her alone in the hut.

Seconds later, two armed men came towards her, their guns in shooting position.

As she pressed back into the shadows, she saw the wolf reappear, this time behind the two men. With a mighty leap, he took both of them down, and they screamed as they hit the ground. Her heart blocking her windpipe, she watched the fight, knowing that Zack was in serious danger. He could have run into the jungle and escaped. Instead, he had stayed – to save her.

He might be a . . . She couldn't say it. Not even in her mind. But she knew he could have abandoned her. Instead he was putting up a tremendous fight, against two armed men. He bit the gun hand of one, clawed at the other. She couldn't let the uneven fight go on.

But what could she do?

Running to the shelves, she grabbed the axe handle he'd mentioned. Too bad it wasn't the whole axe.

Without giving herself time to think, she sprinted out the door, into the heart of the fight. Swinging the handle like a club, she brought it down on the head of one man, hearing a satisfying clunk as it connected with flesh and bone. The man went limp, and she hit him again for good measure. The wolf and the other gunman were still fighting. She would have snatched up the machine gun if she'd known how to use it. Or if she'd been sure she could hit the man and not the wolf. Instead she was forced to step back and wait for an opening to clobber the man, but the wolf was on top of him, growling and snarling. She heard teeth crunch through bone, and then the assailant went still.

The wolf raised his head, looking at her, and their eyes met. All at once, she was too stunned to speak. Stunned by the wolf and stunned by what she had done.

He took a few steps away from her. As she watched, he reversed the process. In seconds, Zack Marshall was standing in front of her.

"You could have gotten hurt," he said.

"So could you," she shot back.

She was still in shock from seeing him change. But that hadn't stopped her from rushing into the fight without thinking – to save him.

Naked, he knelt down and searched the pockets of the nearest man and pulled out a cell phone. "Let's see if I remember the emergency number," he said as he pressed buttons. Punching in a number, he waited for someone to pick up. "This is a guest at El Sol y Enrolla Resort," he said when someone answered. "The resort's been attacked by men armed with machine guns." He listened for a moment then said, "No, I don't know who the hell they are. I managed to disable one of them and take his cell phone. A number of guests and staff are dead. We need help." He waited for an answer, then hung up. "The national police already got several calls from guests. They're on the way," he said, then walked past Jenna.

She followed him into the hut, watching him pull on his pants, then his shirt. Her mouth was almost too dry to speak, but she tried. "You . . ."

"I'm a werewolf," he said, voicing what she hadn't been able to get out of her mouth. "I guess that turned out to be convenient, under the circumstances."

She nodded. "You should have told me."

Turning to face her, he gave a harsh laugh. "You think that's a conversation I have with a woman before we make love?"

"I guess not."

"Until now, none of them has found out because it wasn't important to them."

"But I did, because we were attacked."

"You would have found out anyway." He lifted one shoulder. "I told you I came to San Marcos to outrun my destiny. And I found you here."

"Your destiny?" she asked, still grappling with everything that had happened. It was too much to take in. All of it.

"Around the age of thirty, the men in my family are compelled to look for a mate. When they find her, they bond. Wolves mate for life," he said in a flat voice.

"What if I don't want to . . . mate with you for life? What if I was just looking for a holiday fling?"

His face contorted. "I hope that's not true. I knew as soon as I saw you . . ." He stopped and started again. "I think you're my life mate now."

He was about to say something else, when the sound of gunfire split the air.

Zack leaped forwards, grabbed Jenna, and threw her down to the surface of the bed, covering her body with his.

She felt his warmth. The protective way he covered her. He was shielding her with his body. And something inside her seemed to break apart. He'd told her she was tied to him. Was that really true? Could she walk away from him? Or would that be as bad as death? The notion was absurd. She'd just met him. She'd made love to him once. Yet as they lay together on the bed, she couldn't stop herself from wondering if they truly were bound together.

The gunfire went on for a long time, and she guessed that government troops had landed on the island and were fighting it out with the gunmen.

Finally, there was a long silence.

"What do we do now?" she whispered.

"Wait until we know it's safe."

"How will we know?"

"A wolf could investigate."

She grabbed his arm. "No! It's too dangerous. One of the soldiers could shoot you."

"Would you care?" he asked in a gritty voice.

"Of course I'd care!"

He turned towards her, and she saw the strained look on his face, knowing that what she'd just said meant a lot to him. How much did it mean to her? He'd said she was his life mate. And she'd been too shocked and frightened to deal with that reality.

She was about to speak when a blaring sound startled her. "What?"

In the next moment, she realized it was a loudspeaker.

"This is *Capitán* José Mendoza of the San Marcos military. We have secured the resort. If you are hiding in the hotel or on the grounds, it is safe to come out," a man's voice boomed out.

"Is it a trick?" Jenna asked.

"I don't know. Stay here while I go find out."

"No!"

He looked angry.

"What? You expect your . . . mate to obey you?" She'd said it without thinking. Was she his mate?

"You are precious to me," he answered, emotion lacing his voice.

When he started slowly back towards the resort, she followed. At the edge of the jungle, they both stopped.

On the lawn, they could see armed men, but these men looked different. They were wearing camouflage uniforms.

"Stay here," Zack growled, and this time she recognized an order.

"We're American citizens coming in from the jungle," he called.

Immediately, the man turned towards them. "Hands on your heads."

Jenna stared at Zack. "Why?"

"They don't know we're OK. But it's going to be all right." He put his hands on his head and stepped from the shelter of the trees. Struggling to hold herself steady, Jenna did the same.

Twilight was falling, which was probably a blessing, because she could make out the bodies of the people she'd seen earlier on the beach.

Another soldier with a gun approached them and patted them down. "Do you have your passports?" he asked in heavily accented English.

"In my room," Jenna said.

"Mine also," Zack said.

"Which room is that?"

"We weren't staying together," she answered.

"You're together now."

"Mr Marshall . . ." She started to say that he'd killed one of the armed men, but it was the wolf who'd done it. She finished, "Saved my life by taking me into the jungle."

"You encountered some of the rebels?"

"I hid from them as they came up from the beach."

"We're both pretty shook up," Zack said. "We'd like to collect our stuff and get out of here."

They both gave their room numbers.

"I'm sorry. There's . . . carnage in the lobby," the soldier said. "You'll have to wait outside."

"How many dead?" Zack asked.

"Thirty-two guests. So far. There may be more. And ten rebels."

Jenna closed her eyes for a moment. She would have been among the dead if Zack hadn't come along.

The soldier led them to a patio area where other hotel guests sat in deckchairs looking shell-shocked.

A middle-aged man dressed in a rumpled flowered shirt and green pants glanced up as they also found chairs among the group. "What happened to you?"

"We hid in the jungle," Zack said.

"We barricaded ourselves in our room," he replied, putting his arm around a woman whose dyed red hair needed a good brushing. "The soldiers got here in time."

Others chimed in. It seemed that the guests who had been in their rooms were the ones who survived. Except for Jenna and Zack.

The officer came back with their passports. "We're evacuating everyone to the mainland," he said. "Your bags will be packed and sent to you later. Your rooms will be paid for by the government."

She didn't love leaving her belongings, but she could see there was no point in arguing about it.

Twenty minutes later they were on a helicopter for a short ride to the capital, Santa Isabella. The flight back was noisy. She sat next to Zack saying nothing, trying to work her way through everything that had happened.

They were driven to an upscale hotel where they got in line at the registration desk. Knowing that everyone was staring at the refugees from the massacre, she kept her gaze straight ahead. When the clerk asked if she was registering alone, she turned and looked at Zack.

"Señor Marshall and I are together," she said.

She saw a wealth of emotions flood across his face, but this was obviously not the time for a private discussion.

When the door of their room had closed behind her, he asked, "Did you change your mind about . . . us?"

She swallowed hard. "I don't know," she answered honestly. "I think I need to find out."

He went very still as he stared down at her. In the dimly lit hallway of the room, she raised her hand, touching his face, then his lips, tracing their outline, marvelling at their softness. Just that one touch flooded her with physical sensation and emotion she'd been holding in check since they'd returned to the resort.

His mouth opened, so that his strong white teeth could worry her fingertips, sending heat through her body. He moved her hand, and his lips came down on hers. This time she wasn't as frantic as before. She could let herself enjoy the taste of him, the feel of him against the length of her body.

She spoke against his lips, nibbling the words. "Show me how it is for your life mate."

He gathered her to him, rocking with her as they kissed and stroked each other, each touch, each kiss building the incredible sensual pleasure between them.

His hands shook as they worked to pull off her shirt, then her bikini top, and she helped him with her skirt before tackling his jeans and knit shirt.

Finally, after what felt like an eternity, they were both naked, still standing near the door.

When he bent to press his face against her breasts, turning his head first one way and then the other, she stroked her fingers through his hair and held him to her. He found one hardened nipple with his mouth, teasing her with his tongue, wringing a glad cry from her, then another as he began to draw on her.

She could feel his cock, hard and swollen, pressing against her middle.

"I suggest we get horizontal," he murmured.

They staggered together down the hall, where he ripped back the covers and took her down to the surface of the bed.

With sighs and sounds of pleasure, they rocked together, touching, stroking, kissing.

She had thought the first time with him had been good. Incredibly, this was better. Because she understood something that he'd tried to tell her. She belonged to him, heart, mind and soul.

His hand slid along the curve of her hip, trailing fire down her body. The fire flamed higher as his fingers dipped into the hot, slick core of her.

He took a leisurely trip from her vagina to her clit, teasing her there before pressing two fingers inside her. Moving between her knees, he lowered his face to her, his fingers still working in and out of her vagina as he lapped at her with his lips and tongue, circling her clit, then sliding into her swollen folds.

"You're going to make me come," she panted.

He raised his head far enough to say, "That's the idea."

"Not yet."

She slid away from him, then angled her body so that she could capture the hard, distended shaft of his cock with her mouth. Closing her lips around him, she sucked on him strongly as she slid her head back and forth.

He gasped, his fingers digging into her shoulder.

With his cock in her mouth, she could feel the tremors quivering along his length and judge her effect on him. Stopping before she pushed him over the edge, she lay back on the bed and held out her arms.

He covered her body with his, his eyes never leaving hers as he entered her slowly, inch by erotic inch, the joining a confirmation of the words he'd spoken earlier. She belonged to him.

"Zack. Oh, Zack," she breathed, her arms circling his shoulders with a possessiveness she had never known before.

When he began to move inside her, she matched his rhythm. She wanted the pleasure to last, but she knew the intensity was too great for that. She felt her inner muscles contract around him, heard herself call out his name once more. Then he was gripping her shoulders, pumping himself into her, his whole body shuddering. She felt the power of their climax, like no other in her lifetime, felt ecstasy wash over her.

Afterwards he held her in his arms, both of them gasping for breath. And she silently admitted what she'd known since they'd made love in the jungle. The bond between them was impossible to deny.

"I said it wrong," he whispered.

"What?"

"I said you belong to me. I should have said, I belong to you."

She raised her head, her eyes meeting his. "I think it's mutual. But . . . the wolf part is kind of scary."

"I know. I'm sorry. And you didn't exactly find out the easy way."

She nodded against his shoulder.

"I was trying to tell you when those gunmen closed in on us, and I had to change."

"I know."

"I think it may help to talk to some of the other life mates. It used to be that all of the guys were the head of their own pack. But we've learned to get along together. The women are a big part of that."

"Yes, I'd like to meet them."

"They'll all welcome you into the family, but I'd like to be alone with you for a few more days. First."

She nodded again She wanted that too, wanted more of the incredible feeling of belonging to this man, body and soul. He'd excited her from the first moment she'd seen him. She hadn't guessed what he would mean to her. But how could she? This was a situation so unique that she never could have dreamed it up.

He climbed off the bed to find the covers he'd tossed on the floor. After tenderly covering her, he settled down beside her again. Closing her eyes, she snuggled against him, thinking that she hadn't realized there was something basic missing from her world. She'd focused on her work. Now everything was different. Lucky for her she'd been brave enough not to run away.

"If you'd taken off, I would have followed you," he growled.

She raised her head and looked at him, just a bit warily. "You read minds, too?"

"No. But it's not hard to imagine what's circling through your head. Remember, I was the one who was trying to run away – from you."

"Lucky for me you were there when I needed you."

He gathered her to him, stroking his lips against her cheek. "Lucky for both of us. I think we should celebrate."

"What do you have in mind?"

He answered with a wolfish laugh, and she held him tight, thankful that she had found this incredible man to share the rest of her life.

Carnal Craving

Charlotte Stein

One

There is a man standing in the corner of this loud and seething place, staring at me. He doesn't think I know it, not while my back is turned and I'm so enthralled by the fat blue vein pulsing in the thick neck of the bartender not two feet from me.

But he's wrong. I can feel his gaze as surely as I'd feel his hand on my back. I can even guess the colour of his eyes without turning: a deep blue, like the ocean far out and beneath a storm coming in sky.

It's strange that he's looking, I know – even with my extra layer of allure. Men these days like the waifish, sad-eyed pretty little things, I hear. I've seen them on the covers of magazines and in films with lots of flesh exposed. Men do not like black-haired, short, square-shouldered girls, with sharp cruel eyes and thick hips and stomachs.

And I'm certain that men do not like girls who gorge themselves on blood and then lie fat and lazy in their beds, satisfied by things they cannot always provide.

He's no doubt staring because I am odd. I turn around just to see if my own oddness is reflected in his stormy ocean eyes, or in the way he'll perhaps glance over to something else to show his contempt for me. But when I finally winkle him out amongst the dancing writhing crowd, he holds my gaze admirably.

His eyes are as I thought they would be. But there's none of my oddness reflected in them. Instead his gaze lies open and exposed, like a man baring his throat up to my blade. It's an arresting expression, though I'm certain he doesn't know he's giving it. Perhaps it is only about the rest of the way he looks, that makes me think he looks so laid bare.

He has a dimple in his chin, the way that Tommy did. It isn't much of a dimple, really – it's the kind of thing that only shows when a man turns his head one way or the other. It looks like someone pressed their finger there too long. But it's enough to make a face more interesting, if he has that dull sort of handsomeness that some men do.

I don't think this man is dully handsome. I assess him flatly in a way that obviously disconcerts. He clearly does not expect me to keep staring back at him as boldly as he is staring at me – girls who aren't like those in the magazines are not allowed to stare back. I think they are meant to be invisible in some way – in sexual terms, at least.

Though I hardly know what sexual terms are. I hear it is all about dressing with lots of flesh on show as some of these girls have, and adorning your face with colour, and keeping your shape very lean. The whole process sounds very boring and arbitrary to me and not half as fun as thralling a man into doing whatever you want him to, but I'm sure it must be important when choosing a mate. Perhaps they need their bodies to fit together in a certain way, and one being lean and the other fat precludes this.

Though I have seen many a fleshy man with a slender woman.

This man is sort of fleshy. He seems to be very there in a way that the other men are not, but perhaps that is only because unlike most of them, he is wearing very tight clothes. They cling to his strange shape – his rounded bottom and his fleshy chest. He is lean, but he is also not lean.

He seems very casual, too. He is not posing in silks as some of them do, tops with names on them and trainers with lots of colour. His top his grey and his jeans are black. His jacket is black, too, and he has small flat trainers.

I like his awkwardness – the same awkwardness that Tommy had. He looks as though he doesn't know what to do with himself, here. He looks as though he isn't a part of this.

For a moment I think: vampire. But then the worry recedes – he isn't at all. He's tenderly, obviously human, tall and masculine but with a thread of such exposure running through him that my mouth actually floods with juice. There is something weak and strong inside him, and it makes me hungry.

His gaze flicks away, so suddenly nervous, so completely caught. He licks his lips, bites one of them, then can't stop himself flicking his gaze back. It is such an odd little dance he does that for a moment another wild thought occurs to me: he knows. But such a thing seems impossible; they never know. Not even when they see it.

When he flutters a smile at me, I imagine his blood running down his ivory throat.

It is enough to make me turn away and close a fist down inside myself. I demand my control to come back and wonder at the same time how I lost it so quickly. All that separates me from the ferals and their ilk is this control, and for a moment it abandoned me altogether! And though I can hardly call it the first time this has happened, it's the first time it has happened so strangely.

Just a man looking at me across the bar. With Tommy, it took more. He had to smile a certain way and pursue me like a silly fly and then—

I try to think of higher, more controlling, more calming thoughts, as the music changes. Now it's this coming and going tremulous beat, this beat that says clearly that something is getting close. It isn't a dancing sort of song, and it isn't a slow song, and it lulls them all just the same. It prowls, this song.

I look back at the man and he seems caught, again. I have caught him staring a second time, and he is made uncomfortable by this. Rueful too, perhaps. And then his eyes trail all over me, not rudely but with a hint of unable-to-stop-himself, and I think: You've brought this end to yourself, boy.

He doesn't know it, however. He just follows me when I walk right out of this club, oblivious. Like a good but stupid animal, led to the block. I barely even need to put a leash on him. He gives himself to me of his own free will.

Outside, it's freezing cold. Of course I don't feel it, but it's clear he does. All his blood rushes to the middle of his body, and I can see his nipples peaking beneath the thin stretch of his top. His breath blooms out in the frosty air and I poke out my tongue to taste the moisture in it – like sugar treats and sizzling fat.

Very nice indeed.

He takes my tongue sticking out as something else altogether, however. He laughs, and tries to grab it – playfully, I think. But I give him a little shove, just to offer him a hint of what lurks beneath this nothing-looking outer layer.

His eyes widen. Not for long, though. He recovers himself soon enough, and asks me my name.

I gaze at him over my shoulder in response, steely-eyed, my thick dark hair like a veil cutting across the side of my face.

"I'm Nick, by the way," he says. "Pleased to make your acquaintance." He even sticks his hand out for me – to shake, I believe – though I think he's laughing as he does it. There is something of a joke in all of this, even if I don't know quite what it is.

Usually it's the other way around: the joke's on you, boy. But somehow I don't think so, here, and, unaccountably, that makes a trickle of disquiet ease its way down my spine. I make a fist of control inside myself and squeeze hard, but the disquiet doesn't go away.

Odd, that a mere human boy should make me feel this way. And with nothing at all, really. Just his name, and his hand reaching for me.

His hand reaches for me again as we begin to slide between the glistening cars in the car park. This time, it doesn't ask for my hand. His fingers graze my bare shoulder, instead. Along the line of the material, where it's slid down.

"That's a gorgeous dress," he says, and suddenly I can smell him everywhere, very close. His smell is alien, somehow, and it pushes that unease up a notch. What does he mean about my dress? It isn't a dress at all, but a man's black jumper that I stole from a particularly tasty specimen. It hangs off me oddly, sometimes baring one shoulder. Sometimes riding up quite high on my thighs. I don't think it is flattering, in the way human men prefer. I think it makes me look odd and short and as plump as his lower lip.

When I stop and lean against a metallic blue car on the very outer reaches of the car park, he squeezes right in, in front of me. His breathing is hard and shaky, but maybe that's from having to keep up with me. I could run four times as fast as him without breaking a sweat, though I suspect it looks the other way around, for many people – him included.

I'm sure he thinks he has the upper hand. He doesn't, but it nags at me that I still don't know why he followed me, unbidden.

"Aren't you going to tell me your name?" he asks. "Or is this a no names sort of thing? Did I make a grievous error telling you mine?"

I haven't a clue what he's talking about, but oh I like his voice. He's . . . Australian, I believe it is. His voice lies back as relaxed as anything and just . . . takes it. That's it, I think at him. Just lie back and take it.

Though I must admit, sometimes I like it when they struggle.

"So what now?" he asks – cocky, I think. Hands on hips, jacket pushed back to show off his body to its best advantage. It's almost as though he knows and wants me to bite him.

Of course I've heard of such things: vampire groupies. Vampire wannabes. And yet there's not even a lick of fear in him, of the kind he should be feeling if he knows. There's excitement in his sweat and his heart is pounding, but no spike of terror.

Curiosity thrills through me. "Why don't you tell me?" I ask.

He raises an eyebrow. "Really? Wouldn't have thought you were that kind of chick."

"And what kind of chick do I look like?"

His eyes slide all over me, again. This time without nerves. "Like the kind who tells me what to do, not the other way around."

"How perceptive of you."

His heat swamps me. The contrast between his vibrantly alive body and the cold night air is overwhelming, as is the knowledge of where all of his blood is going. It isn't to the middle of his body, any more. I believe I have misjudged this situation, quite badly.

"So are you going to order me to kiss you, or do I have to just make it happen?"

I don't answer. I'm not sure what I would say, even if I could speak. Of course, I've kissed a man before. I've kissed many men. But I've never done it mouth to mouth.

What would be the point?

He leans down slow, slow, and I follow his every tiny movement with my eyes. Anything sudden and unexpected, and I'll fell him quicker than he can blink.

Though really, all of this is sudden and unexpected. It occurs to me, over and over: I haven't thralled him. He's doing this because he wants to. Because he wants to put his mouth to my mouth, and press his body close to me.

He tries to before he kisses me – move in close, I mean – but I place an iron hand on his chest. I only let him lower his face to mine, and watch him closely all the while. Unfortunately, I think he appreciates the eye contact. Maybe it's the sort of thing human men like, staring and car parks and strange liaisons.

But either way, a pulse is throbbing in his groin. His prick is stiff – I know it without looking or feeling. I can feel it anyway, hot and full and pressing its presence against me through the space between us.

I've felt something like it, before. Sometimes when they're thralled and dopey, and I bite them, their cocks swell. Like a reflex.

His kiss is not like a reflex. It is deliberate and careful, as though I might slap him if he gets it wrong. And maybe I will. Maybe I won't let him ease his mouth over mine, as hot and wet as blood fresh from a vein. Maybe I won't let him brush his tongue over my lips in a soft slippery stroke that makes me want to part them.

What does a tongue penetrating your mouth feel like, exactly?

Like this, like this. Oh Lord, so warm and insistent. I follow his movements – it isn't hard, really – and he grows more excited, more urgent. His wet mouth slants over mine, pushing me and pushing me until his tongue is thrusting into my mouth and his taste is filling me up – that delicious meatiness, the sweet musky tang of him.

It's almost like feeding. I can feel myself falling into that dark place, and soon his working mouth and slippery tongue are going to encounter more than just my soft acquiescence.

But then he pulls away before I can show him where I'm sharp, and burns his mouth over my jaw and throat. He murmurs words about my hotness, my sexiness, how he can't wait to run his hands all over me.

He's lying, however. He can wait. He just chooses not to.

Before I've even had chance to gather myself, he has his big hands on my waist, on my hips. I try to think where my iron hand has gone, but there's so little consideration beyond the feel of his mouth against the turn of my throat. Almost as though he's going to bite me.

I don't respond as I'm sure I should. The correct response to a vampire trying to mark you is to bite back, to snarl and buck and fight. But Nick is not a vampire, and so I'm not quite sure what to do. He isn't going to bite me – it only seems that way. This is a different sort of ritual altogether, and I'm not sure of the rules.

Or even if I want to follow them. At the moment, my body is following them for me, lying limp in his arms and wallowing in the warmth that spreads through me when he licks my throat. I wonder if this is what it feels like to be thralled, though I hardly think I'm that far gone into whatever this is.

Until his hand slides around and down my body, and roughly grabs a fistful of my arse. While I do nothing to stop him – not a single thing. I don't push him or wrench his face to the side, so that I can sink my still unsheathed teeth in. I just relish the tense press of his fingers into my copious flesh, the spark of almost pain and the thrill of his hunger.

I've never felt a human man be so hungry for me. He's rubbing his stiff prick against my belly, over and over. It's like being branded – that's how hot it feels – and the blood that has made his sex so swollen calls to me, constantly.

My own sex blooms and spreads, in answer. I know it does, as shocking as such a thought may be. I can't remember the last time my body succumbed to something like sexual desire, but that's the way he's pushing things and it also seems to be a place I'm willing to be taken.

When he rubs up against me and groans deep and long into my throat, I spread my legs for him readily.

He senses the change in me as I would sense a change in my prey. I'm no longer ready to run or deny him, and so he becomes bolder. He pushes me hard against the chill metal of the car behind, and lets the hand that has a hold on my arse trail around my body, to the thin gap in between us.

Of course I know what he's going for. The pulse that beats between my legs quickens for the feel of his hand, which is ruffling up the material of this thing I'm wearing. His skin is hot against my bare thigh, sliding smooth and sure along the tender inside as his left hand runs up my body to the other things I've long had no use for.

To my breasts, now these heavy and full things with searing hot tips, eager to push into his grasp. If he keeps on this way, I'm going to die. I will die, as surely as if he'd put an axe to my neck. Forced me to swallow silver. Doused me in garlic-riddled water.

Is this what it's supposed to feel like? I can hardly remember. I remember Tommy, but by God that was fifty years ago. More. And Tommy was different, special, he craved me in the same way I crave blood.

"You're so gorgeous," this young buck says, but I don't understand him. I haven't understood humans for 100 years and I can't process the things they like. I'm shaking, I realize, though he hardly seems to mind.

"Jesus, you want it bad, huh?" he gasps into my flesh, and I wrestle against what he means – he means his cock in me. He intends to have me up against this stupid thing that humans drive around in, and force me down deeper into the sensations that just his hands on my breasts and my thighs are provoking. I can feel my sex growing wet and ready to take him, my nipples stiffening beneath his sure caress. He fondles my breasts and then pulls his hand ever outwards, to catch the tip in an agonizing tug.

And oh God, the blood thrumming in his stiff prick. It's deafening. I'm going mad. His fingertips are stroking over the slippery seam of my cunt, and he's exclaiming in his strange innocent-sounding laid-back voice that he can't believe I'm not wearing any underwear, that's so hot, he wants me so bad . . .

I slam him back up against the car behind him. Hard enough to shock. He looks startled, though not enough to bring him out of this lust-addled mess he seems to have fallen into. His cock makes a firm triangle out of the material of his jeans – ridiculous. This is all ridiculous, and yet while his hands are still up in the air – the way people do, when they're about to be arrested by the police – I reach for the buttons on his jeans. I rip them open.

Now, I am in control. I am in control and I'm going to taste that maddening flesh.

He does not in any way complain. Quite the contrary. He urges me on. He asks me incredulously if that's what I'm going to do – suck his cock? And then he turns it into a kind of rough command that only makes these boiling sensations inside me stronger: *God, suck me off*.

I know what he means. He means to have me kneel on the floor and take his prick in my mouth, and then suck and lick and handle him until he spends over my tongue. I've seen it done. I've performed the act myself, when Tommy was fit to bursting and unable to understand what was happening to him.

I did it then, though I can hardly remember what it was like. And I'm sure I'm not about to do such a thing for him, now, here. I only what to sink my teeth into the stiff flesh he has there and drink deep. I do.

I think so even as I sink to my knees before him, and quiver all over to see him shove his jeans to his thighs.

"Oh, man," he says. "This is the hottest thing I've ever done."

He isn't lying. I think, perhaps, that he is not the sort of man who ruts vacantly with any girl who crosses his path. I think he has barely done this kind of thing before in his lifetime, though I should say to him that he doesn't know the half of it.

I don't believe I have ever knelt before any man. And I cannot say what it is about him that makes him so worthy.

He looks delicious, stood above me. Tall and solid, ivory-skinned, wet lips parted. It's starting to rain, a little, and it mists in his softly curled hair. And then there's the thing between his legs. With his black jeans shoved down the way they are, his prick seems framed.

I think it might be deserving of such. It's thick – much thicker than most human men, I know – and longer too besides. He looks pleased with himself, but I can't begrudge him that. The colour of it – as pale as milk – and the sense of its seething core, and the heft of it – all delight even me. The silky skin that wraps that core hugs close right to the very tip, which lies exposed and blood red, like a little secret heart.

Liquid glistens there, tempting me. His already curving prick jerks upwards, eager for my mouth, but he doesn't try to force me. He doesn't grab the back of my neck, as I would do to him.

I admire his patience. Especially when it's employed out here, where anyone could catch us at any moment. That would be embarrassing for most humans, wouldn't it? Shameful and shocking, to be caught with your cock in some woman's mouth.

Still, he makes a very loud noise when I lick away the tiny bead of liquid that's just welling from the slit at the tip. He gasps as though I've bitten him; bliss floods my body.

I had forgotten. It's as good as blood. I had forgotten.

I swallow him down quickly, then. I take the whole of him into my mouth and he groans again, desperate this time. Desperate but grateful, I think. He tells me tales about his gratitude with lovely words that vibrate through me, just as the taste of his flesh does.

"Oh, good girl," he says.

I have no idea why I like him saying such a thing, but I do anyway and, oh, the heat in him. The thrum of his blood, just below such a paper-thin surface. Such fine silken skin, sliding underneath my tongue and then my hands, too.

Of course, I move according to my own hunger and pleasure. I lap at that little slit because it gives me the liquid, and I suck hard on the swollen head because it makes him produce more. When I rub him, too, when I rub and suck and lick him all at the same time – it means that he bucks and spurts little thin trickles on to my tongue.

It's a fortunate coincidence that what I want and like best is also apparently what he wants and likes best. I know, because I can hear his heart rate going up and smell all the hormones surging through his body and his hands are clenching at his sides.

And because his breath comes out of him in harsh splitting-into-groans sorts of ways, and in between he says things like: *Ah, that's perfect, Jesus you've got a sweet mouth. Oh keep doing that, keep doing that, just like that, baby, don't stop, don't stop.*

I could feast on such broken words. I do feast on them. They fill my body up with a humming pleasure, a sweet ache that I've gone years without feeling. And when he tells me that he's going to come, the sweet ache builds up and mingles with all of this heated excitement – I'm going to taste him, really taste him.

He grunts thickly just before he spends in my mouth. He tells me that it's going to happen and I should stop before he does it, but what would be the point of all this work if I didn't get my reward? I suck harder on him, and flick my tongue against all the slippery places I can tell he likes.

In response, he thrusts deep and hard into my mouth. His prick swells and all the pounding and rushing and swirling going on inside him centres in his groin and his tightly drawn-up balls and his trembling thighs. I can almost feel what he feels, as he spurts thick streamers of come into my mouth.

At the last second he tries to get away – I know how humans fret about disease and so on, but he has no worry here – and I hold him fast with one hand on his jerking cock and the other on his thigh. I get all of him, all that lovely cream, tasting exactly like he does – only sweeter, more concentrated.

My senses reel. I grasp at him tighter because I'm so hungry for more, but it isn't like blood. Soon it's all gone and I'm left empty and fizzing, loving the tender feeling of his prick softening in my mouth but angry at the way he tries to prise me away.

I'm going to bite him, now, and get my fill. I even stand up to do it as he tucks himself back inside those black jeans, and looks at me all sort of shamefaced and bashful. What does he have to be shame-faced and bashful about? He's a stupid sort of creature, a wretched little beast. I should have stamped him out immediately beneath my boot heel.

But then, most shocking of all, he grabs hold of me. Just like that, as my eyes are on the verge of turning and my teeth are ready to come out for him. He buries his face in my hair and . . . and sort of nuzzles my neck.

I think this is cuddling. Though I cannot be sure. I don't think humans usually cuddle after illicit car park liaisons.

"Mmpf, that was fucking fantastic," he says. The little sound he makes at the start is very hard to describe. A kind of relaxed, delighted, falling down sort of sound.

It takes me a moment to gather myself, and realize that he's rubbing his hands up and down my back. He's rubbing them, and it doesn't feel at all unpleasant.

"You're so sexy, God you're sexy," he says.

I think he may be mad. But either way, I have no idea what to do. Bite, my body says. Bite now, while he's in this languorous stupor. Even though I'm not the sort of vampire who needs to wait for a stupor. I could smash him against the nearest car bonnet at the height of his powers, with all his faculties intact.

And yet I don't. In fact, after he has next spoken I pull away from him, angry. I step back, suddenly unsure of myself.

"You want me to repay the favour?" he asks.

It's just like with Tommy. I didn't know how to act then, either, and he wasn't half as bad as this. He didn't make me want to switch one pleasure for another. He just made me want, as I'm wanting now. I'm desperate for it, now.

"No," I snap at him. "No, you filthy creature."

And then I am gone. It is as though I was never there.

Two

I dream of Tommy. It is understandable. The taste in my mouth echoes events long over, and sweetness long dissolved. All of it still threads through my mind when I awake – Tommy's dark-blue eyes searing at me from his place, tied to my bed. Tommy begging me to help him, help him, God if only I would say what's happening to him.

I hadn't meant to turn him, you see. He remains the only human I have ever turned, and it was just an accident.

My face is wet. I don't know why. The apartment above isn't leaking and I haven't spilled anything on myself. It's very odd, but then all of this is very odd. Nick, and dreams of Tommy, and this rolling unsatisfied hunger in my belly.

Didn't I stop off at Hottingly Wood? Haven't I eaten my fill? A deer is almost as good as a human, in terms of the meal they provide.

And yet I'm pacing my apartment, wringing my hands. Trying to imagine what he, a human, might be thinking of me. Right now, is he thinking of what I did to him? There must have been something more in the way I look, the way I felt to his touch, that drew him in. Without the safety net of my thrall, I cannot fathom why he wanted me.

Or why I want more from him. I never want more from anyone. I have walked alone for so long that I can no longer see my grandmother's face, though I can still hear her voice: *Fear the things that lie in wait for you, in the forests of the night.*

As you can see, I didn't listen to her. And I don't listen to myself, now, as I go to the window and jump out into the night beyond.

It doesn't take me long to find him. I could find a grain of salt in a mountain of sugar. One measly human – as ripe with scents and flavours as they are – takes nothing at all.

He seems stunned to find me at his door, however.

He lives at the very top of a luxurious sort of apartment block – very modern, very likely to set my teeth on edge. I can hear and feel every single human in the place squeaking and squawking like rats in a labyrinth, going about their ridiculous lives with all the carelessness I've come to expect from them.

They think they're safe, with doormen and locks and security codes. But then the man at their gate took almost no thralling at all and even the best of them just opens his door to me.

I think he is the best of them. He looks stunned to see me, but he also appears . . . pleased. Grateful, even.

"It's you," he says.

There is something I admire in the simplicity of such words. They resonate through me, like words remembered from somewhere long ago. They make me feel like something important, even though that's a silly notion.

I am already something important – more so than he could ever know.

"How did you find me?"

Again, a layer exists beneath his words. I think he means something else. Or maybe he just means something else to me. I think of myself, answering: *I will always find you.*

"Were you under the illusion that you're some sort of master of concealment? Invite me in."

He doesn't have to do so, in order for me to enter his premises. But the old ways die hard, it seems. I want the words, freely given.

"You sound as though I'm going to turn you down. Believe me, Miss No-Name, I'm not going to turn you down. Come right on in."

He steps aside, and I cross the threshold.

His home is as I would expect, from someone who lives in a place like this. Furniture identical to every other moderately wealthy human, awash in a sea of not even knowing that he's no different to anyone else. Paintings with a flair that only a machine can provide, ornaments churned out by factories – I don't understand the need to keep things that mean nothing, absolutely nothing. I have books that have survived centuries. Trinkets that belonged to people long dead.

They seem to have only money and a love of everything bland. Though I suppose they barely have any time at all to accumulate anything of value.

"Would you like a coffee?" he asks.

Perhaps I was wrong about him, after all. I can't imagine, now, why he was worth coming for – coffee! Humans, and all their silly little rituals. Why by God do they need to sit together and drink something they don't really want?

I know he doesn't really want it. I can smell it on him – he's only just finished eating and drinking his evening meal.

And yet I tell him: "Sure."

He gives me this puzzled look that I think has to do with my choice of word, before darting into what I assume is his kitchen. While there he keeps up the talking, however. About how he never thought he'd see me again, and how he'd never done such a thing before, and that I should know how relieved he is to see me, in a lot of ways.

I close my eyes, and block out the soft tasteful glow of his apartment. I only hear his voice, as it spreads out into something beyond meaningless prattle.

"I mean, not just because we . . . and because you're . . ." There is a pause, a silence, and I drift right into it. "You're not like other people, are you?"

Oh, clever boy.

"There was something so dark about you – I haven't been able to stop thinking about it. Kind of like the poem, you know, she walks in beauty like the night, only the other way around. She walks in night like beauty. That sounds insane, right?"

He laughs. The laugh doesn't hold, however.

"It's weird, but usually when I'm with a girl I can't remember much about her, after we've split up. I have a ton of trouble with faces. But I got you completely right – when you turned up at my door, your face was exactly what I'd been picturing. I guess you're pretty distinctive looking, though, right? What are you, Eastern European? I want to say Norwegian, but aren't they more blonde than anything else?"

Whether they are or not, he's right. I shake with the power of his correct guess, and wonder at the same time if he is guessing at all.

"Either way, you should know – you're amazing looking. You seem real confident but kind of like you're not, at the same time, you know? Like you don't know how beautiful you are. But, Jeez, those eyes. Those eyes of yours make me weak-kneed."

It's the openness that reminds me of Tommy, I realize. Not just the way he looks, but the casual way he's willing to share himself in a way that other human men will not – not even when they're thralled.

No vampire can force someone to share their most secret selves, no matter how powerful they are. We cannot force someone to love, or admire, or do anything but follow our commands mindlessly.

When he comes out of the kitchen with two mugs in hand, the urge to turn him into a senseless puppet is strong. But then he lays those stormy sensuous eyes on me, and I am as helpless as I thought to make him. I am helpless.

He puts the mugs down, slowly – as though he knows. I am trying not to show it, but I think he knows it just the same.

"Come to me," he says, and it seems that I must obey. I walk across his glossy wooden floor to him and, as I do, I let the coat I am wearing slide from my shoulders. His eyes widen, but I'm the one who trembles.

I long to put my hands on him. I crave the smell and taste of his flesh, made as bare as I am now. However, he speaks next. In spite of his shock at my naked state, he keeps control of himself and commands me, again.

"Tell me your name."

I think I would disobey him, I do. If he didn't push his hand into the thick fall of my hair while speaking the words. I don't mind admitting: my eyes roll back in my head to feel his fingers draw rough over my scalp. Those same strange sensations roll over me and I cannot resist them.

"Ida," I say. It isn't even a lie. That is my real name, and he is the first to hear it for fifty years.

When I open my eyes I see him looking at me, though perhaps looking is the wrong word. He is watching me, intently, as he twines a rope of my hair around his fist. I try to think of the last human or vampire to look at me the way he is doing, and come up with no one. His eyes trickle over my face and my body in slow fluttering increments that make me weak.

Part of me wants to shove him back against a wall. But that part of me is easily subdued. He subdues it with his laid-back voice. His curling mouth that I want to devour.

"Did you walk all the way here without anything on underneath that leather?"

"Of course," I reply.

"That's pretty *9½ Weeks* of you."

I think he's mocking me. But as long as he keeps rubbing his fingers through the strands of my hair, I don't care.

"Think I might need more time than almost three months though, I've got to tell you."

I snap my gaze back up to him, as fierce as I can make it. He should at least know how large the fire he's playing with is, before it consumes him entirely.

I put a hand on his perfect face, fingers splayed, nails that are not quite razors almost pressing into his skin. Almost.

"How about eternity?" I ask.

He grins. It alters his face from something sultry, to that casual openness that lives in his words. "Anyone ever tell you that you're real theatrical?" he says.

So I give him something to applaud. I show him my strength, and yank his ear down to my lips with just that one hand on the side of his face. And then I whisper, I whisper, "Wait until the big reveal. It's a showstopper, I promise."

"More than being naked underneath your coat?" he asks, and then, oh then, he slides one hand over my back, bristling every nerve there as he goes.

"More than anything you've ever dreamed of," I sigh, though in truth it feels as though he may be the one with the revelations and the things to teach and the worlds I'd never dreamed of. I can feel the power in his stroking hands, and it opens me up.

I bare my neck for him, when he lowers his mouth to kiss it. His tongue flickers out, slick and soft and unbearable against my burning for him skin, and then when he bites . . . when he bites I think I fall. His teeth are only these little blunt things, but it doesn't seem to matter. They push pain and the desire to bite back right through me until I have to squeeze my eyes tight shut against it, and let his arms catch me.

He scoops me up and I can't do a thing about it, because I have to keep my face pressed into his shoulder. My eyes have changed, and for all my talk about the big reveal I don't want him to see just yet. Not before I've had my fill of whatever else my body hungers for.

I think he's going to give it to me. And my suspicion is confirmed when he lays me down on his crisp-sheeted bed in the middle of his golden glowing bedroom, and ghosts his hands the length of my body.

Hardly touching at all, but cleverly so. Such a teasing caress makes me open my eyes whether they've turned back to black or not, and then he puts on a show for me. He looks as though he knows it's going to be one, but I can't fault him for that. Not when he lifts his little clinging top off all in one motion, to reveal the solid body beneath. Not when his skin is the colour of those polished floors, pale and honeyed and sweet.

He is as fleshy as I suspected him to be, though firm at the same time. My mouth floods with juice when I think of such a body littered with the red bracelets of my bite marks, little pinpricks all over to add to the decoration. Blood streaking that perfect skin – ah, just the thought makes me desperate for it.

Though never more desperate than I am for his mouth on me, that swollen flesh between his legs, his body over mine. I lick my lips as he unfastens the buttons on his jeans. I stir impatiently on the sheets when he pushes the material down his long legs.

He isn't wearing any underwear, either. His prick stands up solid and straight, though I don't need it to tell me how aroused he is. His heart rate picked up when he first laid eyes on my body. The scent of his racing hormones fills me up.

I part my legs for him without having to be told or asked. That's what needs to be done – my legs need to be apart, and then he will come between them. I am aware of the mechanics of the thing, though before, with Tommy, I rode over him like a lady on her horse. He lay beneath me, squirming and tortured by his own confused desires.

Then, it was he who couldn't tell bloodlust from the other kind. The kind that is making my sex slippery and my nipples sharp little points.

When he puts a hand on my ankle and pulls me slowly down the bed towards him, I try to regain some control over myself.

Unfortunately, the feel of his firm grip and the teasing look in his smoky-with-lust eyes only sinks me deeper in the mire.

I spread for him without having to be told or asked. It seems as though I don't have to be told or asked anything, even though this is all near alien to me. And he knows it, it seems.

"You really crave it, huh?" he asks. Of course I don't answer. But then, I don't need to. He continues without a word from me. "Searching me out, coming all the way here, spreading your legs for me – yeah, I guess you really crave it. Question is, what do you want me to give you?"

Does he honestly expect me to tell him? He must understand that I have no idea. Though in truth, why would he? I must seem like one of those sluttish sorts of human women who wriggle about the clubs and bars with nothing on, sure of their power even when it exists as only a transient sort of thing.

He kisses my thigh, and I'm reminded what real power is.

"How have you done it?" I whisper, between the trembles that work their way through me at the feel of his wet mouth on my skin in so intimate a place.

He kisses again, higher up. This time I feel his tongue press a slick path all the way up to that neat line between my thigh and my groin. I spread wider for him, eager as a silly little wannabe.

"Done what?" he asks, though I think he knows. I reach out one shaking hand and touch the waves of his rich dark hair, the smooth beginnings of his cheek and jaw. He seems to delight in my faint touch – his eyes flicker almost closed.

"Gained this power over me."

But he doesn't understand. He only laughs, and pokes out his delicious pink tongue to lick another stripe over my burning skin.

"You have the prettiest little pussy I've ever seen," he says. "Maybe that's how you've gained power over me."

I frown, and look down at the object of his affection. It barely means anything to me – it is no longer the place from which I birth children. My mouth and my blood do that. It is not the seat of my pleasure, either, so that cannot be its allure.

Or at least, it could not have been its allure before he followed me to a deserted car park, on a rainy autumn night.

"What is so very pretty about it?" I ask.

He doesn't hesitate. "You don't know? There's nothing like a bare pussy. Especially not when it's so soft and plump and like a mouth. Just makes you want to kiss it. And look how wet you are – you're such a tough cookie and yet you're soaking and I can see how stiff and swollen your clit is. I bet you want me to lick it, right? I bet you're just gagging for me to lick it."

I have a vague idea of what he's talking about. Though my overriding concern is for the heat that's pulsing through my body, and the ache that's in my gums. I'm not going to make it to the end of whatever he is about to do.

And for one of the few times in my long life, I regret that. I regret what I am.

He is staring up at me, waiting. I think it is possible he wants me to beg. If so, he is going to be waiting a long time – and likely I will make him beg before he makes me, though for a different thing altogether.

It's lucky, really, that he has mercy on me. He spreads his big hands over my thighs, thumbs digging into a place I didn't even know was sensitive – those sweet hollows just before the swell of my sex – and then he simply leans forwards and licks the entire length of my slit.

I let my head go back, for that.

I clamp my teeth together against the rising ache in my gums, when he opens that slit up with the next swipe of his tongue. That little bead at the apex of my sex – he almost grazes it. Almost, but wretchedly not quite.

My back arches. My body is entirely not my own now, it seems.

"You like that?" he asks, before the next teasing lick. "You like my mouth on your pussy? Tell me you like it. Tell me you want me to lick and lick your clit until you come all over my face."

I do. I know what he means and I do want it. I want to rise up on a wave of pleasure like the one that comes when blood first bursts into my mouth. I think I remember it being more than that, however – so much more that it's now making me tense with expectation to think on it.

Can it have been? Why is it that I have forgotten such a thing?

Because Tommy is gone, I think, and then I arch again to feel his mouth on me. The hot gust of his breath and the teasing flick of his tongue and, oh please, just go on. Devour me, please.

When he finally licks my clit, I am not ashamed of the noise that comes out of me. It's a gasping sigh of the sort he offered me the night before, and he rewards me for it with another lap at that little bead. I can feel a pulse beating in it and the pulse gets faster and harder to ignore the more attention he pays it, until all my blood and every sensation in me seems centred right there.

I arch on the bed, twisting the sheets into angry knots with hands that are almost claws, clamping down hard on the ache in my gums but knowing I won't succeed. He is going to bring it out of me – and I know it even better when he finds my wet and grasping hole with two thick fingers, and pushes them into me.

Now his tongue lies flat over my clit, rubbing and working at me while his fingers thrust just as his prick might do. I can't recall if this is exactly how it feels to be filled by a man's sex, but I am sure it isn't far away. All this urgency, this pleasure.

And then he stops, and the pleasure is no more.

I snarl at him before I can stop myself, but he only sits back on his heels and looks down on me. Smug, I think. All human men are smug. I snarl again, and this time I don't want to stop myself.

He licks his gleaming lips, as he snatches his jeans up from the floor. Out of his pocket he takes a little square thing – one that I only understand when he strips it open and smoothes a disgusting layer of rubber over his delicious-smelling prick.

I almost stop him. I could thrall him, and stop him – he would forget all about getting me with child or catching diseases or whatever other sort of thing he's thinking of. But of course, there is one disease that I can give him, and though him tasting my cunt and fucking into me might not turn him . . .

It also might. It definitely will if I lose control and bite him in the middle of him being in me and feeling all of my liquid close around his bare flesh. With my taste still in his mouth. With my saliva in his body from having his cock in my mouth.

So I don't stop him.

"Jesus, I can't wait to be in that tight little pussy," he groans, and my hips jerk up to him. My body sobs with a desire I shouldn't feel. When he spreads himself over me, it's as though his heat fills me up before his prick does.

I strain towards my end.

"It's OK, it's OK, shhh," he says, as though calming me. And perhaps he is. His hand strokes over my hip before his prick slides into me and, when the very tip of him grazes my clit, that same hand keeps me still.

The idea of keeping him still sings through me. Oh, the things I could do with him. The pleasures I could show him, how I could train him – it wouldn't go wrong as it did with Tommy. I swear it wouldn't, only let me, let me!

I turn my face away from his eager open one, furious with him. Furious with him for tempting me.

But then he slides that solid length of red-hot heat into me, and I can't feel anything at all, pleasure aside. I gasp and for a second I am certain I have bared my teeth to him, that they're out and he can see them.

A second that soon dies, when he shoves in hard and lets his expression go slack with bliss.

He gets up on his arms over me, working in slow at first but quickly building to something more. Soon, his prick is surging in and out of me in a way I can barely process, his hips rolling against mine and his groans filling my ears.

His hands go all over me, here and there. His fingers skitter over the tight-pursed buds of my nipples, sometimes pinching, sometimes not. When he bends to lick one of them, I fight and squirm against him, desperate to escape these torturous sensations.

But he knows the real score.

"Do you like that?" he asks, but I can't answer. I have to control myself. I have to keep my eyes closed and not think about him jerking against me.

When his hand slides between our bodies to touch my little bud, I think water spills from my eyes.

"You do, don't you? Ah, look how wet you are," he says. "Tell me you want me – God, I want you. You feel so good, baby, so good."

I wish I could tell him how good he feels to me. So solid inside me, waking nerves I didn't realize I had. I cry out, and feel my cunt clench around his prick like a clamping mouth – and, oh, he likes that. Do that again, he begs me, before his expression and his voice are lost in pleasure.

He circles his finger quick on my clit. Tells me hurry, hurry.

He's going to spend, soon. He has no control – his hips are churning and his prick is swelling and he moans my name, over and over. But it's OK, because I have no control, either. When he opens those eyes I know what he's going to see – and I don't wish to hide it any more.

He can look his fill and then run, as his kind always do. I will let him run away, before this pleasure overwhelms me.

Though it washes over me strongly when he finally does open his eyes. I smell the fear immediately spiking through him before anything else, and then he jerks, as though struck. He jerks, but he doesn't try to get away from me. Though his eyes widen and his mouth opens, he doesn't stop driving into me.

In fact, if anything his movements become even more frantic and erratic. He tries to say something, but I honestly cannot imagine what words are going to come out of his mouth. Are there going to be terrified questions, horrified screams?

Humans are so tiresomely predictable.

When he isn't predictable at all, I become the frightened one.

"Oh my God," he says. "What are you?"

But he doesn't say it in a terrified sort of way. He breathes it, in the same way I heard him breathe his desire for me. His eyes are lit with a strange sort of light – a liquid fascination that he can't deny.

It isn't like the drooling imbecilic wannabes, however. It's a glorious, breathtaking thing.

"You're a vampire, aren't you? I knew. I knew you were something. I felt it, inside me."

With such words washing over me, it isn't so difficult to show him my pleasure. I let him see what he is doing to me, in return for his words – I lift my hips to meet his, sheathing him to the hilt in my slippery sex. I tremble for him, all over.

He seems to appreciate both things. His eyes flutter closed, and then open again as though he has to keep drinking me in. My difference swamps him, I know. It swamps him, but in a way I've never seen before.

It is a pleasure to him. It's easy enough to see when I part and then close my lips, part and then close my lips – almost like a bite, taken out of nothing but thin air – and he responds in kind.

He actually leans down to me and makes a little biting gesture, in return!

I wish I could tell him what that means to me. But it is unnecessary, because he then goes one better.

"Oh God," he moans. "Are you going to turn me? Are you going to make me what you are?"

And even worse, he turns his face to one side and bares his throat to me. He shakes, as he does it. He shakes, and not just with fear – I think it may be that the act of giving himself to me actually brings him pleasure. So much so that he suddenly gasps, and starts to fall over the edge into his climax.

I can't blame him. His words, his desire for me – even knowing what I am – they send me over the edge, too. Before I can gather my wits or think about restraint or hate him for bringing me to this, my body goes rigid. Great waves of sensation pour through me, pulling me apart and apart and never letting me come together again, as I once was.

My clit jumps against his still rubbing finger. My sex flutters around his swelling prick, over and over. I call out his name, as he shakes and spills inside me. He is still moaning and shuddering, when I decide. It will be different this time, I know, because no pleasure can come from something wretched and broken.

He will not be broken by me.

As the pleasure ebbs, I let my truest self come out. He keeps his face turned away – so easily submissive! – as I snap my head up, and sink my teeth into his perfect ivory throat.

Three

When he wakes up, he does not look as Tommy did. He doesn't look scared, though I suppose he must be, somewhere inside. He has the advantage of foreknowledge, however – he knew what was coming to him and embraced it.

Perhaps that will make a difference. That, and the fact that I won't make the same mistakes as I did with Tommy. I will be patient with Nick. I will not be impatient with his desires or angry because I cannot understand them. I do understand them now.

He has shown me what my body is, and all of the pleasures it had forgotten.

He strains against the bonds I have fixed around his wrists, but not with any fear. He moves as though sensation is surging up and down his naked body – which I suppose it is. The smell of my blood, the beat of my heart – all will be new and rich to him.

And yet I still don't expect the words he says: "Thank you," he tells me, as his glorious ivory body stretched and relaxes, stretches and relaxes. "Thank you for making me what you are."

Warmth floods through me to hear him say such things. I sit on the edge of the bed beside him, and he cannot resist snapping his new pin-sharp teeth at me. Just a little – just playful. Though with a hint of menace lurking in the background.

He would if he could. But he can't, because I am going to show him the way. Control first, then play. If you do not learn control when first turned, you're likely to go mad.

And then I would have to kill you. I would have to put my hands about your neck, and squeeze the life out of you until there is nothing left, nothing left of my beloved.

"What happens now?" he asks, between straining breaths. "Why have you tied me up like this?"

I stroke his smooth flanks. Smooth the hair from his brow.

"Now I'm going to teach you," I say, and he smiles. He is lovely when he smiles. "You taught me how to remember pleasure, so in return . . . in return I am going to teach you something."

He raises one eyebrow, lips curling – still himself even with the hunger upon him. "And what might that be?" he asks, as I lean down for a kiss he's going to have to plead and beg and work himself into knots for. After all, it's the only way he'll learn. You have to be cruel to be kind.

"Why, how to be a vampire, darling boy," I reply. "I'm going to teach you how to be a vampire."

Rogue Heart

Sasha White

One

Miranda Grey glanced at the lone body in the pub when she came out of the office after locking everything up. The Zodiac was closed for the night, and she was finally alone with the man who'd been driving her crazy for the past two months.

Ex-military man turned pub cook Jake Wolf was the sexiest guy she'd ever met. Blond hair, blue eyes and muscles that bulged even when he was at rest made heat curl low in her belly every time she looked at him. During the past couple of months, the man had made her realize just how hot desire could burn.

More importantly, Jake was the man who made her want to toss aside all the nice girl rules she'd grown up with and become the bold bad girl it would take to tame him. The question was, was she brave enough to actually go for it now that she had him alone?

Damn right she was.

Straightening her spine and pushing out her breasts the way she'd seen so many other women do, she ran a trembling hand over her hair, licked her lips and sauntered towards him. He kept his eyes on the pool table as he lined up a shot then sent the last coloured ball into a pocket.

"Alone at last," she said in what she hoped was a sultry voice. Yes, it was a cheesy line, but it was all she could think of. She wasn't exactly used to making the first move.

Jake's lips tilted up at one corner. "Finally decided to go for it, huh, darlin'?"

Damn it! Was she that obvious?

He'd been using casual touches and seductive smiles to taunt her sensually since the first day they met two months earlier. It was time to turn the tables on him.

Heart pounding, Miranda cocked a hip and studied him, unsure of exactly how to move forwards without looking like the inexperienced idiot she felt like. She'd only had three lovers in her life, and none had gotten her as turned on as she was just standing there with Jake. Lord, how she wanted to get him naked and lick him all over. The heat in his eyes, and the butterflies that swarmed in her stomach every time he looked at her promised that he would open up a whole new world for her.

As if he could read her mind, he set the pool cue on top of the table and turned to face her completely. "Well," he said, holding his hands out, palms up. "Are you going to stand there all night, or are you going to take a taste?"

His challenge sent a ripple of pure hunger through her. Miranda stepped forwards until there were mere inches between them, then stood on her tiptoes, braced her hands on his shoulders and kissed him.

He stood still, his lips surprisingly soft and supple . . . and unmoving beneath hers. Heat built within as she rubbed and nuzzled at his closed mouth until, with a final frustrated growl, she slid her hands into his hair to hold him and thrust her tongue between his lips hungrily. The instant her tongue touched his, Jake came alive.

Firm hands circled her waist and pulled her flush against him as he pressed back and took control of the kiss . . . and of her heart rate.

Fire coursed through her veins and only his touch could put it out. Her sighs turned to moans then to growls as she rubbed and pressed against him. Miranda revelled in the hardness of his cock against her belly as her pulse raced and her insides trembled with her need. She'd done that. She'd made him hard with desire.

Jake pulled back, panting, and stared deep into her eyes. "Are you sure you want this, darlin'? I can't promise you anything."

"Can you promise me an orgasm?"

His lips twitched. "Yeah, I can promise you that."

She slid her hands across his shoulders and pulled him against her again. "Then I'm sure."

With a soft groan and a small shake of his head he kissed her again. Jake's hands splayed across her back then moved up to cup her face as he deepened the kiss. But it wasn't enough; he was going too slow, being too gentle. The fire in her blood demanded more from him.

Tearing her mouth out from under his, she spoke before she thought. "Touch me, Jake," she ordered as she met his heated gaze. Covering his hand with hers, she led it to her aching breast. "Stop treating me like a damn virgin, and touch me like a woman."

His eyes widened for a split second then his lips curled into a devilish grin. "Yes, ma'am," he said before he gripped her hips in both hands and lifted her on to the pool table. Stepping between her spread thighs he proceeded to do exactly that.

Three months later.

Gentle but firm hands stroked down Miranda's back, leaving a trail of tingling flesh in their wake. She moaned softly as she slowly eased from deep sleep to semi-consciousness. "Did you have a good night?" she mumbled to the man who'd just crawled into bed with her.

"Busy," Jake said as his lips trailed over her shoulder to her neck. "You'll be happy when you do the cash."

She rolled on to her back and tilted her head to give him better access, sighing as his soft lips caressed her neck, finding that sensitive spot just behind her ear that made her shiver and bite her lip to keep from begging for more.

"And you?" she asked teasingly, as her hands wandered between them to the hot hardness poking against her hip. "What's made you so happy?"

"You. In my bed when I get home from work."

A large hand skimmed over Miranda's ribs and cupped a breast through the silk of her short nightie, and she couldn't stop another moan from escaping. She loved the way Jake touched her. Her body came alive under his hands in a way that continued to surprise her.

Jake pulled the neckline of her nightie down and lowered his head to wrap his lips around a hard nipple and she arched her back, pressing into him. He wasn't gentle in his suckling, and she liked it. With each tug of his lips another bolt of pleasure zipped from nipple to groin, until she was wantonly riding the hard thigh he'd shoved between her legs. Her pussy clenched, and she pressed against him harder. "More," she moaned.

"That's it, baby," he whispered. "Tell me what you want."

And that fast, she was ready for him. His voice, his hands, the weight of his body on hers had her juices flowing hotly until she writhed against him, gripping his shoulders and pulling him closer. "Inside me, I want you inside me."

One of his hands slid between them, taking the place of his thigh as he pushed her on to her back and rolled on top. He cupped her sex, one long finger sliding deep into her while the heel of his hand pressed and rubbed against her swollen clit. "Like this?"

Scraping her nails down his back, she spread her legs and arched into him. When he didn't move closer she growled her impatience. He'd moved so fast and sure that her desire was white hot, and now he was holding back. Damn the man. He got her so worked up. "No," she panted. "I want *you* inside me. Not your freakin' fingers."

His hand pressed against her harder as another finger joined the first. He wiggled them, pressing deep inside her, but it wasn't enough. She rocked and panted, her nails digging into his back, into his rock-hard butt cheeks, as she tried to force him to take her. When he remained slow and steady, she planted a foot on the mattress and pushed, rolling them over so she was on top.

She leaned down and sealed her lips over his, silencing anything he might have to say, as she reached between their bodies and took hold of his cock. Hot and hard in her hand, she lifted up on her knees, lined him up with her entrance and slid down on to him. His groan rumbled into her mouth and she sighed with pleasure at the way he filled her. They fitted together perfectly.

She pulled back from the kiss, straightened up and grinned down at him. "Now fuck me, Jake," she demanded.

"My pleasure," he said, as his hands gripped her hips and he began to move beneath her.

Her breath caught in her throat as he lifted and lowered her in time with his own thrusts. Bracing her hands on his hard chest, she thrilled at the power of his muscles flexing under them. Tension gathered low in her belly as her sex contracted and clutched at Jake with every thrust and roll of their bodies. Their eyes met and her arousal hit a new high. Curling her fingers, she dug her nails in and scraped them across his chest until she reached his nipples. Watching him closely, she pinched them until his eyes widened and his lips parted in a gasp and his hips began to pump faster and harder. Pressure built deep inside Miranda, she was almost there; she just needed a bit more friction.

"Touch me, Jake," she panted. "Make me come!"

He slid one hand forwards and pinched her clit, sending jolts of sensation exploding from her core to every nerve in her body. Jake's low groan of satisfaction blended with her cry and his cock jerked deep inside her.

Seconds later, Miranda fell bonelessly forwards on to his chest, where Jake cradled her close. Smoothing her hands over his naked chest, she noticed the scratches she'd left when she'd gotten carried away. Deep grooves surrounded his flat nipples and shame rose within her.

"I'm sorry," she whispered, kissing the marred skin softly.

"Shhhh," he murmured, shifting beneath her until they both lay on their sides with his arms wrapped around her from behind. "Don't ever be sorry about doing what feels good."

He pressed soft kisses to her cheek and jaw as she hummed her satisfaction and slowly drifted back to sleep.

Jake lay in bed, listening to the sounds of Miranda going through her morning rituals and his muscles twitched with the need to go to her. While he was often quiet and contained, he was rarely inactive when he wanted something. Coming home to find Miranda unexpectedly in his bed last night had been a pleasant surprise. It had felt so right to have her already there and it brought home how deeply he wanted Miranda in his life, wanted her there permanently. It brought home the fact that he was in love with her . . . and that scared the shit out of him. The shock of it hit him between the eyes. He'd never meant to get involved with her beyond the one night. Not because he wasn't attracted to her. He was. Hell, any man with an ounce of testosterone would be. And not because she was his boss either. Things like that – titles or labels or whatever – didn't bother him. He hadn't meant to get involved with her because Miranda Grey was a love-and-marriage kind of woman, and Jake had given up on finding love after his first wife had died.

Unable to fight the urge to do something, he got up, pulled on some shorts and headed for the small kitchen. Pulling out fruit, eggs, cheese and broccoli he let his thoughts flow as he whipped up a quick breakfast for her.

He flipped the omelette on to a plate next to some sliced melon and set it on the table, just as he heard the drawers and cupboards being closed in the bathroom. Miranda had surprised him with her endearingly clumsy yet bold come on the first night they were alone, and kept on surprising him until somehow, their casual affair had turned into something he'd never thought possible.

He froze with the carton of orange juice in his hand. That was the whole problem. The reason he was so restless and antsy lately. They were together, he was in love, and yet, it still wasn't enough. It wouldn't be enough until she knew what he really needed, even if she couldn't be the one to give it to him.

The light flowery scent of her perfume filled his nostrils a second before her arms went around him from behind, jolting him from his thoughts.

"Can't sleep?"

He shrugged. "Just wanted to make you breakfast. Tea's already on the table."

Soft lips pressed against the middle of his back before she pulled away and went to the table. "Jesus, Jake. You're going to spoil me."

Pride whipped through him as he carried the juice to the table and sat down across from her. "Consider it a thank you for the surprise visit."

"Keep spoiling me like this and I'll never leave." She grinned and forked some of the egg into her mouth.

His heart stuttered and he struggled to think of a witty reply. Before his brain got back online, she finished chewing and waved the empty fork at the empty table in front of him. "You're not eating?"

"I'll eat later. I'm heading back to bed after you leave."

They sat in silence for a few minutes while she ate, and he watched her. Her comment about never leaving had been teasing, but walking in at two in the morning and finding her curled up in his bed had been nice. He'd given her a key to his place above the pub a month ago and she didn't use it enough.

"The salmon shipment should be in today so I'll put it up on the board as the dinner special for tonight, OK?"

"You'll just put it up as a grilled salmon dinner, right? Nothing fancy?" They'd talked about her need to put fancy crap on the menu and his certainty that their simple blue-collar crowd only wanted good food, not gourmet food.

"Yes, I'll keep it simple." She settled back into her chair, her lovely lips twitching as she arched a delicate blonde eyebrow at him. "I'm trusting you to make it good though."

Those words of confidence, combined with the slight command in her tone had his dick twitching, along with his lips. "You know I will, darlin'."

She laughed lightly and he grinned. Oh yeah, she could give him everything he needed, if she wanted to.

"Time for me to get to work," Miranda said with a sigh. She pushed her chair back, reaching for her empty plates as she stood.

"Leave them," he said as he got up and walked to her side. He pulled her close and kissed her. Taking its time, his tongue did a lazy tour of her mouth, drinking in her flavour and enjoying the way she felt in his arms. When he finally pulled back he could tell by her dazed expression that he'd wiped all thoughts of salmon and work from her mind.

Good. He wanted her thinking of him all day.

Spinning her around, he smacked a hand against her firm ass and urged her towards the door with a grin. "Now get. And have a good day."

As soon as the door closed behind her, his mind started going a mile a minute again. He put the dirty dishes in the sink then went back to the bedroom. Sitting on the edge of the bed, he stared at the phone on the bedside table. He wasn't a man who hesitated, and now that he'd accepted that he was falling in love with Miranda it needed to be done.

With a steady hand, he picked up the phone and dialled the number from memory. Fifteen seconds later, a woman answered the phone on the other end. "Hello?"

"It's time. When can I see you?"

"Jake," her voice deepened, almost a purr. "It's been a while, but you know I'll always find time for you. How about tomorrow night?"

"Eight o'clock?"

"That will be fine." There was a brief pause before Suzanne spoke again. "Is it over, or will you be bringing her with you as we discussed?"

He closed his eyes. "I hope she'll come with me."

"I'll plan for either scenario then," she said firmly.

Jake ignored the small tremor that whipped through him. "Thank you."

Her voice was soft, and full of affection when she said goodbye. "Good luck, Jake."

He hung up, and fell back on the bed. Surrounded by mussed sheets and the scent of Miranda, he breathed deeply and tried to steady his heartbeat. He was about to take the biggest risk of his life.

Two

Miranda clicked the mouse over the publish button and her latest "From Boring to Bodacious" blog entry was sent off to cyberspace. The blog wasn't to entertain others, but to use as a sounding board for her own thoughts on the way her life was changing. The online journal had been a godsend in helping her learn more about the woman she truly was, and not just the woman her family had tried to make her.

It was also a great place to voice all her secret fears and desires without sharing them with anyone who actually knew her. For instance, she learned that she had secret desires. In her mind she'd always been a conservative, classy lady, just like her mother and her sister. The reality was that the more she did, the more she wanted to do. If someone had told her a year ago that she'd have sex on a pool table she'd have been insulted. Yet she remembered that first time with Jake with pride, and not a little bit of heat.

Life was good, not only did she have a job she loved, she had a man she also loved. As if her thoughts had called him forth, the door to her office swung open and there he was, larger than life.

"Jake," she said breathlessly.

He closed the door behind him and strode around her desk with a determined look on his gorgeous face. Kneeling down, he boxed her in by bracing his hands on the arms of her chair. "Miranda, I love you," he said.

Joy ripped through her and she gasped. She reached for him but he grabbed her hands and clasped them to his chest.

"Don't say anything yet," he went on. "There's something I need to tell you and I don't think I could handle it if you told me you felt the same, and then changed your mind."

Her heart sang and she tried to wrap her arms around him again, only to have him clutch her hands tighter and block her way again. What was going on? "I'd never change my mind, Jake."

"You might when I tell you what I need from you."

"Need from me?"

He stared at her, silent and intense, before he spoke in a rush, as if the words were shoved out of his mouth by force. "I need you to master me."

"Master you?"

"There are times when I need you to take control, of me, of us, in the bedroom. Sexually." He blew out a breath. "To dominate me."

Her mind went blank. Dominate him? "You want me to . . . spank you?"

He grimaced, and then he chuckled. "That's not really my thing, but either way, there's more to it than that."

Heat pooled between Miranda's thighs and she blushed. She'd never really thought about spanking a man, but the thought of it was a surprising turn-on. "Like what?"

Jake's lips lifted into a relieved smile. "You're OK with it? Just like that?"

"Well, yeah, I guess," she said with a small laugh of her own. "I like the idea of experimenting a little and if that's what you need, then I want to do it if I can."

He stood up, pulled her into his arms and kissed her deeply. "You can do it, Miranda. You're a natural dominant. It's why I've never been able to resist you." His lips pressed against hers, stealing her breath and turning her blood to fire.

Finally he pulled back, moving to the door. "I have to leave before I bend you over the desk." He turned when he had his hand on the doorknob. "I'd like to take you to meet a friend of mine tomorrow night. Suzanne. So you can understand exactly what it is I'm asking of you, before you make a final decision."

"OK," she said softly, coming back down to earth.

He smiled at her, and she watched him leave as panic set in. Jake was the best lover she'd ever had. He'd made her feel things she'd only read about in romance novels. But one of her secret fears had always been that she wasn't enough for him, and his confession had confirmed it. She loved him and hearing him say he loved her was a dream come true.

She only hoped it didn't turn into a nightmare when he discovered she had absolutely no clue how to dominate someone. Hell, she didn't even know what it meant!

Miranda was almost frantic by the time Sable got to her place later that night. "What took you so long? Your shift ended an hour ago."

Sable raised her eyebrows and hefted the brown paper bag in her hand. "I picked up Yow Min's on the way over, they were pretty busy for a Wednesday night."

Clamping her lips together Miranda led the way to the kitchen where she poured them both a glass of wine.

Sable gave her a funny look as she unpacked the Chinese food. "What's up?"

Miranda stood there for second. How was she supposed to say this? Should she even be telling Sable what was going on? Anonymous blogging wasn't going to cut it this time, she had to talk to someone. She had to talk to sexy, confident and adventurous Sable.

Miranda opened her mouth and it all tumbled out. "He wants me to master him, and I'm not even sure what that means. I can guess it means be strong and dominant, but I'm not a strong woman. I'm not bold and dominant and in control. I'm—"

"Stop."

There was such command in Sable's voice that Miranda stopped speaking instantly –then rushed on again. "See? That's exactly what I'm talking about. You're strong and commanding, not me."

"I said stop, Mandy. You're being an idiot."

That hurt. "Oh, that's nice. Here I am pouring out my heart and you're calling me an idiot. You're supposed to be my friend. You're supposed to support me."

"I am your friend, which is why I'm going to smack you upside the head if you keep putting yourself down." Sable glared at her. "Stop with the whining about what you think you're not, and just think about what you've done in the past year. You went against your family and quit a reliable, stable job to run a pub. In running that pub you've learned how to bartend, cook and bounce drunk idiots out the door. You made the first move on Jake, which led to you having sex on a fucking pool table!" She heaved a sigh and stared at Miranda. "The only person who thinks you're not strong is you, Mandy. It's time to open up your eyes and see who you really are."

Well, that shut her up. They stared at each other in silence, then Miranda picked up a plate. "I hope you got extra egg rolls."

"Of course."

"How are the pictures coming?"

And just like that the subject was changed. Sable told her all about the project she was building for her upcoming show and all

was normal. The whole time Sable talked, Miranda listened with
only half an ear as she remembered a time not so long ago when
Jake had interrupted their girls' lunch.

She'd sat in the booth listening to Sable tell Jake about her first
date with Gage, all the while wondering what he'd do if she were to
slip her hand under the table and place it on his thigh. She knew
he'd be surprised, and at that point so would she if she'd have actually gone through with it. She'd wanted to though.

She'd really wanted to.

She'd wanted to feel the lean muscles that covered his whole
body flex under her fingertips ever since she'd seen him lounging in
the leather chair at the lawyer's office during the reading of her
uncle's will. But back then she was still in lockdown mode – a good
girl, and she'd been raised to believe good girls didn't do things like
that. Good girls smiled pretty and waited for the man to make the
first move.

She'd sat there and listened to their conversation carefully,
listening for any undertones or currents of jealousy on Jake's part,
but there'd been nothing. He'd been genuinely happy for Sable,
although he wouldn't even look at Miranda.

That had been her first hint that Jake had been interested in her
too. Almost every day he'd come into her office with some flimsy
excuse and every time he stepped through the door she'd felt the
room shrink around her and fill with his presence. He'd never
touched her or said anything suggestive, but the way he'd looked at
her was so intense that she'd often felt as if her body would burst
into flame at any moment when he was around. It was that quiet
intensity of his that made her dream about riding him long and
hard night after night.

"You OK?"

Miranda smiled at her friend. "Yeah."

"It's obvious you have a lot on your mind so I'm going to head
out and let you do your thinking thing, but I want you to listen
carefully first, OK?"

"OK."

"Don't sell yourself short, Mandy. You've always been a beautiful and intelligent lady, but in the last few months you've turned
into a hell of a woman, too. Don't let your fear cause you to revert
back to less than you can be. It's time to reward yourself with a bit
of bad behaviour with the man you love." She smiled devilishly and
Miranda laughed.

"Now I know why people say you're trouble, Sable."

"Why?"

"Because you make being bad sound so good!"

Sable let out a whoop of laughter to join Miranda's giggles and jumped out of her seat. She pulled Miranda out of her chair and gave her a quick hug.

Stepping back, Sable looked into Miranda's eyes. "There's nothing wrong with being good, Mandy." She grasped Miranda's hands in hers and squeezed them tight. "But maybe it's time for you to do some exploring and discover what really works for you. You might be surprised."

Three

Jake focused on staying calm as he pulled his jeep up in front of Miranda's place the next night. Despite the fact that she'd taken his revelation the day before better than he'd anticipated, he was still worried. She hadn't been waiting for him in his bed when he got home after his shift, and when he'd called her in the morning she'd been pretty reserved.

Thoughts of her backing out, of her losing respect for him because she thought he was weak, or worse yet, that she thought he was a freak filled his head until he couldn't stand it any more. He'd spent the afternoon pounding on a heavy bag at the gym until his mind was completely blank, but as soon as he'd left the gym, the fear that he was losing her had eked its way back into his soul.

When they'd first met it had been clear to him that Miranda was a straight-laced good girl – a hot one, but still not his type. Then she'd decided to keep the pub instead of selling it and, as he worked with her day after day, he'd begun to see beneath her polished surface, and he liked what he saw. When she'd taken the first step, he'd known he was right to think that she had hidden depths. Still, he hadn't wanted to love her, but now that he did, he couldn't lose her, even if it meant burying part of himself.

Kicking all thoughts of losing her to the kerb, he stomped through the snow to her front door and rang the bell. She answered it almost instantly, and his breath caught in his throat.

"I didn't know what to wear," she said, holding her hands out to the side.

Jake's cock rose with his eyes as he drank in the sight of her from the shiny black heels covering her feet to the silky blonde hair pulled back in a sleek high ponytail. Her pert breasts and smooth skin were showcased with a black strapless corset, and black dress pants skimmed over her hips and down her legs. She looked classy, strong, and too fucking hot!

He cleared his throat. "You look beautiful."

"Sable gave me the corset as a gift last year. I've never worn it before," she said as she stepped back and reached for her coat.

Jumping forwards he took it from her hands and held it for her, fighting the urge to kiss the back of her exposed neck when she turned.

Fuck it, he thought, and pressed his lips to the soft spot behind her ear. "You're amazing, darlin'."

She turned in his arms and gave him a small smile. "So are you."

He touched his lips with hers, barely a kiss, more of a promise, a wish for it all to work out. Before he could do more or say something to fuck things up completely he urged her out the door and into the jeep.

"Where are we going?" she asked after a few minutes had passed in silence.

"As I said, we're going to see a friend of mine, Suzanne. Leslie introduced me to her, and I've been seeing her on and off for the past couple of years."

"Seeing her?"

Jake heard the hurt in Miranda's voice and spoke quickly to soothe her. "I haven't seen her since you and I hooked up. And even before then it wasn't like you think. It's not romantic, and she's never had a piece of my heart. She's simply an outlet when I need one."

He waited while she digested that, ignoring the knot in his gut and concentrating on the road as snow began to fall lightly.

"You said Leslie introduced you?" Miranda asked tentatively.

He'd only ever told her about his wife once. He'd never been one to talk about his feelings, but she'd asked and by then he'd cared enough about her to answer. Leslie had been his childhood sweetheart and his best friend, and she'd died only three years earlier, while he'd been out of the country on a godforsaken peacekeeping mission. She was in remission when he'd left, and her death had come as a devastating shock.

But now he had Miranda, and she deserved to know it all.

"Sort of. She'd left me a letter with her final thoughts and it included Suzanne's name and phone number. I found out later that Leslie had met with her and talked to her about me before she died. She wanted to be sure I was looked after."

Neither spoke again for a few minutes but this time the silence was almost comfortable. He knew that Miranda would be shocked a few times before the night was over, but hope was alive inside him that it would be in pleasant ways. She was inexperienced in any sort of kink, but it was such a deep part of him that he'd subconsciously eased their sex life in that direction right from the start. The first time he'd tied her to the bedposts and eaten her pussy until she screamed she'd been shocked all to hell and he'd been thrilled to discover that the ropes held an attraction to her, too.

He realized now that it had been that night that had opened a crack in his heart for her to slip through. He just hoped that tonight didn't turn that crack into a complete split.

Jake stopped the jeep in front of a Victorian-style house in an old neighbourhood and Miranda waited while he jogged around to help her from the vehicle. Her heart pounded and her palms were sweating, and if she were honest with herself it wasn't just fear that had her so anxious.

She'd felt a lot better after her time with Sable the night before, but it hadn't been enough. She had to deal with things in her own way, and she had spent the day in her office doing exactly that. Research and educate had always been her motto so she'd pushed aside her work and typed "master" and "dominate" into the search engine . . . and what she'd found both excited and terrified her.

She'd spent more than three hours surfing articles, blogs and BDSM websites with a notepad right next to the keyboard. There was so much information to take in. Dominants, submissives, tops, bottoms, switches and slaves. There were degrees of power and control and even contracts!

Some of the things she read were purely academic – full of rules and with little emotion. But then there were the sites that were all personal. Not really pornographic, but erotic and sensual and full of pictures and stories that did more than intrigue Miranda. They'd sent visions of tying Jake up and doing all sorts of wicked things running rampant through her mind until she'd begun to hyperventilate. Her pulse pounded and hot blood rushed through her veins, her nipples peaked and her mind balked to the point that she'd finally shut down her computer and left for home.

Now, as Jake led her to the door of the woman his dead wife had set him up with doubt crept back into mind.

The door opened and Miranda got her first look at Suzanne. The breath she hadn't even been aware she was holding rushed out and Jake gave her arm a squeeze through her jacket.

Suzanne was tall, brunette and pretty in a very soft feminine way. She wasn't dressed in leather and studs, she didn't hold a whip, and she did smile warmly.

"Miranda, I'm so glad you came. Jake's told me all about you."

"All about me?" she asked as they stepped inside.

Suzanne took their coats with a laugh. "Not all I'm sure, but enough to know that he thinks you're very special."

Miranda glanced at Jake. "I think he's pretty special too."

"Shall we sit down and have a chat first?" Suzanne gestured towards the front room. "Greg will be happy to serve us."

It wasn't until then that she noticed the almost naked man kneeling in the corner of the room. Miranda's heart jumped and she stared for a minute before tearing her gaze away. As nice as Suzanne seemed, they weren't there to sit and chit-chat. "I'd rather we just get started with the session."

Miranda held Suzanne's gaze until she nodded and looked away. "Of course. Let's head downstairs then, shall we?"

Suzanne called Greg to her and they led the way down the hall to some stairs. Miranda wanted to look at Jake to see what he was thinking, but she was desperately afraid he'd be watching Suzanne lead the way instead of her.

At the bottom of the stairs, Suzanne opened a door to her left and led them into a small room with a plush leather loveseat in front of a huge tinted window. "This is the viewing room. You're welcome to watch me work with Greg. All I ask is that you don't interrupt us. Please have a seat here, and Jake can kneel at your side."

Jake had moved to the side of the sofa and Suzanne was almost out the door when Miranda finally found her tongue. "No."

They both stopped, staring at her. Jake's expression was grim, Suzanne's surprised.

"You don't want to watch?" she asked.

"No. I mean, yes, I'd like to watch." She faced Suzanne and, heart thumping in her chest, she spoke clearly. "What I meant was no, I don't want Jake to kneel by side, and if or when I do, I'll be the one to tell him so, not you."

A small smile played at the woman's lips and she nodded. "Of course."

When the door was closed and they were alone she turned to Jake. "Are you OK with that?"

He smiled. "Absolutely."

"OK, then." Restless heat swam through Miranda's system and she really didn't think she could sit. She blew out a sharp breath and moved towards the window. She'd read a lot about proper etiquette that afternoon, and she wasn't sure if interrupting Suzanne that way was a breach or not, but she'd been unable to stop herself. Tying Jake up and playing with him was one thing, but she didn't want to make a slave out of him.

The other room was large, open and well lit. Along the walls and in the corners were some odd pieces of furniture that made Miranda's pulse leap: a huge padded table with gleaming chrome legs and buckles all around it, a large wooden X and padded vault or horse of some kind.

Hanging from chains in the middle of the room was a steel bar with padded cuffs attached. As she watched Suzanne finished locking Greg into the cuffs and stepped back.

"If we're here for me to see what you need, why aren't you out there in the cuffs?"

Jake stepped up beside her and spoke softly. "Because I won't bottom to anyone else but you, until you tell me you can't, or won't, do this."

She stared at him. "But you've done this before, let Suzanne . . . top you?"

"Yes."

"But not in the last three months?"

"That's right."

She turned away from him and watched the couple in the other room. Suzanne had a flogger in one hand and was twirling it lightly so the ends brushed against Greg's chest with each upsweep. The swings sped up, and his chest turned pink, then she set aside the flogger and picked up something that looked like a metal-tooth comb. She imagined Jake in those cuffs, his body open and bared for Suzanne, and determination set in.

Jake was hers.

★   ★   ★

Every muscle in Jake's body was taut as he drove the jeep towards Miranda's house. She'd been entranced by the scene of Suzanne and Greg, he'd been sure of it!

The pulse at the base of her throat had throbbed and he'd listened as her breathing had gotten more and more excited. Watching the play had aroused her. He'd seen it in the way she clenched her hands as if she were the one holding the tools and the way she'd rocked back and forth on her feet in an effort to contain herself. He knew her, and he'd known she was aroused.

He hoped she was aroused, because just seeing her there, dressed as she was, amongst implements of pain and pleasure had raised a primal hunger deep inside him.

When the play had ended and Suzanne had come back to the viewing room, Miranda had asked to speak to her privately. They'd left him alone for quite a while, and his certainty about her reaction had begun to fade. When she'd come back to the viewing room all she'd said was, "Take me home now, Jake."

His heart had dropped into his stomach, and stayed there ever since. Maybe he'd just projected his own wants and desires on her. Maybe it was just wishful thinking that she'd been aroused. He wanted to ask her what she thought, but he was scared of her answer.

Fluffy white snow was still falling lightly when he parked in front of her house and he rushed to open her door for her.

Once they were inside her house he couldn't take the silence any longer. "Miranda," he said.

"Stop," she commanded, holding her hand up in front of him. She met his eyes and spoke firmly. "I want you to go upstairs, strip naked, lie down on the bed and wait for me."

Blood rushed to his cock and his head swam with the implications of her words. "Then yo—"

"No talking yet, Jake. Just do as I tell you." She shrugged out of her coat before he could move and glanced pointedly at the stairs. "Go. Now."

His brain caught up with his ears and without hesitation he kicked off his boots and moved up the stairs. Heart thumping, dick throbbing, he moved quick and sure. He wasn't naked on her bed for more than thirty seconds before she strode into the room wearing a short silky robe and nothing else.

She stood by the edge of the bed for a moment, her dark eyes unreadable, before leaning over to grab his wrists. Stretching his arms above his head, she pressed his hands against the headboard of the bed. "Don't move from this position, Jake."

"Yes, ma'am," he said, watching her carefully.

Her head jerked at his words and she stared at him, eyes wide. A heartbeat later her lips curled into a slow sensual smile that hit him right in the dick.

Fingertips barely touching his skin, she ran her hands down the insides of his arms, over his ribs and down his entire body. Then back up as she began talking. "Suzanne suggested we start with where we're comfortable, in the bedroom. She made me realize what exactly you've been doing in the past, Jake. Sometimes taking complete control and tying me up, and other times simply teasing me until I wrested control from you." She licked a nipple, sucking it gently into her mouth before biting down sharply. Pain and pleasure blended, rippling out to every nerve ending. Miranda shifted, staying close enough that her hot breath brushed teasingly against his skin as she talked. "I'm supposed to take it slow, but I find having you like this too hard to resist."

Straddling him, she swung around until they were in a classic sixty-nine position, her pretty pink pussy right over his face.

Her scent filled his head and he licked his lips. His mouth watered and his arms trembled with the need to cup her hips and pull her down on to his face. But she'd told him not to move, and he did not want to disappoint.

She kept her hips raised, but lowered her front until her silk-covered breasts brushed his torso and her lips circled his cock. She licked, sucked and swallowed him, as he writhed beneath her, sweating with the delicious effort of not moving.

He turned his head, nibbling on her inner thigh, licking every inch of soft skin he could reach until finally he pulled his head back and begged. "Please, Miranda. Let me taste you. Let me please you."

She straightened up, her mouth releasing his throbbing cock with a loud pop. Looking over her shoulder at him she met his gaze. "Only because you said please."

His chest swelled. She was enjoying their play.

"Make me come, Jake, and keep those hands on the wall." She spread her legs wider, lowering herself slowly closer to his waiting mouth.

When she was close enough he took a long slow lick before delving in. She tasted so good, so sweet and true. He stiffened his tongue and slid it inside her, going as deep as he could and slurped up the juices that flowed from her cunt. He pulled back and bit so he could circle the rigid clit that had popped out from its protective hood. He flicked and nibbled at the knot of nerves, loving it slowly and surely for just a moment before going back to work.

Thrusting his tongue into her entrance, he nuzzled his chin against her clit and began to work. Soon she was rocking against him, grinding down and moaning.

"More, Jake" she encouraged as her nails dug into his abdomen. "I love it when you eat my pussy."

Her words of praise made his heart sing, and he redoubled his efforts. She rocked forwards, her thighs trembling as she started at his thighs and scraped her nails up over his hips and belly to his chest.

He groaned at the sensation, as his balls tightened and fire gathered at the base of his dick.

"Oh yeah, you like that, don't you?" she whispered. "Look at your beautiful cock waving in the air. So hard and red . . . so hungry."

Her hand wrapped around him and his whole body jerked. He struggled for control, only to gasp when she ground her hips down harder. "Don't stop, Jake. You don't come until I do."

He redoubled his efforts. Stiffening his tongue, he worked a steady rhythm, pulsing it up and down, in and out of her juicy hole as he rubbed his chin against her clit. Soon she was rocking on him and jerking his dick with a strong hand. She'd always been so gentle in the past, but as her pussy grasped at his tongue, she rocked faster and her grip on him got tighter. Her fist twisted up and down, as she began to bounce on top of him.

"Yes, that's it. Don't stop!"

He grabbed her hips and used his thumbs to spread her slick pussy lips and open her up. He thrust his tongue as hard and deep as he could and her insides tightened and spasmed around him as cream coated his face. The hand around his dick tightened and his whole body jerked. When the spasms of her pussy slowed, her grip loosened and he exploded, crying out as he came with dizzying ecstasy.

When he came back to earth, Miranda was curled up against his side, one leg thrown over his as her hand stroked him from collarbone to hip.

"Wow," she whispered, looking deep into his eyes.

"Yeah."

She pulled back a bit, lifting on to an arm and looking down at him, her face serious. "Jake, as amazing and freeing as that was, I don't think I can do it all the time."

Love washed over him.

"I don't want it that way all the time," he explained. "And I don't want you to think I'm submissive to just anyone."

"Oh, I know that!" She laughed.

He chuckled, happy that she could see him for who he truly was. "It's just one aspect of things, and I needed to know that you were open to it before you broke my heart."

"I could never break your heart."

He lifted a hand to her cheek. "I love you, Miranda Grey, and I wanted you to know all of me."

Tears welled in her eyes and she smiled down at him. "I see all of you Jake Wolf. I know all of you, and I love you too."

Joy burst deep inside his heart and he moved, rolling over and pinning her to the bed. "Good," he whispered as he placed his lips against hers, "because I'm never letting you go. We're in this together now."

When he lifted his lips from hers, Miranda smiled up at him, her eyes gleaming as she blushed. "And I have to admit that I'm looking forward to tying you up and playing with you a lot."

Heart full, he grinned. "Anytime, darlin'. I'm all yours."

Inspiration

K. D. Grace

One

If he had been wearing a toga, Donna could have easily mistaken Jake Anderson for Apollo. Instead his shirt was tucked and ironed and his trousers creased, which was no small feat for someone who had just driven all the way from Texas. He was tall and well muscled with golden hair and a sensual smile any woman would want to eat like ice cream. But alas, Jake Anderson was not Apollo. Jake Anderson was the new English teacher for Golgotha Christian School.

If she'd had a choice, she would never have rented the spare room to someone who had been raised on a diet of Bible Belt right-eousness. No doubt he would be no more comfortable with her than she was with him. But since Golgotha School and Church were conveniently located next door, Jake had rented the room, sight unseen. More importantly, he had paid the first and last months' rent in advance as well as a hefty cleaning deposit, return-ing Donna to a precarious state of solvency that would allow her to eat until she got her first pay cheque from Sirens.

Jake shook her hand tentatively. "I was expecting someone older."

She was expecting someone a little less yummy.

He offered her a win-friends-and-influence-people smile. "Uncle Ed says you're an artist."

"Ed Tandy's your uncle?"

He nodded enthusiastically. 'He's the president of the school board, as well as the senior evangelist at Golgotha.'

'I know who he is.' She forced a smile between bared teeth.

He continued, all sweetness and light, "Teaching's only temporary, you know, to give me some experience. Then I'll . . ."

"Follow in your uncle's footsteps?"

"That's right, and my father's and my grandfather's." His glory hallelujah smile spread tight across perfect teeth. "No self-respecting male in the Anderson family would consider anything else."

As soon as she could, she excused herself and returned to her studio, not because she didn't want to linger and look at him, but because she knew his kind only too well. Better to keep a safe distance. In spite of herself, as Jake banged up the stairs with his luggage, she thought again of what a lovely Apollo he would make. Apollo was her favourite god from Greek mythology and the one who inhabited some of her hottest fantasies. It was sad that her fantasies were peopled with mythological beings in the absence – very long absence – of the real thing.

She busied herself sketching the preliminary drawings of Apollo and Daphne she hoped to use for the mural at Sirens. Apollo's hand caressed Daphne's breast just above her ribs while his other hand slipped low down her stomach. With the hurried glance over her shoulder, Apollo's lips almost but not quite found purchase on Daphne's as his powerful embrace engulfed her.

"Excuse me." Donna jumped at the soft knock on the open door. For a second it was as though her sketch had come to life, as she turned to find Jake peeking around the corner. Quickly she flipped to a fresh page on the sketch pad.

The dusting of sunlight filtering through the window, made him look even more like Apollo, and his voice had that honeyed resonance one would expect in a deity . . . or a preacher, she reminded herself. "You got settled in then?" she asked breathlessly.

On the blank page, she sketched him rapidly, surreptitiously, feeling like a voyeur watching the god unawares, wishing wickedly that she could see beneath his clothes. There was no doubt that the Apollo now coming to life in her sketches, and in her imagination, would be Jake-inspired.

But Jake's gaze was locked on a half-finished canvas near the back of the studio. It was a large painting of a nude, legs open to the explorations of an enormous swan whose wings mantled the object of its affection. The woman's arched back forced ripe fruit breasts heavenwards in a struggle to escape. Her arms were flung open as she tumbled backwards into folds of tapestry and silk. Her eyes were wide, and her mouth was an "O" that suggested both ecstasy and terror.

"That's Leda and the Swan," Donna said.

"Who?"

"Greek mythology? Never mind. I'll lend you the book."

His jaw stiffened and the sides of his nostrils pinched as though he'd just stepped in something nasty. "Doesn't sound like the sort of book I'd read."

Suddenly he didn't seem at all like Apollo.

"Is that your work?" He sounded as though he were accusing her of breaking the china.

"My mother started it. When I get the right inspiration, I hope to finish it."

"Your mother did that?" Neutrality could not quite mask his distaste.

"That's right. I'm surprised your uncle hasn't filled you in on the notorious Ellen Jenkins." She slapped the sketch pad shut and glared at him. "This was the last thing she painted before she died."

His face flashed red and he shot a quick glance towards the door as though he'd like to run. Then, as if God had answered his prayers, his cell phone rang, allowing him a quick escape. Good riddance, Donna thought, wadding up the sketch she'd been making and throwing it in the trash. She knew renting to him was a stupid mistake, but she just had to have regular meals, didn't she?

That night, she tried to work with little luck. It felt strange having someone else in her mother's house, the house she herself was still getting reacquainted with after her return to Denver. As a child, the old Victorian heap had been full of students, full of laughter, full of creative energy and free thought. Ellen Jenkins had rented rooms to students at affordable prices. Back then the house was a magical place, a place full of inspiration. Sharing it now with someone employed by Golgotha after what had happened to her mother felt wrong somehow, and yet she saw no alternative. Before she closed up the studio, she dug the sketch of Jake out of the trash, smoothed out the wrinkles and stuffed it into the back of her sketch pad.

Sleep, when it finally came, was laced with dreams of Apollo and Daphne, of Leda and the Swan. In the early hours just before dawn, she woke to the sound of running water. It was pretty inconsiderate of his holiness to shower at this hour. Cursing softly to herself, she threw on her robe and stomped down the hall to the bathroom, where she found wafts of steam floating through the open door.

The surprise barely had time to register when the water stopped running, the shower curtain drew back and there he stood like Apollo just up from the sacred baths.

"The shower woke me." She forced the words through her tight throat, struggling not to let her eyes go exploring,

"I couldn't sleep." He seemed not to mind his nakedness or her inability not to notice. The bathroom floor creaked anxiously beneath his feet as he stepped from the tub, moving with the regal grace of a god, brown eyes locked on hers. His hands came to rest on the sagging lapels of her robe and, over the scent of deodorant soap, she breathed in the wood-smoke tang of male arousal. Her nipples stiffened against silk as she realized he wasn't the only one who was wet.

Your stature is like that of the palm, and your breasts like clusters of fruit.

That wasn't right. Why would Apollo be quoting "Song of Songs"?

With a flick of thumb and forefinger, he undid her robe and slid it off her shoulders.

I will climb the palm tree; I will take hold of its fruit.

For a long moment he stood looking at her, his gaze falling like a caress against the tips of her breasts and the lower reaches of her belly. Her eyes dropped to admire the weighty erection pressing anxiously towards her.

He lifted her hand to his lips and placed a searing kiss against her palm. A step closer and he guided her fingers to encircle him, then he took her mouth with a soft grunt of pleasure at her touch.

While his tongue mesmerized hers, he pressed her back against cool tiles, then lifted her on to him and began to rock his hips, slowly at first, allowing her to feel with each movement the shape of him inside her before picking up speed and force with the growing intensity of need.

May your breasts be like clusters of the vine.

She circled his neck with her arms and clung to him as he thrust, feeling the rapid expansion of his chest against hers, hard muscle beneath hot skin beaded with moisture.

And the fragrance of your breath like apples, and your mouth like the best wine.

They both had stopped breathing, she didn't know how long ago, but then gods surely didn't need to breathe, did they? Mortals, however, did. As they clawed and pushed at each other until neither of them could hold back, she figured the ringing in her ears was surely from lack of oxygen.

She woke with a gasp. Sunlight blazed through the windows of her bedroom, the sheet was tangled and damp from sweat. Every inch of her ached for the release the dream had promised, but not delivered. Outside somebody leaned heavily on the doorbell.

She cursed under her breath, threw on her robe and raced down the stairs to find her bleary-eyed Apollo standing on the front porch in nothing but his jeans. Her heart nearly stopped at the sight. As she fumbled with the lock on the door, she found herself struggling to memorize as much of the magnificent torso as she could for her painting. She was amazed at how perfectly she had dreamed the shape of the young teacher only minutes before.

When the door opened, and he stepped inside, she couldn't keep from noticing the tightness in the front of his jeans. She knew it was impossible, but somehow she felt as though he'd been privy to her dream.

If he wasn't blushing already, he certainly did at the sight of her in the short silk robe, cleavage well exposed and nipples still at full attention. With what must have taken a great deal of effort, he respectfully kept his eyes locked on hers. "I'm sorry. Uncle Ed conned me into doing next Sunday's sermon. I went to get my notes from the car." He strategically moved the black leather briefcase he was holding to obscure his telltale bulge.

"My fault," she breathed. "I forgot to tell you it locks automatically."

His nipples mirrored hers with mini erections of their own, raised above well-muscled pecs in the cool morning air. "I thought you were painting."

A glance at the clock told her it was nearly ten. "Guess I overslept. Did you sleep well?" She didn't know what else to say.

He shifted uncomfortably from foot to foot. "I had . . . unusual dreams." He blushed again.

For a second they stood staring at each other, both struggling to keep their eyes from wandering, neither quite knowing what to do next. At last, Donna found her voice. "I need coffee. Want some?"

"No thanks. I'm expected at Uncle Ed's for lunch." He turned and fled up the stairs banging the briefcase against the banister as he went.

By the time the coffee was brewing, she could hear the shower running, and her mind was catapulted back to the dream. The strength of his muscular body had seemed so real as he pinned her against the wall. She had been so close when the damned doorbell had rung. And from the strain on the front of Jake's jeans, it hadn't been a sermon he'd been thinking about either.

Her mother used to say this house had powerful magic, that people who stayed here often had visions that inspired them in ways they never could have imagined. Standing in front of the counter with her back to the stairs, she found herself pressing against the hard wood, rocking hypnotically, feeling the pressure deep between her thighs. She slipped a hand inside her robe to cup her breasts, stroking her heavy nipples.

The other hand sought familiar territory, still slippery from the dream and fragrant with her own salty sweet scent. She shifted her hips back and forth against her working hand and was soon holding her breath, bearing down harder and harder until her knees nearly gave as orgasm exploded through her, and she couldn't hold back a startled gasp of pleasure.

"Donna?"

She froze, fingers still buried between her legs. She could just make out Jake's reflection in the window above the kitchen sink. He stood on the stairs in a blue terry robe that barely covered his damp chest. She didn't dare turn around. Even an innocent would surely figure out what she'd been up to.

"The bathtub isn't draining."

She fought to control her breathlessness, while pretending to watch something fascinating out of the window. "It's just slow. The plumber is coming tomorrow."

Once he had disappeared back up the steps, she slumped against the counter, cursing herself for getting so hot over a dream, and a dream of a future preacher boy, no less.

Two

The next day, she arrived at Sirens early. She could hear Irv cursing in his office about profits being down. He always came in before hours to fondle his account books and bitch about profits, even though the place was usually packed as soon as it got dark. The attraction of the strippers aside, she knew she was partially responsible for the crowds. Most of the time she worked during the day when the club was closed, but on Thursday night she painted atop the scaffolding during regular business hours, oblivious to the gyrations and pole dancing of the strippers below, the only female employee who worked with her clothes on.

The progress of the huge mural was a big draw, and Irv knew it. In fact, he had commented that when she finished, he might have her whitewash the whole thing and start all over again. The crowd was always anxious to see what titillating bits she had added to the Roman orgy unfolding on the ceiling and walls.

It wasn't a bad job. The pay would be good, and Irv allowed her plenty of artistic licence, so she painted more than a few of her favourite seductions from Greek mythology. Roman, Greek, Egyptian – Irv didn't care as long as there were plenty of voluptuous women on display, and men with enormous cocks fucking them.

She climbed the scaffolding and settled on to her back to paint a sexy romp unfolding in front of the temple of Apollo. She wondered what Jake would think if he saw what she was painting. A few touch-ups with just the right colours and the statue of Apollo surveying his realm looked warmer, more human, admittedly more like Jake. Then she turned her attention to a well-endowed suppliant kneeling in front of the statue of Jake, er, Apollo. The best part about painting the mural was that Donna got to experience the orgy vicariously, which was about as good as it got for her these days.

Once she settled in and began to paint, the strip club and the scaffolding quickly drifted away, and her mind painted at least as many details as her brush did. It was easy to imagine herself the flame-haired suppliant offering herself on the altar of Apollo. In fact she could almost feel the warm breath of Apollo on her neck as he asked what she sought from him.

Of course the answer was simple. In her mind's eye, Donna always sought the same thing she sought every day of her life – inspiration. And, as always, with her heart pounding her ribs, she would offer herself, unconditionally, without reservations, in exchange for that gift of divine inspiration. It was a bargain really. Inspiration was priceless and, when it was there, when it surged through her mind and body to manifest itself on the canvas, she was never closer to the gods – whoever they were.

"Donna, you got company." Irv's voice brought her back to reality.

She looked down over the edge of her perch to find Jake – this time the real Jake – staring open-mouthed at the painting of the supplicant before the watchful eyes she hoped he didn't recognize as his own. Damn it! He always managed to interrupt at the worst possible time. She scrambled down the scaffolding and motioned towards the bar. Jake followed, stumbling over his feet, his neck craned to look back at the mural on the ceiling. "It's a strip club. You work at a strip club?"

"Yes, Jake, I work at a strip club. So?"

"And that's what you're painting?"

"Yeah. That's what I'm painting." She poured them a couple of Cokes and slapped one down in front of him.

"Are you . . . You know?" He made a motion like he was taking off his shirt.

"You kidding?" Irv interrupted before she could say anything. "I can't even get her to show a little cleavage."

"I'm an artist, Irv," she growled. "You've got chicks with implants for that. Now what's going on?"

"Found this slinking around in the shadows watching you," Irv said. "He says you're his landlady?" Her boss gave Jake a doubtful once-over. "Lots a perverts would love to handle their junk while they watch you paint. He says he's a preacher or something. That true?"

"I told you, I'm not a preacher. I'm a teacher at Golgotha Christian School."

"Preacher, teacher, I don't give a fuck. You wanna watch artsy-fartsy here work, you come Thursday night during regular business hours like everyone else. And you–" he turned his attention to Donna – "make it brief. I'm not paying you to chit-chat."

Irv strutted away like he was cock of the walk and, when they were alone, Donna downed her Coke for courage, then turned to Jake. "What are you doing here?"

With some effort, he pulled his gaze away from the orgy on the ceiling. "The plumber says there's some work that needs to be done. He needs your permission. I couldn't get you on your cell phone, so I came here. I'd really like to shower without fear of a flood."

By the time she called the plumber, Jake was already long gone, and he wasn't at home that evening when she got back.

That night she awoke with moonlight flooding her room. She shoved back the blanket and let the gossamer light bathe her breasts and stomach. Her mother always said bathing in moonlight would inspire creativity. She might have drifted back to sleep if she hadn't heard something. She rose from the bed and slid into her robe. For a second she wondered if she was dreaming, but she followed the sound that seemed to be coming from her studio.

She tiptoed into the hallway over the threadbare carpet her mother had laid when she was a child. The sound grew louder as she drew nearer. Slowly, carefully, holding her breath, she peeked around the cracked door. There in a shower of moonlight sat Jake draped over the model's chair. The open blue robe cascaded on to the floor around him exposing the slope of his belly. The carved planes of his chest rose and fell like bellows. One hand clenched a volume of *Bullfinch's Mythology*. The other stroked the substantial length of a heavy erection. His gaze was locked on her mother's painting. For a brief second she felt anger that he had invaded her private domain, but he seemed so vulnerable, so lost in his own need. She stood frozen at the door watching him.

The artist longed to memorize the symmetry of his body; the woman longed to go to him, to open herself to him, as Leda had done for the swan. The sound of his breath, heavy and quick, filled the silent room. The muscles of his stomach tightened as he arched upwards until the curves of his buttocks and the straining elongations of his thighs were visible off the chair. His lips parted, his fingers curved and tightened around his penis. His pubic curls glinted in the moonlight. She could imagine their softness as they grazed his stroking hand.

He was too far gone to notice anything but his need to come. The chair creaked beneath his undulating weight, and he could no longer hold back the soft groans and grunts of his pleasure. The book fell to the floor with a muted thud, freeing his other hand to caress the distended bulge of his balls while he pumped harder. His body looked brittle, as though the strength of his need would shatter him. His back arched as though it were breaking. A strangled cry escaped his throat and he came in heavy viscous spurts on to the bare floorboards.

She caught her breath, flooded with a confused sense of tender longing at seeing him so exposed. She fled back to her bed. There she writhed in the hungry caress of moonlight, not certain what was dream and what was real, touching and fondling until she came, burying her face in her pillow stifling cries as rip-tide waves of pleasure broke over her, pulling her downwards into sleep.

Three

In the week that followed she saw little of Jake, and when she did, he was always fleeing off to some church function, grading papers, or locking himself in his room to work on the imminent sermon. It was just as well. The less they saw of each other the better.

Saturday morning they found themselves making breakfast at the same time, moving cautiously around each other, speaking in nervous short sentences about the weather or the much improved drainage in the bath. She had just finished toast when he dropped a cup of coffee, shattering the mug and nearly scalding his leg.

As they knelt to pick up the shards of ceramic, she noticed his hands were trembling. He forced an embarrassed laugh. "Guess I should lay off the coffee."

"Are you all right?'

"Just nerves." He avoided her gaze. "Sermon's tomorrow. I'm not as ready as I'd like to be."

She wiped the spill with a sponge, and he tossed the shards in the trash, then moved to the window, looking out at the grey brick of the school and church building glinting in the morning sun. "Uncle Ed doesn't like me living here. He says it's a dangerous situation."

Before she could do more than bristle, Jake continued, "I don't want to be isolated. I think it's important to be in the world but not of the world, like the Bible says."

"Is that why you came to Sirens? My cell phone wasn't off. You could have reached me at any time. Besides, the plumber had my permission to do what he needed."

He blushed hard and offered only a helpless shrug.

She thought about Jake masturbating in front of the painting of Leda and the Swan and couldn't fight back the sense of déjà vu. Reverend Tandy knew what he was talking about. In this case, he just might be right. Then she quickly pushed the thought out of her mind. She wasn't her mother, after all. She wouldn't make the same mistakes.

* * *

Sunday morning Jake was gone before Donna woke up. He had planned to go to Golgotha early so he could practise his sermon in the auditorium. As much as she disliked Golgotha Church, she hoped everything went well for him.

She painted for an hour before breakfast, trying to convince herself that her Apollo wasn't looking too much like Jake, then she padded off to the shower. With the drain fixed, she was looking forward to lingering in the hot spray. But she had barely gotten wet when she heard the door slam downstairs. Jake surely wasn't back. She dripped across the bathroom floor and peeked out the window. The church parking lot was still filling up. It must be almost time for the main service.

A knot tightened in her stomach. With Jake about to give his sermon, whoever had just stumbled into her kitchen certainly didn't belong there. She slipped the silk robe around her wet body and yanked the sash tight, willing her hands not to tremble. As she stepped out into the hallway she definitely heard movement in the kitchen downstairs. Leaving wet footprints on the landing, she grabbed the baseball bat she kept at the top of the stairs.

An elongated human-shaped shadow snaked across the kitchen floor, moving towards her. Flattening herself against the door of the spare room out of the intruder's view, she held her breath, baseball bat cocked against her shoulder. The shadow moved up the stairs, making no attempt to be quiet. Whoever it was must think no one was home. She drew back for the strike, then let out a little yelp, pulling the bat just before she bashed her tenant's forehead.

"God, Jake, what are you doing here? I nearly brained you. You're supposed to be preaching."

His face was white, but not from the bat, which now hung limp in her hand. "Jake? What's the matter?"

He jerked his head towards the church. "I don't think I can do this. There are so many of them. I was up half the night working on the sermon, and Uncle Ed is expecting me to . . . " His voice trailed off.

"You've got to do it. They're counting on you."

He grabbed her hand in a vice grip. "Donna," his eyes were locked on hers, "you don't understand. I couldn't get inspired. The sermon's crap."

"It'll be OK, I promise." She reached out and gave his shoulder a squeeze, and the sash on her robe slipped open revealing her breasts and the humid path down her belly. With a little gasp, everything shifted into slow motion. Almost as though his hands were on auto-pilot, he reached out and slid the robe off her shoulders.

She didn't push him away, she couldn't. Suddenly she wanted nothing so badly as his admiring glances caressing her body, as they had in her dreams, in her fantasies.

"They'll be singing the opening hymn soon." He cupped her breasts and moved his thumbs across her nipples. Instinctively, she arched against his touch, feeling it in places far removed from her breasts. He continued, "Then Uncle Ed will read the announcements. Then . . ." He took her hand and laid it against the fly of his black trousers and moved against her palm, at first timidly, almost as though he hoped she wouldn't notice. But he quickly abandoned caution and rocked against the pressure of her touch. His eyelids fluttered shut and he moaned softly.

Intrigued, she moved in closer to the heat rising off his body, to the scent of nerves and maleness she could almost taste. "What do you want to say to them?" The words trembled off her lips.

He undid the button at the waist of his trousers and guided her hand inside, manoeuvring it into his shorts. She was surprised to feel silk boxers rather than practical white cotton.

"I want to talk to them about love." He lowered his mouth to hers, while shoving at his trousers with the hand that wasn't cupping her. "I want them to know that nothing else matters, not really. The rest is just ambiguous doctrine and politics." He spoke against her mouth, words fading as he made an awkward attempt at a tongue kiss, pressing too hard, his breath hot and suffocating as he pushed her against the wall.

She shoved him back enough to catch her breath. "You can't tell them anything if you don't get back over there, and you certainly can't go like this." She ran a hand down the length of his erection, figuring she had about five minutes to get him back in shape and back to the pulpit. Anger blazed at the thought that he had suddenly become her responsibility, but as his hand slid down the flat of her stomach and insinuated itself between her legs, she forgot all about being angry. The world around them slipped out of focus and all that existed were their hands pleasuring each other – Apollo coaxing Daphne, who was more than a little tempted to yield.

But this Apollo was awkward, nervous.

There was almost no movement. They both stood with their backs braced against the door frame shifting and rocking against each other's hands in tight little thrustings that would have been barely noticeable if they had been clothed, if their hands hadn't been in each other's crotch. And yet the pleasure of it was electric.

She took his mouth, using her other hand against his chest to regulate the pressure, teaching him by example the pleasure of the tongue on the hard palate. He was a quick study. Too quick. Fantasy was one thing, but this shouldn't be happening, and yet his mouth now made all the right responses, and she needed this, just this little bit. And the way he stroked her pussy felt so wonderfully naive that she just couldn't pull away. She wondered if this is what her mother had felt all those years before.

The movement of his hips intensified until he was pumping hard against her encircling hand. The stretch of his cock felt feverish and tetchy against the curve of her fingers, and his body felt as though the very muscles beneath his trousers were spring-loaded. It only took a couple of thrusts before he came. With a groan he tried to suppress, his penis convulsed against her hand, and she felt the sticky heat of him on her palm.

She figured he'd been taught it was wrong to masturbate. If so, then what they had just done would only add to the guilt he must be feeling for the other night's episode in front of Leda and the Swan. Just another reminder of why they shouldn't be doing this. But somehow the reminder of how naughty their behaviour would be perceived in Jake's world was enough to send her over the edge, and she clenched and shuddered against his stroking fingers.

At last he came to himself. "I'm sorry! I'm sorry!" His face turned crimson, and he pulled away gasping. "Oh God, Donna, I'm so sorry!"

She ignored him, quickly wiping her fingers as best she could on the inside of his boxers. Then she grabbed him by the hand and hurried him to his room, nabbing a towel from the bathroom on the way. "Quick! Get cleaned up. You can still make it, and don't worry. Everything'll be just fine."

He stood almost as though he were in shock, unresponsive to her commands. She tugged off his trousers, practically forcing him back on to the bed in order to get them off over his shoes. Then she rummaged through his drawers until she found his underwear, completely oblivious to the fact that she was still naked.

He simply sat on the bed watching as she knelt in front of him and hurriedly cleaned him. As she slipped the fresh boxers up over his thighs, he reached down and stroked her breasts. "Did you come?" The words sounded so strange from his mouth, and he blushed again and lowered his eyes.

"I did, I came." In fact, she could have come just thinking about what they had done. She couldn't tell by the pained smile on his lips if what she said had pleased him or caused him more internal suffering. No doubt there would be a battle with his conscience and plenty of guilt, but she couldn't be blamed entirely for that.

Once she had him tucked and zipped and inspected for any telltale signs of the morning's escapades, she sent him back over to the church, a bit shell-shocked, but just in time to give the sermon. As for her part, she said a little prayer to Apollo and kept her fingers crossed. She hoped he regained his nerve, and his inspiration.

It was almost ten that night when he came to her studio still dressed in his preacher suit, but looking much calmer. She was adding the final touches on the feathers of the swan's wing where it caressed Leda's breast. "How'd it go?"

"Good." He came to her side. "It wasn't at all the sermon I intended. The words were just there, and it felt right." He nodded to the canvas. "Working on your mother's painting?" This time there was no judgment in his voice.

"Almost finished actually."

"Guess you were inspired too." He watched her for a few minutes as she painted, then heaved a sigh. "About this morning. Nothing like that's ever happened to me before."

She braced herself for the guilt-riddled breast beating and apologizing she figured he was about to unleash upon her, all of which was exactly the reason she had wanted to stay away from him. She was already mentally preparing her response to his guilt when the total silence got her attention.

Jake stood slack-jawed in the middle of the room, gaze locked on the sketch of Apollo and Daphne that she had finally gotten on to canvas. He craned his neck for a closer inspection. The muscles along his cheeks tightened then relaxed, and he squinted closer. There was no disguising the resemblance. Donna had become brazen in her surreptitious use of him as a model. The jig was up.

Four

"You're using me as your Apollo?" The muscles along his cheekbones twitched. For a second she thought he was angry.

"It had nothing to do with this morning." She lay the brush down and wiped her hands on her cut-offs. "I've thought you'd be the perfect Apollo ever since you walked in the door, I swear."

His laughter surprised her as it erupted from deep in his chest. He couldn't stop laughing. He fell uncontrollably into the chair and wiped tears from the corners of his eyes. Then he doubled over, grabbing his sides. "Me as Apollo? That's hysterical."

"Why? Why's that funny, because you want to be a preacher?"

"You think I want to be a preacher?" He practically exploded in another fit of laughter, nearly falling off the chair before he regained control. "Apollo's the god of wisdom, the sun god, who has quite a way with the ladies." He nodded. "Yes, I've been reading up, and I've read enough to know that I'm definitely no Apollo. I'm naive, short-sighted, opinionated, ignorant and, as far as women are concerned, well, how pathetic is it that I had to come in your hand?" Suddenly he was blushing fiercely, unable to meet her gaze.

"You inspire me," she said.

"What?" He blinked hard, and looked up at her.

"I said you inspire me."

For a long moment they held each other's gaze. Donna could swear she heard both their hearts drumming in the stretched silence.

With a movement so sudden that it startled her, he jerked his tie from around his neck, then clawed at the buttons of his shirt and shrugged out of it. She could hear his accelerated breathing. She could see his fingers fumbling as he undid his trousers and slipped them down over his hips.

His voice was a harsh whisper, rasping at the still air. "I'll be your Apollo, or at least I'll try." As he stepped out of his trousers, he paused only briefly before slipping out of the boxer shorts as well. A quick glance at his crotch, and his face reddened again. There was no disguising the erection popping up between his legs. He offered a sheepish grin. "I don't suppose you've got a toga?"

Donna moved on unsteady legs and fumbled through the pile of fabrics folded on a nearby table. She chose a soft white cotton. As she unfolded it, she was reminded of the swan's powerful wings. The room felt tight and airless. She was surprised at her own nerves. She had drawn hundreds of nudes with a practised, profes-sional eye, so why was Jake any different?

She eased him down into the chair and knelt in front of him, trying to see him through artist's eyes, but she felt like the suppli-cant kneeling at the feet of Apollo. As she leaned over him to drape his groin, his hand came to rest on her head. He curled his fingers in her hair. Then he caressed the nape of her neck, looking down at her through lowered lids, making everything in her skittish and quivery.

Carefully, as though not to startle the preacher or anger the god, she planted a kiss low on his belly, just above the base of his cock, and felt him shudder. The sight of his heavy penis so close to her mouth was more than she could resist. She cupped his balls gently in one hand and with the other guided him into her mouth, running her tongue in feather flicks along the underside of his cock.

"Oh God," he groaned, thrusting so hard he nearly gagged her until she lay a controlling palm against his hip. "How can anything feel so good?" Then his hands came to rest on her shoulders. "Wait. Stop. I want it to last."

He half lowered himself, half fell on to the floor next to her, taking her face in his hands, taking her mouth. Then he pulled away and searched her face. "If you had been Daphne, what would you have done?"

She held his gaze. "I would have let Apollo seduce me. I would have offered myself to him for his inspiration. You can't put a price on that."

With awkward fingers he undid the buttons of her blouse. She helped him with the hooks of her bra and pulled him to her breasts as she lay back on the floor.

"I'm not very experienced," he whispered, sliding a hand down the flat of her belly and into the front of her cut-offs.

"I'll show you what to do." She shifted until he could wriggle his fingers inside her panties and over her pubic curls, where he lingered to stroke, and she rocked against the pressure of his palm.

"I want to look at you." He spoke through barely parted lips. "I was too embarrassed this morning, too nervous."

She undid her shorts, lifting her butt so he could slide them off. She watched the play of muscles along his broad shoulders as he freed her feet. When he opened her legs, his breath was warm against her heavy pout as he inspected her folds, sliding fingers over her contours, spreading, stroking until his forefinger pressed against her and she jerked and caught her breath.

"Is that—"

"My clit, yes." She rose on to one elbow and took his fingers in her mouth until they were wet, then she guided them back against her. "This is how I like it. Wet and slippery. Circles, small tight circles." She shuddered and gasped as his movements became less awkward. "Yes, that's it. Now use my own juices. That feels even better." She guided his fingers into the slickness of her cunt, then back on to her clit, undulating against his touch as she did so.

"It's like a pearl," he whispered, easing back the hood for a better view. "I never knew it would be so hard."

She squirmed. "Keep that up, it'll get still harder."

"Can I taste?" His voice was breathy, hot against her vulva.

She thought he only meant to sample her flavour on his fingers, but instead, he pushed her legs apart further and lowered his face. At first he licked gingerly with just the tip of his tongue, sampling carefully, unsure of himself and, she figured, probably a little frightened.

"Do you like it?" She was suddenly, painfully aware of her own vulnerability.

"I do, very much." He opened her wider, his tongue following the path his fingers had splayed. "It's different than I expected, soft, almost sweet, but not. Does it feel good, the way I'm doing it?"

"Mmm." She pressed closer. "Like I never want you to stop."

It was as though he had suddenly been given permission. He cupped her buttocks in his hands and buried his face in her. In spite of her best efforts to stay still, lest she intimidate him, she found herself moaning, moving against him, curling her fingers in his hair, and crying out when the first wave of orgasm hit.

She pushed him away for those few seconds when she was still too sensitive to be touched. But he watched, his head resting against her thigh. "Everything shudders when you come. It's like small earthquakes."

She could feel him rocking against her, the press of his own arousal becoming more urgent. He raised himself to look at her face, struggling to breathe. "Donna." His voice was raw, exposed. "I need to come."

"Wait." She reached into the drawer beneath the credenza, found a condom and helped him into it. Then, still trembling from her orgasm, she took his penis in her hand and guided him, reassured him. She shifted her hips and parted her swollen labia until, with a little thrust, he was completely inside her. He let out a sharp moan that sounded almost like pain or maybe fear, then grabbed her shoulders hard and held her. "Don't move," he gasped. "I'm too sensitive. Give me a second."

She could feel his body straining for control. It was only a minute, but in her impatience it felt like an eternity. She longed to bear down, she ached to thrust against him, desperate to know how it felt to come with him inside her. And when at last he was ready, she wrapped her legs around him and met him thrust for thrust. They were hard, hungry thrusts, inexperienced, elated thrusts accompanied by a duet of grunts and moans.

The veins along his neck pulsed. Every muscle tensed. The in and out friction of his cock had her on the edge again. She dug her nails into his shoulders and threw her head back. Just as her second orgasm hit, she felt him convulse as he shoved in deep and then he cried out, ejaculating in hard, grinding thrusts that threatened to bruise her coccyx.

For a long time the room was awash in the desperate sounds of respiration, which gradually softened and lengthened into post-coital drowsiness. At last he shifted so his weight wasn't fully on her and pulled her close, nestling her against his chest, stroking her hair as he dozed.

Then the artist in her took control. She pulled away and reached for the sketch pad. She sketched rapidly. This time it wasn't the curve of his neck and the slope of his belly she drew. She drew the way his penis, once freed from the condom, rested in its nest of blond curls, the way his balls bulged against the hard muscle of his thigh, the half-domes of his buttocks, the straight lines of his hips.

"What are you doing?" he asked sleepily.

"Drawing your cock." The very awareness of her efforts made his penis heavy against his thigh, and he reached down to stroke its length as though he had only just now become aware of it. He fondled unselfconsciously, much more comfortable with himself than she would have imagined. He caressed his balls and shifted to give her a better view.

She sketched feverishly until he leaned in and nibbled her ear. "If you want to draw Apollo seducing Daphne, then perhaps you should do a few groping sketches. Come on. Bring your sketch pad." He half crawled, half scooted across the floor to sit in front of a large mirror

He positioned himself behind her until she could feel the press of his penis against her back, then he cupped her breast and stroked until the nipple was fully engorged. "Now open your legs. That's good." He curled the other hand down over her pubis, fingers dipping teasingly into her pussy. "Surely this is what Apollo would do if he caught Daphne."

As she sketched, he nibbled the curve of her neck and her ear lobe. She imagined Apollo whispering softly to Daphne, making her promises she couldn't resist until she succumbed to his desires.

The sketching became more difficult with growing arousal. Jake wasn't very sympathetic to her art. He probed and caressed, giving her exquisite views of her vulva, dilated and anxious for more of his cock. He teased her clit from behind its hood to be sketched and fondled.

"You're hard," she grunted, straining against his fingers, nearly dropping the charcoal.

"Of course I'm hard," he said. "I'm touching you."

"Get a condom. I want to draw you inside me."

When he was properly outfitted for the occasion, he pulled her into his lap and entered her face to face so they could both see the point of pleasure. With the help of the mirror, she drew from every angle – he took her from behind, he took her in a spoon position, he pulled her on top of him. All the while he teased and caressed until at last she threw the sketch pad aside and pulled him on top of her. They came amid scattered sketches of cocks and breasts and pouting cunts, sketches of all the acts they imagined Apollo and Daphne might do together.

At last he pulled the drapery over them like a blanket, like the wings of the swan, nestling her into a spoon position, and they slept.

She awoke chilled and stiff, with anaemic dawn filtering through the curtains. Jake was gone. His room was empty. She showered and moped over coffee. Of course the guilt would eat at him. It would be hard for him to face her. Her stomach knotted, and she swallowed back anger. He had come on to her. She would have happily let him remain pure and untouched if that's what he wanted.

But hadn't she wanted him from the beginning, and hadn't sex with him been even more exciting than she could have ever imagined in her Apollo fantasies? He wasn't Apollo, she reminded herself, and she sure as hell wasn't Daphne.

At Sirens, nothing went right. Her satyr looked more like a cow than a goat. Everything she painted reminded her of her night with Jake, and she fought back the niggling fear that she had ruined her inspiration by having sex with him.

But it was more than her lack of inspiration that bothered her; it was the deep raw ache that wouldn't go away. How could she have been so stupid? Hadn't she learned anything from her mother's miseries? Jake was not for her, end of discussion. Finally she gave up her efforts to paint and went home to an empty house.

In her studio, she flipped through the sketch pad of great new ideas, all sketched fast and furiously, all done since she met Jake. The canvas with the sketch of Apollo and Daphne was ready to paint. There were several other canvases that had preliminary sketches, not all involving Jake, but all somehow inspired by his presence.

She studied the painting of Leda and the Swan. The swan nearly flew off the canvas. She could almost see the rising and falling of Leda's breasts in her effort to breathe. The painting was alive in the way she knew her mother had intended it to be when she started it so long ago.

In the foggy recesses of her mind, Donna remembered coming home from school in the afternoons to find the handsome young reverend and her mother sequestered at the kitchen table arguing politics and religion over some exotic blend of tea.

Time passed, and she found them in her mother's studio, her mother painting Reverend Tandy as Hermes or Zeus or Endymion. She thought nothing of the preacher's varying stages of undress. Her mother often worked with nude models.

Then one day she came home from school unexpectedly early. She was old enough to understand what the sounds coming from her mother's bedroom meant. Her mother had taken lovers before. But this lover had been different. This lover had ripped their world apart. The church found out. Soon after that they moved from Denver without saying goodbye to the nice preacher.

Now Reverend Tandy looked sad and old, like her mother had before she died. A heart attack, the doctors had said, but Donna was certain her mother died of a broken heart. She blamed Tandy.

And yet her mother had seen Endymion in the man. He had kindled that spark of inspiration in some of her best paintings, something Donna hadn't understood until Jake waltzed into her life. She'd always said she'd willingly pay any price for inspiration. After what happened to her mother, she, of all people should know just how high that price might be.

When Donna left for the club the next morning, there was still no sign of Jake.

As usual, it was only Donna and Irv at Sirens. The rest of the crew straggled in much later in the day. She had been painting several hours when, from beneath the scaffolding, Irv called her. "Donna! Get your ass down here. The Reverend's here to see you."

For a frightening moment, Donna feared she'd hyperventilate. She peeked over the edge of her fortress to see Irv and Jake, both nodding enthusiastically then shaking hands before Irv went back to his office without his usual warning that he wasn't paying her to chat. Trembling so hard she feared she'd shake the scaffolding loose, she lay staring up into the eyes of Apollo as though she were praying, struggling to calm the cocktail of emotions now slamming her heart against her ribs. When at last she found the courage, she looked down over the edge of the scaffolding to find Jake gazing up at her.

He smiled his greeting as though nothing had happened, as though he hadn't just vanished for two days. Then he nodded to the painting of Apollo. "You'll ruin my reputation painting my face all over town like this, not to mention my other bits."

"What do you want?" she called, annoyed at the tremor in her voice.

The smile disappeared from his face and he was suddenly serious. "Please come down. We need to talk."

She eased herself over the edge of the scaffolding, finding the descent more difficult than usual in her unsteady state. Jake's heavy gaze on her back did little to settle her nerves.

Before she reached the floor, her foot slipped and she would have fallen the last few feet if he hadn't moved quickly to brace her securely against the metal rungs. His hot breath against the back of her neck made her nipples ache and her breath catch. Why did it have to feel so good to be near him?

With more willpower than she thought she could muster, she pushed him away and stepped down. "You said you wanted to talk. Glad you finally got around to it." She folded her arms across her chest.

"I'm sorry. But I needed time to think."

"And how did that work out for you?" she huffed.

He raked her with a hungry gaze that came to rest on her face. "I'm not going to seminary."

"What?" The shock of his words forced her back against the scaffolding, and anger rose in her throat along with no small amount of panic. "You can't put this kind of responsibility on me. I wasn't the one who—"

Suddenly it was as though he could stand the distance between them no longer. He stopped her words with an earth-shaking kiss, pinning her against the scaffolding with his body, chest pressed hard against her aching breasts, groin raking her pubis.

She made a valiant effort to push him away, but he held her tight, his tongue snaking along her hard palate exactly the way she had taught him, exactly the way she liked it. His raw strength shocked her, frightened her, then aroused her, until she gave up the struggle and found herself fighting to get even closer to him.

At last he pulled back just enough to allow her to breathe, then he spoke. "Didn't you hear me the other night? I never wanted to go to seminary in the first place. I was only trying to please my family. You were just my wake-up call, nothing more."

"Nothing more?" She shoved her hand hard against the flat of his chest. "So glad I could be of help."

"That's not what I meant." He grabbed her hand, but not before she jerked away and gave him a resounding slap across the cheek.

"That's for disappearing for two days without a word." She fought back an angry sob and slapped him again. "That's for making me care one way or another." As he recoiled she turned and headed back up the scaffolding.

"This is not going to happen." His voice came out a frustrated growl. He was on her before she could make the third rung, wrapping his arm around her waist and pulling her off the scaffolding like she was a rag doll. She came around fighting and struggling, but he held her tight and kissed her again. She bit his lip. But still he held her. "I'm not leaving until we've cleared this up." His breath was ragged as it tore through his chest, and his grip on her was bruising. "You said I inspired you. I've never inspired anyone before." He pulled her closer, holding her so tight she could barely breathe. "Did it ever occur to you that you inspired me too? That just maybe you gave me courage to pursue my own dream and not what everyone else had planned for me?"

In their struggles her skirt had come up until only the thin crotch of her panties separated her from the obvious bulge in his trousers. The subtle rocking of their hips made it clear that their bodies knew what they both wanted long before their minds could settle on a plan of action.

"Don't push me away." His words came out a harsh whisper against her throat. "Not when I've only just found the courage to come to you."

The roil of emotions forced its way out in a heavy sob that shook her whole body. Suddenly she hadn't the strength to fight any longer. She wrapped her legs around him feeling his penis surge beneath his trousers. The rocking became blatant dry-humping. She grabbed the rungs of the scaffolding for support and leaned back while he undid her blouse, popping two buttons in his anxious efforts. Then he shoved aside her bra, bathing her breasts in the heat of his breath as he suckled and caressed.

With her legs still wrapped around him and his face still buried in the valley between her breasts, he cupped his hands under her bottom and lifted her away from the scaffolding. Then he carried her to the bar and eased her back on the smooth wooden surface.

"Irv will catch us." She made a weak effort to push him away.

"Let him." He nipped the inside of her thigh with his front teeth making her clench and swell. He pulled her panties down over her hips and let them drop to the floor. When he slipped a finger between her heavy folds, she was already slick and responsive to his probing. He pushed her legs apart and his tongue took over what his fingers had begun, snaking along the engorged lips of her pout, making her groan and bear down against his face while he nibbled and tugged.

The sound of his fly opening was followed closely by the crinkle of a condom wrapper, and her pussy grasped expectantly. She opened her legs wider, brazenly exposing herself. Her whole body ached to be filled, just like the supplicant offering herself on the altar to Apollo. And when Jake climbed on to the bar between her legs, it was as though her painting had become reality.

He fingered her lips apart, then with a deep-chested grunt, pushed into her, stretching her around his thickness almost, but not quite, to the point of pain. She gave a sharp cry and caught her breath. Then she wrapped her legs around him, grabbed the edge of the bar for leverage, and they both began to thrust and hump and writhe, like the satyrs and the fauns who frolicked in her mural.

Beneath the watchful eyes of Apollo, the room was filled with the urgent sounds of sex, and the smell of arousal dominated the smell of fresh paint.

After two agonizing days of anticipation, neither of them held back. There was no lingering, no exploring, only hard shoving and pushing to get to what they both needed.

They came together convulsing and shuddering so violently that she feared they'd be ripped apart by the sheer pleasure of it. She could think of no better way to die.

She wasn't sure how long they lay on the bar spent and oxygen depleted, unable to do more than gasp. From behind the not very soundproof walls of his office, they could hear Irv cursing the damn government for all the damn taxes.

Later when they were once again clothed and enjoying a Coke at the deserted bar, she asked, "What will you do now?"

He studied the larger-than-life image of himself on the ceiling. "I'll finish out the year teaching English. That gives me some time, and money. But I know I won't follow in Uncle Ed's footsteps." He turned his gaze on her. "I asked him about your mother, though I suspected the answer. He told me everything." He looked down at his hands now folded around his drink. "Uncle Ed had a chance to be Apollo, and he threw it away. I feel like I've been asleep until now, only dreaming my life. You woke me up. And now that I'm awake, I want to stay awake with you. I don't want to miss out on anything."

Her stomach did a little flip-flop as his words sank in. "Then you still want to be with me?" The words trembled from her lips, lacking confidence, but not hope.

His grip was nearly painful as he took her hands and held them to his chest. "I actually came here to make you an offer. After everything you've been through with your mother and Golgotha, and with me being such an idiot, I'll understand if you don't want to take me up on it. But I'm desperately hoping you will." His pulse fluttered against his throat. A deep blush rose up his cheeks, and he offered her a shy half-smile. "I'd like to be Apollo for you, or at least try to be. If you want me."

She spoke around a tingle of barely controlled nerves. "Apollo's always welcome at the Jenkins house."

"I'm extremely glad to hear that," he said, folding her in his arms. "Because I know who inspires Apollo, and she lives at the Jenkins house."

That night, as they lay in each other's arms bathed in moonlight, she couldn't help thinking that her mother had been right, and she had been right too. Inspiration was worth the price, whatever it was, and she had gotten off easy this time. This time, it was a price she was only too happy to pay.

Just Ask

Lilith Saintcrow

Of course it was raining.

The cold didn't bother Selene Thompson; Nichtvren were largely immune to temperature and, in any case, it was much warmer than it had been half a world away. But stepping off the transport and on to the concrete of Santiago City's dock, she shivered. The chill radio-active heart of this felt no different, even though she'd spent a century on the other side of the globe. Her body tingled, adjusting to the change in ambient Power, adapting in seconds instead of the day or so it would take if she were still human.

What a laugh. She'd be long dead by now. She bared her fangs at the thought, a swift flash of sharp white, then caught herself.

The rain didn't reach down here below ground level, but cold stray flirting breezes touched her long dark hair as the anti-grav. on the transports played havoc with air currents. She suppressed the urge to hunch her shoulders. In her coat pocket, the medallion gave a small fluttering pulse against her finger. She hadn't even been aware of touching it.

Nikolai's hand polished the curve of her hip, something cool and metallic sliding against her skin. He drew it up over her ribs, under her breast, then the medallion lay where it used to, half the chain spilling down to pool on the sheet. He fastened it at the back of her neck, one-handed, and flattened his other palm against the silver lying between her breasts.

"This is important, Selene. Without it, you're at risk. This gives you protection. *You cannot throw it away. Understood?"*

She'd left it on his riven, bloodless chest as he lay on his death-bed, a hundred years ago. And yet, two days ago it had arrived at her Nest in Freetown New Prague. A cedarwood box, the medallion on its tarnished chain and a note on expensive linen paper. Two words in fantastical calligraphy: *Come home.*

Her boot heels ground the concrete as she turned in a full circle. The flight had arrived after dark, but the new transport well was deep enough it didn't matter. A calculated risk, travelling by hover transport . . . but calculated risks were what she did best. Or at least, what she did now that she was a functionally immortal blood-drinker and very hard to kill.

There really wasn't that much difference, she reflected, between being a sexwitch whore and a Freetown mercenary. Both accepted money, but performed for a darker need. In Selene's case, it was all the cloned blood she could drink and the leeway to find the limits of her preternatural body and mind on the battlefield – because she hadn't had a Master to teach her about being a suckhead. The one who Turned her was dead. She'd seen as much, sent him to his afterworld with all the offerings she could manage.

So who sent me this, then? Her fingers touched the warm metal. *Oh, what the hell.*

She drew it out of her pocket. A hard silver gleam, the full moon rising. Spiked runic writing on one side, the figure of some odd animal scratched on the other. A lion, perhaps? Who knew? The fastening was tarnished shut, but she slid the chain over her head and dropped the medallion down her shirt. It felt like it belonged, cold metal warming and nestling against her breastbone. The Power in the medallion thrilled along her nerves, a small zing lilting biting tinfoil.

Let's hope someone's noticed that. The languor of dawn approaching weighted down her fingers, a warning.

There was another feeling. Anticipation. It ran along her veins, pooling in her lower belly. She hadn't felt the swimming weakness, the hunger, the *need* in so long. She didn't miss it – after a whole human life spent as a slave to a sexwitch's need, it was impossible to regret its disappearance.

And yet.

Nikolai.

There. She'd thought of him. Dark eyes, his fingers, the soft curl of dark hair that fell over his forehead. The sense of contained power and grace, the utterly frightening control he took of every situation she'd ever seen him in. Other memories crowded in, and the lump of cold iron in the bottom of her belly warmed. His blood in her veins, her curse in his; the *need* didn't rule her any longer but with no prospect of it ever being satisfied, it was best not to taunt it.

I hated him, she reminded herself. Then, judging she'd stayed on the transport dock long enough to be noticed by *someone*, she gathered herself and melted into the crowd of humanity. Up above the rain would blur her scent . . . but she would take care not to blur it too much.

The geography of Saint City hadn't changed out of recognition. Spread, of course, and there were different peaks and valleys. Cities aged as slowly as Nichtvren, even in the New World.

How anachronistic of her, to call it the "new" world. By the time she'd been born, it was already old.

The International District was still rough trade. She remembered hunting in these alleys to feed her human curse, sailors and soldiers while her brother stood guard. Time healed plenty, but it didn't ameliorate the sharp shame or disgust.

Even boom towns had abandoned buildings, and she found what she was looking for after a half-hour's worth of wandering. The warehouse slumped against its bones, dispirited under the strengthening rain. Water falling from the sky bleached everything here, turned it grey.

Not really. Things had been grey since she left. She'd lost her curse, but also lost the hurtful colour of the world.

In any case, it was child's play to break in past the maglocks and recon. She could have found a hostel downtown, one that catered to her kind . . . but why? *Make it difficult for whoever wants to trap you*, that was a rule of survival. She planned to make it just difficult enough.

She dug in her bag for the small rolls of tripwire, spent a precious twenty minutes laying surprises. A hard delighted smile lingered on her lips as she worked; spending fifty years as a mercenary was good training for booby traps. And they had such delightful little toys nowadays, like the plasbursters and the new vaston explosive; light, easy to carry, wouldn't blow up unless you primed it but once you did, watch out!

Her fingers and toes were full of lead by the time she finished and settled in her chosen resting place. No chance of sunlight, even if they came after her; the explosives would take out the support structure and bury her safely.

She was counting on whoever-it-was wanting to capture her alive. If that wasn't the case, well . . .

Selene curled into a corner, her back braced against concrete. The sun pressed against the horizon like a boil, she *felt* it with the queer inner clock every Nichtvren possessed. How long would it be before she could walk around by day but not in sun, like Nik—

Sunrise. The blackness took her. And as always, she dreamed. Of *him.*

At least the space inside her head was her own. "Go ahead and feed," *she whispered, and closed her eyes, shutting him out. Hot tears trickled down her temples, sank into her damp hair.* "Don't mind me." It doesn't matter to you, it never matters to any of them. Christos, just hurry up and take what you want, the sooner you do the sooner you'll leave me alone.

"You're weeping." *As if surprised.*

Selene went limp under him, pliant. Just get it over with, will you? Fuck me if you have to, but leave the rest of me alone. "Of course I'm crying," *she said, her body gone hot and prickling with a sudden flush of Power.* "My b–b–brother—" Shut up, Selene. That's not his business. *The bed was soft underneath her, she sank down helplessly.*

"I did not want you to see . . ." *He sounded, of all things, uncertain.*

Nikolai, uncertain? No. I didn't hear him right. "I had to. He's my brother"

And it's my fault, sucktooth. Someone else tore him into bits, but it's my fault. And for once I'm not fucking blaming you, either. Even though I am, you got him involved in whatever killed him, but if I wasn't what I am you never would have been interested in me and—

He freed his fingers from her hair long enough to stroke her cheek, a gentle and completely unexpected touch. "A bargain is a bargain, dear one," *he whispered. But still he didn't move, though she could feel him pressing against her inner thigh, hot skin against slick dampness. She was wet and the low constant ache had started again. She wasn't drained, but her body wanted completion now.*

Again. My curse. *Selene's throat was blocked with unshed tears.* "Just get it over with." *It took work to force the whisper out.*

"Do you still hate me?" *He kissed along her throat. His teeth scraped above the pulse and Selene's heart slammed against her ribs.*

"Don't," *she began.* "Nikolai – don't!"

"Too late," *he whispered, and his hips came down. She was so slick and wet with need that he had no difficulty – and, at the same moment, he drove his teeth into her throat.*

There was no laying in bed half-awake for Nichtvren. When the sun sank, consciousness returned with a sound like metal breaking.

No. Metal clashing against itself. Chains, and fiery pain in her wrists.

Selene opened her eyes. Not quite a glare, but the light was painful. She disregarded it, stretched out her senses. Power swam in the air, a heavy weight against breath and heart and mind.

Another Nichtvren. She inhaled, tasted the air.

That's not Nikolai. It's female. And old.

The vaulted ceiling was stone. Softness under her, a type of padded platform. And the chains, clasped at wrist and ankle, pulled tight. Chill air against her bare skin. The medallion shifted against her breastbone.

Well. This is interesting.

"Don't bother testing the chains." A high tinkling voice, the Merican accented broadly. Something Eastern Europa, if Selene was any judge by now. "You'll just be damaged."

The burning at Selene's wrists intensified. She already had scars there, from Grigori's little mixture so long ago. He'd chained her too, but not for very long.

Selene blinked. The light scored her eyes, brought hot water out to trickle down into her hair. Her ankles began to prickle, too. Something was smeared on the insides of the restraints, an oily residue.

"You cost me eight thralls, with those little explosives." That high sweet voice smoked with contempt and absolute power. "But I caught you, nonetheless."

You were supposed to, you idiot. Well, at least this part had gone according to plan. Now she would find out who this was, and what they wanted.

A shadow in the light. It leaned over Selene, two blonde braids falling over her slim shoulders. A fair clear complexion, dainty fangs, half-lidded blue eyes and naked skin dusted with golden freckles. She'd probably been Turned because of that fresh, freckle-faced look, like an Alpine milkmaid on an advertising holo.

Jesu help me, I've been kidnapped by Heidi. A rill of laughter rose in Selene's throat; she didn't even try to contain it. Her laugh came out as a harsh caw, bouncing off stone. The echoes gave her the dimensions of the room – large, a high vaulted ceiling, and it *felt* underground.

Blondie's face twisted itself up a little, smoothed out. She didn't like being laughed at. That was the problem with so many Nichtvren Masters. So *touchy*. That prickly pride made them predictable, as far as Selene was concerned. It gave her an edge. And as a lone Nichtvren, she needed every edge she could get. Particularly since she was chained down and naked.

Funny how things don't change. Spent a lot of my life naked at someone's whim. Her lips peeled back from her teeth, exposing her own fangs. It was a show of aggression, and likely to madden this bitch, whoever she was.

It worked. The little nose wrinkled, and she slapped Selene hard enough to bounce her head off the padding. Selene didn't even strain against the chains. The Power in the air drew close and stifling, ice cubes against every exposed inch of her, and she calculated the little blonde girl was at least as old as Nikolai. But she didn't have Nikolai's sheer suffocating will, or his strength.

Hmmm. Again, interesting.

"Bitch." The woman climbed up on the platform, gracefully. She wore her nakedness like another woman would wear expensive silk; she'd been Turned right in her prime and she knew it. "Of course, this is what I expected from *his* inamorata."

Something in Selene stilled. The other Nichtvren must have felt her reaction. She leaned down, those blonde braids slithering down to brush against Selene. "He never spoke of me, I would hazard. I am Marya. *You* are Selene. His precious Selene. So easy to catch, and my vengeance is complete." Her lips brushed Selene's cheek, fangs scraping lightly. Instinct warred with will; Selene tensed.

Marya smelled of cloves and old rusted blood. Her breath was a little foul; she must have just fed because her skin was bloat-warm. Fed from something drugged, most likely, that would be the acridity in her mouth, her metabolism burning through whatever her victim or thrall had been high on. Loathing crawled through Selene, even as Marya's mouth met hers.

She *could* have bitten the bitch, she supposed. Her own teeth were just as sharp. But this woman had a script she was working from, and letting her play it out would get Selene further than violence at this point. Her fingertips played over the canvas cover of the padding, her hands twisting to feel at the cuffs. Whatever was smeared on the inside of the metal was beginning to hurt like hell, and the coppery-sweet scent of her own blood rose in the charged air.

Marya's tongue slid into Selene's mouth. Obviously nobody had taught her to kiss, she just shoved it in like Selene was supposed to be grateful for the privilege.

Oh, Jesu. Nothing ever changes, does it? Selene restrained the urge to roll her eyes and accepted it. She even went loose under the woman's dense weight, a Nichtvren's heavier muscle and bone pressing down. Her knees were on either side of Selene's hips, she settled like a dog crouched over a bone.

Marya broke away. "Once a whore, always a whore." A bitter little laugh, her young-old face contorting. You could have mistaken her for a teenager in certain very dim light, except for the mad, ancient thing peeking out through those bright, bright blue eyes. "Except I know you were *tantraiiken*, you filthy little . . ." A long rumble, the growl filling Marya's chest. She pushed herself up, settled her weight firmly on Selene's hips. She ground down, and Selene went utterly still.

Her script's changing. Huh.

Marya turned her head. "Bring him in," she snarled, the *command* unmistakable. There was a sound – ah, her thralls would be outside the door. Close enough to hear their Master, by flesh or mental call.

Selene tipped her head carefully to the side, a few millimetres. The other Nichtvren glanced back down, and she leaned forwards. Her long, capable hands – they felt too broad and strong, rough as if chapped – closed around Selene's throat. But gently.

"What is the best revenge, *kallike*?" She smiled gently as a scraping sound filled the room. A door, opening. Selene didn't dare turn her head further to look. She kept her mouth shut, watching like she would have watched a client in her human days. When she would have been waiting for a cue, her curse throbbing through her flesh.

"The best revenge," Marya continued, her thumb stroking along the side of Selene's throat ever so gently, "is to kill the thing your enemy loves before him. While he is helpless."

What the hell is this bitch talking about?

"Look," Marya whispered, and tilted Selene's head to the side. "Look at him."

Selene did as she was told.

The scraping had been double doors, iron-bound and made of some dark wood. They were pushed open now, and the darkness behind them was absolute. A huge hideous creaking, and the shape became visible. Selene blinked again, fresh water trickling from her eyes. How did the other Nichtvren stand it so bright in here?

It was a low wooden cart on broad iron-rimmed wheels. The thralls – huge muscle-bound men with empty stares, their will erased by their Master's dominance – pushed it forwards, straining. It barely cleared the opening, and threatened to tip over because a massive X of plasteel beams crouched on it.

And there, spreadeagled and in rags, his face and body horribly mangled and seeping thick sluggish black blood, was Nikolai. A glitter of eyes under filthy hair showed he was conscious.

So he *was* alive.

The shock grated through Selene, her entire body frozen, pinned like a butterfly. Marya laughed and settled her hips more firmly. Her hands tightened just a little on Selene's throat.

I don't need to breathe, Selene reminded herself. But if I don't, I'll burn through my cellular stores more rapidly and my body will start cannibalizing. Great. She's bound to have another means of killing me, this is just theatre.

"Demoskenos Kirai Nikolai." Marya's laugh was a chill little giggle, high-pitched. She sounded so *young*, it was the worst thing. "This is going to take a long, long time."

So you think. Selene gathered herself. Nikolai's eyes glittered. He hung there, and she could see the iron bolts driven through his wrists and ankles. The pain would have been excruciating.

But he was alive. *Alive.* All this time. How had he . . . He had been *dead.* She had been so certain.

There were more dragging sounds. One of the thralls was heaving another wheeled thing towards the platform. It was an iron frame, and the things stacked and hung neatly on it would have turned Selene's stomach if she hadn't spent so much time seeing the different ways a body – even a preternatural body – could be broken.

It had lost its power to shock. She wasn't sure if she should be grateful for that. The medallion flared with heat against her breastbone, a familiar old sensation.

Marya's fingers bit down. "This is just for beginnings," she chortled, and her hands turned into a crushing vice. "First I'll take your voice, so you cannot even scream. Then there will be the irons, and the rack, and the open flame—"

Selene pitched aside, every muscle tightening. The chains were strong and the cuffs were tight, but you don't spend your human life as a sexwitch without learning how to slip out of tight hand-cuffs. It would mean stripping flesh off the bone, but she'd heal.

If she escaped this.

She *yanked*, her skin ripping and the pain like a red bolt of fire up her arm, and her claws bit into the other Nichtvren's face, unloos-ing a gout of blood.

The pain was a spur, and she welcomed it. Her other hand ripped free, leaving a significant amount of flesh behind, and she *shoved*, getting good contact on the other Nichtvren's chest and heaving with every ounce of preternatural strength she owned.

Which was considerable, and battle-hardened as well. Marya went flying, a shattering wail of rage trailing behind her and threatening to pop Selene's eardrums. Selene curled up, her claws slicing through padding and closing on the chains holding her feet down. The metal parted with a screech and she was up in a flash, crouching on the platform and taking in the entire circular room with one sweep. *Know your ground*, another cardinal rule of survival.

Another exit over there. And . . . Christos, that is *an actual rack. She wasn't kidding.*

Selene threw herself aside, tucking and rolling. Stone grated against her naked back, bullets chewed the platform bed. Explosive ammo, meant to bleed her out. At least some of the thralls were free to act in an emergency. She gained her feet, moving smoothly through the roll, her legs bending and releasing as she *leaped*, twist-ing to avoid another spray of bullets. They were thralls, yes, but they were only human.

And Selene . . . was not, now.

She landed behind the knot of thralls with submachine guns, her claws out and the growl filling her chest. Blood flew, bones splin-tering, and there was a shattering, ripping sound. Marya's howling changed pitch, and Selene bent backwards like a gymnast, her foot flashing up and catching the last thrall under the chin with a sicken-ing crack. She rolled aside again as the blonde bitch arrived out of thin air, her clawed face splattering blood, blue eyes rolling with mad hate.

That's going to hurt as it heals. The thought was a flash. Selene's body did the work for her, once she got out of the way and let train-ing and instinct take over. *Goddamn, she's fast.* Her feet slapped the floor, cuffs and broken chains jingling musically, Selene's claws sank into the stone roof and she twisted, agonizing pain in her wrists, her hands spattering more candy-smelling blood. There was enough of the red stuff here to craze a newly Turned; the thirst threatened to close a veil of red over Selene's vision. She landed on the floor, whirling and throwing her hands out in flat palm-strikes, Power burning through her as she connected.

Hit me with flesh and Power both, Selene, Nikolai whispered in the dim recesses of her memory. *Anything else is useless.*

The medallion burned, a sudden sharp spike of heat, a jolt of pure Power. Surprising, but Selene welcomed it. Any tool to do the job at hand.

That was, she thought briefly, the biggest difference between her human self and what she was now.

Marya flew back again, but not as far as Selene had hoped. The blonde hit the iron frame with its torture instruments, everything collapsing and flying with musical jangles. The noise was incredible – Selene's instinctive growl and the howling the blonde was doing, more gunfire somewhere outside the room.

And a deep, powerful thrumming underlaid every other sound. It was coming from the plasteel beams where Nikolai hung. His head was up, the mad glitter of his eyes suddenly scorching, and Selene's heart gave an amazing leap.

Stop staring at him and mo—

It was too late. The blonde had gathered herself, and she collided with Selene. The sound was like a good hard break on a hoverpool table, and Selene *flew*. Claws tangled in her ribs, pulling – the bitch was trying to pull her heart out the hard way.

Selene punched her twice before they hit the stone wall, a shock wave jolting through her abused body. A life spent disassociating herself from the omnipresent swell of desire a sexwitch was prey to was good practice for learning to disregard pain, but she was losing blood fast now and hadn't fed in four days.

Stupid, silly, goddamn it, Selene, start thinking!

It was too late. Marya's claws sliced further in, and the queer floating feeling of too much blood loss began in Selene's flayed fingers and bare toes. She brought her knee up before they landed, her back scraping the stone wall. Another punch, blood flying from her knuckles as they fell. Hit the floor in a tangle, Marya's flesh feverish against hers, and Selene's chin snaked forwards. Her teeth champed, a bare inch from the other woman's throat. Naked blood-greased skin slid, straining, and if she didn't end this fight soon, Selene knew she would lose.

Over Marya's blood-slick shoulder, Selene caught a flicker of motion. A familiar shape fell from the plasteel beams, the X toppling backwards with a heavy clangour.

Chaos. Screaming. The red haze of bloodshed. Selene's teeth clamped home, breaking through the hard crust of a Nichtvren's skin, just over the *carotid minora*. A hot flood of candy-spiced blood filled her mouth. She didn't precisely want to drink, just to bleed. If she could weaken the bitch enough—

More screaming, more gunfire. Selene's eyes rolled. She hugged Marya close, arms and legs pinning the other woman, disregarding her rapidly weakening struggles. If she could just hold on long enough, swallowing what she could of the other woman's strength, it might be enough . . .

Marya tore free, howling. The sound battered Selene's damp hair back with clawed fingers, sharp spikes against her sensitive eardrums.

"Let *go!*" he yelled, and the *command* rang through her, a gong inside her head.

She fought, of course, the instinct of her own Mastery rising to deny him control. But he was older, and he had Turned her, and her arms and legs loosened of their own accord. Her teeth slid free of Marya's flesh, and the other Nichtvren hissed feebly as she was jerked back, her blonde braids looped around a bleeding, broken fist.

"You," Nikolai snarled, his gaunt dirty face contorted. He dragged her as she writhed, somehow avoiding the wild strikes of her claws. "*You.*" A sudden movement, preternatural bones crunching, and more blood flew. His fangs were out, and a cold prickling weight settled over the room.

How had this crazy blonde beast ever held him?

Selene blinked. She lay on her side against cold stone, her fingers twitching as the flesh repaired itself. Candy-sweet blood burned her tongue, sank into her parched throat. She'd always loved sugar – any child growing up in the camps learned to take as many calories in as possible, the sweeter the better – and this was so *good*. The best candy-spice burn was from the blood of another predator.

How much did I take? There was a lump of warmth behind her aching breastbone, another answering it from above.

Nikolai's chest swelled with the growl, a wall of subsonic vibration. His mangled hands tightened, swollen pale fingers, the ring and middle fingers terribly crunched and distorted, and he twisted sharply. There was a crack like well-seasoned wood, and Marya's body convulsed.

Nichtvren don't throw up, Selene told herself, swallowing hard. The habit of nausea was strong, even after all these years. One day, she supposed, she'd outgrow it. If she survived.

Nikolai straightened. He drew one wasted leg up, the knee a grotesque knob of bone and skin, and the fury twisting his face turned Selene's stomach even more. You wouldn't think it was the same maddeningly gentle, inflexible, always controlled Nikolai she dream-remembered every time the sun rose and waking consciousness fled her.

He stamped down, *hard*. There was a sound like a stone watermelon breaking, and the screaming outside the room took on a frantic quality. Of course, every one of Marya's thralls would feel her skullspatter-death. They were condemned to an agonizing death of their own without her animating influence, unless Nikolai took them under his wing.

Or Selene. Or any other Master.

Marya's body twitched, her misshapen head lolling as Nikolai drew his foot away. Blood spread in scallops, a crimson lake. Selene swallowed again, hard, and flexed her fingers.

Nikolai stood, staring down at the body. The remaining rags of his clothing fluttered, but he was utterly motionless. The tension leaked out of him bit by bit, and Selene gathered herself.

He lifted his head. The mad twin gleams of his eyes, reflecting differently than a human's, were a flat catshine as he studied her in return.

You were dead, she wanted to say. Her lips twitched. But in the end, she said nothing. There was no use in stating the obvious. She tensed, slowly, one muscle at a time, and when she was certain everything was more or less functional, she pushed herself upright.

A soft breeze touched her cheek. Selene flung up a hand, her claws extended, their razor edges a hair's breadth from his *carotid minora*. The *majora* was more deeply buried under the changed structure of the throat; she didn't have the right angle for a strike.

There was no need. He simply watched her.

He was on his knees. Right next to her. The faint breeze died as the gunfire spattered to a halt. There were other sounds she recognized – the calls and short bursts of mopping-up instead of an actual battle.

Nikolai's thralls, she realized. Why had Marya left any alive? Or had they staged an assault?

Of course they had staged an assault, probably from outside. Once Nikolai, bleeding and bound on that iron X, had *told* them to.

Well now, don't I feel silly. She swallowed, roughly. Her hands were still raw, her ribs ached, but the worst of it had stopped. The wounds were closing over, and if she found a bar with a cloned-blood counter she would be right as rain in a few hours.

Another survival.

She eased away, along the wall. Twinges and vicious little nips of pain rang stitched through her. The trickles of blood slowed. Her exhaustion was a human habit, but still. Even a Nichtvren could get tired.

"Jesu Christos," she whispered. "That was entertaining."

Nikolai crouched, staring at her. His face didn't ease, and his eyes were now dark holes.

Selene sighed. So many things changed as the years passed, and so many didn't. "You could have killed her at any time." She braced herself against the wall, leaving a long wide smear of blood as she pushed herself to her feet. "You were waiting. For me to show up, apparently. Whatever morality play you put together is concluded. I'll be on the next transport out. Nice seeing you again."

"Selene." Everything in the room rattled as he said it, from the wheeled carts to the scattered implements. Broken bodies lay everywhere. The blood seeping from Marya's broken body ruffled along its liquid surface. Someone was going to have a hell of a time cleaning that up.

She tested her legs. They would hold her up. The broken chains rattled as she took one step away from the wall. Another. Thirst prickled in her throat; it would rapidly become unbearable.

He likely wouldn't begrudge her hunting live prey here. But still.

"Master?" A thrall at the door – a tall bald man with a familiar voice, his submachine gun pointed at the floor and his well-cut suit spattered with fluids it was probably best not to think about. Selene almost shut her eyes. If she blinked every time something here reminded her of the past, she was going to look like a narcoleptic vox-sniffer.

"Jorge." Nikolai sounded like himself again. "Attend her."

Selene took another step. Really doing well, she congratulated herself. *Now let's find some clothes.*

Nikolai was suddenly there next to her, his mangled hand closing around her upper arm. "You need blood."

The first touch, after so many years – and her traitorous body lit up like a marquee. A different weakness spilled through her, and her breath caught. Selene tore her arm away. "I need a lot more than that, Nikolai." She could have sounded irritated, she supposed, but the only thing that came out was weariness. "Leave me alone."

"There is—" he began.

No comfort in alone. She could have finished the sentence in her sleep. "Shut. Up."

Miraculously, he did.

"Since you're so bent on being *helpful*, I'll need clothes. And cloned blood, preferably cut with cafetrol. Then I'll be on my merry." Her eyes fixed on the floor. She took another step, another. Did not sway.

"Very well." Chill and hurtful, now. "I owe you my thanks, after all."

Selene shrugged. "You could've killed her anytime you wanted to."

"Yes. But you came."

There was no answer to that. She put her head down, her naked skin prickling under the blood absorbing back into its surface tissues, and headed for the door.

A short, scorch-hot shower restored her. Her wrists would scar once more, from whatever Marya had painted the cuffs with. They flushed an angry red, traceries crawling down her hand and up her arm. She'd never tanned anyway, and now she was marble pale; the crimson spider webs as her flesh reacted to the mixture was shocking contrast.

Selene took three long swallows of cloned blood, the sting of cafetrol hitting the back of her throat. She'd never drink espresso again, but the half-second jolt as her body burned through the artificial additive was enough.

It made her feel almost human.

She would have preferred jeans and a T-shirt, but Jorge brought her midnight-blue silk, a long flowing skirt, low cut, with spaghetti straps. It fit perfectly, which was . . . thought provoking.

It also showed the medallion's gleam, and the mottling on her arms as the flush of nutrition from the cloned fought the allergic reaction. Her ankles weren't too bad, just a mild itching and a pink-ish bloom on the skin.

Of course, the wrists were the most vulnerable. Her weakest point, the delicate structures of the claws and hand still not fully settled from her Turning.

She set the tankard down with a click. The table was a restrained ebony wood piece, and the room was done in oak, restful dark-blue velvet swathing the bed and hanging on the stone walls. Still under-ground, of course, and dust in the air. Had Nikolai changed his Nest, or was this Marya's doing? This looked like a female's room, with more delicate furniture and that massive, choked-velvet bed. The bookshelves ranked along one wall were mostly empty, except for some little tchotchkes. Two brass elephants, their trunks raised. An antique crucifix on a stand – it had to be pure gold, and the rubies dewing it were probably worth a pretty penny.

A gleam of blue caught her eye. Selene let out soft breath, brush-ing past the bed and its hangings. Silk rustled as she reached up, her aching fingers meeting cold glass.

It was the glass apple. It had fallen from her bag in the tunnel under Nikolai's Nest, the passage behind the bed she'd arranged his dead body on.

Dead body. Well, he's looking pretty alive to me.

At least now she knew this was one of Nikolai's abodes, and Marya had invaded it.

Selene tapped the apple with a fingertip. She could still remem-ber the panic at the bus station, the familiar weight missing from her canvas bag. It was, she reflected, the last time she'd had a wholly human reaction to something. Even though she had been Nichtvren then.

Afterwards, simple survival had taken the place of human fear. She'd run as far and as fast as she could, as if something had been chasing her.

Maybe something was.

It would be ridiculous . . . except for the note. *Come home.* And this, waiting here for her.

The storm-tingle in the stillness warned her, so she didn't flinch when he spoke. His breath touched her hair. "You look lovely."

Selene's fingers curled around the glass apple. The bracelet of pain around her wrist sent a sharp jolt up her arm.

"I did not think you would come. I told *her* you wouldn't. That you cared so little for me, and indeed believed me dead." Still the same voice, soft and inflected a little oddly. He spoke the Merican of her human life, as if he knew what a thorny pleasure it was to hear.

No to the first. Yes to the last. She shrugged, silk moving against her skin, her arm up and the glass apple cool against her fevered palm. She would run warm until she metabolized the blood. Then it would be time for more, possibly before she stepped on the transport to take her away from this goddamn town.

Anywhere in the world, now, you could walk into a bar and get a tankard of cloned. A Nichtvren always had money. The biggest change?

Saint City was no longer *home*. Now that she knew he was still alive.

"This has been . . . educational." She sounded steady enough, even to herself. Her fingers uncurled from the apple. It was the only thing she had left from Danny, but if she left it here, it would be safe. Nikolai would keep it until the dust drifted up over it. "But I've got a transport to catch."

"Unsafe." He stepped closer, and the heat from him told her he'd fed too. Cloned? Or from a willing thrall? Since this had all been a game anyway.

"They don't usually drop paying customers into the sunlight, Nik." It was just the right tone, she congratulated herself. Light, flippant and with enough distance between them to need a transport to cross it.

She half turned. He stood too close, and he was staring again. Yes, he had fed – and quite a lot, by the look of it. He was no longer filthy, the clothes were new: jeans and a black sweater, paper thin but still palpably expensive. She didn't raise her eyes to his face, but the mottled bruising would be going down. His hands were still twisted into claws, but the fingers were crackling as they healed. The glaring wounds in his wrists were filling in, livid where the fresh blood was soaking through ageless tissues.

"Stay." Peremptory command. That, at least, was the same. He was never one to simply ask if he could demand.

She made a little clicking sound, like a mother with an over-enthusiastic child. "I have a job to return to. Not to mention a life, Nikolai. Or unlife. Whatever."

"Mercenary." He made a restless movement, a simple flicker, and Selene almost flinched. "Must I pay you for your time?"

A few decades ago, it might have stung. Now, she laughed. "Why bother, when there are so many willing ones around?"

"You are not willing?" He said it like he didn't believe it for a moment.

Of course, he could hear her heart hammering, a Nichtvren's strong irresistible pulse faster than usual because every nerve in her body had tightened. The weakness was back, shortening her breath and turning her to liquid.

Well, if he could be hurtful, she could too. Or at least, she could *try* to hurt him. "When did that ever matter to you?"

"Always." Another small movement, just a twitch before he restrained himself. "How could you think it would not?"

Because I remember how you forced me, and how you didn't care if I cried as long as you got what you wanted. Here I am, a Nichtvren, just like you wanted me. I even came to take part in this ridiculous little setpiece, whatever it is. "Goodbye, Nikolai." A single step forwards, her hip dropping in case he moved, and she was past him. He was fever-warm, a self-repairing furnace. "Next time, I won't answer."

His hand closed around her bare upper arm, the prickle of his claws a delicate reminder. "Selene." The dark tone that promised trouble.

A bolt of heat lightning crackled through her, each vein with its cargo of fresh cloned lighting up. She inhaled, sharply, the human habit of breathing too strong to break. There was that, of course – her response. A sexwitch's response, to only one man instead of everyone. Was it any better?

"What could I offer you?" His breath touched her cheek. Leaning in, his warmth against the surface of silk and the suddenly more responsive canvas of her skin. "The city. Blood. Spectacle. More, if you want it. What will it take?"

Everything except the one thing I want. Selene froze, the gnawing in her belly easing for the first time in years. She had the chance now. She might as well use it. And perhaps, just perhaps, it would hurt him.

Selene turned her head, slowly, shower-damp hair sliding against her shoulders. He watched her from under his mask of bruising, dark eyes glittering. Like a hawk in a cage, perhaps.

Her fingers slid between his as she moved his bruising grip away from her arm. "Come here." And she led him, step by step, to the bed.

It was a new thing, to push him down on to the dusty mattress and slide her hands under his sweater. Hard skin, muscle flickering under its stony surface, perfect and poreless. The shallow dish of his stomach, the angles of the ribs responded under her fingers. He submitted, his eyes half-lidding and his bruised mouth, flushed with his own feeding, opening just slightly.

He didn't object when she slid her palms down his arms, the sweater's texture alive under her own skin, and pulled his hands up. Spread his arms, as if he were on the cross again. Pushed them down. "Don't move," she whispered. "Your hands stay here."

The slightest approximation of a nod – his chin dipping just a little, his mouth softening even more. There were swiftly healing wounds all over his torso; she wondered what Marya had done to him.

"Why her?" She leaned down, touched a particularly vivid bruise. His entire body tensed, but he didn't move his arms.

"She was . . . Grigori's, too. She betrayed me to him, the first time I sought to escape." Nikolai swallowed, hard. "Selene . . ."

"Ah." Selene kissed the bruise, a butterfly-stroke of lips. Her tongue dipped, tasting; she could smell the blood under the surface and her fangs tingled.

It was actually pleasant. The swimming feedback of sensation echoing between them, the curse now a drug in her veins, her fingers working at his jeans.

So many things change, but a pair of Levi's is forever. She caught a laugh in the bottom of her throat; it turned into an inquisitive purr.

"I escaped Grigori." Nikolai's whisper touched the walls. "She did not. And she blamed me for it."

"Mm." She slid the zipper down, one small tooth at a time. "Lift up just a little . . . there. Good boy. I think that'll do." *Huh. Were you hopeful, Nik? Because I seem to remember you used to like boxer briefs instead of commando.* For a moment she wondered if a zipper would break if a Nichtvren male got something caught in it, and the laughter threatened to spill free.

"Selene—"

She decided to leave the jeans tangled around his knees. "Nikolai, unless I ask you a question, *shut up.*"

He did.

A tongue-touch, just a slight lap, like a kitten. Her tongue was rougher now, the barbs on the surface meant to help with the anticoagulant, meant to keep the blood flowing. Her fangs ached, sensitive razor points, and she toyed with the idea of distending her jaw and *biting*.

It would be a revenge, but not the type she wanted. So, instead, she set herself to learning him again.

He hadn't changed, of course. Still frozen in the same narrow-hipped body, a slim line of dark sparse curls from his belly button down, the same long legs and broad shoulders. The glaring welts and jagged lightning shapes from cuts were flushed, but once she was close enough they weren't ugly. They were simply different, a road map of suffering. She played with them while the trembling pushed through him, his arms stretched out and his body making little betraying movements when she hit a sensitive spot.

Was this what it was like, to control someone? Had it been like this for him? Except she'd been truly helpless, and he . . . was not.

Selene's claws prickled. She ran them up the outside of his thigh, slowly scraping the skin. He actually shook, and a small sound escaped his throat.

Well, now. Wasn't that interesting.

"Your blood in my veins," she whispered. "My curse in yours. Is that what happens when you Turn a sexwitch, Nik? I didn't get a chance to ask, before."

"Yesssss—" The sibilant turned into a gasp as she moved, sliding snake-like up his body, her knees settling on either side of his hips. "It burns." His throat moved as he swallowed again. "I don't know how you stand it."

"It was worse when I was human. And now it's just . . . you." Selene considered his face. Eyes closed, mouth slightly open as he breathed in short gasps, the charcoal fans of his eyelashes lying obediently in their proper arc, his hair still damp from washing away the filth of confinement and torture. "It's not every man who wanders along," she whispered against his lips, sipping his breath.

Then she slid herself down, exquisitely slowly, and closed him in her flesh.

Still the same. There was nothing like the first thrust, her body closing itself against the invasion and yet accepting at the same moment. Nikolai's back arched slightly, but he stayed where she'd placed him.

Selene settled into a slow, rocking rhythm. The blood was burning through her, but it was the warm, slowly rising aura of sex, like oil against her skin, that would feed her now.

Nikolai was actually sweating. It took hard effort to make a Nichtvren perspire; Selene's mouth turned up in a smile and she closed her eyes, her fangs touching her lower lip. His hands blurred up, but her reflexes were just a fraction faster and she caught his wrists, slamming them back down on the bed. Dust rose, and the change of angle made her gasp. His hips tilted up, Selene gasped again. Still-healing bones ground in his wrists as she squeezed, and Nikolai stiffened.

White fire raced through her veins as he bowed upwards, his spine arching and a low throaty sound escaping. The bed shook, flesh and Power both quaking, and Selene rode the tide through, energy spilling through her skin as the curse, for the first time since she'd left, fed itself to completion.

It settled into a warm glow. Bones crackled, shifting, and new strength spilled through her entire body. She shuddered, half-wishing he'd been able to hold off for longer. But almost a century was a long time, and she had the notion that perhaps he hadn't been using sex to feed for a while.

And her own completion didn't matter. This was about power, and about him.

"There." She opened her eyes, silk sliding as she moved. "You can say *you're welcome*."

"Don't leave." This time the rumble of Power was more definite, and the entire room resounded like the inside of a bell.

Selene sighed. She levered herself aside carefully, the skirt falling down with a whisper. She held his wrists until the last possible moment. It must have hurt, but they were whole and healed now. The rush of Power had restored him to himself, and eased her own hurts. "That's the trouble with you. You're too old. You don't learn a goddamn thing."

He had nothing to say to that. Selene slid off the bed, the silk draping soft and slick around her, and decided to look for some more reasonable clothes.

The transport hove into sight like a gigantic grey bird, the whine of hover tech settling into Selene's back teeth. Her fangs itched a little, responding to the vibrations. The rain flashed, little jewels sparkling through street-lamp shine, and the wet breeze touched her tangled hair.

She'd found jeans and a T-shirt, and a jacket. The medallion was warm under her shirt, and she had thought of leaving it somewhere

. . . but, this way, it couldn't be used to lure her back. The glass apple, perhaps, but that was a different story.

There was another job waiting as soon as she stepped on to the dock in Freetown New Prague. It was a good place to work, especially since the paranormals were driving all the human mercs out. On the other hand, it meant nothing was as easy.

She suspected she didn't want an easy job for a while. Something complex would keep her occupied enough to forget.

Her entire body glowed, her skin fluorescing a little under her clothes. The feeling, she suspected, wouldn't last long. The wanting would settle back into her lower belly, and she would endure it.

Nikolai stepped up to the yellow line beside her. She'd chosen the most shadowed part of the dock, watching the endless flow of humanity as they filtered past.

Christos, couldn't you leave it alone? She spoke first, to forestall him. "You don't need to see me off."

"I am not willing to see you off." Quiet, but with an edge. "I have waited, and waited. If you will not stay, I have no choice but to follow."

Well. "Does it ever occur to you to just *ask?*"

He was silent for a few heartbeats, digesting this. "Would it matter if I did?"

"It would."

"If I asked you to stay, Selene . . ."

How can you be so old and still not understand? "I would say no, I have a job I'm contracted for. But after that, if you sent me a letter asking me to come back, I would. If you asked me to stay, I think I could manage it." *There. That's as far as I'm going.*

Another long pause. He was strung tight, a sharp hurtful readiness. "Is that all that is necessary?"

"Probably not. You're a petty dictator." She idly calculated the best angle of escape, wondering if she could move quickly enough to escape him.

"Do you ever grow tired of bringing me to my knees?" Lower now, and rough.

Now there's an idea. "Do you ever get tired of ordering me around?"

"You will come?" A pause. "If I *ask?*"

Hallelujah. We've penetrated one of the thickest skulls on earth. "Yes. If you ask. Not command, or demand, or manipulate. You're going to have to learn this skill. It's going to take you some time."

He obviously didn't think much of the idea. "Selene. Please."

She stepped out into the rain. Soft chill little pinpricks touched her cheeks, her chin. "You know what to do, Nikolai."

"Selene . . ." As if he'd run out of air. Finally, she'd reached him.

"Don't make me wait too long." She strode through the rain as the transport's upper doors opened. Another good thing about being Nichtvren – she didn't have to wait for boarding.

He was silent behind her. But the words came, laid softly in her brain like a gift, the blood-bond between them pulsing once, silently.

I will ask.

"Good," she whispered.

And kept walking.

The Mammoth Book of Women's Erotic Fantasies

Edited by Sonia Florens

UK ISBN: 978-1-84901-451-9
UK price: £7.99
US ISBN: 978-0-7624-4002-3
US price: $13.95

What do women *really* want?

A collection of over fifty intimate personal stories by ordinary
women from all over Europe, North America and Australia. In
these erotic accounts – sometimes light-hearted, occasionally
shocking – women reveal their most sensual dreams and
innermost desires. The result is a revelatory snapshot of
the often mysterious nature of female sexual desire which
smoulders beneath the mundanity of everyday life.

Erotic and illuminating, these are stories
for open-minded, sensual readers.

The Mammoth Book of Paranormal Romance

Edited by Trisha Telep

UK ISBN: 978-1-84529-941-5
UK price: £7.99
US ISBN: 978-0-7624-3651-4
US price: $13.95

Fall in love with the otherworldly

If love transcends all boundaries, then paranormal romance is
its logical conclusion. From the biggest names around, here
are twenty-four tales to take you to another time and place.

Let Alyssa Day, Sherrilyn Kenyon, Cheyenne McCray,
Jeaniene Frost, Ilona Andrews, Kelley Armstrong, Maria
V. Snyder, Carrie Vaughn, Allyson James and others
show you powers beyond your wildest imaginings.

Within these pages, mythical beasts, magical creatures of
all shapes and sizes, heart-stoppingly handsome ghosts,
angels and mortals with extra-sensitive sensory perception
play out the themes of extraordinary desires.

The Mammoth Book of Paranormal Romance 2

Edited by Trisha Telep

UK ISBN: 978-1-84901-370-3
UK price: £7.99
US ISBN: 978-0-7624-3996-6
US price: $13.95

Love is the drug

Paranormal romance was never going to be content with just vampires and werewolves. The fantastic stories in this new collection lay claim to much, much more: paranormal serial killers, gaslight Victorian rendezvous and the urban mayhem of fantasy and steampunk.

Here you will find well-loved, bestselling authors writing under new pseudonyms, fresh stars and steadfast favourites, together offering a feast of mind-bending subgenres . . .

'To Hell with Love' by Jackie Kessler
'The Majestic' by Seressia Glass
'Fragile Magic' by Sharon Ashwood
'The Getaway' by Sonya Bateman
'Spirit of the Prairie' by Shirley Damsgaard

Paranormal romance will never be the same again.

The Mammoth Book of New Erotic Photography

Edited by Maxim Jakubowski

UK ISBN: 978-1-84901-384-0
UK price: £10.99
US ISBN: 978-0-7624-3999-7
US price: $17.95

A stunning new collection of over 500 erotic images from some of the world's leading photographers

Expertly compiled and beautifully reproduced, these female nudes and erotic portraits – some of them self-portraits – represent the best new work of over seventy of the most outstanding photographers in the US, the UK and the rest of the world who have made names for themselves with their nude and erotic work.

This massive compendium, the third volume in a truly ground-breaking series, brings together an impressive array of talent within the covers of one book. It reveals the individual photographers' unique and innovative ways of capturing and bringing fresh eroticism to their subjects. Above all, these are pictures which tell stories.

The Mammoth Book of Threesomes and Moresomes

Edited by Linda Alvarez

UK ISBN: 978-1-84901-019-1
UK price: £7.99
US ISBN: 978-0-7624-3994-2
US price: $13.95

Threesomes, foursomes and moresomes

Erotic fantasies for lovers hungry for more

Why be forced to choose between two lovers when you can have them both – at the same time? The truth is . . . we all want it. Take a walk on the wild side with this unforgettable, mind-blowing collection of erotic experiences from bestselling author Linda Alvarez. Here you'll find a window on a whole new world – two women sharing a single man, two men dedicating themselves to pleasuring one woman, swingers, insatiable nymphomaniacs, ménage a trios . . . a quatre . . . each story's a sure-fire turn-on.

A couple looks to spice up a jaded relationship; a woman attempts to satisfy veracious lusts with her lover . . . and his friends; and three friends slip unexpectedly into something more than friendship.

Too much of a good thing? Never! When it comes to erotica, three is definitely not a crowd – nor is four . . . or more.

The Mammoth Book of Time Travel Romance

Edited by Trisha Telep

UK ISBN: 978-1-84901-042-9
UK price: £7.99
US ISBN: 978-0-7624-3781-8
US price: $13.95

Time has no meaning for true love

Twenty tales of swashbuckling adventure and passionate romance from some of the most exciting names in romantic fiction, including Margo Maguire, Autumn Dawn, Sandy Blair, Michelle Maddox, Patti O'Shea, Holly Lisle, Kimberly Raye and Madeline Baker.

Join the heroines in this delightful anthology as they step backwards – or forwards – in time, transported to the Scottish Highlands of yesteryear, the Wild West and the distant future. Propelled through time into situations rich with possibility and fraught with danger, these sexy, sassy heroines each seek their dreamed-of happy ending.

Will souls separated by time be reunited – or separated for ever?

The Mammoth Book of
Regency Romance

Edited by Trisha Telep

UK ISBN: 978-1-84901-015-3
UK price: £7.99
US ISBN: 978-0-7624-3992-8
US price: $13.95

**23 wickedly witty, racily romantic,
and sublimely sensual short stories**

A rake by any other name is still a rake, no matter how
handsome . . . or sexy. A duke, on the other hand, an earl,
or a marquis – now there's a suitable man to capture a
girl's affections. A man and a marriage, that's on the cards,
but what to do about all those dashing scoundrels?

Caught between family, intolerable longing, and impossibly
tight corsets, the young ladies of the Regency era navigate the
fashionable waters of High Society in the name of love and
desire. Keeping one eye on their reputations and the other on
their fragile hearts, they cavort with devilish rogues who attempt
to charm them out of their gowns and into impropriety – will
any of them escape with their innocence intact?

The Mammoth Book of Scottish Romance

Edited by Trisha Telep

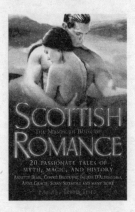

UK ISBN: 978-1-84901-452-6
UK price: £7.99
US ISBN: 978-0-7624-4003-0
US price: $13.95

Real Men Wear Kilts

Enough to make even the hardiest Highlander blush, here you will find the steamy romantic history of Scotland laid bare. With swords, through sorcery and in the course of some of the hottest nights ever experienced on the Inner Hebrides, Scottish heroes stake their claims, both in the bedroom and out. Dreams come true and legends are born as ancient prophecies are fulfilled by time travellers from the future, in a Scotland where real historical figures exist side by side with pagan magic and werewolves. Dashing lairds and Scottish barbarians fight for love and honour in a wild, magical world.

Let Julianne MacLean, Patricia Grasso, Lois Greiman, Marta Acosta, Donna Grant and many more lead you into the fierce, sexy, irresistible heart of a Scotland that is, was, and might have been.